Best wishes

fr P- O'Do

Larry's Law

by

Patrick J. J. O' Doherty

**Grosvenor House
Publishing Limited**

This book is published by
Grosvenor House Publishing Ltd
28-30 High Street, Guildford, Surrey, GU1 3EL.
www.grosvenorhousepublishing.co.uk

A CIP record for this book
is available from the British Library

ISBN 978-1-78148-764-8

Acknowledgement page

To Love:
Love is our only God,
our only Prophet,
our only priest, church and altar.
Love and care of each other are humanity's only future.

Patrick J.J. O' Doherty.

About the Author

Patrick J. J. O' Doherty was born in Ireland in 1940 and orphaned with his brother Tony as an infant to the care of the Sisters of Charity in Blackrock Co Dublin to whom he attributes a debt of love and gratitude. He was moved to St. Patricks Upton, Co.Cork, at the age of ten under the strict supervision of the Rosminian Order of priests and religious brothers. He experienced those last six years with frightening anxiety to his very sensitive nature. He was reunited with his mother, two sisters and two brothers after sailing to England in 1956. He had many Jobs and eventually settled into general building work involving him in many trades.

He was ordained priest at age 48 in England in 1990 for the Nottingham Diocese. He has since retired and is now aged 72.

Index to Chapters:

Introduction

An infant slipped quietly into our turbulent world, an innocent, most humble soul, a gift to parents of no seeming importance. The child's name was Larry. Physically, he was an adult; mentally he was something of an enigma, a mixture of genius and child together. Many close associates knew him as a lovable innocent child. Others would call him a simpleton and a dreamer and yet he would eventually unite the world in a way no other human being ever thought possible. It was not with any new knowledge or innovation that he would achieve this seemingly impossible goal but with the simplest of all directives – the love and care of all peoples. To that end, he would change the world for ever.

CHAPTER 1

The Birth and Childhood of Larry

From the day he was born Larry was absolutely adored by his parents, Brendan and Mary Walsh. From the onset the tiny tot was a gurgling, happy child for ever smiling on the two beloved faces that looked upon him with radiant affection. He revealed a remarkable sense of affection for both his parents, never feeling comfortable out of their sight. It wasn't sufficient that one or other parent gave him their singular attention – baby Larry wanted both of them before he would settle or play with confidence. This was a small inconvenience for both parents, given their deep love and worship of the infant. They considered his birth as a gift from heaven, the very fulfilment of their dreams. They had long since given up hope of ever being blessed with a child, given their age – both parents were in their middle forties.

As the baby passed through all the stages of infancy to primary school it became evident that there was a distinct problem with his physical coordination and his sense of normality. Doctors from Cork City Children's Clinic attributed these peculiar physical and mental abnormalities to the advanced age of his parents in relation to the conception of their child. It was affirmed by the Children's Clinic that in their experience, concerning late parenting, such abnormalities were not unusual. The child spent many hours of hospital time undergoing various tests and therapies as his development progressed. At the age of fourteen, and after several years of tests and observations, Dr. Oral O' Connor consulted Larry's parents with regard to their son's future potential. Her diagnosis was both cautiously encouraging and yet bearing a distinct sense of foreboding for the family.

'We don't think there is any real need for immediate concern. Larry is remarkable in his affections towards all the staff, including those whom he has only just met – you are already quite familiar with this pattern of behaviour.' Both parents smiled knowingly at the doctor while Larry held their hands as though he was still in infancy. Larry beamed his infectious smile at whoever was speaking. He would look full into the face of each speaker forcing their attention. Doctor Oral, as she became familiarly addressed, knew that this degree of attention, this expectation for such intense attention was far from normal. This very characteristic was already noted as extremely odd among other school children and his teachers. Even so, his beaming happy nature was invariably a road into the most stubborn hearts. Dr. Oral drew the parents aside to speak to them in private, leaving Larry with another of the staff to distract his attention from his parents ... he was fine as long as his parents were close by.

'I'm afraid his physical coordination will prove a serious problem for the lad as he develops into adulthood. You will have noted from his school reports that none of the children want to play with him because he is extremely clumsy due to his coordination imbalance. While attempting to help other children to jump inside a skipping rope, he either lashes the rope into their faces or fails to keep a consistent loop with the person at the other end of the skipping rope. He is actually dangerous even though he does not intend to harm anyone.' His mother, Mary, was in tears at this last revelation. Both doctor and Mary's husband, Brendan, took hold of Mary together to console her.

'There now, Mary, there now …. We have a wonderful boy. We'll teach Larry to do things ourselves. Why, he can help his poor old daddy to make some things in the shed. Sure, I will make a fine carpenter of him yet.' Although Brendan's banter stemmed the flow of Mary's tears, causing her and the doctor to smile in appreciation of his willing acceptance of the situation, she knew in her heart that Brendan didn't believe a word of it. However, Mary knew perfectly well how much Brendan loved their son. Larry was for ever in the shed with his dad passing him his tools or picking up bits of wood shavings to show to his daddy just to have his attention. Bernard had the patience of Job with him, simply because they loved each other so much. Both parents had already agreed, wholeheartedly, to keep the lad at home in the event of Larry's inability to hold on to a job. Their most haunting concern was Larry's long term happiness and security when and if both parents died. That was a horrible haunting thought which both of them had to face as a distinct possibility and to try to make whatever provisions they could for his future. Larry would be in his forties when both of them would be in their eighties.

Dr. Oral continued, 'He studies very well on his own. His teachers consider him something of an eccentric genius. He eats books. It appears that his school cannot keep up with his reading ability. In fact we have ascertained from various test, as you know from our reports, that his intelligence in well above average. However, let another person come near him, he just drops what he is involved in and gives that person his undivided attention, whether the other person desires it or not. His concentration is remarkable while on his own. He becomes completely absorbed in literature and shows excellence in written composition and comprehension. Yet he has no interest in personal praise from his teachers. He only wants to relate to them on a personal level all the time as though every stranger was an intimate part of his family. He can exhaust people with this extreme need. It seems he just loves people.' There was no real need for Dr. Oral to relate that characteristic to his parents. They did not begrudge Larry's demand for their love and constant attention. He was the very sunshine and joy of their lives. They were all too willing and prepared to give themselves over completely to their son's needs. Both felt certain that they could face anything in order to keep their beloved child in a secure, happy home. That was all they cared about.

When Larry attempted to enter the world of work, early predictions of his problems were soon realised. Larry lost job after job in the city due to his inability to stick to his work. He just wanted to be friendly with people at work, distracting them from their own duties. Eventually all Larry could do was to stay at home with his Mother. Both spent many hours walking the streets. Shopping for Mary was a tremendous and prolonged ordeal. As she shopped and walked the streets she was always held back by Larry's constant banter with every one he met. He would pull his mother back each time just to introduce himself and his mother to complete strangers. Both became known all over Cork city. The trying thing for his mother was the fact that Larry was genuinely interested in all people. His conversations with complete strangers were very personal and disturbingly intimate. Most people responded to his intimate enquiries quite openly, usually addressing their remarks to his mother, by way of saying we realise your son has put you in this embarrassing situation. Most strangers were convinced that they were responding to a disturbed but loveable child. This situation continued for years and was very draining for Mary. Every one in the city, who spoke about the wandering mother with the wandering child, spoke of her as a saint. Eventually Mary felt that her son would be safe enough to wander the streets on his own. Her confidence in peoples' love and acceptance of Larry had grown over time. Very few teenagers mocked him. There was always someone ready to protect Larry. The city had taken him to its heart.

Larry's street wandering continued happily enough over the years. He haunted the city libraries devouring books. He was given his own study section in order to keep him away from distracting other readers. For all his eccentric behaviour and the impositions it created, he was genuinely and lovingly cared for. He brought out the best in most people. He was also a regular visitor to the local police station just to chat to the Garda. Most officers treated him with respect and a genuine sense of endearment. Larry was also devouring more library books at home. He had an insatiable interest for ancient history and the general development of humanity from its early primitive development to the great civilizations of Egypt, Greece and Rome.

Now in his early thirties he was considered by his parents a remarkable biblical scholar ... this in view of his complete lack of academic background. His parents had introduced him to the bible since they had always regarded it of immense importance to their own lives. Both were good-living Christian parents with a simple piety. Larry took to the Good Book like a bee to the flower, firstly because his parents loved the book and secondly, because he became fascinated by its characters and stories. His parents were not really theological Christians, not in the strict academic sense; although both were familiar with various commentaries on the bible as Judaic religious history and its multitude of other writings such as Wisdom literature, poetry and military exploits; the reported conquests among their pagan neighbours. All these interests were naturally passed on to Larry by default – he copied his parent's activities with utter abiding affection. Larry would devour any book that related to human enterprise. His parents encouraged Larry to always show a deep respect for people and to develop a meaningful prayer life. They need hardly have stressed the point. The questions he regularly posed to his parents assured them that his prayer life was well in advance of their own. At the age of fourteen he once asked his parents, 'If God made everything out of nothing, where did he get all the material from since he is called a person? How can all the material of all the stars and the entire universe come out of a person? I simply don't understand that.'

'Ah, Larry, son,' his mother replied, 'you will have to get into a mighty long queue with those who ask the same question.' His parents had taught him not to accept everything he read as actual fact; that many stories, while not actually true, still contained much wisdom. Larry had a distinct gift for meditation and a penetrating curiosity for learning. He never discussed religion with people other than his parents. They had advised him to keep his own counsel because posing controversial questions to many people who believed everything they read about, or were taught about, regarding religion would do more harm that good. Both his parents were widely read and yet they too kept their own counsel for precisely the same reasons. They knew all too well that many people had to have plenty of time to accept disturbing facts about their long-held beliefs and faith which were held as sacrosanct.... They were aware also, that to force ignorance to the well of truth against its will and dunk the head of hostile resistance into its waters would invariably do more harm than good, wilful ignorance being a powerful tool when reinforced by blind unquestioning authority. Larry's parents adhered to the practical aspects of the Christian message, having a decent kindly respect and regard for other people. Their way of life had no hardships for Larry. Indeed, he worshipped his parents and loved the life he had with them. They were a firm anchor to his life.

His parents were partially successful in finding him a place in the city university to study literature, however, he caused so much disruption with his wanderings into the study rooms of other students that he was forced to leave. However, Professor Rodger O' Rourke who was so impressed with Larry's written work insisted that the lad be given the opportunity to work at home with his mother and be enrolled as a member of the Open University. Larry did study enthusiastically at home but never handed in any of his work. As far as the city university was concerned he had dropped off the planet. This was a great disappointment to both his parents. When they enquired as to why he ignored the wishes of the university? He replied with a most mysterious and cryptic reply,

'Yerrah, mammy, they only want the fruit; they don't want the tree.'

That same night when Mary and Brendan lay in bed Mary asked,

'Brendan, what do you make of Larry's reply to our question concerning his indifference to the university?' Both parents had their backs to each other as they spoke speculatively into space.

'I can only think that he feels unwanted there as a person in his own right, with his own character and his own particular need.'

'You could be right, Brendan. But it's not a bit like him to dismiss anyone – I have never known the like of that in him before. It's just not his way.' Mary's face was a stage of confusion as Bernard remarked:

'Yerrah, Mary, maybe our boy is growing up, becoming more aware of his own standing in the world. Sure, when all-said-and-done, even saints have some spots of rust on their halos.' Bernard smiled teasingly at his own mischievous remark. Mary gave her husband a back kick.

'Don't you dare defame our precious boy, yeah great lump.' She smiled knowing Brendan was not going to lose any sleep over the matter.

'Be serious a minute, Brendan. I'm thinking of the long term .... You know what I mean; we're both getting on in years. What happens if he ends up alone, without either of us, what then?' Mary's eyes gazed into the dark of the room; it seemed potentially as dark as the future if Larry was to end up alone.

'Mary, sweetheart, if worrying helped I would order it by the cartload. There are good people in the world,

Mary. Look at the Maddens next door to us, how they love Larry and are always looking out for him. Sure doesn't Larry nearly eat them out of house and home when he's with them? Then there is our parish priest, Father Kevin, and his house keeper, Nell. Sure, they love Larry as if he was their own. No, Mary. We can't live forever; we're not gods. I will admit, though, it makes my heart gasp and tremble to think of being separated from either of you.' Mary was in tears sobbing quietly. Brendan couldn't know that in the darkness. Hers were tears of love. She felt Brendan holding her very life in his own dear heart. She experienced a deep sense of safety and love from his words. He had always been a very practical caring husband. He had a little money put by in an insurance policy for Larry – Mary was aware of that. It wouldn't be much. The carpentry trade in Ireland, given the state of the economy, was not paying that well. In any event, and coupled with Larry's basic welfare money, he would be able to scrape by. Larry lived very frugally. He would go naked in the street if left to his own designs. He didn't care a fig about gadgets or clothes, only people. The government was stretched financially and Larry's parents, as well as most of the Irish population, believed that the members of the government should be strung up with most of the bankers for all their incompetence. What did any of that lot give a damn for the likes of Larry or for any struggling family? No, Brendan thought, his mind scurrying about. Our little island was drained to the dregs. Once more a forsaken island bereft of its migrating youth, too costly to employ many, too wretched for dignified welfare. All this heartache and prolonged misery for her sons and daughters because of greedy speculators and self-serving bankers who sold Ireland to the four winds, making it a pauper whose hands were forced to dig deep into the pockets of quaking Europe.

Both parents continued talking out the humour and events of the day. Invariably their beloved Larry was in every carriage of their thoughts.

'Did you see the dance of himself this evening in the kitchen? Sure he frit the very life out of me. All this spinning of his body with his long arms flaying the air like some demented jet swooping and diving in all directions. Like a top he was, spinning faster and faster, and me ducking and screaming for him to stop. He seemed to be in a drunken demented ecstasy and then to end flat on his bottom, his great long legs nearly in the oven … and then to finish up holding his spinning head and grinning from ear to ear.'

'Will yeah give over, Mary Walsh. The pair of you will be the death of me.' The bed was shaking with both parents convulsed in laughter. After a while, and conscious of the open bedroom door, they fell back into whispers. This dance of Larry's was a strange phenomenon for one with coordination problems. Usually he reserved such behaviour for his walk in the Mardyke parks nearby. Just occasionally he would go into his spinning dance in less appropriate places. It seemed to his parents that he just loved the utter sensation of motion. The strange thing was that other local city children were copying his twirling dance, not in mocking mimicry of Larry, but because they discovered their own exhilarating sensation from it. This oddity came as no real surprise to his parents. They knew from their own experience of youth how motion was an absorbing thrilling sensation for most youngsters. How often they were both reminded of this fact when watching the city kids swooping up and down on their skate boards at break-neck speed on the high concrete slopes in the parks. Eventually, a contented sleepy silence washed over them. Both their hands clasped each other from behind their backs.

'Good night Mary. Sleep well, my love, and pleasant dreams.'

'God bless you, Brendan and our beloved child. Good night.'

CHAPTER 2

The Death of Larry's Father

Larry was now in his thirties, still jobless and living on welfare. His father, Brendan, worked to keep the home going while Mary looked after the household or wandered the streets with Larry. Startling news came from Brendan's employer of his sudden death from a massive heart attack. He died in the ambulance while being rushed to the City Hospital. This news nearly killed Mary; she was demented – beside herself with shock, disbelief and tearing grief. There had been no warning to cushion the tragedy. Brendan was a solidly-built man, over six feet tall. He had never been known to have taken time off work. True he was a pipe smoker. Yet many pipe smokers lived into their nineties and beyond – he was just unlucky. Mary was lost in her bewildered world. Added to all her troubles was the terrible effect it had on Larry. He was completely lost mentally. Mary could not console him. She had to call the doctor for him. Larry was diagnosed as suffering for deep depression and severe shock. He wouldn't speak to a living sole, not even to his beloved mother. It felt to Mary that she had lost both husband and son together. The tablets prescribed kept Larry in a constant state of stupor. He had no interest in anything. Doctor Joe O' Brian, the family doctor, had to come several times to the house much as he would for a problem ailing child. Larry had to be fed on special liquids since he ignored all food. Even the liquid diet had to be forced-fed to him. Larry had grown into a tall solid adult like his father, yet never gaining an ounce of weight. Now, however, he was getting thinner. This tragic situation continued for some nine months after the funeral of his father, which Larry was in no condition to attend. Eventually Larry recovered. Only now he was even more clinging to his mother. He was never far from her. Mary didn't object in spite of having to bring Larry to her own workplace where she was employed as an office cleaner. She had to keep the home going on her own now. He dutifully handed over all his welfare money to his mother each week, not that it was much. He had no personal interest in money apart for collecting it to help his dear mammy whom he treasured. She was his entire world beyond the books he devoured from the library. He tried again and again to find work but he could never hold on to any job. His distractions were like a curse on him at this time, he desperately wanted to help his mother to ease her burden. Inwardly he cursed his afflictions and the burden of his liability. In all this time and in the passing of the next decade Mary laboured stoically with her beloved Larry still clinging to her as a dependant child. Her all consuming love for Larry never waned in the slightest. All her hardships, and they were many, given Larry's extreme dependence on her and his constant presence wherever she worked or shopped, were considered a reward for having such a wonderful loving child.

Life for Larry and his beloved mother seemed to settle into calmer waters. She was forced into retirement but managed to live comfortably on her state pension and on a small investment left to the family by Brendan. Mary grew weaker with the passing years. Eventually she was taken seriously ill. Over the weeks she became bed-ridden. Many called to her house, the Madden family next door, saw to her meals and shopping. The doctor and priest came in turns. In the end her weakness and age overwhelmed her waning strength.

CHAPTER 3

The Death and Ascension
of Mary Walsh

Larry's hysterical screams reverberated throughout his mother's bedroom as he gripped the back of his head with both hands like some demented soul. His aged mother, spent and withered from her eighty years of life, was now in the slow process of dying. Her selfless attendance to her forty-five-year-old innocent child was closing swiftly on the final calendar of her days. Her pending departure to death's cold indifference would set the seal on world-changing events for her poor inconsolable son.

Mary's eyelids fluttered rapidly in her ashen withered face, as even now, she tried, with torturous effort, to console her beloved boy. Scream after hysterical scream, his words yelled out as one in raving madness.

'Don't leave me, mammy! Don't leave me! Mammy! Mammy! Mammy! Don't leave me! I promise I'll be good; honest to God, mammy; I promise – I promise – I promise. Mammmmmy' His screams were mind-rending. Fortunately they were only just audible to his dying, most cherished mother. He leaned over gripping and shaking her disfigured gnarled hands – they might have been the leavers of an ancient pump as he yanked them up and down in a frenzied effort and hope of preventing her death. His face was red with raging panic and desperation. His rage seemed like erupting lava, his fierce crazed eyes burning and awash in blinding tears.

'Shush Larry, shush. Don't do this to your mammy. You can't be a better son than you already are. Shush, son, shush.' Her voice was little more than the breath being forced from her throat, her eyes growing heaver and heaver. Larry flung his arms round her neck still screaming into her blood-drained face. He lifted her up bodily in an attempt to keep life within her. The effort making matters worse. 'Shush, son, shush.' She kept straining in whispers. 'I'll be back to help you Larry. I promise. I will ask holy God to let me come back to see you.' There was a long strained pause. Mary continued her voice barley audible. 'Go to the Maddens next door, they will see to your food until I come back. Now remember all the instruction I wrote down for you.' Mary's mind was wandering back to Larry's childhood days as she struggled to speak. 'You must keep digging in the garden, the same as I taught you.' [The holy Bible was for Mary and her son always referred to as the Garden. The reading of it and its study was fondly considered digging in the soil of its deeper more pertinent wisdom]

'Now be a good boy. Say your holy prayers every morning noon and night. Continue to read your holy Bible until you know it off by heart. Think about what you read, see if you agree with it, and then put it all into practice, you will want for nothing. Always hold the hand of holy Jesus in sweet virtue. Be good to people always, as best you can.

Harm no one. It's all there in the holy garden; treasure it son, as you have your dear old mammy.'

'Oh, I will mammy, I will. Promise me, mammy ... promise me you will come back to help me. Promise me.' Suddenly she was silent and deathly still. What happened next was scarcely comprehendible. She simply disappeared from the bed. Larry was left face down on the bed screaming into the empty sheets. The poor lad demented out of his mind.

They lived in the city of Cork, Ireland, in a terraced house on Shandon Rise, part of a long narrow cobbled side street of similar dwellings. The house was painted externally in a light pastel blue. Shandon Rise ran off the main Mardyke River road in the city. It was quite a picturesque area, in spite of some of its poorer dwellings. The main road was well known in a time old song which the natives of Cork lovingly referred to as the "The Banks" in which the Mardyke River was mentioned as being in the "...leafy shades of its old elm trees..." It really was a picturesque road at times, especially when spring bedecked its many trees and shrubs with transparent veils of virgin foliage. hanging like veils, softening the skeletal forms of passing winter. Such beauty, when delicate virgin blossom of every subtle hue graced every park and avenue ... where fresh scented flowers danced in the breeze across its many gardens and parks. But now, the elm trees were stripped to their skeletal forms, swaying and crying wildly in a bitterly cold November, where the city was being battered in wild gusting winds.

CHAPTER 4

Mary's Missing
Body – Investigations

Larry's good neighbours, the Maddens, were first to hear
of the tragic event, for tragic it was, given the unique
relationship and dependence of Larry on his beloved
mother and the great love each had for the other. They
came to visit Larry and his dying mother. She had been
bed-ridden for some weeks. When Larry opened the front
door his face was red, strained and awash in tears. The
Maddens guessed that the worst had taken its course.
The poor lad flung his arms round the necks of his loved
neighbours and friends who were by this time in tears
themselves. They had always loved Larry for all his
innocence, his open friendliness and childlike ways.
No words passed between them for some time. They all
remained in a clinging, supportive bond.

Seamus was the first to break the silence. He spoke in
whispers. 'May we see mammy, Larry?'
   'She's gone to heaven, Seamus. She's gone to Heaven!'
His pathetic face wrenched once more as though ready
to explode into a new wave of hysterics. Both looked

into Larry's wretched face and drew him in more tightly than ever, rubbing his back. Eventually Seamus said:

'We know that mammy is gone to heaven, Larry, where else would such a wonderful mammy go?'

Little did Larry's friends know the literal truth of the words which he spoke.

'I can't show her to you now, he spluttered in tears ... but I will show her to you when she comes back from heaven. She promised me that she would come back.'

Seamus and his wife, Lil, turned to each other. They were wiping away their own tears. Each looked quizzical at the other. Both knew something was not quite making sense. Larry was childlike, they knew that all too well, but he was not an inarticulate fool. He saw the confusion on their tearful faces and without more ado he brought them, almost dragged them, into the house and up the stairs to the bedroom. All they saw was an empty bed. All three stood there in deafening silence. Larry repeated what he said only moments ago, 'Mammy has gone to heaven. She was just taken up.'

By now both friends were standing either side of Larry, still facing the bed. As all three stood staring down at the dishevelled, empty bed, his friends grimaced at each other, raising their shoulders in expressions of total incomprehension. Lil sat beside Larry on the bed while Seamus sat on the only chair in the small bedroom.

Lil drew Larry close to her breast, her long fair hair fell perfuming across his tear-run face. Seamus in the meantime was absorbing the utter simplicity of the room. The carpet was worn and threadbare, its pattern all but worn away. The room, though taking on the semblance of utter poverty, was at the same time perfectly clean.

It might have been a cell in a convent comprised of a double bed, and small bedside cupboard and chair. On the cupboard were placed a framed coloured photograph of Mary and her deceased husband, Brendan, and Larry as a ten year old holding the hands of both parents who were smiling self-consciously. Beside the photograph lay a well worn copy of the holy bible, a most treasured companion to both Mary and the family. Mary liked to call the study of her bible digging in the Garden, a phrase that Larry had also adopted. On top of the faded blue cover of the bible lay Mary's time-worn spectacles, a set of red rosary beads, a biro and beside these a reporter's spiral notebook which she habitually used to take notes from her prayerful thoughts and studies. Seamus sensed an atmosphere of reverence in the humble room. Indeed, he was not in the least surprised in linking the atmosphere and humble contents of the room with Mary's holy and sincere but unassuming nature. Seamus had always been aware of the simplicity of the entire house. Yet only now had that same humble state made a strong conscious impact and impression on his thoughts. Hers had always been a quiet piety. She was only noticed in her church, St. Patrick's, through her son Larry who made a point of greeting everyone who passed by his seat at the very rear of the church.

Lil had calmed Larry to a lower level, his sobbing now less hysterical. She felt broken-hearted herself and could not control her own streaming eyes. The friendship between the three was more deeply rooted due to Larry's open and expressive innocence. Since the death of Mary's husband, Brendan, Larry's immediate neighbours, the Maddens, took Larry more and more under their care and concern. Words could not describe Mary's gratitude to the Maddens for their genuine love and care of her vulnerable son. Indeed, she considered herself and Larry blessed to have the good fortune to have such good neighbours. In point of fact, they were more like intimate family members than mere neighbours.

Lil was speaking in whispers over Larry shoulder as she continued to hold and console him. She felt it was time to move the situation forward without seeming to hurry.

'Did Father Kevin come to visit mammy, Larry, before she went to heaven?' Lil was trying to be as sensitive as she could and endeavoured to go along with the assumptions put forward by Larry.

'Father Kevin came lots of times to bring mammy Holy Communion and give her the anointing of the sick.' Lil and Seamus were already well aware of that point. 'But, no,' Larry continued. 'He was not there when mammy went to heaven.' His words were a little stronger now as his mind was a little more focused away from himself. Talking to his beloved friends helped distract his pain.

'You know he will need to come, Larry, so that he can be satisfied that all is well with you. You like Father Kevin, Larry, don't you? He has always been friends with mammy and yourself, hasn't he?'

'Yes.' Larry replied. 'We like Father Kevin.' He spoke in the present tense as if his mammy was still with him.

There was a strong contrast in the voices of Lil and Larry. She was a native of Dublin and Larry had the strong, lilting, sing-song Cork city accent.

As Lil released her hold on Larry she rummaged through her russet-coloured bead handbag for her mobile phone. She touched in the numbers of the church to call Father

Kevin. In the meantime Seamus went below to the kitchen to make some tea and coffee.

Seamus was a native of Limerick. He was quick-witted and naturally of a confident and generous disposition. He was a well-built man in his forties, with grey-black receding hair. His round plump face bore a small moustache. He was a warm confident person, energetic in a relaxed way. Nothing seemed too much trouble for him. His was a lively mind – one given to puzzles and besotted with sports, especially of the Gaelic kind. He could be totally absorbed in these activities. Yet let there be a call for assistance from anyone, he could switch into an accommodating mode and drop of all his own plans and interests as though they were of secondary importance. His eager generosity was selfless and unaffected. He had been a teacher but now worked mainly in the training of others in market economics.

His wife Lil was very much a close family person with a very large extensive family who were constantly in touch with each other. Perhaps it was because of this innate characteristic that her house was usually a hub of activity with visitors and parties of one sort or another. She was also very fond of animals. Seamus thought she was too fond of them sometimes. He was always grateful that the house was not a field otherwise she would have added to the three dogs and four cats that had free reign in the house. Like Seamus, she too had a very generous and accommodating nature. She was an avid reader and blessed with a remarkable sense of humour, a great story-teller in her own right, which she claimed to have inherited from her father, Christy. Her calmness and broad mindedness seemed to have come from her mother's side, though in truth her father also shared the same trait. Lil worked locally as a part time teacher of children with special needs, while Seamus worked mainly in the city. On occasions his work took him all over the country and sometimes he had to go to England on one course or another.

Fr. Kevin Noonan wasted no time in coming. He simply dropped all his work at the St. Patrick's Church presbytery. He had expected this call for some weeks now. Lil did not elaborate on the mysterious nature of the call. However, she made it clear enough that his presence was essential, given the very odd nature of the situation. A missing body was going to throw up real problems. These thoughts were paramount in the minds of both Lil and Seamus. The Priest, doctor and police would certainly have to become involved. How could poor Larry prove what he claimed to have occurred?

The knock on the door was gentle. Seamus was already alerted to the situation since he heard the priest's car pull up and the sound of the electric bleep of the door's locking mechanism. Seamus opened the heavy, green-painted door. The tall solid figure of the priest was ushered in by an inward pull from Seamus' hand, an action expressing an established intimate friendship. Fr. Kevin was certainly that. He was very popular with his people as well as a long-standing personal friend of the Madden family. His was a late vocation. His early working life had been spent in the building trade. He was very much at ease with people having had to earn his own living among the rough and tumble of the many building sites across Ireland and beyond. He was now in his fiftieth year. He had a very simple approach to his faith. He was profoundly attracted to the simplicity and practical nature of Christ's life and teaching. He never felt the need to wrestle with the big questions of the mysterious nature of God. Christ's life was all he needed to concern himself with, in spite of all the torturous theology and philosophy of his formation days as a late vocation to college and seminary.

'Fr. Kevin, you're most welcome. I've got some tea on the go, just as you like it,' said Seamus, smiling in his familiar way.

'God bless you, Seamus,' said the priest returning his smile. He whispered to Seamus, 'I take it she's gone?'

'Gone I'm afraid, Father Kevin, is a little bit too close to the truth.' Seamus arched his eyebrows handing the priest a mug of steaming tea making the mug ring as the spoon propelled its amber liquid. The priest arched his brow, his free hand spread out before him in a questioning expression.

'There isn't a body, Father. I kid you not.' Seamus added the latter with serious emphasis since both were used to a bit of a leg pull and banter. Seamus' face was earnest. The priest continued in whispers. 'What has happened?'

'I'm afraid you may have to work that one out for yourself. Larry claims she was taken up to heaven and that she will be coming back to help him. He is absolutely convinced that is true.' At this stage Seamus arched his shoulders and extended the upward palms of his hands, expressing utter incredulity and mystery. The priest was staring into Seamus' face. He too was totally bewildered … he didn't, as yet, want to give serious focus to the implications and consequences of a missing body. It wouldn't surprise anyone if Larry tried to hide the body to keep his beloved mammy, he loved her so much.

They brought some more mugs of tea and coffee upstairs to the bedroom where Lil continued to hold Larry close to her.

'Larry.' The priest greeted the tear-reddened face of the Lad with a single word. Larry's pathetic wretchedness was all too evident of his loss. Fr. Kevin's greeting was made with his head bowed, his eyes looking upward. It was difficult for him to face Larry full on. It was not a situation where politeness and solemn formality could suffice, no matter how sincerely such gestures may have been expressed. The good priest knew that he was in every sense in the company of a very distressed child whose unique world of love and dependence was ripped away. Larry's dependence on his cherished mother was one thing; her complete departure Left Larry in a very vulnerable position in a hard world. The undisguised love that he held for his mother was indeed the main root that anchored his life and made him the most loveable, most open individual.

'Father Kevin.' Larry's brief greeting was offered with a smile, a smile radiating from his reddened eyes and face. The priest had always been a good friend to the family. Presently he sat at the other side of Larry for want of a chair which was occupied by Seamus. The priest greeted Lil with a silent touch on her arm which was placed round Larry's shoulders. Father Kevin was in no hurry to speak – small talk was not appropriate in the circumstance; the pain had to be bourn by all. Only slowly did he skirt round the subject.

'No doubt mammy has gone to heaven, Larry. No doubt about it. God bless the good woman.' The priest was quite prepared to just speak to himself and hopefully draw Larry into conversation at the lad's own comfort and time. He continued looking across Larry's face into Lil's. 'I'm sure you will see to Larry's meals, Lil, now that we have to wait for a while until mammy's return.' This was said in a very matter of fact way as if the extraordinary circumstances were perfectly natural and in order. The priest knew all too well that the Maddens had already made provisions for Larry's temporary welfare with regards to meals and whatever else may be needed.

'He's our lovely boy, isn't that right, Larry?' He smiled as Lil gave him a gripping hug. He then turned to her almost involuntary and gave her a big kiss on the cheek. By slow degrees Father Kevin grew bolder with his conversation.

'Tell me, Larry, did mammy have the doctor to call before she left the house?'

'Yerrah not at all, Father Kevin, sure, they weren't friends at all. Sure, isn't he fierce with his manners all the time?' This reply held no surprises for Father Kevin. He knew the doctor well enough, a man who seemed to be forever on a short fuse with expressions of pomposity and waspishness. It was not usual for Larry to speak in derogatory terms of any person. His reply only served to emphasise the general poor opinion in which Dr. Joe O' Brian was held. Of course this knowledge did not help the priest in any way. He knew that Larry was obliged by law to have a doctor call, body present or absent! This fact was going to prove very difficult. Further complications were inevitable when the police would have to be informed. A missing, person, a missing body, no matter Larry's claims to celestial intervention, the Law was, and remained, god on earth even in these mysterious circumstances.

The priest patted Larry's leg as he arose and beaconed silently to Seamus to move downstairs for a private word. Once below, Father. Kevin shared his thoughts concerning the need to have both the doctor and police pay a visit. 'This is going to prove very difficult for the lad, Seamus. I will contact them myself and try to lay the groundwork for the necessary enquiries. God, Seamus! I could do without this at any time. But in these circumstance, given the lad's condition and emotions – what with making references to an ascension into heaven. God! The more I contemplate the implications, the more I see the Lad being caught up in a mockery of public ridicule, especially when the Media get hold of the story. I can't see any way in which it can be avoided.'

'Father Kevin,' said Seamus, placing a consoling hand on his friend's shoulder, 'we will stand by him come what may. I think you will find he will receive far more sympathy and respect in the city than you might believe.' Seamus took a deep breath as he held his head backward and continued confidently, his eyebrows arched expressing utter conviction. 'We have walked the streets of the city with Larry and his beloved mammy. They were invariably hailed with the greatest respect and courtesy. Let's face it Father, what will be, will be. I'm sure he will not be as negatively exposed as you might assume.' The priest, feeling somewhat consoled with his shared concerns, patted Seamus on the back.

'You're a brick, Seamus, indeed a real consoling support – what with Lil and all. We're fortunate to have you both behind us.' Father Kevin kept nodding his head appreciatively as he stared vacantly at the tattered carpet of the front room. Seamus sensed the weight of his concerns. A missing body would inevitably involved the priest in controversy, ridicule and God knows every annoying inconvenience with the media, which was bound to produce the inevitable pack of snapping hyenas wherever the Church became involved in controversy.

'I'd better call the doctor first, Seamus, even though it must, in the end, be considered a matter for the police.' The priest took a deep breath while raising his eyes heaven-ward.

'Would you like us to be present, Father?' Seamus searched the priest's downward face for a reply.

'I think that would help, Seamus. But I'm sure you have loads to do, what with your children at home and having to get their food ready …. Look at the time. I think the, quare fella,' [meaning the doctor], 'will not be best pleased considering it being a Sunday and lunch time to boot.' Father Kevin, normally a placid, easy-going man showed all the signs of irritation with himself. His round friendly face showed his annoyance.'

'Look, Father, let's all go to our house with Larry and make an appointment to see the quare fella after we have eaten. We can all march back to Larry's house afterwards. He can't chase us out of the house since he has nothing to perform on. He can only question our Larry.'

'I won't eat with you, Seamus, if you don't mind. My housekeeper will be none too pleased if I do. However, I will have a cup of tea aside from you and wait it out as you so kindly suggest. I'm sure it will be a great support to Larry if we are all here by his side.' The priest let out a hysterical laugh. 'God, Seamus! Isn't it some carry on that we should be acting like nervous children ganging up to confront a blooming doctor.' Seamus smiled and called up to Lil and Larry to join them for their midday meal.

All four marched next door. Once inside, Father Kevin made the dreaded call to the doctor. He kept the message as brief as he could, speaking only of his concerns for Larry who had just lost his mother. The doctor's waspish voice, its irritation, was no less than Father Kevin expected.

'Yes, doctor. The visit is essential – The lad needs to be seen – No, doctor – I haven't seen the corpse – No – I can't say how I know that the lad's mother is dead. I have been called out myself. It is every bit as inconvenient for me.' In all his replies to the doctor's questions the priest's voice was mounting in volume, irritation and defensiveness. Father Kevin replaced the receiver with a clatter and at the same moment burst out with uncharacteristic fury. 'God! That blooming man is a blooming pest.' He put up his hand to Seamus and Lil, as if to say, don't worry, it's all over, the deed is done. Father Kevin was more annoyed at himself for being annoyed. The truth of the matter he knew lay in the fact that he was attempting to shield an innocent, hurt, bereft child from further hurt. He knew that this situation was not going to be easy for anyone. It didn't help when such services came with needless pomposity and insensitivity from a supposed servant of the people.

The homely clatter of plates and cutlery during the preparation and eating of the meal lent an easing of the foreboding and tragic mood of the earlier moments. Larry demolished the beef stew and mixed vegetables with his usual speed and absentmindedness. He was quite at ease in the company whom he loved so much. It was very unlikely that he would have taken food from anyone else in his depressed condition. Three dogs nudged at the feet of the diners hoping for titbits while four cats wandered to their eating bowls sniffing indifferently at the contents. Lisa, the family's fourteen year old daughter, sat beside her brother, Andrew at the large round table. Andrew was twelve; his long fair hair and his slim build were in contrast to his sister's dark hair and her sturdy proportions. Both looked under Larry's face from time to time. They could see his reddened eyes and the strain on his face. It hurt them deeply to see Larry in such a state. Both loved him for his utter simplicity and uncomplicated nature. Father Kevin sat apart leaning forward on a hardback chair beside the open fire staring into its flickering coal flames. He was cupping his steaming tea with both hands his mind racing to the future and its impending difficulties. Lil, as usual, was covering several tasks at once with serving and eating. She took it all in her stride, being naturally used to a lot of company. As the meal came to its conclusion, the children and dogs were affectionately ushered into the lounge out of the way. The remaining company sat for some moments looking out from the glass doors that ran across the wall of the rear spacious garden. It began to rain. Tear-like streams ran down the tall glass panels. The sky became overcast and a gusting wind whipped at the tall tree-line surrounding the rear garden. There was a distinct dreariness to this portentous October day; portentous, because one individual, a doctor, for God's sake, the priest thought, who was capable of making a bad situation all the worse with his unhelpful attitude.

The four moved back to Larry's home to await the doctor's arrival. Fortunately they timed their return perfectly. No sooner had they entered the house out of the rain and seated themselves at Larry's kitchen table when they heard the slamming of a car door outside. The four friends looked at each other in turns with hunched shoulders and mouths opened with expressions more familiar on mischievous teenagers fearful of the wrath of some overbearing teacher. The clatter from the metal knocker on the door resounded throughout the house, making the friends twitch with tension. It was hard to credit how one man, supposedly in the service of the public, could create such an atmosphere of unease and, dare it be said, apprehension. Seamus, now riled and ready to confront this arrogance, seeing its effect on the supporting company, pulled opened the door with such force that the slipstream of the door all but sucked the irate doctor into the house.

The doctor stood for some minutes, his dark suit showing glittering signs of rain. He stared at Seamus and saw the riled, unwelcome expression on his face. The doctor leaned his dripping umbrella by the wall, which immediately fell over in a puddle of water. He marched arrogantly across the room and laid his scuffed black medical bag on the kitchen table. As he raised his face to confront the remaining trio, something very strange occurred. As his penetrating light grey-blue eyes beamed into the drained, sickly face of Larry, the doctor covered his own face as though some unseen force had punched him in the face. As he attempted to speak through his hands, his muffled voice quavered and his tall skeletal frame vibrated with involuntary sobs. The four friends turned to each other, their faces expressing utter bewilderment, their mouths drooped open. Seamus' expression was a stage of its own. His mouth lay open, his nose and entire face screwed in sneering bewilderment and disgust. He simply could not comprehend the distraught figure before him. As he stood behind the doctor, Seamus, his hands splayed outward, gesturing towards the company as though to ask, what the hell is all this about? The doctor struggled to compose himself with the aid of Lil's sympathetic arm around his shoulder she seated him on one of the dining chairs and took no more notice of the company, placing all her comforting concern on the distraught doctor.

'I'm so sorry. I saw my poor wife in the lad's eyes. She was all I ever had in life.' A long awkward pause ensued. 'It is twenty years ago, now. My wife was knocked down by a lorry that had mounted the pavement where we walked together. I never forgave myself for being on the inside of her when the dam lorry struck.' Another long pause .... The doctor's thin, pinched face was in tears .... There was an awkward gripping silence among the company. The doctor continued. 'I have never spoken of this to any living soul before. I can't imagine why the memory of it should flood from me now. Larry's distraught state seemed to act like a mirror of the event. I'm sorry. Forgive me for imposing my personal troubles on you.' Lil, to her credit, kept rubbing the doctor's back. He showed signs of appreciation for this undeserved comfort so freely and compassionately given. The company in general found it extremely awkward to compose themselves in this unexpected and extreme change in the doctor. Although the company listened intently to the doctor's account of his past traumatic events, the awkwardness remained. After a considerable time in which the poor man gained composure and self-control he moved from the chair to his bag but not before placing his hand on Lil's arm as a sign of appreciation for her unsolicited kindness. He turned to the priest each looking full into the face of the other. The doctor's eyes were very red and his flushed face showing an embarrassed unease for his untimely revelation.

'Please forgive me, Father, for my earlier rudeness. It was completely uncalled for and very unprofessional. If it is any consolation, my own colleges at the practice have put up with much worse consistently over the years. I know I have been a right pain to them and to all my unfortunate patients. I just couldn't seem to let go of the tragedy.' His latest narrative was half-spoken into his bag with embarrassment as he rummaged about inside. The priest, in spite of his discomposure, splayed his hands apart, his eyebrows arched revealing an expression of conciliation.

'You have carried a great deal of pain for many years, Doctor O' Brian.' The doctor cut him off before he could finish what he wished to say.

'Please, Father, Doctor Joe is fine.' The priest smiled, his physical gestures taking on a more relaxed expression. He could see that the medic was making every effort to reveal a warmer side of his nature.

'Love can crucify us sometimes, Doctor Joe, and you have obviously had your share of it. If we could dismiss our loss just like that and be spared the trauma, we could never speak meaningfully of having loved at all.' The doctor looked full and intently into the priest's face, he realised that this man really did understand human suffering. It was a kind of revelation to the doctor for which he expressed his sincere appreciation by nodding his head knowingly as though the priest had really hit a spot deep within the doctor's harrowed thoughts.

'Thank you, Father, for your patience and understanding. I hardly deserve it,' he said with an air of self-reproach. The priest simply spread his hands, indicating in their expression his absolute understanding without any need for an apology.

The doctor beaconed with both his hands for Larry to come closer to him. His voice was gentle and sensitive to the lad as he inquired after his departed mother. Larry moved towards him in slow uncertain movements. His past experiences with this doctor were far from endearing. When he was close enough the doctor rested his thin arm on Larry's upper back by way of comforting him. He was well aware of the lad's discomfort and guardedness. The doctor's words came almost in whispers as he peered into Larry's face much as a caring parent would. 'I need to ask you what happened to your mother. Where did she actually die?' Larry was still feeling raw and vulnerable. He was uncertain as to how to respond to the doctor. He showed no signs of being at ease with the medic and so indicated somewhat coldly with his head to the stairs above. The doctor removed his arm from Larry and indicated to the priest to accompany him upstairs. As they arrived in the simple bedroom the doctor turned to the priest and said softly. 'Is this where his mother died, Father?'

'I must be honest, Doctor Joe, I haven't seen her since my last visit when I brought her Holy Communion and anointed her,' the priest replied with his shoulders and facial expression indicating his own incomprehension. 'I have examined the entire house myself unknown to Larry. I was trying to spare him any more pain than he was going through. Anyway, there was no sign of her body anywhere. I don't know what to make of it, short of believing Larry's account of the matter, which in itself carries with it even greater problems.'

'In what way?' the doctor inquired thoughtfully.

'You can't imagine the reaction of the Church if this story breaks out in public. And break it will if no body is discovered.'

'Why should the Church concern itself with a missing body? Surely that's a police matter, Father?' The question was innocent enough on the doctor's part. The priest guessed that if the doctor had not stopped practicing his faith when he lost his wife in tragic circumstances, he would be more attuned to the religious implications. The priest put his hand on the doctor's shoulder and smiled whispering softly,

'How would the Church deal with a second ascension into heaven?'

The doctor stabbed his own forehead with his middle finger and raised his eyes. The penny suddenly dropped.

'O, for heaven's sake! Not another Church inquisition on top of everything else!' The priest nodded slowly and knowingly, his face, though attempting to smile, fell to resignation. The last thing in the world he needed was to be central to this situation. Both stared hard at the bedside cabinet which bore the simply framed photograph of Mary, her Husband, Brendan, and Larry as a child. Neither of them really took in the details of the photo; they were reflecting on their own troubled thoughts, imagining the problems ahead. Both stood for some time collecting their jumbled thoughts. Each of the company was aware of a very distinct perfume wafting throughout the room; neither took too much notice of it, both presuming that it most likely belonged to Lil. The doctor broke the silence as he moved silently into Larry's bedroom and small play room. There was nowhere on the upper floor capable of hiding a body, short of the attic which was only accessible through a ceiling hatch. He paused for a few moments considering whether or not to look within it but considered it really to be the duty of the police and not himself. The doctor, content that he did all he could to satisfy himself that no deceased person was present above stairs, went below again with the priest following. The doctor continued his search throughout the ground floor as unobtrusively as he could. He was satisfied that there was no body in the house and so turned to Larry.

'Larry,' the doctor began, his hand on Larry's upper back and his voice much softened, yet sufficiently loud for the rest of the company to hear. 'I need to ask you some questions concerning your mother. Do you understand me?' Larry searched the faces of his friends and rested a deferential gaze in particular on Father Kevin's face as though he expected him to answer the doctor's enquiry instead. The priest, smiling encouragement, nodded his head upward in an expression indicating that it was safe to co-operate with the doctor. With a little hesitation and awkwardness he complied.

'Yes, doctor. I do understand,' his lilting Cork city accent was at a higher pitch than the doctor's. For all his discomfort there was a growing assertiveness in Larry's voice. The doctor continued.

'Did your mother die upstairs, Larry, in her own room where she had been sick and confined to bed for several weeks... the same room where I came to see her?' Larry searched the faces of his friends once again before answering, his forehead lined and quizzical. The company too was wondering where his line of questions was leading. Again, Larry was hesitant with his answer.

'Yes. Mammy died upstairs,' he paused before adding with deliberate stress on each word, 'in – her – own – room.'

'What happened to your mother, Larry, since we cannot find any trace of her?' The doctor was looking directly into Larry's defensive face.

'She said she was going to heaven and she just disappeared from under me.' He said all this without the slightest attempt to justify himself.

'Disappeared from under you .... Can you explain that, Larry?'

'I was on the bed with her. I was holding on to her.' Larry's voiced raised and became more emotional as if reliving the tragedy. 'I didn't want her to die. I thought holding on to her might help to stop her dying.'

'Yet, she did die?' the doctor repeated for emphasis.

'Of course she died.' Larry showed his annoyance and shrugged away from the doctor's comforting hand. The lad went straight to Lil who immediately continued to rub his back and spoke to him in consoling whispers.

'It's ok, Larry. It's ok. He has to ask these questions. It will be all finished soon.' She was not convinced as to where the questions were leading. However, she felt that she had reason to trust the doctor who had earlier shared his own traumatic troubles with the whole company. Larry became somewhat more at ease in Lil's embrace.

The doctor persevered with his questions but not before moving his eyes across the faces before him and spreading his hands apologetically for the necessity of the sensitive nature of his questions. The company indicated their understanding sympathetically. So the doctor was given a general agreed consent to continue.

'Larry have you ever been to the funeral of a friend or relative before?'

'Yes, I have, my father's and his two brothers, Uncle Liam and Uncle Terry.' The names meant nothing to the doctor.

'Were they buried or cremated?' The doctor's questions grew shorter. He was attempting to hurry away from the obvious strain visible on Larry's face.

'Yerrah, they were all buried, doctor! What else would they be?' Larry annoyance heightened.

'You understand, then, Larry, that the usual end for any person who dies is to have a funeral and be buried or cremated?' Larry looked into the faces of his friends once more. They could see his vexation. His expression seemed to say, does he think I'm daft or something? His answer was somewhat hostile.

'Of course I know that they have to have a funeral and be burred or cremated!'

'So, you would agree, then, Larry, that in the case of your mother's death that the situation we find ourselves in is far from being accepted as normal?'

Larry shrugged his shoulders and replied sulkily, 'Of course it's not normal.'

The doctor smiled. The company could see the burden of his task fall away from him. They realised now that the doctor's line of questioning was an attempt to ascertain the mental capacity and state of Larry's mind and his general ability to comprehend the true reality of the situation in hand.

The doctor waited for some time to allow Larry to calm down. During this period he spoke in whispers to the company stating his intentions to examine Larry physically and enquire after his general health, much as he would do for any of his patients. The lull was an opportunity for refreshments. The general clatter of china was a welcome break from the intense atmosphere that had prevailed over the past hour. Father Kevin's stomach was beginning to rumble. He smiled at Lil and Seamus who were aware of the sound. The invitation to have a little to eat was written on their faces. 'A little sandwich wouldn't go amiss. I better not risk more with a meal prepared and waiting at home.'

The physical examination of Larry offered no concerns. His heart was sound, throbbing out a good strong beat. His pulse was also regular and his leg reflexes were sound. The doctor smiled as he patted Larry's back and moved aside indicating both his satisfaction and the completion of his work in the house. He deliberately caught Father

Kevin's attention and surreptitiously signed to him with a slight beaconing movement of his head.

'Father Kevin, you realise we have to call the police in the absence of a body? Whatever Larry claims both of us need to act within the expectations of our office.' The doctor spoke in whispers as he repacked his scuffed medical bag and took hold of his umbrella that left a pool of rain water where it had fallen over. 'If you wish me to hold on until the police arrive, Father, I will do so willingly so long as they are able to accommodate us with their presence reasonably soon.'

'That's very kind of you doctor Joe. I think that would be helpful in the long run. It may save us all being called at a later date to go over the whole unhappy episode again.' This agreed, the doctor volunteered to call the police. He informed them of the bare facts and that he and the priest would appreciate a visit at their earliest convenience.

It took the police little more than twenty minutes to arrive, to the express appreciation of both doctor and priest. It was now almost 2.30pm in the afternoon and as the officers entered the house they carried all the signs of heavy rain with them. They wiped their heavy boots on the threadbare piece of door matting. Poor Father Kevin felt like Judas, the betrayer. Yet for the good of all concerned, he thought, it was essential to be absolutely certain that nothing underhand had taken place. Two hefty uniformed Garda faced Father Kevin. He bowed slightly in respectful deference to the professional necessity of their presence. The two officers, a man and woman, removed their dripping peaked caps and returned their own silent nod to the priest, who indeed, was well respected and popular in the town for the very reason of his being with Larry in his time of trouble. Such typified the general pastoral concern that the priest had for all his charge. Their greeting for the doctor was more formal and curt since the severity of his character was widely known throughout the city.

'Doctor…' both officers voiced their greeting in unison and with a slight nod of the head. Their greeting then extended less formally to Seamus and Lil.

'Would you like us to leave?' Seamus addressed the officers.

'Are you related to the family?' The young woman officer inquired, her brow raised, her question put with professional courtesy.

'I think you will find their presence necessary, officers,' the priest suggested. 'It was their initiative that brought our attention to the situation. They are also as close to the family as if they were blood relations. They have been a great and intimate support to the family for many years.'

Since Larry was being comforted at the kitchen table with Lil's arm about him, the picture spoke volumes to the officers. Larry remained relaxed though still showed all the facial redness of one in recent tears.

'Enough said.' The male officer agreed.

Larry was well known to the Garda. He often waved to them or passed the time of day with them on the streets. They knew instinctively, before ever a word was spoken, that this innocent lad before them was incapable of the slightest malice. The truth was that they admired his open innocence and disarming child-like honesty. It was as though Larry anticipated the intention of their visit.

'Hello officers. Mammy is gone to heaven so she can't see you just now. But she will be back soon.'

It was a strange phenomenon, Father Kevin thought, as the Garda entered the house, how the authority of uniformed officers always seemed to fill the house with a sudden tangible gravity, as though some unseen omniscient presence manifested itself upon the entire dwelling.

'God bless you, Larry,' said the lady officer. 'Is that an invitation for us to wait for your mammy?'

'By all means, you're both welcome to wait, very welcome indeed ...' he added speculatively, 'but she didn't say how long she would be.'

'And how long do you think we might be waiting, Larry?' The measured question was posed with calm and unhurried sensitivity.

'Yerrah, she didn't say how long ... but she did say that she would be back soon.'

'Her male colleague realised that they had to examine the back garden for any signs of a burial. He whispered to his female counterpart to examine it while he would go up to the loft to see if there was any sign of a body there.

'If you don't mind, Larry, I will examine the loft above in case there was any damage to the roof from your poor departing mother.' It was doubtful that the lad would have grasped the irony of the remark. Certainly the officer did not mean it as a cheap jibe or mockery. He used a small wooden domestic type double extension ladder to climb into the loft. He didn't expect to find anything untoward. He moved about carefully among the wooden beams with the aid of his torch. There was nothing in the slightest way suspicious, nothing more than a collection of cobwebs and trunks full of discarded toys and rusting carpenters' tools. When the lady officer returned from the back of the house she whispered to her colleague, who was now descending the stairs.

'The back is a yard. There is no garden. There are no signs of any disturbance.'

The officers examined all other rooms in the house. They found nothing remotely suspicious.

'That beautiful fragrance, what flowers have you had in here?' The question was posed by the lady officer.

'It came when mammy left me and has been here ever since. Isn't it grand and all?'

'Grand indeed, Larry,' she replied, adding, 'Isn't it a pity we couldn't bottle it?' The whole company laughed at the unintentional witticism; it served to relieve the awkwardness created while the official search proceeded. The sweet aroma was so distinct that the woman officer, a very attractive fair-haired woman in her early thirties, though exaggerated in bulk with her padded and protective uniform, put a further related question. 'Did no one notice the aroma before me? It is very distinct,' she added. The entire company looked towards Lil. She expressed questionable surprise with her splayed hands and with one quizzical word leaping from her startled voice.

'What?'

The company smiled again, all except Larry who failed to grasp the speculative inference. All agreed that they thought it was Lil's perfume. To which Lil replied, 'I wish.' More laughter as her husband Seamus remarked teasingly,

'Never mind, Lil, I still love you as you are.'

'Seamus Madden. Are you making impertinent suggestions about my deodorant, or what?'

'Would I dare, Lil?' He received a fair kick below the table which took some of the smirk from his face. However, it was all light-hearted banter. Even Larry smiled; he was well accustomed to their teasing.

The male Garda addressed the priest and doctor in private. 'Well, Father ... doctor ... we can't do any more here. We will visit some more neighbours to ascertain when the good lady was last seen by any of them. If all agree that the disappearance cannot be explained. We will be forced to put her on the missing person's list. Sorry Father. No matter the innocence of Larry's account, we have to keep our feet on terra firma. I'm sure that should suit you too, Father. I know,' he added with some concern. 'The later you are forced to accept the lad's account, the more the Church will be spared one heck of a hullabaloo.' He scratched his head and added with a frown: 'A second Assumption into heaven is, I'm sure, without president, Father, would I be correct?' He was only reminding the good priest of what was already racing through his mind.

'We are actually talking about ascension, not an assumption officer. In either case I quite agree with the unwelcome consequences you refer to.'

The departing male officer added, as he held the door open for his colleague,

'There would be no merit in allowing this to go beyond the few souls that are familiar with the family.' All agreed with the officer and bid them both good day. The officers replaced their caps and hurried through the rain to their waiting vehicle. Shandon Rise was by now a virtual river running swiftly into the main road as the officers sped away.

Doctor Joe prepared to leave the company after excusing himself in a somewhat discomforted manner ... Although much changed in attitude from the traumatic and unexpected experience suddenly thrust upon him, he felt exposed and alone. This experience was not new to Father Kevin who surreptitiously observed the discomfort of the departing doctor. The priest's heart reached out to him. Father Kevin hurried across the kitchen to make a deliberate point of saying a very personal farewell.

'Doctor Joe, I would like to thank you for your much appreciated sensitivity to all concerned. I know it cannot have been easy, considering Larry's state and condition. I hope you might give me the pleasure of an unofficial visit at the presbytery; we might have a jar together?' The priest looked directly into the doctor's face with utmost sincerity, followed by a warm inviting smile.

'I would be happy to accept your invitation, Father Kevin. It's a long time since I paid a visit to any Church. I feel indebted to you for all the assistance you have given to me today. You have helped much more than you perhaps know. I felt you understood what I have been through. I am sorry it all came out involuntary in a very unprofessional way.'

'Please, doctor Joe; you have no need to excuse yourself for an involuntary outburst of grief.' The priest paused and added with gravity, 'God forbid that any of us should be unfortunate enough or forced to imprison such pain!'

'The poor doctor was close to tears when he replied, 'you are a very understanding person, Father Kevin – I feel humbled and fortunate to have met you. It will certainly be my pleasure to come and have a talk with you; and as you say, "to have a jar together."' The priest closed the door behind the doctor and gazed absentmindedly at the hallway floor, his thoughts engaged about the doctor's life. He hoped that the doctor was not going to an empty house and a life void of intimate friends. Presently, he broke away from his immediate thoughts, convinced it was pointless speculation. He felt sure that the doctor would be as good as his word; although he knew he needed to be philosophical about it. Long experience taught him that to hold one's breath for every one who promised to meet him, but never to be seen again, would be to die waiting. Yet he had a strong feeling about the doctor. He hoped that feeling would prove to be well-founded since he believed that both would benefit from the experiences of each other's work. The priest gave a warm but hurried farewell to the rest of the company. Assuring all that he would call again soon or when needed. With his blessing on all, he departed into the wet October streets. It was now 4pm by his watch as he sped away to his late afternoon meal, a hazard to which he had grown accustomed.

CHAPTER 5

Delilah Ferret Reporter Investigates

The news of Mary Walsh as a missing person, gleaned from the police report, was given a good deal of coverage in the local newspapers, television and radio. The main coverage fell into the hands of Delilah Ferret, a young unmarried woman of twenty four years, a reporter of remarkable bearing and competence. She was, however, one of those nasty probing individuals with a quick, sharp intelligence, a perfect body ... generally used to solicit her trade in any way she could. She drew all her energy and sense of existence and purpose by digging her literary talons deep into her vulnerable prey. She seemed born for that side of the media that had its conception in the gutter of human folly. She was a bully from her earliest days ... a manipulator of the most horrid and dangerous sort even during her school and university years. She had a genius for generating trouble, setting friends against each other by telling tales, petty remarks, normally of no consequence among friends, but in her hands, and revealed out of context and proportion, enough to have the most intimate friends at each others' throats. To think that she actually took the greatest pleasure in such perversion and in the generating of general mayhem, havoc and unease. She lived for this. Her only friends were those who had unwittingly become caught up in the net of her bile, all of whom were broken in turn and made the messengers, the tools of her poisonous pursuits. She knew that she was the object of other's hatred, yet this knowledge too was a source of perverted pleasure and power for her.

In the office of The City Vanguard, the most widely read Cork city newspaper, Delilah Ferret was considered the backbone of it's modern liberal views of life. No matter what the issue or story was she was given first choice of coverage. She was a kitten to the editor, both in his office and in his bed; though her sexual permissiveness was no more than a begrudged necessity. He was well aware that she didn't like sexual intimacies. She would lie as limp as a dead fish. He found the absence of her sexual response both frustrating and infuriating; yet he was ever drawn to her incredible beauty. She refused all kissing on the lips. Not that she was saving herself for someone more worthwhile; she simply experienced the whole sexual thing as disgusting, and especially kissing. She could just about bear to be kissed on the face. Ferret didn't have the slightest love for the editor; he was a necessary evil and convenience so long as he served her need to retain her status as goddess of the gutter in the news office. The editor Brendan Hawkswood, a forty-five year old married man with two adult children, was well aware of the atmosphere of hatred against her among the other journalists in the newsroom. He believed that she kept the other run-of-the-mill-reporters in their place and in competition with each other. All her fellow journalists, men and women alike, were not just weary of her, they were terrified. Jobs were scarce. Her colleagues acknowledged her presence with grimacing deference and sickly smiles. For her part she gloried in their deference and fawning subjection. She took the greatest pleasure in setting them against each other simply to gloat over their discomfiture and fall out. This was the vampire set loose on the story of Mary Walsh, the missing mother of her son, Larry.

She knew in her gut that there had to be mileage to the story of this particular old Lady with the peculiar halfwit-of-a-boy, as she referred to Larry. Ferret was very shrewd. She avoided calling at Larry's Mardyke home. Every sinister instinct of her twisted mind calculated that he would have able friends to support him. No. She knew it was only a question of time when she would meet him alone on the streets. It seemed to have been Larry's lot in life to walk the city streets with his mother or his with his close neighbours, the Madden family. Larry's neighbours usually took Larry for walks when his mother was unable to. Larry was free with his greetings to all. This, Miss Ferret had gleaned from street gossip. It took her the whole week of a very cold December to fall upon her prey. She spent several days waiting in a small inconspicuous old Volkswagen snooping car, usually parked in alternative spots along the narrow road of Shandon Rise. She only used her silver lotus for pleasure. She wore a dark blue padded weather coat, and faded light blue jeans and a light grey thermal head covering. Her silken blond hair hung from under her head-covering. The clothing did not flatter her exceptional and distinct beauty. Normally, her appearance was the kind of image you would expect to find posing seductively on glossy magazines or on the catwalks of high fashion. Her disguise was in keeping with her trade and personality. Even her natural beauty was little more a door to hell for the unsuspecting fool unfortunate enough to solicit her charms. There was no pressure put on her time by the editor. When she decided to hand in the copy of her story, he knew it was guaranteed to blast off on the front page; she never failed. Her success meant money, position and power for Ferret, the newspaper and for the editor, in that distinct order. Hawkswood, the editor, had a secure future so long as his marriage to the owner's daughter remained intact.

Ferret's waiting paid off. One frosty morning in early December Larry left the house alone. He wandered by the Mardyke River wall that ran along the main road. It was a beautiful setting. An avenue of swaying elm trees gave the road a distinct elegance. Larry was dressed in a dark blue, warm padded jacket with broad white and red stripes. He wore a black thermal head cover pulled over his ears to keep out the early December frost. The water running along the river's course was so clear that Larry could see the sparkling stones glinting from the riverbed. He leaned with both arms on the frost-covered stone wall – his hands clenched in a double fist. He watched strips of emerald streaming weeds ride the playing waters. These floating streamers suddenly engulfed his distraught mind as he thought of Christmas … Christmas without his beloved mammy. Suddenly he saw a vision of his mammy and daddy and himself swinging happily in their outstretched arms. They were all laughing in delight. Tears streamed down his face. The sparkle from the rippling river was hypnotic. It seemed to his swirling mind that even the river was sharing tears for his mammy. It was early Saturday morning with very few people about. As Larry leaned over the frosty wall he was only half conscious of the talking voice of his family coming from the crystal waters. As the vision of his family faded into the running waters he left out a piercing scream. His forehead now buried into the gloved fists of his hands. Scream after hysterical scream rang out into the streets. Passers-by thought him a drunk or a druggie suffering the horrors and aftermath of his own folly. His face was red and awash in blinding tears. Never in all his life did he feel as alone as he did at this very moment, more so because he couldn't even hold onto the phantoms of his visions. The poor lonely soul was utterly demented out of his mind, beyond all control. Added to his present wretched state, he was experiencing a recurrent nightmare ever since the death of his poor mother, and so found it impossible to get his usual uninterrupted sleep. His disturbing dreams cast him on a desert island all alone without shelter or food. He was aware of many ships passing both day and night. He could see that the passengers and crews of the ships were aware of his predicament, but all they would do was wave to him as he waved back franticly for help. They were always too far away from him to be of any help. His frantic nightmare always ended in the same way. The captain of one particular ship would stop and send a motor launch to the beach to pick him up. The crew always comprised of his next door neighbours, Seamus, Lil and children. The family would take him on board, their faces beaming with joy and offering him all the food and drink he desired. Then all would make their way back to ship, at which point Larry would wake up, usually soaked in perspiration. Larry felt so alone. Although his nightmares varied in detail, he had a gut feeling, an understanding of his own, that the only people who he could really rely upon were the Maddens. Every one else was friendly but too busy with their own lives to care with any degree of intimacy. People in general, Larry felt, were like ships passing in the night. Such was his general feeling of isolation and utter loss and sense of despair.

'How's your dear mother, Larry ... Any news...?' Ferret, the journalist, forced her attention on him as he leaned on the frost-covered wall; her intrusion into his grief shocked him out of his distraught turbulence. She looked down into his face with the sweetest smile. Her voice was inviting and warm. She read his startled face and could see the discomfort in the furrowed lines between his grey blue eyes. There was no reciprocal smile on his tear-run face. Although Larry was usually open and exceptionally friendly to most people, he was taken off guard by Ferret's intrusion. His expression was one of total confusion and loss; he couldn't quite figure out why.

'I don't think I know you,' he remarked still wearing a tense expression, which was really out of character for him; usually he was the one to greet strangers in his innocent mannerly way.

'Of course you don't know me, Larry. I do apologise for my intrusion.' She stuck a gloved hand almost into his face as he was turning around to face her. Involuntary, he stood erect and took her hand but not before he removed his thermal glove as a habitual sign of respect taught to him by his beloved parents.

'Delilah Ferret, Larry. We printed the news of your missing mother in our newspaper .... Glad to meet you.' Her smile was icy, little more than self-asserting intrusion – a total indifference to his utter bewildered state of grief. She had heard his piercing screams but brushed them aside as the ranting of a lunatic, which she believed him to be.

'... Any news at all, Larry? You know that you are both widely known throughout the city ... you and your dear mother.' Her flattery was put as a carrot before a stubborn donkey to make it advance forward. That was how she considered him. Larry simply shrugged his shoulders and remarked curtly,

'So what...?'

'Odd though ... don't you think, Larry ...? Gosh!' She exclaimed in childlike pretence, 'if it was my mother who was missing, I most certainly would not be leaning on this frosty Mardyke wall early on a Saturday morning. Gosh ...!' She exclaimed once again in pretence of concern. 'I would be out looking for her myself. I certainly wouldn't depend on the police or anyone else, I wouldn't be looking into a river hoping she might turn up there.' Her remarks were beginning to peel at Larry's smarting wounds. Something deep within his instinct that he could not articulate in his state convinced him that his first defensive reaction to her intrusion was well founded.

'Of course I'm not looking for mammy in the river,' he snapped. 'She's gone to heaven and she is coming back to help me, mammy promised ....' This comment and Larry's snapping at her ignited an explosion of contempt within her. The fruit of the nut was revealed, she thought. Attack the Church for filling an innocent's head with manipulating nonsense, she thought. She had an angle of one aspect of the story, if all else failed. She knew the Catholic Church in Ireland was awash in scandal and with ever-dwindling congregations.

She took no notes ... used no pen or pencil ... didn't bother with any journalist's jotter; she relied solely on a tiny daisy broach barely visible on the lapel of her padded jacket. The yellow centre of the daisy was a clever little microphone wired up to a small digital recorder in the inner pocket of her coat. Miss Ferret didn't miss a trick. In fact her private recordings were kept in a secure vault which contained all the poison of every person of consequence that crossed her path; it included the editor of her newspaper. He too was recorded and filed; their most intimate conversations in bed were to Ferret an assured investment, dare he dismiss her on any pretext ... he too would be in for a rude awakening when it suited her. Scandal was the life blood of her existence ... the fangs of her depraved world ... a world where she was the shining light at the expense of her prey's dark follies. She also kept a small digital camera in her jacket pocket.

'How do you know that your good mammy has gone to heaven?' She continued probing with provocation. 'I mean, did you see her ascend ... go up like a rocket or something?' She wanted Larry to snap again – hoping for some more nonsense to distort.

'I know she disappeared from under me as I lay on the bed crying and holding onto her. I didn't want her to die, to be taken away from me. I loved her so much. Now I have no family. She just died and disappeared. The doctor examined the house; the priest examined the house; the officers examined the house; and my friends Lil and Seamus, my next door neighbours, they too examined the house. Mammy just disappeared. She could not be found. In any case,' he added matter-of-factly, 'she said she had to go to heaven to ask holy God to help me.'

The more she heard of this crap, the more she felt utter contempt for all who put this nonsense into his head. Not that she cared a tinker's toss for Larry or his grieving predicament. Ferret, a Catholic by upbringing, was by choice and lifestyle a vehement atheist and equally as vehement an opponent of the Church and every other religion having a supposed Creator God in its creed. Her life's creed was instinctively Darwinist and evolutionary and all stations to outright and unadulterated Atheism, vehemently expressed in "The God Delusion." by Richard Dawkins, the "mechanism man," as some Creationist's mockingly named him, because they saw in his science a purely genetic view of humanity; how man came into being through evolution ... man who was capable of great things but ultimately was no more than a collection of genes surviving for their own ends. But this, according to the fundamental Creationist's camp, was utter nonsense. They saw genes as no more than the machinery, the slaves, the mechanisms at the service of the driver, human intelligence. Genetics didn't do anyone's thinking for them.

Delilah Ferret used her atheist conviction as a means to live on the outer edge of every virtuous norm. Her conviction told her that since there can't be a God, all human morality, ethics, Law and order, human virtue, were all no more than a bit in the mouth to control the ineffectual. Her motto was, Grab all you can, any way you can, because you pass this way only once; and since there is no ultimate consequence to one's behaviour beyond the grave, you might as well live life as if you alone were its most important subject. Obstacles, human or otherwise, were there to be pushed aside or walked upon if need be. Her belief was that any kind of order usually favoured the rich, powerful and privileged few who controlled its boundaries. That is where she wanted to belong; even in such a privileged society, she would use it for her own ends and by every means possible. She was, in short, very much drawn to nihilism, the rejection of all religious and moral principles; the doctrine that nothing has real existence.

Ferret, now filled with utter contempt, wasted no more of her precious time with Larry. She didn't even bother with the courtesy of bidding him good day; she just walked away to her Volkswagen and sped away, leaving Larry to his frosty scene and to stare after the black smoke billowing our from her snoop's car. He looked after her ... his mouth open ... his face a total stage of incomprehension. Inwardly he thought that she must be the rudest woman he ever met. What would mammy and daddy make of her? He thought quietly to himself.

Later in the morning Ferret visited Larry's doctor after making an appointment to see him, making pretence of her concern for Larry. Once the doctor realised that she was form The City Vanguard, he showed her the door out very swiftly. The only information she gleaned from him was that, 'Yes, he did see Larry. Yes, he was aware of his loss and his missing mother.' He offered no more and made her aware in a most waspish expression, of a patient's right to privacy. She left his practice in grimaced irritation. He would be another target for the future. With all the patients in the practice, with five other doctors, there was bound to be a slip up sooner or later. She had all the time in the world, she thought. His fall would await the pleasure of another day, she considered with neurotic venom.

Later in the afternoon Ferret visited Larry's neighbours. When she introduced herself as a reporter from The City Vanguard, Both Seamus and Lil scowled at her. They were raging with vexation.

'You're some fecken bitch!' said Lil, the veins in her neck rippling with white anger.'

'Don't you dare call me a bitch ... you don't know me from the man in the moon,' Ferret retorted with equal vehemence.

'Don't know you ... you little brat,' said Seamus, equally outraged. He continued – his face red with temper. 'You left that poor lad in a right mess this morning after poking your snotty nose into his grief and his personal business. God woman! You've got some bloody gall! Go on, feck off out of here before I set the dogs on yeah. You bloody hard-faced bastard.' Lil pulled her husband from the door and slammed the door in her face but not before she shouted after her:

'Go back and wipe your arse with that rag you call a newspaper. Go on with yeah; you bloody bitch; feck off.'

The Maddens were not in the habit of being so rude to strangers. They were normally very welcoming to all. It was their natural way. Their large circle of family and friends rooted them in a hospitable culture and character. Parties were thrown in their house at the slightest excuse. However, when Larry came to them for his lunch the same day after encountering Ferret, he was in tears; he revealed his meeting with some woman from a newspaper. It left his good neighbours and friends picking up the pieces of Larry's shattered day.

Miss Ferret left the Maddens in a state of white rage. She was half crazed in broiling temper as she sped off to her home. She didn't want anyone to see her so out of control. As she entered her lavish apartment and slammed the door shut on herself; she removed her fur-lined boots and flung them at the wall; she ripped off her padded coat as if it were a personal enemy that dared embrace her and flung it across the apartment, then burst into tears; still shaking in rage.

She had no certain plans for the evening and decided to stay in for the night to try to regain her lost composure.

After slamming her digital pocket recorder into the security of her combination safe, an instinctive defensive habit, she grabbed a bottle of whisky from a well-stocked bar and poured out a half tumbler of the amber liquid, spilling a good quantity of it as her hands rattled the bottle and glass in pulsating spasms. Her mind spun out of control. She craved to do damage…to make someone pay for this day. She could never have foreseen that the earlier success she had achieved with Larry's vulnerable condition would backfire on her and leave her sense of self-importance in such shattered discomposure. She had met her match in Larry's neighbours.

As she slowly regained some semblance of control, helped by the effects of the amber liquid, she tried to focus her mind on all the connections, as she thought of them, in any way related to Larry Walsh and his missing mother. She meant to visit the priest later on the Saturday evening, but since it was late and the priest would have a vigil service for the weekend, so she figured; and given her unexpected rejection from the Maddens, she thought she would leave the priest until Monday. She presumed, rightly or wrongly, that he might be more amenable to an interview if she avoided his workload on the Sunday; it was for her own advantage, not the priest's.

Ferret had no real friends. Anyone who got close to her she made subservient and deferential; they became mere objects of her use rather than the subjects of her love or affection; all were kept at arm's length. To any other person in her position in life, one might be able to speak meaningfully of their loneliness. However, in her case, she was too self-possessed ... too self-indulgent ... too wrapped up in her own imagined self-importance to experience a conscious sense of loneliness. It was akin to the lunatic having no concept of what most people considered "normal". She alone stood firm while the rest of the population were kept in orbit round her; she was the sun in her own universe where all else depended upon her existence; a solipsist to the core ... her own existence being all there was to life.

She fell into a drunken sleep before the TV. Even in her dreams she was fighting a war with the world outside the impregnable fortress of The City Vanguard; naturally she was the heroine, slaying all before her with un-wavering energy and confidence. She was young, for sure; even so, she was a classic candidate for a mental institution at some stage in her life. Her neurotic existence, would eventually, burn out like any overloaded fuse. However, like so many who are young and lacking the experience of age in body and mind, convince themselves of their own invincibility.

She awoke late on Sunday morning with a hangover. She gazed with bleary eyes at the half used bottle of whiskey. She cursed her abuse and set about making breakfast. Her watch, after several bleary-eyed attempts to focus on it, told her it was 11.30am. She raised her hands defensively to shield her eyes from the bright December sun. The pastel-blue vertical window blinds had been left open all night. Under normal circumstances she took pride in keeping her luxurious apartment in pristine condition. Now she just kicked aside last night's debris from the floor where she had flung all her outer clothing. She decided, with tottering deliberation, to leave the cleaning until she felt more composed. She forced herself to eat some buttered toast and finished two mugs of steaming coffee.

The aroma of the toast helped in part to take away the stink and staleness of her alcohol-fumed breath. She was usually fastidious about her meals and personal cleanliness, even though she always dined alone. She finished her skimpy breakfast with her eyes closed the whole time, the coffee mug in one hand and the other hand propping up her chin. After forty-five minutes on her watch, which she removed after reading it, she stripped off completely and went into the wet room to have a shower.

She had a perfect, beautiful body. Hers was not the skeletal beauty of the catwalks that belonged to high fashion. It seemed such a wasted gift on Delilah Ferret who was so rotten to the core on the inside. No amount of washing could ever cleanse her character. As the suds of the shower gel and steaming spray slid swiftly down the contours of her beautiful body, her hands were pressed into her hair with some force as if she was washing the hateful world out of it. After drying off, she put on a beautiful blue, Chinese-patterned, silk dressing gown and set about blow-drying her silken blond hair. Fresh coffee followed in the process. The noise of the dryer and boiling kettle irritated her strained nerves.

Her lounge comprised of a long black settee and three easy chairs to match ... all square-shaped; a glass oval-shaped tabletop carried by glinting brushed aluminium legs ... a flat silver-coloured T.V. set and music centre to match. She rarely fully opened the vertical powder-blue blinds that swept across the walls of glass surrounding her apartment; instead, she walked about in their striped shadows like a camouflaged prowling cat or sat listening to documentaries on T.V. or listening to soothing relaxation music or Gregorian chant which contradicted her nasty character. It was as if she was at home with the symbiotic contradiction of religious hatred, yet cherry-picking from the genre of its music so long as it fulfilled her own ends. The doors of her apartment were painted to correspond with a general powder blue theme. Light coloured cushions served to prevent the apartment from taking on the atmosphere of a funeral parlour; the entire flat took on an elegant appearance with the use of ultra modern materials. The apartment rarely appeared to be used; it usually gave the strong impression of pristine newness and a certain sense of luxury mixed with a distinct coldness. The entire floor space comprised of hardwood parquet flooring highly glossed in a very tough coating; there were also some white crescent-shaped mats close to her seating.

Her personal choice of reading comprised mainly of three areas of interest: ancient world histories, from the primitive to the ancient civilisations and cultures of Egypt, Greece, Rome, China and other emerging cultures of the period; the second group of literature was modern and some ancient philosophies and primitive religions: she was particularly conversant with the likes of Jean-Paul Sartre, usually associated with being an atheist existentialist, Friedrich Nietzsche, who was explicitly opposed to Christianity as involving a slave morality; she also had works on Darwinism, and the more recent works of Stephen Hawking, A Brief History of Time; and several works by Richard Dawkins including The Selfish Gene; River Out of Eden and The God Delusion, the latter's books usually works deliberately written as polemics against all religions, especially those that specifically believed in a divine God as the origin of creation and as a Divine Being of human worship She was by choice and character a Nihilist, one who rejects all established authority and institutions. From these works and her general attitude to life, it was plain to see where her insatiable diet for anti-religion was fed. The last category mainly consisted of the lighter side of life. She had many videos of rugby, football, and boxing.

She had no interest in sports usually associated with women. In fact her general hostility towards women as the giggling playthings of men and the painted clowns of the cosmetic industry filled her with a loathing that was seriously neurotic. She avoided parties in general, refusing to hide her icy irritation with frivolous small talk. She preferred the company of men, but not for their benefit. For all her anti-social traits, she would endure any situation that promised to further her sniping career supplying the victims that had fallen from grace to be cremated in the acrid ink of The City Vanguard. She rarely failed to come up with the metaphorical corpses of human folly ... nor did she fail to meet deadlines. That was not for the benefit of her editor ... he too was a pending corpse when it suited her to destroy him. No. It served her needs to kick life in the face at her own indulged convenience. Human misery was the blood she sucked for the stimuli of her own depraved existence.

CHAPTER 6

Ferret visits the
Priest –Nell's supporting role

Monday came with a bitterly cold and powerful wind storming its way across Cork city; blasting at every swinging sign and tearing madly at demented flags, whistling and screaming through every building. Miss Ferret was driving along the wind-battered streets to keep an appointment she had made with Father Kevin Noonan at St. Patrick's Parish Church presbytery. She purposely used her second car, a silver-grey Lotus. She was sure that its appearance outside the windows of the presbytery would be an irritation to the priest, of whom she was informed, on good authority, lived a frugal existence in a spirit of empathy and solidarity with the starving poor of the Third World and for the poor of his own unemployed people of Ireland in general. His world was lived in the spirit of the call from the wider Church to live simply. As she pulled up outside the presbytery windows, so she gave the horn a good strong blast to create as much attention as possible of her momentous arrogant arrival and better for the car to be seen. The net curtains of the house were drawn apart, much to her delight. She waved a mocking gloved hand to the priest with an attitude of utter indifference to the polite norms of a visitor. Father Kevin allowed the curtain to slide and reposition itself, but not before he took a mental snapshot of the silver Lotus. He noted the quality of the visitor's ankle-length morning-grey overcoat with its generous fur-lined hood and the flaps of its pockets and lapels tastefully contrasted in black velvet. She wore high comfortable fur-lined boots, those too in a beautiful light shade of grey. She was every inch the lady of luxury and very self-willed. He noted too her rich sparkling clear blue eyes. He took his time in answering the constant noise of the doorbell where she fixed her gloved finger. As well as keeping her finger on the bell she knocked loud and constantly hoping to cause as much upheaval and disturbance as possible. She was certainly making a bold statement of her arrival, the priest thought.

He opened the heavy bottle-green door and offered his hand saying with a dismissive smirk, sufficient to deflate her arrogance, 'Mrs. Murphy, Yes? Is it about the church cleaning, or are you her daughter?' The priest held his smirking expression; a battle of wits had instinctively begun. Ferret was taken aback. She refused to take his hand, which the priest promptly withdrew. She could not have imagined a priest putting her down like that.

'I have an appointment with you, in case you have forgotten. My name is Ferret, Delilah Ferret.' she retorted, visibly irritated.

'Ah, yes; from The Ireland's Own, Yes?' The priest was really mocking her now, all the while braving the blasting wind at the door so that she would be made as uncomfortable as possible. Ferret snapped at the priest.

'I am not in the habit of reading comics,' she retorted contemptuously. [Ireland's Own was a simply-produced, non-glossy weekly magazine, a favourite among traditionalists across Ireland and way beyond its shores. It had something for everyone; it was aimed specifically at family entertainment and interest with something for all ages including very young children who could join in with colouring simple pictures. It contained many traditional pieces, including ghost stories; contacts for pen friends; outstanding potted biographies of the renowned world and local characters; there were facts on science and world cultures. It's most guarded and prized character which was held in great esteem both by its owner, editor and readers, was the fact that nothing smutty, not even a hint of it would be allowed onto its pages. That was the main point of the priest's deliberate sarcasm. The contrast between Irelands Own and the supposedly sophisticated newspaper, The City Vanguard, were worlds apart]

The Madden family, the new guardians of Larry had already warned the priest concerning Ferret's meeting with the vulnerable, grieving Larry.

'I work for a mature paper – The City Vanguard – designed for intelligent and mature discerning adults.' Ferret spat out each phrase pausing between each.

'Ah, yes.' Father Kevin returned with pretence at being harmlessly philosophical.

'There is always that, maturity and discernment ... like the need to leave the meat of a shot pheasant to hang and rot before considering it suitable for human consumption. I suppose 'tis all a matter of taste, eh?' By now the priest was fully prepared to swap insulting inferences with her.

Ferret made no reply; instead, she brushed past him in the dark hallway to force her way out of the powerful, blasting wind. The priest stepped back in exaggerated fashion to emphasise her lack of manners, respect and common decency. It seemed to him that no amount of his obvious displeasure was going to make one iota of change to her arrogant manner.

He pointed her to the lounge, the room from where he had been made aware of her arrival. She was ushered to a hard dining room chair; his usual ploy for those he hoped would not be staying long. He also favoured such a seat for himself as a support for his troublesome back – a relic from his building site days before he joined the priesthood. The priest's gesture for her to take a hardback seat was wasted on her since he shared the same choice for himself. Before she sat down she removed her warm coat and flung it aside onto a nearby faded-brown, leather easy chair.

As she placed herself on the hard chair the priest was forced to swallow a great lump in his throat. Miss Ferret, with her breath-taking beauty was virtually naked in her choice of dress. Not only was the cleavage in her silken white shirt little more than a bikini top, the transparent silken top also revealed quite plainly that she was not using a bra at all. The warm glow of her youthful firm breasts and nipples were clearly visible. To add to the priest's further discomfort and distraction, she wore the flimsiest of grey skirts, little more than a pelmet. As she sat there, her silk white panties clearly showing, she pretended to be looking about her as though eying up the character of the old fashioned dark polished furniture in the room. She suddenly turned to stare directly at the priest. She could see without any shadow of doubt that he was totally transfixed with distraction.

Before either of them opened the meeting, Nell, the elderly housekeeper, entered the sweetly-perfumed room.

The priest, fortunately, had taken precautions to arrange for her presence. Indeed, whenever there was the least cause for concern, as with the present situation, Nell would naturally be included in the meeting. The half naked Miss Ferret had never reckoned on or made provisions for the likelihood of such an event. That in itself indicated that she was not a regular attendant at church, or she would have know about the presence of his housekeeper.

Nell took one glance at the half-smirking and surprised young woman in the chair and immediately left the room to return within seconds with a red-patterned travelling rug which she promptly wrapped round the visitor in a flurry of pretentious motherly concern.

'You poor child ... you must be frozen to the bone. Father Kevin, why do you keep the place so cold on a December morning with the wild wind outside strong enough to blow the very house asunder?' As she spoke, Nell winked surreptitiously at Father Kevin; he knew perfectly well that the room was comfortably warm and that all Nell's antics were elaborate ploys for Father Kevin's benefit and dignity. All the while Nell spoke she could feel the beautiful visitor wriggling to remove the blanket. Nell held on as if wrestling with a wilful child. Nell's actions, which would be considered extreme under most circumstances, were eventually accepted as the youthful journalist found it too embarrassing to continue the struggle.

'You poor child, did your mammy bring you here in the car? Dear! Dear! Dear! Imagine the kind of a mother who would allow her little child to come out at all in this weather and only half dressed. Oh dear! Oh dear! What kind of times do we live in at all? Would you like some hot milk, or a glass of orange?' Nell continued to hold on to the visitor and yet at the same time to pat her cheek as one might a little child. All the fuss and motherly exaggeration only served to exasperate the journalist. However, Ferret had two choices, as she read the situation; either she stays, but wrapped up like one rescued from drowning, or fling off the blanket and storm out. One thing was certain; she knew instinctively that if she dared to uncover herself now in the presence of this formidable over-protecting silver-haired, old grandmother, she would be tossed out on her beautiful arse. To add insult to injury Nell continued to make much of sniffing around the journalist purposely to provoke her in the hope that she might loose all sense of control and storm out.

'Child,' said Nell, with her brow lined in quizzical mockery, 'has someone washed you in disinfectant? Gosh! It's fierce powerful and no mistake.' She turned to Father Kevin who was fit to burst a gut trying to contain his inward hysterics. 'Do you not get the smell, Father? Aren't you quick enough to complain if you can smell the fish cooking from the kitchen?' The truth was that the perfume worn by the journalist was not just outrageously expensive: it also had the most beautiful fragrance. This pretence of scolding the parish priest seemed in some extraordinary way to pacify the journalist; who really wished that the old grandmother-of-a-housekeeper would just drop dead and leave herself to deal with the priest. Before sitting beside Father Kevin, the old silver-haired housekeeper pinched the journalist's cheek in mock imitation of an act more in keeping for a child. The journalist took a deep breath and put a strained damper on her mounting irritation before she gained some semblance of self control. Now she spoke with some deliberation and sarcasm.

'Now, hopefully, this bloody pantomime is over, we can get on with the reason for my being here.' She didn't wait for a reply. As dazzlingly beautiful as she was, her expression was of one ready to spit poison. She continued. Her beautiful silk, shoulder-length blond hair swung about her pouting, sulky face, animating her irritation. 'I had a meeting with the son of the missing woman, what's her name …?'

'Mary Walsh ….' The priest interrupted her immediately and added grimly, 'ah, yes, the unofficial meeting by the Mardyke River wall early on Saturday morning. Yes, indeed. The Madden family, his neighbours and friends, were forced to console the tearful lad for the rest of the day.' The priest grimaced. Nell was well aware of the incident; she too looked severe and added:

'A terrible shame that. I didn't realise your superiors allowed a teenage apprentice journalist to carry on in such a fashion.'

'Look, I came to interview you, Father Noonan, not your grandmother too.' The housekeeper held back from reacting to the journalist's designed insult. The priest responded.

'You don't attend St. Patrick's church, do you Miss Ferret?'

'What the hell has that got to do with anything?' she snapped angrily.

'Well, Miss, if you were using our church, or any Catholic church in the city, you would know that a priest is not accustomed to being left on his own with under-aged teenagers on their own, unless of course, you wish me to hear your confession, in which case you may come to the church and have open confession. Nell, here, would be glad to facilitate without overhearing either of us. This … for both our protection, you understand.'

'I'm no teenager, nor am I in need of confession to a God who doesn't exist.'

'Now there's a surprise for us all, Father Kevin,' Nell intervened. 'She hasn't left her teenage years yet ... Imagine that! You know, Father, I always knew that one day I would meet up with a perfect saint; free from all stain of sin. And now I have met one, so beautiful and all; sure 'tis no wonder she doesn't need confession. She doesn't need to believe in God; sure, isn't the child already saved ... I mean, being free from all stain of sin. Isn't that a grand thing to encounter on a cold December Monday?' The Journalist didn't react to the housekeeper's mockery.

'Of course you're not in need of confession,' the priest intervened. It is a pity really, Miss Ferret.' Father Kevin was now studying her face as he pursued his point. 'You know, Miss Ferret, confession is a great relief to the soul and in the hands of the right confessor, it can lead to a deeper appreciation of one's self and one's motives for doing the things we do. We can all benefit from it either at a psychological level that promotes self-understanding, or at the spiritual level that brings us closer to an authentic sense of closeness to the God who draws us to himself in a communion of love. You see, Miss Ferret, none of us can love God when we are full of hate within ourselves for other people.'

'If you have quite finished your sermon ...' Miss Ferret's face was now contorted with utter contempt for the company; her attitude was aimed at both of them. She resented their smug offensiveness and their superior attitudes. 'Confessions!' she spat the word out with utter revulsion; more so because she had already made her atheist position clear.

Nell's jibes and sarcasms were completely out of character for her; she was usually the soul of discretion with long-practiced courtesy, even more so with strangers. Her present attitude to Miss Ferret was really in support, respect and protection for her friend and priest. Nell was far from feeling comfortable with her own defensive attitude; it came as if the priest was a little child in need of protection from Ferret's designed seduction. On Ferret's part, she never missed a trick to compromise her prey.

Nell had the deepest love for the priest in a motherly way. They had been staunch friends from the onset of his first appointment after his ordination in his thirtieth year. Now in his fiftieth, she was as close as ever to him. As housekeeper she always moved with him whenever he was expected to take over a new parish. He didn't treat her like one of the housekeepers of old who were kept at arm's length. No. In Nell's case, he shared with her the deepest and lightest conversation ... as intimate as sole friends will.

Ferret returned to pursue her subject. 'This strikes at the very purpose of my being here,' she pressed onward with her dismissal of the priest's patronising attitude, as she experienced it. 'That poor distraught Lad ... what's-his-name ...?' She paused awkwardly, to her own embarrassment.

'Ah! Of course,' the priest intervened sarcastically, 'your deep concern for Larry, no doubt, is the cause of your temporary lapse of memory.' Nell's chin dug deeper into her chest in an effort to prevent her from smiling, but not before Ferret became aware of her supporting mockery. Ferret didn't react outwardly to either of them; inwardly, her hatred was given yet another layer of her bitter compost. She pressed on:

'This, lad ...'

'Larry,' the priest interjected.

'This lad ...' she repeated, ignoring to the priest's goading. 'He insists that his mother ...' she stumbled over her name.

'His dear mammy, Mary, God be good to her.' The priest was just slightly less mocking.

'Anyway .... He insists that she is gone to heaven and is coming back to visit him. My problem with all this, Father Noonan,' she dragged out his name contemptuously; 'is the false support that the Church gives to his likes in their loss.'

'Of course, Miss Ferret, your gracious concern for the family may be misunderstood, given that your initial coverage of Mary's death inferred the likelihood of foul play, even murder; and your goading of the grieving lad by the Mardyke River seemed more like your hope of entrapping the innocent lad into compromising him in order that you might animate the columns of the slop bucket you refer to as a newspaper. Your deliberate speculation, with regard to the innuendos in your article, created a large shadow of suspicion on the grieving lad's life ... as if his pain was not already more than he could bear.'

The yokes of respect and decency were removed from the Priest's and Ferret's vying minds; both were now in the front line of confrontation and insult ... trenches had been dug by both hostile parties.

'No, Miss Ferret,' the priest continued: 'I think that Larry will be shown more love, care, and support and respect from his supporting community that has his best interests at heart; these are people close to God.' The priest's grey-blue eyes burned in his unflinching hostile glare at Ferret.

'What part of, there is no such person as God, do you both fail to understand? I mean ... really.' She struggled to free her hands from being wrapped up like a mummy in the red-checked travel blanket. It was all very comical, the priest thought. When she did manage it, she was careful to keep her provocative semi-nakedness covered; she didn't want a repetition of the earlier wrestling match that resulted in a farcical embarrassing pantomime. Once free she extended her delicate hands in an expression of incredulity as she continued in mocking contempt. 'I mean to say ... evolution is proven and scientifically established without any shadow of doubt to any intelligent person. Let's face it, we are all no more than intelligent animals, at least some of us are,' she added, directing her insult and contempt at the two facing her; considering them both as roving dinosaurs who should be hung up by now in a museum. To nail her point home she added: 'No brain, Father Noonan, means no after life; we are our brain. You only get one bite at this life's apple. When was the last time you heard of anyone come back from the dead?' Delilah Ferret was on home ground now; her confidence beamed in the smugness of her contemptuous grimace.

'Of course you will not be familiar with the Holy Bible, Miss Ferret, will you?' the priest remarked provocatively. How Jesus appeared to witnesses ... his followers, after his death.'
    'Bible ...! Bloody bible ...! Holy ...! Holy be damned! The only thing holy about that collection of mumbo jumbo is that its holiness goes with it being full of holes ... a

collection of fairytales … Jewish tribalism … mere Jewish propaganda designed to intimidate their surrounding neighbours and control their own gullible, fear-subjected nation; an autocracy of religious zealots and dictators, taking their cue from the Egyptian pharaoh's who kept them in slavery and subjection for decades. Don't you realise that most of the troubles in the Middle East today have their roots in the history of those so called God-favoured, God's chosen people? Occupying by force the lands of the surrounding pagans at the so-called consent and direction of a slaughtering war-hungry God? An authority hell bent on justifying their nonsense merely to prevent intermarriage with uncircumcised pagans. And yet it was quite in order to put all the conquered pagan inhabitants under the ban! Put simply, Father Noonan, the ban meant the butchery of innocent men women and children.' Her very expression was one of utter contempt and rage … her voice echoing loudly in the room. The expression of disgust on her face was sufficient to burn holes in her antagonists opposite.

'Ah!' said the priest mockingly,' when she had paused from her diatribe, 'so you do believe as factual, some events at least in the Holy Bible. Maybe you could be accused of cherry-picking the passages that serve your contempt for God and all who believe in the Son who came to reveal his character of Love for all peoples. Perhaps you have never considered that if it had not been for Jewish prophetic wisdom and their ongoing development, that we might all be still worshipping the images and idols of animals, human figureheads of authority such as the dynasties of the pharaohs, the pantheon of Roman gods and emperors and kings, the planets, and all Greek mythology; all of these believed by the masses to have divine status, as many still believe in today. Have you never read John's Gospel where God is said to be Love, that never to have loved was never to have known God? Or have you never experienced the development of the Jewish people who came to understand that God, indeed, "... has no favourites?" These being the words of Peter, himself a Jew, as he spoke to Cornelius and his household who had converted to faith in Christ. Or have you never read Paul's words, and he one of the staunchest of Jews of his time; how he came to the same conclusion when he acknowledged that, God makes no distinctions between Jew or Greek; male of female; slave or free?'

'And who is cherry-picking now, Father Noonan? We all know how much your own Roman Church makes many distinctions between the status of men and women.' She took a perverse and mocking delight in drawing out his name in contemptuous syllables. She added. 'Would this be the same Son of God who promised to burn God's created creatures in Hell, in a fire that will never go out?'

Ferret added: 'all this, because this so-called Creator gave us a natural disposition for imperfection? Do me a favour!' She let out a long teeth-clenched hiss. The expression of contempt on her face was like a spill of red-hot lava.

'You know, Miss Ferret, we all change as we come to understand more. We move from positions that were once considered sacrosanct. Surely there is no shame in discarding the dirty water of error so long as we keep the child of wisdom for further cleansing.'

'You are quite the philosopher of convenience, Father Noonan, but wisdom is not the preserve of Christianity, if it has any wisdom at all.'

'Well, Miss Ferret, I will concede that Love and care for all people is not the preserve of any particular denomination; but your atheism, seems to me, to be the worship of a genetic god that gives function to the mechanism of our physical nature. We do not consult our genetics as to where we wish to go; nor would the driver ask the donkey where it wants to go. We design our own way forward and learn from our errors.'

Father Kevin felt that he could be teasing out so many metaphorical details of the Holy Bible all night. It was obvious to him that Miss Delilah Ferret had no desire or willingness to discuss with a deeper understanding the nature, composition, and wide expanse and contextual circumstances in the compilation of such a complex collection of books that made up the Holy Bible. In his heart he knew that her visit was not about concern for the grieving Larry; it was really about a contest between the two camps of Evolutionists and Creationists. This he could handle and hold his own; what he did not wish to get involved in with her, just now, was the bait she was cleverly offering him. He knew that she was goading him to say something controversial such as admitting that he, and most, if not all fellow priest with half a brain, did not accept the bible as a book of facts; but that it was an ongoing history of the development of one particular people and their interpretation of Jewish, prophetic understanding and historical interpretation.

'I think, Miss Ferret,' the priest said looking at his watch, 'that we could be trading disagreements all day and night on the subject of the Christian faith. Though I respect your views, I most certainly do not share them. You put your faith in science and evolution and that no God lies beyond our world or in it. Certainly we nominate for ourselves who or what we believe God to be. Modern

Christian faith, as many conclude, rests on the fact that Love is God. It is obvious to me and to any thinking person, that if we are no more than a collection of replicating genes evolving into ... God knows what, human life itself would have no ultimate moral or ethical meaning beyond this life. In which case, there would be no point to our ultimate virtuous, moral or ethical actions. Murder, rape, robbery, violence, would be the better way ahead for those without power position or influence, since all would have only "one bite at life's apple", as you insist. What possible purpose would there be to living a good life? What would it all amount to? As one of your advocates insists, "...The universe owes no one comfort." If you wish to plant your field of life with the seeds of atheism, you will reap what you sow. It will not take long for the followers of your creed to realise that nothing they do has any meaningful relevance beyond the grave; that even the worst hedonistic debauchery would have no ultimate consequence; that living a good life would be for fools and the feeble-minded. Kill, take all you can, any way you can, since you only get to bite the apple ... No, Miss Ferret, you may share that perspective of life; we Christians, at least those of us who try to live authentically Christ's life and direction, put our simple faith in the life, teaching and example of Jesus. St. Paul spoke of himself as being a fool for Christ. So we too only share in faith and so share Paul's sentiments of being fools for our faith.'

'So you admit to being fools then?' Ferret said with contemptuous smugness; 'you concede to that at least.'

'A fool with hope in their faith, Miss Ferret, no matter how tenuous that hope may seem to you, for some of us at least, is preferable to being certain of a life that has no purpose beyond our own temporary existence and hedonistic appetites. Even the poor primitives sought extension to life; it is the yearning of those who loved and lost their loved ones. Even you with your atheistic claims must concede to the fact that even the ancient world yearned for an after-life; their burial methods and rituals tell us as much. I'm sure you don't share those sentiments, Miss Ferret, I can't help wondering why? Perhaps even Journalists have someone special to love and miss?' The young Journalist's face, beautiful as it was, now wrinkled in sneering contempt for the umpteen time; yet Father Kevin's words hit home; and Ferret knew they touched a raw spot, as the priest and Nell were to learn later.

'Well Miss Ferret, unless you wish me to hear your confession or perform some other priestly duty, I feel I can be of no further use to you or your newspaper.'

'Confessions, be damned' Ferret interjected, spitting out the poison that the word and its implications held for her. Such contempt led the, already weary priest, to push himself, involuntary to one last effort for one so young. He felt, instinctively, that there might be some remote hope of disengaging her contempt for the Lord's offer of healing forgiveness. He was prompted by his recollection of an incident involving a volunteer to a city community dealing with homeless and problem teenagers: He related the story of a young lad named Michael to Ferret.

'Allow me, Miss Ferret, to make this last point on the benefit of confession, with the example of a poor unfortunate, very damaged teenager, who was left homeless after the death of his alcoholic father and mentally-institutionalised mother. He was picked up off the streets by the police for his own protection since he was being bullied because he himself inherited some of his mother's mental incapacity. The boy was totally without confidence and incapable of making friends or defending himself.

'The lad was accepted by a First Step charity that took in homeless drug addicts, young people abused by violence at home, or those just thrown out of home for being impossible to manage.' Miss Ferret listened intently, hoping the priest might compromise himself with some confessional matter; in which case, she could make the priest very unpopular among the people and be in serious trouble with his bishop for breaking the seal of confession. The priest continued his account: 'The lad showed no interest in any of the activities aimed at self-improvement that the community offered until one day a new volunteer, an artist, offered his services free for a two hour session each week. The sister in charge of the centre explained Michael's predicament and asked the new volunteer if he would give the lad a chance. She explained that she did not put much hope in the lad's response but that it might be his last opportunity; in which case, she explained, that the community would have to lose him or have him forced into psychiatric help. The sister explained that she was very reluctant to go down that road unless it was absolutely unavoidable.

'The artist, after several weeks of one-to-one tuition, managed to get Michael to produce a very worthwhile painting of a rose in a common Jam jar. The painting created quite a stir and resulted in one member of the staff making a reasonable offer to purchase the work. Michael refused the offer in spite of several attempts to pressurise him into a change of Heart'.

'No! No! No! I just want my painting ... it's mine.'

'Before the week was out, someone had stolen Michael's painting. He went on to plague every member of the staff, including the artist, demanding of each, whether they had borrowed the painting? No one owned up to the missing or stolen painting. The artist attempted to pacify Michael by helping him to see that someone must be very envious of him and his work; that this was a back-handed compliment; meaning, that he was someone to be jealous of. The artist promised to continue to help him with more paintings to compensate for the missing one. Michael was too distraught to be pacified.'

'I want that painting; it's mine; it belongs to me, not anyone else.' The lad was raging.

'This story has an end?' Miss Ferret interjected with sarcasm and impatience.

'Here,' Father Kevin ploughed on regardless, 'we come to the point of the story.'

'Not before time,' Ferret interrupted with deliberate goading and deliberate disrespect; she only wanted the floor for her own agendas. However, the priest persevered.

'The point of the story, or at least of the lad's involvement in his tuition, was that all the staff believed that Michael showed no promise or interest in anything going on in the small community. The artist pointed out to the staff how Michael made such a hullabaloo over the missing painting that he did, indeed, care strongly about his achievement.

This situation led on to Michael being introduced to work in a local supermarket in the city on the understanding between the community and the store manager that the community would be responsible for his behaviour. Michael up to this point had no record of wrongdoing.

Within two months of working at the store, Michael was discovered to have stolen a tin of meat. Once discovered, he was dismissed on the spot and the community was contacted. The community pleaded with the store manager not to have the police involved; that his dismissal and the recovery of the tin of meat might resolve the matter for the greater good of Michael. The store manager agreed reluctantly, and gave the reason for his reluctance.

'Look,' he said, 'Michael was well-liked at the store, in spite of his sulky and forbidding character. He was quiet, good-mannered and got on with his job. In view of his background and limited finances, most of the staff had offered him gifts of food at their own expense; he refused every time. He just preferred to steal what he wanted and as far as I am concerned I interpret that as being bloody-minded. It's was akin to putting his two fingers up at people's generosity and good nature. How on earth could anyone befriend someone like that?'

Back in the community Michael appeared before all the staff, including the artist. The artist didn't like the way the lad was being interrogated by four adult volunteers and yet the artist too had to learn an important lesson.

'Have we got an end in sight to this monologue?' Ferret asked, looking at her watch and added we have been here over an hour already. It's now eleven o' clock.'

'Your turn to speak will come, Miss Ferret,' the priest replied looking at the wall clock, 'I am sure we will not interrupt you so frequently,' he added with resignation, and continued.

'The lesson that the artist learnt was that stealing was something completely new to Michael's character and history in the community. What also came to light was the fact that you could not put your arm round Michael to show friendship; he would always pull away, no matter who the person was, that including the artist. The lad had never known love in his life; he simply couldn't handle intimacy. Now the point, Miss Ferret, which I felt was worthwhile your perseverance, was that if Michael was to come to me for confession, no doubt all he would be able to tell me was that he stole a tin of meat from a supermarket and he would naturally expect to be forgiven for that sin.'

'And why not...?' Ferret interjected in a matter-of-fact tone; 'it was only a bloody tin of meat, after all; you can hardly call that a capital offence, can you?' She added sarcastically.

'You are missing the whole point about the purpose of confession, Miss Ferret,' the priest replied to counter her sarcasm.

'Pray, put me out of my misery, what point is there beyond forgiveness of sin, not that I believe in that either. All offences belong to the realms of the Law of the land,' she added contemptuously.

The priest allowed her contemptuous opinion to pass him by and continued.

'The purpose of confession, Miss Ferret, if you will allow me to continue, is to help the person to look at the cause of the sin. In Michael's case, if he was to receive the healing of confession, he would have to ask God for help to heal his brokenness ... to heal that injured aspect of his nature and upbringing which was unable to accept love and support. He was not responsible for his nature or his upbringing. He never chose to be born or inherit the nature that he was inflicted upon him. His only freedom and healing would come from understanding his own brokenness and being able to realise that is where the basis of his sin lay; not that it is his fault. Yes, he would have to stop stealing. However, his real task would be to face that deeper brokenness within himself. There would be no future in blaming a shortage of money as the motive for his stealing. In his case he was offered help in that direction and it didn't work. That is why the Church is asked always to forgive sins by Christ himself. The point being that none of us have the full picture of anyone's life or how badly any individual may be injured by Nature itself. Nature, Miss Ferret, is not a precise entity; it is difficult to account for all its many deformities, whether we speak of plants, birds, fish, animals or humans.'

As Father Kevin concluded this account and having made his point on the purpose of confession, he really hoped, inwardly that Delilah Ferret might, on the off chance, wish to take advantage of the moment to seriously consider making a confession of her own pains. It was just a passing thought that came natural to a priest who really did care for his people, especially those who seemed to resent all he stood for.

He was more than a little surprised when he realised how silent the journalist had become since he was not looking directly at her during the latter points of his account; he was looking at the carpet carried away on the wings of his own thoughts and concentration. However, when he looked up to focus on her face he noticed that her eyes were glazed; she was taking in deep gasps of breath. The priest's face grew anxious. He couldn't be sure or not if she was having some kind of a bad turn. Nell, the housekeeper, knew better; she moved from her chair;

walked to Miss Ferret; put her hand briefly on her shoulder and said, 'will it be tea or coffee?' She didn't wait for Delilah's reply. 'Come with me; it's a bit stuffy in here.'

The journalist left the blanket drop to the carpeted floor; picked up her fur-lined overcoat and covered her scantily-dressed body and followed Nell to the kitchen holding her head downwards to conceal her tearful face. Father Kevin was very concerned for her. Was she having a fit? He thought. He knew that she was in good hands with Nell; she would call the doctor if the need arose.

Nell reappeared alone with a cup of coffee for the priest and whispered to him, 'She won't be long; she's ok, you just hit a sore spot.' Presently Nell returned once more with Delilah. It seemed from her reddened eyes that she had been crying. In the silence that lasted, seemingly forever, so far as the priest was concerned, he decided to break the awkward and potent atmosphere.

'You ok, Delilah?' The priest's voice was more conciliatory. Delilah sensed an authentic priestly and compassionate concern; not alone because of the concern he now showed to her, but for what had preceded; in the story of Michael the priest's revelation of deeper aspects of understanding resulted in her inadvertent fixation on the personal implication in the details for her own hidden life and deeply buried pain.

'Father Kevin,' the sound of his name coming from her lips took him by surprise; it seemed that she too was in a more conciliatory frame of mind judging from the softer tone in her voice. There was a distinct calm to her face; the icy aggressiveness had disappeared. 'I mentioned that I have no belief in God, however, I have no wish to pick a fight with you over the matter.' The priest hoped that this was a more progressive and amicable footing for them both. 'It is this whole business of Larry's indoctrination; this belief that his mother has ascended to heaven ... that she will come and visit him again in his own lifetime!' She added with her hands extended in an expression denoting the utter incredulity of such an expectation. 'I don't mean to make a mockery of his grief, but should the lad be left in so delusory a frame of mind when you and I know that is not how things are, even from a religious perspective. It seems reasonably clear to me that you, Father Kevin, have a great gift of perception, perhaps even of healing, I am willing to concede to that; even if the concession, for my part, inclines towards a healing based only on a purely insightful psychological level. The point is will the lad be left without being counselled away from such a bizarre and delusory expectation?'

The priest thought that this young, beautiful journalist was now genuinely going down another avenue for her story. Her tack, however, was potentially just as embarrassing for the Church; he could imagine the mocking headlines: A New Ascension into Heaven ... A New Resurrection Expected ... A Mother Returns From The Dead. The priest's mind spun in half dread; he had every reason to believe that he would be in the thick of it all. He would become the Church's closest scapegoat. No doubt, his church and its parishioners would become a laughing stock. Worse would be the coach loads of misguided pilgrims, those with dubious piety ... miracle-hunters of the worst kind .... Father Kevin shuddered at his own bizarre imaginings.

He was in her hands now. She owed the Church nothing, considering her revealed contempt for its Creationist and

God-centred nonsense. He couldn't help wondering how one so young, and considering her Catholic upbringing, could be so attached to her atheism. She didn't sit on the fence as some agnostics do; hers seemed to be full-blown atheism. This put her into the distinct anti-Christ camp, a growing movement spawned by the evolutionists, coupled with Reason over Faith. In this spawning camp, hard-nosed science saw faith as a dinosaur in the Age of Reason; it hoped for the God camp to dissolve into speedy extinction so that science alone would hold the magisterial throne of human knowledge ... the empirical world over spiritual imagination and interminable speculation in the guise of Faith that seems fatally driven to suicide by walking too close to a mountainous landslide of imponderable supposition. Science in our time, so many believed, acted as the authentic broom of reason sweeping away the chaff of speculative theology. There appeared now a coalition of scientific voices and minds, with the likes of university professors banging on the drums of reason over spiritual speculation and supposition. Where Delilah Ferret was going to run with her story was anyone's guess. The priest could do nothing about it. As she gathered herself to leave, for some inscrutable reason she looked long, even affectionately, into Nell's face. Both looked into each other's eyes; there was no malice in either. It was the unexpected and prolonged pause that seemed so enigmatic. She seemed to tell Nell something in the reading of her face. Nell's expression bore the countenance of a loving mother. Father Kevin stood by the partially-opened door to save the wind blasting all asunder. He noted the inexplicable delay and the strange expression on Nell's face; he could not read what it might mean nor could he see the Journalist's face since she stood with her back to him. Ferret seemed to shake herself out of her hypnotic thoughts and walk towards the door but not before turning her head back for one last look at Nell. It was just a brief glance and yet when she turned to face the priest, she was actually smiling, but not for his benefit. Father Kevin spoke, almost involuntary. 'Delilah, if you wish to come again for a visit or a chat, hopefully not in your capacity as a journalist, you will be most welcome.' He couldn't think for the world why he gave the invitation; it just seemed to slip out. There was some semblance of acceptance or at least, a consideration of one, in the thoughtful movement of her head and how she spread her gloved hands. Their faces met in shared cordiality as he took her hand and held on to it tightly to prevent her departure before he said what was on his mind. However, before he could speak she burst into hysterical laughter, her eyes a little glazed as she remarked, 'not the blanket treatment again, Father surely?' With that both Nell and the priest broke into delayed hysterics, the priest face now a blushing tomato. When all grew silent again, Father Kevin spoke his troubled mind.

'Delilah, we are both sorry for our earlier hostilities; regardless of fault or blame, Nell and I had no right in our professional roles to exchange insults.'

'Father, say no more … we journalists live on being a pain. I promise if ever I do visit again I will endeavour to be more cordial and less dressed for club life.' The priest's head fell in embarrassment. As she stepped out into the storm-blown afternoon, the priest bade her farewell.

'God bless –Delilah.' The expression was emitted from pure habit, even though sincerely meant. She looked back through the demented wind and smiled … her beautiful silken blond hair fluttering like a flag in the wind; she knew instinctively that it was no mocking farewell. She moved away sedately, an act not too familiar to her silver Lotus. Both priest and housekeeper waved from the drawn net curtains as The Lotus veered into the main city road.

'Well; well; well; Nell; this has been some morning; she certainly knows how to leave her mark.'

'So it's the morning, you think it is, Father Kevin; we had better settle down to our lunch.'

'You can't be serious, Nell; it's never that time, surly be to God!' He looked at the lounge clock the black hands of its vivid white face stood out like soldiers at 2.30pm the priest could scarcely believe his own eyes; he was so deeply lost by the intensity of the swift-run hours.

Nell served up some piping hot spuds running in tears of butter. As they tucked into the cabbage and bacon, and as the priest sprinkled salt liberally on his potatoes absentmindedly, so the subject of the visitor took up the topic of the meal. It was Father Kevin who opened the conversation, between mouthfuls of food.

'What did you make of her earlier anger, Nell?' the priest asked thoughtfully. Nell didn't reply at once; quite apart from dealing with a mouthful of food, she was also mulling over the question. Nell was in a kind of reverie. In her mind she was still facing Delilah before their departure; there was that seemingly long mysterious meeting of faces; she also called to her reverie their time in the kitchen away from the priest when unknown to him, she had held the tearful child, as Nell experienced her, in her arms. Nell spoke consoling words to her while she stroked her silken hair and back. All this prolonged Nell's reverie. The priest knew that Nell was measuring her words ... she always did. Presently Nell grew more earnest than usual.

'She is full of bitterness and hatred, Father.'

'But, why, Nell...? She began all the hostilities and blatant disrespect,' he replied with incredulity and defensiveness.

'Ah! No, Father. We are back to your story of Michael ...' Nell's face was somewhat cryptic.

'I don't follow you, Nell; what's the connection?'

'Her confrontation and disrespect for us was only concealing her own personal hatred and bitterness.'

'Sorry, Nell; you've lost me completely. What has she to be so bitter about? Is it because of her atheism and her contempt for Catholic Ireland or what ...? Surely that is a road she has chosen for herself.'

'I seriously doubt that, Father; I am not convinced that she is happy with her claim to be an atheist.'

'Well, Nell, she certainly convinced me with her disgust for Christian views, let alone what she thinks of us Catholics and the Jewish faith. I must be honest, Nell, I did have some doubts myself considering her age and her early roots in Catholicism. It is an unusual choice in one so young. I did hope, even now, to at least give her the opportunity of a way back in case she was bullied into her position.'

'Do you recall Father when she denied the existence of God; how all of us only "get one bit of the apple."'

'Yes, Nell, I recall those words, more or less as she said them.'

'That tells me, Father Kevin, that she is not a happy atheist. Both of us have met non-believers who were happy enough with life; perhaps because they didn't feel the need to think whether life had any ultimate meaning or not. But in her case,' Nell added with some conviction, 'she is not at ease with it. She seems to be using it as a weapon; as though she is shielding an even greater soar.'

'But she has everything in front of her ... a well-paid job – that's obvious enough ... her incredible beauty will take her to any height in a secular superficial world....' Nell cut him off mid sentence.

'Ah! No, Father...' There was a long potent pause. 'You are, I'm afraid, very mistaken about her beauty. That is at the heart of her bitterness and hatred.'

'Has she told you something in private? If it is meant to be between the two of you that's fine; but I am still baffled as to how you conclude that her rare beauty is a problem.' The priest's face was frowned from incomprehension.'

'I did comment on her beauty when we were alone in the kitchen, as you might to a pretty daughter or friend. She still clung to me in her tears, yet hissed so vehemently at my complement on her beauty. I could feel the hatred and resentment. It was no fawning pretence, as some women instinctively practice, as a means of soliciting further complements to inflate self-conceited egoism. No, Father Kevin, she hates her beauty; she hates being a beautiful woman; she hates being a woman at all.'

'Ah! Nell; come, come; I know you are a perceptive old Kerry goat; but I think you have overreached yourself with that tack.'

'Father, what makes any of us what we are? Our body doesn't do our thinking for us, does it?'

'Come on, Nell, enlighten me; tell me what you think you know.' the priest was being a little philosophical but also resigned to accepting Nell's perceptive experience.

'She was born wrong,' Nell remarked as she started collecting and clattering the dirty food dishes from the table and was heading for the kitchen when the priest cut her steps to a halt.

'Ah! Nell! Nell! Nell! How can you say that she was born wrong? We hardly know her for more than a few hours.' He was waving his hands about in gesturing incredulity.

'Father, she's a girl ... a woman in her body; but she was born a boy in her brain. She's been given the wrong driver.' The priest was dumbfounded; his mouth and face aghast as he fixed his incredulous expression on Nell who stood there briefly with a tray full of dishes, her head nodding solemnly; her sagacious face inviting humble acceptance of a terrible and disturbing truth.

'You really believe that, Nell, don't you,' the priest remarked still stunned by Nell's challenging revelation. He knew deep down that Nell did not offer anything of which she was not fully convinced. Who was he, he thought, to doubt her about this, incredible as it was to accept. Nell had rarely been wrong about people, concerning serious matters. Yet, this revelation was so shocking for what it must have meant to the journalist's every-day life.

'Nell, If what you say is true, that poor creature has been through hell most of her life.'

'I know what you mean, Father, I don't doubt you in the least on that score.'

'Well! Well! Well!' the priest nodded his head, staring into nowhere. He was now talking to himself. 'The poor child; what a hapless misfortune ... such a cruel fate – cursed with contradiction – polarised in duality – a pawn to distortion.' Father Kevin just couldn't take it in. In spite of the journalist's grating manner, his heart was truly wrenched for her. Whatever could please such a soul?' he thought.

Many cruel aberrations came to his mind; those more obvious to the human eye and experience. He was well aware of the poor misfortunate hermaphrodites ... or children born joined together in the most hideous ways; dwarfism; poor souls forced by fate to earn their existence as the objects of freak shows for the callous entertainment of frivolous curiosity. How many animals like the many cows he had seen born in the fields with extra legs protruding from their backs or sides; which was all very sickening? How nature could be so imprecise, so cursed for some poor creatures. It was difficult now for the priest to dismiss the whole rotten situation from his mind. He shuddered to dismiss his awful train of thought.

All this time Nell was in the kitchen, her hands immersed in suds washing the dishes and staring out from the window at the flowers in the containers of the backyard – not that she had any conscious awareness of them. She too was pensive, carried away on a reverie of her own. She too had Delilah in her heart; tears came to her eyes; the tragic deformity of the young lady in her thoughts was tormenting her motherly nature and instincts. Father Kevin entered on her tears as he helped to dry the dishes. A tangible silence descended on them both. This was made more acute by the forlorn sound of the old chiming clock from the lounge and the wind moaning through gaps in the old, ill fitting sash windows, rattling, animated by the blasting whistling wind. When both had replaced the clattering dishes and cutlery to their respective cupboards, Father Kevin held Nell in his arms for a while. He was all the family the silver-haired Nell now had. It was obvious that she still hadn't been devoid of a mother's heart, for all her age, her instincts for a wounded soul never deserted her; God bless her, he remarked to himself.

CHAPTER 7

Ferret's Childhood and Background

Back in Delilah's home, she too was in tears. Nell, in spite all the earlier aggressive encounter, had touched her deeply. Delilah missed the only friend she thought she had in the world, the mother of her childhood. Unfortunately her mother had separated from her father and walked out on them both. Ferret was only five years old then. She blamed herself for the break up, as children often do. She believed that she could never be the daughter her mother wanted; she just couldn't act a daughter's part. Although her mother, a very immature person, knew that her child was very much the tomboy, she never considered that a problem; she believed, like many parents, that it was no more than a stage of development; that one's dominant sexual orientation was not in all cases an immediate definitive reality. There was no real happy medium with her mother; one moment she would play with Delilah and make her as happy and as high as a kite; at other times she would ignore her entirely as if her daughter never existed; that hurt Delilah deeply. The countless times she went to bed left alone and weeping without as much as a fleeting story or kiss to help her to sleep and feel loved. No. Her mother was more interested in the city clubs and bars; she had always been too flirty for her besotted, indolent husband. It was not to be wondered at that the child became the terror of her schoolmates as she moved on from her unhappy, unloved childhood to the world of school.

Delilah's father was never one to give time to his child. It was as if he didn't know what to do with her apart from feeding, clothing and washing his young daughter ... all of which was an utter irritation to him. There was no enterprise in the man; no particular enthusiasm for anything. He had fallen for the charms and beauty of his wife, and seemingly paid the price for his skittishness and lack of discernment. He too was void of love from his wife; she was really little more than a fairy light only switched on at parties. All these painful thoughts bubbled in the festering cauldron of Delilah's lost childhood. The only credit to her father was the fact that he hung around long enough for his daughter to make university. She was grateful for that stability at least. Ultimately he too drifted into a new relationship; he never once came back to visit his grown daughter. The only celebrations, such as Christmas, or birthdays, that she knew, were what she did for herself. She was too damaged, even in her university days, to grow close to anyone. She simply studied with a vengeance and became an outstanding Journalist. Unfortunately for all, she carried her festering cauldron of damage about with her. It was no wonder that the story of Michael, related to her by Father Kevin earlier, had pealed the scab off her festering history. In fairness to the priest he could never have known how close-to-the-bone his revelation was; how like a living parable it had become, acting like a key opening up a lock in the dark crypt of Delilah's life.

Father Kevin was locked in his thoughts. Lord, let there be some simple explanation to Mary's disappearance. I know you took Elijah the great prophet and carried him off to heaven in a chariot of fire driven by fiery horses and had him vanish in a whirlwind. Then there was the priest-king Melchizedek, another speculative candidate, who seemed to have vanished without trace. Then there was Enoch who was taken up without experiencing death because of his faith. However, I didn't have to deal with the consequence of those God-fearing souls. Father Kevin knew that his mind was clutching at straws. He didn't want to have to deal with Rome on any account. He was a simple priest caring for a people he knew and loved. Another assumption, or more precisely, ascension into heaven, he needed like a portrait of hell hanging over his bed.

CHAPTER 8

Life in Heaven. Mary
and Maureen Meet

Mary's arrival in heaven coincided with the preparations of a great musical festival. She found herself in a grand amphitheatre. The scale and luxury of the place were breath-taking in the extreme. It was impossible to grasp the true number of people, men women and children, seated in the tiers of seats rising to so distant a point above the glittering floor of the theatre that they appeared to be lost in the utter scale and dimensions of the vast scene. Gigantic wall-to-wall TV screens were used for all who were too distant from the floor of the theatre. Enormous capacity floor lifts surrounded the theatre on each floor level. Food and refreshments were available for those who preferred not to bring their own. The seated figures, the thousands that could be seen clearly enough for description, were attired in their best clothing. Indeed, Mary, though quite unconscious of her own attire, was dressed in a powder-blue silk, sari-like dress and sandals. The last she knew of her arrival in this majestic place was in the bed clothes of her recent earthly departure. As she now became more conscious of her own presence, seated at the lower stage level, so, she turned to face a beautiful companion who had come to sit by her side. Both seemed to be seated alone; the many seats either side of them were relatively empty for some inexplicable reason. That seemed odd to Mary since all the seats above her were full to capacity. The crowds were eating and drinking, all at ease with each other. Mary came unprepared; or so she thought, since she had no food with her. However, the beautiful young lady beside her offered her some of her food and drink from a rather generous hamper which she had brought along for the occasion. Mary was somewhat uncomfortable at her companion's familiarity; she thought the stranger to be someone very special; perhaps some important celebrity and that she, Mary, had taken someone else's seat. Her beautiful companion could read her discomfiture and so introduced herself.

'I'm so sorry, Mary. I didn't mean to make you ill at ease. My name is Maureen. You obviously do not remember me; you couldn't be expected to, given the extreme change in my appearance. Do you recall your young sister who died from leukaemia when she was twelve years old? We were always so close. You were so good to me, so patient when all others, even mammy and daddy gave up on me. I understand now that they couldn't cope with the inevitability of my death. It was all too hurtful for them to know that there was no more hope for me. They couldn't have realised how much I needed them to be with me in the hospital. Yet they left me to die. I felt so frightened and abandoned. But you Mary, you never failed to visit me right to the very end, even when I was incapable of conversation with my beloved and precious sister. Thank you so much Mary. Thank you.'

Mary burst into tears, gripped in uncontrollable emotion from the memory of it all. The details of her past experience and earthly childhood; the unimaginable pain and loss of her beloved sister, Maureen, came flooding back as though it was only yesterday, it all took on a new reality, a renewed sense of shock and pain, a love now surging through her entire body. She clung to Maureen as though she might once again lose her in the vast new world in which she found herself and in which she could not yet even begin to comprehend. So, they clung to each other in the purest bliss, both experiencing a cascading tenderness of love surging with an all-consuming belonging. Slowly, as two lovers will, once they are convinced that the other will not suddenly disappear, the embrace loosened. Both sat face into face, not wanting to ever again lose sight of the other. Both wiped away their tears. Tears of unimaginable happiness, even disbelief, that so much love was even possible for any living being. So they sat, now hand in hand, in a blessed gratitude and wonder, intoxicated with each other's physical love and presence.

There came, suddenly and without warning, the majestic call of countless clarions. The sound rang out seemingly from every brightly illumined terrace that surrounded the heights and depths of the vast theatre. The sound, the call, could only be described as petrifying. It demanded with its majesty and power, a gripping sense of importance and the immediate attention of the entire gathering. There could be no estimate as to the vast number of scarlet-clad figures that stood in perfect symmetry trumpeting their attention.

As suddenly as the calling clarions came, so there followed a tangible silence, a silence that seemed to have a solidity, a form, of its own. The lights that had illuminated the clarion figures now dimmed suddenly a new burst of lights came from countless other stage-like alcoves surrounding the entire edifice. It all seemed like mystical moonlight. Then there came the cascading lilting cords of what sounded like a billion harps rising and falling like the hypnotic sounds of a tinkling brook babbling and cascading over a myriad of rocks. A river of silver appeared, pulsating, cascading downward from the heights of the theatre. The flow moved in perfect unison with the rise and fall of the hypnotic harps. At first it seemed like some beautiful ode to the glorification of Nature itself. Only when the pulsating river of silver came within ground level in line and view with the seats of Mary and Maureen, did the true reality reveal itself. With the awe-inspiring, intoxicating sound of the harps came a million haunting voices. These sang the awesome Sanctus, the Holy, Holy, a chant-like hymn that Mary had heard on earth. It was a beautiful hymn that gave solemnity to the sacredness and glorification of Christ. Yet there was no Christ here. As the white pulsating mass continued in Mary's direction it gradually became clear that this great white mass was not an artificial pulsating silver waterfall; but rather the tiny figures of countless children, all were no more than eight years old. What had earlier appeared to be a mass of pulsating silver water was indeed the rise and fall of children's arms. It might have been a scene from an earthly ballet. Yet the shear scale and delicacy of the scene was other worldly, truly awesome. It could only be of the numinous; and yet these children were real; they were dressed in white transparent veil-like costumes.

Mary could not take her eyes away from the scene, not even for a moment. She was transfixed, awestruck by the breathtaking spectacle of voices, music and children. The slow motion of the hundreds of children slowly and gracefully waving their delicate arms, as though they were the wings of a majestic albatross, the words of the Sanctus, which the children were singing to the rhythm of countless cascading harps were utterly heart-gasping in awe and reverence. The delicate arms of the children would be drawn across their breasts, held for a while; then the backs of their hands would be drawn across their foreheads as though to shield them from a blinding light, their subtle bodies, bowing and rising in solemn worship; their delicate angelic faces, now smiling, now in solemn expression. Again their arms would spread out, rise and fall in unison, in perfect symmetry, beating the air in slow majestic motion. Once again Mary was in a flood of tears almost chocking for want of breath. There was not one single soul in the seats above whose eyes remained without tears. Their tears were of indescribable adulation. Words alone could not suffice for the scenes and sounds that brought gasps of wonder from the entire spectators. All eyes were gripped by the scene's indescribable magnificence.

Without explanation Maureen took Mary from her seat and walked forward to meet the oncoming children. Mary was delirious, astounded, giddy, fainting and terrified all at once from the utter spectacle, the delicate, enthralling magnificence and solemnity of it all. She clung more tightly than ever to Maureen to prevent herself from swooning into total collapse. It was all so astonishing – so other worldly.

A neatly-dressed figure in a light-grey suit and open white shirt emerged from behind and parted the two friends and put his arms round them both. Mary felt a new surge of sensuousness course through her body. She wanted to withdraw from the figure, her feelings seemed so inappropriate to the solemnity of the events unfolding before her. At the same time she wanted this sensuousness never to end. She could not tear herself away from it. It was the same surging sensation that she experienced earlier from Maureen's embrace. It still seemed to Mary that this overpowering feeling belonged to personal, intimate, physical love. The man bent his lips to Mary's ear and whispered.

'Don't be fretful, Mary. What you are feeling is natural to all of us here. It is as essential to our nature as the very air we breathe. It is what unifies us in a bond of love that keeps us inseparable from each other. You will experience the same unity and feeling with everyone here. You now belong to all of us. What you feel from each person is exactly what they experience from you.'

This new knowledge drew an immediate reaction from Mary. It seemed to be a green light to her to embrace the stranger with such a surge of kisses that it made both Maureen and the stranger break into echoing laughter as the stranger spoke over Mary's shoulder to Maureen. 'It seems, Maureen, that your companion wants all the love held in eternity to be released in a single moment.'

The spell of the music and angelic voices were broken as the music faded. All the children lay prostrate before the three figures in the centre. The entire theatre thundered into rapturous applause. The stranger clapped his hands, at which cue, the entire bird-like lake of children rose as one to their ballet-dressed feet. The delicacy of their crisp translucent veil-like dresses might have belonged to angelic beings. These cherubs were, however, very real, their angelic young faces smiling at the adults before them. They were also fluttering the fingers of their upheld hands as though they were the wings of hovering birds. They kept calling our 'Mary! Mary!' This repetition was taken up by the entire Theatre. Her name thundered throughout the vast theatre. She was suffused with utter astonishment. She looked away from the beautiful spectacle with their beaming joyful faces and their fluttering, greeting fingers. Mary turned and looked quizzically into the smiling faces of the stranger and Maureen.

'This is your hour of glorification, Mary, The evening may belong to all present, but the hour and occasion belongs in a very special way to you. These little cherubs before us have trained very hard to welcome you home, Mary, as indeed have all who have contributed to such an outstanding and glorious welcome. It is your hour of glorification in which we are all proud to share. Thank you so much, Mary for all you have struggled with on earth. You have been found worthy of our home here. Be assured, Mary, that never again will you experience the slightest sadness or pain once you have settled in with us. Sadness has no place here.'

'Are you, Jesus, then, or are you God?'

'You don't know what you ask as yet, Mary. In our world, here, your new home, we all share in what or who you understand to be God or Jesus. I will put it this way for the present for simplicity sake. Imagine Love to be God. It follows that all who give their lives over to love, live exactly as God lives. There is no difference. However, for your sake you may call me God or Jesus – yet always remembering that such names are only language, symbols, and attempts to express living realities beyond the power of words. To call a tree a tree is not to grasp it as a living reality. But, never mind all that for now, all will become clear to you in time.'

'Can I ask to whom the children belong…? They do belong here, do they? I don't want them to be angels who will just vanish before me ... Will they? They are so beautiful. I want them to stay forever... Can they?' Mary's torrent of questions made Jesus smile knowingly.

He called four of the children forward the first leapt straight up into Mary's arms and kissed her with great passion so much so that one of the other little cherubs pulled at the leg of the one clinging to Mary saying frantically, 'I want to kiss her too. Come down now, you had enough. And so all four had their turn at kissing Mary who then looked at the stranger and said,

'What about all the others. Won't they be cross if they don't have a turn? They all look as though they want to rush forward.' Mary loved them so much. She knew that she could never tire of their love.

'There will be time enough for them all, Mary. They will have to go to bed soon. However you can visit them any time you wish, either in their homes or in their school.'

'Do they have to go to school here?' Mary asked – her face revealing a mixture of regret, disappointment and incomprehension. 'I mean, what could they possibly need to learn in their wonderful state?'

'It is like I said to you earlier, Mary. All will become clear to you in time.'

'Will I be able to meet their parents? I would love to thank them all individually for the most wonderful and indescribable welcome that they put on for me.'

Jesus' face was unsmiling for the first time. He kissed the four little cherubs and when Maureen bade them good night with a shower of kisses also, he whispered softly to them to go home. Off they scampered, skipping away like so many feathers in the wind, all the while looking back with the most angelic beaming smiles. Mary could see that they wanted to be up all night.

'They have no parents, Mary, in the sense that you mean. I will tell you this only once since no one here knows of their origin, they have been spared such sadness and knowledge.'

'Spared!' said Mary in a startled voice.

'Yes, Mary – spared…!'

'These cherubs, as we like to call them, were once the aborted of the earth. All were sacrificed on the dark altar of hedonistic perversion, where the ordered end of love, its fruit, the birth of life, was crushed for one blind compulsive act of selfish gratification … where creative unity gave way to evil's most demonic act … the horrific destruction of the innocent in the worship of lust and licentiousness.

Did ever the lowly earth fail to bring forth her food, the trees their fruit, the sun her light and heat? Did ever the lowly animals not suckle their kind with joy and pride? Did ever the fretful birds ever fail in frantic haste and labour to build a home to secure their chicks and nourish them from the trials of on-coming winter? Did ever the rain fail to fall freely to the benefit of all …? Did ever the planets and stars fail to keep to their ordered time and end? Yet all these supposed inferior forms of life put to shame those who were given the gift of knowledge to discern between right and wrong, truth and lie … between reason and madness, freedom and slavery. That those blinded by moments of sensuousness should choose murder for a moment's pleasure. And for the supposed learned and dispensers of Justice … ministers of the Law, ministers of the courts … high parliament … should, all in their degree of authority and power, legitimise the death warrant of the innocent for the expedience of those who claimed ownership of their own bodies, their own lives and destiny, as if they had some holy right to such a contemptuous claim ... with blind indifference to the most abominable distortion. Like minds and voices banded together to support the blunt instrument of godless democracy as though numbers could ever replace the throne of sacred truth. For if only one taught what is true and sacred, how could a million billion ever justify what is plainly a disfigurement, a blatant distortion? Were these hideous deeds to be the response to the Messenger's call to creative love in the gift of one life to another ... this call for all human life and human action to reach its ordered end?'

When Jesus had finished speaking he apologised to Mary.

'I should not have troubled your attention with all of this, Mary. I know that within a short time now you will forget these things of the earth and experience a completely new beginning, free from all that is capable of hurting you.' Mary wished to disregard the apology for this shared intimacy and pain. She could almost feel the weight of it all. After all, she thought, the children in question, however God managed to renew their existence, were so loving, so beautiful, so unblemished, in a phrase, so perfect. How could any person sentence such innocence to death? What seemed even more insulting to Mary was the fact that the very person she was listening to gave his earthly life for the guidance and salvation of such offenders. She was well aware that any offence, no matter how grievous, only required contrition and a request for forgiveness and it would have been freely given because true love knew all too well the fickle nature of humanity. These thoughts prompted her next question.

'The offenders, will they be punished?' Mary asked with some trepidation since she could discern from the sorrow on Jesus' face that he did not seem consoled by the fact that Love, God, or mysterious Nature had indeed given new life to all these martyred souls.

'They will not be Judged by me or by God personally, Mary, nor by any part of heaven's life,' he replied with an expression of deep personal pain and regret. 'Their punishment, Mary, is of no consolation to me, nor of any benefit. I simply feel that we lost the battle ... the fight for the renewal of all souls, for the salvation of the whole of humanity. After all Mary, no one chose to be born; no one chose their own nature; that is why Love existed in the form of a Messenger; it was always there to be known, to intervene, to instruct, to sacrifice and forgive all.'

'But surely, you gave us all free will and freedom to discern between right and wrong. I above all people could never claim to be extraordinary clever, or highly intelligent, but I do know what you taught, what you wanted, no matter how difficult it might have been at the time or on various occasions. Sure, didn't you give us the right to forgive and be forgiven, even on earth? We all had the opportunity to turn from our sins and wrong way of life. Why should you still be burdened with the pain of those you gave your earthly existence to redeem? Surely your offer of help was too easily ignored, dismissed by pride and twisted self-indulgence and self-importance?'

'All of what you say is indeed true, Mary. However, it will always remain my own concern. Love is not glorified in the damned.'

'If you or heaven's life have no part in their punishment, who or what, carries out their punishment?'

Jesus looked into the Mary's face and drew her apart from Maureen.

'I will show you their punishment, their judge. Once again I must say to you, Mary, you will forget everything you are about to see because there is an everlasting gulf between their world and ours. There is no crossing over either way.'

In an instant Mary found herself transported from the halls of her celebration. She was shown a man on his own in a vast landscape. He was so busy and frantic in his purpose and occupation that great beads of perspiration fell from his haggard face and stressed body. He was in the frantic pursuit of moving something bright from the base of an enormous range of high, glittering mountains. His actions were frantic as he continued to shovel some glistening rocks into a barrow, all the while looking over his shoulder as though expecting someone to pounce on him at any given moment. He would then hurry away with a barrow load to some great distance and bury the load. His was a twilight world, a dark forbidding landscape with not another living soul anywhere to be seen, neither bird nor animal.

Mary shivered at the sight and asked Jesus, 'What is he doing there on his own? Is he a slave to someone, he seems so terrified?'

'He is shifting a mountain of gold from one place to another in an attempt to hide it. However, his task is really impossible and futile.'

'But who is he hiding it from?' Mary asked. There is no one else anywhere near him.'

'You are quite right, Mary. He is alone and will remain alone for all eternity.'

'But why?' she asked. 'How can a person live for ever in a physical body? You say that God has no part in this. Surely God made every world, including this one? Isn't that what we have been brought up to believe?' Mary's face was grimaced in disbelief.

'His is not a real world to you or to me, Mary. It simply does not exist in the sense that you understand existence. This is a world of a troubled spirit, a troubled conscience. Human nature, Mary, unlike that of the animal world, is naturally imbued with a heightened sense of awareness between right and wrong. Conscience reveals and exposes itself in dreams; at times it becomes the world of the nightmare, fabricated by the man's own guilty, his unredeemed conscience. He is in a dream world. We all know what the nightmare world is like, how frightening, how horrible, how demonic and threatening it can be. However, for the living these are dreams with lessons behind them for our own benefit and growth. In the case of the man you are watching, unlike the living, he will never wake up, because he does not physically exist. He belongs to the world he created for himself.'

'How did he create such a world?' Mary asked, still deeply affected by all she was witnessing.

'He was a very selfish man in his lifetime. He lived for money. He worked all the hours at his disposal and sought every avenue of investment for his own furtherance. He was what you might consider too self-regarding – too self-important. The world for him was the rise and fall of the stock exchange. He was most proud of his status as the most highly commissioned worker in the company of his employment. He was so seldom at home that his family scarcely knew him. His grandiose home, his top of the range cars and gadgetry, his handmade clothes, these were all tokens of success; yet in reality, no more than masks in a market place selling self-delusion. He became what he possessed ... deliberately erecting a screen between his higher sense of right and wrong with regard to his conscience and his irrefutable connectedness to other human beings. Yet he knew from his earliest days the teaching of possessing the world and losing his very self.

'His was the choice of one who chose pride for his mistress. And, she, if you can comprehend, Mary, gave birth to a child. And the child was death ... a mouth, and appetite impossible to satisfy. He wanted human admiration in spite of despising those who fed his own self-glorification. He craved acknowledgement only to swell, gloat and nurture the ghoul that gradually took possession of his life. Yes, Mary, he was free; he had sufficient knowledge, warning enough for any heeding soul.'

'So he will be at this futile labour for all eternity?' Mary shook her head in a slow motion of disbelief to her own question.

'Is there no glimmer of hope for him ever again?' Her head was still moving, still expressing incredulity; it was all too difficult to accept. 'Jesus, I can't grasp this! Surely it was better for the man never to have been born, never created. Have you no power over this since you can see it and reveal it to me? You have always taught that the essence of God is love. So, how can this be even possible? It all seems to me a kind of revenge.' Mary tried to remain composed. However, she experienced anger welling up within her. She was well aware in one part of her mind that she could not sympathize with the expression of the man's lived experience, but he was once a child of God, surely!

When she turned to face Jesus, he was in tears. 'I tried my best, Mary. I only had my life, my love, my knowledge and my teaching to offer. I was only the Messenger, like the thousands of messengers that followed or came before and after me – I had nothing else. All this will be wiped from your mind Mary.'

She put her arms round Jesus, both still sobbing. She could not be consoled by the knowledge that she would never have to remember this revelation. She felt forced to ask one more final and frightening question; this she asked while pressed into the intimate arms of Jesus.

'What of the parents of the aborted souls?' She never looked up into his face. The question sailed over his shoulder. Mary's eyes were enlarged and tense. She was convinced that the answer would be even more unacceptable, unbearable and more horrific than the last revelation still tormenting her mind. It was some while before Jesus answered her. Both stared at the landscape where the lone frantic soul hurried about his futile task, shifting non-existent gold. However, the dark silent scene, broken only by the noise of the man's grating shovel and squeaking barrow before them was now melting away just as it had appeared. The grating metallic sounds seemed to linger on like some haunting horror belonging to another time; like a bell from hell, clanging to call its damned to suffering. In the closing stages of the spectre apparition a new, even more gruesome, heart-rending and sickening vision appeared of a lone woman searching through an endless deserted and bombed-out city. Her worn out body and ragged clothes appeared as one who had survived a terrible holocaust. Her face was frantic as she searched everywhere, constantly falling over the rubble piled along the indistinguishable streets. Her world too was only one of half light. From time to time she levered up slabs of broken debris and strained her aged body to peer below. Sometimes she would scream and then stop up her own ears.

Mary turned to Jesus, again both were in tears. 'What is she doing? What is she searching for? Why is she screaming? Why is she shielding her ears all the time?' Jesus explained that the woman was searching for her lost child. Her screams are answering the imaginary cries of her aborted child.'

'But I can't hear a child crying or her screams.' Mary replied, her face a stage of frowns and horror.

'Of Course you can't hear her, Mary. We cannot enter her world. It is a fabrication of her own soul, her own self-accusing conscience; her former memory, her restless guilt. She will never find the child. This is her hell, a nightmare world she created for herself. Too late she discovered that her lovers had no real concern for her as a person or for the ordered end of love ... the creative gift of motherhood that was passed on to her by her parents. There was no such return of gift from her to her child. Instead she chose the blind slaughter of the innocent by the most horrible means of abortion. She had all her life to ask forgiveness just as the other tormented soul you saw earlier had the same opportunity. Neither of them gave Love's redemption and forgiveness a second thought. Many have turned to their conscience for help and received it, no matter the crime, even so late as to implore for that help and forgiveness on their deathbed. We know the difficulties of the human condition; I too shared them once as you know, Mary. There has to be a direction for humanity to follow that is universally understood and universally applicable to every human soul, no matter their race, colour or creed. That direction is based on Love of others. Every person can clearly understand that as an evergreen teaching, a universal truth that is indisputable. It is the very ordered end of human life and existence, to love and be loved; to forgive and be forgiven.'

'But why not just wipe such offenders out of existence?' said Mary, 'even from the dimension we have just now witnessed? Would that not be more worthy of a loving caring God? Surely, Jesus, you have the power or the influence to do that, Have you not? It seems to me that these damned, suffering souls point to a limit on God's forgiveness and love. Again I am conscious of the fact that no human being ever asked to be created, to be born, to be saddled with our imprecise and wayward nature. I know too that many have aspired to great saintliness in spite of that nature, through prayer and grace. However, for numberless others, human freedom has been nothing but a curse, a kind of sentence to be damned, even on earth.'

'Mary.' Jesus replied with understanding for her line of thought and deep concern. 'There has to be a consequence, an outcome caused by disorder. How could you understand anything or even be directed if licence, disorder and destruction were allowed ungoverned and meaningless expression. I say again, Mary, the torture of these lost souls are not God's will as a person. God, Mary, if you can comprehend it, is only a Messenger; yes a powerful one, but still only a Messenger of the greatest and highest good expressed in the love and care of all people; that is humanity's greatest and highest good. It is fatal to ignore this message. The message and the Messenger are one and the same thing, Mary. There is more to God than simply referring to God as person.

Nature is a part of who God is or can be. It is Nature that gives God to human sensibility not the other way round. Nature is the great giver of everything. It has its own rules and consequences. God as Creator is written into human nature in the form of Love. Love, Mary, does not exist outside of animated existence, otherwise it would have no purpose; any yet it is an essential part of human existence, if human existence is to be directed creatively.

'It is similar in concept to mathematics which is an important means for humanity to build and create or destroy; it too does not exist outside man's being except as pure potential. It is a part of what is understood as a creative force capable of order or disorder and self-destruction, or self-extension. Nature too is open to self-expression; it has judgement written into its life or being; it too teaches and displays its own consequences when subjected to infringement and abuse. Abuses of the climate, the earth, the seas, the trees, the animals ... the very air; none of these will tolerate indefinite abuse. Is Nature then to be accused as being a cruel Judge or totally without justice in the protection of itself?'

'Are you then saying, Jesus, that what we have seen in these damned souls is a natural judgement, an act of Nature defending itself from abuse?'

'As difficult as this may seem to you, Mary, that is how it is. Conscience, Mary, has it own world, its own reality, its own rules, its own retribution; it has its own punishment. It co-creates with what it understands truth to be and to mean; in like fashion, it comprehends the lie and distortion and will react accordingly.'

'But surely God governs Nature, or are you inferring that Nature governs itself by its own rules separated from God as Person?'

'Yes, Mary, Nature is self-governing and yet it is always attempting to reach a creative perfection through renewal because within it there is a shared mind capable of conceptualising the idea of the holy, the sacred, or capable of self destruction by misuse of its life forms.'

'Shared mind ...?' Mary replied with some surprise.

'Yes. Mary. Every living thing from vegetation, roots, insects, trees, the fish of the oceans, the animals, humans, all share some degree of consciousness or awareness of itself, even though in many cases some, for convenience sake, refer to it as instinct. For example, Mary, take the simple leaf butterfly. It has developed to imitate the bush it lands on. The bush did not change the butterfly except by default ... there had to be a sense of consciousness or awareness in the butterfly to reach out to Nature to make this defensive change. The preservation of life is inbuilt even at such a seemingly unimportant form of life. Nature too teaches us the need for values. It can teach us how wars, violence, revenge, lack of forgiveness, are never solutions but perpetuate further destruction. As I say, Mary, Nature is an important part of what you understand God's life to be. It is Life itself that gives life. Life relays all life from itself. Life is the Great Giver. It is imbued with its own consequences which are comprehendible to its own mode of intelligence. Nature if you wish to understand it this way is full of messages and messengers. Any deliberate offence against Nature's life-giving creativity is also an offence against the creative law of Life or Love as it affects humankind, when the offence affects the spiritual and moral growth of humanity. Universal love, Mary, is its own messenger to humanity. It is not a magical source. It is clearly comprehendible to any soul willing to grasp its truth. In the same way, human hatred, lack of forgiveness, self-destruction, war and so on ... none of these are inevitable. Nature, Mary, co-creates with all its life forms. The bad choice, like poison, is the fools own folly. Is the fool to be complemented for being a fool, for being asleep to learning?'

'Can God, then, never be totally known? Is that what you are attempting to say?' Mary continued as baffled and bewildered as before by all that was revealed.

'Yes, Mary.' Jesus replied, his hands spread in front of him and his shoulders rose in an expression of resignation. 'That is what I am saying, Mary.' His voice was gentle and yet accepting what to him was both mysterious and even beyond his own knowledge, since there is no boundary to knowledge, no more than there is to creative life. For Jesus this was an act of faith. God, or Life, can only be known to humanity in the greatest and highest good of humanity's own fleeting existence. 'Although the later prophets and your theologians spoke of me as being "seated at the right hand of the Father" after my passion and resurrection, such a conclusion issued merely from human theological speculation and supposition, incomplete knowledge; although such speculation was offered with commendable pious metaphor in the absence of absolute knowledge. My resurrected life is really like the position of the most trusted person chosen by an earthly king or queen as an advisor. It is only Truth and Love that can advise each other. Lies cannot advise Truth; no more can Hate advise or counsel Love. To that extent it is an important comparison. Yet since only Life and Love can be considered as God, then the only trusted servant who could remain at the right hand side of Life or God as an adviser is one who lives in absolute love as the essence of his or her own being.' Jesus continued his explanation.

'Creation, with its natural infinite universes Mary, does not require a God beyond it, a First Mover; or maybe it does, or maybe it doesn't. It is foolish to give definition to that which is too vast and mysterious in a point of time, too far from reason and clarity. This is always a problem for many who make statements about life and the unknown when they have neither the insight nor the development to justify such speculative definition. To understand this, Mary, really means that ascending virtues are what reign in heaven with power at the redeemed side of virtuous Love and care for all. The whole of my life was a physical and spiritual manifestation of Love. I, as Messenger, made this teaching on love my life's work – short as my earthly existence was.'

Jesus concluded that his earthly message of the Commandments hinged on love of God and neighbour. And that this dual or concomitant commandment is the entire message of the whole of scripture's purpose, meaning, and true human direction. The latter commandments were clear enough to be understood by any thinking person. However, to love God in the way just expressed, considering the mysterious nature of God, could be more easily understood by loving Love or living in love. Since that is the most indisputable and universal direction for all humanity. It was these and other such revelations to Mary that helped her to have a deeper understanding of God and Jesus than she ever had before.

Jesus returned to the subject that troubled Mary. 'Although you cannot know God in totality since you cannot fully grasp a impenetrable creating force, Mary, as far as humanity is concerned, to live for Love is all any of us needs to do or know. That is the most fulfilling and worthwhile direction for all humanity. And that, Mary, is exactly what my life is still concerned with. You remember my earthly prayer: 'Our Father in heaven?'

'… Heaven in this case, Mary, is a higher state of love. It is Love that co-creates with Nature or Life. It is always endeavouring to bring harmony and cohesion to all living creatures. Love, Mary, in the mind of a living being asks for its needs, Nature then provides – given time'

'And yet you speak of God as Father?' Mary was confused.

'It is virtue that fathers or parents the soul of humanity, Mary, not a mysterious un-knowable or male-gendered God.'

Mary's eyes never left those of Jesus as he continued, patiently to explain, as best he could, to what troubled her. She posed one last question. 'The fathers of the aborted children … what of them …?'

Jesus was not keen to show her any more of the gruesome and despairing world of eternal nightmares, the unredeemed conscience, this self-made hell, as he described it. However, Mary's curiosity, or to put it more precisely, her need to understand the terrible dilemma of a lost soul left without the possibility of help or cessation of despair and suffering. Human nature, simply put, was far from perfect. To Mary It still seemed like revenge, like a sentence. It all felt so wrong from a loving God. Mary was still in total confusion about her indoctrinated concept of God. Since Mary was not going to remember these horrors, Jesus decided to reveal the last vision.

There came immediately before them both a naked man, again in a twilight world … a dream state. Again the scene was that of a bombed-out city. The man was wandering about searching for a woman. Every woman he encountered was naked and exquisitely beautiful. They were all beckoning him to come in to their rooms. Each room in the dilapidated city was draped in cobwebs. Their beds coated with years of dust. The man was not put off by the horrible conditions of their bombed-out dwellings. His aroused senses blinded him to all but his depraved sense of lust. As he attempted to penetrate each woman in turn, they in turn would manifest into the most gruesome savage creatures that would bite mercilessly into his face and body. The man would run screaming in terror. Yet within moments, the same depraved vision would continue to repeat itself.

Jesus noticed Mary turn her face away. The entire scene sickened her. The horrible revelation disappeared as quickly as it had appeared. Mary kept her eyes tight shut and shaking her head from side to side.

'No more! Please! No more!' When she had recovered she turned to Jesus, her voice quavering: 'you can't allow this to continue; you can't! It's not worthy of God.'

'I'm sorry Mary. Life is what Life is. This is not of the imagined God that humanity has fabricated for itself. It is that soul's own fabrication. Nature is what Nature is, Mary. None of us, even I do not live in a magical existence. The lost soul created his own nightmare world when he refused to live by the messages, the rules that Nature itself reveals. He chose his own rules, his own direction. He turned the potential of creative love into destructive lust and life into abortion. Nature, Mary, is Life. Every life that deliberately deviates from its ordered end for the purpose of perverting that ordered end will eventually build its own destruction, its own hell. The world of dreams, Mary is a consequence of Nature attempting to reveal its own ordered end. It is forever teaching and struggling for harmony.'

'But some human beings are driven by excessive appetites,' Mary appealed. 'I know you expected us all to be responsible for our actions and to have control over our thoughts, to be people of grace by the power and help of meaningful and contemplative prayer. But, some people seemed incapable of any of these virtues. You know, Jesus, quite well, that we are all driven by so many appetites. It is these very drives which some cannot control. After all, are there not shadows of these in so many of the animals on earth? Is not the fox a perfect example of the drive to kill for killing sake? After all, few would begrudge a fox eating one chicken to feed itself and its young; and yet when it breaks into a chicken compound, it kills everything within its reach. Surely there is also the animal nature in humanity, men and women; and is not that same imprecise nature a shared reality for all? The point I am making in defence of those damned souls is how imprecise, how imperfect human passion continues to be for so many. Surely you cannot put the responsibility for such imperfection, such driven forces on the human condition? I still cannot see why you simply could not just cut them off from all life and memory so that they could no longer exist in any dimension, imagined or real.'

'I understand your reasoning, Mary; I understand your strong sentiments and your abhorrence for what you believe comes from the power of God. Again, I can only say to you, Love has its own laws. Life will protect its own creativity; it will not suffer the deliberate disfigurement of any ordered end. Free choice is always there, no matter how tenuous it may appear at times. Free choice is not void of grace, or the ability to know the outcome of choice. There is always the instinct to choose between the good thing and the bad, between the right course of action and the wrong one. If a consequence to any human act could not be known, either by instinct or by conscious knowledge, all life would end in chaos. Life is its own teacher, Mary, its own judge; it reveals its own lessons, its own good and bad choices. It is its own Messenger and reveals its own consequences. Just as the compulsive killing of the fox results in itself becoming the hated and hunted. All sin has a natural consequence, Mary.'

Jesus went on to explain. 'Sin, in the military sense of the word, Mary, comes from the use of the bow and arrow. The arrow is meant to hit the target – to miss the target is given the term, "to Sin," which really means to "miss the mark." The bowman or woman has control over the bow; strict training is required to achieve the ordered end of the act; hence the preoccupation with Sin when it comes to understanding the Holy or Sacred aspects of life. Every human act has an ordered end – its true aim or purpose in a given period of time, the act's highest and greatest good: to deviate from that purpose is to miss the mark of the act's ordered end and so to Sin. Because of the serious consequence and vital nature of all human action, practice at virtue to achieve the right ordered end of all human acts becomes critical; it demands purposefulness, deliberation and self-control. Indifference to such directives will inevitably destroy the careless soul; it will punish itself.

'Now, Mary, we have indulged enough in the dark world where neither of us can enter since it cannot possibly exist for us. As I told you earlier, you will forget that you ever experienced what I have shown you. You have a new life here, Mary – the old one is gone for ever.'

Suddenly all of Mary's earthly concerns disappeared; all but one – her concern for her promise to help her earthly son Larry. She was prepared to keep that concern on hold for a brief spell from her mind as Jesus took her by the hand to rejoin the celebrations of her entrance into Heaven. Maureen had already laid out the food on some of the spare seats. Maureen offered them both some meat pies and some white wine; heaven or no heaven, Maureen was not keen on red wine. By now the floor of the theatre was crowded with dancers as the cascading music continued late into the evening. After the shared meal, Jesus said to Maureen,

'You can show Mary to her new home and sort out what kind of work she wishes to follow. Give her a tour of the local area ... I'm sure she will approve. Both of you can take a month's holiday if Mary is able for it after all the excitement.'

'Work!' said Mary. 'I can't be expected to work, surely. I'm over eighty years old, or have you not noticed?' Mary was very much taken aback. She instinctively looked at her hands and dress as a means to emphasise her age and condition. However, Jesus and Maureen fell into fits of laughter. Mary's mind was still fixed on earthly experience. Jesus said to Maureen.

'Show her a mirror.' Maureen produced one from her handbag. When Mary saw her face reflected in the mirror she was dumbstruck. She was every bit as beautiful and of similar age to her sister.

'How is this possible?' she all but ripped the small compact mirror form her sister's hand. Jesus and Maureen continued laughing good-naturedly.

'I will let you do the explaining from here on, Maureen, you will find her a myriad of questions. Believe me, she will drain you. It is our good fortune,' he added teasingly, 'that we have the rest of eternity to enlighten her otherwise we might die in the process.' Jesus turned and kissed them both before departing for the night.

The theatre was some distance from Maureen's rural home which was set in deep sparsely inhabited farmland where she worked as a teacher and cared for two children. She took Mary by the hand and left the noisy theatre driving home in a jeep-like, rugged vehicle. As night fell and the crowds departed for home, Mary and Maureen were exhausted. It seemed as if they had chatted to every living soul in the vast theatre; all wished to welcome the new-comer personally; that included her earthly parents and every other one of her family relations and countless friends. Mary was highly animated and yet exhausted all at once. With the windows of the vehicle opened, the gentle night breeze was a refreshing relief after the crowded atmosphere of the theatre. A sweet scent of corn wafted from nearby fields, which gave the two exhausted sisters a sense of the time of year ... early autumn. They came upon the dark shape of two thatched cottages; both were very old fashioned dwellings; they were like picture postcards once familiar to Mary's diminishing earthly memory.

As they alighted from the jeep, Mary was first to open conversation:

'Are these our homes, Maureen?' Mary whispered in the moonlight as if she might disturb a neighbour, although they were quite a distance from the next dwellings in the village.

'Yes, Mary; that's us home.' Maureen dropped the empty food hamper and put her arms round her sister and kissed her; a great surge of love coursed through their bodies. Maureen whispered in her sister's ear: 'We are together again, at last, Mary; never to be parted again.'

'Never ...?' Mary asked with disbelief, clinging lovingly to Maureen.

'Never!' replied Maureen in a whisper that held all the assurance of a lover's promise. Both were in a stream of tears and an indescribable bliss. They didn't want to part; they were quite content to cling to each forever. However, Mary, always the one with questions, broke the silence;

'Are we a bit backward here Maureen; I mean in time?'

'Backward in time, Mary; whatever can you mean?'

'Thatched cottages ...! Straw roofs! Are we the poor relations in the village?'

'Mary Walsh! You are the end. Of course we are not poor. Everyone has a dwelling, a home of their own, if they want to. We have no use of money here; it has no relevance. Yes we all have to work; but that too is a pleasure since you choose the work suitable to your ability and what you wish to contribute to the good of all.'

'It's not like I imagined heaven to be.' Mary gave her sister a reassuring cuddle and added; 'I'm in bliss, Maureen, love; I suppose I imagined heaven to be out of this world, if you will forgive the pun.'

Maureen smiled and replied: 'It is out of the Earth's world in many senses; you will understand that in time. However, love, it is like the Earth in the sense that Heaven is not a magical world with flying angels with harps or other such images. Heaven, here, only means a higher state of advancement, socially and spiritually-speaking. We are held responsible for our own welfare, our own advancement and stewardship of our environment. Although we have everything we need and everything is free; even so, we do not waste things as they do on Earth. We are one big family sharing all resources in common; and, indeed, delighted to do so. On Earth, the reality of our life here could only be imagined as an ideology.'

Mary picked up the empty hamper to allow Maureen to open her cottage door. There was no need of keys or locks in their new world. Maureen was somewhat taken aback. 'You left the door unlocked; is that wise out here in the village at night?'

'Mary! Mary! Mary Walsh! The old World is too much with you still. You have a lot to let go of here. No harm will come to any of us. Everyone here, as I told you before, is family; there are no strangers to fear. All animals are friendly. People who we may meet from time to time are all family even before you get to know their character. Mary, love,' she added for reassurance, 'the way we two feel about each other is the same way we feel about every other living soul here; it's the way we have naturally evolved and developed.'

Once inside the old stone-floor cottage, Maureen switched on the light and put a finger to her lips as a sign for silence. Mary's instinctive reaction was to spread her hands in a quizzical gesture as if to ask, what's up now? Maureen put on the kettle for some tea and pointed in silence to the ceiling and whispered, 'The two children are asleep.' The fact that her sister revealed this in the most casual manner, so matter-of-fact, took Mary aback; indeed she felt more than a little disappointed in her sister's silence on the matter at the theatre and on the way home. She never mentioned anything about a husband ... or about being married, or about having two children. Mary was a little vexed when she revealed her thoughts in whispers. Maureen almost turned puce as she struggled to keep herself from laughter. Through the noise of the boiling kettle, Maureen threw her arms round Mary and whispered:

'Gosh, Mary! I'll be glad when you know more about the birds and the bees up here. Of course the children are not solely mine; they belong to everyone; it is just that we are all responsible for being family to our children. There are no husbands involved; there are no marriages here.' Mary stood there dumfounded before asking another of her innumerable questions, though still speaking in whispers.

'Does God or Jesus make the children, then?' Maureen shook her head patiently as if to say, she's worse than a young child for questions. But of course Maureen understood her strangeness to the place. One thing Maureen was deeply grateful for was the fact that Mary was presented to her in the theatre at the age she was and not as a baby. However, Maureen had not the faintest idea how this came about; she only understood the natural circumstance of her own birth and of the people in her world. The entrance into heaven, or the more advanced world that Maureen inhabited, was very much a mystery to her; not that she lost any sleep over the question. After all, the ocean doesn't ask itself where it came from or what it is made of; it is what it is. However, Maureen couldn't answer the question of her own emergence in heaven; she just woke up there and became conscious of her life at a very early age much as the children of the Earth eventually develop an awareness of their own existence.

'We are unlike the Earth's people, Mary; our bodies regenerate themselves; they get to a certain age and a whole series of biological changes occur; the adults near by see the signs long before this happens and so we are taken into care by the nearest person or persons close to us and so they take care of the new life that is born. It's a bit like the seed in a flower. In fact our whole gigantic world here regenerates itself from tree to every form of animal. But before you ask me how that is done with your next two million questions; I'm for bed after this drink; there's always tomorrow ... it's guaranteed, Mary; be assured and don't lose a night's sleep worrying over it.' Maureen was smiling good-humouredly and added, 'You best sleep here with me for the night. We can sort out your cottage in the morning, if you wish.' Mary was all too eager to agree; she continued to experience a state of bliss while with her sister. Although there was a spare bedroom for guests, both undressed and climbed into Maureen's bed where they fell into a blissful sleep clinging to each other. Many thoughts trickled through Mary's dreams, but she didn't hold on any of them until she recalled her promise to help her son Larry. That was disturbing for her. However, she let the thought pass as she convinced herself that his neighbours, the Maddens, would be taking good care of him. She really wished that Larry was here with Maureen and herself.

As the light of the morning beamed through the gaps in the closed curtains, so the sisters awoke a little bleary-eyed. The two seven year old children, Primrose, the girl, and Pody the boy, were already scampering playfully downstairs, still in their silk pyjamas. Maureen, after showering with Mary, called to the children to come up and be washed also; both adults were by now dried off and in powder blue, silk dressing-gowns; both garments were very beautiful. The children took to Mary in an instant, jumping all over her by way of greeting; it was as though they had claimed instant ownership of her. Maureen stood there enchanted by the ecstasy written all over her sister's face. It felt to Mary as if these were some of the children whom she met in the theatre the previous night; both had fair hair and slim delicate bodies.

'My name is Primrose,' said the little girl wiggling about in Mary's arms with a proud sparkle in her grey-green eyes, and added for emphasis, I'm called after a flower.' As she finished her solemn introduction she looked straight at Mary with her angelic face drawn back and nodding as if to say, what do you think of that, then? Primrose had the habit of milking attention, so little Pody was pulling at Mary's gown and straining upwards with his hazel-coloured eyes to be noticed and said:

'My name is Pody. Maureen says that I am called after the peapods ... I always help her to take the peas out of the pods for the cooking ... and nobody knows how the peas got into the pods because they're always closed and it's a mystery.' Primrose looked down at Pody from Mary's arms and shook her head saying sagaciously:

'You most certainly are a mystery, Pody, and no mistake.' Mary couldn't prevent an outburst of laughter and turned to Maureen:

'You have some lady here in Primrose.'

'You can say that again. That little one would make a nest in your ear if you let her land there.'

Mary put Primrose down and picked up Pody. She couldn't help but notice that same powerful feeling of utter ecstasy when she embraced the children or Maureen. It seemed as if she could not get used to the utter surging sense of loving attachment. She could see the same effects in the children as they were washed in the bath, both clinging to each other as often as possible; it was such a wonderful thing to experience. Angelic as they appeared, it did not prevent them from splashing about staining the silk gowns of the two sisters with suds and water. They had to be chastised from time to time, to be taught appropriate behaviour. However, for most of the time the children were given a wide latitude for fun. Like any form of higher intelligent life, there had to be a guiding force, a philosophy for living. Here in heaven, that philosophy was love and care of all people, a living philosophy that was central to the whole of their existence.

It was difficult to speak of heaven regarding its size. Its landscapes being so varied from the tropical to glacial, from prairie to vast mountain ranges soaring for miles upwards. Its oceans were so vast that they are yet un-traversed by many apart from their indigenous inhabitants and wildlife. Its lake-lands and rivers are too many and vast to name and numerate. Its beaches too run for kilometre to kilometre. Its soaring granite cliffs, in places, stand like giants defying the roar of exploding waves below. The sheer magnitude of its worlds; its verity of jungle, forest and woodland defy comprehension, a vast living creation within creation. Its peoples, the chosen of many worlds and times, are as many and varied in colour and character as the planets they inhabit. Their populations couldn't be counted; there are people there from every age to the dawn of human existence, and each one is family to all. It shares other vast planets of like character in it own unique universe. Though many would never have met other inhabitants from across its vast shores ... or never even knew of each other's existence, except by news from the various T V relay stations; none of that mattered. Heaven was a compilation of many worlds that were earned by all who had shown care and concern for others in their own lifetime. Only the essence of good souls were allowed to penetrate its vast womb and take on a more perfect nature and continue to grow more and more in that perfection. Spirit beings, or souls took on material existence just as thought process on earth generated brain material.

Since Love was Life, and Life had no limit, neither did perfection or knowledge have a boundary. Creation was what it was ... a creation ... a Life-giving life in unlimited diversity. Whatever the human mind might care to envisage, it would come about by the very act of imagining it; to will it was to create it; even though it would take the passage of eons of time to bring it about. Life had a shared mind; even the butterfly could ask to be camouflaged as the leaf of a bush; or to have wings to fly. The one distinction in this heavenly planet was that all its life was eternal and without harm or malice. In short, life rewarded creative life; destructive life had no home or existence here. This was the home that Mary inherited.

Primrose and Pody were delighted to learn during breakfast that they were allowed a few weeks off school so that they could go with Maureen and Mary to visit some special places and go to the beach to make sandcastles and have some ice cream. Both piled into the utility room to search for their buckets and spades.

'Mine's the yellow one, cried Primrose; you can have the red one, it's yours; it's got a hole in it; you did that the last time we were on the beach – so it's yours.'

'Before you go any further you must sit quietly; say your grace, and show Auntie Mary how good you can be.' The two children just beamed playful faces at Mary while Maureen placed some scrambled eggs on toast in front of them. They were too excited to sit still and eat slowly; instead they wolfed down their food and swallowed their tea with great frantic gulps and galloped to the utility room to search for their water wings so that they could swim in the sea. However, Maureen called them back. 'What do we do after we eat? What do we say?'

'Thank you, mammy, for the lovely food.' The two little cheeky faces turned from side to side with mischievous grins at the two smiling sisters.

'But who do we thank first?'

'We thank Heaven ... at least I do; I don't know about Pody, I think he forgets sometimes,' said Primrose with the indifferent air of an old woman.

'...Course I say thank you to Heaven,' said Pody defensively and added: 'maybe I might get a new bucket from the shop, mightn't I mammy?'

'You might, but only if you are a good boy Pody. We don't want to make Heaven sad now, by being naughty, do we?'

'If Primrose was really good she would give me her bucket; mine's got a hole it. But she won't swap; therefore she can't really be so good after all, can she?' With that matter-of-fact deduction he gave his head one big nod at Primrose as if to say; sort that lot out, then.

Maureen wagged a playful finger at both of them; she knew all too well that all their talk was nothing but banter and teasing – a playfulness with language. The truth was that they were really inseparable friends. One moment it was all banter; the next they would be clinging to each other like limpets to a rock.

Maureen prepared a large hamper for their outing. There was a variety of meats: chicken, duck, beef, ham and some stick-loafs; butter and jam. The children's favourite drinks of orange and other fruit drinks were included; a large flask of tea; a bottle of white wine; some current cake and all the utensils to complete the hamper. There was a good possibility that they may be away from home for three or four weeks, in which case they planned to make use of whatever facilities were available.

All places of hospitality were generously furnished for sleeping over and for dining. Those whose duty it was to work in such establishments did so with the greatest enthusiasm and unstinting generosity. The fact that everything was free did nothing to detract from the professional and homely service and a comfortable sense of belonging.

Maureen took visual stock of the clothing in her wardrobe. Mary helped to choose suitable items for both sisters and the children. There were rugged cloth for travel; swimwear for the beach; silk dresses and trouser suits for the warm autumn evenings. Since the climate was characteristically stable, the sisters dressed the children: a light delicate sea-green silk top for Pody; it was his favourite; and light tan kaki shorts, white socks and sandals; she packed a pair of trainers as backup. Primrose was always another question. It could take a month to dress her if the sisters didn't cajole her into wearing what they really believed most suitable. In any event she settled for a silk pastel-cream suit; white socks and light russet-coloured shoes. She insisted on wearing her outrageously wide-brimmed, bottle-green hat that would take up half the space of the jeep. To all this she added a granny's grey shawl. She looked a character indeed; she might have walked off a stage from a part as an outrageous wilful old woman. Both sisters wore bottle-green blazer jackets and powder-blue slacks; these showed off their ruffled white silk shirts. And both chose to wear white trainer-like canvas footwear; both donned white-peaked caps to shield them from the bright autumn sun. All the suitcases, hamper, buckets and other holiday paraphernalia were packed neatly into the jeep to allow maximum room for the children's comfort..

'It will do you good to see some of the local facilities and people before you settle down, Mary; it will give you complete confidence in their goodness and genuine love and care for each other. Whatever you need, you have only to ask for it and it is yours. As I mentioned before, we all work and live for each other's needs and benefit.'

Apart from the children playing at slapping each other's hands in some complicated rhythm, the sisters were quiet. Maureen was aware of her sister's tears even though Mary was looking out from the opposite window in the front of the jeep. Maureen took one hand from the steering wheel and gently took her sisters hand. As Mary turned to acknowledge her sister's gesture of concern, so she saw the tears streaming down Mary's face. The sight of her sister's tears tore at Maureen's heart; she knew instinctively that these were not tears of joy or bliss.

'I'm sorry, Maureen; it's Larry. I can't help it. I know he is in good hands with his neighbours, but I miss him so much. I promised I would come back to help him. Now I realise I couldn't have known how I would be estranged from him in this beautiful world.' Maureen had to pull over to the side of the road; Mary was truly in a terrible state. Added to Mary's distraught state was to see Primrose and Pody in tears. She felt miserable because she blamed herself for spoiling everyone's holiday.

The jeep had barely stopped for more than a few moments when Jesus pulled in alongside them. He was riding a scooter-like machine, a popular form of transport for general use among the younger inhabitants; Jesus himself was only in his mid thirties. His body too was subject to regeneration and yet lost nothing of his innate powers as a unique powerful being He knew perfectly well what Mary's problem was before he took her aside. He greeted Maureen and the children in such a calm leisurely way in spite of their tears. All three clung to him as if he was their father. He held on to them until they overcame their distraught state. He moved Mary away some distance from the others so that the two of them could be alone. After embracing Mary for some time and calming her, he spoke into her ear over her shoulder as he continued to embrace her.

'Larry is quite safe; quite happy with Seamus, Lil and the children. I am well aware of the promise that you made to him before you passed over from his world. Your promise will most certainly be fulfilled. His future is already in our hands.'

'I'm sorry, Jesus, to be such a worry to you and everyone else. It is just that I know he cannot hold onto any work, he's just not quick enough for it; he wants to be talking to people the whole time; he loses concentration; his employers invariably consider him a nuisance or unemployable; he is just too friendly for his world.'

'We know the love in the heart of your son, Mary. One thing we can promise you is that Larry will become an employer himself; you can take my words as absolute,' Jesus said reassuringly.

'You keep saying "we," Jesus. Do you mean that you and God are assuring me of his welfare?'

'I am referring to the spirit of our world here. Of course we are deeply concerned about Earth's peoples. The spirit by which we live here is what we are at pains to instil in the Earth's inhabitants and in the entire creation so that all can eventually come to join us here or in a like or neighbouring world. Your son, Larry is such a developed spirit but not according to Earth's expectations. He is full of love for other people. His soul, or essence, is already with us here; only his physical presence and time delay his being with us – Be assured Mary, his spirit and soul already belong here.'

Of a sudden Jesus showed Mary a living presence of Larry before them. He was eating breakfast with Seamus' family; all were busy eating while the dogs and cats were wandering about the kitchen. It shocked Mary to see her son and his friends in real Earth time. She looked startled into Jesus' smiling face; he prompted her to continue observing what was before her, reassuring Mary that she was not in some magical dream. After being reassured of Larry's happiness Jesus said to Mary:

'Now, I want you to visit Larry to reassure him of the promise you made to him. He will see you as you once were, his elderly mother. He would not recognise you in your new nature. This will be your only visit after which you must let him go, Mary, to develop in his own way and circumstance. As I mentioned earlier, do not worry about his employment; that is all in hand. The whole world will know and acknowledge your son in a way you could never dream possible.

'Walk now into the picture that you see before you. Whisper to Larry to excuse himself from the table, and walk with him to his own house next door. Once there, you may manifest yourself before him and leave this parcel for him; it contains a message for him to remind him that your visit was more than a mere vision of a phantom or dream. The message within the packet refers to the work we have requested him to undertake.' With these words Jesus took a simple brown paper package from his scooter. The parcel was tied up with string. He said reassuringly. 'I will leave this picture window open, Mary, I will be watching over you all. I will hold on here with Maureen and the children; they will not be aware of what you are about. Now go to your son with our blessing.' With his words Mary dissolved into the picture and was with Larry in a fraction of a second.

Mary carried out Jesus' instructions to the letter. She was overjoyed to be among her wonderful neighbours; to see them ... to hear them ... to smell the familiar aroma of cooking... the scent of the animals ... the strong aroma of toast ... the radio giving out the weather forecast and the news of the day, sounds once so familiar. True to instructions, she whispered in Larry's ear to go to his own home. Although the family was a little startled at Larry's sudden departure and his unexplained exit from the meal table; it was not like him, giving his natural good manners. The family accepted his few words of parting as sufficient reason to leave the company.

'I have to go now but I will be back. Don't let that savage, Andrew, finish my meal.' The family laughed at his good-natured banter.

Once back in his own home, Mary appeared to him as she was formally, his elderly mother. Larry ran to her; tears streaming from his eyes as he screamed on the top of his voice.

'Mammy...! Mammy! Mammy! You've come back; you've come back.'

'Hush, Larry, hush. You keep this up and you'll be the death of me. I see you are well and looking strong.' Larry's heart was pounding and overjoyed to see the old familiar loving face and her silver hair; to hear her own familiar voice. He was dancing from foot to foot unable to be still with his joy-filled emotions. He even did his aeroplane dance swooping with his long extended arms about the house. Mary smiled ... glad to see him so happy again. She wore her old heavy grey shawl and simple long working dress; the same threadbare canvas slippers so much a part of his old mammy. They held onto each other for what seemed an eternity but in truth it was no more than a few moments. Finally, Mary spoke in her old familiar Cork accent.

'Larry, son, I am delighted to see you well. You must thank Seamus, Lil, and the children for looking after you. Tell them all that they are all in my prayers always. Now I have had a word with Jesus and he is going to find you a nice Job where you cannot be dismissed any more. He didn't tell me what the occupation is but that you will find the instructions in the parcel that I have left in my old bedroom. When I leave you again, it will be proof that I have come back as promised and that you will have all the help you need. Now Larry, son, you must promise me not to get upset when I leave you this time ... will you promise me?'

'Oh, mammy; I will, I will, I will.'

'Don't make me sad now Larry, will you? Don't break my heart again. I am truly happy where I am and especially since Jesus has promised that you will join us when your work on Earth is done. You will always be near to me wherever I am.'

'Oh, Mammy, I promise; I really do; thank you for coming back to me. Now I know you are safe and happy I will be fine. Are you really in Heaven with Jesus?'

'Of course I am, son. Bernard, you daddy, sends his greetings too. Jesus is looking after your mammy and your daddy and many more of our family; everyone there is so kind, so wonderful.'

'Oh, mammy; I'm so delighted.' Just as quickly as she came, so Mary disappeared with her parting words.

'God bless you Larry; I will love you always.' Suddenly Larry was alone looking about him as if he was in a dream. He seemed to remember something about a parcel to be opened with a message inside it He took the parcel back to his neighbours to show them that his mammy had returned; he felt he owed them that much for never questioning his claim that his mammy had been taken up to Heaven.

Mary reappeared in heaven walking back into her new life and company. Reassured by her earthly visit, she promised Jesus that she would let go of Larry now and put her full trust in Jesus to carry out what he had promised her. The promise was solemn and accepted in that spirit. With that done, Jesus said farewell to the company who were now calm and more themselves again. It had all been very traumatic for the family and not at all supposed to be a part of normal life in Heaven, nor the beginning of a holiday.

The family continued on their journey passing beautiful lakes and woodlands; great numbers of men, women and older children laboured away with scythes, sickles, pikes and rakes bringing in the harvest. Mary thought this very odd and could not avoid another spate of questions.

'Maureen; I don't understand this,' Mary remarked quizzically.

'Understand what, love?' said Maureen.

'Why are there hundreds of families gathering in the harvest by hand? It is all so odd. I mean, here we are travelling at ease in this motor jeep; why are they not using mechanical means for bringing in the harvest; surly that would be more efficient, wouldn't it? Are these people behind the times or what?'

Maureen smiled as she answered her sister. 'We don't rush things up here and we prefer to work together. We only have the use of the jeep because of the distance our village is from regular transport. Those workers will be singing away merrily; they will be dancing in the evening and having a rare old time of it. They are all volunteers; they do have other regular jobs of their own. Life here, Mary, is just simple ... lived at a leisurely pace most of the time. For all that the harvest is taken in by hand, we haven't lost one yet; there is never a shortage of volunteers.' As they passed the workers in the fields all waved enthusiastically back to the jeep. The families in the fields were too distant to make out individual faces. Maureen added, 'To answer your question those people are very far from being a backwater people; you will find many educators, professors, lecturers, musicians, scientists, chemists, biologists and every other discipline among them. We could bring in the harvest mechanically if we so wished or were forced to by unfavourable weather. Time is not terribly important here, Mary. It is not linked to money, as it is on the Earth.' Mary let her lower lip protrude and nodded her head appreciatively with a mixture of surprise and appreciation. The children were by now kneeling on some soft cushions with their faces pressed against the windows of the jeep.

They passed through various villages and towns without stopping. The company in the Jeep was quiet as all took in the bustling activity. Mary, in particular, was once again surprised by the old world buildings; she might have been back in ancient Ireland with all the dark timbered buildings with their whitewashed walls and diamond-shaped lead and glass windows. At times these distinct earthly details caused Mary to shudder as if someone had walked over her grave. She had that disturbing feeling that heaven was no more than an illusion, a figment of her imagination. In point of fact she always did prefer the old world where things were built to last by people who took pride in their various crafts. The towns were jostling with a wide assortment of horse-driven coaches; bicycles; electric scooters and four-wheeled electric vehicles for the very old or semi-incapacitated. Cream-coloured busses for the masses of inhabitants seemed to be the most popular form of transport; all of them pulled a carriage behind that held the shopping of the passengers or their bicycles. As Maureen had mentioned earlier, the people just ambled about at their own unhurried pace. The only real sense of pace was to be seen in the playful teenagers and children who darted about as if in a world of their own. Even these, with their helter-skelter activities, only drew favourable smiles from their older counterparts.

After three hours travel and having stopped for several short breaks to stretch their legs and picnic, they came upon a great seaside town. Many cliff-top hotels and private dwellings looked out onto a vast turquoise ocean. They experienced a distinct freshness to the bracing sea air. There were very few motor vehicles about so that parking the jeep at the edge of the long promenade caused no difficulty. There were regular convenient breaks in the railings that ran the length of the seafront; from these, stone steps led down to beautiful silver sands. The beach was not very crowded. There were several young families with their children playing away contentedly with excited yelps intermingling amid the sound of the pounding fall of the tide. Some older folk dozed in the brilliant midday sun; some with large-brimmed hats covering their faces. Most of the people were naked apart from the very frail and elderly who preferred to be covered in light clothing to shield off the intense heat of the sun. Self-consciousness was unknown to the people in so far that it related to any kind of sexual consciousness. As mentioned before, the population was constant through self-regeneration. Although other earthly members were introduced from various other worlds besides the Earth, in the same way that Mary had entered Heaven; even so, this planet of Heaven remained un-crowded. The Heaven in which Mary had entered was not the only higher form of intelligence or existence; there were others, even more advanced planets of equal vastness in the same universe and far beyond. To that extent, intelligence, perfection and knowledge, like God or Life, were on-going creative realities

The family emptied the jeep of all its seaside paraphernalia. There was a mad dash from Primrose and Pody to be first on the beach; both wanted to be the first to build their sandcastle; both filled their buckets with such force and speed, you would think that there would not be enough sand left to complete both objectives. Unfortunately for the two seven-year-olds, and to their consternation, both their efforts fell apart as soon as they pulled the upturned buckets away; neither considered, in their wild excitement, that the sand nearest the promenade was running dry. Primrose dug her delicate hands into her naked ribs in a gesture of frustration. Pody, always the one to laugh when things went wrong threw his new bucket and spade up into the air just for the sheer fun of it. Maureen whispered in the ear of the disappointed Primrose:

'You need damp sand, dear, or it will keep falling down.' With this reminder of past visits, Primrose, always the great achiever grabbed Pody by the hand and headed some way from their guardians to reach the wet sand nearer to the incoming waves. There were piercing screams of joy, spade waving to get their guardians' attention. Maureen and Mary waved back enthusiastically; it gave them an absorbing sense of happiness to share in the children's sense of innocence and joy in such simple pleasures. The children continued more creatively now to decorate their sand castles with white beach stones and lengths of seaweed. Pody, ever the one to investigate, kept sniffing and bursting the pods of the seaweed just to see if there was anything inside them; occasionally he would put a pod under Primrose's nose for her to smell it. She would look into his mischievous face with her sparkling grey-green eyes, tighten her delicate lips and shake her head like some old granny endeavouring to chastise a naughty child. Pody would just grab hold of her and cuddle her. Primrose would always give way to smiles and cuddles in the end. There was no getting away from their utter love for each other.

Their guardians were watching all their antics. The children moved on to some rock pools that were covered in wet moss and seaweed. They were finding it slippery underfoot as they clambered with all care among the mossy rocks; some were great sturdy boulders that were once a part of the land but now, the mere play things of the relentless crashing and ebbing tide. Now kneeling, by a sizable rock-pool created within the seaweed-covered boulders, the children gazed with all concentration into the pool's sparkling and shallow depths. Small fish, no more than a few millimetres long darted about from time to time with such speed that the children couldn't afford to blink an eye or they would miss a second of this hypnotic activity; tiny lives marooned perhaps until the next incoming tide. Occasionally the children could be heard in competition with each other, 'There's one; there's another; this one is silver; that one is brown; look at the size of that one, it's a monster;' and so it went on. They both stayed riveted to the pool transfixed and mesmerise by the miniature world below the sparkling water. The sudden spurts of sand at the bottom as a basking tiny fish would suddenly dart from its hiding place or chased by another, a little bigger than itself. The bottom of the sandy pool also revealed a myriad of the tiniest shell life. All the while the sound of the pounding ocean and the crying of the wheeling gulls overhead became the orchestration that would take root as loving memories into the treasure chest of their endearing childhood. These roots so unconscious now, would ever bind them in an unbreakable bond of their love of the precious gift and diversity of life; like young May lambs jumping in sheer joy for just being alive.

Pody was for pulling at the many limpets clinging to the rocks but Primrose put him off the idea.

'They're fish too, Pody, mammy won't like you to kill them.' There was genuine concern in Primrose's appeal.

'How can they be fish, Primrose, they are stuck to the rock; I don't see them swimming about and neither can you. Look there is some of the same shells in the sand and there are no fish in them.' Pody was very confident in his simple deduction. However, Primrose made another appeal.

'...please Pody.' That was enough to forgo his intentions; his fondness for Primrose always took president whenever he was convinced that she was serious.

Primrose was not a sibling sister to Pody except by upbringing; just as no one in heaven was related by blood, though all were more intimately bound up with each other as one vast family totally dependant on each other. Here, it was virtue that parented all the children. It was the virtues of love and care of each other which drove and motivated their very instincts. It did not come from any conscious religious fervour. Their physical evolution went way back into the annals of pre-history.

'Will we go for a swim in the sea now I feel burning under this blazing sun?'

'Ok, Pody, let's go back to mammy and Auntie Mary and put on our water wings.'

After leaving the rocks and saying goodbye to the little fish pool that had absorbed their impressionable minds for so long, they ran across the sands to their family. Leaving aside their buckets and spades, they pulled on their arm bands. Before they were allowed to go to the water Maureen wanted them to have something to eat and drink; they had been absorbed for some two hours without a bite or a cool drink. They sat quiet for a while eating some ice cream which Mary got from a beach service shop. While absorbed with this cooling ice-cream on their tongues, Maureen was busy applying sun cream on the children's sun-burnt bodies. She was sufficiently concerned about their exposure to the sun that she insisted that they both wear swim wear, including head covers and vests to prevent any further serious exposure to the blazing midday sun. After some half-hearted protests, the children ran darting to the crashing waves and plunged into the cool waters. Maureen and Mary joined in the fun; they too wore protective clothing. Many strangers nearby joined them in a game of punching a large multicoloured beach ball among them. The ball being fairly light was ideal and so kept in close proximity within the group; its large size presented no difficulties for the many children who came to join in the fun. It was taken for granted among children and adults alike that no one required any formal approach to join in any public activity; unless, of course, if it was a specific sport purposely designed for a team of players.

It was 4.30 pm when the incoming tide put an end to all play on the beach and time to pack away everything in the jeep. It was also time to arrange accommodation for the night. The family climbed the many wide steps to reach the gaily-coloured dwellings that formed part of the lengthy sea view. Maureen was used to using these facilities; she knew it was going to be a difficult choice of guesthouse since all offered the same generous hospitable services. Everything was free and the management of these holiday dwellings was in the hands of very capable and enthusiastic staff. In fact they acted as extended family. The service was always very professionally undertaken with enthusiasm and pleasure. It was easy to get to know everyone at a very personal level; indeed, both guest and host were almost indistinguishable apart from the duties carried out by the hosts. It really did come down to a choice of the colour of the outside of the dwellings, hence Maureen's question to the family.

'Which colour front do you like?' Maureen asked with a philosophical smile and with her arms spread as if to remark, how else can you choose?

Mary was puzzled as if the question was a little inappropriate, even frivolous.

'Shouldn't we look at the menus first?' She asked.

'We have been here before, Mary; I can assure that every hotel offers the most comprehensive choice of food, drink and accommodation. The only real reason for passing by any such hotel would be the fact that it had a "Full" sign, or "Closed for Improvements" displayed in its window. Needless to say, the children chose the hotel by its external colours or other decorative features. It took a little time and patience before lady Primrose won the day. She chose a pastel green-coloured building because it had a beautiful starfish embossed on the front and picked out in blue and sliver speckles.

'Ok,' said Maureen, and added, 'Pody, if we move from here you can have the next choice.' This was accepted by Primrose with a mischievous side-long glance at Pody who, in turn, stuck his tongue out at her and emphasised the acknowledgement of this privilege with an affirmative robust nod of his head. Primrose roared with laughter at the exaggerated antics of her brother. What might have appeared as competition among the children was no more than a bantering, good-natured game. Maureen and Mary could only smile and shake their heads at the antics of the children. Within seconds all interests went into choosing something to eat.

A youthful waiter helped the family to settle at one of the tables, which faced a view of the rolling ocean. He welcomed each member of the family with a warm kiss and hug as if he had known them forever. He introduced himself as Sean. All the family introduced themselves in turn. Mary felt like putting her confidence to the test; as yet she was not quite settled into her new life and identity; so it was something of an experiment when she opened conversation with Sean.

'How long have you worked here, Sean?' Mary asked with a smile.

'Oh! Gosh! Mary, I would need to think about that one; let's say for now that it has been years.' It seemed as if it was not a question that was ever put to him before.

'You don't seem very old, do you, Sean? What are you … our age perhaps or less than twenty-four?' Sean turned to an older lady serving behind the drink's bar.

'Elizabeth, how old am I now, can you recall?' Sean appeared as if he hadn't the slightest clue to his own age. Elizabeth greeted the company warmly and shouted across to the family good-humouredly.

'That one would forget the day of the week if we didn't have a calendar to consult. Yet ask him about fish and he could name everything outside in the ocean.' Elizabeth added, 'he is twenty-two going on twelve.' Sean radiated a beaming smile and replied.

'Never mind Elizabeth, I will remember their order, have no fear.'

'So you're big into fish, then, Sean?' said Mary in a teasing manner, taking up Elizabeth's banter. Sean moved his head from side to side expressing only a minimal interest in fishing. He waved his outstretched hands about in a sea-saw motion to indicate that his interest in fishing was no more than a moderate passing fancy. Elizabeth, Sean's guardian-parent, a beautiful lady in her early forties and dressed in a white shirt top, which was all you could see of her behind the bar, was not going to let Sean get away with such exaggerated modesty. Her dark black hair and sea-tanned skin appeared every bit the epitome of health as she pulled drinks for the guests.

'That one sleeps and dreams fish. Even if we were never supplied with our fish, he could supply us with his own efforts. He spends most of his evenings and days off on the pier below with some of his friends just a batty as himself.'

'Would you not prefer to go to sea and fish with the big trawlers, Sean?' The question posed by Maureen seemed to her to be the obvious thing to do since Sean was deemed to be so keen.

'Sea ...! Him ...! Elizabeth retorted mockingly, nodding her head towards Sean for emphasis. 'He gets seasick when he turns on a tap. No, Maureen, he prefers to fish from the pear or beach, on terra firma. Dragging in fish nets by hand or by machine onto a deep sea trawler in storm and exploding oceans is not his idea of fun. He likes it here, don't you, Sean? He is a kind of pain we love to live with.' Sean pointed his wagging finger at Elizabeth – they were obviously very dear to each other.

'I want to go fishing with Sean,' said Pody without the least knowledge of what was involved.

'So do I.' rejoined Primrose, not to be left out. Maureen and Mary smiled at Sean and remarked.

'Now look what you have started, Sean. It looks like you're going to have more company than you realised.'

'The more the merrier,' Sean returned, with his arms and hands imitating the reeling in of a big fish on a rod. 'Let's see how keen they really are when they see all the other amusements that are on the promenade to amuse the lovely children.' Sean made this remark by looking exaggeratedly into the faces of the children in a gesture of a tease and a challenge. He knew perfectly well the hundreds of amusements along the sea front would most certainly absorb their time. Sean soon became a favourite among the family; he was always so playful, like a little child himself.

All through this, lively banter, the restaurant's ambient atmosphere enveloped Maureen's family and the several other families that drifted in and out. Beautiful atmospheric music filled the air and mingled gently with the periodic excited voices of many other children engaged in their own playful games with their guardians while waiting for their food. The voices of adult guests were also raised in their enthusiastic greetings and conversation with the hotel's serving staff. In spite of bursts of sporadic busy service, a distinct relaxed and friendly spirit remained with a calm professional efficiency. The staff, while having a professional service to carry out, simply mingled with the various families as if they were lifelong extended family members.

These details enveloped Mary's acute consciousness. So much was new to her; like the mind of a child or youth, every new experience had an absorbing freshness to it. Maureen on the other hand took it all in her stride; her face, though rarely without a smile, was as tranquil as if she was in her own home. Mingled with all the atmosphere was the cries of the wheeling gulls from outside the open hotel doors; the autumn sun blazed through open windows and doors and yet there was a very comfortable coolness circulating throughout hotel. Occasional bees flew from flower to flower on the fresh replenished flower vases that decorated the many tables; this, in spite of the many beautifully manicured flowerbeds that ran from the steep heights of the hotels to the edges of the road that ran along the promenade. The colourful impression of the myriad of flowers, the workers carefully watering them, the deep blue sky and gentle white passing clouds formed a vivid scene in Mary's mind. The holiday was certainly beginning to fill the world of her senses.

Mary was surprised and deeply thoughtful concerning the different characters of the people in Heaven; for most part they seemed very much like Earth's people in their humour, character and activities, including their work. She felt at times that she had only exchanged worlds of similar character. What stood out from everything else, here in Heaven, was the utter inseparable bond between every individual. The care each person expressed for one another was without pretence or conscious effort; it was innate to all, much as you would expect to see a tail to a dog as a natural part of its evolution. It was that very word, evolution that struck Mary forcibly in the depths of her many reveries. Heaven, she was convinced, was a natural evolution even though it was a more advanced world than the Earth of her former life. Not that Heaven was more consciously ethical or moral than the Earth's inhabitants, all of that was simply innate; not requiring any special or demanding effort. Certainly learnt behaviour was taught and involved from the children's earliest days of development. Primrose and Pody had to be controlled and formed in Heaven's ways; there just didn't seem to be so much effort to it all by comparison to the people of Earth so Mary was beginning to realise.

She held these two worlds in the balance of her speculative reveries. On the one hand she had figured out that the old world of Earth was going nowhere in particular, at least not as a whole; it was too fragmented and divided for a common purpose to evolve. Even its diverse religious character was fragmented, and at times part of the problem. The very fountainhead of Earth's leaders was so corrupt ... so self-serving ... power-driven and grasping, that most of its myriad minions shared the same poison chalice. Yet for all the division, injustice and outright abuses of the nations, there were signs ... tokens, of some degree of co-operation. Perhaps, it seemed to Mary, it was a case of one step forward and ninety-nine percent back. There were heroes and heroines who gave their blood, their devotion, the totality of their lives for a more noble future and ideal, Earth's graveyards were full of them.

Mary shuddered to think that the old world had one eye on vacating the Earth to occupy worlds beyond itself and carry with them the old hostilities, division and no doubt the same poison that would sow the seeds of violence, division and corruption across the far reaches of outer space and spread its contamination, perhaps, indefinitely and to infinity.

Maureen broke into her sister's daydreams.
'Hello, Mary ... we are here too, remember we are on holiday.'
'I am so sorry, Maureen; I was fathoms below.'
'Back to Earth again ...?' Maureen asked teasingly.
'Yes and no,' Mary replied, showing both embarrassment and yet a sense of heightened interest.
'I was just thinking how alike the people of Heaven and the people of the Earth are in terms of diversity and character. Just observing Sean's antics and Elizabeth's banter with us and the various people in the hotel and on the beach, we could be back on Earth.'
'Are these regrets, Mary, or what?' Maureen asked feeling a bit left out of things.
'Certainly not! I can never remember being so happy, especially with you and the children. Believe me; I would never like to experience the Earth again. Certainly I feel for its divisions and its troubles and particularly for Larry; but no, I would never exchange places. Once I know that

Larry is with us up here, I will feel that I am a complete woman at last. In any case, Jesus assured me that I would forget all about the Earth in time.'

'Mary, love, you are a dear sister and beloved friend to me and I am delighted that we have been given the privilege to be together at last. However, it is only fair to warn you that things will not stay like this. We will have to move on from here. We cannot love each other more than anyone else here in Heaven. We cannot have favourites, nor can we be less personal with others, in the same way that we were on Earth. We love everyone here in a very personal and dependant way. That does not mean that we will love each other any the less. Your Earthly nature and ties will diminish with time, as Jesus assured you. Our new nature commits us to how things are up here where everyone is family; everyone is special; and no one is more special than another.'

'I can understand and appreciate that, Maureen. I see the sense of it in the interaction of all the people I have met so far.'

'We will always be together Mary,' Maureen offered in consolation; 'but, we cannot expect more from each other than others are capable of giving. Larry, if he were to come here tomorrow, would lose all his Earthly connections, including your good self, Mary, in time; not because he loved you any the less or was in any way spiritually detached from you. The truth is, he would love you more, but not in a solely dependant way as it needed to be while on Earth. Larry, when he arrives, Mary, will be shown the same love by all in our new world; he will belong to all. All exclusivity will be a thing of the past. We are not unified by blood here, Mary, but by Love alone.

'The two worlds we have known, Mary, are different in character where personal relationships are concerned. It is not easy to explain how this is the case; it is a question of having to live with the difference of experience. It is like having to explain to a child of six years old what it is like to be an adult. The explanation might mean something to them but the lived experience would be totally incomprehensible to a child of that age and of limited experience.'

Mary absorbed Maureen's enlightened conversation like a sponge; though her clear, light blue eyes seemed to be gazing into a deep lake, or in a labyrinth of many unsigned passages. What she heard would need time to gel in her understanding; it was like that with most new arrivals in Heaven. Some, like Mary, took longer to detach themselves, given their pressing concerns of their unfinished business, as Larry was with Mary.

Mary decided to do her utmost to prevent herself from allowing these untimely flashbacks to take hold of her attention. However, Earthly motherhood and its unique bonds seemed to live on in the spirit long after human physical death had taken place. Better alive in Heaven than a tormented ghost in a self-perpetuating nightmare, Mary thought privately.

The sisters decided to order a salad lunch for themselves and a cooked meal for the children, since that is what they preferred. Primrose and Pody played with the children of the other guests while food was being prepared. When the food appeared and placed in front of each guest, the drone of voices ceased as the clatter of metal on plates took precedence in the ambience of the dining room. The salad was crisp, cool and fresh; the meat slices of ham and chicken were beautifully presented on separate platters along with a variety of other local vegetables. There was a variety of sweet sauces for the meet and for the children's food. Needless to say, the children were shaking dear life out of the sauce bottles. Sean was giggling at the strenuous efforts of Pody as the lad's whole head vibrated violently in his attempt to get the sauce from the bottle. Sean eventually took the bottle from him and calmly tapped out the thick fruity sauce for him. Pody's radiating smile was sufficient thanks and acknowledgement to Sean. The children were totally absorbed with Sean's tales of his many fishing exploits. While he shared the meal with them, Elizabeth was shaking her smiling face in fond incredulity at Sean's stories. She saw him as little more than a child himself. The meal for the sisters was consumed with a smooth white wine for Maureen and for Mary, while the children drank a mixture of sparkling water and fruit juice. There followed a variety of ice cream, fruit and cake, a mixture of soft biscuits and a choice of cheeses. Everyone had their fill but were too settled to move from the dining table and so lingered for some time conversing with new guests and with the chef himself who came out to sit with the family for a while and have a refreshing drink. The chef was a large heavily-built man with a red beaming face smiling energetically from ear to ear. He was dressed in gleaming white protective clothing including a tall classical mushroom-shaped hat. His crystal clear green eyes were given to frequent smiles; like all the people Mary met, he exuded a calm, happy and fulfilled disposition. Maureen had met him before and so renewed her acquaintance with him while at the same time introducing him to Mary.

'I hope you enjoyed our cooking, Mary?' The indirect question was hardly worth mentioning since all the plates were clean; nonetheless, Mary chose to offer their compliments and satisfaction merely as a means of engaging him in conversation. The chef picked up quickly that Mary was new to Heaven and by way of assurance he held both her hands in his across the table and remarked.

'You will like it here Mary... you will grow into our ways in no time at all. Certainly we hope to see you here often;' and he added sensitively, 'with no disrespects to our many neighbouring establishments; you will find a warm welcome in all of them without exception.' It pleased Mary to hear this said quite openly and without the slightest trace of solicitousness. The chef was only stating what was beginning to be patently obvious to her now. The love, care and innate spontaneity of these virtues were so unlike anything within Mary's experience. She was beginning to feel enveloped in their love the more she became exposed to such unpretentious and unsolicited hospitality and care.

Mary was curious to discover how the many hotels and guest houses were supplied with their food considering everything was free and that money did not exist in Heaven. With these thoughts engaging her curiosity she put the question to James the chef who informed her.

'Most of our food is delivered direct from the farm suppliers, Mary. We usually order our requirements by telephone or through the internet.'

'But who are the suppliers?' Mary retorted with persistence; she was enthusiastic in her enquiries hoping to get a clearer picture of how such basic essentials were organised without the aid of a monetary or bartering system.

'The bigger picture, Mary, works like this: people who like the outdoor life and farming care for the produce on the land. All labour is professional by training. Many work the land by hand, others by machine; people like to work in different ways. The important point is that every individual does some responsible and necessary work. We don't produce what is not necessary or undesirable; we take stewardship of the environment very seriously. All work is done for the benefit of all just as our work in the hotels is for the benefit of all. To get back to your first question: once the harvest is brought in, all the produce is delivered by road or by rail ... by trains specifically designed for the preservation of the various foods. These in turn are delivered in prime condition to vast refrigerated stores. These stores are in turn staffed by people committed to such work. There are also various factories dedicated to processing, preserving, and packaging and labelling the produce; fleets of transport deliver the various produce to local stores where individual families collect what they need either on a daily or weekly basis. As to meat, the farming and care of animals follows a similar process of production.'

When James the chef had covered the process of supplying the food, Mary was thoughtfully silent. Maureen was half-listening to the conversation while also keeping her mind on the children who were playing with other children. Maureen shook her head slowly; she was amused by the many questions Mary put to James. It was something of Mary's past characteristics that had grown and developed rather than diminished. It wasn't long before she put a new question to James.

'I thought every major life form in heaven regenerated itself?' she posed the question indirectly.

'So, they do, Mary,' the chef replied quizzically. James wasn't sure where she was running with her comment at first until it suddenly dawned on him.

'Ah!' James exclaimed with dawning comprehension. 'When farm animals produce their young the old animal ceases to live; the carcass is then removed and butchered for its meat.'

'But how is the calf or the young animal weaned?' Maureen intervened smiling.

'She will have you on this all night, James,' said Maureen. The chef just spread his hands indicating that he had all the time in the Heaven. He turned from Maureen back to Mary.

'Any nearby animal will instinctively go to the young calf and wean it; that is the way they have developed. They share similar characteristics to us.'

'What happens to human bodies after they regenerate?' Mary was dreading the answer to her own question.'

'It simply withers as if made of dust and the bones are crushed and used as fertilizer.' James related the details in a very matter-of-fact expression. He continued. 'The process of regeneration in humans is so draining on the body that by the time the regenerated life emerges it is quite advanced in its weaning; this is unique to humans.'

Mary was ill at ease with the knowledge concerning the crushed human bones being used as fertilizer and with this knowledge engaging her mind she felt driven to pose yet another follow up enquiry.

'Why are human remains not buried as a mark of respect?'

James looked at Maureen quizzically; the question was beyond his comprehension since he had no awareness of the traditions of the Earth; he had been through regeneration several times.

Fortunately, it was given to Maureen to understand where Mary was coming from.

'Mary, love,' said Maureen calmly, 'death means nothing up here. There are no graveyards in Heaven. You do not regard what doesn't warrant respect. It is like the chaff of an ear of corn; the seed is what matters the chaff that protected it is of no consequence once the seed is safely evolved and removed. Similarly, the human body, though having a life of its own, is of no consequence without a driver within it. It is the mind, the soul, the spirit using the body for life's higher creative purpose that matters.' For once Mary was speechless. Her mouth was open and her face expressing awe and wonder. Her expression brought a big smile to Maureen which seemed to infer, at last something has occupied her sufficiently to shut her up.

The family moved from the table as the chef got up to serve a new family of arrivals. He embraced the sisters and children, his face full of smiles. After greeting the new arrivals enthusiastically he disappeared from view to his kitchen. With his departure Mary was left with so much introspection.

It was now late evening although it was still light outside with a bright glowing sunset. Maureen suggested that they settle in this hotel for a few days. When this was agreed by all, another member of the staff, Collette, a young woman of similar age to Sean, was called to give the family a helping hand to unload the suitcases from the jeep. Even the children helped out as best they could with the lighter packing. The steps up from the promenade made the family grateful for the extra help.

Collette was a dear, cheerful soul. She was a temporary member of the hotel staff as she was on leave from university where she was studying archaeology. She wasn't due back to the university until late autumn. She was what could be considered the daughter of the chef, James, who brought her up from childhood and so she liked to be close to him when she had time off. These friendships formed from the intimate bonding during childhood development were very special and unique and yet these intimate relationships never diminished an individual's love of strangers. It was every one's instinctive inclination to adopt. This same instinct also served to feel intimately close to all other individuals. It had a similar effect to that of a drop of water falling from a tap into a bowl already half full of water; the new drop simply merged with the rest and disappeared and yet made the body of water more powerful. Like the power of the ocean, it was comprised of many related droplets. Love and care in a similar sense were inexhaustible and powerful realities. The whole could never exist without its smallest parts.

Collette settled the family into their rooms. Everything was spotless and beautifully furnished. Heaven was highly advance in technology. It had its own version of the internet which was just as well considering the vastness of the planet. The computer screen in each room was part of the wall and totally wireless. It appeared as if it was a mirror and had outer sliding protective doors. It was touch operated and voice activated for writing and capable of personal visual communication. It was especially programmed for teaching, learning and searching for every kind of need, interest and speciality. There were facilities for making drinks; light snacks too were also provided in case the guests required refreshments during the night.

Once settled in, Mary was once again driven with curiosity concerning Collette's studies as a student of archaeology. You could always count on Mary to ask the most unexpected question, and she didn't fail with Collette either as she posed another of her innumerable question.

'Collette, dear, you say you are studying archaeology. Would you by any chance know how old this planet is? Or have your studies not taken you that far yet.'

'That is a basic piece of knowledge, Mary,' Collette answered with a simple smile and added:

'It is many billions of years old. I can't quite remember the actual age.' She smiled as she remarked, there are so many zeros after the number that I leave it recorded in my study books rather than in my head.' The sisters smile at her remark. But Mary was eager to follow on from her original question.

'Have you had any chance to help out with a dig anywhere yet?' Mary's question was a metaphorical dig of her own; only here she was digging into Collette's knowledge.

'Yes I have had many opportunities and occasions to dig in some remote regions of our planet. Students usually do so in order to see if they are suited to the work and that the work suits them. It can be very slow work sometimes in extreme conditions; it can demand all one's patience, endurance and dedication, since success or discoveries are few and infrequent.'

'Has anything interesting or surprising ever been found that you know of, like the remains of past civilisation, animal fossils and the like?' Mary was fishing for specific answers. What was really on her mind was the fundamental question: was Heaven built by God, as she was formally brought up to believe, or was Nature the author?' She was trying to be sensitive in her approach, not being certain how such a question might be received. She had no desire to upset either Maureen or Collette in case she was treading on holy ground.

'Yes there have been past civilizations and yes many different developments of human life and also extinct animal species clearly shown in the many fossils found. You seem to have a thirst for archaeological knowledge, Mary.' Collette deliberately leaned her head sideways to look into Mary's face and displaying an appreciative expression with regard to Mary's obvious interest. Collette, although still very young, gauged that Mary was not just making polite conversation but that she was genuinely interested in the subject. Mary's next question touched the bones of what she really wanted to know.

'Is Heaven a natural planet or did Jesus or God make it?' Mary held her breath and half expected her sister to call a halt to such questions. To her own surprise Collette answered with utter bewilderment as she turned to Maureen for an explanation.

'Heaven…! God! … Jesus …! What are they?' Collette asked.

Maureen intervened as usual, given her unique understanding and knowledge of Mary's condition and transition.

'Mary, love, Collette wouldn't know the meaning of Heaven, God or Jesus. To her, like all of the inhabitants here, this is just a highly developed planet; it evolved the way you experience it. And the Jesus you and I know is unique to our past experience. He, like many others, was a Messenger, though a unique one. Every one on this planet is an expression of what we understand to be Jesus. Jesus was only an ancient Earthly name which described a unique person power, a spirit being that is essentially a part of all our lives here in Heaven.'

'But what about the Jesus we met when I first came up here? The one who made it possible for me to see Larry and come back again? The one who promised me that Larry would eventually be with me up here? The one who made me young again? You know what I'm talking about, Maureen, don't you? I didn't dream all that up, surely?'

Mary was feeling vulnerable as though her entire footing and understanding was being removed from her. Collette showed concern for Mary who was clearly upset. Maureen was given this unique position of understanding Mary's old world and the one she was now reborn into. This understanding was given to help Mary until she was able to let the old world go. Right now Mary was far from that advanced state.

Maureen continued to disentangle the confusion both for the sake of Collette as well as Mary.

'On this planet, Mary, people live in a certain way. Jesus, the Christ we once knew on Earth, was more than just a Jewish individual. Christ was the spiritual office he came on Earth to carry out. Every messenger and message can be described to be, or to hold, an office of ascending virtue or guidance ... a teaching reality. He spoke of himself as being "the Way, the Truth and the Life" of the world. In other words he was showing the world its true beneficial, ordained direction. His teaching which was universally true and applicable to all peoples and generations was neither popular nor widely accepted. By truth he meant, all that directed life in a good and ordered way, rather than cause its destruction. The Way he spoke of was the recognition of Love and care as the only possible future and fulfilling direction for humanity. Love is part of who or what God or human life is. It is a dynamic way of being. Love was the only path or way to advance humanity on its ordained or most beneficial advancement. Jesus as Supreme Messenger to human existence and direction descended from what love's life is and took a sacrificial crucifixion as a means or gateway out of human self-destruction. The Heaven he spoke of was the advancement of perfection through the path and reality of love and all its virtues. He was put to death for his teaching. However, you can't kill the Way or the Truth, or the Life he spoke of, they would always exist. No matter how Truth becomes distorted, it would always remain the Truth. It is an eternal reality. Heaven, as we know it, is just another expression for the Way – the Truth and the Life. Heaven, Mary, is a natural consequence of reaching out to it. You reach for it, Nature provides it. All Nature shares in its own degree of mindedness or awareness, even if only at an instinctive level. Jesus' physical nature ... the body he possessed, was not an eternal reality – it had no reason to be. He said himself that the flesh had nothing to offer. It was the body's spiritual driver that gave his life and expression its true meaning and self-worth. The spirit of each of us is what we really are, that which drives us with a kind of sacred wisdom ... it gives our lives its most meaningful expression, be that expression good or bad. The good spirit will drive the physical body to do good things ... be attracted to goodness. In opposition to that, the bad spirit will drive the physical body to do bad things ... to be attracted to badness. The former, goodness, is a creative force or power; just as the latter, badness, is a destructive force blindly harnessed to its own fate. Physical nature, Mary, is merely a biological mechanism. It is not its own driver. At least not in more advanced moral nations.

A human body without a developed mind and spirit would express or reveal itself as what we understand a mad person or zombie to be. While we cannot share the same body, we can share the same spirit. What makes one spirit good and another bad is a combination of free will – the influence of others – discernment – appetite and wisdom. We can either make our physical nature work for each other or against each other. Here in the planet we call Heaven is simply the development or consequence of choosing goodness as the essence of all our actions. The goodness developed is always directed towards a greater perfection, all of which is a natural consequence of reaching out to Nature in goodness, harmony and at one with its higher laws. So, Mary, there you have it as best I can describe it for now. The Jesus or Christ that you once knew is simply an essence of goodness. He or it cannot be other than he or it is. We become what we take within ourselves so that in the end of our development we cannot be other than what we have become. We either co-create with the good or co-destroy with the bad. Here in Heaven all co-create with the good so that everything is directed towards a greater creative perfection.'

Collette understood all of this as patently obvious. It was no wonder, after Maureen had finished explaining, that she looked on with a certain degree of bewilderment. All Collette could ever remember was the life she now lived with a people who embodied what Jesus was at pains to instil in the people of the Earth. Heaven could exist and develop on any planet given the essential realities just described. Collette could never imagine a world without love and concern for others. What Maureen had just explained was stating the obvious. To Collette, every person in her world was the Jesus ... the Christ ... the Love

... which Maureen spoke of. To Collette, it was like saying that water is water. In fairness to Collette, it was the first time that she encountered anyone in Mary's condition, with one foot in two worlds and not completely in either.

There was a lingering silence as the family bid Collette good night. She embraced all the family warmly in turn before departing for something to eat herself. Primrose and Pody slept together as usual as did Maureen and Mary. There were no more questions from Mary; she had plenty to digest and so fell quickly to sleep clinging to Maureen.

As the morning light seeped through the gaps in the curtains so its beams fell on the pillows of the sleeping sisters – the brightness causing them to wake. They kissed each other good morning and slowly emerged from the sheets. After showering together and dressing, they went in to wake up the children; both were fast asleep still with their delicate arms entwined across each other. Maureen prepared their shower and had them dressed afterwards in fresh clothes. The soiled clothing of yesterday was left for Collette to have laundered. As usual, Primrose was always picky about her choice of clothing. Fortunately the limited choice, by nature of being away from home and restricted by what could be carried in the Jeep, made the choice a little less time-consuming. She decided, reluctantly, to settle for another light blue suit and stuck with the same outrageously broad-brimmed bottle-green hat. Pody was happy in fresh short kaki trousers and fresh silk blue shirt; he stuck with white socks and trainers. Both children looked very smart and fresh when at last they entered the dining room for breakfast. They ordered and ate a good hearty breakfast of bacon, eggs, mushrooms, tomatoes and lots of toast. Maureen was advised not to bother ordering any food for the beach after she let it be known that they would not be travelling today and would spend the day partially on the beach but mainly among the shops and places of entertainment. They were assured that there were many places to take refreshment throughout the day.

The light mist that had earlier hung over the ocean in the distance was now dissipating and the clear blue sky was appearing as though the curtain of mist was being drawn away by an invisible hand. The gulls swooped screaming and skimming over the slow receding tide, they were also following the many huge fleets of fishing trawlers setting out to sea. By now the heat of the bright sun was beginning to warm everything as the family prepared to go on the beach. Both sisters wore light kaki trousers and white shirts. After spending a couple of hours on the beach and taking to the water, the family returned all the beach paraphernalia to the jeep and headed for the entertainment arcades of which many abounded the several widely-constructed piers. The colourful merry-go-rounds were already well occupied with the happy voices of many families. Horses, chairs, train carriages, swing boats; helter-skelter rides; gaily-coloured gaming stalls of every possible kind of entertainment abounded the place. The cacophony of exciting sounds was a kind of discordant madness: exhilarated human voices – train whistles – bells being struck – the rush and crashing of dodgems – the antics of clowns – the screams of tiny tots watching mischievous puppets – ball games of every description – boat rides and fishing. It was difficult to cover the hundreds of fun-pact stalls and activities.

The children enjoyed the variety of rides and games, with Maureen and Mary dragged in toe as if the dog took the owner for a walk for a change. The sisters didn't object; they saw it as the children's time. Eventually, and in between refreshments, the children settled for the quieter and more skilful pursuit of hand-manipulated, glass-encased cranes that could pick up beautifully crafted handmade prizes of figurines, small bags of sweets; perfumes; broaches with every kind of animal, bird, fish and insects, beautifully crafted miniature cottages and gaily-coloured miniature flowers and glass water balls with every conceivable object encased within them. Because the prizes were so masterfully-crafted, so they were made all the more difficult to win. The crane for reaching and gripping them purposely demanded patience and skill from adult and children alike. It took some two hours before all the family gained various rewards. All the other families engrossed at other machines were deep in concentration, in spite of the carnival-like sounds surrounding them. It was the middle of a swelteringly hot afternoon before they decided to snack once more. Once refreshed and the treasured prizes in the safe keeping of Maureen's shoulder bag it was unanimously decided to go fishing from one of the smaller pleasure launches . This decision did not come spontaneously but from the umpteenth reminder of Pody who wanted to get one over on Sean, the fisherman at the Sea View Hotel. Both sisters smiled instinctively at Pody's motives.

The three crew, two women and a man, of the small launch were hospitality itself. The sisters were happy to leave the children to be instructed on how to fish with rods purposely designed for young children. One lady, Helen, who was dressed in brilliant white uniform and peak cap, was at the helm of the launch; her deeply tanned face was set in a constant smile as she turned from time to time to look at the excited antics of the children learning the rudiments of casting the lines. Pody took to the skill very quickly; he was 'naturally dexterous,' as the crew commented. Primrose seemed to be more interested in making a neat shape to the arching rod and line and in doing so accidentally gained a certain style and competence of her own.

It was time to bait the rods for a catch. The hooks and bait used depended on whether the catch was going to be kept and brought home or returned to the sea. Pody didn't care for any of that wasteful nonsense. 'Not on your life,' he was heard to exclaim passionately. His line was prepared with a barbed hook while Primrose's was prepared with a smaller barb-less hook to facilitate the easy removal of the undamaged fish. Pody would have settled for a stick of dynamite, if that is what it was going to take to get his fish as a trophy to wave victoriously in front of Sean at the hotel.

It was Primrose who got the first bite. She reeled in as instructed shouting at Pody all the while:
    'Pody I've got one! I've got one!' her beautiful little face was grimaced in strain as if she had at least a shark on the end of the line. Dermot, the male member of the crew, held on to Primrose as she was half leaning over the side of the launch with the tugging on the end of the line. Her rod was bent like a hairpin with the fight. Eventually the other lady of the crew, Paula, helped to net the catch; it was a reasonably sized mackerel and still struggling and thrashing in the net. The trophy was photographed by the smiling crew with Primrose holding the catch with a beaming smile all over her sweet, joy-filled face. She would haunt Pody with this photo for the rest of his life; that was at the centre of her joy. She was the first to catch!

There was no getting out of that for poor struggling Pody who was grimacing his face and baring his teeth at the water which had the crew in hysterics. He didn't think much of Primrose being first to net a fish and have a photograph to prove it. If he could jump into the water and drag a fish out by the tail he would do so without hesitation. However, it was not many minutes later when a mighty tug on the line almost pulled Pody over the side of the launch. Fortunately, Dermot had a good hold of him and helped him with the straining rod. Pody's thin arms and tender face revealed their very bones with the grimacing tension he put on them. Once again, Paula came to the rescue with the net. The big fighting mackerel trashed about in the net as if it might rip it apart. When Paula suggested, mischievously, winking at the other crew members,

'Shall we put it back in the water?' Pody shouted in wild desperation,

'No! No! No! That's our supper tonight at the hotel.' The crew roared with laughter. They knew perfectly well that the lad had no intention of putting it back. Primrose, who was latched on to Dermot's arm was half teasing and half pleading with Pody, to have the fish released.

'I let mine go,' she said mischievously and with an air of self-righteousness.

'Well,' said Pody in defiance, 'you left your supper in the sea; mine is coming back to the hotel.' The crew could only smile at the teasing banter between the two children.

After the crew inquired how many were in the family and given the number as four; they decided to catch another two mackerel.

'One is hardly enough for all four of you, is it?' Pody was elated, jumping up and down in wild excitement, while Primrose put on a face of indignation. Once again, the crew was in hysterics at their competing banter. The last three fish were netted within the half hour to Pody's wild cheers. His shouts of triumph and his air-fisting punches had the crew once again in hysterics. Primrose wrinkled her nose mockingly at his boisterous behaviour. The crew again beside themselves as the triumphant Pody now put his rod on his shoulder and marched up and down the launch singing at the top of his voice. He made up the words of the verse on the spot and attempted to sound like an older man:

'I caught three fish; they're for the dish,
They're for the dish; they're for the dish;
'I caught three fish; they're for the dish,
And Sean will tear out his hair.'

Pody's voice and song were about as tuneful as a croaking pheasant. The scene that fell upon the return of Maureen and Mary was the last strutting images of Pody marching and singing as the launce pulled in and tied up at the quay. The crew was falling about in hysterics at Pody's elated antics. They lifted the children out of the launch. Maureen could see plainly from the faces of the crew that more than a quiet pleasant afternoon fishing had occurred. Her natural caring concern prompted the question.

'I hope these two have not made a disgrace of us?' Maureen addressed her question to the smiling crew.

'You can bring these two lovely fisher children on our boat any time you wish. I don't really know who got the better day's entertainment the children or the three of us. They are truly delightful children. It was our greatest pleasure to have them.' The family waved appreciatively to the crew as they headed home. The children turned back several times calling out the names of the crew in turn as they repeated their goodbyes. The crew, even now at a distance, was still in fits of laughter. They could still see Pody trying to force Maureen and Mary to look at the four big fish in the bag. All they could do was shake their heads and smile. The lad was so beside himself with excitement. Primrose on the other hand completely disassociated herself from him, much to the amusement of the sisters.

It was 8 o'clock in the evening when they reached the hotel. Sean was the first to greet them as they made their way into the dining room to dispatch the fish to James the chef. Pody stood proud and as erect as a mountain in front of Sean and opened the canvas bag with a look of absolute triumph on his face. Sean played along with the exaggerated pride written all over Pody's face.

'You mean to tell me that you have caught all these huge monsters yourself? Boy! I declare, I have never seen such monsters in all my life!' Pody most certainly had the floor as all the staff gathered round to examine the catch. The lad was gloating and glowing with pride, with a grin reaching from ear to ear.

Primrose had to get in her piece of due attention. She wasn't having her brother taking centre stage without putting some damper on the praise surrounding him.

'I caught the first fish before Pody and I put it back in the sea.' Primrose held up the photograph which showed her kissing the fish. Her efforts were a little half-hearted since the adulation Pody indulged in seemed impenetrable. However, the gathering soon realised that Primrose felt left out of their attention. Suddenly all eyes turned on her and the photograph which she held aloft for hopeful attention. Her earlier disappointed face soon took on a radiant smile as high praise was lavished on her victorious catch. Pody's ballooned-ego was soon deflated.

James, the chef, in his white uniform, took the fish from Pody and set about preparing the meal, but not before giving Pody a big hug for being a very clever boy. Needless to say the lad had his fair fill of pride and praise. As the family seemed to reek of mackerel, all went to their rooms to shower and change.

The meal set out before the family was expertly presented. James didn't do much to flavour the mackerel; he didn't want to spoil the true flavour of the fresh-caught fish; apart from some pasted bread crumbs on the outside and a little honey on the inside. The grilled mackerel was a feast for all including all the staff who came over for a morsel; not that they were particularly hungry, but rather to make the occasion all the more memorable for the children. Even Primrose forced herself to indulge.

Of all the praise that was heaped on Pody he was most impressed by Sean who said:

'It was the best fish he ever tasted.' The family slept like rocks that night after all the excitement and sea air.

They stayed on for a week in the seaside town. There was much to explore in the shopping precincts and the theatres. Although everything was free in the shops, Maureen felt it wise to explain to her sister that nothing was manufactured that did not have a practical use. Small items such as toys and little trinkets for the children to play with were the exception. All important household conveniences were manufactured to last and be easily repaired if beneficial to do so. Craftsmen and craftswomen took a pride in whatever trade they followed; this also applied to motor vehicles, whether built for the road or for industrial use. With regard to road vehicles, whether passenger vehicles or for road haulage, the emphasis was on comfort safety and practical use and every part easily replaceable at any major garage. Most people used public transport simply because they preferred to be among each other. Traffic problems were unheard of since there were very few private vehicles on the road. Shopping was always a practical thing in the sense that people only asked for what was essential. The entire population of Heaven was people-centred and virtue-centred, rather than material-centred. Even so, shopping was always a pleasant pastime since new useful creations were always on display. Do-it-yourself was always a popular store for its wealth of new ideas on every conceivable topic and interest. There was a strong, natural, creative character in the people.

Even the contents of the various book stores were manufactured to endure. All books, whether for enter-tainment or instruction, were digitalised and convenient to download. You could have the print any size or font you preferred. You could also have the pages in a variety of ornamental designs at the touch of a button. Each digital book-reader contained a dictionary as well as many other useful multiple features. The convenience of these digitalised books lay in the fact that you let the store staff know what books you were interested in and they would download them from their own inexhaustible data storage onto your digital book-reader. The frame cover of the book could also be changed to an illustration that either related to the particular story you were reading or to beautiful illustrations of scenes, animal or a host of other pictures. You could also choose to have videos run throughout the various reading matter which made the reading of novels all the more a realistic and enjoyable experience. When an author described a scene of a village and its surrounding countryside, you had the option of playing a video clip of the scene or just relying on your own imagination. It was also possible to plug these books into your home computer to install new material. The digital book was also used as a photo album.

Pody wanted to have a new fishing rod of his own to use when he went back home to the cottage.

'If you think we are going to spend the rest of our holiday with you marching up and down the streets or riding in the jeep, or travelling on ship, bus or train with a great fishing rod stuck up our noses, you can think again, young Pody. Yes you can have one and a net for the lakes at home but you will have to wait until we are on the return journey.'

'Ok.' Pody answered with a big beaming smile as he danced drumming his feet into the pavement with wild excitement and then clinging on to the hands of Maureen and Mary.

'And what does our little Primrose want to bring back home?' Maureen looked down on the outrageous hat with its overhanging brim and with Primrose straining to look up from under it. She was like a walking mushroom. Primrose, ever the cautious and calculating one, said sedately and with her brow in wrinkled consideration,

'I'm not sure yet. I think I will just wait nearer the time of our return to our cottage.' Mary pulled a face at Maureen and shook her head, as if to say, she is a wily old granny, as cute as a bucketful of monkeys.

'Well, Primrose,' said Maureen, 'don't be too long in choosing because we may be too far away to return for something you really want or you will have to order it by post afterwards.' Primrose was smiling contentedly because she knew that she had the remainder of the holiday to choose; whereas Pody had already made his choice and it might not have been his best one, she thought smugly.

The remainder of the week at Sea View was spent with walks along the costal road, fishing with Pody, and on Tuesday with Sean from the hotel. When Sean took the children fishing Maureen and Mary would relax on the beach; they could see the children and Sean fishing from the pier; he preferred pier fishing to the boat or launch. Primrose would have preferred the entertainment arcades or visiting the shops; however, she was not very content without being in her brother's company, even when there were other children of her own age to play with. Pody seemed to give her a sense of security; a sense of roots. Although strangers were always intimate and friendly with her, whether young or old, they would always be going away eventually. Some evenings the family would go to the theatre to see a play especially created for children; sometimes it would be a hilarious comedy which would have the theatre in roars of laughter; on other occasion it would be some simple but interesting story. Theatre-going was very popular for both adults and children alike. Since there was no cost involved in the world of theatre or movies great epic stories with fantastic scenes and voyages drew awesome gasps from all. Acting was a highly respected and skilful occupation. Since there were no costs involved, great epics were given spectacular production and unlimited casts.

As the second week of the holiday began there were a lot of tears shed as the family said goodbye to all the hotel staff individually. All the members of the staff were very emotional as they too did not know when Maureen's family might visit again. Parting in any case was always emotional for all visitors such was the closeness of the people in general. Sean had to give a deal of extra attention to Pody as the two had grown very involved and close. It helped a little that Sean, Colette and Margaret assisted the family with their luggage to the Jeep. As the Jeep moved slowly away from the promenade, all hands waved to the top of the steps where James the chef with his tall white hat and white uniform was waving vigorously from the doorway of the hotel. Primrose was comforting Pody in a way no one else could. He too felt secure with her arms around him. Maureen could see them from the mirror; she was half choked with emotion. She put her hand on Mary's knee to bring her attention to the two in the back with a slight backward nod of the head. The children didn't look up; they were too engrossed in each other. Mary felt a lump in her throat and turned back to look into Maureen's face whose eyes were fighting back the tears. Mary placed her hand gently on her sister's arm to avoid interfering with her driving and whispered,

'You ok, Maureen?' She didn't answer but kept her eyes on the passing traffic. She glance quickly at Mary and gave her a couple of brief nods to confirm she was coping ok. Seeing the sadness of the children caused Mary's mind to go back to Larry on Earth, in spite of her best efforts to leave things in Jesus' care. Even so, she battled on trying desperately not to allow her mind to remain focused on it; especially in these circumstances, since it seemed very selfish of her to allow her thoughts to wander off so. Sometimes when such thoughts took hold of her she wondered if she could ever settle fully into the intimate life of Heaven; she knew that she had to keep trying.

Maureen had not laid out any definitive plan for the holiday other than making it possible for Mary to get a good experience of the countryside around her and in the process to give the children a similar experience of the vast lands. She took the notion of spending the next two weeks travelling by train and liner across the continents. This turned out to be a most satisfactory decision and allowed Maureen to relax even more without having to drive great distances in the autumn heat and mists. The trains were all air conditioned and luxurious, with sleeping accommodation and beautifully arranged dining cars. The trains were very roomy, silent and smooth. They rarely exceeded speeds that would spoil the fantastic views of the passing mountain ranges, sea and wild countryside during daylight hours. The family never grew tired of watching the vast changing landscapes. The scenes were breathtaking at times with the glorious gold and reds of autumn everywhere; at other times the shear scale of the mountain ranges with their snow-capped turquoise summits.

However, at night speeds would increase considerably especially on very long journeys of several days duration.

They boarded an intercontinental liner with six levels for the passengers. These too were the very height of luxury. The cabins were generous in size with every convenience of comfort. The crew, dressed in immaculate white uniforms and blue caps with gold braid trimmings that inspired a real sense of security and professionalism. The entire crew, no matter their duties, was kindness itself. Mary in particular was more impressed than ever with the people of Planet Heaven. It didn't matter how far away the family were from home, which by now was over four thousand miles, she found the people, even perfect strangers, to act quite naturally as if they were intimate family. It all seemed so incredible to her. The gigantic liner provided every kind of interest imaginable, given their limitation as ocean-bound vessels. There were theatres and plays, concerts, dancing; onboard swimming pools; film shows; games and entertainment to spoil the children. The food, its freshness and quality, had to be experienced to be believed. It was served in the most luxurious dining rooms. There were even gymnasiums for the more actively inclined, or long uncluttered walking passages along the sides of the various decks. There was no such thing as divisions of class only quiet areas for those who chose to sit quietly or read.

Pody was always looking into the sea and never tired of seeing the massive whales that appeared from time to time or the looping dolphins riding the waves. The gulls overhead were a constant presence incessantly calling or swooping down to snatch the scraps of food being jettisoned from the liner.

There was something forlorn about seeing other liners passing by in the distance at night with all their lights like stars floating on the ink-like swelling seas. The family would watch together along with other families who had come out for fresh air. Many stood leaning on the rails watching the billions of stars glinting in the night sky. Mary was constantly awestruck and forced into reveries by the utter scale of the universe that twinkled in the vast reaches of space overhead. To Mary's sense of wonder, the vastness and scale of creation was utterly beyond comprehension.

The second week passed in leisurely routine. Sometimes they would dock to investigate the various ports of interest while the liner took other passengers and supplies on board. One of the things that struck Mary as strange was the fact that all the peoples they encountered, no matter how far they had travelled, spoke the same language, no matter their race or colour. Maureen assured Mary that it had developed like that to make all communications immediately inclusive to all. Only the customs were different from place to place; there were as many different ways of fishing, cooking and building as the lands they discovered for the first time. Interests and sports were also very diverse from continent to continent. The character of the people was as diverse as Pody was from Primrose. Yet all had an innate love and care for each other.

The other thing that struck Mary was that she never encountered a single church nor had she seen Maureen or the children at prayer. She couldn't help putting this point to her sister.

'Maureen, why have we not come across any churches here in Heaven, above all places? Where do people worship God? I never seem to see people at prayer or blessing themselves.'

'Ah, Mary, love, you are back on Earth again, aren't you?' Maureen had infinite patience with her sister since it was given to her to understand Mary's difficulties in her state of transition from the old world of Earth to one of Planet Heaven. 'The Church on earth is specific to its own needs,' Maureen continued. 'However, here everyone is in constant communion with whom or what you consider God to be, the life of Love we live. That is our highest and greatest good and direction, our love and care for each other. There is nothing more advanced or higher in virtue and quality than that. It is the equivalent to your so-called

Church on Earth. That is the big distinction between our world here in Planet Heaven and the old world of Planet Earth. That is how it is with your Larry. He is marked for this place, thanks to you and his own co-operation with you. I only know that by Jesus' own assurance.' It gave Mary a great sense of Joy and even greater security to experience Maureen's utter conviction in the certainty of what she just related. She hugged her sister over and over with shear joy. Such reassurance from her sister was actually an aid to feeling less incomplete in her transitional period. In a sense her pain of motherly love and her bond with Larry was growing less acute; but Mary would not have been conscious of this taking place within herself; except when she became aware from time to time that she experienced longer periods of time passing in between thinking of Larry at all. Mary too had to learn, in her transitional period, that her exclusive love for her son was insufficient in itself to be fully part of Heaven's life where exclusive love would have to develop more and more into an all-embracing love of every person in Heaven. However, that was now taking place in Mary by the help of the very nature and love of the people whom she now shared her new life with. The very same transition would eventually be a part of Larry's new life also. He too would have to be weaned off his exclusive love and dependence on his mother; not that he would love her any less but rather love her in an even more perfect, fulfilling way. Earthly love was an important stepping stone to Heaven's life and love. It was really the fact that the life of love in Heaven was the very ordered end of love itself. It was Love's own life; like a living language everyone grew into as vital and as inescapable as blood was to the life of the physical, human body. Heaven's life and love was an indescribable bliss.

By the middle of the third week into to the holiday it was time to return home; it would take the remainder of the holiday to return to their village which was now several thousand miles away. The family was all very tanned and relaxed. There was no sense of time with them at all apart from the routines of life on the luxurious liner. They docked for the last time on their outward journey and changed liners for home. They would have to retrace their steps to catch the train to where they left the jeep and so to Home.

It had been a great adventure for all the family. There would be so much to talk about; so much to recall. The final journey took the family back to the Sea View Hotel when they had picked up the jeep. It would only be an overnight stop to feel fresher for the last three hundred kilometres or so home. The overnight stay was like a family reunion. Pody couldn't wait to tell Sean about the whales, the biggest fishes he had ever seen, and about the dolphins and everything else he had seen; he couldn't get the information out quick enough so that every half sentence began with 'and' there were stars everywhere ... and ships with thousands of lights ... and the moon as big as Heaven ... and our liner was high up ... and it was going very fast ... and their were flying fish ...'

'Wow! Wow! Wow!' Sean said. 'Catch your breath and slow down – you'll make me giddy trying to remember all those wonderful things.' Pody was too excited, too full of all he wanted to share with Sean in particular and so he went into another rush of memories and incidents. Sean took a firm grip of him and held him lovingly to himself. The lad was full of smiles and half unable to breathe as Sean pulled his little face into his chest to keep him from spurting out more events. At last he calmed down. The last thing he blurted out was,

'...And mother said that you would help me choose a fishing road and a net to bring home with me if it isn't too big for the jeep so I can fish in the local lakes back home in the village.' The lad looked up into Sean's youthful face and grinned with expectancy and pleasure.

'Of course I will help you to choose a road and a net. I have the very ones in mind; and they will both fit into the Jeep without the slightest problem.' Pody gave him and even bigger hug and was delirious with excitement.

It suddenly struck Primrose that she hadn't chosen anything as yet to take back home. She really didn't need anything. However, she realised that if Pody was going to be away fishing for a lot of his spare time, it meant that she would be either stuck on her own at home with other school children from their village. As much as she loved her many school friends, Pody was still almost part of her own body and mind. The truth was, that they couldn't bear to be separated from each other for long periods. She turned to Sean and asked, 'Will you choose a rod and a net for me too, Sean. 'cause I can fish with Pody too in case he falls in the lake every time he catches a fish, 'cause he gets too excited and goes into a big dance every time?' Sean looked to Maureen and Mary, his hand shielding his face from Primrose's view as he tried to fight off his need to burst into hysterics at her reasoning. Both sisters smiled their approval to Primrose's request. Both just raised their eyebrows and gestured with their hands to Sean who turned immediately back to Primrose.

'There's your answer Primrose – your mammy and Mary think it is a splendid idea and I know Pody will be delighted to have you with him so you can look after each other as proper fisher folk should.' Pody was delighted with her choice; he was delighted that Primrose wanted to share in the pastime. True to his word, Sean brought them both to the shop the following morning and chose two telescopic rods and two telescopic nets. He also chose all the other bits of equipment, hooks, line, floats, and weights. He rigged up all the tackle so that they were ready for immediate use. He also chose a DVD disc which showed every aspect of fly and course fishing in easy stages. He also assured them that if they could not find anyone locally to help, that they were to telephone the hotel and he would do what he could. Both children were delighted. Sean was already beginning to feel sad at the prospect of their return home. It was always the same when guests were leaving – everyone was special in their own unique way.

Saying goodbye to all the staff at Sea View Hotel was a little less painful for all concerned as they waved vigorously to each other. Pody wanted Sean to come home with the family. Both were in tears. It helped in some way to have been through the worst of it before. Even so, the journey home was very quiet, for most part. The children were huddled together as usual but without the upset they had been through previously. They also felt that they had a personal contact with the hotel having its telephone number and its e-mail address. The children would certainly find excuses for contacting the hotel just to hear the voices of the staff.

It was good to be home, back with the familiar, although Maureen's cottage felt very small in comparison to the hotel and the ocean-going liner. They had a distinct sense of the cottage having shrunk. It would take a while to settle down after being away for four eventful and amazing weeks.

CHAPTER 9

Larry's Work on Earth Begins

Larry brought the parcel that Mary had left into his neighbour's house. He was full of excitement;

'She came back! She came back! Mammy came back as she promised. She sends her love to you all and wishes to thank you all for looking after me. Oh! It was lovely to see her again. And she said that she is very happy in Heaven with her family and friends; and she said I will join her in Heaven when my work on Earth is done.' He opened the parcel in front of the family and found all Mary's old bedclothes; the ones she had disappeared in when she died. Seamus, Lil and the children were familiar with the old bedclothes; they had seen Mary wearing them when they used to call round when she was taken ill. As the family scrutinised the familiar clothing, Larry was more interested in the work list that came with the packet. He took the whole event in his stride as if such things were every day events.

'What does the note say, Larry; or is that too private?' The question was put rather sensitively by Seamus. The jubilant, but somewhat perplexed Larry, passed the note to Seamus. Its contents caused Seamus to furrow his brow as he looked back at Larry.

'Do you understand what this means, Larry. It's a tall order and a very difficult one, and perhaps an impossible one to carry out on your own without a good deal of professional help.' Seamus read out the contents as the family was gathered round the dining room table, all wearing expressions of intense interest. 'It states here in the letter:

"Larry, your work for the future is to bring about a new era on earth by assembling together a single world government, and your duty is to be at the head of that government. Do not be intimidated by the enormity of the duty laid upon you; I will be with you always. No one will be allowed to harm you, though many will try to subvert your efforts. You, Larry, will be the final prophet to humanity. After you, there can be no more direction for humanity. If your message of love and care for all people goes unheeded, there can be no other hope or help for the world, neither in your time nor in any generation to follow. Humanity will remain unredeemed and fixed in its own self-made hell."'

After reading the note Seamus and Lil felt a deep concern for Larry. If there was anyone left on earth to undertake such an impossible task, the last person you would choose would be Larry. He was not a complete idiot, in spite of his simple ways. He had a certain way with people in an innocent fashion; even so, he was no politician. He was, as things stood, quite incapable of leading a birthday party, let alone a political one. A very creepy, scary feeling came over Seamus and Lil. If Larry took the note to heart as an actual command, he could become the laughing stock of the community and the world, let alone his native city and his friends. There was no name attached to the note; not even Mary's. Certainly, if all was to be believed, Mary was only the messenger and not the source of the commanding letter. There was also a sense of solemnity about the wording; it had a kind of biblical context to it, in a similar way to instructions given to Moses and Aaron; how they were sent to lead the Israelites out of slavery and out of the land of their abusers, the pagan Egyptians. But who on earth, Seamus and Lil thought, was going to help Larry on what realistically seemed to be beyond the compass or ability of any one human being no matter how clever or influential? Such an enterprise would require an international army of soldiers and the need to set up a powerful world government and most likely the need of a dictatorship. Who on earth could ever possibly get all the nations of the world to come together in agreement and work together for a common cause or for the common good of all? Most nations have forever been in one struggle or another for supremacy over their neighbour or continually in defence of their own nation and its people. It would appear that there is something innate in humanity that makes it extremely divisive and violent in its fight for power, supremacy, position, and the suppression of all to gain control over the world's resources. No, this all seemed like the request of an extreme idealist or of one given to utter fantasy.

Seamus knew perfectly well that an animal's instinct to survive in competition for food and territory was written deeply into its genetic awareness and drives. These same characteristics and drives were all too common in the human animal also – even though more modified in some advanced moral and ethical souls. Nonetheless man the animal was still a long way off from an all embracing care and concern for others. Our history and present brutal conflicts worldwide only differed from the wild animals in humanity's greater knowledge and ability to utterly destroy one another. Dominance was written into the human psyche like a perpetuating and mutating disease. Such reflections streamed instinctively into Seamus' thoughts. Survival of the species took eons of time to reinforce its driving forces and character on every living thing. How could humanity change in order to live in harmony under one international government, unless by the very characteristics and drives that imprisoned it by force fear and dictatorial domination? Was there another way? Certainly Seamus didn't think so. It was not a question of cynicism on his part but by having his feet firmly anchored on terra firma.

None of this affected the children except in their innocent and genuine offers of help if Larry was to ask them. Seamus and Lil smiled at the innocence of their children's ever willingness to help and show their love for Larry. They hadn't the faintest conception of what was involved. It was more like the beginning of an exciting game to them. Seamus and Lil felt instinctively that if Larry was to act without serious advice on this grave matter, he would be leaving himself open to ridicule and accusations of being totally neurotic. The Madden family was too fond of, and too protective of Larry to allow this seeming madness to be acted upon without the strongest advice from Father Kevin at St. Patrick's church. Quite what Father Kevin could do about it was very doubtful?

As it was early Monday morning Seamus and Lil decided to call Father Kevin in the evening after Seamus had come back from work. Anything of this nature, the possibility of Larry becoming an utter laughing stock was bound to have repercussions on Father Kevin if he allowed Larry to even attempt to carry out this unimaginable lunacy laid on him. If Larry attempted to expose himself to such ridicule without Father Kevin's intervention, then the whole population of Cork City and the media would have a field day at the Church's expense. The bishop too would come down on Father Kevin like an avalanche and bury whatever priestly future he thought he had.

That evening Seamus and Lil went to the church presbytery and showed Larry's instructions, to Father Kevin. After reading the note and hearing of Mary's return with the parcel of old bedclothes and the attached letter, he couldn't make up his mind as to which was the more troublesome, the actual return of Mary or the message she brought with her. The priest had no hesitation in believing the truthfulness of the innocent Larry, though inwardly he really wished that Larry might be suffering from an imaginary visitation – a kind of compensation brought on by his grief.

Father Kevin sat down in the lounge with his visitors, these personal friends whom he trusted completely to keep this whole mysterious and serious event to themselves. He had known and trusted them for years as souls of utter discretion. All three were served drinks by old faithful Nell, both friend and housekeeper to Father Kevin. The priest kept rubbing and squeezing his chin with the message held up in the other hand and yet not continuing to read it but to stare bewilderedly beyond it. Occasionally his eyes and mind would go back to the message with a kind of desperation, willing the message to reveal some rational clue or way forward ... something less demanding ... something more attainable. No matter how hard the priest scrutinised the message, it couldn't even be made to fit into the convenience of a metaphor. The message spoke of Larry being in command of "a world government." It was too difficult for the priest to conceive of such an impossible enterprise. The more he scrutinised the message, the more perplexing it became. Father Kevin took the tiniest glint of hope from the words, "Do not be intimidated by the duty laid on you..." Perhaps it was only wishful thinking that some miraculous set of interventions would manifest themselves. Father Kevin saw some vague glint of encouragement in those reassuring words. It was as if the writer was putting a kind of confidence in innocence. If the expected duty was laid on someone more able to comprehend the utter scale of the task, such an individual, no matter their ability, would simply crumble under the utter complexity of the imposed duty. There was also some profitable hope in the passage, "... I will be with you always ..." Was this God's or an angel's assurance? The priest shared these thoughts with his guests and with Nell. The next passage that came under the priest scrutiny was: "No one will be allowed to harm you, though many will try to subvert your efforts." There was obviously a strong sense that Larry will be protected in some mysterious way. The final point of the messages clearly indicated that the writer is all too aware of opposition to the enterprise. The end of the messages was too frightening to contemplate. Was God about to abandon humanity, the priest thought?

'So, one and all, there you have it!' The priest exclaimed with outstretched hands from where he was seated, his face a stage of perplexity. 'What are we left to do aside from developing ulcers with the worry of it?' Father Kevin was smiling but not in his usual easy manner; he didn't fool any of the company for a moment and his guests were all too aware that he knew he was fooling no one. 'Nell, what do you think, have you any notion in that Kerry reservoir of yours, because I'm lost for the moment?' Nell was standing all the while with a tea towel draped over her shoulder and both her hands resting on the back of Father Kevin's upright dining chair, the hard chair acting as a support for his troublesome back. Her head was bent as she appeared to be speaking over his shoulder to the linen-covered dining table.

'There would be no point in calling Doctor Joe O' Brian again,' Nell remarked; 'he gave Larry a clean bill of health the last time, that was only three weeks ago. The bishop needs to be warned at least, in case this whole thing goes askew and breaks over our heads like a storm. I know the bishop is not the easiest person to deal with, however, we should warn him at least since he will be the immediate target to feel the full force of the media if all this goes wrong. He is, after all, the head of the Church locally. The Media will descend on you both with all its mocking power and machinery. They will have a field day with this and consider it a blessed duty well done.' The priest joined his hands as if in prayer and pressed their tips into his chin, thoughtfully gazing beyond his companions. Nell interrupted his thoughts when she added: 'There is one other thought that came at me from the moment that message was read out.'

'What do you mean, Nell?' The priest enquired, side-glancing at her.

'You know, this message, if it did come from heaven, and if we try to suppress it, we could find ourselves fighting against God's will; not that any of us here could know his will in an absolute way.' She continued reflectively.

'Wasn't there a similar predicament encountered in the book of The Acts of the Apostles?' Nell continued, 'when the apostles were arrested for preaching in the name of Jesus Christ to the people … how they were arrested with the intention of killing them. They were brought before the whole Sanhedrin, the entire religious authority of Israel who had gathered together for the sole purpose of preventing Jesus' disciples from carrying out their work. These religious authorities, the entire Senate, were hell bent on silencing the disciples one way or another. However, the intervention of Gamaliel, a highly respected Pharisee and a doctor of the Law and also a member of the same Sanhedrin, reminded them to recall another period of time when other leaders had gathered followers around them only to be killed and their movement to fade away. Therefore he gave this advice, which I recall indirectly, "… leave the situation as it is. If the command is not from God, it will fail of its own accord. However, if the command is from God and anyone tries to interfere, we could find ourselves fighting against God Himself."'

Nell continued, 'I suggest we take that same advice. The worst we can suffer over this is a red face for a while. We've been mocked before and survived. Or as one Jesuit put it years ago,

"The enterprise has begun… It's for God; it can't be stopped."

Father Kevin turned about to Nell behind him and gazed upwards into her face for some time without comment. Seamus and Lil sat there in anticipation awaiting the priest's decision. The priest knew all too well that Nell read her bible regularly and quoted it freely when she needed to do so. However, to just pull a seemingly obscure quote out of the New Testament just like that amazed him. Her memory, considering her seventy-eight years, was indeed remarkable. He was aware that some people had that gift. In Nell's case, she had it in abundance, she was truly inspired. She was instinctively a very spiritual person yet one who didn't go on about it to others unless she had serious need to.

'You're right, of course, Nell; that is the wise way ahead in spite of all our reservations.' Father Kevin felt more assured and less distracted as if Nell's suggestion came straight from Divine authority. He looked to Seamus and Lil and asked, 'Have you any suggestions of your own?' His friends puckered their lips simultaneously and turned to each other. Seamus spoke for them both.

'I'm sorry, Father Kevin, I don't believe we can suggest anything wiser than Nell's inspired words.' The trouble is, he added guardedly, 'you just never know who Larry is going to talk to as he wanders the streets. I think we can only do the best we can to advise him of the need to be careful of what he says to strangers when they ask him if there is any news of his missing mother. Other than that, there really is not a lot we can do apart from coping with events as they unfold. We cannot shadow Larry day and night as we all have to get on with living. Obviously he continues to have his meals with us, and Lil calls round to his house to help him to keep the place clean; not that he needs too much assistance there, since he has been brought up to be tidy. However, it is always a good reason to drop in on him to see that he is ok. Apart form this mysterious problem, he is no bother at all to anyone.' Father Kevin was deeply appreciative of his friend's indispensable and generous help to Larry. In fact, without that help, the priest would have a good deal more to concern himself with.

'I'll warn the bishop, as you say Nell; it's only fair that we do so. The Lord alone knows how he will react.' The priest joined his hands and looked up to heaven for divine inspiration. Lil laughed at his light-hearted mockery and commented smilingly,

'He's not on your Christmas card list, then, Father Kevin.' The priest smiled, wagging his forefinger at Lil's perceptive remark. They all smiled with relief at the relaxed banter after the intense gravity of the earlier more serious matter.

'Well, let's sleep on it for tonight. I will phone the bishop shortly and make an appointment to call on him as soon as he can see me.' The guests made their way home in their black four-by-four.

Bishop Paul Duffy was a solidly-built individual. Everything about him was stern – his piercing light grey-blue eyes had a fixed penetrating character from years of his hostile and aggressive attitude towards his fellow priests. Even his thick steel-grey head of hair seemed ridged as if it was composed of barbed wire. His hands were those large muscular kind inherited from generations of a farming background. His fingernails, though manicured and clean, had a distinct sterility about them since his own career avoided all physical contact with his parent's land. His hands were not accustomed to being extended to his priests. He was tolerant of religious sisters, only because of their guarded and fawning deference in his company. They had the good grace to absorb his bullying nature. He was less hostile to the laity which he met from time to time; however, for most part he kept people at arm's length.

It was hard to imagine him ever having an original thought of his own. Strangely, that was his strength; much as the concomitant brutes of ignorance and insensitivity are often a powerful force against ill-positioned intelligence. He dealt with the media by being dogmatically orthodox and protected himself and his ignorant attitude in doing so. Canon Law was his indisputable bible. It had always been his favourite subjects at college, and he used it defensively, as a dumb soldier uses the right to kill as an excuse to bury conscience. His manner of speaking, along with his grating Northern accent, immediately raised one's hackles Every comment or contribution to a conversation was bawled out with his loud arrogant, grating voice; his opinions, as black and white as a dictator's.

Father's Kevin's meeting with the bishop was not one he looked forward to. Each had a history of irritating the other. On Father Kevin's part it was the fact that he wouldn't tolerate the bishop's bulling manner. On the bishop's part it was how he saw this priest as insubordinate and too diverse in his thinking. As far as the bishop was concerned, this priest only confused every situation by looking into too many imponderables.

Bishop's House was one of those grand palatial buildings with a very impressive heavily gravelled entrance that ran in a wide crescent-shape road with its own exit at the other end. Its many religious statues and tall stately cedars and beach trees gave the visitor a distinct impression of luxury and grandeur. Because of its present incumbent, a visit to this grand edifice and its grounds always seemed to create a distinct sense of intimidation and apprehension. Its many rooms, furniture and offices were lavishly decorated with some of the finest antiques and wall coverings belonging to a bygone period of classical art and the finest craftsmanship, beauty and luxury. Its high domed windows, with their expensively draped curtains, seemed to bring the outer landscape into the light-filled, airy rooms. The bishop emphasised his farming background by leaving all the windows wide open as though he were in the middle of a field with the curtains waving inwardly as frenzied as the hidden madness in his own head. It would have surprised no one if he let a herd of cows loose on the lawn. As a compromise, he kept a few hens and a cockerel at the rear of the palace Just to hear their cackling and the cock's shrieking call to remind him of the land and ambience of his childhood days.

When he received someone really influential and important at his palace, the result was skin-crawling to watch the bishop's hand-wringing, his fawning subservience, with his thick head leaning to one side and his body and eyes lowered, shamefully making a mockery of all attempts to fain humility. It took no particular intelligence to see beyond his pretentiousness. His extreme orthodoxy was his only friend and defence to his literary incompetence. His attitude to fellow clergy and people below his rank and status reminded Father Kevin of a line from Milton's poem, "Paradise Lost," where Satan cries to God, "Better to reign in hell than to serve in heaven...." And that quote or motto might well serve Bishop Duffy on a coat of arms, signifying the spirit of his forbidding, autocratic ministry.

Prior to his grovelling elevation to bishop, he was renowned as a vocation-breaker. He once held the office of vocation's director. From that position he went on to snake his way to canon and then monsignor. Many a young priest pulled out of the priesthood due to his bullying and abusive attitude. He was also directly responsible for the mental breakdown of some of the older priests as well as some of the younger ones. Some blame for this man's position and attitude must inevitably be laid at the door of his predecessor, Bishop Dwyer, who was as black and white in his opinions as the one whom he positioned to replace him. This then was the unwelcome tyrant that Father Kevin had to confront on a most sensitive matter.

As Father Kevin's old black Ford Corsair crunched its way on the heavily-gravelled, crescent-shaped driveway, he couldn't help feeling ill at ease. He wasn't looking forward to this meeting with the inhospitable bishop. In spite of the priest's discomfiture, he experienced a distinct awe in the grandeur and richness to Bishop's House. The building's imposing features were spoiled only by the thoughts of the incumbent occupying the grand edifice.

A middle aged maid answered the doorbell almost instantly. As she pulled open one of the two massive oak doors, he was met with her warm smile and welcome.

'God bless you, Father, if it isn't your good self. I'm very pleased to see you, and no mistake. Is it himself you want to see?' He didn't answer the question directly since he was taken aback by the last person he expected to find in this imposing palace, a smiling welcoming face. The priest leaned back emphasising his surprise and to get a closer look at the beaming smiling woman before him. He didn't really recognise her at first; she was dressed in such a formal way, wearing an old fashioned, starch-white maid's apron over her black uniform, and a brilliant white head covering to match. Even the black stockings and glistening black, thick-healed shoes seemed to evoke another bygone age.

'God bless your soul; if it isn't Molly McGuire herself in all her grandeur.' The priest was smiling warmly; it seemed to release him from his earlier foreboding thoughts. She might have been an angel from heaven sent for his own very comfort and benefit.

'Now, Father Kevin, don't be teasing a poor woman; sure, isn't it mockery enough to wear this degrading uniform in this century. I feel like I'm stepping into an old Dickensian story; God help me in me troubles.'

'Never mind molly; whichever way you look at it, you still look as beautiful as ever, God bless the mark.'

'Ouch, away with yeah, Father, 'tis not kissing the Blarney Stone you have, but eating it.' They both had a hearty laugh at their own banter. Whatever might unfold from his meeting with the bishop, he felt he had some supporting spirit in Molly, one of his own parishioners; not that she could be present in any capacity to comfort him; it was just the calming thought of her presence under the same roof.

'Well, to answer your original question, Molly, yes; 'tis himself I've come to see.' Molly joined her hands and her eyes looked up to heaven just as Father Kevin raised his own eyes heavenward in unison with hers, except he just shook his head as one who was in dread of the next hour or so.

Molly ushered Father Kevin into the bishop's study and whispered discretely, 'Good look, Father, I'll say a prayer for yeah.' Even now the priest had to smile as Molly, kind creature that she was, scampered off as quickly as she could after announcing Father Kevin Noonan's arrival in her most formal, polished Cork accent. It was so comical to see Molly half bent with her head just poking round the study door as though she couldn't wait to be off out the bishop's line of fire. She literally ran up the stairs like a scampering rabbit to get out of sight and danger. As Father Kevin entered the study he could feel his whole body contract. If there was one man on God's good earth that he would rather avoid, for everyone's benefit, it was this bludgeoning-farmer-bishop before him, seated in contemptuous pomposity.

The bishop didn't even look up in acknowledgement of Father Kevin's entrance; nor did he make the slightest attempt to answer him as the priest said, 'good morning.' Instead, he barked out gruffly.

'Well. What is it?' Looking up he added, 'Oh! It's you, is it?' This pretence at not knowing of his appointment was typical of the bishop as a means of intimidation and to belittle the priest. Father Kevin could feel his temper rising. Before anything else was said there was a knock at a panelled door behind the bishop to which he responded with a peremptory roar in prancing authority and aggressive impatience.

'Come in, for God's sake, come in and be done with yeah.' In popped another Dickensian maid and laid down a cup of tea in front of him. She was about to ask if there was anything else he wanted, when he dismissed her with a backward sweep of his hand, almost swatting her as if she was an annoying insect. She gave a hurried courtesy, raised her eyes to heaven for the priest's benefit and disappeared as quickly as she could. This apparently trivial event – the refreshment, was yet another ploy designed purposely to demean the priest standing in front of his desk. The bishop knew perfectly well the time of the appointment; yet, he deliberately connived that the visit be interrupted. He had arranged for a cup of tea to be brought for himself without the slightest attempt of offering his visitor any refreshment. Nor did he offer him to take a seat. In any event, Father Kevin was in no mood to prolong his stay in this bishop's degenerate presence.

'You know perfectly well why I am here from our telephone conversation where I outlined my concern about Larry Walsh's situation and his missing mother, whom he claims to have ascended to Heaven, and of her return with this message. The priest handed the bishop a photocopy of the original message. He was dreading the mockery that he knew would ensue. True to the bishop's sneering and dogmatic character, it came by the cart load. He read the message holding the copy at distance with a grimaced look of distain as if the paper was utter filth. Without looking up he spoke contemptuously at the paper.

'Ah, ha...! I see they use photocopiers in Heaven these days.' The bishop wore a contemptuous grin on his grimaced face; his red neck showing the protrusion of his veins which further emphasised his inner anger and contempt at what he considered a complete waste of time and the rantings of a religious lunatic. He moved a little way from the desk pushing on the mobile office chair. He now sat in a position with his two hands gripping the arms of the seat, one leg crossed over the other, leaning back pompously as one in complete command of his office, his eyes and face still fixed in disgust at the page he had now thrown down contemptuously on the paper-strewn desk. The floor too was littered with papers. He wouldn't allow anyone to disturb the disorder he himself considered order. He prided himself of knowing where everything was, like a drunken fool in a fog.

'Look, bishop; I'm here for one purpose only. I'm not concerned or intimidated by your mockery. It is no more than I expect from you. My sole purpose is to let you know what may break over the Church's head if this situation descends on the media. At the very least this notification, no matter its authenticity or otherwise, allows you space and time to be prepared in the likely event of your being bombarded by the press for your opinion on the matter.' Father Kevin was determined to get out of this bishop's presence as swiftly as he could before loosing all sense of calm, dignity and patience. However, the bishop was determined to complicate the issue still further.

'Where is the supposed original note?' the bishop enquired contemptuously, 'or is there one at all?' he added with a sneer.

'It is in safe hands,' the priest replied defensively and continued to look down at the bishop's bent head. Suddenly the bishop raised his head to confront the priest's face. The bishop's light grey eyes glared with utter hatred and contempt as he spoke.

'O, dear ...! So the bishop is not to be trusted! By God! How dare you keep important papers from my authority? Are you now making yourself the sole authority of the Cork diocese? You think again, Noonan. I will have your bloody removal from this diocese if it is the last act of my ministry, you can stake your arrogant life on that.'

Father Kevin lost it as he responded with some anger of his own. The faces of both clerics were now white with rage, their eyes locked on each other like two rutting stags in a fight for supremacy.

'Look here, you bloody half-wit. It's bad enough that you haven't the wisdom that your office requires; you're a fucking disgrace to the priesthood, never mind the diocese. Don't you ever wonder why you are so hated in the diocese by the clergy and religious? Even the people detest your presence when you visit the various parishes to perform the sacrament of Confirmation and the visiting of the sick, which you inevitably try to avoid. The plain truth is that most, if not all, of clergy can't wait to see the back of you because of your domineering and bullying attitude. I'll tell you point blank, you will never see the original letter because I know from long experience that as soon as I walk out of here you will shred it. Quite apart from not trusting you, you only need to know the contents of the letter that is my only duty to you here. You have a copy of the contents. As far as I'm concerned my duty to you is done, and thank God for it; I couldn't abide in your presence a second longer than I have to.'

'Look here, Noonan, there are many apparitions and heavenly visitations across the world that have been accepted and authenticated by Rome. This nonsense of yours hasn't even reached the Holy Father and yet you expect me to accept it on your say so – you who have neither respect for my authority nor for my position as the legitimate shepherd of the diocese of Cork.' The bishop was seething with hatred and sneering in face-snarling contempt like an attacking wolf.

'You.... A shepherd of the diocese of Cork! God help us all, if that is how you really see yourself. You, bishop, should have stuck to shepherding sheep on your family's farm. Those poor creatures might have saved us all the hell you create all over the diocese. Just as I see an angel in Larry Walsh's face and innocence – so I see Satan in yours. You may wear the bishop's pectoral cross around your neck but you use it as a cudgel to bludgeon and oppress both clergy and people into blind obedience to your own ignorant dictates.' Both clerics were shouting into the other's rage-racked faces.

Even the servants of the house grew frightened. They had never known Father Kevin to lose control as he had now. They were used to the bishop's fiery temper, his rages and impatient arrogant ways. Now the servants covered their mouths in utter disbelief as they looked at each other gathered in a cluster on the upper landing. They stood transfixed as the upheaval raged on below like a relentless storm.

Father Kevin continued, 'As for those apparitions or heavenly visitation you say have been authenticated and accepted by Rome, all I can say to that is, thank God your were not responsible for their approval or even Christ himself would have been burned at the stake as a heretic.' With those words still ringing in the bishop's ears, Father Kevin stormed out of the study slamming both the study door and the heavy oak entrance door. The slamming of the outer door made the whole building vibrate as though it were the result of an earth tremor.'

True to form, the bishop, shaking and half blind with rage grabbed the photocopy of the message as though it was a filthy rodent and put it in the shredder; he even watched the process of the machine as if the thing wasn't ripping the paper fast enough. He returned to his seat trembling with rage. His heart was pounding in his chest as if some inner blacksmith was hammering on it as his anvil.

In the meantime, Father Kevin drove away on the gravel driveway leaving deep tyre ruts in his wake. He too was shaking with rage. He pulled in off the main road and stopped for some time with his hands covering his face; his mind racing and utterly distracted. Somewhere at the back of his churning mind he knew that there would be serious consequence to his actions and outburst of rage, for the unacceptable language used in front of a bishop. However, at the moment, given his distressed state, he couldn't give a damn.

When Father Kevin returned to the presbytery Nell already had the door opened. When she saw his ashen face, her first instinct was to put her arms round him and hold him for a while as she pushed the door shut with her foot. After some moments he whispered in her ear,

'Nell, please bring the whiskey and soda and give me a few minutes before we have lunch. I need to calm down.' Nell was very upset herself to see such a kind caring priest and dear friend in such a state. This was not the first time that he returned from a meeting with the bishop in a state of utter distress. However, she had never known him to touch the whiskey bottle at this time of the day; wine yes, with the meal? Whiskey? Never! The truth be told, he was happy with one can of larger in the evening and the odd whisky and soda as a night cap; even that was followed by coffee. However, even now she trusted her friend with the whiskey.

Eventually, he revealed all to Nell, telling her how ashamed he felt concerning the language used and his total hatred for the bishop. He even questioned his own vocation and worthiness as a priest.

'How could I stand up in church, Nell, asking people to love their enemies and forgive them when I was as near to murdering the bishop as a man could get?'

'Father Kevin,' she replied across the lunch table, as she rested her wrinkled hand on his, 'you will have to get into a mighty long cue for that privilege.' She added, looking under his downcast face. 'None of us are spared our nature, Father Kevin, even you, one of the most patient persons I know. Didn't the good Lord himself rant and rage in his several indictments of the scribes and Pharisees? Didn't he also chase the money changers and market sellers out of the Temple with a whip for their abuse of the House of Prayer?

'Now if what you have done to the bishop is held against you, I will quietly remind Holy God Himself of his Son's rage.' Father Kevin looked up at Nell's wise old face and smiled between his own tears.

'You're a great comfort to me, Nell. I know that if you were in charge of Heaven I would have no doubt of a secure place.'

'Ah, ha…! Exclaimed Nell; you see before you the face of God.' Father Kevin nearly fell off his seat with laughing.'

'Nell! Nell! Nell! Please don't make a joke of something like that.' Father Kevin tried to be serious.

'That, Father, is no joke. Nell rarely referred to her friend and priest as "Father" on its own; it either meant that she was a bit cross with him or, that she wanted to make a serious point. She continued.

'My late mother, God rest her good soul, told me time and time again that if I wanted to put a face to God when I prayed, that I was to think of a person, living or dead, who loved me for myself. When I asked her why I should do that? She replied, "Because God is love and that I can count on the Holy Scriptures for the truth in what I am telling you." Now, I took all that to heart as a child until I became familiar with the Holy Scriptures myself and then I realised that mammy told me the truth. Sure, didn't Saint Paul himself – God bless the man – arrive at the very same conclusion in his First Letter to the Corinthians; don't I know the passage well; it always meant so much to me personally since it emphasised mammy's view of God.' Nell gave her white head a emphatic nod as though it was the full stop of all full stops; she all but head-butted her friend. There was a big smile radiating from Father Kevin's face as he remarked.

'And whose face have you put on God since, I wonder?' There was a teasing mischievousness in the priest's question.

'It was always my mammy's as a child; she was so loving and patient with the whole lot of us. Sometimes I imagine your face on God, but not today; you have been naughty and laughing at poor Nell; may my mammy forgive you.' With that final remark from her quick wit, Father Kevin was in tears from laughing; indeed, Nell herself was smiling. However, that is how she really came to associate Love with God – no matter where she encountered kindness in others.

With the New Year there came the disturbing news in a correspondence from Cardinal Roger McGuire, Primate of all Ireland. The letter read:

"His Lordship, The Right Reverend Paul Duffy, Bishop of Cork has retired due to ill health and is presently being cared for in Saint Magdalene's, in County Down. Please ask your congregations to keep him in your prayers.

On no account is he to be contacted by any parishioner; his doctors are most emphatic that he is in need of rest and quiet. Any communications whatsoever are to be sent to the newly installed bishop, The Right Reverend Mark McCann; he alone will be in communication with Bishop Duffy."

This communication would play on Father Kevin's mind for several years after. He found it difficult to live with the idea of having demonstrated his utter contempt and hatred so emphatically to a fellow priest and bishop. The guilt affected both his prayer life and his preaching for a long time afterwards. He never felt confident in either but always felt a deep sense of his own hypocrisy. Nor did his burden find relief when in a later communication from the new bishop that Bishop Paul Duffy had passed on. Father Kevin felt the last piece of news as an even greater shock as though he himself had driven a steak into the bishop's heart. He already knew from the first communication from Bishop Mark McCann that Saint Magdalene's in County Down only cared for, and specialised in, the care of diocesan clergy and religious who had been sectioned and in need of urgent psychiatric help. Father Kevin's only consolation lay in the knowledge that the new bishop knew all too well of the extreme and widespread damage inflicted on the clergy and religious in general by the recently deceased Bishop Duffy.

At the funeral of the late bishop, it struck many of the clergy, as well as the laity, in a powerful way, just how solemn and awe-inspiring a bishop's funeral could be. The crowds that packed Saint Peter's Cathedral, beyond its normal capacity, flowed out into the main city thoroughfare and expressed in its numbers its own awesome sense of importance and solemnity, even grandeur. The importance of the occasion, its impact on the crowd's sense of gravity, was a great breathtaking-spectacle due to its utter scale and pageantry. To add further to this already overpowering sense of solemnity and importance came the seemingly endless liturgical procession comprised of thurifer, cross-bearer, acolytes, altar servers, priests deacons, canons and monsignors, followed by the newly installed bishop and his Master of Ceremonies. Two hundred clergy processed past the coffin and went on to reverence the altar. Nell, who was also present on one of the outside pews, prominent by her white head of hair, watched Father Kevin's face as he looked up after kissing the altar. He appeared haggard, worn and red in the face, strained from the utter tension of the occasion, his probing conscience, and due in part to his awareness of the TV cameras broadcasting the ceremony live throughout Ireland. There was insufficient room for all the clergy on the sanctuary and so most were ushered to several rows of pews in front of the people, the seating reserved for that very purpose. All the while the swelling sound of the great Cathedral organ piped its powerful cords over the heads of the singing congregation and choir.

The gravity of the elaborate ceremony from start to finish seemed as if the departed bishop released from all life's cares, lying before the foot of the great altar, could only be received in one place, his final home in Heaven. It was as if the very grandeur of the occasion promoted the bishop to sainthood. Few would ever be conscious of the fact that it was not the bishop nor the man that was being honoured, but the importance of his high office. It was akin to the funeral of all great men and women who held or reigned in high office, kings, queens, presidents, whether tyrannical dictators or renowned princes of the people. The death of such dignitaries – the scale and spectacle of the final honour bestowed to them seemed to overshadow the fact, that no matter their importance, they too would have to face a final judgement. As much as Nell tried to cast such unworthy, judgemental thoughts from her mind, she couldn't help the truth, that the deceased bishop haunting her memories with the all too significant hurt he had inflicted on her dear friend and priest. She prayed silently, desperately, for forgiveness for holding on to the faults of the deceased bishop. She knew as well as any that no one, but God alone, had the whole story and circumstances of any individual's life or worthiness.

The homily at the requiem Mass was all too predictable; the entire homily predicated the office of bishop and emphasized the importance and gravity of that important office. It did, however, refer to the sixty years of service Bishop Duffy had given to the Church. The celebrant spoke of the many parishes that the deceased bishop had served throughout his long ministry from his earliest days as priest to his elevation to high office. At the end of the rather clerical homily, mainly emphasizing the office and role of bishop, no one was really any the wiser about the deceased's personal life. All the appropriate things that were expected to be said were given due emphasis. However, it was really the scale of the event, the music, the singing and pageantry that gave the occasion its sense of solemnity, grandeur and magnificence.

After the ceremony the casket was carried and placed into a low glittering black, Mercedes limousine. The bearers of the casket stepped aside while the new bishop splashed the sign of the cross over the casket with holy water. The glass side panels of the hearse were decked with flowers and also seated six coffin bearers, three either side of the hearse. The limousine inched slowly away from the cathedral until it was safely past the danger of the vast crowds of people that spilled precariously off the overflowing pavements. The Hearse was followed by one lone funeral limousine that conveyed the chauffeur, new bishop and his secretary. The deceased bishop had no surviving family and so it was decided to keep the final internment strictly private.

Once out of the city, the hearse and following limousine followed the route north to Derry. The Journey took several hours in driving rain, the windscreen wipers were at hammering speed and barely able to keep up with the deluge. The vehicles arrived in an ancient country graveyard. Its old crumbling church, half hidden in dense ivy, clanged out its doleful bell. The terrible call of death's authority carried along the sober thoughts and final words of the new bishop who was now half in shadow under the large cascading umbrella held by his secretary. Both clerics were in their black cassocks and white cotters; their purple stoles and clothing flapping franticly in the rain-lashed wind. The bent heads of six bearers, not spared the rain, holding the webs that would lower the heavy casket awaiting the bishop's nod. After the blessing of the grave the gravediggers let the casket down with some haste so that they could to be out of the rain as fast as possible. The cold wind and rain was greater than their sense of dignity. The bishop's voice droned wearily on:

'Man that is born of a woman
has but a short time to live
and is full of misery;
He is come up
and is cut down like a flower
He fleeth as it were a shadow,
and is never long in one stay.
The days of man
are but as grass in the fields,
As soon as the winds blow over
it they are gone
and the place thereof
shall know him no more.
In the midst of life
we are in death O Lord
For whom shall we seek
for succour but to thee O Lord ....'

It was quite apparent to the gravediggers that the bishop missed out on a few prayers given the extreme conditions and for the benefit of the living as he watched the gravediggers huddled under a tree which cascaded its waters like a waterfall in spate. Then came the last words to the relief of all, including the bishop and his faithful secretary, they were bursting to relieve themselves. The rain was playing tricks with their biology.

'...earth to earth; ashes to ashes;
dust to dust. The Lord gave;
The Lord has taken away.
Blessed be the name of the Lord...'

Within moments of the burial both bishop, secretary and all six coffin bearers rushed to find some bushes to relieve themselves as there was no available toilet in the desolate and dilapidated ancient burial place. Human nature took no account of status or occasion – biology had its own authority.

It was very dark now although it was still early evening. None but the gravediggers remained behind to backfill the grave. It was a macabre scene in the dim remaining light. The four dark figures shovelled the earth in frantic speed to be away as quickly as possible from the misery and freezing conditions of the dripping cemetery. The dull thud of earth thrown on the wooden casket became more muffled and silent as the hurried shovels threw their final load smacking the mound of earth with loud impatient slaps shaping it into its final mound. The gritty sound – so ghostly – so final. The men left the dark dripping scene as mere shadows. They too might have been no more than spectres themselves as they disappeared, dissolving into the darkness, their macabre duty done with cold indifference.

There he lay – a silent new resident in death's orchard; a stark mound of raw earth amid the overgrown grass and tangle of weeds, with ancient stones leaning in all directions – their crumbling faces flaking and void of all inscriptions. The world's forgotten ... The forlorn wind rising and falling like the ancient voice of mocking phantoms calling through the trees and hedgerows to the new resident to come up and take a place among the dripping branches and moan with them. All the man ever had, or was likely to have, had been now stripped away without warning. Finally, the night fell like a pall of death. Never again would this soul glimpse the stars or the moon of night. This eerie place grew all at once so terrible – so final.

The impact of Bishop Duffy's death affected Father Kevin and Nell for a long time afterwards. As they sat companionably in the visitor's lounge at home they often pondered on why he was the man he was. They made earnest attempts to fathom the complexities of his life. The best that they could conclude between them over the years was that the poor soul's original identity was lost completely .... His mimicry of a preferred personality had him totally lost in self-rejection. He couldn't possibly develop and mature in himself since what he wished to be was utterly beyond his natural abilities. Perhaps if he had acknowledged his farming roots and kept to their humble strengths and familiarity, he might have been a different priest and person entirely. The truth was that he tried to be someone that he had neither the talent nor the sensitivity to achieve. It was like a vulture trying to mimic a swan. Nell and her friend knew perfectly well that we all have notions of our own self-importance ... our own degree of self-conceited grandiloquence, and our own vain aspirations that cunningly solicit admiration of those we believe to be our inferiors. However, to bury his own simple personality in blatant imitation of the unreachable was to scramble his own true sense of being. What did he achieve in the end but a living torment and misery? A few moments of glory on a pilgrim's throne-of-office, gained with fawning subservience from another's reckless authority where his predecessor, who placed him in office, was equally at fault.

'Ah, sure, if the truth be told, Father Kevin, 'tis only pride and pretence gone amuck.' Nell nodded thoughtfully into the worn carpet. Father Kevin took up her enigmatic remark, his head drawn back in utter incomprehension, his face and lined brow a stage of confusion.

'Whatever do you mean, Nell?'

'The primitive male banging his chest to show his presumed strength to a watching female ... all soliciting courtship ... a display of coloured feathers to draw a partner on ... rutting violence ... to show the female doe how strong the stag. These you know, Father Kevin, are powerful primitive instincts in all animal and bird life. However, in our so-called civilized times, our soliciting displays are more concealed, more cunning and complicated. The smile on a face signifying an open door ... an invitation ... a pretence at indifference ... We all grow up with the addiction of approval ... we seem never to stop pleasing mammy and daddy. Sure 'tis no surprise at all that most of us continue most of our lives as slaves to approval. Need I go on?' Nell was smiling into his face as she added mischievously, '... No need to bang on your chest for me, Father Kevin, I'm all yours.' He broke into fits of laughter at Nell's remark.

'You're some flower, Nell, and no mistake.' There was a thoughtful silence between them for some moments before Father Kevin remarked with considered deliberation. 'You know, Nell, there's a whole ocean of meaning in what you have just said. I see now that we often want to impress each other without always knowing consciously why. I can even see how we can be acting to impress out of our own desperate drives to make our mark, to keep up with the tribe even though we don't always know where we are going or what we are about, or what it is that is driving us. Pride, no doubt, Nell, has many masks. We can even be conceited in our own pretence at self-deprecation ... displays of false humility, while all the time soliciting hopes of self-elevation in the esteem of another's regard. We are not always comfortable with feelings of being left behind. I think I will always refer to this phenomenon, as of now, "Feathers of promise", and inscribe it in my own little book of wisdom as a tribute to my dear sage, Nell.' She dismissed his complement with the swipe of her hand, any yet smirking.

'Ultimately no one could judge the poor soul but God alone.' With these words, Father Kevin and Nell agreed to avoid any further attempt to make sense of Bishop Duffy's life.

'It is far better to keep the man in our prayers and hope that God might be patient with our own short comings.' These were Nell's last words on the subject.

CHAPTER 10

Love Affair between Larry and Dee

Larry thought he was having more nightmares since he was constantly being haunted in his mind by all kinds of difficult problems concerning the work that he was supposed to undertake. He seemed to be organising the entire world single-handed, that in itself was disturbing enough. However, what disturbed him even more was his being pestered in his dreams by the Journalist, Delilah Ferret. A voice in his dreams kept insisting that he go and visit her with the view to seeking her help. He would wake up in a cold sweat feeling that he was going out of his mind. Added to all his disturbance was the fact that during some periods of each night he would be forced out of his warm bed to write frantically whole loads of instructions in the spiral jotters by his bedside ... 'Oh Lord...!' He would exclaim aloud; 'I wish all this worry to be over.' He would appeal to his mammy often. 'I miss you so much – I wish you were here.' And some times he would see her as she used to be. She would smile and console him and tell him not to worry in the slightest, that he would get all the help he would need from the most unlikely places. He didn't mention to her about the journalist, he was fearful of her haunting his dreams. Eventually he made up his mind to go and visit her even if it would only bring him more restful nights. He never mentioned the journalist to his friends, his good neighbours, Seamus and Lil; he didn't want to upset them again because she made them very angry the last time they met; and he didn't like to see the family he loved being angry again. He had a half-baked notion in his head that he was supposed to receive some kind of help from the journalist; at least that is what the voices in his dreams seemed to be telling him. It was with gritty determination coupled with a real sense of foreboding that he visited her apartment.

After ringing the bell to her flat he heard a female voice speak rather impatiently. The voice came from an intercom on the wall; the wall-intercom was at his shoulder level but he couldn't make sense of the gadget since he had never come across one before in his life. Larry looked up and down, all over the wall, but to no avail. The woman's voice grew angrier by the second.

'Who the bloody hell is there? Press the f...n green button to speak, if you're too bloody ignorant to know what it's for.' With a good deal of effort Larry eventually got the hang of the talking wall and announced his presence. To say she was surprised and taken aback was to understate her sudden silence. The first thought that came instantly to her mind when her surprise diffused was, Like a lamb to the slaughter. She felt she owed him a deal of grief for all the problems he caused her, particularly from his neighbours.

The heavy glass door opened automatically after the electronic lock was released. Once in, the door locked behind him. He grew even more apprehensive than he was already; he didn't like the idea of being locked in with her.

The ambiance of the rich marble interior gave the intrepid Larry a sense of intimidating luxury. He tried to reopen the heavy glass door but it was firmly locked. She called down to him to come upstairs. Her voice sounded different; there was no anger in it now but a gentle seductive invitation that meant nothing more to the innocent Larry than the imagined calming of her prior irritation. The front door to the inner sanctum to her apartment was already open to receive him. Nobody, but nobody – not a living soul, was ever allowed into her private rooms, not even the editor she worked for. In fact, apart from handing in copies of her work to Brendan Hawkswood, the editor, she generally gave the office as wide a birth as possible and preferred to work from home sending her finished work by e-mail for last minute corrections if needed. Her work rarely needed even the slightest alterations since she was at the very height of her profession – streets ahead of her rivals.

She was blow-drying her silken blond hair as Larry followed the direction of her voice. He crept about gingerly to locate her, his head turning this way and that around each door. He could hear the blow-dryer mixed with, what sounded to him like, church music. It was her favourite Gregorian chant disc. Larry, in his innocence thought the chant a very odd choice in such a place and for such an odd person. He certainly never saw her in Saint Patrick's church. Now he met her in her bedroom from where the voice drew him, she was sitting on the end of the bed with the hand-held, hair-dryer. She was dressed in her favourite blue patterned, silk Chinese dressing gown. Even with her dishevelled hair she was truly beautiful. Larry had time to appreciate this fact since she wasn't being her usual nasty self on this occasion. He seemed to tower above her as she sat grooming her hair. She sat framed on a bed of glistening light blue silk. He felt instinctively uncomfortable in her luxurious bedroom. He had never in his lifetime been inside the bedroom of any female other than his dear mother. It made him shudder with unease. It felt all wrong. Her body exuded a beautiful freshness from the shower gel. She knew perfectly well that he was looking at her in a new way. She couldn't be certain if he was aroused in any way – she looked for obvious signs, convinced that no matter his idiotic innocence, the animal instincts rarely left the man – even in a lunatic. Larry, however, was unaffected by her subtle attempts at seduction, even when she allowed her silk dressing gown to slip and reveal the upper parts of her bare thighs. By this time he had turned away taking an indifferent interest in some abstract art pictures on the walls of her bedroom. She noted his lack of response.

She had finished grooming her hair by the bedroom's vanity suite and turned to him after spraying herself rather heavily with her favourite sweet-scented perfume. She put out her hand towards him and said in her soft seductive voice.

'Larry dear, give me your hand to pull me up from the bed.' Though her voice was gentle, there was a distinct command in her tone. She thought to herself that she would get a story out of this imbecile if it was the last thing she would do this day. She withdrew her hand since Larry was paying no attention to her for the last few minutes.

'Come into the sitting room, Larry. There's a good boy. Have a drink while I fetch something from my bag. Would you like some whiskey … sherry … wine … what?' She placed all three bottles before him on the glass table top along with two generous cut glass whiskey tumblers. She poured out two overly liberal whiskies and pushed one in front of him and then made her way, not to her bag, but to the safe from where she withdrew her small digital recorder with its little daisy microphone, which she clipped onto the lapel of her beautiful silk dressing gown. She placed the small voice recorder on the tie of her silk robe. She sat some way from him in on one of the square-shaped black armchairs. She allowed her silk covering to slip once more from one of her bare legs so as to reveal a good portion of her beautiful thighs. Larry lifted the cut glass with the amber liquid to his lips but before he had a chance to taste it he got a strong nasty whiff of the alcohol and placed the heavy glass back on the table with a clatter. He screwed up his face in disgust and utter revulsion. His face still grimaced as he said,

'That smells horrible. I only drink what my mammy used to call soft drinks.' Ferret, in her disappointment and irritation said to herself.

'Am I surprised? It's a wonder she didn't feed you from a baby's dummy.' Presently she offered him some lemonade instead and removed the bottles and glasses from the low glass table. She didn't even take a sip of her own drink, she rarely, if ever, took alcohol before a day's writing. She made herself a coffee and placed in on the glass top drinks cabinet at arm's reach from her seat.

Ferret couldn't fully explain why a sudden feeling of guilt came over her as she watched Larry sip from the tumbler of lemonade. Her mind suddenly swung back to her partial reconciliation with Father Kevin Noonan and his aged housekeeper, Nell. In no way did she want to risk hurting the lad for their sake. Yet she was a journalist through and through. She had to make a living. However, in Larry's case she wondered how she might write something worthwhile but trying her utmost to keep to some degree of damage limitation to this innocent child.

Larry was looking all over the room not quite knowing what to make of the apartment. It exuded a strong impression of a rather posh dentist's waiting room or even a surgery. Ferret was eying him up from under her lowered beautiful face. None of her attempts at seduction worked on Larry. He still didn't know what he was doing visiting her in the first place except that a voice in his dreams told him to go to her, that she would help him. Eventually he decided to speak his mind and get away from her as he felt more and more uncomfortable in her presence. She was not slow to see his unease.

'I was told to come to see you, that you will be able to help me.' As he spoke, his brow was lined with an expression of confusion and unease. He simply didn't know what to expect from her. He was well aware of how nasty she could be; and he wasn't at all convinced that she would be any different now.

'Help you, Larry! Sure there's no better woman for the job.' She was half mocking and teasing him at the same time. She was trying to be more light-hearted, allowing a sweet smile to light up her beautiful face. She was so different when she smiled, Larry thought.

'Who did you say sent you, Larry? Was it dear Father Kevin and Nell his housekeeper?'

'No. I didn't say who it was.' He was not trying to be smart – he usually stated the obvious.

'So, who told you to come to me for help, Larry?' Her voice was really soft now and her smile and expression more attuned to addressing a little child.

'It was an angel in my dreams. Several times I was told to come to see you and I didn't think that you would ever want to see me again because of all the trouble I caused you with my friends Seamus and Lil.' Ferret winced at the mention of his neighbours. However, she tried to brush aside the memory of the confrontation that she had with them. She pursued the strange line of their conversation convinced that they were veering away from reality.

Ferret could sense that he just wanted to be out of her company as soon as possible; so in an effort to make up for the past she forced some tears from her eyes and apologised for her past rudeness and lack of understanding. As the words slipped from her practiced pouting lips she said:

'Let us be friends now, Larry, and let bygones be bygones.' She came close to him on the large settee where he sat at one end of it. She offered him her hand which he took, this time because of her tears. No sooner had their hands touched when she was literally thrown across the room. She slid involuntary across the highly glossed wood floor ending with a muffled thud at the opposite wall near the entrance door to the lounge. Larry himself passed out but remained slumped in the settee. It was as if a bolt of lightening had struck them both at the same time.

Larry was the first to wake from his unconscious state. He was attempting to bring moisture from his throat to his very dry mouth. It took some while before he regained sufficient composure to realise that he was in complete darkness except for some dull striped amber lights from the partially opened Venetian blinds – the light coming from the street below. He tried to stand up and move across to a wall. Any wall he thought, where he might find a switch. He crashed into the heavy glass table sending the tumbler flying across it and crashing to the bare parquet floor. With the help of the little light from the windows he managed to find a dimmer switch which he had to fumble with for some time to get it to work. He tried pulling it and pressing it. After several attempts he succeeded in turning the switch and saw the light gradually come to life. He had never seen such a contraption in his life. He looked about him and was utterly bewildered and couldn't make any sense of where he was until his eyes came to rest in a state of utter shock and alarm when he saw Ferret's unconscious body in a heap against the wall.

His eyes were wide and staring in utter panic at the beautiful crumpled body in a disfigured heap on the floor with one of her soft limp arms half hanging from the wall while her other arm was trapped underneath her soft body. Larry put his hand to his mouth and kept repeating through his muffled fingers: 'My God! My God! What have I done? What have I done?' he was terrified out of his wits. He kept staring at the unconscious figure repeating the same thing over and over keeping his hand across his mouth in shear terror as he stooped down hoping that she would suddenly come to life. He hadn't the faintest notion of what to do.

After what seemed an eternity to him, he decided to straighten up her body because he knew instinctively that she could never get up by herself with her legs and arms so misshapen. As he straightened up her limp body into its regular shape, he couldn't help noticing her nakedness. Her Chinese silk robe slid from the front of her still smooth body. He was even more shocked than ever when he realised that her private parts were missing, so he thought. He had never seen a naked woman before since he lived a very sheltered existence with his mother, Mary. Now he looked across the floor in an attempt to find her missing private parts. He even moved the settee and armchairs to see if they had rolled underneath them from the crash that must have occurred. He returned to her body. He rubbed his hand in panic across his mouth and bared his teeth in and expression of sheer terror. He used his other hand at the same time to rub the back of his neck with quick panicky moves which only served to add to his frightened and confused state. He noticed that there was no blood where her missing private parts should be. He moved her legs apart and grew even more concerned as he began to believe that the crash must have been so bad that she was split where her private parts should be. He replaced her legs together and covered her nakedness. He stood for some time not knowing what he should do next. Suddenly he remembered how his mammy used to move the heavy dustbin from the back of the house by dragging it on a piece of carpet to the front of the house for emptying. Although Larry was strong enough to lift her bodily he was nonetheless very clumsy and he was afraid of the damage already done to her. He took the large white, crescent-shaped mat and placed it under her bottom while lifting up her legs at the same. He pushed the mat under her with his foot, his face grimacing from the effort. He dragged her by the legs into the bedroom using the mat as a slide. He then rolled back the duvet and hoisted her on to the bed and rolled her about in order to cover her nakedness with her Chinese robe. He removed what he believed to be some kind of music device from her dressing gown and placed it on the bedside cabinet. He then covered her over with the duvet and pulled her hands free to lay them on top of the cover, just as he used to help his mammy when she was sick. He gazed down on her beautiful sleeping face in spite of it being fixed in an expression of shock. Once again he set about rubbing his mouth and the back of his neck panicking as to what he should do next. He tried to use the telephone near the doorway but he couldn't manage it because it wasn't like an ordinary phone, he needed to press 9 for a line out but he couldn't have known that.

He was beginning to think that she might be dead. He went below stairs to the entrance door but realised it was still locked. He banged at the heavy glass in an attempt to get free and call for help. The glass door was too solid to part from its locking mechanism and it was very late in the night or in the early hours of the morning – he couldn't be certain of the time. He knew his neighbours would be very anxious. He had already missed his meal with them and he was really in need of coffee, tea or a cold drink as well as some food. He returned to the apartment once again and helped himself to some more lemonade. He looked in on the figure on the bed but there was no sign of life in her. He eventually found a partially used loaf of bread, some butter and cut off a big lump of cheese. He was ravenous with the hunger and scoffed the food and hoped Miss Ferret wouldn't be angry with him for helping himself.

'Well, I have missed my lunch 'cause she locked me in. It's her fault really,' he spoke aloud to the room. He took a dining chair from the kitchen and brought it in to sit beside her bringing with him the bottle of lemonade and a tumbler.

When it dawned on him after some time of watching her face closely, he realised that she too must be thirsty and hungry. He remembered that he had to feed his poor old mammy when she was bedridden in the final weeks of her life. But then his good neighbours, Seamus and Lil had given him the food to feed her. He put some of the lemonade on a teaspoon which he found in the kitchen and lifted her head up from the bed in order to put some of the drink into her mouth. He was delighted to see his achievement as the liquid slid from the spoon. After several successful attempts he noticed her face beginning to grimace with discomfort. She opened her eyes suddenly and spat out the drink in a jet, straight into his lowered face. He let her blond head flop back on the pillows with a mixture of pure fright, shock and relief.

'What the bloody hell are you doing here in my apartment?' She was still a bit delirious and confused.

'You locked the door, so you did! I couldn't get out and I couldn't use your phone to get help – it doesn't work.' Larry screwed his nose and gave a nod of his head in the direction of the white phone. 'I wanted to call my friends, Seamus and Lil, to get help 'cause I couldn't find your missing private parts and you split your private parts between your Legs, and I was frightened 'cause I might get the blame for hurting you and I didn't. You must have done the damage when you fell over against the wall.' All this came from Larry's mouth in one cascading torrent.

Miss Ferret was still a bit groggy. However, the situation before she had passed out was gradually beginning to return to her. She remembered that she took the lad's hand as a ruse to making friends and apologising for past disrespect. She remembered her crocodile tears, the touch of his hand and what seemed like a bolt of lightening or an electric shock come between them. This recalling of the event made her look at her right hand to see if she was actually damaged. The impact was terrifying in its strength. As she took a brief glimpse at the palm of her delicate hand she noticed a very distinct and sharp indention of a perfectly shaped triangle. It was very red as if she had been branded with a branding iron. However, it was only just slightly stinging. After viewing her hand she turned to Larry who stood close to the bed and asked him in a curious tone.

'Let me see your right hand, Larry, will you?'

'Why, what you going to do to me?' He was still very wary of her.

'Sure, I'm not going to do a thing to you. Do you not understand; I wouldn't hurt you; remember we agreed to be friends and forget the past.' He turned up the palm of his right hand and showed it to her. She felt a mixture of fear and bewilderment. There on his hand was an identically-shaped triangle, with the odd distinction, that his was a raised shape as if he himself did the branding. She looked up into his face. He was perplexed with the sudden gaze of her sparkling blue eyes. Her brow was furrowed ... curious ... questioning. Larry spluttered out.

'What?'

Ferret asked him patiently and calmly trying to deal sensitively with his obvious unease,

'How long has your hand been like that?'

Larry looked at his own palm and brought his head back in amazement. 'Good God? I've never seen that before.' He looked startled.

'Does it hurt you?' Ferret asked curiously; she avoided any desire to touch his hand again. One disaster was quite sufficient, she thought to herself.

'It only tickles a bit.' he replied as she displayed her own raised hand to him. 'Gosh! You've got one too.' She didn't bother explaining the difference; none of it made any significant sense to her anyway. She returned to some of Larry's early comments.

'You were saying earlier, Larry that you were going to call your friends to come and help; did you mean your neighbours, Mr. and Mrs. Madden?' By now she was sitting upright in the bed. Before you answer that, Larry, will you please bring me a cup of coffee and a slice of toast, can you manage that much?' She smiled at him to encourage his confidence and yet half expecting him to say that he couldn't manage that either. She was very fortunate to have requested those two very items since they were about his limit apart from beans on toast or tins of soup or stew – or anything from a can that only required opening up and heating in a saucepan. She shouted instructions to him, much to the discomfort of her spinning head – he was asking where everything was kept.

'Can I have some toast and coffee myself?' he asked enthusiastically in his raw city accent.'

She smiled to herself at his thoughtfulness, his refreshing simplicity. She could guess that he was not one to take people for granted – plain good manners, she added to her thoughts. He was not at all your average city wide-boy but a genuine humble, innocent soul. She was beginning to warm to him in some, as yet unexplained way. When he brought in the tray, like he used to do for his dear old mammy, he put in on her bed laying it down very carefully so as not to spill anything. The tray had a cushioned beanbag base and she managed quite well. She was just about to eat some of the nicely done buttered toast when he prevented her from biting into it. Her mouth was opened, her sparkling teeth ready for the hungry bite when he froze her action by suddenly exclaiming.

'No! You mustn't do that! We haven't said the grace, the blessing yet.' She looked positively startled – her face frozen in utter disbelief. It was the first time since being at her Catholic primary school that anyone bothered to remind her to say her grace before meals. She was too hungry and thirsty to argue with him and said.

'You be a dear, Larry, and say it for us both.' He did so with great elaboration as though his long arms would reach the ceiling and three walls with such a mighty sweep in the shape of an enormous cross.

She returned to her earlier question concerning the possibility of a visit from Larry's neighbours.

'Yes.' He replied in between munching his toast. 'I was going to call them, I know their number,' which he reeled off without the slightest hesitation. She waved this information aside as if to say that she hadn't the slightest interest in the detail. What she did say instead was,

'Don't you ever bring your neighbours to my home, Larry … do you understand me? They are your friends, not mine. I hardly know them and they have been very rude to me.'

'But they would only help,' he replied innocently. He knew that she had upset them. However, Larry had known other people to have upset his friends but they never let that stop them from being friends again. He simply couldn't understand her reticence to forget what happened in the past. He persisted a little further to try to clarify why he wanted them to help and said.

'They could bring you to the hospital and get your private parts stitched up.'

'Private parts …?' A startled expression of utter confusion fell across her beautiful face. 'Private parts …!' she exclaimed once more. 'Whatever do you mean, Larry Walsh?' She considered his comment lewd and indecent.

'It is just that when I found you on the floor your silk covering fell from the private parts of your body and I noticed that they were missing and that I might be blamed for the damage.' As he spoke, Larry held his toast to his mouth, a mug of coffee in his other hand, both paused in mid air; he was eager to bite into his toast, he was so hungry. However, her tone of voice and the obvious vexation harrowing her face had terrified him.

'How can my private parts be missing? I don't understand you, Mr. Larry Walsh.'

'I am very sorry to mention it. My daddy and mammy said that I must never be rude, ever, especially in front of a lady.' Ferret was still baffled. Larry could tell that much from the look of incomprehension on her face. He continued a little more directly. 'I noticed that you didn't have a willy like me and everyone else.'

'Have you never seen a lady naked before in your life, Larry?' She couldn't believe her ears. This was the kind of innocent remark that she would have expected to come from four year old brothers and sisters. Larry replied with self-righteous conviction.

'My mammy said that I should never look at a naked lady; that it was rude and against modesty, unless, if I ever had to change a little girl's nappy, which she said would be very unlikely anyway.

'Was it rude to see me naked, then, Larry?' she asked teasing the lad. She could tell he was well brought up to respect women.

'I couldn't help seeing you naked, 'cause when I picked you up I tried to look away but I couldn't take my eyes off where you missing private parts were supposed to be and then I saw the split under your private parts when I moved you to your bed. I didn't want to be blamed for hurting you, 'cause I know I never meant to hurt you.'

'O never mind all that now, Larry. I know you couldn't help seeing me naked. Let's just forget about that. In any case, we are friends now, aren't we?' She was about to extend her hand to him again and quickly thought the better of it. She withdrew her hand swiftly in case she got another bolt of lightening, or whatever it was that knocked her unconscious. Then, she suddenly thought to ask, 'you had to touch my skin when you moved me, Larry, didn't you?'

'I had to,' he replied defensively.

'O, I'm not complaining, Larry. Can you pull back the duvet, I want to see if there is a red mark where you touched me; you know, like the one on our hands.' Larry complied gingerly, only rolling back the minimum for modesty sake. He scrutinised her beautiful bare legs but could find no trace of damage. She now thought to risk the renewal of their friendship again with the shaking of hands; she was still keen to get the story of his mother in its entirety and to find out what kind of help she was to get involved with. She offered her hand quite gingerly and said: 'Now that we have renewed our friendship, Larry, I think it's about time you called me by my special name which only my dearest friends are allowed to use.' She didn't have any friends to speak of. Nor did she have any special name. Larry was not to know that.

'What's that?' replied Larry, with an expression of surprise; he didn't realise that she had any name other than Miss Delilah Ferret.

'You are my special friend now, Larry, you must call me Dee. Never call me anything else only Dee,' she repeated with strong emphasis looking straight into his face with a solemn expression.

'Alright so, Dee; if that is what you want me to call you.' To her blushing astonishment he gave her the biggest, warmest hug and kiss on the cheek that she ever had in her life; she was so taken aback by the unexpected display of his instinctive affection that she nearly threw the dishes off the tray. She was in tears. Larry released her and stood there with the biggest smile on his face because he knew in his heart that he had made another special friend, like his good neighbours, Seamus, Lil and their children Lisa and Andrew. To Dee's surprise she actually felt a sense of affection for Larry, something very distinct that was utterly new to her and entirely unique to her life.

She began with a little flattery with a view to opening him up for his account of his story. 'You must be a very strong man, Larry, to have lifted me from the sitting room to my bedroom. I can't imagine how you managed that.'

'Yerrah, that was easy, 'cause I put a mat under your bottom like my mammy used to do when she had to move the rubbish bin out of the house.' Larry continued to bite into his toast with an expression of pried in his own ability for having managed to move Dee. She began to tease him with no intended malice.

'What a wonderful comparison, Larry, you might make a PR man for a newspaper yet.' Her comment passed over Larry's head like a shooting star.

Ferret realised that the police would be out looking for this lad, given the likely worry and concern of his neighbour friends. After all, he had missed his usual meal time and his company in the evening before he was due to go to bed. She realised the urgent need to make contact with his neighbours so that they could inform the police and have the inevitable search for him called off, with that in mind she said to Larry.

'Now, Larry, dear, I want you to phone your friends and tell them that you met a nice kind friend named Dee; that you are safe and well and that this nice Dee is looking after you, and that you will see them all later in the morning after you have had a rest with your new friend. You tell them also that you have had something to eat here and that you will also be having your breakfast here too. Now, Larry, dear, can you remember all that? Don't worry about the phone I will make the connection for you.'

Larry removed the tray from her bed so that she could arranger herself. He returned to her bedside to help her in case she might be dizzy as he himself was when he awoke for his unconscious state. She took a few tentative steps away from the bed holding on to him. Once again she felt a warm comforting sense from holding on to him. She began to feel a very distinct feeling for Larry; it was a feeling that she couldn't quite articulate at the moment; however, it was such a comforting and sensuous feeling that she didn't ever want to lose it.

Dee pressed 9 on the dial to get an outside line; she also took the precaution of protecting her own number from being traced. Larry was faithful to the message that Dee had composed for him, after which she returned his earlier hug and kiss. Only when she meant to kiss his cheek by drawing him down a little, he turned his face to see what she was doing, with the result, that she placed her lips inadvertently firmly on his own. Both experienced the same surge of passion towards the other. They stayed interlocked in each other's arms for some time; not in a display of reckless passion, but in a tenderness that brought both of them into floods of tears. The held each other in an embrace that neither wanted to end; it was a new experience to them both. The few unhurried minutes seemed to enfold them in a sense of reverence for each other. Slowly they released each other looking solemnly into each others face. Both knew for certain that something very special had occurred. They stood facing each other, their heads lowered in a kind of strange embarrassment peculiar to new lovers.

They moved slowly away from each other in a tangible silence, a kind of reverence. Dee looked back to Larry who was now seated on the long settee not quite knowing what was happening to his innocent inner world. She was smiling through tears she knew that came from a new joy in her lonely and embittered life. Now she experienced a deep sense of pure love, and wonder. She Just couldn't believe that something so wonderful could happen to her from someone, who less that an hour ago, was little more than the means to an end in her guttered world of vindictiveness and sensational muck-racking.

After some more coffee and a sandwich they bedded down for the night but not before they embraced each other for what seemed like a timeless ecstasy. It was early morning before they settled down. The cold of January glistened on the road outside and the amber lights of the street filtered between the gaps in the horizontal window blinds. Dee snuggled underneath the covers of her bed while Larry settled down with some blankets on the settee. She would love to have had him in the bed with her but realised it was all too early for his modesty and very sheltered upbringing. Dee was gradually beginning to admire these qualities in

Larry; whereas, only a short while ago she saw him as some sort of imbecile. She was still glowing with that very distinct feeling of love coursing through her beautiful body. The sensation of it all was one thing; however, she kept wondering how it all came about. It was in this state of wonder that she drifted into a state of deep sleep and ecstasy.

Dee was up before Larry as she seemed to have had more rest. He was exhausted with all the worry and panic of the previous day. Dee cooked a breakfast for two, something she had had never done before in her twenty-four years and she was very conscious of that very detail as she went about the task with so much delight and pleasure. When she called Larry out of his slumber she kissed him. Larry looked gawkily at her wondering if he was seeing another angel, only this one wearing a blue-patterned, silk Chinese robe. The look of unease that was clearly visible on his face made Dee's heart slumped in disappointment. Her beautiful face appeared distraught. She wondered if the previous night was too wonderful to be true. Her spirits soon regained her sense of wonder when Larry, having recovered his focus, smiled into the beautiful face bent over him.

'Ah, Dee...! You're about early.' She was so delighted to know that he recognised her and remembered her name. Nothing else mattered to Dee now. She gave him another big kiss and hug while the blankets covering his half naked body were tangled in a heap about him. She smiled at the sight. She made a mighty fried breakfast of bacon, sausages, mushrooms, tomatoes, white and black puddings all topped with two beautiful clean fried eggs, a rack of fresh toast, and steaming coffee. Dee was pickier; she had some fruit drink to start and she settled for scrambled egg on toast. Before eating, Larry once again interrupted the flow of the drink about to descend between her soft lips when he put up his hand to stay Dee's action.

'We must always say the grace before meals – that's only right and proper. Again the great exaggerated sweeping sign of the cross all but filled the kitchen dining room. The expression on Dee's face was a sight as she paused, her expression frozen ... her soft lips open and the glass too stuck to her fingers as though her whole body had in a single moment being turned into petrified stone. After breakfast Larry expressed his enthusiastic appreciation for the wonderful feast. Both showered separately. Dee now turned to him and instructed him earnestly:

'Now, Larry, love, I want you to go back to you friends to show them that you are ok. And after you are finished what you have to do. I would like it very much if you would come back here. By all means take your lunch as usual with your friends, because they are very special to you, she added. However, I think it best for now that you do not talk about us until we all get to know one another better and get over past wrongs.' Looking up into his face she said kindly, 'will you be able to do that for us, Larry.'

'Of course I will. I am really happy to know that you will become a friend of my friends too. Don't worry. I won't mention you except by you new name, Dee, and I won't explain anything. My friends, Seamus and Lil never make me say anything that I want to keep to myself.' Dee was delighted to hear his confidence in her.

'After you return, Larry, I will give you the number of the lock outside the door so that you can come in and out whenever you please, even when I am out on business, she added trustingly. Larry had a strong feeling of being enwrapped in her love and affection. He felt giddy from it all; he never wanted to be away from her for long. He stooped to kiss her and hold her in his arms never wanting to be parted from her until she gave his behind a friendly smack and said, 'Now Mr. Larry Walsh, you get off about your business too and when you return we can talk about how you want me to help you; ok?'

'Ok, Dee,' he replied with his kind disarming smile and added: you be a good girl too, you hear.'

'Be off with you Mr. Walsh,' she replied to his teasing. She threatened him good-naturedly with the frying slice.

With the return of the prodigal, all three dogs barked furiously. The bark of Dillon, the golden Labrador, was enough to frighten any stranger with its deep volume which filled the house. However, when the dogs saw that it was Larry they circled round his feet sniffing curiously because they knew well that he had been to some strange place. Indeed, Larry had still the distinct whiff of Dee's sweet-scented perfume about his clothes. Lil was one of those people who could smell a gnat's wind from a hundred yards. She also noticed how he held himself more upright than usual. Although he wore the self same clothes as yesterday, they now appeared to be even tidier than usual. Even his soft-coloured grey tie with its russet knot looked sharper and neater. Lil didn't make her observations obvious. That didn't deter her keen interest in the lad. Larry settled down to his usual midday lunch with Lil who was on her own, Seamus was at work in the city and Lisa and Andrew were at school. Lil could see that Larry was miles from her in his thoughts. He wasn't one to conceal emotion. Lil noted the smirk on his face. Although he ate his stew with a spoon and stared into the food, he never really saw it consciously. Presently he spoke to Lil while petting the three dogs in turn, Murphy, the Jack Russell; Dillon the fair-haired Labrador and the other, a short-legged excuse-of-a-dog with a cantankerous yapping nature, and the last, Julie, some kind of French breed.

'I wont be home this evening Lil, I promised my friend that I will call back because she has been asked to help me with my work for the angels.' Larry was still petting the dogs; partially using them as a means of avoiding Lil's eyes. Nonetheless, Lil's ears picked up on the word "she." For the life of her she couldn't imagine who Larry might have in mind. He never was one for chasing the ladies ... although he always spoke to any lady he met. His mammy had told him that it was only good manners and politeness to greet people. It was this innocent and open way with people across the city that made him such a popular character. Although Lil was now more curious than ever to get a few more crumbs or clues, she avoided pressing him on the matter. She knew perfectly well that he would tell all when he was good and ready.

Lil. Mentioned about the police search for him and so he promised to go to see them by way of thanking them for their trouble. He knew that he could honestly say that he had passed out and that a kind friend had taken care of him. Knowing Larry to be an honest and reliable lad, they would have no trouble accepting his explanation for their report on the matter.

Larry moved from the table and stood erect like a soldier to give himself the grace and blessing taking in the whole kitchen with the grand sweeping motions of his long thin arm. He gave Lil a bigger hug than usual and planted a big kiss on her cheek. Lil instantly got the whiff of the perfume about him; it was stronger that ever, given his close proximity. Lil was good on perfumes and knew only one person who had worn that scent and it wasn't among any of her friends. The nasty journalist came straight to her memory. However, knowing what had passed before; how she had really upset Larry and the family, and because of that knowledge, she discounted Ferret completely as a likely candidate that would be called upon to help him.

He bid his good friend, Lil, goodbye for the present and went next door to his own house to change into his blue suit, his Sunday best – polished shoes and all. He put on a clean white shirt which Lil had ironed and he chose a very light blue tie. He sat at the kitchen table for a while. He became conscious of keeping things from Lil. It began to play on his mind. He stared at the floor thinking how his loyalties seemed to be changing. He couldn't for the life of him explain why he was so suddenly protective of Dee, who was by comparison, a complete unproven stranger. Yet he felt certain that something as yet unexplained had taken possession of him in Dee's presence. He looked again at the red triangle on his hand; he wondered what it might mean. He knew with some guilt that he had hidden this too from Lil. He didn't like this guilt surfacing within him, this need of secrecy – especially keeping things from Lil. And yet the pull of his growing fondness for Dee was beginning to fill his mind and felt in a distinct way to be a different kind of affection, a more powerful pull drawing him away from his Neighbours who were always his dearest friends.

Presently he rose from the chair and climbed the stairs to his bedroom with slow ponderous feet. He deliberated as to whether he should bring his bundle of spiral notebooks

with him to Dee. He wondered if she could do anything
with them or even make sense of them. He knew that all
the writing in the jotters was from his own hand, yet he still
found it hard to believe it. There were notes on every
conceivable topic you could imagine: money matters;
farming; fisheries; prisons; Law; justice; religion; housing;
in short, every political and social concern imaginable.
Larry stood shaking his head in disbelief and rubbing the
back of his neck in confusion at what appeared to him at
the moment as utter madness. He knew that he had been
only half conscious, half asleep, while emptying his
overburdened mind onto those jotters. He now asked
himself consciously, 'were these notes really the dictation
of angels? Could they be from the demented murmurings
of his own grieving mind at the loss of his dear mother? Or
was he simply mad?' He couldn't really be sure which. He
was weary of the entire enterprise before it had ever moved
from the paper to even the vaguest form of action. Maybe
… just maybe … he thought to himself. Dee might be able
to make some sense of it all. The thoughts of Dee made him
abandon his troublesome thoughts and the warm feeling
made him hurry from the oppressive bundle of Jotters that
seemed to be haunting him. With further deliberation,
he decided not to inflict the jotters on Dee. He considered
that they created their own acute sense of foreboding,
even oppression. Why should he carry them off to Dee's
flat, and in doing so, be unable to escape their oppressive
attention. He knew he had to do something with the
messages within the jotters, but what? He couldn't be
certain. He considered briefly, three overpowering aspects
of the notes that stood out from all the rest …There was to
be a world without money with every essential need of the
people worldwide to be given freely as a fundamental
entitlement …There was to be full employment to all

without exception ... Lastly, and most troublesome of all, that he, Larry was to form the first world government, with himself at its head. On these three commands alone, he was convinced would make him appear a lunatic in Dee's eyes. Larry was beginning to feel a greater sense of himself. It felt as if his sense of himself had risen to a higher scale of self-awareness. He decided to leave the bundle of jotters where they were. Then he remembered that he needed to go to the police station to explain why he went missing the previous night. He climbed the stairs to his mammy's bedroom, took up the photograph of the family and kissed them. He embraced the photo to his chest in childlike enthusiasm and called softly into the empty room: 'daddy and mammy I love Dee. You hear ... I love her!'

Larry had to wait for some time at the Garda station enquiry counter where the duty officer was attending to a middle aged woman who was in a wheelchair. She was in a state of shock and fiery agitation. Larry too was very disturbed and concerned for her as he couldn't avoid overhearing the vexed account of her troubles. She was rattling on aloud in her strong city accent:

'... in the church, I was ... in the church, mind ... St. Patrick's. The church, I ask yeah ... and this Catholic Ireland ... me own country ... and me in a wheel chair from birth ... is there a God in heaven at all to stand by and see a poor defenceless woman robbed of her invalidity money ... all I have to get me through the week.?' She looked up into Larry's face and addressed him while rotating her shoulders for emphasis. '...In the holy church of God ...! Catholic Ireland ...!' Her head was nodding in a torrent of exclamations. 'There you are now ....! In God's holy church mind … not in the street …! Oh no! Not even on the beach ….! In St. Patrick's church ... mind … here-in-Cork City!' She threw back her head with the most emphatic nod to Larry, that had his head been bent down any further in his sympathetic gesture for the poor distraught woman, he would have been knocked senseless. She continued now to address Larry since the duty officer was busy scribbling the gist of her account of the incident. She milked Larry's attention as he showed no signs of indifference to her plight. The furrowed lines on his face only encouraged her to continue the incoming tide of repetition, exploding on the rocks of his hypnotic attention. At last she came to an explosive conclusion with her last spill of exploding surf.

She spat the words into the downward head of the duty officer. '... Catholic Ireland! …Cork City! Bah! And where were you when you were needed – scribbling on bloody paper as usual? Bah…to the lot of yeah!' With those last words she sank deeper into her wheelchair totally exhausted from her exploding tirade.

'Now, then, Miss Cassidy; we can't be everywhere at once, you Know.' The duty officer's voice attempted to be consoling as he was genuinely sympathetic for her plight and her condition. However, she was in no mood for his patronising attitude and so retorted.

'Wouldn't it be grand indeed if you were anywhere at all ... Never mind – being everywhere at once?' Larry felt sorry for the officer since he knew all the station staff. After all, he thought, he was only doing what was forced on him by his superiors and someone had to record the publics' complaints.

The officer looked to Larry and raised his eyes heavenward as if to say, some days we can't win at all. By way of consolation, Larry put a sympathetic hand on the poor woman's shoulder with the results that she went into some kind of wreathing convulsion and was thrown headlong from her wheelchair almost knocking herself unconscious as Larry grabbed her before she smashed her head off the wooden counter.

'What the bloody hell happened?' The duty officer shouted and came in rapid strides from the other side of the counter only just in time to help Larry to lift the poor crumpled woman back into her chair. Her eyes fluttered wildly drifting in and out of consciousness. Without further hesitation the duty officer telephoned through for an ambulance and Miss Cassidy was rushed to the City General Hospital.

Larry's words to the flustered duty officer came from his lips as cascading torrents of defensiveness.
    'I didn't mean to harm her... I only put my hand on her shoulder... she leapt out at me for nothing ... I didn't say anything to upset her....'
    'All right, Larry ... calm down. Calm down. I was here; I know what happened; she had some kind of fit, that's all. It wasn't your fault. You have no reason to blame yourself. It just all happened so suddenly. All we can hope for is that she will be alright in hospital. I'm sure they will get to the bottom of her problem.' The officer knew Larry well and chatted to him in a general way in order to allow him the space to calm down. He asked him where he was living since his mammy had disappeared and was there any further news from her.

'Well, I still live in the same house at Shandon Rise; but I spend most of my time with my good friends Seamus, Lil and their two children Lisa and Andrew.' Larry was more composed now, more connected to his natural unselfconscious character. He made no mention concerning his new friend and love, Dee; nor had he any desire to do so. He did mention in passing that his dear mammy came back from Heaven to see him. The duty officer just smiled at his presumed innocent remark and let it wash over his head as he beamed a fatherly smile at Larry over his spectacles. The duty officer was thinking to himself, if ever any individual on God's good earth was worthy of a visitation from Heaven, it was that innocent and endearing soul. Larry was now leaning over the counter. His child-like character was a breath of fresh air and a joy to witness in a city that at times seemed to have sold its soul to the devil, to self-destruction in drugs, violence, crime and materialism.

'Of course, I did come to explain what happened to me yesterday when I was reported missing by my friends. I want to apologise for all the trouble I must have caused. I didn't feel very well and so I slept at a friend's house and the phone wouldn't work so we couldn't let my friends know. But I have been back since to explain what happened.' He added in passing. 'Do you think Cork will beat Dublin in the All Ireland this year?' The officer smiled at the sheer disconnectedness of his train of thought.

'I'm sure we will; I'm sure we will,' the officer replied with a smile; and added, 'but the Dubs are never a formality.'

'Will everything be ok now that I have come to explain what happened yesterday?' Larry asked with some anxiety. He had a very deep sense of always doing his utmost to avoid causing any kind of trouble; at times his efforts to avoid giving offence to anyone bordered on the neurotic. He grew up more in need of his mammy's love than any desire to have his own way. Her love, her smiles and happiness meant everything to him. Her happiness was the very soil of his existence. He also loved his daddy dearly and would spend hours with him in his shed just content to see the pleasure that daddy derived from his love of carpentry. His parents were always conscious of their son's innocence and simplicity. They saw it as something special and not as a handicap, even though they were almost certain that the boy would never be able to take on any kind of work that would bring him in a worthwhile living wage. Larry nearly died of remorse at the early death of his daddy. It was equally hard for his mammy since she had to grapple with the loss of a most loving and caring husband and soul friend as well as coping with her beloved distraught son – Money was scarce.

Presently the duty officer answered Larry's question with a smile as he pinched the lads cheek in fatherly affection and humour as he said. 'I'm afraid, Larry, that we will have to lock you up for two hundred years on bread and water.' Larry gazed into the face of the smiling officer not quite certain for a moment if he was serious. However, the officer gave out such a hearty laugh and said in his exaggerated city accent, 'Larry, boy, if they ever lock you up anywhere, and I can assure you, they never will, they will have to lock me up with yeah.' At this, Larry wagged his finger at the mischievous office and smiled with his one word reply,

'You,' he said, knowing that the kindly officer was only teasing him with his banter.

The duty officer said quietly, 'Don't worry, Larry, now that you have dropped in we can clear up the report here.

You go home and God bless you.' Larry shook hands with the officer and gave him the biggest smile as he bid him goodbye.

It was 4pm when he arrived at Dee's apartment. The sound of her voice over the intercom on the wall outside made him go giddy with excitement and yearning for her. As the heavy glass door moved aside he ran clambering up the marble stairway to her apartment. The door was open and she was calling out his name. Her voice was like a wonderful melody that he wished would never stop. He was all but fainting from giddiness and want of her, she no less as she plunged into his open arms. Both were entwined and wild in their kissing. Her perfume washed over him sending him into a trembling ecstasy; her own feelings of desperate yearning for him caused her whole being to go limp and giddy too. Neither dreamt that such an all-consuming love for each other was remotely possible for them. They didn't want to let go of what seemed meant for more worthy souls than themselves. Their thoughts and senses were tossed about like two small corks clinging together in the wild ocean of exploding love. It was all a kind of pristine newness. Could it really be that this same nature that had in dumb imprecision blighted their earlier lives suddenly become aware of the folly of its lost purpose and design and now paid compensation in full by the love and wholeness that each was now experiencing?

Dee, though busy covering a prison riot in County Laoise could not empty her mind of her love for Larry. She couldn't explain what had happened within her only that there was a distinct and powerful pull towards him. She didn't experience him any longer as some unenlightened insensitive, imbecile, all she experienced now was a beauty that came from within him … his innocence … his courtesy to all … his manners … his simple sense of fun … even his naivety had a grace of its own. She came to learn later in their continuing closeness that, indeed, he was actually very well read. This she had gleaned slowly over time. He never opened up the world of his own reading and learning to others until he felt safe to do so with Dee. She helped him to develop his own confidence to expose a greater conscious sense of his own intellectually ability. At times she thought back to when she first imposed herself on his grief by the Mardyke River and the shame and hurt it brought her since – she was reduced to tears more than once.

It was Larry himself who broke the domestic silence as both were seated in the kitchen-diner. He looked concerned as he said, 'Did you have to get involved with the prisoners, Dee?'

'Gosh! No Larry. My work as a journalist demands having many contacts. I am not always obliged to be at a particular incident unless it is worth our while giving the story important space and coverage. Don't look so concerned, love. She placed her soft hand on top of his across the table, at the same time leaning her beautiful sweet face to look up into his lowered concerned expression. Her smile wiped away his trouble as he continued eating the meal of roast chicken.

'What happened in the prison, then?' he asked with some curiosity.

'Ach … It was the usual silly stuff that just got out of hand.' Although Larry was listening with interest to her, he kept telling himself, Dee, you are so beautiful, I love you so much. Dee continued: 'All the prisoners were out of their cells slopping out. One of the inmates threw a bucketful of toilet slop over one of the wardens who was shouting at him. The warden retaliated and punched and kicked the offender to the ground. After that all hell broke loose with an entire corridor of prisoners who were in the process of slopping out. All joined in the fray so that there was skin, hair and dust flying all over the place. One corridor was running with blood. Several inmates and prison officers were taken to hospital. As you can imagine, the prison was swarming with police and fire fighters for hours afterwards. There was considerable damage done to the prison's internal fabric with several wings being set on fire and with black acrid smoke billowing out form the hundreds of barred windows. The screams were terrifying, so my witness reported from within the prison. It was one of the wardens whom I knew who filled me in on the details. He even sent me some digital pictures of the burning prison. This all came via my mobile phone. We usually pay our contacts well, when and if the story comes off our press first. This one was a scoop for me through that contact. So everyone was pleased at The City Vanguard. There is a copy of the article in the paper on the lounge table if you wish to read it. I can tell you now that there is very little to add to the account that you have just heard from me.' As Dee finished relating her day's news, both retired to the lounge. Dee poured herself a whisky and lemonade as Larry settled for a coffee.

He was very thoughtful as they both sat close to each other with their arms about each other's shoulders.

'You're absent, love; what's wrong.' Dee was worried; she saw furrowed lines on Larry's boyish face.

'It's wrong you know, Dee.' He looked straight into her beautiful blue eyes.

'What's wrong, Larry? What's bothering you?' She was more concerned than ever discerning the serious tone of his voice.

'The story is wrong ... not the account of it that you wrote, Dee. The real story has not been written.'

'Larry, love; I have just stated the facts as my witness gave them to me. They are reliable.'

'No, Dee. He cupped her face tenderly and added. You only got the end of the story. The whole system of the prison is wrong. Wardens who provoke prisoners should not be employed there; just as the prisoner should not have the indignity of having to slop out his own dirt. It is degrading.'

This was a new side to Larry. She knew now that he was, indeed, a deeply thoughtful person. Dee was shocked; her eyes took on a fixed penetrating stare as if she was suddenly compromised in the company of a complete stranger. The words and expressions that came from Larry seemed to belong to someone entirely different. He could see that he had disturbed her normal calm self and rushed his words to calm her.

'I saw this incident in my mind as you spoke, Dee. Not the details that you have related to me. But I was shown that the whole prison system was all wrong; that it had to be changed.

'Wow up! Larry! Wow up!' Dee put up her two hands to his strained face. 'I can't change the prison system, love. Some of those prisoners are the nastiest animals alive; in fact, prison is too good for many of them.'

'Please, Dee; don't say that. They are all God's children.' Larry's innocent attempt to pacify Dee with such an irritating platitude incensed her deeply. She was all too aware of the horrendous crimes committed by prisoners – not alone in Catholic Ireland, but across the world. Some men and women, she thought, were not even fit to be called human. Sure prisons housing hardened criminals were little more than the containing cesspits of a nation at its wit's end as to how it might cope with the brute and savage mentality of some of its worst inhabitants. Their rottenness was no more than an infection spreading from one inmate to the next like an unstoppable mutating plague.

Larry interjected. 'But some of the younger ones only come from bad homes, poor neglected areas, and poor parenting, homes where so many are out of work … some from socially deprived areas with many of its youth who live only to belong to street gangs as a means of identity and security. People who are loved, Dee, are less likely to be drawn into criminal relationships. Love itself acts as their ground, their inspiration and conscience … their sense of belonging. To that extent people who feel loved know far greater freedom than those unfortunates who are not absorbed and held in love. I'm sure you are all too familiar with that already Dee, with your work as a reporter.' Dee's conscience surfaced painfully when she considered her own background and the bitter hateful person she had become as a result. Larry's use of the word, "reporter," was the first time she had consciously taken in the wider implications and meaning of the word. She wasn't quite certain that she was comfortable with the title and its more negative implications. Larry's gentle and innocent kindness was having a profound effect on her thoughts and identity. They were both changing each other without necessarily being totally conscious of the gradual influences. Dee seemed to wake from her distracting reverie as she continued.

'Look, Larry; your told me enough times that you couldn't keep a job down yourself ... how your mammy had to keep you both because of the pittance you were bringing home from welfare benefit. Yet in spite of all that you didn't hang around with gangs or get involved in thieving, drugs, violence on the elderly or swearing on the streets or the abuse of young girls or women.' Dee was trying her best to bring Larry around to the idea that we all have to be held responsible for our own behaviour, even from our earliest days. That same responsibility demanded that we choose our own friends rather than allowing others to impose themselves on our friendships. 'The point is, Larry, love, that if anyone oversteps the mark by deliberately causing harm in any way to innocent and law-abiding citizens, then they must suffer the consequences. If you cannot handle the moral right and privilege of liberty without making another's life a living hell, then the iron fist of justice must come down on the perpetrator of such offence with the whole weight of the Law and Just punishment.' Larry was still not convinced by the gist of Dee's views and insisted on a more benevolent disposition from the Law and just punishment as he added.

'But, Dee, no one would have me in their gang when I was young; even though I wanted to belong to young people my own age. I didn't understand it then and it caused me a lot of pain and frustration. It seemed no one really wanted my company except daddy and mammy and older people. I understand the reason for it now. What I'm trying to say is that I was only lucky; it was little more than an accident that I avoided being in trouble. Sure, daddy and mammy used to say that I was a good boy to keep out of trouble and that I was better off for not being accepted in any gang. I realise that now but I was very miserable in those early school days away from my parents. I never wanted to do bad things; I never wanted to bring trouble to my parents because I loved them dearly. But now I have learned that not all families are so close or so loving.'

'Larry, love; I grant you that there are many extenuating circumstances such as good young children and good older ones who come under the influence of bad and dangerous company. And I do believe a young person who has come under the influence of bad company should be handled carefully in the prison system. However, nothing is that straight forward, there are no simple solutions. The Cost of running prisons on the law-abiding tax payer is not just a scandalous failure of society in general; it is also imposed on us by the deliberate neglect and irresponsibility of some people who create a great burden of expense and manpower. Some prisons do try to separate the chaff from the wheat, the less bad from the downright evil. However, all such attempts to facilitate such measures put more and more costs on the taxpayer, that's you and me, Larry. Now, you tell me why we, the innocent victims of irresponsible criminals and thugs, are forced through our taxes to keep such scum in idleness and relative comfort while they continue infecting each other with even worse attitudes than they had before they became a part of their own collective sewage system?' Dee spoke through her teeth with an expression of disgust and intolerance.

It was easy to see that Dee's life as a journalist made her quite uncompromising in her views of law-breaking. However, Larry had become far more perceptive since his nightly scribbling and coupled with his knowledge of Jesus' teaching with regard to prisoners. Indeed, he was recalling such passages to his mind even as Dee expressed her very forthright views. He was thinking of a passage from Matthew's writing concerning the Last Judgement where Jesus himself speaks of his own life being intimately bound up with the marginalized of society; the passage was very clear to Larry and for Jesus, it was not open for debate or compromise. It all led him to see that all people were family to God – even when they acted completely against God's directives for life. In that passage of scripture Jesus speaks of himself as a prisoner and of those who visit as the true family of God. Larry knew that even good parents have troublesome children ... they would not be happy to see them in a prison with hardened criminals or under guard by vindictive prison wardens who saw all prisoners as the scum of the earth.

Larry knew from the teachings of the Holy Book that we are all asked and expected to do good to others as we would have good done to ourselves. He expressed these thoughts to Dee but she pulled him up sharp.

'Look, Larry, love, many rich people give generously to charity for selfish motives ... sometimes for their own vainglory ... sometimes to get back more than they give. It's akin to politicians kissing babies for parental votes ... it is all solicitous ... they don't give a dam about families once they achieve their goal. Families will still struggle to find homes, while those for whom they voted live in security and with wages that make them incapable of identifying with the struggles of the poor or less well-off.'

'I realise that, Dee. But surely the good done for those in dire need is no less good for those who benefit from that goodness, even though the motives of the donor are in some way expression of vainglory or solicitous as you say. Wrong motives in virtuous action have often been the stepping stones to inner conversion of conscience.'

It was conversations on these lines and on the passages on Christ's teaching that gradually made Dee think more openly on the other side of the Holy Book. And what such passages indicated to Larry was that the way we treat others is the way we treat God or betray Love itself. Larry was also aware of another of Christ's teachings where it states that to have seen Jesus is to have seen God ... and that the true name of God was Love. It was clear enough to Larry, that the way we treat others, no matter the extenuating circumstances, is the way we treat God or the way we betray or compromise Love. Yes, he knew that we are all Love's very imperfect children. That was the fact that Dee couldn't get her head round in spite of all Larry's appeals to Jesus' teaching. To bear wrongs patiently had never been a part of Dee's creed; in spite of the fact that revenge and retaliation would always be a vicious unbreakable cycle that had so many nations, families and individuals at each other's throats. The old adage held true for Larry, that, "... an eye for an eye would blind the lot of us ...." Dee's position made her all too aware that Jesus' teaching of loving enemies and forgiveness of offences were all grand ideals but not practical for the darkness of savage and brutal individuals, gangs and governing tyrants who were capable of the most horrendous evil. In spite of Larry's lack of exposure to the wider world about him, instinctively he was very much drawn to Jesus' life and teaching even though he did realise that it was not always easy to follow as Dee knew only too well. Although he was growing more and more deeply in love with Dee, something deep in his gentle instinct was unwilling to compromise his love of Jesus' basic teaching, all of which he received from his loved parents. That teaching had been the very foundation of his childhood years. He experienced a great deal of rejection from his classmates at school because of his coordination problems and his inherent naivety. Yet in spite of all his hurt he was imbued with a forgiving nature. Conversely, Dee had never cradled the child of forgiveness in her life – quite the opposite. In fairness to Dee, her early home life and childhood were hapless misfortunes. She could hardly speak meaningfully of having parents at all. Her young heart reached out to a cold world for love; she was returned an oppressive indifference and loneliness. She learned to survive by inadvertently choosing to hate any form of dependence, and so set her perverse estranged mind to challenge authority. Without knowing it, she was rebelling against her parents for their neglect. In consequence she lashed out at everyone in her writing. She had been weaned on cold indifference and so was spreading her disease everywhere she went. She was like a carrier of a contagious disease, all she touched turned rotten. Larry on the other hand was not given a favourable nativity, given his early physical and mental impairments. However, he was blessed with parents who could surely be described as two in a billion. It didn't bother them greatly that their son had such defects; that their son would be totally dependent on them throughout their lives; they reached out lovingly and totally to their son and carried him in their own loving hearts as pure gift and to that end made their home a heaven for their son, a sanctuary of pure bliss. Whereas, poor Dee was cradled in neglect – and her home was little more than a boarding house. It was a situation where she had a home but felt like an orphan in it.

It must be understood that Larry was given a very different understanding of Jesus and of God than the great majority of Christians around him. The love he experienced from his parents and other kindly people was a living tangible experience; it had a tangible power and immediate influence and a firm anchor to his life. God was not a concept but a living reality expressed in the reality of love. The loving influence of both his parents left him with a very unique understanding of love as something absolutely essential to human life. His parents had told him as he matured mentally and spiritually, that Christ gained nothing by loving humanity. He gave everything and lost nothing except a pilgrim's physical life. His love remained indestructible since the reality and power of love could never be anything other than love itself. He was free to love, free to die. It was a case summed up in the words, "You can kill the messenger but not the message." Love was like Truth to Larry. You couldn't destroy either even though you may destroy the physical bearers of both.

The sudden intrusion of the phone ringing brought the rather involved debate to an abrupt end but not before Dee gave Larry a big hug and kiss as she swept in one swift movement to the telephone. She listened to the familiar voice of Brendan Hawkswood, the editor.

'Can you get down to the City General Hospital as fast as you can?' There was urgency and gravity in his voice.

'What's happening there?' Dee's voice was alert and curious.

'Some old lady had collapsed in the police station and was rushed to hospital, a Miss Mary Cassidy. There is a bit of a disturbance, a hullabaloo. Ask for Doctor White; he's a friend; make sure you mention my name or you won't get a thing out of him ... confidentiality and all that Tommy rot. It seems the bloody woman is running amuck up and down the hospital screaming in some demented way. She's terrifying the staff and patients. Just get down there … there may be mileage in the story if the police are responsible for her dilemma. She was brought by ambulance from a police station by all accounts.'

Dee dressed swiftly and excused herself to Larry after both embraced swiftly. She grabbed her voice recorder from the safe and hot-footed it out of the apartment dressed in her blue winter padded jacket. Her parting words to Larry were: 'I won't be long love; please stay until I return.' Larry nodded in agreement and closed the apartment door behind her fleeing figure.

The weather was extremely cold on this dark February evening. Entering her Volkswagen was like placing a piece of meat in a fridge. All the windows were heavily coated in condensation. The vehicle spluttered into action, billowing out black acrid smoke as her snoop vehicle set off backfiring towards the city hospital. She introduced herself at the desk but not as a reporter but as a friend of Doctor White. She explained her presence to the doctor on the phone and he beckoned her to come to his private office. She only caught the tail end of the commotion as she watched a middle-aged woman screaming past her to the utter bewilderment of the crowd who were making their way peacefully along the busy corridors.

'I'm cured! I'm cured! I'm cured!' She was raving hysterically and chasing up the corridors like a woman possessed. Some visitors were laughing, believing her to be an outright nutter. Others were terrified as though they too might catch whatever it was that was wrong with her. Eventually four burly hospital porters grabbed her, though she continued to wrestle from them like a powerful lioness. With a great deal of effort she was secured and brought into Doctor White's office to ascertain what all the commotion was about. The doctor made Dee wear a white coat to look like she was his personal assistant. In this way Dee was privileged to the entire story first hand. After listening to Miss Cassidy's account of events from start to finish and discreetly recording the entire interview, she took a photograph of the woman in a hospital wheelchair and afterwards with her jumping about. Miss Cassidy was only too happy to accommodate Dee with all the photographs she wished to take. She also invited Dee back to her home to fill her in on the family background.

The story was a sensation across the city. The only one important detail that Dee left out of the story was the name of the stranger and a description of the one, whom Miss Cassidy claimed, with absolute certainty, had cured her lifelong paralysis. Dee knew at once the identity of the healer since she knew from Larry that he had gone to the police station to explain why he went missing the previous day. However, the story had made such a stir as rumours and speculation echoed across the bars of the city pubs and from the news stations on TV and radio.

It was around 9pm when Dee entered the dark and silent apartment. Larry was out cold sprawled on the black settee. She turned on the dimmer switch to a low light so as not to blind Larry with the sudden contrast of the light. Dee looked at his peaceful figure stretched out with his long arms crossed over each other on his chest as though he was a sleeping soldier or corpse ready to be buried. She stood over him in the semi darkness wondering about the power to heal that was coming from him. Why her Larry?

she thought. She considered her own question as she gazed lovingly down at him. The expression on his sleeping face was that of an innocent and peaceful child. God! she thought, I love you so much, Larry. 'But who are you, really?' she whispered over him, shaking her head in wonderment.

It was the gentle ringing of a china cup being stirred that drew Larry out of his sleep. She had made a late supper for them both and drew the sleepy-eyed Larry into the kitchen-diner. He was stretching and yawning fiercely. Dee was glad that he was so well rested. As they ate the chicken stir-fry, Dee could not keep her eyes from Larry's face. At first he was not conscious of her as his habit was to eat with his head down. Eventually he became aware not only of her silence but also of her gazing. She was smiling and shaking her head slowly as one who was in awe of something wonderful and yet also mysterious. Much of her wonder lay in her confusion concerning her atheistic nature and the odd phenomenon of miraculous healing. It brought to the fore of her atheistic mind the question, was their some power available, or at work outside of natural events? Or were miraculous events perfectly natural human powers or phenomenon but not yet quite fully understood? She felt deeply confronted and somewhat disturbed. It was as if there had existed some superior power or being to mankind. There were no doctors involved in this situation, she told herself. Presently Larry smiled quizzically and said, with a fork full of food near his mouth,

'What?'

Dee explained about the events at the hospital and their connection with him at the police station; how the woman had to be rushed there. Larry immediately dropped the loaded fork on his plate with a clatter and jumped to his own defence. His expression was furrowed as he said rapidly.

'I didn't mean to harm her. I just touched her shoulder to help her to calm down, 'cause she was angry with the nice duty officer. Then she jumped out at me and the officer helped me to put her back in her wheelchair … and he said that it wasn't my fault … that she might be having some kind of fit or something. He definitely said that it wasn't my fault.' He finished his defensive tirade with short assertive nods of his head to emphasise his innocence.

'Wow! Wow! Wow! Larry. No one is blaming you for causing her any harm or damage. On the contrary, love; you healed that old woman when you touched her.' She came round the kitchen table and cupped his astonished face to calm him and said softly. 'Remember, sweetheart, what happened to us when you first touched me … how you collapsed into the settee and I was thrown across the room?'

'I wished it wouldn't happen the way it does, Dee. It frightens me.' He clung to the security of her comforting hands.

'You needn't be frightened of good things, Larry. There must be a good reason for the gift you have received, from heaven-knows-where …' she added introspectively.

'But I don't like to hurt people. Why do those I touch have to go unconscious? It's really frightening; I can't be sure if they are going to get better or not. I was so worried when you passed out that time when I first came to see you.' The expression on Larry's face coupled with the distinct fear in the tone of his voice told Dee that he really was not comfortable with this new and dramatic aspect of his life.

Dee continued to console him as she put things in a new perspective for him.

'Larry, love; you know when people are taken to hospital for an operation?' Larry nodded his head. Dee continued. 'Well, then, the surgeons have to put the patient to sleep and sometimes when they wake up they may suffer some pain for a while afterwards. But eventually they get better. What I am saying, dear, is that sometimes you have to hurt people to make them better.' Larry looked into her eyes and said with a more confident smile.

'You are right, Dee, of course. I remember reading from John's writing in scriptures that the terrible suffering of a woman in childbirth is soon forgotten at the birth of a male child. Yes, you are right Dee.' She was speaking quietly to herself as she walked into the lounge. It didn't take much to send Dee into a tirade of embittered reverie. 'Of course, it would have to be a bloody male child; it couldn't possibly be a girl child. Typical ....' She thought of all the horrible Eastern and Jewish bigotry, in fact, the bigotry of most nations against women and all their patriarchal nonsense. She kept these irritating notions to herself since the whole patriarchal history of human kind was not instigated by the Jews. It evolved as far back as primitive man. Dee knew such history intimately from her love of reading ancient history. While she found it absorbing in itself and in the development of civilisations; nonetheless she always approached such history from the general bias against women and from her rebellious atheistic perspective. She had found enough evidence for herself to be convinced that God, or all reference to a divine and benevolent being was no more than the concoction of powerful men feeding the masses with their own designs, indoctrinating the ignorant and powerless underclass with a diet of fear, tyranny and notions of their leader's immortality and divinity. From the wild claims and antics of tribal painted chiefs and their witchdoctors, to the great dynasties of Egypt, the Greeks, Romans, the Vandals, Vikings, the British and all the other vanquishes empires of the past. Has anything really changed? Dee thought to herself? She shook her head almost spitting out the venom of the disgust and intolerance lodged in her mind. Dee's wide reading was akin to an arm's fair where the nations bought the latest in weaponry. She kept mental notes of Church abuse and questionable teaching from its long historical development not as points of interest to be wondered at or avoided in the future, but as metaphorical muck to smear into the face of religious authority and respectability. It had been her dearest and most enthusiastic pleasure to lampoon the Church, the accepted norms of its tradition and privilege, and all that held woman and sisterhood in the chains of contempt and deference.

Larry was not aware of her so-called atheist liberation. She knew that she could tolerate Larry's strong attachment to the Bible of his formative years; how it held him and his loved family together and formed the ground of their convictions and character. She had no intention of pulling that sacred ground from under him since it was all part and parcel of the loving person he turned out to be. Indeed, she knew other saintly Christians in her short lifetime ... people like Nell and Father Kevin who were really sincere in their care of others. And yet she valued her own atheist perspective to life. She made her position by free choice – or was it free choice? She knew that she hated her early existence where her only real pleasure lay in the power that she had as a gifted and outstanding journalist. She had her own power over people. Was she no less a tyrant just because she only used ink to kill and destroy reputations?

Larry now pressed his need for Dee's attention. 'Dee, will you help me to do something about all the notes and jotters that cause me so much trouble in my sleep? I can't get proper rest from them making demands of me. I just don't know where to turn next. And the angel said that you were the one to help me.'

Larry was really tired again in spite of his earlier sleep. It appeared quite evident that all these disturbed dreams were putting a great strain on him. Dee could see clearly by his pleading eyes and expression that he was being tortured by these revelations, imagined or not. She sat on his knees on the big settee sipping a weak, diluted whiskey.

'What is it sweetheart that you want me to do for you, can it wait until tomorrow? You look all in.'

'Oh yes, it can wait Dee, if I you say that you really will help me.'

'Of course I will help you, Larry Walsh. She kissed him teasingly. He smiled at her use of his full name and remarked,

'You see I have to form a world government and I have to be in charge of the whole world. I received a message from Heaven when my mammy came to see me and that's what the message said.'

'Ouch! Is that all you are worried about? Crikey, I thought it was something big and important.'

'You're laughing at me Dee. I can tell now when you are not being serious. Your face changes you know. You pretend to be calm when you are not.' Dee laughed and kissed him again only longer now as she removed the whiskey glass from her hand.

'I tell you what we will do. Tomorrow we will drive to your house and see what can be done. Will that suit you Mr. Walsh?' She knew that he would be delighted and that they were both ready for sleep. Larry once again settled into the settee. Dee really craved to sleep with him. However, true to her earlier instincts she felt sure that she didn't want to destroy their love for each other by rushing things forward for her own passionate needs and convenience. Larry was the one decent thing in her life and she had no intention of ruining it through selfish haste or insensitivity. Larry had not yet made any attempts to fondle her in an overly sexual way. She was sure that giving him the respect and time that he deserved all would fall into place; though being truthful to herself, she really did hope that it would be sooner than later. She knew that Larry had awoken feelings of passion in her that she had never experienced in her life. She also knew as certain as she could be, that there never would be another love in her life beyond Larry.

Dee picked up her copy of the City Vanguard posted through her letterbox. She smiled with great satisfaction as she read through her own scoop regarding the Miss Cassidy healing sensation. It was front page news in great bold letters and a variety of photographs in full colour depicting before and after scenes of Miss Cassidy's lonely existence being confined to her wheelchair and the poverty of her dingy flat. They were also pictures of her early childhood as a paralytic with her parents. Then bold red arrows pointed to the after pictures with the hysterical woman jumping up and clipping her two legs together. The main headlines ran:

Mystery healing at City Garda Station!!!
Victim of Robbery Loses More than Money!!!
City Hospital Confirm Miracle Cure!!!
Search for Mystery Healer!!!
Sensational Story by our Leading Reporter: Delilah Ferret.

Dee had piled on a barrow load of sensational clichés adding all the spices of her trade to lift the sensational story leaping off the pages. It spread like wildfire throughout the cities of Ireland and beyond its shores. Her account of events had it all … the miserable existence of Miss Cassidy's poverty-stricken childhood … her isolation due to extreme mobility difficulties … her living from hand to mouth on welfare payments … the hatred Ferret's story generated for the heartless thief, the thug, who snatched the poor woman's welfare money in the street. Oh, she played her public well and milked the story of every drop of its potential. It was the envy of every other competing newspaper in the city. All of this was to the great credit and benefit of Dee's secure future with the paper. It seemed that year by year she was multiplying the readership of The City Vanguard. Hawkswood, the editor, although peeved at times concerning Ferret's avoidance of his personal company, he remained more than happy by the frequent praise and congratulations that he received from the owner of the Vanguard. After all, Hawkswood was married to the owner's daughter and his position was only tenable so long as he remained devoted to her needs and kept measurable growth in readership. The editor knew that he needed Ferret much more than she needed him. Whatever it took, he knew he had to keep Ferret sweet at all times. He knew that he was absolutely reliant on her journalistic talents and her uncanny nose for a sensation. Of course Dee knew this all too well. She had a recording of his love-making that would destroy him in seconds of its exposure. This situation gave her all the security and freedom that she needed. She had need of that security. She knew that she had to protect the vast sums of money that her position warranted as a proven, dependable and outstanding reporter. She could name her price from any other of the city newspapers. However, she was quite content with how things stood at present and especially as she enjoyed all the freedom and liberties that she took from the noisy and stuffy city office. She had no fears of not coming up with the goods. She had enough paid snoops and contacts from every walk of life. These essential costs were passed on to the editor who never dared question their legitimacy or accuracy.

CHAPTER 11

The Collation of Larry's notes

It was past 10am when they arrived at Larry's home. Dee was glad to get away from the busy city traffic. The day, though bright and cloudless, was, nonetheless, a very cold February day. Larry's house was comfortably warm considering that he had not used it for a couple of days. His neighbours had set the heating timer for him.

'Gosh, Larry, your carpets are a bit threadbare or are they some new kind of fashion?' Dee was teasing him any yet truly shocked.

'Yerrah! Stop it Dee; they're not that bad. Mammy wouldn't change them 'cause she said it was better to help the poor people in the Third World instead of bothering about something you have to walk on. In any case, Dee, they are clean; they're not dirty 'cause Lil hovers them,' he added for emphasis. Dee's face flushed scarlet because of her crass remark. She began to cry because without meaning to she had insulted not only someone so precious to her now but also inadvertently causing insult to the extreme charitable sentiments of his mother.

'Don't cry Dee ... please don't cry .... I know you didn't mean to offend me; really, Dee; I'm not offended ... I love you so much.' Dee was beside herself throbbing and shaking with shame and grief as she threw her arms round Larry in loud sobbing tears. Her words were shaken in her attempts to apologise.

'I'm so terribly, terribly sorry, Larry. I don't deserve you; I don't deserve your love,' she repeated in all earnestness. 'Sometimes my mind and ways betray human decency. I'm sorry, love; sometimes I can be so superficial – so thoughtless.' Larry brushed all these explanations from his thoughts; he was too in love with her to harbour her faults. He wasn't so backward as to consider her a saint. He simply loved her. This incident, however, had a lasting impact on Dee's life. She began to question the validity of her own lifestyle ... her own response to the poverty of the world around and beyond Ireland's shores. It took her a very long time to get over what she now considered the crassest and most imbecilic insult she had laid in the heart of someone who was far more mature than herself as a decent human being.

It was with blurred tearful eyes that she thumbed through the bundle of spiral notebooks in Larry's bedroom. There was something pathetic ... something childlike in the movements of her body as her shoulders rose and fell jerking in attempts to control her sobbing. She realised that she had never felt so deeply ashamed of herself in her short lifetime. Larry took her gently from behind her trembling body and popped his head in her front as though he were peeking round a hedge. His mischievous smile brought her own tormented face into the shy, deferential smile of a child who was emerging from a serious upset. She rubbed his face with her free hand; that was all Larry needed to give her another one of his big lingering hugs.

She knew perfectly well that these scribbled notes were a serious and perplexing torment to him. Had she encountered these in any other person's house, given their subject matter, she would have considered that person an outright neurotic and little more that a hair's width from insanity. In this case ... in this house ... knowing how Larry was irritated and sick of the entire imposition thrown on him, she was certain that he was no lunatic.

'Will you be able to do anything with them?' He asked with a frustrating grimace on his face as he bared his teeth sensing that it would all be mere gibberish to Dee. She didn't answer him straight away; instead, she took one of his hands in her own by way of reassuring him that she was giving the matter her full and undivided attention. He relaxed a bit more as a result. Dee's head went into twists and turns as she continued to speed-read the hundreds of notes that were crammed into the jotters Every now and again she would squeeze his hand as a means of reassuring Larry that she was actually paying attention to the problems facing him. So far as he was concerned the entire problem was beyond him, even out of rational control. At last Dee broke her silence and asked.

'Are these all of the jotters that you have?' He didn't answer directly. His instinct told him that she couldn't work for a newspaper and not have some extraordinary talent. He had read enough of her work by now to realise that in a very clear way. He would read anything that she had written if for no other reason than the fact that the work carried her name and he loved her so much. He didn't always agree with what she wrote. He held on to his own family ideals of always being kind and considerate to all people; that was instilled into him from his earliest days and was the Christian way and his basic inescapable creed.

He assured her that the bundle of notebooks before her were the complete collection. Her next question caused him some unease.

'Can you recall where you began all these notes, Larry, love?' Which Jotter did you begin with ... can you remember, only they are not numbered ... It might help if you could remember?'

'I'm not sure. Once one jotter was full, I just flung it into my bedside cabinet to get it out of my sight and out of my head.' Larry was now concerned that the mix up of the jotters was going to put a real strain on Dee. After all, she had her own work on the newspaper to cope with.

'Will it all be too difficult for you, Dee? I know I am asking a lot from you. It's only that the angels who sent the messages said that I was to come to see you ... that you would know what to do.' Dee didn't know what to make of Larry's remark with regard to his reference to angels. She was aware of the complexity of the human mind, especially the world of the dream state or unconscious. She was certainly sceptical of the presumed world and existence of angel beings. She decided not to remark on Larry's bizarre revelations.

'Don't worry too much over it, Larry, love. I'll get to grips with the jotters. It will simply take a little time to put the notes into coherent order. Once that is done, we can face the next possible step ... whatever demands they may place upon us.' Dee seemed to be calm about the matter. Putting things in order and perspective were part and parcel of her journalistic profession.

She went about the house searching for the possibility of any more notebooks that might have been overlooked. She was fit for crying again as she went upstairs on her own. Larry was below making some coffee. The house and all its rooms had just the very bare essentials of furniture, They might have been a family that were just beginning to set up a home rather that being established in the house for over forty years of their marriage. The combined furniture would scarcely be adequate to facilitate the needs of a poverty-stricken student, let alone a family. Mere bits of odd, well-worn carpet and mats were placed by the bedsides. The built in wardrobes with their clothing might well have been the bare essential of a family of refugees recently re-housed. Granted the father's clothes were missing since he had passed away some years ago. Nonetheless, all that was there belonging to Larry's dear mother were a couple of half decent outfits that might, with a discerning stretch of the imagination, be classed as best. The rest of the clothing, though carefully and tidily hung, was mere rags. Dee's head was moving very slowly; her eyes fixed in trance and disbelief; this was the wardrobe of a saint or of an impoverished refugee. The clothes were almost speaking to Dee; telling the story of Larry's life among simple saintly people. She knew from Larry that he used to go on holiday with his daddy in their large old garden shed where daddy would be quite content to do his carpentry while Larry would be making him laugh all the while rubbing his daddy's arms and back and keep telling him he loved him and mammy. He had the father in hysterics most of the time; his daddy having to tell the lad to stop or he would die laughing. The family had just the one day out by the seaside in Garrets Town and that was really more of a treat for Larry's sake than for his beloved parents. The strange thing about Larry was the fact that he never wanted anything for himself except to be with his mammy and daddy always. The love Larry received from them had to be unique of its kind. They lived for each other and yet could find every reason to reach out to others in greater need than themselves. Dee was beginning to believe that she was in the presence of something sacred in this house and that she was being given an undeserved share in the best of it, the offspring of those saintly parents.

She noticed the family photograph on top of a homemade dresser on the mother's side of the bed. Larry had left the photograph in his parent's room, as he related to Dee much later, because he felt that it still belonged to them because they told him they liked to kiss it when he wasn't with them. Dee's eyes were smarting again as she held the photograph tightly to her breast and said quietly to herself, 'I will look after him; I promise; although I think he is really looking after me.' She now held the photo at arms length to study the picture of Larry as a child being swung from the hands of both parents. She replaced the photograph and continued to go through any likely place that might conceal a forgotten or misplaced notebook. Larry appeared with two mugs of coffee and some chocolate biscuits. He noticed that she had been crying again. The smiling expression melted from his face and with a strained brow asked,

'What's wrong Dee; is it all too much to sort out? Don't worry about it any more we can get other people to help.'

'Ouch, Larry, it isn't that. I'm just a silly little child who just cries over nothing at all.' She pressed his hand and smiled to reassure him that there was no real cause for concern.

'I don't like to see you crying, Dee; it makes me sad; I love you so much.' His head looked under her lowered face and she smiled at the very way he gazed so fondly at her. He reminded her of a faithful old dog who was forever looking into its master's face and wriggling its body and wagging its tail in its own language of devotion and happiness. Larry just wanted to give and receive love and affection the whole time. Dee felt in her heart that he didn't belong to this world at all or that our world was incapable of being as his was. She was slowly coming to realise that he was far more advance as a human being than anyone she had met before. His was a world lived entirely content with love and friendship, nothing else mattered to him.

When Dee had been through all the written notes in the entire house she said to Larry. 'We can take them home if you wish and I will sort them out there. I can tell you now, having read most of them swiftly, that they can be put together quite easily. They won't be any great problem. What happens after that we can sort out in easy stages? What they amount to is really no more than the notes of someone drawing up the details of an enormous manifesto for the formation of a kind of political dictatorship. There are details on housing; food and its manufacturing and distribution, welfare; fisheries; farming; finance; etcetera, etcetera. I can say now love, that it is all very controversial, even though it will not be too difficult to write up.' Dee was trying to treat the task in a simple matter-of-fact way for Larry's sake. The pattern began with basic human needs such as, housing, food, medication, work; fuel; transport, followed by more involved sets and subsets of instructions and expectations The entire bundle of notebooks were placed into a bin liner which she placed in her old Volkswagen car.

Dee was about to speed off when Larry's friend and neighbour, Seamus, pulled up in front of them in his black four-by-four. Ferret experienced a frightening sense of foreboding as Seamus' vehicle cast a shadow over her Volkswagen. Seamus could scarcely believe the scene before him. He felt confronted. Ferret, for her part, froze as though stuck to the wheel – her eyes were wild and wide, expressing instant panic and terror. Seamus was frozen too in utter disbelief. His door was partly opened but his face was fixed in a menacing glare at Ferret. He barely paid any attention to the smiling and waving figure of Larry. Seamus experienced an immediate strong feeling of hostility rising from the pit of his stomach – he was remembering how the bitch had used Larry before. He stepped down slowly from his motor with a distinct menacing deliberation, straining to compose himself. He was still struggling to master his temper when he felt his back being rubbed and heard the sudden friendly voice of Larry behind him. He never noticed Larry's advances towards him – his hostility was blinding.

'Hello, Seamus, is it yourself?' Larry was grinning all over his face, delighted to see his good friend.

'Ah, no, Larry boy, it's me twin you're looking at,' Seamus said smiling but then added gruffly, almost in a whisper, 'what's that bitch doing here with you?'

Larry winced at Seamus' cutting remark. He put his hand on Seamus' arm in a pleading manner.

'Oh! She's my friend now, I love her; she's helped me with all the notes in the house. They are all gone in the car.' Larry was still full of confidence and smiles. Seamus took a sly sideways glance at Ferret, who was now locked inside her own car not daring to come out. She looked terrified. Larry forced the next move on the unprepared Seamus by dragging him enthusiastically by the hand to Dee's side of the door. She winced in fear as he approached with Larry still holding his hand. Larry knocked on her door. Ferret winced and jumped for a split second. Slowly she unwound the window, just sufficient to hear their voices. Larry saw the fear on Dee's face, so did Seamus. Larry's voice had some urgency in it as he said to Dee.

'Please open the door, love; it's Seamus, my friend. I know he will like you now just the same as I do.' Larry looked pleadingly into Seamus' face as if to say, you wouldn't hut my friend, Seamus, would you? Seamus put him at his ease by placing his arm round his shoulders and whispered in a slightly tremulous voice.

'Of course I won't hurt her, if she really is your friend now.' It suddenly came to Seamus that this was the new friend that Larry had stayed with on the night that the family had reported him missing. Typical of Seamus, to give her the benefit of the doubt, he invited her into the house for a coffee. She really didn't want one after the big mug-full she had with Larry. Besides, her fear was playing havoc with her biology – she was now bursting for a pee. However, her mind swung into a swift spin and said yes to the invitation; she was hoping that she might recover the lost ground created from her previous encounter and behaviour.

Lil was inside with the children. The dogs barked excitedly as Ferret and Larry walked in. She glanced at her husband who still looked very sheepish. Lil signalled to him with the parting of her outstretched hands, as if to say, What's that bitch doing here? No one saw Lil make the unfriendly gesture and Seamus shook his head in short rapid movements signifying to her not to challenge Ferret.

It was Larry who made the introductions after he had given Lil a big hug and kiss and greeted the children in like fashion. The three dogs were leaping all over Larry as if he had been away for years. The animals sniffed cautiously at Ferret's legs.

'Lil, this is Dee, my new friend; I love her!' Lil's eyes nearly popped out from her face at the mention of that blunt and unexpected word, "love!" which she could never associate with Ferret in her wildest imagination. Seamus wanted to laugh at Lil's reaction but thought better of it. Lisa, the older of the two children, pushed out her lower lip and brought her head back amazed by the sudden and intimate announcement. Andrew, who loved having a knock-about with Larry, put his hand to his mouth to prevent him laughing. It all seemed strange and inappropriate to him ... it seemed out of character for Larry from the perspective of Andrew's inexperienced mind ... he just couldn't get his head round that at all. But he said to his mammy afterwards.

'She's a real beauty, ma, isn't she.' Lil had to smile and agree.

Seamus faced Dee and asked: 'Will it be coffee? Or, would you prefer something stronger – a whiskey, wine, sherry, beer, what...?' It was Andrew who replied to the question out of pure instinct.

'Of course she doesn't drink beer like you, do you Dee?' She smiled at his innocent comment as did Lil. Lisa chimed in.

'How would you know, Andrew, you've only just met her?' Lisa was often a bit surly with her brother to keep him in his place. Andrew could be a bit forward at times. In spite of all, he replied to his sister who looked down her nose at him.

'Well. Dee doesn't have a big beer belly like me da, does she?' Dee couldn't control herself any more and burst into involuntary hysterics putting her hand to her mouth, as much from nervous tension as from the unintentional impertinent comments from Andrew. The whole family cracked up with laughter as all the tension seemed to diffuse itself. Dee was glad to settle for a strong whiskey and a little lemonade and ice. Lil and Seamus stuck to wine as they were preparing to sit down to their evening meal. Dee asked to be excused and was directed to the toilet by Lisa. She returned to the company feeling like an intruding, unwelcome stranger. Seamus addressed Dee.

'You're very welcome, Dee, to stay and eat with us; we are in the habit of cooking more than we need as we never know who is going to drop in unannounced. While that was true, Seamus was not trying to be overly polite or straining generosity. Dee felt that she was not in a comfortable position to refuse. Deep within her memory she was still smarting from their first encounter when she had proven to be a selfish, uncharitable bitch. She felt that she needed to build a bridge to help both her and Larry's concerned friends to cross safely over the troubled waters of her shameless and degenerate past.

'It's very kind and generous of you both; I would be delighted to join you if I am not really imposing on your kindness. But, please, call me Dee!' She sounded quite posh and sophisticated to the family, which created a distinct response of polite and guarded formality. She noticed that the family was using both Delilah and Dee alternatively.

'I don't care for my real name, it was my mother's choice; she always looked upon the name Delilah as having a strong character.' Dee was all too conscious of the biblical story of Delilah's betrayal of Samson. In her early years Dee took a perverse delight in that account of the destruction of Samson. It accorded with her own nasty development, her own self-loathing. However, in only a very short time, and in no small measure due to the influence of Father Kevin and his elderly housekeeper,

Nell, but most of all through Larry's influence on her, she was now gradually veering away from her dark, self-serving past.

Inadvertently, Larry chimed in to confirm his own detailed knowledge of the name and the story when he added to Dee's remark.

'Oh! .... A really nasty one, that Delilah! She's not like our Dee at all.' He turned his smiling face to Dee. She was now sitting beside him, her face a blushing tomato – she looked and felt mortified. It was Lisa who saved the day by innocently re-enforcing Larry's remark as she noted Dee's mortified face.

'Of course Dee is not like that. She couldn't shave me da's head, 'cause there's only fluff there now!' The whole family roared with laughter; even more so when Seamus remarked good-naturedly,

'Two children, not too far from me, will be on bread and water; and lucky to get that. First I have a beer belly and now I'm almost bald.' This only made the family laugh the more.

He suddenly put a friendly hand on Dee's shoulder as he added, 'you wouldn't like to take these two brats off my hands? I'll pay you well for your troubles?' Dee smiled self-consciously; her face smouldering in mortification.

There followed a steaming hot stew for all, Just the right meal for the cold February weather; it was washed down with red wine for the adults and mineral water for the children. The three dogs were nudging between Larry and Dee; they usually nudged strangers at meal time knowing that they were more likely to get a tit bit from them … they knew that the family usually ignored them during meal times. Naturally Dee fell for it and offered all three dogs a small piece of beef each, after which, Lisa, sent them packing so not to pester Dee any more. She took it upon herself quite instinctively to protect and comfort Dee.

When the meal finished Andrew and Lisa were sent off to their own interests. Seamus managed that by drawing their attention with his eyes and waving them away with his head. He didn't want Dee to feel he was dismissing his children on her account. The children understood immediately, excused themselves, and went off to their own distractions. Seamus and Lil raised the matter of Larry being away for so many hours. They put it sensitively so that Dee would feel comfortable with it. After all, they felt that they had the responsibility for him as his long established friends and as their unofficially position as his adopted parents. It was Lil who posed the question indirectly; she directed it at Larry but really meaning it for Dee's attention.

'We hope you are good, Larry, when you are with Dee and helping her in her home when she asks you? We know you are always good here at home except when you go chasing Andrew and Lisa all over the place.' The children liked poking fun at Larry and messing about with him. When Larry could get a hold of them he would tickle Andrew so much it always brought him screaming to stop it; they were almost inseparable friends. He was gentler with Lisa. Larry was smiling now as though he was caught out at being mischievous. Dee spoke a little coyly looking directly at Larry and smiling.

'He will never be any trouble to me; we are too fond of each other even though it has only been a short time since we became actual friends. In fact I love him dearly. I am only saying this to put you both at ease. Yes, I was only using him at first for a story concerning his missing mother.' She stopped suddenly and burst into involuntary. heaving sobbing. It took a good deal of time to calm her. All three put their arms round her at the dining table. Eventually she continued.

'I now feel so ashamed of what I was to him then and how I upset both of you and your good friends, Father Kevin and Nell, his housekeeper. I can only apologise now for my uncouth behaviour. When I say I love Larry, I mean just that. We have suddenly been thrown together in a literal sense.' She explained at length what had happened in her apartment and showed them her hand and Larry showed them his hand. Dee added, 'I wish to keep this matter private between ourselves. I have no objection to Father Kevin and Nell learning of the situation. We are both serious about this relationship and its development. I will do everything in my power to see that he comes to no harm while he is in my company. I also intend to help him in every way concerning this strange cycle of events that is imposed upon him. You must also realise that he will be hounded from time to time over his ability to heal people. You probably don't know that he has healed a woman in the city police station.'

'Well we know it's the talk of the city and still hot news throughout the various media outlets,' Lil offered as comment. She continued. 'However, we had no reason in the world to associate Larry as the healer.' Seamus and Lil were astonished at what they were hearing. Had Larry not been present, they would have been hard pressed to believe her on her own merit. However, Dee was flushed and deadly earnest. She was not entirely comfortable with her personal revelation. Yet, she felt she owed these good friends and neighbours of Larry every assurance of her motives for her sudden and intimate attachment to him. Her need to be reconciled with Larry's neighbours was as if they were really his natural blood parents. Their care of Larry had always been above and beyond any strained charity or duty; they simply took the lad to their bosom from the very beginning.

Dee turned to Larry handing him her car keys and said, 'Larry love, can you nip outside to the car and bring in a copy of the newspaper; it's on the back seat.' Larry returned with it and handed it to Dee who in turn opened it and handed the broadsheet to Seamus. He gripped the broadsheet as he usually did with newspapers, stretching it like a drum. His eyes indicated that he was speed-reading the article. Seamus was very proficient at that. If he considered any article worth more attention, then he would give that attention with a second more studied read. As it was he didn't give the article another read nor was Larry's name mentioned in it. This made him return the paper to Dee and comment.

'So you believe that his nibs here is the mystery healer?' nodding his head to Larry who was still sitting beside Dee.

'Well, Dee replied; I told you what happened to us in my apartment and how things have changed dramatically between us; let him give you his own account of what happened at the police station and the conclusion of the hospital; the woman was crippled from birth,' she emphasised.

'You're serious, Dee.'

'I have never been more serious in my life. He didn't know anything about it himself except when he placed his hand on the woman's shoulder by way of calming her in the police station, she was very distraught and angry at the time; she was thrown out of her chair and all Larry experienced was a degree of weakness at the time, but never passed a comment to a soul except when he related his account to me afterwards. The woman described Larry almost photographically down to the very clothes he was wearing. The description was so good that I felt it necessary to omit any reference to it for Larry's sake, otherwise he would have been hounded by the rest of the media and crowds would continue to flock in their hundreds, if not thousands from all over the city and all over the country. No, I wasn't having any of that.'

Larry gave his account to Seamus and Lil of the events that had taken place at the police station; although he made no claim for the healing, he was entirely oblivious to it. Seamus and Lil couldn't help turning to Larry in sheer wonder. Dee continued.

'Later on the duty officer at the police station confirmed Larry's account of the event. The same officer was convinced that something strange did happen to the woman in the station at the time; though he would not go as far as to say that Larry was the source of the healing. He too didn't want any more hassle than he had already from reporters and the general public who came flocking to find out the identity of the mysterious healer. The incident report filed at the police station was removed from the book at the approval of the station sergeant for the good of all concerned. A wall of silence was brought down on the incident and no one claimed to know a thing about it. The woman herself got so enraged and sick of the pestering that followed from her claims that she too eventually asked for police protection to rid her of the crowds of visitors that made her life unbearable. Even genuine parents and adults with handicapped children or with serious health problems of their own were eventually turned away by the police who were forced to endure the boring task of their daily presence at her house.'

Dee returned to the immediate matter in hand concerning the mysterious and troublesome duty imposed on Larry from on high. She was uncertain about the notes that burdened Larry. She asked Seamus and Lil for their thoughts on the matter.

'To be quite truthful, Dee, we are as baffled as you are. I mean...form a world government! One man without one iota of politics! And excuse me for saying it, one who has never had to run his own home – or had the benefit of any acknowledged secondary education other than a brief spell at one of Cork's Universities ...Though we have to admit that he is astonishingly and widely read. Crikey! It all sounds like one of the exaggerated tales from the Book of Genesis in the Bible where Joseph the Jew, his father's pet; one who could interpret dreams and eventually make Pharaoh completely dependant on a Jew to govern Egypt. No, we can't make head not tail of it. What about you, Dee, what do you make of it?'

'It is like you say, Seamus; It's all a bit of a mystery. I promised I would do all I can to help. According to Larry, he had specific instructions from some angels or other to come to seek my help. Me...! Who chose to be an atheist in consideration of all the suffering and injustices that I have experienced in my brief lifetime ... to come to seek my help ... it doesn't make much sense to me at the moment. To be frank, I find it quite scary personally ... It's like I'm being watched or marked out in some way by an actual power able to influence me and Larry directly.

However, considering the healings, my own included, I am keeping an open mind, while at the same time, hoping divine inspiration might come to my rescue too.' Dee turned to all present with a smile, one that suggested that she doubted her chances; she had always been a pragmatist from her earliest years. She added, 'I can only do what is in my power to help.'

'Have you some inclination, some plan or other as to what to do with the notes?' Seamus asked a little baffled and added, 'I have read some of them ... they seem to cover every social subject in creation. I wouldn't know where to begin, aside from their collation.'

'That is the cue I have taken from the notes,' Dee said in agreement. 'They seem to be an intricate social manifesto for a revolutionary form of world government, not like any government, national or otherwise, that has been attempted before. Just to take one command from the notes. It states clearly that: "The use of money and all forms of bartering worldwide is to discontinue immediately ... that money was only sending humanity round in circles ... and continuing to divide peoples not uniting them." Can you imaging,' Dee remarked, with her hands extended over the dining table, 'to seriously voice such a concept to any existing government across the international world? You would have to conquer the entire globe first in order to achieve your aims by some form of dictatorship. At least that is the way it seems to me at present. Of course there is much more to be said on the subject of money as one single issue in itself.' Dee shook her head slowly as she concluded her brief and sketchy summary of the situation. 'As I said earlier, I can but try to put the notes into some coherent order and shape, then find some able publisher who could handle the work on a global scale. The other related point is to get some international voice to give credence to what such an international manifesto proposes.'

'Well,' said Seamus, 'you seem to have given it some considerable thought already, Dee; good for you.' He added, 'I have been a school teacher for several years and I must be honest, I couldn't bring myself to make credible sense of the notes. They seem off the scale of plausibility altogether.'

'You may well be right, Seamus,' Dee replied as she rose to leave the table and prepared to return home. 'It is as I remarked earlier; I can only do what is in my ability to do. I am keen to spare Larry every possible worry and concern. I have a gut feeling that if my help was truly requested and legitimate from on high, then no miracles are expected from me; I find a strange consolation in that thought.'

'Well, Mr. Walsh; are you coming home or not?' Dee smiled at the seated figure of Larry who seemed mesmerised by the entire debate floating over his head like so many clouds. It was only when Dee realised the significance of what she said, so innocently and so instinctively, that she bent her head and put her hand up to shield the side of her face in the act of hiding it from the embarrassing presumption as if she was now the real family of Larry. Lil and Seamus looked at Dee and remarked together:

'What? What's up?' They were baffled but quite amused by the strange action expressed in her embarrassment.

'I'm so sorry for making the presumption, that I had some priority over Larry.'

'If Larry is happy to go with you, Dee, then, you both have our blessing.' It was Seamus who spoke and he added for reassurance, 'only remember that he is welcome into our home at any time to treat it as his own.' Lil added a special invitation to Dee. 'As we are at it, you are also welcome to drop in whenever you wish, Dee. We will be delighted to have you.' Dee burst into sudden tears again and had to be consoled by all present. She was so taken by their forgiving nature. Once Dee had calmed down they took their arms from her.

'Well, Larry,' it was Lil who now put the choice to him with her hand openly extended, 'what do you wish to do, go with Dee or remain here?'

'Oh! I'm off home with Dee.' He added with an expression of absolute certainty: 'I love Dee.'

'So, we're being abandoned, then Larry?' said Lil mischievously. Larry ran to Lil as though he was going to lose her. He put his arms around her and gave her a big gripping hug saying,

'No Lil! – Never! Never! Never! I will never abandon you or Seamus, nor Lisa and Andrew. You will always be family to me... whatever may happen in the future.' Although Lil was only teasing him she couldn't help crying; not with disappointment, but with a sense that a loved child had flown the nest and making a life with someone else. Her tears too came from the utter expression of Larry's love for the family. They certainly were not tears of regret; she didn't feel in her heart that she was losing him completely. The family have always kept in close contact with all intimate friends; that was how they were; it was part of their warm generous character.

Before Dee moved off with Larry, she scribbled out her address and telephone numbers which included her mobile. She handed the note to Lil and afterwards put her arms around her and kissed her cheek. Lil wasn't slow to remember the perfume. Dee kissed Seamus in similar

fashion. His embrace of her was warm and prolonged ...
it brought fresh tears to her; she never felt so loved in her
life. She knew in her heart that she had met and been
accepted by a real family at last. Lil called the children to
come and say goodbye, but only Lisa came thumping
down the carpeted stairs. Andrew, as usual, was outside
... you couldn't keep him indoors. Dee caressed Lisa.
The fifteen year old blushed because she had never been
so close to anyone so beautiful. As Dee and Larry set
off, well wrapped up, into the cold of February, all
the family congregated outside to see them off from the
cobbled street of Shandon Rise. Lil was remarking to
Seamus as the old Volkswagen moved away into the main
Mardyke road,

'You know, love, I know she is just wearing a padded
winter jacket, and God knows she looks stunning in that
– but I declare to God that if she was to wear a dirty old
sack she would still turn heads – she's got to be the most
beautiful young woman that I have ever seen in my life.'

'Never mind, Lil, you can't help being as you are.' Lil
gave Seamus a smack on the arm and replied,

'Well, Mr. Madden, you have the face of a man who fell
off of the ugly tree and none of the branches spared yeah.'
Seamus gave his wife a consoling, teasing hug.

Dee put hours of her spare time into the orderly collation
of Larry's notes. To say that the manifesto for a world
government was very controversial was to put it mildly.
Dee had no intention of watering down the contents
and comments of what was clearly stated, even though
the directives seemed more like the expectations and
commands of a dictator. Even his own Catholic Church
and its institutions were not to be spared massive changes
and upheavals. Other faiths came in for changes also and

their various authorities curtailed. There was no room for compromise. The entire project could be summed up as a social manifesto but not like any other Dee could call to mind. Looked at from a purely philosophical view point, it amounted to a world that was no longer allowed to operate on a monetary system or on any commercial basis. The new world that Larry was to govern was to be based on the principle values of "Love and care of all peoples." The notes were very Christian in their essence … that hardly surprised Dee, given Larry's claimed source for the material. Here there was a need to have a fairly close look at the term "principle values."

Money was to be completely done away with according to the new directives as one of the great curses that have divided humanity and its individuals as well as humanity's collective talents from the earliest times of human moral and ethical development. It was the first time that Dee had looked into the origin, history and development of money. She concluded from her study of the subject that the entire concept of money was a very challenging one. It was not at all as straight forward as it may have seemed from the point of view of common sense.

Larry's notes directed attention to … so-called recycling and refuse centres where the likes of TV sets; computers: refrigerators; old radios; bicycles; relatively new computers; manufactured metals of all sorts; house irons: old furniture; timber and furniture that had been ripped out of houses because of a fad for change or because of the need to manufacture new fads to keep the economy going; children's toys that only needed repainting or a little repair, the list of mass-produced waste was staggering. The question that Larry's notes inferred was, why were these things not being repaired? The answer was straight forward enough; because it cost too much in labour and parts to make it worthwhile. Two points arising from that conclusion were, because repair and labour costs made it unprofitable, it was all too convenient to dump items that were quite simple to repair or upgrade. Other points arising and related to such dumping were that the labour that could be trained to repair such scrapped items would be considered too costly. So it could be clearly understood that money linked to the cost of labour, time and materials was creating an unbreakable cycle of unemployment and waste as well as the continuous production of unnecessary items and draining natural resources of all kinds. Over-production of unnecessary items was done to serve and circulate money and to bolster up the economy. It was small wonder that looking at the above issues alone, the obstacle of money was nothing short of destructive to the possibility for full employment. It was also a plague on the environment and its diminishing resources.

With money linked to every conceivable aspect of human living, As Dee could see from the notes before her, it was clear enough to her that it was doing more harm than good to the higher dignity and aspiration of humanity as a whole. Some privileged classes or individuals would benefit from the use of money at the expense of the basics needs of the majority. A classic example showed the owner of slaves whom a rich individual could buy and force them to work for the very minimum, barely sufficient to survive on, so that the life of a slave was one of absolute misery from their capture to the happy release of death. That some slave owners were less cruel than others was in truth a mere degree less abusive. Of course the latter was an extreme example. However, the terrible injustices and the disparity created by individual wealth were widespread and worldwide. One of the major problems with the use of money, even bartering, is that humans are more divided in the process. Obviously bartering was necessary in the primitive development of humanity ... it was better than continuous and hostile struggles for the need to survive, where lands claimed by settlers who occupied and claimed them in ownership and developed them ... and on which their animals were raised for meat and basic survival. In such primitive times there was no social network of development to safeguard the less fortunate savage wanderers who were not developed sufficiently to own or cultivate land. Even flocks of birds lay claim to and defend trees as their own; dogs and many hundred of animals mark out their own claimed territories, defending them with ferocious violence. That had always been the Real world. Dee was thinking of these realities as she delved into the rather utopian expectations running through the veins of Larry's notes. She weighed the balance between the less powerful and less privileged. Was life always going to be a constant self-serving vicious war between the animals and primitives that arrived first? The powerful that controlled others in shameful subservience...? The privileged from birth...? The ultimate question in all of this ... the note's very foundation and premise appeared to ask, could the love and care of all people on an equal footing ever be possible in a world of human beings still operating from their natural reactive self-asserting brutish instincts? It was patently obvious to Dee in her spinning trammelled mind, as she considered the possibilities of Larry's impossible mission, that putting a suit of clothes on the human monkey and dragging it off to school and Church had in several thousand years of history made very little impact on equality and fairness to all. So-called great civilisations and empires have come and gone and human greed and innumerable abuses remain the dominating features of animal humanity in spite of the saintly good of the few that give some glimmer of grace and signs of tenuous redemption.

One often hears the expressions: How much are you worth? How much is an old master painting worth ...? .... A so-called priceless diamond ...? A prostitute ...? The list is endless. In short, one has only to look at basic human needs such as housing and the general distribution of wages from the top end of society to the bottom to realise the enormity of disparity and the injustice inflicted on the majority of society both nationally and internationally. Frontline workers such as the basic services of nursing, farm labourers, fire fighters, the lower positions of police workers, cleaners, refuse collectors, teachers and so forth... most struggled to be able to purchase basic housing or starter homes. Invariably they would spend the greater part of their working lives paying off their mortgage while the privileged classes and this includes royalty, nobility and most, if not all, politicians are living in luxury on the backs and efforts of the poor and powerless. Imagine the terrible disparity of an Irish president in Dail Eireann earning more than the president of the United States of America. How was it possible for such individuals to really appreciate the struggles of the so-called lower paid classes?

Dee could see clearly, as she burned the night lights in the collation and study of the notes. She could see that Larry's directives were very utopian in their expectations and in their commands. After all, she thought, you cannot remove thousands of years of brute nature and development or its lack overnight. It was like trying to take the bird out of the cat's brain; or the killing out of the fox's instincts ... or the hunter and brutality out of man. And yet the directives were really the only possible salvation for humanity, both in the world it occupied and whatever possibility mankind might have in the future. It made clear sense to Dee, as she studied the notes and their comments "... that all future space exploration was to be put on hold until every nation had all its basic needs and a fair share in the world's goods before using all the efforts and best talents on the exploration of space. All nuclear weaponry as well as all machinery of war was to be dismantled and recycled." The notes clearly stated that mankind was not yet ready for the occupation of the universe outside of Earthly orbit. It was bad enough that our divided nations kept the whole of humanity in constant aggression, war and turmoil with each other on earth. To allow mankind in its present state of development to occupy worlds beyond the Earth was to contaminate the worlds of the future. According to Larry's notes, it couldn't be allowed. Fear, distrust ... suspicion ... the need for control by one nation over another was still too destructive to be allowed a greater licence to exploit the outer reaches of space. The outrageous cost of it all was a scandal to the starving and homeless millions worldwide, and in particular the scandal was all the more contemptuous in charity-funded impoverished nations whose governments were themselves blatantly pursuing space projects and nuclear weaponry while its desperate homeless and starving were forced to scavenge among infested rubbish dumps and live in the most ghastly squalor in shameful shanty towns. Many Third World despots were pocketing massive amounts of international aid and putting into private accounts and building many great luxurious palaces for themselves while their own people were starving and homeless.

The notes also pointed to the abuses of the class system, both at home and on the international scene; this was also hinged on the accumulation of wealth. Privileged classes were inclined to avoid mixing with the lower classes, often avoiding them like the plague. Such divisions were a deliberate choice of privileged individuals and societies. Their status and circles of society were more important to them than any concern or obligation to wider, less privileged, less educated peoples. They had the power and influence and where-with-all to avoid paying taxes which the less positioned and less influential had to find in increasing demands.

Historically, the privileged classes, often deferentially referred to as "high society" usually made it their business to see that the oppressed lower classes were kept ignorant especially the servants of the great mansions and houses. Such servants, historically, were treated more like skivvies or slaves ... they were not even allowed to be in the same company as the privileged members of such mansions and great houses; in fact there was a pecking order deliberately designed to function in the under classes. The terrible irony was that such supposedly educated and privileged families would have considered themselves Christian examples and pillars in their own faith – even pillars of society. What did sophistication mean when contrasted with Christian ideals of love and care of neighbour? It was power and position alone that perpetuated such blatant hypocrisy. Now under the new laws, according to Larry's directives, all such divisiveness was to come to a complete halt with every person given the same opportunities to advance in care and love of each other. All titles of privilege bestowed by royalty or by any other public institution, either religious or secular, were to be considered an abomination and a mockery, a crime against human love and the respect due to all Love's children.

"The acclaimed portraits of the rich and royalty, the nobility of all the esteemed great palaces and mansions of the centuries, captured in all their finery, posing pompously in shameless vanity from their ghostly times were to be considered a criminal outrage, a disgrace, and to be burned in public. Their painters too were to be considered no more than the hapless fawning prostitutes of their art, since such works could never be considered to have glorified the good in humanity, but a blatant mockery and disfigurement of what it really means to be truly human. They disgraced the artist almost as much as the so-called influential figures of their hapless prostitution. For these were the privileged families, who, in truth, were merely white-washed tombs attired with the outer robes of respectability ... mere empty shells vying for power, position, privilege and high office. In truth, they were the very excrement of human hypocrisy ... blinded by pride and their own shameless self-aggrandisement, ever expressed with inflated expressions of pomp and bombastic ineptitude.

Such was the sired decorated excrement that fell as sewage from a mighty height to cover the minions, the lowly chamber pots of their fellow beings, hapless slaves to fate's misfortune. These privileged who were handed great wealth and property so wrongfully bestowed on them by corrupt governments and tyrannical royals and despotic leaders ... all who were given grand houses and great estates in conquered foreign lands or at home ... those who at the same time held the innocent native peoples in serfdom and, indeed, their own people too; the majority oppressed by fear, suppression and hunger ... those privileged who took rent from the poorest of the poor while their own privileged offspring lived in palatial mansions off the graft and misery of the powerless and ill-positioned ... those privileged who were given the opportunity to attend the best establishments of private education and given entry into the great colleges and universities of the nations. Their memories are to be wiped out from history. For they stood idly by in shameful and mocking parasitic grandeur, while the masses they ignored or abused struggled to the days of their death. The horrible poorhouses of the past across the so-called more advanced civilised nations were a terrible blot on humanity's inhumanity to its poor and deprived. To claim that the poorhouses were at least a safety net ... an orphan's ragged coat as a means from outright starvation, was to ignore the very selfishness of the privileged that created such conditions in the first place.

Larry's notes warned of "... a consequence of the deliberate abuse and neglect of the less fortunate." That the privileged will recall their own folly in the ghostly afterlife, in the haunting slime of their own memories; they will crave for the barest crust and most ragged human company but find no solace ... they will have made their own punishment ... their own wandering hell ... their own curse upon their heads. Ultimately the presence and use of money among the world's population, according to Larry's message, is to be written out human history.

Dee's eyebrows were raised very often by the new demands made on the world of the future. She could see clearly that with the publication of this manifesto for world government, under one leadership, was going to cause all kinds of mayhem and immediate protests from every quarter imaginable.

"All banks, building societies and stock exchanges, across the nations, are to be closed down as edifices of commerce and re-established for more suitable social purposes. With the termination of the use of commercialism all buildings once devoted to dealing with money are to be used as dwellings for re-housing, medical centres, and other such places for the purpose of social and general benefit and care of the people; the same applied to all estate agencies. There will be no more buying or selling of any properties under the new directives. All housing is to be made available free of any charge. To put it in a nut shell: money is of now, immediately," the notes stressed, "to be a thing of the past and considered the greatest error and blight on human history and on its moral, ethical, and spiritual development.

"All food distribution is to be issued free to all working people and to those unable to work due to severe disability. Any healthy person able to work but refusing to do so, for whatever reason, will be classed as a criminal since his or her offence will be considered against the love and care of all people. Work cards will be distributed weekly from an official source replacing the wage packet. Work cards will be activated each Friday as proof of actual work undertaken in a satisfactory manner. Proof of work undertaken and of its quality and acceptability will be the responsibility of a working overseer. The overseer will be replaced by a competent senior worker or crafts person each month as a shared duty and responsibility. Any deliberate attempt to activate a work card fraudulently by an overseer for his or her own benefit, or for the fraudulent benefit of another worker, is to be considered a betrayal and crime against the people and against the law of love and care . Punishment will be severe and in proportion to the amount of times the offender has appeared before a tribunal composed of other fellow workers. A third offence by any individual will be considered so serious that the offender will receive a term in a psychiatric house of correction.

"Prison work will be of a beneficial nature to all; it will also be demanding. The general working of prisons will be dealt with as a separate issue.

"The distribution of food will continue in the usual manner from supermarkets as a convenience for all. The one major exception will be the fact that it is the people who will control and operate the supermarkets. All other shops such as mini-markets existing simply for emergency supplies to those unable to shop at a supermarket, will also operate free of all charge.

"Furniture and clothing suppliers will also supply their goods free to all working people. Only essential items may be produced and sold until such time that every person worldwide has the basic comforts for living, including proper educational establishments.

"All farms are to be run and owned by all the people of every nation. There will be no private ownership of farms ... no private or privileged ownership of land ... no private ownership of any description. Care of all beasts used in the food chain will be given the best possible conditions for life. The harvesting of crops will be done from special villages built to house rural labours. All rural buildings must be built to complement the nature and materials surrounding the local countryside. Right of way to all aspects of the countryside will be marked clearly and maintained in such manner as to be safe for members of the public to visit at will. Certain restrictions will come into force regarding the right of way open to the public when certain conditions arise such as the case of an outbreak of animal disease and infection; or in the case when to walk in certain situations would prove to be unsafe for the public. During the winter months where some farms do not require so many labourers, such labour will be required to follow other essential work for the community.

"Essential sea fishing on a large scale for the supply of fish to the people must cease every three years for the period of one year; unless it can be absolutely established, without all trace of doubt that it is quite safe to continue for an extra year. No nation will have the right to encroach on its neighbour's waters or endanger its own by over-fishing. To keep all sea-going fishing trawlers in good working order during a year in which fishing has ceased, some of the crews of the trawlers will be expected to help out in other useful employment while other crew members may take it in turns to use the peoples' trawlers for rod fishing as a form of pleasure for the public. Any catch must be limited and catch and release of fish may be unrestricted.

"All lifeboat crews are to be supplied with the best of equipment for the purpose of saving lives. The people will show the greatest respect for them since they are risking their own lives for the good of all; this will also apply to all guardians of the public such as fire crews, medical staff, and those responsible for law and order.

"Education will be free to all. No grading of pupils will be allowed or tolerated, except and solely for, the benefit of each individual; with the sole purpose of giving each person, especially the slow learner or those with severe handicap, the best possible opportunity for personal advancement and achievement ... Higher education is to be open to all irrespective of any physical or mental difficulties or other obstacles. Specialist teachers will be trained to help the advancement of those with special needs. There will be no privileged classes under any circumstance. Primary education will deal with the love and care of all people from the earliest age. All very young children will have their innocent years protected and guarded from all unseemly influences. All subjects of learning will be directed towards the happiness, love and devoted care of all peoples both nationally and internationally. All teachers will be given the highest respect for their devotion to their charge. All parents will have a duty to help their schools in every way possible especially by being the first teachers of their own children. Any difficult children will be assessed for special help; this may involve special help and assessment of parental ability and attitude.

"Primary subjects for all schools and higher education will be those that have a direct bearing on the care of all as the primary contribution to society as a whole. Subjects of secondary importance such as science, history, the arts and philosophy will be reserved for individual study outside of the national curriculum and made available free to all on the internet. Specialists with a gift for the more advanced subject of science, physics, mathematics, biology, genetics, chemistry, medicine and so on, will have special colleges and premises devoted to such disciplines. However, all such disciplines will be strictly devoted, dedicated and accountable to the well being and advancement of the dignity and care of human life. All internet access will be free of private servers and be open to all. Any content discovered on the internet that is considered harmful to others will be considered a serious crime and offence against all people; its perpetrators will be traced and receive a prolonged period of incarceration in a corrective psychiatric institution and the offending material removed from internet access.

"Only one religion will be taught universally. And that is the love and care of all people. No other concept of God or religion will be tolerated. As to who or what was responsible for Creation? The question is to be considered too enormous, complex and lost in immeasurable time. Love and care of all people is to be considered the supreme reality and example of universal wisdom. That reality has been embodied in many outstanding peoples throughout the world; and most supremely in the person of Jesus Christ ... since universal love of all people never existed in the world until his appearance. His Love was un-earned by humanity... it was also indestructible. It was not his Judaic roots or his male gender that offered this unquestionable universal example of Love. The sacrifice of his young life was for all people of every time and nation. His sacrifice, his teaching, was not limited to the example of soldiers giving their lives for the salvation of their own nation, commendable as such sacrifice has been, given the circumstances forced upon them at the time. No.

His sacrifice was for all – it gave a universal seal of applicability for all nations to follow.

"What then was the right book or books of religion for human guidance? It has been decided under the new law that the absolute essence of the Christian message in the writing of Matthew 25: concerning the final judgement of humanity where all offences against another human being is to be considered as an offence against Love and Care of all. This teaching, this creed, was to be established as the most authentic expression of the sacred and holy...that every individual practice it as an un-questionable imperative."

Considering all the above; Larry's notes were clearly directed to having the whole of the bible reduced to its essentials ... namely the love, care and protection of all people. His source commanded that he get rid of all the passages that contradicted love for all peoples. Many of the old books of so-called sacred scripture were to be considered as no more than historical cultic rituals and traditions ... the exploits of warring tribes ... the enslavement of one nation by another ... the capturing of pagan lands ... the slaughter of pagans put under Yahweh's ban were now understood as no more than national propaganda, military strategies that attempted to justify one nation's right to slaughter so-called foreign tribes at the behest of a warring god – and all that done for the sole purpose of the occupation and suppression by a so-called "Chosen People." All such claims and their justification were to be written out of ancient history as utterly irrelevant to the present time and its greater understanding of the primitive past and its superstitions, which, unfortunately, still abound and are quite inappropriately referred to as religion.

Larry's directives clearly stated that

"....All schools throughout the world were to be taught and trained to Love and care for all peoples of every nation ... that humanity's primary concern and ultimate goal and direction for all human life was written into this fundamental and unchanging truth. Love and care was the true Christ or saviour of humanity ... that Love was the true "Anointed One..." that salvation of all humanity was only possible through love, care and concern for every individual, no matter their race, religion or colour. Love had to be all seeing, totally connected to all in a completely new stewardship, not just of people, but of the entire environment and its own connectedness to all human life and its entire ecology.

"All trades such as carpentry, plumbing, electricians, bricklaying, mechanics, engineering and manufacturing were to be open to all men and women without discrimination. All training and apprenticeships in the various trades and manufacturing were to be thorough and of the highest standard possible. Pride of craftsmanship was to be re-established and the old creed of "bodge-it- and-flog-it" which was the creed of monetary greed and misuse, were to be relegated to humanity's shameful and erroneous history.

"There will be no less respect for the tradesperson or the labourer than for the more able and advanced disciplines, as in the sciences. All workers, in whatever field of employment, will be in the direct service and benefit to the people, not for their own vainglory or individual advantage. All work will be chosen freely; or in certain cases assigned to individuals with special qualities for the greater benefit of all. In such cases, every care and attention will be taken to be absolutely certain, by trials of various kinds and duration, to see that the outcome is the best possible for the dignity of that individual. As mentioned earlier, everyone is expected to work enthusiastically for the good and benefit of all. There will be no attempt to overwork any individual beyond his or her natural balanced capacity. However, any individual neglecting to do their work without grumbling or creating a bad spirit and disharmony among fellow workers, will be severely disciplined and go through a period of disgrace among his or her own colleagues and family. Persistent offenders with regard to disruption at work will receive a period of isolation by being incarcerated in a place of psychiatric correction devoted to the strictest readjustment and discipline of offenders."

Dee continued to plough on regardless with the collation of Larry's notes and their demands; they were not couched in words that could be watered down; they were as definitive as mathematics were to a builder, 1+1 always made 2 no matter how much one wished to distort the truth of the sum for any other purpose.

" All offences against Larry's Law would be considered as offences against the love and care of the people. Such offences will be dealt with in specialized psychiatric hospitals devoted specifically and entirely to the problems of social offences.

"Serious alcohol abuse will be seen as personal neglect and one that renders the culprit a danger to the community. Therefore, it will be treated as a serious crime of personal neglect and warrant a period of incarceration and appropriate correction in a psychiatric place of correction, if considered beneficial.

"Obesity, caused by proven neglect will be considered a neglect of personal control and responsibility. If the latter fault is discovered in a young person, then the parents too will have to join their offspring as part of the corrective treatment, except where it can be proven, without shadow of doubt, that some genetic abnormality is at fault; in which case the patient will receive help in a normal hospital specialising in that particular illness; such help will be extended to the parents also. Very young children belonging to a family of offenders will be taken into specialist care to safeguard them from destructive parental influence. They will be treated with all the love, care and protection that are possible in such unfortunate circumstances.

"Any individual found to be using unlawful drugs or participating in their manufacture and distribution will receive a lengthy period of incarceration in a psychiatric institution and be subjected to corrective treatment until such time that all involved in such serious violations are proven beyond all doubt to be safe, and can be safely reinstated back into the community. Even if the corrective treatment means that such offenders are no longer capable of following any but the most venial occupations normally reserved for the severely neurologically handicapped. These will be considered extreme self-inflicted corrective punishment.

"All deliberate offences against innocent children and vulnerable minors, the elderly and including adults considered to have abnormal mental development will be considered the most serious of all offences. All those who commit such heinous crimes will sacrifice their own liberty by receiving corrective neurological treatment which may mean the severest cessation of their liberty and be reduced to the most venial useful occupations that will benefit the community in some way. It will be considered one step away from total loss of life by execution.

"Any individual found guilty of premeditated and unprovoked murder, will receive the same cessation of liberty as those found guilty of crimes against innocent children and vulnerable adults. Incarceration and severe psychiatric correction will follow.

"Any individual found guilty of manslaughter, due to proven serious neglect, will receive a period of cessation of liberty by being incarcerated in a psychiatric place of corrective treatment; where the individual will be judged by a team of competent psychiatric specialists and doctors to ascertain whether the offender should warrant severe correction, or just partial correction. Proven genuine remorse will always be considered."

CHAPTER 12

Marriage of Larry and Dee

Dee was trying her best to keep the collation of subject matter in some kind of thematic order and keeping to priorities of importance. As the days swept off the face of May and were in the sunny climes of June, Larry and Dee decided to get married. Until now there had been no sexual intimacy between them. That was a decision taken earlier by Dee for the sake of Larry's innocence and moral upbringing. Dee was feeling more and more in need of Larry's physical love and yet at the same time she broached the subject of marriage with patience and sensitivity. On Larry's part, he had never mentioned any desire to marry. Dee felt that if left to him, she would die an old and disappointed maid. However, the desire to marry was initiated by certain signs of sexual arousal in Larry's instinctive behaviour. Larry's response to Dee's hint on the subject of marriage brought such an amazed and immediate reaction from him that Dee was reduced to hysterics.

'You mean that I get to keep you for myself – that no one else can have you, like my mammy and daddy?'

'Yes. It's like that, Larry, love.' She managed to speak while at the same time being deeply touched by his innocent reaction and his clear demonstration of his absolute love of her. Larry knew that you could not own friends because anyone could have lots of friends. He also knew that marriage was different to friendship. However, in modern times, he was not quite sure of how permanent a relationship was between two people in marriage. Dee continued to smile at his reaction; she never quite realised that he doubted his ownership of her. Now she saw clearly that Larry was beside himself with delight as he grabbed hold of her and jumped up and down with her in his arms as though he was shaking dear life out of a bottle of Champagne. This bizarre shaking released all Dee's earlier instincts to break out into open hysterical screams of laughter. She felt so happy, so relived at the positive outcome of what she couldn't quite be certain of earlier. They held each other for a long time kissing tenderly, and leaning the cheeks of their faces together for some considerable time. They felt a deep enfolding loving ecstasy radiate from each other. The question now was where the marriage was to take place? This would certainly concern Dee more than it would Larry. Dee gave it a deal of thought in the days and weeks ahead. She thought that the sooner it was done the better for all.

Out of respect for Larry's simple faith and his strict but loving parents and their Catholic background she felt that it would only be fair to him to have the celebration in a Catholic church – but which one? She asked herself. She wasn't a native of Cork City. She was in fact a native of Bandon in County Cork. She had not practiced the Catholic faith of her upbringing for about seven years. She was still drawn to her atheist instincts and human reasoning, since her beliefs came through her intellectual influences and wide secular reading. Now however, her encounter with Larry and the events surrounding him, new doubts were gradually having their effects on her earlier convictions. She was making things complicated for herself by wanting a degree of anonymity. She knew that she was not popular among the general public in the city because of the scandalous exposures in her columns in The City Vanguard. She denounced and wrecked the lives of many important people. She was both widely feared and hated.

She wanted Father Kevin from St. Patrick's Church to take the service, if possible. However, she was more than a bit dubious about using St. Patrick's; it was a very popular church which was open all day and frequented regularly at all hours. She decided to meet with him in private; she was also well aware that Larry was a regular parishioner, that Father Kevin was very fond and attached to Larry as if he was family. Who better to marry them? She thought. She wanted the occasion to be special and yet, very private. She considered who to invite. She had no contact with her parents for several years. She then thought of the Maddens. They were a must, considering all that they had done for Larry and the love they still shared with him. Larry had no family to speak of so there were no demands from that quarter. Obviously she had to consider Father Kevin's housekeeper, Nell. It seemed strange to Dee, as she pondered on it, how much of her recent life was encircled with so few people and how all were so closely bound up with St. Patrick's church.

Another perplexing thought floated into her mind. Where were they going to live? She liked her own apartment and Larry's house was too surrounded by rows of houses. Shandon Rise was cobbled and narrow; giving a sense of another bygone time, it seemed to Dee to be too claustrophobic. She wanted space … simply that … space! Naturally she liked neatness about her too and a sense of quality without wallowing in luxury and without being overly elaborate, or ostentatious. Quality was her main focus. She didn't feel ready for Larry's house nor its hermitic or rustic furniture and minimalist comfort. She respected what his home came to mean and stood for, she was benefiting in a direct way from its undeniable and unique development of the love of her new existence. There was also the proximity of the neighbours he loved and cherished. She would have to lay all these concerns before Larry. She put the question to him as openly and as honestly as she could without the slightest commitment to either place.

'Larry, love, have you ever thought of where you might like to live?' The question stopped a fork-full of ham and salad going into his mouth as though he had just been set in stone through sudden petrifaction. When he got hold of the question more clearly, he said in a tone of uncertainty,

'…With you of course. Who else…?' The question actually frightened him. He had a sudden feeling that Dee was having doubts about him and their pending marriage. She wanted to break out in laughter but she kept the joy of his answer to herself as best she could. She was all too aware of the seriousness and gravity of the details for both of their positions. Dee continued.

'Of course we are going to live together, you daft twit.' She was smiling and gave his fork hand a reassuring touch. 'I mean, you have your house and I have this apartment; we both like our own homes, don't we?'

'Well, of course we do. But listen, Dee, I don't care if I have to live in a cardboard box so long as you are in it with me.' He appeared stressed and with a grave seriousness of expression; she rarely experienced such a perplexed face on him; in fact she could only remember such and expression once before and that was by the Mardyke river wall where they first met; the thoughts of that cut deep into her sense of guilt and shame now.

'Please Dee,' he added; 'don't frighten me like that again. Your place, my place. it doesn't matter to me ... really.'

'But what will you do with your house? It meant so much to your daddy and mammy and to you; you were born there ... it is part of your personal history.' Dee wasn't too sure if she was doing the right thing by bringing all these elements of his background into so sharp a focus. Larry's next comment took Dee by complete surprise.

'You have often said that you would like to move deeper into the countryside since the city and its creeping suburbs were beginning to close in on you.' His face now wore a reflective expression. The gentle sound of classical music in the background seemed to wash a sense of peace and tranquillity over them both. They were finishing off the meal with a light fruit trifle with cream on top of a bed of custard. Larry was focused on the red cherries on his plate while Dee too kept her head lowered.

'Yes, Larry, I have often wished to move deeper into the countryside but not too far from the city because of my work and the need to keep abreast of what is going on.'

'Well, then. Couldn't we just sell both places and buy what we can afford from the sales?' Both raised their heads in unison to gauge the reaction of the other. 'People do that kind of thing. I've heard them talking about it from time to time. Couldn't we do that?'

That was a thing about Larry, Dee thought, he always seemed to state the obvious when she really didn't expect it. The solution was obvious to her in a flash. The reason why she never thought of it before now was that she considered the wrench from his security to be unbearable. After all, it was more than a pastel-blue painted terraced dwelling ... there was his loved neighbours, the Madden family to consider... the memories of his parents. It all must mean so much to him and here he is ready to let it all go; not for the sake of moving, but for his love for her. She was very touched by Larry's decision. That thought sealed it for Dee. If Larry was willing to sacrifice his own home and all it meant to him ... as well as moving form his cherished neighbours, then she was not going to quibble about moving from her apartment, as much as she was at home there. It even meant more to her since Larry graced the home with his endearing presence and love.

Dee worked on these two basic necessities: the arrangements and preparation for their marriage and for the search for a new home. The Latter she put in the hands of an estate agent to come up with several choices to view. Larry's terrace house was at the lower end of the market and was valued at 170,000 Euros; while Dee's freehold apartment was valued at 445,000 Euros. Dee was also worth 800,000 Euros in savings. Larry had no savings since he lived on welfare. Between them they were worth 1,445,000 Euros. On top of that princely sum, Dee's job guaranteed an average annual wage of 970,000 Euros. Money was certainly no problem on paper. However, and this was a frightening thought at the back of her mind, what if Larry's commands regarding the elimination of money and commercialism ever came about? Dee couldn't see it as a possibility. The more she thought about it the more convinced she became that the whole concept was too utopian, too futuristic. And yet, what happened between her and Larry, and Miss Cassidy, the middle-aged woman healed at the police station, kept a big 'what if?' in the back of her mind. Mysterious powers, miracles, the possibility of their reality frightened Dee. It was one thing to dismiss a belief in a supreme being or power as a primitive concoction. It was quite another to explain what had happened to herself, Larry and the healing of Mary Cassidy at the police station, all of which brought on thoughts of the miracles which Christ performed in scriptures. Were these no more than metaphors and not really true? Were they the wild claims of his followers in order gain converts? Was the account of the receiving of the Holy Spirit in the Book of Acts in the New Testament a complete fabrication? Were the miraculous experiences of St Paul in his letters to the churches also no more than Christian fabrications and propaganda? Dee's doubts were disturbing and challenging her own cherished atheism. She concluded to herself, that if by some freak of nature that such a world-changing event was to take place, there would be nothing any one could do about it. There were times, Dee thought, that serious and prolonged world recessions had taken place many times across the nations ... what if the world's populations themselves saw the sense in getting rid of money as no more than a millstone round their necks and preferred a global world family where all did indeed come to see the sense of living for each other rather than being shackled to individual employers, nationalism and the mistrust and divisions that went with such destructive identities? Everything in Nature itself seemed to favour unity of peoples over their divisions. Ultimately there was no divine right to any nationality. Personhood was, after all, what you wanted it to be ... it was not a fixed unchanging truism or sacred cow that could lay claim to be unalterable. Ah, well! Dee thought – one problem at a time.

Dee found that the days and weeks were falling from the calendar swifter that she could complete Larry's notes. She felt that she just had to have a clean break from all the concentration that this duty added to her own work on The City Vanguard. In all this time she had made bits of sketchy plans for their wedding and their future life together. Now she considered it time to focus on their needs and lives whatever the consequences might incur or the temporary cessation of her collation of the demands made by Larry's notes. The more she brought the demands of the notes into fine detail the more she felt frightened of the controversial response of the so-called free world. There was bound to be the most awful uproar and protestations from every conceivable area of society both nationally and internationally against such dictates. Sometimes Dee just wanted to burn the whole lot of such extreme demands. However, she could not be sure how such a decision might affect Larry. Surly, she thought, if these directives are of a divine or heavenly origin, she was certainly very sceptical about their influence and their source; surely Larry would be given a reasonable time to sort out his own life and needs with her. Crikey! She exclaimed to herself, the notes just couldn't be the absolute concoction of Larry's mind ... he was too loving – and from her knowledge of his parental love and background, coupled with his normal inability to compose such controversial stuff – he would have to be possessed to have written all those dictates of his own accord. The notes were too involved, too vast in their scope and without more assistance than she, Dee, could provide or manage, it would take a miracle and a vast international army of personnel to get such a venture off the ground.

Whatever the consequences, Dee decided to have a complete break from the entire project. She made the decision to go and have a word with Father Kevin and his housekeeper. Dee found someone special in Nell, the housekeeper. She trusted her wisdom and concern for others. She would have made an excellent priest on her own merits. However, coupled with, and committed to Father Kevin, they made a formidable ministry of genuine devotion to their people.

The meeting took place in the sitting room of Father Kevin's presbytery. Both he and his white-haired housekeeper were taken aback to see both herself and Larry together. Dee hadn't made the nature of her business clear to the priest over the phone, except to say that it was very personal. She had reassured him that it had nothing whatsoever to do with her work on The City Vanguard; a fact that brought great relief to him and a deal of hopeful speculations that she might be open to the re-establishment of her Catholic, Christian roots. He was ever the hopeful one. He would have been a mighty odd priest if he had not entertained such hopes, no matter how unlikely or tenuous they might be. She was the last person that he would ever expect to land in his presence with Larry. It caused father Kevin to throw back his head in an expression of utter amazement and surprise. It made him tense and a bit frightened as it did Nell. They were asking themselves privately with a swift torrent of thoughts. Was this about to be another confrontation?

Instinctively Father Kevin invited them both to be seated in the more comfortable chairs while he was in the process of sitting in his own preferred hard-back chair for the sake of his troublesome back. However, before he was quite seated, Larry sprang across to Father Kevin and nearly lifted him off his feet with the biggest hug he could manage for the occasion. Before the startled and partially relieved priest could say a word Larry burst out into a torrent of elated news:

'You're going to marry us, Father Kevin, 'cause Dee and I are going to be married; and we agreed between us that you are the only priest that we want to celebrate the ceremony.' Dee by this stage was a blushing radiating tomato. She would have preferred a leisurely circuitous route to the intimacy of the subject. But, as always, you got from Larry what you got from Larry. Although Father Kevin was used to Larry's directness, this bit of news left him completely dumfounded. His thoughts were racing in their attempt to meet up with the reality and implications of what he was really hearing. It was disquieting, to say the least, to take it all in. Dee's silence and discomfort only partially convinced him that this most unlikely match was even remotely possible. He was half convinced that Larry, in all his innocence had mistaken something Dee might have said and inadvertently taken it all out of context. It didn't improve matters when Dee left the room. The priest thought that she was in need of a comfort visit. Father Kevin, himself, needed a comfort visit, not to the loo but to a generous measure of whiskey blessed with the slightest amount of lemonade, would be more helpful. Larry did his usual rapid hand-rubbing and feet-pounding dance when he was truly excited. It made Father Kevin laugh aloud, as it usually did, to see Larry so excited; it also gave his racing mind a chance recollect and calm his thoughts. He was now thinking that Dee was a long time gone considering that it was she who set up the meeting. It only appeared to be a long time. The truth was that his mind was all too eager to get to grips with the full implications of this personal meeting. The whole business still seemed so bizarre to him – he was all sea-ships-and-shells, like a drunken mariner in a stupor. When Dee did return it was to bring Nell by the hand into the lounge as if she was introducing her own mother. Nell brought some semblance of sobriety to Father Kevin's cascading thoughts.

'I've heard the good news, Larry, aren't you the lucky one, eh!' Nell was smiling broadly, her lips pressed together and nodding cheerily. 'Did you hear that, Father Kevin? Larry and Dee are going to be married and she wants you to do the honours; and wait for it … I'm to give her away in place of her parents. Now Father Kevin, what do you think of all that on this bright sunny June morning?'

Father Kevin was still in shock. The match, he thought, was like that of a spider inviting a fly to share its webbed home. They shouldn't have been the thoughts of a priest, yet he was also a man of the world. He felt a fatherly love and protective instinct for Larry's innocence. It was very difficult for any rational person to accept what seemed too contradictory to him. The experience of past events is, after all, the tried and tested bedrock of credulity.

When Father Kevin felt more at ease in Dee's company he managed to take in her attire. She was wearing a beautiful light material, a pastel-grey trouser suit and cream satin shirt; her highly polished black shoes had all the appearance of class and distinction. She looked good enough to be married there and then. Larry too was looking his best, he too dressed in a morning-grey suit of a heaver cloth yet light enough for the very warm June weather. He even sported a new tie. His shoes were also new and sparkling. Father Kevin was beginning to believe that they wanted to be married on the spot; even though he knew that was out of the question. Dee was stunningly beautiful at any time, even if she was to wear old sacking; however, what Father Kevin was now looking at was breath-taking. Dee became aware of his fixed gaze on her clothing and on her whole countenance. The words slipped out of her mouth before she could prevent them.

'Please! No ... Father Kevin! Not the blanket treatment again!' Her expression was startled and apprehensive until there came a delayed eruption of laughter. Father Kevin and Nell were puce with the strain of their own spontaneous hysterics. There was a certain sense of guilt and self-accusation in the minds of the priest and Nell as they were both reminded of what had taken place on their first hostile meeting with Dee. Then Dee herself realised what she had said. She flushed like a radiant tomato and smiled covering her embarrassment with her hands. Father Kevin left his chair spontaneously and took Dee by the hands out from her seat and gave her such a big hug that she was buried in his arms and body as he said,

'God bless you Dee and Larry – congratulations to you both.' Their faces touched each other, like father and daughter. He whispered into Dee's ear, but loud enough for all the company to hear, 'and I make a solemn promise, no more blanket treatment.' There was another roar of laughter all round except from Larry who was just smiling bemused by all the carry on – he hadn't a clue what it all meant. Dee had never mentioned the incident to a soul; and because of the unsavoury nature of the past incident it would not have been easy or suitable for Larry's ears.

Although it was a morning meeting Nell brought out a bottle of sherry to celebrate the announcement of the impending marriage. It was unusual for Nell, in particular, to have any form of alcohol so early. This was also true, for most part, for Father Kevin and Dee. However, this was a rare event and its like, very rare indeed, Father Kevin was thinking. He raised the toast.

'Here's to you both. May God bless you and keep you safe and happy always.' The words were all too much for Dee, she became a bubbling well of tears. She felt that she was already married, such were the effect of Father Kevin's words and sentiments, along with their sense of solemnity. Larry's face flushed. It was his first taste of alcohol and from the way his face coloured, it might have been a glass of red die that he sipped.

When all had regained their composure Dee went through all the events that had led up to the present time. There was gravity on the faces of Father Kevin and Nell as Dee explained all, such as the marks imprinted on her hand and on Larry's, her sense of healing and her falling deeply in love with Larry; the healing of Miss Cassidy at the police station, the notes and their demands made on Larry. These she could only summarise in the briefest detail along with some of the more important contents of the commands and their possible unearthly source. She laid out their plans to move from both their properties and to live some miles further from the city and her reasons for the move.

The gravity of all that was said, with its far reaching controversial implications, caused a tangible pall of silence to descend upon the room. Even Nell's white head seemed buried in the upper part of her gaily floral pinafore, her lower lip protruding and her face studious. Father Kevin too was in similar expression with his greying head nodding which emphasised his own concentration and occupied mind.

Without lifting his head, Father Kevin spoke, almost mechanically, 'Of course, Dee, there will be no problem with the actual wedding, we hope.' The latter aspiration was added only as his thoughts concerned themselves with the inevitable paperwork and arrangements that went along with any wedding. 'The other issue,' the priest remarked soberly, 'the notes you are collating – they are a more serious matter for all concerned; they have all the controversial implications of very explosives issues if the work and its ideas ever reach the publication stage.' Only now did he lift his head to see how his comments had affected Dee.

'Tell me about it, Father!' There was a long potent pause before Dee continued. 'The only way I have managed to regain my normal pattern of sleep was from the decision I took to remind myself that these demands were not my own and that I was helping Larry at the same time to unload some of the burden, which I believe was unfairly placed, on his inadequate shoulders.' Dee's voice reflected the general gravity of concern of all present.

'Well, Dee; I must admit that I am pleased to hear that you too share my own sentiments concerning the explosive implications of what you are intending to have published.' Father Kevin turned to face Nell who was seated beside him. She took his attention as an invitation to comment on what was said. As of old, she always seemed to lead the battered ship into calmer waters as she reminded the company, particularly Father Kevin, what she had once quoted before concerning the first note that

Larry had received. She now reminded the entire company of the important points of the original message.

'Can I just remind all, what was first communicated to Larry?' She allowed her white head to fall once more to her chest as a means of avoiding distraction as she spoke.

'Now, Father Kevin, any you too Dee and Larry; you must put all this worrying behind you. It is as I mentioned before. If this enterprise is of human origin we will soon find out; but if in fact it comes from God or a higher power than our own, we will not only be unable to ignore it, but we might find ourselves acting as obstacles against a higher and more powerful influence than ourselves. One other thing we need to remember,' Nell added thoughtfully, 'we may think that someone like Larry may not have the capacity for this awesome duty imposed on him, however, he is not being left to his own devices, if you ask me, what we have heard from Dee this morning, convinces me at least, that he has been deliberately chosen for this work for the very reasons that we express out doubts. How often have we heard sacred scripture point out that most people prior to their conversion to Christianity were lacking in true wisdom and influence. And yet God chose the foolish to impart the message of human salvation and direction. The worldly wise were seen as obstacles to God's will as we glean from St. Paul's First letter to the Corinthians.' Nell continued, 'at least they are my thoughts on the matter.' Nell's conclusion seemed to lift a great weight from the company – she always seemed to be the voice of calm inspiration and common sense.

'Well, Nell,' said the priest, 'as usual, you are the voice of our wisdom, God bless the mark.'

'Yes. Thank you Nell for making us feel a little more confident and trusting about this problem.' Dee was sincere in her thanks. It had been a great burden on her shoulders since she took the task of collating the notes for Larry.

'And so, to the other less intimidating matters, the impending wedding – where do you both wish the celebration to take place? Which church?' Dee answered Father Kevin's question with raised eyebrows, conscious of needing a favour from him.

'Well, we were hoping you might be able to carry out the service in a church outside Cork. Is that asking too much? We want a quiet affair since neither of us have any contactable relatives. Apart from yourself and Nell, there will only be the Madden family and their children. We were hoping that the wedding could take place on the first Saturday of next May; that allows us ten months to make all the arrangements concerning moving house and having it decorated.' Father Kevin made a note in his diary and asked Nell if she had any plans or obstacles for that date? Nell made the company smile when she said:

'Well I had made an earlier appointment to go to Mars,' she added resignedly. 'And where might I be going on me own on that day or on any other day, can you tell me?' The affectionate smile on Father Kevin's face spoke volumes as to his appreciation of Nell's selfless generosity in the service of others. 'So we have no problems with that date. Now all we need to find out is if that date is free in the diary of Seamus, Lil and family,' Father Kevin added. 'As regards the church, leave that one with me. I know a nice little place in Garrettstown in county Cork. You could do worse than stay there for your honeymoon if you wish. There is a beautiful cliff hotel there looking out to sea, Oakley's Hotel. The silver beach is rarely overcrowded except for the occasions when the mackerel race in to feed on the shoals of sprats. On those occasions the waters are trashed in a feeding frenzy ... then you will see lines of local fishermen and women just as active as the thrashing mackerel, but they will be no bother to you. The little convent church there actually belongs to a small community of Saint Clare sisters whom I visit regularly as friend and priest. They are all very elderly, but they will be only too delighted to accommodate us with the use of their chapel. How does that sound for a solution?'

'It sounds absolutely perfect to me, Father,' said Dee. She looked at Larry beside her, his smile was answer enough. All he was concerned with was the fact that it was now becoming less than a dream and more of a reality. He gave Dee's hand a big squeeze.

'Well, you two, said Father Kevin in a resigned and happy tone; all there is left now is the paperwork.'

After viewing many different properties for sale in various locations in the county of Cork, Dee and Larry settled for a property well set in from the sea at Garrettstown. It was more sheltered from the high winds that came billowing in at times from the open expanse of ocean. It was a very secluded spot with three acres of land surrounded by rolling hills and good rivers for fishing. The general area was good farming land both for livestock and arable produce. The house itself was a new build and had a Spanish feel and design to its outer appearance. There were three arches to the front. Hanging from the four pillars that framed the arches were beautiful displays of floral hanging baskets in an exciting spill of colours The external walls of the house were painted in a hue of deep rich yellow that aided its continental appearance, so too did the orange-red, pan-tile roof. There were five bedrooms to the house; not that they were needed; Dee had always been a very private person prior to meeting Larry. The extra rooms and space pleased Dee; she was very orderly by nature. The various rooms meant that she could spread herself out without being forced to pack her belongings into a limited area that would only generate an irritating feeling in her of being hemmed in by clutter. Because of its location, even though well set back from the sea, nonetheless, all the windows and doors were tripled glazed to keep in the warmth when the bitter cold of winter would set in. The continental character of the house was also evident with working shutters to give added protection from the very worst costal weather.

Dee had the entire house decorated by a team of specialist; she demanded the highest standard of work. Prior to purchasing furniture, she removed all her own from her city apartment and studied Larry's, basic-style, handmade efforts, before deciding what to take. She came to the conclusion, after much thought, that for the sake of what his simply-furnished house contained, she would take most of it with them to help Larry feel that he would have some of his cherished history in the new place. The old brass-barred bedsteads would give the newly decorated bedrooms a bit of character; they only required new bedding. His parent's old dining table, basic as it was, made up of old floorboards and left unpolished had, nevertheless, a precision of workmanship about it; it would obviously hold fond memories for Larry; he helped his daddy in the building of it; even though he was only passing him the tools which his daddy encouraged him to do. The table was constructed at a time when his parents had little or nothing in the way of luxuries, a time of prolonged recession in Ireland's less affluent days. Dee looked upon the old table with a kind of loving reverence.

It seemed to evoke the spirit of an altar in her mind, taking on the sacredness of endearing voices that could speak their love in an enduring communion with the son who was nourished and cherished at its face. To Dee it now seemed like a gift that would always remain as its builder meant it to be, simple and functional ...able to bear the spoilage of years without fuss or complaint.

Larry was left with his old brass-barred bed; it was fitted with all new bedding. His bedroom, while they remained unmarried, was decorated in a very light pastel blue, his favourite colour. All the woodwork was painted in a beautiful, deep butter-cream. Some of the old furniture from his former home was left in its unpainted condition to help Larry to feel more at home miles away from the city. These comprised of a high chest of drawers, a bedside cabinet, complete with the photograph of his parents and himself swinging from their arms. His old battered bible lay on by the bedside with some pens and spiral jotters kept neatly in an old cardboard box. There was a very old hard-backed elm chair with its scuffed legs and rails. The vertical window blinds were in a deeper blue than the walls. His bedroom windows looked out onto rolling fields, now in their harvest colours. The bed belonging to Larry's parents became what would be the master bedroom once they were married. It was at present occupied by Dee. Her room was tastefully finished in a light sea mist hue with all the woodwork in brilliant white. The vertical blinds of her windows were also in sea mist, the lightest of green hues; even the raised and diamond patterned embroidered bedcovering was in pure white giving the entire room a sharp pristine appearance yet softened by the cosy appearance of the bedcover's raised pattern.

It took many weeks to settle down into some semblance of comfort in the new property. Finding a new home for every item seemed to take forever. Dee was that kind of soul – she constantly experimented with the repositioning of furniture, lamps and pictures. She instinctively made the positioning of furniture, pictures, vases and all other smaller pieces of furniture and mats into an art form. She had to have a distinct reason for every item to be exactly where it was positioned. Even her music centre was not spared its many moves. In all this time she did very little work on Larry's notes. The irritating and overpowering smell of paint and newness of the house was beginning to disperse and it took on the more homely aromas of personal use. It was good to smell the lingering aroma of toast. They could even smell the sea air now and hear the seagull's piercing cries overhead as they flocked inland to scavenge for food from the autumnal-ploughed fields. There was always some new activity to distract Larry and Dee; each window offered a different view of the rolling landscape, the flocks of sparrows, the song of blackbirds, the thrushes that frequented the beautifully landscaped garden ... the forlorn call of flocks of crows. Dee had taught Larry how to attend the garden ... when to water ... how to weed and feed the various containers and flowerbeds surrounding the house. The area ... the views ... the quiet ... the aromas ... all lent their various elements to make the position a heaven of its own; and all this unimaginable happiness to be crowned and complete with her devoted love for Larry. Dee had never known such happiness as this in her entire young life, it was pure bliss. Sometimes she felt like bubbling over with utter love and contentment. It seemed like a gratuitous compensation for the dark pattern of her early life. Larry too never looked healthier since he left the city. He was looking even more hansom and relaxed. He took to everything that was shown to him. He was even learning to fish from the fishermen and women that frequented the seashore ...They soon picked up on his coordination problem and quickly learnt to give him a wide berth. He too couldn't have been more happy and content.

As good as his word, Father Kevin made all the arrangements for the celebration of the wedding. The elderly Saint Clare sisters decorated their beautiful little intimate chapel as if Larry and Dee were of royal importance. The entire chapel was gleaming, sparkling clean; it was a credit to the wonderful spirit of generosity of those good simple souls who devoted their latter days to a life of prayer. The cleanliness of the chapel obviously could not have happened over a short period of time. It was patently obvious that this had been the effort of years of devotion. Nonetheless, with the addition of so many flowers, given by the couple themselves from their own garden; the scene was both breath-taking in both simplicity of gleaming polished pews and the feast of floral arrangements. Dee, now in tears, was dressed in a light rich cream trouser suit and white silk shirt. Larry wore a morning-grey suit with black velvet trimmings. Dee had chosen and paid for the entire needs of the wedding. The beautiful little chapel took her by complete surprise. Who better to appreciate its neatness and quality than Dee herself. The small isle, no more than ten pews in length, displayed glistening cream and red ochre tiles for flooring. The isle seemed regal in its quality and decoration. The isle-end of each pew was decorated with small delicate posies of mixed coloured flowers tied together in bows with white silk ribbons.

Father Kevin surprised Dee by informing her that the celebration was to take place during Mass. She was a little taken aback to say the least. It actually bothered her since she really did not feel worthy of such a celebration since she had abandoned the practice of her faith altogether. After expressing her concern in private to Father Kevin she decided she might as well go the whole distance and receive the sacrament of reconciliation as well. She had remembered the offer once made to her by the priest under very different circumstances – a period of time that she felt she had put behind her for most part. Her confession took place in a small room off the chapel since Dee decided to have the sacrament face to face. By now she had an entirely new relationship and fondness for Father Kevin – he was more like family to her. It was a painful and tearful revelation of her past life; the story of her parents...her schooldays ... her bitterness and deep sense of her lost childhood ... and darkest of all the distortion of her very gender and its bitter results of her hatred of all people and of her total disbelief and rejection of her nation's God. It took a long time for Dee to become calm enough to take part in the wedding celebration. The elderly sisters provided some tea before the service to give Dee that extra time she needed to compose herself. The entire company also took some refreshments in the parlour of the sisters' house beside the chapel. There was an intimacy to the small company as everyone had stayed overnight in Dee's house, Father Kevin, Nell, Seamus and Lil, their children, Lisa and Andrew.

Nell, who was giving Dee away, was given final instructions with Dee at the entrance of the chapel door by Father Kevin. Larry was in the outside of the front pew nearest the altar. Seamus was to act as best man and

Lil was to present the rings for their blessing and exchange. Lisa and Andrew were to act as altar servers while two of the more able sisters were to carry up the offertory. When all were ready to begin, Dee got an even bigger surprise as the sound of the chapel's organ burst into the wedding march. Everyone stood at the first few familiar notes of the march; even the elderly sisters, with the exception of Sister Bridget, who was unable to stand. In spite of the latter's infirmity, she wore a very happy and enthusiastic smile. Nell walked arm in arm with Dee down the isle to the music. As she approached the front pew where Larry was anxiously waiting, as if he might miss a bus, he emerged form the pew, as practiced, as Nell withdrew into the pew opposite. The couple continued the walk to the two waiting chairs in front of the altar. These were two beautiful oak chairs with white silk cushions on their seats. The Mass followed its simple form with the exception that the dear sisters insisted on singing the various parts of the Mass; they gave their angelic best in spite of their aging voices. It was all very moving and emotional for Dee and for her friends. Even the children, Lisa and Andrew, acting as altar servers, wore expressions of awe, interest and solemnity. One young novice from a sister convent in Dublin volunteered to be there for the purpose of capturing the entire ceremony on video camera which was to be later edited on a DVD and presented to Larry and Dee as a special memento of the celebration and occasion. The Novice was very discrete so that the two were completely unaware of being captured on film.

The readings for the Mass were appropriately chosen to emphasis the nature of a true Christian marriage. The First Reading was taken from St. Paul's letter to the

Corinthians which emphasised the priority of love over all other considerations and Christian virtues.

The response to the psalm emphasised the need for the home to be built on God's love. The Second Reading taken from the First Letter of John's stressed even more the fact that God is love itself. The final Reading was taken from John's Gospel, Wedding feast at Cana. The importance which Father Kevin placed on this reading in his homily was "...the best wine being kept 'till last." In other words, he explained, 'When we grow old and seem useless to the world, that we have an even better future with God after out death, so long as we remain faithful to Christ. The only way that we could remain faithful to Christ was to remain faithful to each other in love and in the love and care for others; married love could not remain at the level of self-serving – it had to be extended beyond the home to others.' In his homily, Father Kevin left much to ponder on as he offered some insights to relationships.

'None of us own each other, not even in marriage. We absorb each other only in love; we don't own. There has to be a healthy detachment from each other. Real love of the other person whether in marriage, community or in friendship, allows the other person to be and grow in themselves ... to mature at their own level. In our efforts to change people we are really saying that our own sense of being is superior to the other person. We become manipulators and imprison people in the service of our own selfish needs. That is not being free to love. "Love," as Saint Paul teaches, "... seeks nothing for itself ..." Christ himself teaches us,' Father Kevin continued, 'that unless we turn away from everyone and everything, we cannot belong to him. That prompted the question, what did it mean to belong to Christ if there could be no ownership between two people who had become one in marriage? The answer to that was quite clear. That belonging to Christ is belonging to love, or being free in love. It is love shared that makes two people one. Dee can never be or replace Larry; nor can Larry ever be or replace Dee. Love of its very nature cannot be dependent on anyone or anything – it is its own life. And in its life we find the true source of our own freedom, fulfilment and meaning. In practical terms, we depend on doctors and nurses, teachers and friends ... yet we do not need to own them or be owned by them. The whole purpose of our life is to be in and with love.'

Father Kevin continued. 'There is a need to care for the poor and all in need of comfort. But our love must not depend on their needs and condition to find its diverse life and expression; otherwise we are not motivated by love or living in love but rather feeding our own vainglory, even if our caring is beneficial to the needy. We are all pilgrims. We have to learn to love without dependence on the other person for our love. Our own love is sufficient of itself. We cannot be driven and motivated by someone else's love in complete dependence on them. That would be the ruination of a child's maturity for itself. We all have ourselves to give. Sometimes we have to discover ourselves before we can give ourselves in love. Yes, love has to be discovered, taken into ourselves. It is not a magical reality that suddenly comes from nowhere. It has to be discovered and absorbed by all by degrees.'

When Father Kevin had finished his homily it was obvious to all that there had been a deafening silence in the chapel. There was a profound and enigmatic content to his words. The sisters, of course, were quite used to his profound homilies. He usually gave them something for their contemplation which they were always grateful to share in. The sisters knew from their own living together that every member of their diverse community over the years had to learn that very lesson of giving themselves graciously and realising at the same time that each member of their community was special in themselves no matter how inadequate any member might feel. Each individual's constellation was unique ... each personal world had something to offer and be thankful for. His words left a lasting impression on Larry and Dee as well as the entire company. His words were very provocative and required taking home to chew over. Larry in particular tended, by upbringing, to be overly possessive and dependent on his loved parents. Dee too began to be overly protective of Larry as if she was the only person capable of holding him in her heart and life. That was to completely forget how much the Maddens had been to Larry and continued to be to him. Many other people in Cork city had also embraced Larry's innocence and held him in their love ... individuals like the station sergeant at the police station where Mary Cassidy was healed. So it was that Father Kevin's words were very thought-provoking. He knew from much of his prayers and meditations that Christ himself gained nothing from humanity by his sacrificial love. He simply demonstrated the ultimate purpose and direction for humanity. Love of its very nature always was a sacrificial giving and living of its own life. The only way that Christ could be present in the world to all people in every age was in living love itself.

At the exchange of Vows Nell was called out to present Dee's hand into Larry's as the final sign of her being given to Larry with everyone's blessing. Nell, with her distinguished white hair, her beautifully flowing silk pastel-blue dress and white silk shoulder-throw looked exquisite; her aged face rippled in smiles and appeared so fulfilled and proud for being lovingly invited to take such an important role in the life of two beautiful people. She too was fighting back tears but failed in the effort; Seamus and Lil fared no better; nor were the good sisters spared being caught up in the moment of so much emotion. Only Larry remained without tears – he never cried when he was happy, only when he was very sad. It was in his nature to smile most of the time among his friends and among people in general. When Lil was called out to hold the small silver tray which held the two glistening wedding rings, her tears were all but blinding her. Instinctively, Larry put his hand around her shoulders; which only made her more emotional. The roots of her love for Larry went very deep as it did with all her family. As Lil stood there so Father Kevin blessed the rings; he asked the couple to face each other with a gap between them so that the small gathering of sisters in their pews could see more clearly what was taking place. The priest was aware of them straining their necks to see this aspect of the exchange of rings, otherwise they would only have seen the backs of the couple. Larry repeated the words after Father Kevin:

'Dee. Take this ring as a sign of my love and fidelity:
In the name of the Father;
and of the Son; and of the Holy Spirit. Amen.'

As the words of the exchange were spoken by each in turn, so they placed the ring on the finger of the other in three movements signifying the sign of the cross. Starting at the tip of the finger saying, 'In the name of the Father,' the ring was pushed gently forward on the finger, 'And of the Son,' the ring was pushed gently onward, and eventually into its final position on the finger saying, 'and of the Holy Spirit. Amen.'

When the marriage vows were complete and the couple kissed each other the little community burst into spontaneous applause. The rest of the Mass followed its usual pattern except when it came to receiving Holy Communion. At this point Father Kevin invited the newly weds to come forward to the serving side of the altar. The priest explained why each of the newly-weds were to give the Body and Blood of Christ to each other.

'This was an act to signify that it is the husband and wife who minister the sacrament of marriage to each other, not the priest.' That particular point had special significance for the community of sisters as well as for Seamus and Lil. In marriage, as the priest explained. 'The two become one person spiritually by living in love. This was Christ's own teaching on the significance and the solemnity of the marriage bond. In the crucifixion Christ married the whole of humanity in one supreme act of love, giving himself completely in love to all.'

At the end of Mass, Father Kevin had the couple kneel at the foot of the altar to receive the Nuptial Blessing. After the entire company received the final blessing and the priest thanked all the sisters for the use of their lovely chapel the organ struck up for the final procession out. Once outside, Dee buried herself in Larry's arms and chest. She was in a flood of uncontrollable tears. Larry's face wore an expression of utter confusion and deep concern; he couldn't understand why Dee was so upset when they were both really impatient for this very day and occasion to arrive. Larry turned to Nell, Seamus and Lil, with a questioning expression painfully etched on his face. The three friends formed a circle of comfort putting their arms around the couple. It was Nell who whispered in Larry's ear.

'That's true happiness, Larry. This day has been so special for her in many ways that she cannot explain to you right now; but she will when you are alone and away from everything that has taken place. Just hold her and let her have her tears; they are priceless to her.' Lil just shook her head at Larry indicating that there was nothing to be concerned about; the fact that Lil's face was also streaming in tears gave him a little more assurance since she managed to smile, indicating that all was well.

After Father Kevin removed his service vestments he joined the company. The elderly sisters shuffled their way back to their house. Words of praise and thanks were exchanged by all in a babble of excitement and a sea of smiles from everyone. The company joined the sisters for light refreshments. Although the sisters' brown habits seemed somewhat drab compared to the brightness of the wedding attire worn by Nell, Lil and Lisa, even so, those dear sisters glowed with a beauty that could only be seen with the mind. Their beauty couldn't be painted by cosmetics or enhanced by clothing.

Dee was more composed two hours later when all the company came back to the couple's new home where all had stayed overnight. It was Nell and Lil who had prepared the main courses of the banquet that followed. Father Kevin suggested ordering the food from Oakley's Hotel which was little more than three miles from the house. However, Dee felt that there would be too many questions asked as to what was being celebrated and by whom. The priest saw the sense in this as the couple really did need their anonymity until many other pressing matters were resolved. The priest was concerned with saving the company from the work involved, especially on this unique occasion. Nell and Lil brushed aside all such concerns ... they were delighted to be involved in something so special and so personal to them both.

As the friends parted late in the evening there was a sense of warmth and satisfaction all round. There was also a feeling of tiredness falling on the company as they said their goodbyes. It had been a very emotional day all round. Father Kevin felt especially drained; secretly he had arranged so many details with the sisters, the couple and all the friends present. He wanted everything to be perfect. The fact that the entire celebration was very much out of the ordinary routine of things had kept him on a high and more concentrated than usual. He was ready for home and a good rest; Nell too was more than ready to put up her tired aching feet.

The first night of married life looked like it was going to prove very difficult for Larry as he had to be brought into, what he considered to be Dee's bedroom. She had already stripped off and was wearing a transparent white silk nightdress. She stood for a while smiling down at Larry as he sat on the bed fully dressed. She knew perfectly well that he was too shy to undress in front of her so she began removing his clothes until he was completely naked. He was feeling intoxicated by her overpowering sweet perfume. As he bent over, climbing into the bed before she left his side, she gave him such a whack on his bare bottom that he went into a fit of hysterics and so began a frantic wrestling match. Larry was more relaxed now as Dee guided him into their love making. Once he got the hang of it he didn't want to stop. Several times he kept saying to Dee,

'Can we do it again?' Dee looked into his smiling eager face and replied:

'Mr. Larry Walsh; if you think that Mrs. Dee Walsh, here, is doing this for a sponsorship to repopulate the whole of Ireland overnight, you can think again. You can hang that thing up for a few days at least. Larry burst out laughing and did a little jig in the bed kicking his feet in the air. 'My God, Mr. Walsh! What have you been eating all day? Where do you get your energy from? Crikey, mister, I swear I will burn your energy out in the garden if I have to make you break rocks all day for a month.' Larry grabbed hold of her again and kissed her as if he had never seen her before this night. They clung lovingly together and eventually fell into a deep satisfying sleep.

For several weeks married life was pure bliss for both of them. However, there began a kind of brooding in Larry's mind as he seemed once more to be tormented by dreams concerning his future role as leader of a world government. His dreams were deeply disturbing and made him restless and talkative in his sleep. This eventually had Dee in tears. She couldn't be certain if Larry was really deeply disturbed mentally; that this crazy notion of leading a world government was all a kind of neurotic fabrication of his own disturbed mind. And yet she felt that the way he had healed her in her flat and Mary Cassidy at the city police station were no fabrications. Both were not only real events that had actually taken place, but of their very extraordinary nature, had to be classed as miracles in their own right. After all, Larry had no special knowledge or abilities to have engineered these things himself. Dee felt no other alternative but to bring the whole thing to its conclusion.

CHAPTER 13

The Publication of Larry's Law – Early problems

Eventually Dee did get round to completing Larry's notes, working furiously but carefully to fulfil her promise to herself to see the thing through as complete and as coherent as she possibly could. She took some semblance of comfort in the conviction that she would let matters take their own course as they evolved. The odd thing was, that as she set about in earnest to bring the notes into their final orderly shape and ready to be published, Larry's disturbance ceased completely. Although this pleased her beyond words, at a deeper level she experienced a certain bitter resentment for whatever, or whoever was responsible for offloading such a mammoth task onto such an innocent and inadequate person as Larry. Why, she thought, it was all the stress and concentration that she could handle on her part to just construct the ideas and concepts of the crazy enterprise into an orderly, coherent and structured form.

By October she had the work in the hands of a large printing firm. She used Larry Lee as a pseudonym for the writer since she wanted to keep both their names from unwanted publicity. The addition of "Lee" to the name came along with thoughts of the River Lee in Cork city, Larry's home and birthplace. Both were too easily identified, Larry as the mysterious healer, which the media were still keen to trace. They knew already that he was a native of Cork City. Dee was even easier to identify as the leading journalist for The City Vanguard. She spent a substantial sum on the publication and distribution of the book. For Larry's sake she wanted to give the book the widest possible distribution and maximum publicity without disclosing the identity of either of them. She was depending heavily on the controversial nature of the book to sell itself. She had no intentions of making Larry or herself available for signing session as with most authors. It was not, however, a case of vanity or personal publishing; nor was she afraid that it might be too controversial and risky for a publisher to handle. Because of the personal cost involved and the critical need for anonymity she considered it just as well to get maximum profit from the book for Larry and herself. If the book failed to sell widely, it would mean at worst a small financial loss. Her Job was a reliable one, so she had no doubts or fears concerning their future finances. Right now, getting the book out of their hair was all she cared about. It was as if she was telling the source of the material: Look, we've done our part; now give us some peace and get an army of other helpers to do the rest. Dee, however, knew that in her heart of hearts she was also saying – If only! She was also ignoring or contradicting the book's insistence on the abolition of money from the entire international world.

The title of the book posed a slight problem. After discussing these details with Father Kevin, Nell and the Maddens, it was agreed to use the title, "Larry's Law." It was a simple title and easy to recall.

When the book hit the high streets and supermarkets the media had a field day with it. It seemed that it upset so many groups and self-interested individuals that the book was declared "lunatic, dangerous, revolutionary, and seditious." The more the book was denounced, the more people wanted to get hold of it and read it to see what all the fuss was about. All Dee's fears of its failure were groundless in the end. After just eighteen months the book went into multiple reprints; it was also translated into all the major world languages.

Ironically, the book made Larry and Dee multimillionaires. It was a further irony when realised that the book demanded the total withdrawal of the use of money from the international world. So what would happen to the multi millions made on the colossal sales of the book? That was a thorny question in Dee's Mind. She would have to deal with that event when and if the need developed. She did agree for most part that money favoured the rich, the privileged and gifted. It had always been the most fundamental divisive curse on humanity, especially on the lowly poor and disadvantaged; it favoured the privileged classes of every hue ... the criminal classes ... the drug producers and suppliers ... the casinos ... the prostitution rackets ... the tax evaders ... the fat-cat bankers ... the privileged politicians ... the art world at its top end ... the diamond and jewellery merchants ... the vice racketeers ... the arms and war industry ... the list was endless. In a nutshell, the abuses of money and bartering of every sort drove a deliberate wedge between the real love and care of individuals, families and nations.

The ideas and contents of the book were seen as a new kind of Communism; one which attempted to rid the entire world of all institutionalised religions and base its philosophy on a kind of humanist's pretence of love and care for others, which was really considered by most intellectuals to be no more than a slipper in the door before the real boot of the tyrant was brought to bear down on all. There seemed to be sufficient reason to give credence to this opinion since the entire communist world saw absolute sense in the broader scope of Larry's Law. It wasn't too eager, however, on such topics as the insistence of withdrawal of all nuclear weaponry since it was convinced that no nation with nuclear capability could be trusted completely to take such a risky step.

International authorities were now taking Larry's Law seriously, not because they agreed in principle with its fundamental, utopian ideas of a world based on a philosophy of love and care as the abiding principle for all human life. No. It was because fierce rioting and mayhem was breaking out across the globe, especially among the lower classes and those struggling to keep up payments on the mortgages of their homes ... and because of the astronomical costs and the debts that ensued from having a university education. It meant the vast majority of peoples worldwide struggling with the effort to make some kind of dignified living and career. Dee was thinking to herself, was this the real army that was needed to actually establish Larry's Law? She couldn't help her gut feeling that this reaction by the majority of the world's population was no accident but resulted from some unseen influence giving the people the impetus, power and means to unify themselves and thereby achieve what under normal circumstances would be absolutely impossible. The new law had its own charisma as millions worldwide flocked to do it homage and activate it as essential to their own lives. For many it meant a personal and radical turnabout of their lives, a kind of desperate last stand to their human dignity and a riddance once and for all of oppressive and abusive authority.

The people's rebellion was gaining new momentum each passing week. New revolutionary leaders, with advanced powers of communication which seemed to spring from nowhere, inspired and rallied the working and unemployed classes worldwide. Soldiers were terrified to turn against the people; they simply absconded from the army and joined in the rioting mayhem of civil disruption. Banks collapsed, no wages were being paid. The worldwide media was taken by force as were the governments and all institutions that once served them. Ordinary people were now controlling the Law. Their clenched fists of liberty punched the air with screams of revolt and vein-swelling shouts,

'We want Larry! We want Larry! We want Larry!' No one knew who he was and yet the revolting world screamed out his name. It became the sacred mantra of the common peoples across the international globe.

Pressure was put on the Irish government right across the world to hunt down the author of the book and silence him by any means. Every detail of Larry's manifestos was read out in punctuated and dictatorial detail, line by line; theme by theme. The BBC broadcasting institution along with all the other international broadcasting networks, including the Internet, was taken over by able-bodied communicators and highly advanced technicians. Royalty were condemned for their blatant luxury and indifference to the poverty and struggles around them. They in turn demanded that their governments hunt down "this Larry individual," and silence his supporters at all costs. Governments across the world demanded that the broadcasting of Larry Law manifestos be codemned, shut down. It was all too late.

One by one each country that comprised the European Union released its grip on authority by the sheer force and numbers of the now highly organised, motivated and determined common people. They were angry at the way they were made the slaves of the privileged classes ... they saw the utter futility and abuse of money and what it had done to the people across the world for so many hundreds of years. Ireland itself was the first to lead the revolution. It sacked its government and every other financial institution and organization, including its local councils, who had never been more than privileged parasites, elitist, privileged puppets of national government. Dail Eireann, prior to its being reorganized for other social purposes, stood empty and ghostly as if its former occupants had all died. Its floors were strewn with papers that were once considered of the utmost importance. The massive debts of billions owing to the International Monetary Fund and to neighbouring countries were no longer deemed redeemable as the people's rebellion advanced and grew in number and power. There was a certain amount of sympathy for the immediate families of the bankers and politicians – most in those once lucrative positions took their own lives in a spate of mounting suicides.

Everyone came to realise that Ireland was indeed the womb that gave birth to Larry's Law. And the world was pleading with Ireland to reveal its new god, the true voice of reason and the justice of the nations. However, there were other scheming minds skulking in the shadows of malevolence who craved ardently to spill the blood of this Irish instigator of democratic destruction. Across the media airwaves of TV, raido and the World Wide Web came the voices and comments of the common people. Many spoke with courage and venom in retrospective terms as the voices of the once downtrodden and abused peoples of the world railed at the now fleeing privileged and affluent. One such voice from America came across the airwaves railing wildly: " We the majority of the world have been until now without influence or privileged position. Now with the help of Larry's Law we have seen through prostitute democracy, the thin veneer of so-called civilisation. After all," he continued shouting at the top of his voice, "what was democracy? What had it ever been to the common man or woman? It was never any more than evil's fawning seduction of its minions; prostituting us, its gullible voters, with a cartload of promises that could not or would never be delivered. The so called great names of politics – of democracy – were nothing more than the self-seeking egotists hell-bent on power and influence. The common people were mere prostitutes to the lords of so-called democracy. It was invariably a case of the prostituted paying the pimp of democracy for protection, and then being left to a lifetime of feeding the insatiable cuckoo of self-perpetuating power and dominance." The people were cheering worldwide, punching the air emboldened by the railing voice that spoke for millions.

Within one decade the entire world had succumbed to an entirely new way of life. Larry's Law was practiced religiously and widely. Several nations held out for some time before their inevitable capitulation – among them were the oil rich nations of Sadie Arabia, many of the Islamic states where their ruthless authority had once kept its minions in suppression ... Nigeria, America and England, eventually these too capitulated, being overrun by the force of their own revolting peoples.

There was an irony in all the disruption of the statue quo: the rioting achieved the establishment of justice for all.

"Democracy was never more than prostitution by numbers and self-interest," as one speaker put it. "It was a number's thing, implanted by the strongest, most able, most manipulative leadership, whether tribal or highly developed, or so-called civilized." Larry's Law established itself as a kind of metaphorical chieftain that empowered and armed its heroes and heroines with fearless and heroic valour.

The creed of love and care for all peoples of every nation was steadily deepening it roots. True, it was another expression of worldwide indoctrination forced on the nations as a living and working ideology. Its utopian inception cultivated itself by means of enduring and intimate familiarity and unquestioning devotion by the now powerful majority of the common people. Its greatest claim to widespread success and acceptability was that the majority of people expressed a living and vibrant sense of happiness and a distinct sense of self-worth and fulfilment. Larry's Law was not a panacea for all nature's imperfections. However, it had all the ingredients of gradually elevating humanity to a greater level of enduring happiness than it had ever known in any previous civilisation. It was in essence the ascension of humanity onto a far higher level of socio-spiritual development.

The early problems of Larry's Law were manifold. The rich, the privileged classes, vocational classes such as those in the higher ranks of the Judiciary, private medicine; surgeons, university lecturers of the various privileged institutions ... entrepreneurship; investors of every commercial expression, these were racing to countries they hoped would be still open to their self-serving, and private advancement. However, no matter where they ran with their hoard of investments or services, they eventually came to a embittered end forever coming up against a stone-walling by fanatical advocates of Larry's Law. Terror, panic and utter bewilderment seized such individuals who lived for the accumulation of money and self-aggrandisement. Stock exchanges, building societies, estate agents, banks, loan sharks ... their world had collapsed and disappeared ... their kind of security had gone for ever. Many took their own lives in a plague of suicides across the entire globe. Diamonds, art investments, high position and status, all these that were once the investments of future security for the privileged few were now worthless commercially and had no place of admiration in the new world governed exclusively by Larry's Law that put the essential needs of justice and fairness for all peoples first.

The great lucrative mining industries for gold, silver, diamonds, and other once precious metals and minerals abounding in Africa and beyond, were finally silenced except for the use of their raw material in essential and necessary industry. Such material had no commercial value. Naturally, all jewellery made of precious stones or of any other, once considered, precious metals had no value whatever; in fact, to wear such things for personal decoration or to draw attention to oneself in that way was considered vulgar, frivolous and immature. There was no more indiscriminate cutting down of forest which all too often resulted in floods, mudslides, and the destruction of the lives of so many poor. There had previously been thousands of deaths, mainly of the poor, because the stewardship of nature was indiscriminately exploited for the shameful exploitation and greed of the rich and powerful. The whole ecology of nature was now under the stewardship of responsible people across the world. People worldwide displayed absolute loyalty to Larry's Law, because they realised its care and consideration for all, and because they also realised that it was the last chance for the whole of humanity to work with Nature and each other before that same Nature turned against them through their own indifference and abuse.

The need for uniformity of purpose, personal security, and sense of direction meant that a new dependable centre of authority needed to be established urgently and on an international scale. This was eventually achieved by the establishment of a computerised network of communication set up in a multi-story office block in Cork City, Ireland. The centre was devoted entirely to the communication and the establishment of all Larry's Law. All new laws were relayed across the globe by this authority alone. Any attempt by any nation, group or individual to infiltrate and corrupt this authority was dealt with swiftly and severely. This system also formed the absolute authority and reference point for local government. Those who formed local government were not in any kind of privileged position. Their only authority was to communicate locally what was addressed to them by the voice of Larry himself from an international perspective. There were special guardians over the law to make sure that all considerations and alterations were founded on the basic principles of love and care for all peoples.

CHAPTER 14

World Employment for all

There was no longer any reason for any nation or individual in it to be without employment. Since money was absent from the entire system of work, every person was able to be employed in useful and essential occupation. Things that were once dumped, because they cost too much to repair by skilled labour, were now repaired by those trained to repair and specialise in such work. Nothing was allowed to be produced that was not of real benefit to all. In the old world where products were specifically designed to rust or break down so that new products could be sold ... that wasteful and scandalous world, that way of living, was now gone forever.

Gradually there was international co-operation regarding the sharing of raw materials essential to the smooth running of all nations. Oil, gas, the generation of electricity, all these resources were shared in similar fashion. Where skilled labour, be it technical or scientific, was required internationally, then such help was given willingly and generously. This global response and attitude helped people worldwide to discover a new-found happiness and unity ... a new trust which had never been attempted before created a new pride and confidence, particularly in strangers. The international world had, by the voice of one individual, albeit an inspired one, awoken in humankind, not what was once nominated as Fallen, but that which in humankind had ascended from natural brutish tribalism onto the spiritual plane of a new development and vision. There always had been a strong sense of the spiritual in humanity, right across the globe, however, that too had often expressed itself in primitive form ... a kind of totem worship led by quackery and witch-doctor priests ... they being the first steps on the ladder of the spiritual. It was easy to laugh at and dismiss such practices from the distance and questionable enlightenment of our own time.

All employment in the food chain continued much the same as before as if nothing had changed at all, whereas there was no cost to the supply of food. So long as people were in useful employment, it entitled them to take what they wished from the shelves of the superstores or from the smaller stores which served the rural areas. Proof of employment was essential before any entitlement to shopping. Such proof was given on a weekly basis through the workplace. Attempts at fraudulent production of legitimate proof-of-work cards was considered a most serious offence against the care and concern of the people. All such deviancy or crimes would be considered, rightly so, as crimes against the people. Punishment would be severe and the naming and shaming of such individuals would carry a prolonged stigma among good upright people. Certain strict sanctions were also imposed on such offenders and on their household.

There was no longer any form of private ownership of land, irrespective of who had responsibility for the smooth running of the peoples' farms; the same was also true of the fishing industry. All sea-going trawlers which now belonged to the people were built by the skilled labour of the people and were now held in common by them. All transportation, whether by air, rail, land or sea, also belonged to the people. The designing and engineering of such transport was shared among the nations for the benefit of all. Housing production too and its supply were also constructed for the benefit of all. No swapping of housing was allowed unless a particular family or individual was forced by change of employment to move out of his or her natural work area to pursue similar or specialist advancement in employment elsewhere. Any attempt to take advantage of another individual in any way was considered a most grievous offence whereby punishment and sanctions would be swift, severe and prolonged where necessary.

The shipping of goods from one nation to another was for the benefit of all. Here again, there was no private ownership by any of the serving lines or routes. The building of ships included the workforce of all nations. Responsibility for the good repair and smooth functioning of shipping was the responsibility of all the crew at their various levels of position and skill as well as the dockyards responsible for repair services and dispatching of cargos. There was to be no hierarchy on board any ship just a mutual respect for each person's position and contribution in order to promote the smooth and safe management of the ships. Holiday or cruise liners too belonged to the people for their use and recreation when their holidays were due.

No passports were required for entry into any country. However, indiscriminate and unnecessary permanent movement from one country to another by indigenous peoples was not encouraged for the sake of population control and the smooth running of indigenous cultures. Security with regard to emigration was to concentrate on matters of a medical nature so that the prevention and the spreading of infectious diseases and other issues of concern were addressed in a dignified and courteous manner, always keeping the traveller's best interest in mind.

No child was to be used to do adult's work; they were to be protected and allowed to enjoy their childhood without adult interference. The chastisement of naughty children was the responsibility of parents; excessive punishment of children that bordered on cruelty or disproportionate chastisement would not be tolerated. Love and care of our children was to be the primary and fundamental duty in their upbringing.

Religious leaders too were forced to conform to the basic principles of Larry's Law. All religious leaders were expected to serve their communities on the fundamental criterions of Larry's Law, the love and care of all peoples. Palatial mansions occupied by religious leaders and their luxurious lifestyle were removed. No religion was to be spared a complete cessation of abusive authority. The primary essence of Larry's Law concerning what might be termed Religion was that of the love and care of every individual; this stricture was to be upheld right across the world without the slightest deviation or compromise. To any thinking person the essence of Larry's Law fulfilled the absolute criteria of every faith that could rightly be considered worthy of human concern and adherence. There was nothing lost from any of the truly great religions of the world by stripping them of all their laborious and superfluous theologies, much of which were mere superstitions concocted in the dark ages of humanity who lived in fear and a general collective ignorance. Even the greatest of all religious figures could only be followed as to how they lived for the common good of all. In fact the ultimate judgement for all mankind both in the present world and in the promise of a new tomorrow was how it treated others. It mattered not a jot as to how any individual was connected to a specific religion, nor did it matter how many rules a person might or might not keep concerning such religion if the essential one was ignored or inactive on a daily basis, that of the love and the care of others.

CHAPTER 15

The Birth of Ruth

Married life with Larry and Dee had, up to this point, continued in a simple bliss. Because of the accidental fortune they had made from the publication of Larry's Law, Dee had ceased to work for The City Vanguard as their leading gossip and slush writer. However, she remained with the Vanguard in her chosen capacity as their leading political writer. Hawkswood, the editor, tried his utmost to keep her as a slush writer, since that was how the paper generated its money up to the present. Now, however the world had changed rapidly so that The City Vanguard was forced to change its entire image. It now had to deal with current affairs in a dignified and informative way. The editor felt some consolation in the fact that Dee was willing to remain with the Vanguard as an international correspondent covering current world affairs and international development. Although these were demanding areas of coverage, even for her proven talents and reliability, nonetheless, Dee had fed her own blood with the need to write – it had always been a therapy for her; only now she was more concerned with a new spirit to her writing. She leaned more and more on the developing spirit of Larry's Law and it many influences across the international world. Her writing reflected this new spirit and people in general turned to the Vanguard as a paper worthy of their respect, patronage, and interests.

Hawkswood had every reason to be happy and to admire Ferret's talents even more. Although Dee now wrote under the pseudonym of Dee Lamb, the editor would always refer to her privately as Ferret for all the wrong reasons, and for the remembrance of his old relationship with her. The choice of her adopted name, Lamb, would always mean something special to her. In meeting Larry she came to experience softness, a very gentle, even vulnerable side to her new nature. She attuned herself to the world at a much deeper and meaningful level than ever before; where once all the tools of her talent were honed to mercilessly destroy some individual or group, her new approach was in support of the less privileged and exploited. Her writing took on a cleaner concise factual insight into current events. She was no less penetrating and professional for this new approach to her career. She let the reader pass their own judgements on the facts set out clearly before them. That was the key to her new expression of journalism. It was in the compilation and writing of the book, Larry's Law, which had given her a taste for clarity, brevity, precision and personal unobtrusiveness to her writing which became her new benchmark for which she was widely admired and respected. Yet, for all her neutrality, her writing lost nothing in its power and influence. The readers of the City Vanguard knew that its new writer, as they were introduced to her, was someone distinct and special from the former lot of journalists that had given the Vanguard its nickname, "The Slush Bucket." Now the growth in readership reached a wider, more discerning group of people and became more widely read in many other Irish communities across the globe. In general there were far less newspapers in circulation as digital-media continued to overtake and dispense with the wasteful and inefficient old newspapers.

It was on the stroke of midnight, now passing into the great festival of Christmas day, that Larry was presented with his best Christmas present ever from Dee. It was all wet and clammy. This screaming bundle was passed on to Larry by the local village midwife who had attended to the birth of the infant. Dee was exhausted after the struggle. Their marriage was by now in its tenth year, making Larry aged fifty-five years and now the proud owner of a new baby girl named Ruth. From the moment she was first put into his arms he nearly flooded the poor creature with his own tears of joy. Dee could scarcely get a hold of the child afterwards except to breast feed the little mite. Larry held on to her so much. He was besotted with little Ruth; he wanted to keep her in bed at night with Dee so that he could keep hold of her. Dee had to be firm on that point, she was frightened, rightly so, that the poor little tot might be squashed. Sometimes Dee thought that Larry treated little Ruth as a puppy – he wanted her to be with him everywhere he went, including when he was working in the garden ... whether it was hail rain or burning heat, or going down to the beach to see his fishing friends. Dee had a major job on her hands trying to teach Larry about the delicate and vulnerable nature of little infants ... that they had to be protected, kept warm, not burnt, fed and cleaned, not drowned in play while being washed. All she seemed to get from Larry was, 'I'll do it.' In many ways Dee was delighted with Larry's obsession with little Ruth, it meant that she had a wide latitude in order to recover and face her many jobs. As the weeks past by Ruth took centre stage of everything. Her carrycot would be taken into the garden or into the house ... her pram would be wheeled onto the beach or on the country lanes for walks. All the while Larry would be filling every moment with his incessant chatter to little Ruth. He would tell her about the flowers, their colours, the trees and their names, even the signs of the changing weather and the passing clouds above them. He was even more affectionate to Dee, if that was possible! He was so grateful to her for the gift of their little daughter. Both were all he seemed to desire in the world.

In due course the question of Ruth's baptism had to be considered. This was not a straight forward matter for Dee. Prior to falling in Love with Larry, her own baptism meant nothing to her beyond the certificate that her family received, which was needed to prove her legitimacy as a Roman Catholic and to be recorded as such in the records of Baptism kept in the parish registers. In fact she considered her infant baptism in her later years as a personal liberty, an offence forced on her by very indifferent parents who had showed her no love at all, and whose own religion could never have meant very much to them both, since they had ultimately walked out on her. During those years she treasured the liberty that she experienced in her chosen atheism. Much had changed for her since then. Yet in spite of the many changes in her life since she freely returned to her basic Catholic roots, she certainly did not compromise on questioning every aspect of religious ritual. She did not always make her opinions known, mainly out of respect for Larry's simplicity of faith and because of the family's closeness to Father Kevin and Nell in Cork city. Nonetheless, because she now gave serious consideration to the implications of accepting baptism for Ruth, she delved into the origins and meaning of what was considered an essential sacrament of the Catholic Church, which claimed that without baptism no spiritual salvation was possible. She was familiar with the New Testament's demand for the acceptance of Baptism. However, her research and study on the subject revealed many controversial and contradictory issues. Firstly, Baptism was not unique to Christianity. Its immediate roots were Jewish since they established the first converts. Even with that revelation, Dee discovered to her surprise that an earlier form of baptism actually preceded Christianity and Judaism by centuries. In fact it had its roots in paganism.

The early controversial nature of baptism or for its legitimate necessity may be illustrated when some Jews reacted against Jesus for chasing the market dealers and money-changers out of the Temple. The Jews asked Jesus, why he acted so controversially towards them? He answered with a troublesome question .... He asked them "where John's baptism originated, was its origin human or divine?" They could not answer his question since they would be in trouble for saying its origin was divine. In which case they would be asked, why did you not accept it? If they said that the origin was from a human source, then they feared being attacked by the people who considered John the Baptist a outstanding prophet. Since they refused to give an answer, Jesus refused to tell them on whose authority he acted so controversially.

Although Dee realized from her research that Baptism of one form or another went back to ancient pagan times the very significant distinction with John's Baptism over that of the pagan or Jewish versions was that Jesus believed that it came from God, a divine source and not from human tradition, and as such, it was essential for salvation. It was not meant to be a ritual washing for the purification of the body, as in many ancient practices. John's Baptism, which Jesus accepted for himself, was meant as a spiritual cleansing for the remission of sins. That is what John believed. It became the first time in history that a baptism for the forgiveness of sins came into practice.

Dee discovered that as the years progressed the Catholic Church put an unfortunate emphasis on the actual mark left by the water that no one could see except God ... that the water had to be poured over the baby's or convert's head to signify the flow of the river Jordan where the first Jewish, Greek and gentile converts were bodily immersed in the River Jordan. Another unfortunate emphasis was that of the convert wearing a new white baptism robe to signify the purification that had taken place. Dee discovered from her research that in the course of time too much emphasis was placed on the outward forms and material trappings of the baptism while the spiritual essentials of a living virtuous and holy life were all too frequently obscured. Many simply accepted baptism to get their child into a sought-after Catholic school or other institution; or as an occasion for a big family and social get-together to have a great party to mark the occasion. One of the more obnoxious practices in child baptism was that of the priest being called into a hospital or home where he would insert a syringe of holy water into the vagina of a pregnant woman who was believed to be in danger of losing her baby. Here the object was for the water to reach the baby's head. In more enlightened times

that most obnoxious and ignorant practice ceased as the
Church turned more and more to the spiritual meaning
and significance of Baptism as a spiritual conversion
experience; so that a child's entire life had to mature in
virtue and not depend on a magical understanding of the
outward form and material nature or liturgical elements of
baptism. In the end Dee came to realize that wanting to
belong to God in the spiritual sense, meant that a person
had to be baptized through Christ's life ... it demanded
living Christ's life in virtue. The recording of a baptism and
the certificate of proof were simply the external matter of
the institutionalised Church. Dee realised from her studies
that Baptism could not work by some form of magic. True
consent to be baptized could only be authentically given by
a genuine willingness and personal effort to live a good and
virtuous life. Parents could only stand in for their child as
a kind of spiritual credit. They could only guide the child
with love and example – they could not live the child's life
for it. At some point in their physical and spiritual life each
maturing child or adult had to live the actual life of
baptism laid down by Christ's own example and teaching.
That example and teaching were summed up in two
concomitant virtues, love of God in a total way and one's
neighbour as one's self ... which amounted to the entire
teaching of Holy Scripture. Loving God in a total way
meant living virtuously in Love itself. Finally she asked
herself the question, was material baptism necessary at all,
since its true life was really an internal spiritual reality? In
simple terms, only the one seeking baptism could really
perform the reality of the sacrament by living out what
baptism is meant to achieve. From a comment of Jesus on
the difference between physical circumcision [another
form of tribal belonging and necessity] which was essential
in order to belong to the covenanted Jewish people, and

circumcision of the heart, she concluded, that the material or outward manner of circumcision and of Christian baptism were not essential for a genuine virtue-committed Jew or virtue-committed Christian who were determined to live a virtuous life under the guidance of their respective teachers. She was also convinced that many baptized Christians of the various denominations gained absolutely nothing by being materially or institutionally baptized if they showed no inner belonging or conversion to the virtues of Christ's life, since baptism did not work by magic. Dee had wrestled long and hard with the question of Ruth's baptism, now it only remained for her to accept or choose to ignore the actual rite of material Baptism. Larry was delighted to hear that she had decided to go ahead with the baptism of Ruth and to accept all its familiar ritual – the full institutional menu laid down by the Church. Larry appreciated Dee's questioning of the physical need for baptism. He experienced her delving into the question as something once familiar to his parents, who had taught him not to accept what he had read in scripture as indisputable fact. Larry was also looking forward to the opportunity of visiting Father Kevin and Nell as well as his friends and neighbours in the city. The name Ruth, already chosen for the child, was considered by both parents as a wonderful symbol of love and devotion – based, as it was, on the biblical account of the Book of Ruth.

Ruth was well known for her devotion and faithfulness to her mother-in-law, Naomi, who had lost her husband and both of her sons; she also believed that her God too had raised his hand against her. Naomi tried to dissuade Ruth and her sister from following her back to her own people after the deaths of their husbands – Naomi's two sons. It was Ruth's reply to her mother-in-law that revealed her devoted and dedicated nature. She insisted on following Naomi even to the grave if necessary.

Dee had been very impressed and moved by this passage of scripture from the Book of Ruth. Indeed, like Larry who had never neglected the promise to his mother to keep up his prayerful reading and study of Holy Scripture, Dee too fell into the practice with much enthusiasm. What she had once rejected as pure mumbo-jumbo, Jewish politics, and their bizarre religious tribal and political history ... their strange religious rituals ... their obsession with the notion that they alone were the chosen race of people of God. The claims they made on pagan lands as privilege gifts from their God put them in constant religious feuds among their so-called pagan neighbours. Dee now showed a new appreciation of the Bible. She could see so much wisdom in its various parts; and yet she did not accept all its claims since she knew perfectly well that the Bible was not a book of facts, even though at times its various composers might give that impression to the uneducated who accepted the entire book on a fundamentalist level ... convincing themselves, that indeed, it was all sacred truth. The Bible, she learned, was really a kind of library composed of some sixty-seven books; these being divided into seven groups: The Pentateuch, Historical Books, Wisdom Literature. The Prophets, The four Gospels, The Book of Acts and finally the Epistles or Letters.

Dee had learned that many religions around the world held on to primitive beliefs and rituals as fundamental truths. She came to realise, through her wide reading, that almost every avenue of human knowledge in the distant past that was believed to be sacred truth was no more than the actual development of knowledge and new insights over time. It was like the Aborigines' belief in the sacred rocks of Australia. It didn't take a genius, with present day insight and knowledge, to understand why they were held as sacred and given such reverence. The permanence of these rocks and their presumed sacredness became woven into their minds and passed down through oral tradition to many primitive generations. It was the rocks' great size and age which gave them a sense of permanence in comparison to the fleeting world of passing generations of humans and their insignificance that was at the heart of the Aborigine's sense of their rock's sacredness. Change in understanding over time is akin to a point that St. Paul makes of knowledge as something that changes with time as we come to have deeper insights of how we understand ourselves, our concepts of God and the world around us. Such did not demean the primitive's knowledge of the past, nor did it mean that they believed in lies and fairytales. They had no other means of knowledge at the time, what they believed and lived at the time was the truth to them. It is simply that human knowledge and understanding keep moving on from new insights over time.

That was how Dee came to understand the two versions of the story of the creation of the world in the Bible given the title "Genesis." The stories of creation in Genesis were quite an advance from the creations stories fixed in the minds of the people living at that time. Earlier creation stories from Mesopotamian and Canaanite myths help to realise and make sense of why the creation story in Genesis took the form it did. The old Mesopotamian myth speaks of creation's beginning by coming out of chaos. The known universe was considered as the result of a great battle between two monsters that had emerged from chaos ... how one monster called upon the four winds to inflate his opponent. The victorious monster used a spear to puncher its enemy thereby causing an enormous explosion. The exploded bits of the defeated monster resulted in the formation of the known material universe.

Now, anyone with the briefest memory of the Old Testament stories of God's creation of the world and in view of the brief account of the Mesopotamian myth above should see similarities. The very distinct difference between the old myth and the new is that in the creation stories of Genesis is given a distinct order. The sun was created for the day and the light of the moon for the night. The main point of the later myths of Genesis is that there is distinct purpose and order to all that was created. From the use of the words put into the mouth of a supreme being referred to as God by the authors of Genesis, we begin to see an enormous leap away from the old Mesopotamian and Canaanite myths where there is constant war between the gods; and that the gods themselves have to be renewed annually like the seasons. Life in the old myths is simply repeating itself. The writers of the Genesis' creation myth didn't like the content of the old myths. Genesis can easily be seen as a polemic against most of what went before it and all that kept the ancient peoples in fear and in the worship of a pantheon of warring gods. For the writers of Genesis, there could only be one God responsible for the whole of creation. To that end, Genesis could be understood as an effort to evangelise the people of its time away from the earlier oppressive fears and superstitions ascribed to the warring gods of the cosmos. Of course Genesis ascribes the light of the sun and moon to be created for the benefit of all humanity even though these great planets were well established before the emergence of human life on earth. The Ancient Greek and Romans, including their more educated and positioned leaders, were all caught up in the ancient belief system of the ancient myths; many allowing their lives to be ruled by the accorded influences and presumed powers of such warring planets.

The Egyptian Pharaoh Akhenatan and his renowned queen, Nefertiti of the 18TH dynasty BC; [1580-1350BC; 1550-1295BC the dates ascribed to them] had attempted a similar effort away from a pantheon of gods. He insisted on the worship of the Sun god only. He was considered the first monotheist. To enforce his creed, he closed down all the temples of worship that were dedicated to the countless other pantheon of ancient gods. He only ruled for seventeen years and some Egyptologists believe After Akhenaton's death the people had their old temples and pantheon of gods restored by the Pharaoh's nine year old son Tutankhamen. To reduce all the gods to one was quite alien to them. The deceased Pharaoh was openly considered a heretic for having abandoned all the other gods of the people.

Dee came to realise how gullible people can be, how easily indoctrinated, even in our own time, when royalty and leaders of rank and influence impose their own beliefs and convictions on the ignorant masses below them. In our modern understanding of the creation story we are more reliant on scholarship and science in which the Hebrew God of the bible was now, attempted at least, to be replaced by the god of the Science ... or the genetic makeup of our physical nature. Dee saw how Darwin was given a prominence that couldn't be ignored. What might we learn in the future? Such thoughts occupied important periods of Dee's life and further understanding. The problem she considered with over-emphasising our genetic makeup was its tendency to claim too much, as if that is all we really are. To her it was like a train driver asking the engine where it wanted to go, or the donkey telling the driver where it wanted to go. Our genetic composition, Dee came to realise, is merely the means at the service of the driver's mind and aspirations. Yes, she realised that we are driven by our natural make up and composition; she understood that perfectly well. However, she realised also that most of us have our own sense of purpose, vision, and a self-educated sense of moral, ethical, and spiritual choice of control. We find ways of preventing the worst excesses of overpopulation. The powerful drives of our passions can be tamed and regulated by our own efforts to a substantial degree ... making our sense of freedom and choice our own, thus avoiding, for most part, being at the mercy of brut nature. What we may be in the future is largely in our own hands. She was convinced of that truth.

Now all of the above came to the fore in Dee's studies of her newly reclaimed Catholic roots – all of which she shared patiently with Larry. Larry may have been cack-handed physically, lacking even average dexterity with work tools and such like, hence his inability to find work. Yet he was studious. He consumed books even more now under Dee's influence. They were his chief private companions. And yet he rarely made his knowledge known. Apart from Dee and his close friends, the Madden family. No other person ever credited Larry with his wide latitude of learning. Dee was the closest one with whom he would discuss matters of learning at any considerable depth. He preferred silence and listening rather than voicing his own opinions. He was people-centred and mostly light-hearted with them. He had a natural propensity to quiet deference, an innate humility and love of people. The prestige and position of others held no attraction for him.

Dee now felt confident in accepting baptism for Ruth and to that end had made an appointment to see her priest and friend in Cork City. The drive down from Garrettstown to the city was a welcome break for both Larry and Dee. He was easily entertained in the passenger seat with his favourite toy, little gurgling Ruth. Dee was glad for the opportunity to empty her mind of international events in Egypt in which she was currently engrossed as The Vanguard's leading international journalist. The situation there was very volatile with its dictatorial government, and the people entrenched in a battle for liberty under Larry's Law.

Dee's speeding Volvo with its droning tyres was a welcome tonic away from the clattering keyboard of her computer. The rolling hills and spring-bedecked countryside helped to relieve her mind like a refreshing balm. Larry was giving a running commentary to baby Ruth on everything he saw as the Volvo purred onward; it was Larry's playful way of conversing with Dee too in his familiar indirect way.

'That's a thrush, singing on the bush, little Ruth; did you know that? Yes it is. And the brown and white horse looking over the gate at you is saying hello. Look at all the lovely daffodils. Will we pick some for Auntie Nell? She would like that, little Ruth, wouldn't she? Of course she would.' Dee had to smile at Larry's comment – she knew that he meant it for her. She was actually delighted to be reminded to buy a bunch of flowers for Nell. She reached over from the driving wheel and tussled Larry's hair and said.

'Thanks, dear, for the reminder. That's a good idea.'

'You see, little Ruth, isn't your mammy very kind to Auntie Nell. Maybe she might buy some sweeties for you too – would you like that, little Ruth?'

'You mean for yourself, yeah great gannet ... sweets for little Ruth ... I'm sure.'

'Did you hear that, little Ruth? Your beautiful mammy is going to buy you lots of sweeties and you can eat them all when we get home. They're all for you.'

Dee was amused at Larry's indirect requests. She knew how he loved and enjoyed this playfulness. She did stop at Gerry Winter's Garage and mini provision store along the way to pick up a bunch of beautiful white roses and some sweets for Larry. His wide mischievous smile was all the thanks she received – words were not needed in their little playful intimacies.

After two hours or so the silver Volvo eventually came to a crunching halt on the gravel driveway outside of the priest's house. The crunching sound was enough to have the heavy dark green door of the house to swing open for the expected friends. Beaming smiles and prolonged hugs were exchanged enthusiastically. No one spoke. Words were not needed while the family and friends locked each other in an affectionate embrace. Larry and Dee felt that they were reunited with family; Father Kevin and Nell experienced the same joyous intimacy.

It was Larry who broke the silence, as he usually did when in company. 'Now little princess, you remember Father

Kevin and Auntie Nell? Of course you do.' The little mite just kept smiling in her daddy's arms. 'Did you know that they are going to wash your head and make you all smiley for holy God? And you're going to have the whitest shawl and dress in the whole world. And then we are going to have a big, big party afterwards because you will have three fathers – Father Kevin, father Larry and holy God. And you will have four Mothers, Mother God, holy Mary, the mother of Jesus, holy Dee, although she's not always good when she gives out to your daddy ... and holy Nell, 'cause she will be your God Mother. What do you think of that, then, little princess?' The group of friends broke into fits of laughter as they huddled awkwardly in the narrow entrance hall.

'Come away in to the front room,' Nell said invitingly, 'before we knock the hall pictures off the walls.' The old familiar pictures were beautiful landscape paintings of the Kerry Mountains and old thatched cottages. Dee left the company to help Nell with refreshments; not that Nell required help ... it was a good opportunity for the women to be together and to catch up on events. Dee filled Nell in on the political writing she was covering for her newspaper. Much of what they shared was really old news since both were regularly on the telephone to each other. Nonetheless, the little changes and nuances of their daily lives and interests were of special interest to both. It made their separate worlds come together more immediately and intimately. They also shared a lot of extra hugs and kisses in-between sharing the washing up of the pots and pans from the ready-prepared meal for the visit. These were special moments from Nell and Dee. They were very much mother and daughter, more intimate and loving than the blood mother who had abandoned Dee as a child.

They never tired of looking into each other's face; both experienced an intimate feeling of love radiate from one to the other.

Father Kevin, Larry and child waited in the lounge while the women prepared the meal. Little Ruth, only weeks old, was bright-eyed and smiling contentedly. Larry, as usual, wanted to know how every one he ever knew in the city was keeping. He threw out a cascading litany of names and asked after each one individually. He was not simply making polite conversation ... he had a genuine interest in all those he had known prior to moving from the city. Father Kevin was somewhat embarrassed; he couldn't keep up with all the details associated with the names that came so fluently from Larry's recall. What Father Kevin forgot temporarily was that Larry once walked the streets of Cork with his mother. He was known over the entire city as a character who spoke to everyone. He would usually arrive home with his mother in those far off days and have the entire avalanche of his encounters cascade on his daddy's head, much to the amusement of his mother, Mary. They were both aware of his phenomenal memory and the very ease of his recall. At times Father Kevin felt that he was being milked dry as he stretched his busy mind to keep up with the intimacies that Larry recalled so endearingly. It was small wonder that Father Kevin welcomed the women's return to the sitting room, both laden with trays of food.

'Father Kevin, I hope Master Larry has been good while I have been away helping Nell? I know he can be a right old chatter box.' Dee was speaking over her shoulder as she helped Nell to set the dining table for lunch.

'Ah, sure, we got on famously ... we were just catching up with every soul in Cork City.' This comment made

Larry wag his finger at Father Kevin. He knew his friend was having a bit of fun with him.

'Oh, his memory is it … tell me about it…!' Dee's voice and expression spoke volumes. 'He's the very same at home with little Ruth. If our little princess doesn't finish up as a professor at least, it won't be for the want of information from that long-drink-of-water-of-a-father who keeps her little ears and mind as busy as bee hives.' Larry stuck out his tongue at Dee good naturedly and brought laughter to the table because of his child-like ways.

Father Kevin offered up the grace before eating, and only just in time as Larry was in the effort of making one of his gigantic signs of the cross, which usually went from ceiling to floor and took in the four walls to boot. He never did moderate this childhood means of showing mammy and daddy how well he was able to make the sign of the cross. Dee had helped to moderate many of his other childhood actions, such as walking with his knees somewhat bent in an effort to stop other school children from mocking him for his extreme height. However, she never really tried too hard to moderate his sign of the cross … she just stayed well clear of his sweeping arms. There was innocence about the gesture, a kind of intimacy, which seemed to Dee, to enwrap both his adorable childhood days and his parents in a kind of loving sacred bond. He always appeared so proud and determined, giving the sweeping movements of his long arms his very best effort – it was as if he was doing it for Dee also, enwrapping her in the same sacred bond.

Nell had prepared two meats for the occasion – boiled bacon, served traditionally with jacket potatoes and Savoy cabbage … the greens being cooked in the bacon water; she also presented the white, linen-dressed table with a sumptuously-cooked roast chicken, Dee's favourite meat. The heavily roasted skin of the bird lay glistening on a white oval platter. The chicken begged to be torn apart as its roasted aroma wafted among the friends. Steam rose from the table and from best willow patterned china dishes as their lids were removed to reveal honey-roasted parsnips, roast potatoes and fresh cooked garden pees. The medium sized joint of bacon was ready carved and was the choice of Father Kevin and Larry; both were always hearty-eaters. There would be sufficient bacon meat left over to provide Father Kevin with late evening sandwiches and, with a bit of luck and a fair wind, if Larry hadn't scoffed the lot, provide some meat for the following day. Nell and Dee tucked into the chicken and the lighter vegetables. Larry, as usual, plastered his jacket potatoes with lashings of butter. In spite of his ravishing appetite, he never put on a feather's weight. He kept Ruth's carrycot close to him which was placed on an old leather armchair. He kept turning to little Ruth and making funny faces at her causing the little mite to return with beaming smiles and waving her little clapping hands. They never tired of each other. Nell too was so proud of the baby; it meant so much, with her intimate love for Dee. Father Kevin looked over at the child from time to time, never ceasing to wonder at the fact that Larry had become a father. It was not something he could ever have envisaged in his wildest musings. He also found it strange to experience Dee at perfect ease with her domesticity. He always experienced her in the capacity of a high-flyer, which she certainly was now as the Vanguard's leading political journalist. Even he now read the Vanguard since his relationship with Dee was on a totally different footing; like Nell, he considered her family along with Larry and Ruth.

When lunch was finished and the dishes removed, the company sat back in the lounge. Dee once again assisted Nell with the dishes; more as an excuse for more small talk. Nell felt that she had to know every little nuance of information of Dee's rural existence; not that there was much to relate on her simple lifestyle. Her work as a top-flight political journalist was the more interesting as it involved many flights abroad covering many domestic and dangerous political situations across the globe. She invariably travelled as leader with a team of camera and sound crew. She explained to Nell how difficult it was to cope with leaving Larry and the child for days on end; how Larry found those times difficult to cope with. It wasn't that he couldn't manage; he most certainly could. It was simply that he hated being apart from Dee. The trouble is, she explained to Nell, 'he is terrified of flying; so what can we do?' Nell was very pleased to hear that Dee had exchanged her racy lotus and now used a family-sized Volvo instead. Nell's own influence gave Dee a more homely and wider mature sense of herself. Nell had hinted enough on the subject in her subtle ways.

'Wasn't it a terrible shame and discomfort for Larry's long legs to be crushed up in that silver sardine tin and have poor little Ruth to see nothing more exciting than the smelly exhaust pipes of cars and trucks.' Dee used to laugh at Nell's subtle hints. She knew perfectly well that she was really concerned for her safety. Nell hugged her more than ever when she realised that she had seen the last of that silver sardine tin – it had never impressed her one little bit.

Presently the women rejoined the company after coffee and tea were served and the washing up after the meal being leisurely completed. It was time enough, Dee thought, to get down to talking about the arrangements for Ruth's Baptism.

'Well, Father Kevin, as you know from our phone call, we wish to have our little Ruth Baptised. We would appreciate it greatly if the baptism could take place in Saint Clare's Convent, Garrettstown. Naturally we are very happy to wait until an occasion that suits your good self, the convent, the Madden family and ourselves. We have grown to love the sisters there and the small farming community that attend their little chapel. We could get one of the supply priests that usually say their Masses for them. However, we would much prefer you to do us the honour, as we consider yourself and Nell as our second parents.' The priest and Nell beamed smiles of appreciation in the realization that they were both held so warmly in Dee's affection. 'We realize it cannot be a weekend without burdening you with extra work and a long journey on top of that. A weekday would suit us fine if it also suits yourself and the convent.'

'Dee! Dee! Dee! Don't fret about choosing a weekend or Sunday. I will gladly come to Garrettstown to see my old Sister friends and say the Mass for them. They are certainly due a visit from me. I will arrange for a supply priest to cover my weekend parish Masses here so that I can spend a few days break with you all and take in the lovely sea air at the same time. Indeed, I feel sure that a weekend would be more convenient for Seamus, Lil and children since they have to work weekdays and the children have to attend school'

'Father Kevin, that is so generous of you.' Dee was delighted, especially since it meant that her friends would stay at her house. Larry too was thrilled; for him it meant that there would be lots of friends around him to reacquaint himself with.

Dee asked for a moment of privacy to Speak to Father Kevin alone. Nell, Larry and the child went off to a side office where Nell was given the honour of holding baby Ruth for some time. Larry, as was his way, kept his long right arm around Nell's shoulders while she cradled the baby with such beaming fondness on her face. Baby Ruth was at ease in the arms of comparative strangers ... not that many strangers were entrusted with the child. It was the first opportunity for Nell to hold the infant. The child looked so innocent, smiling and adorable in her white wool wrapping; her little face beaming out from her hooded cover like some angelic miracle. Indeed, to Nell, this tiny tot was indeed a miracle when thoughts of Dee's earlier years surfaced to her mind; not that she purposely held on to or deliberated on such dark years; it was simply the miracle of two of the most unlikely characters being brought together by such a strange twist of fate and circumstance.

'She loves you Nell, you know.' Nell suddenly blushed, which was quite unlike her. She knew inwardly that it was the guilt of her surfaced thoughts that flushed on her conscience. It felt to Nell that Larry was saying to her in a perfectly innocent manner, that Dee loved her. It was strange how conscience could compromise our waking thoughts, surfacing, as they did now for Nell, like the dreams of sleep surfacing with troublesome or cherished events of our past days or years. Larry released his embrace of Nell and walked leisurely to a sash window which looked onto a rear view of the back garden. The sight of the well-attended lawn and flower beds with so many clusters of flowers and oriental foliage brought a deluge of chattered from Larry.

'Gosh, Nell; aren't yeah grand with the garden an' all? Will yeah look at the lovely roses; the wild daises; beautiful clusters of primrose and my favourite pansies an' all; that's limonium or sea lavender, statice ...' Larry chattered away with his litany of garden flora. He gave all the Latin names of everything. In any other person, Nell would have suspected a show-off. However, she knew of Larry's obsession with details and his wide reading interests. She had already been primed from her many conversations with Dee on the phone, how he haunted the mobile village library since he left the city. Nell also noticed Larry's personal care of himself both in his dress and his physical deportment; she could see the long-term effects of Dee's general influence on his appearance. She had often related to Nell the patient battle she had with Larry clothes. He was happiest and most at ease in old working clothes, holes or no holes. However, like a fussing mother and sophisticated woman, Dee would draw the line at Larry's outward appearance when he was visiting or going out somewhere important. Dee never lost her instinct and desire to have all things that she cared about and that surrounded her to look their best; she found a virtue in natural beauty and order but vulgarity in wanton neglect. She allowed for Larry's rustic attraction as long as he expressed it in his shed.

In the meantime Father Kevin and Dee had a long and engaging discussion on the subject of Ruth's pending baptism. Dee had deliberately set the parameters of the discussion to spare her friend from all the normal instructions expected of parents who contemplated the baptism of their child or of themselves. Such instructions, for what was considered a very important and primary sacrament of the Church, would rarely be neglected, even where the parents or guardians of the child were only interested in using the local church as a rite of passage to one of its desired schools or other institutions that brought other desired benefits with it. Dee prepared her friend.

'You know, Father Kevin, I have researched the entire history of baptism from its pagan roots up to our own times. I really wasn't sure if I wanted Ruth to have a Catholic institutionalised framework and religion imposed on her. I never did like the guilt and fears it imposed on me in my younger years. In fact, for all my years as a practicing atheist, I still never managed to completely release myself from all the earlier fears and abhorrence of so much of the Church's guilt-obsessed theology on sin. Certainly, I have learned over the last decade or so to acknowledge my own understanding of sin and the need to avoid it and seek forgiveness from those I have injured in any way. I have experienced a deep sense of relief in doing so ... if only at a purely psychological level. You know me, Father Kevin, as well as any one can over the years of our friendship, and in view of your intimate fatherly support which I cherish dearly.' Dee's openness caused Father Kevin to blush; it wasn't from embarrassment but from the unexpected intimacy of the complement. Dee saw his mild discomfiture and reached out from her seat to pat his knee in a gesture of affection. He immediately reciprocated her gesture by covering her hand with his own. Dee continued. 'I have looked into the Church's present instruction on the Sacrament of Baptism just to put you at ease. In fact, I even dug up a very pertinent passage on the true reality of Baptism which bears out my own fundamental beliefs on the sacrament. It was a comment by Saint Cyril of Jerusalem [315-386] a bishop and doctor of the Church, no less.' Dee smiled good naturedly at digging up such an old text. 'Cyril remarked in his instructions to those candidates preparing for conversion and baptism into the Christian Faith,

'"...Make yourselves ready, then,
equip yourselves,
not with shining white garments,
but with devotion of soul and a good conscience..."

'I realize that the only person I really wanted to be
instructed by was your good self. However, because of the
mileage between the city and our home in Garrettstown
and because our own busy lives, I took the trouble to look
up the instructions on the Sacrament from the Rite of
Christian Initiation of Adults, or as it is usually referred
to as the RCIA. I am in the possession of a book of
instructions, entitled "Faith Alive", which I have borrowed
from the local convent at Saint Clare's. As you know, they
have a wonderful up-to-date library of essential reading on
the Faith.'

'Yes, I am keenly aware it,' he replied, 'since they
usually seek my advice on most purchases and they place
their orders through the parish for their own convenience
and advantage.'

'Yes; the good Sisters told me as much,' Dee replied,
nodding in appreciation concerning his interest in the
Sisters and their mission.

'Well, Dee, my little heart throb, it seems once again
that you wish to spare us all a good deal of work and
personal help, not that we would ever begrudge it to such
a dear friend. We know perfectly well that you can be
trusted to do the right thing for our lovely Ruth. I'm sure
you could teach us all a thing or two about our Faith.'
Father Kevin nodded knowingly with an expression of
sincere confidence and respect. He, more than any other,
knew that she was a woman of learning.

'I hope you really do not feel put out in the slightest
concerning my own wish to self-instruct. As I say, if you

or Nell were closer to home I wouldn't hesitate to come to either or to both of you to discuss matters. I haven't troubled the convent ... I wouldn't care to express any of my thoughts that might cause those dear elderly Sisters the slightest unease since I hold them in the highest regard.'

Father Kevin rose from his chair and helped Dee from her seat by taking her hands. He embraced her for some time and spoke over her shoulder.

'I am not put out in the slightest by your proposal, my precious angel. On the contrary I am deeply appreciative of all the trouble you have already taken on our account and on little Ruth's behalf.' He squeezed her more tightly and with affection as he added, 'If all our own candidates for Baptism would take half the trouble that you have gone to, I would be a very relieved priest indeed.' Dee released herself from his hug but not before she planted a lingering kiss on his cheek.'

'Well my little angel, you just let me know when it is convenient for all parties to get together and we can celebrate a very happy event in our lives.'

'I can't thank you enough, Father Kevin, for your generosity. We are very fortunate of have someone as dear to us as our friend and priest. You and Nell mean a whole world to us.'

'You'll have me blushing again, Dee Walsh. Now, away with yeah Dee...' She gave him a final embrace and kiss.

The date for the baptism arrived on a beautiful sunny June day. The convent grounds were at their blooming best. There was a little sadness to the weekend in some ways as the party of friends ambled slowly and reflectively round the pristine-kept cemetery grounds of the convent. Unfortunately, three more elderly sisters had passed on in the ten years that Larry and family had settled in

Garrettstown. Three relatively new graves stood marked in stark white stone with crescent-shaped tops. Each plot lovingly and simply displaying a small posy of delicate pansies flapping their delicate faces in a slight summer breeze. The utter simplicity and beauty brought tears to Larry. There seemed to hang over the quite half acre of immaculately-kept weed-free lawn a distinct sense of the holy. The deep blue sky overhead had a mere few puffy white clouds passing timelessly by and the beautiful song of blackbirds high on a row of fir trees calling in verse and chorus to each other. It might have been the reincarnation of the souls of all those beloved sisters living in a new bliss. The visit to this peaceful place became a treasured experience in Dee's heart especially. It was more difficult for Larry he would take the loss of those elderly holy souls to heart far longer than his wife. He found it extremely difficult to deal with the death of any one that had touched his life in a significant way. Dee accepted the fact that Larry was not at ease around death, even though the graves before them were a few years old. His recall for the personality and character of people he knew was profound and sharp. She remembered, with a stab of guilt, his poor distraught face and countenance when he stood alone grieving for his mother by the frost-covered wall by the Mardyke Road, staring into the river and her knifing into his grief with the hope of filling up a column or two in the Vanguard's slush bucket. The thoughts of it, even now, ten years or more on, brought her burning painful tears. She loved Larry so much that those past memories hurt her all the more because of that love. In those past distant days she had mistaken Larry's gentle humility and simplicity for crass imbecility. Such shame-tormenting memories came to haunt her when they floated upward from what she thought of as the buried depths of her dark and disfigured past; they seemed to emerge from a deep fetid swamp in her past. Dee knew that the life she lived now was a miracle and an undeserved miracle at that. Her eyes glazed as one in deep reflection. She thought, how many times more worthy of receiving some distinct miracle or sign from God were these good Sisters laying here? Were they ever given a sign that they were intimately loved by God? Perhaps they witnessed that love and deep sense of being loved without the need for miraculous events in their lives of utter devotion. Dee hoped that was the case. She often pondered on the Christian faith, and every other faith, as somehow delusional ... wonderful in its core teaching of love of others and for much of its wisdom on a life of virtue ... and yet open to so many questions on prayers for the suffering that were rarely if ever answered...? That a Divine person was responsible for the entire material creation of all the universes...? No. Faith for Dee would always be difficult in spite of miracles. Yet for the good Sisters, now departed, their lives from novice to fully professed Sisters could not always have been a bed of roses with the many thorns of suffering and trials that come even to the best of us. Dee felt that she owed these good souls a debt of gratitude for all their kindness and prayers for Larry and herself. She hoped earnestly, for their sakes too, that their simple faith would prove to be founded in reality in a new tomorrow – their sacred life and service to the wider community and each other deserved it.

It was only fitting that the Baptism of Ruth should take place among them with their prayers to bless the occasion. Their utter devotion to prayer and the intimate friendship with each other made that little convent of Saint Clare Sisters holy ground.

Eventually the baptism took place as planned with the little community of Sisters. Nell acted as God Mother to the child; Seamus and Lil, Larry's city friends, acted as witness. The children, Lisa and Andrew acted as altar servers. The entire event was witnessed by the surrounding villagers. Once again there were tears all round. It wasn't due to the occasion alone but more to do with the sense of being among the holy. All who were present remarked on this very distinct and tangible presence in the little chapel. As Father Kevin poured the water over little Ruth's forehead, a shaft of light lit up the family and priest as though the entire event took on a celestial nature. There was something so remarkable about those moments. A sceptic might say that it was mere coincidence ... nothing more than the sun suddenly breaking out from its concealment behind a passing cloud blown across the Summer-blue sky. And certainly no one could argue with such a view. After all it was just a sudden sun-burst that lit the scene. And yet the picture of it, the very spectacle, given the contextual importance of the event taking place, a new soul consecrated to God in faith, created an unforgettable experience for all present – a moment of transfiguration.

Once again there was a big party afterwards which Dee had arranged for the good Sisters and all the friends present. Little Ruth had never been passed into so many different arms. Everyone, without exception, took a turn in holding the adorable smiling child. Her big glistening blue eyes beamed smiling into the face of each person as she was passed from one to the other, to ruddy-faced farmers and sea- tanned fisher folk all beaming down on the infant in their own adoring expressions and smiles. It seemed as if baby Ruth was giving her own very personal greeting and recognition to each individual. Larry's eyes never left little Ruth. It wasn't that he didn't trust any person present; it was more to do with the fact that he felt naked without holding or playing with his own beloved daughter. Everyone was dressed in there Sunday best. The food afterwards was excellent; it was brought from Oakley's Hotel. They had some wonderful chefs working there who produced only the very best in a professional way. The party went on until early evening when the six remaining Sisters excused themselves to return to the chapel for their usual evening prayers. The local farming community dispersed slowly after sharing a fine feast. They reminded Larry and Dee's group of friends that Baby Ruth was a villager. The remark came to the family as a surprise. They had always thought of themselves as city folk. Did it really take this special event and ten years residence to be accepted as locals? The strangeness of the remark struck Dee; they had never really been treated as outsiders since they first arrived – that was mainly thanks to Larry with his immediate way of entering company without the slightest effort or hope of advantage, and completely void of affectation. There was also the added and immediate acceptance of Father Kevin who visited from time to time and endeared himself to the locals with his manly, unpretentious ways. He was, after all, a man with a working background in the building industry; one who had to fend for himself as he travelled at home and abroad in search of work prior to answering the call to priesthood. Dee consciously pondered on her seemingly new identity with a philosophical smile of acceptance. She experienced a distinct conscious sense of having just arrived locally.

CHAPTER 16

Larry's Preparations to Meet Pope Dominic Ubutu X11

About two months after the baptism of baby Ruth, Larry experienced a recurrence of disturbing nights due to his dreams. He was ordered in his dreams to go to Rome with Dee to carry an urgent message for Pope Domenic Ubutu X11, the first African pope, a native of Kenya. Pope Dominic was extremely popular with the world's Catholic population; he was found to be sincere in his faith – one who lived simply, and a man of profound prayer and wide learning. All who knew him intimately considered him to be a truly holy and saintly man. He was a lean man whose actions were slow and deliberate. He conversed in slow deliberation, measuring every word. For all his hesitant manner in conversation he always beamed a deceptive smile. It was easy to be mislead by the notion that he really was unable to answer fairly simple questions when address to him by the media. The truth was quite the contrary. He was gifted with a very calm nature and a penetrating intelligence. His gracious smiling eyes never left anyone with whom he conversed. His face instinctively radiated a most gentle humble smile; a smile so warm that it immediately put people at ease. Yet, beneath his gentle accommodating nature was a mind, an intellect, as deep as any gifted and privileged scholar, and yet he had never been privileged to grace the corridors of any distinguished or hallowed university. His early existence, and that is all his early life had ever been, an existence; had by some twist of fortune plucked him out of the mire of raging misfortune and set him on the many byways to Rome. His early struggles, seemingly without hope, in a tribal community in the bush-lands of Kenya, had, fortuitously, salvaged him from the dross of inhuman misery and waste and from all its grinding pitiless poverty. The inspired choice of the hard-pressed Missionary Fathers had been his salvation. He had known ravishing, gratuitous tribal violence, merciless disease and pain-racking hunger. Such were shadows that would haunt him to his dying day. He had suffered the most inhuman indignities from his own people. How love ever remained in this holy man only some more powerful mind could know. Many others, including his family, were left behind, un-chosen, un-called. They were left to the ravages of brute nature and its pitiless fate, where most were little more than the compost of tribal savagery – thrown wasted to the earth like fallen leaves, mere compost, withered and twisted, ground underfoot into their jungle's bloody earth.

Dee had the task of arranging an audience with Pope Dominic through various clerical channels with the help of Father Kevin. He approached his Bishop Mark Mc Cann, bishop of Cork. The bishop himself arranged for Larry, Dee, and Father Kevin to go to Dublin, the capital, to have the matter put before Cardinal Christopher Dwyer. The cardinal took some persuading before he considered the visit to be both genuine, critical and of distinct value. The cardinal was not a man to countenance time-wasters. The eventual meeting with the cardinal was spread over a four week period in which Father Kevin was required to be present. It meant that the priest could only visit his parish on weekends to celebrate the parish Masses due to the distance from Cork to Dublin.

Dee reversed the Volvo from her garage, taking charge of the driving from Garrettstown to Cork city. They had a delightful break for refreshments with Nell when the family had reached Cork city. Nell was clinging to her beloved Dee as if years had passed since last they met. Larry gave out all the local news in a flood of details. None of the local fishermen or farmers was excluded. Father Kevin and Nell were at home with his phenomenal memory and his insatiable enthusiasm for details. It was hard for all to leave Nell behind as they headed for the Capital, Dublin, over a hundred miles away. She waved from the old green door; her floral dress was worn especially for what she considered Larry and Dee's homecoming. She liked to look her best for Dee especially – it was also an attempt to disguise her feeling of age.

The journey to Dublin was deliberately extended to five hours to fit in a leisurely meal with Nell and Father Kevin. The chatter along the journey, mainly catch-up on both their separate home fronts, gave a distant buzz and warmth to the ambience in the silver Volvo. Larry, as usual, was full of chattering bubbles. He loved Father Kevin as if he was a replacement parent. Larry sat in the back with baby Ruth, his bundle of joy and favourite toy. When the green hills and fields gave way to the busy roads and houses of the city of Dublin a sense of apprehension descended on the family.

'God help us all, Dee. It's not every day I have to face a cardinal.'

'Ouch! Don't be bothering yourself with him, Kevin. No matter his reputation for his inflexible resolve, he's only one man at the end of the day.' Dee smiled at her friend to calm him.

'Crikey! Dee. Are you trying to calm me or terrorize me? "Inflexible resolve!" Couldn't you just say he's out to murderer us and be done with it!' The good-natured banter took some sting from the potent mood-change. Dee was more familiar with Cardinal Dwyer than Father Kevin. There was history between them when she worked as a slush reporter. She covered many controversial scandals among the clergy of the past. The cardinal was involved with covering up for fallen priests while serving as bishop in his early days. She withheld that knowledge from her friend – it was not a conversation to rake over at this juncture. Being a mother, wife and political writer widened her focus on more meaningful matters. She planted a big kiss on Father Kevin's cheek while temporally held up in the crowded city traffic. He gave her a big lingering cuddle, her sweet perfume wafting all over him and the entire Volvo. Both were reassuring each other of their support. Larry was totally unfazed in the rear. He was telling baby Ruth all about Dublin.

'Look at all the big green busses, little Ruth – they have a downstairs and an upstairs. You won't see them in Garrettstown. Look at all the people and all the cars ... millions and trillions of them. They have all come out to see you little Ruth, so you must wave to them all.' The little child just gurgled away contentedly, charming her beloved daddy with every smile and her big glinting eyes like crystal pools.

The cardinal's address lay off a series of private roads which were all secluded in avenues of trees. As yet there was only a delicate veil of virgin green to soften the harshness of their wintry forms. Presently they came across a very imposing building with a wide wrought iron gated-front and gravelled crescent-drive. The wrought-iron work above the gate with its bold design of a white bishop's mitre with a broad golden cross set on a crimson background imposed itself on the visitor's view, declaring its own magnificence. Dee inched the Volvo in with great care. Two other vehicles were parked within, both gleaming black Volvos. There was ample parking space for several more vehicles if needed. A great white statue of Saint Patrick in the centre of the drive looked out in the direction of the city. The cardinal's palace, and such it was, could easily have been built by the Greeks some two thousand years ago. It displayed all the characteristics of that civilization's classic features complete with seven typical columns spanning a deep weather-inset portico all capped by a classical Grecian facade. The great oak doors forming the imposing entrance stood open inwardly above a short flight of stone steps. They climbed the steps and walked within, all feeling a bit apprehensive. They found themselves faced by another less grand set of internal doors which were closed. A large white porcelain push-bell was used to declare their arrival. The family were greeted by a very energetic and smartly dressed private secretary, her suit, a pristine sober black. She appeared to be in her thirties and every inch a professional and competent Lady. Her smile was as infectious as the warmth of her greeting.

'You are expected and very welcome. I'm Oral, the cardinal's private secretary. Please let me show you around the important bits of the house.' She avoided using the word, palace. It was as if she was keeping the imposing grandeur of the palace in its place by placing all her attention on the importance of the guests. She spoke with modesty and a distinct kindness, taking their hands in both of hers. It was plain to detect from her relaxed and warm manner that she knew nothing of their business here. That seemed to indicate that she was not in the cardinal's more intimate confidence. She ushered them to a small spare dining room which was to become very familiar over the next four week while their business with Cardinal Dwyer lasted. They were served hot refreshments after being guided to conveniences and powder room. These oozed grandeur and luxury. Dee, in particular appreciated the class and utter splendour of all she saw. The palace was well maintained. Every little item, down to the neatly hanging pink towels, richly woven and neatly hung on their glinting heated holders. There was a pristine white crescent-shaped mat below a classical, pedestal wash bowl.

After their refreshments, Oral guided her visitors to a great study and introduced them to Monsignor Sean O' Rourke, Cardinal Dwyer's mentor. Oral left the company. She had barely vanished from sight along a dark wood-panelled corridor when the family felt isolated, estranged and nervous. The palace and their reason for being there descended on them like an oppressive weight. Father Kevin put his arms round Dee and Larry to reassure them of his guardianship, in spite of his own distinct sense of discomfort. The general ambience and atmosphere of the place gave off a strong aroma of scented wax polish and the fumes of warm ink wafting from the hub of a printing room near the study.

The visitors were ushered into an intimidating office by the cardinal's private mentor, Monsignor Sean O' Rourke,

a cleric of portly proportions in his early sixties. His round
red face and dark grey eyes smiled warmly at the guests.
And yet, Dee and Father Kevin sensed a certain degree of
unease in him. He directed the visitors to their seats with
a tangible sense of foreboding, displaying an over-
cautious degree of what could best be described as
deference. Since Father Kevin and Dee did not consider
themselves of any particular standing in these hallowed
halls. Both realised that their business here was given the
greatest degree of courtesy and importance. Father Kevin
had already contacted the cardinal's secretary of his need
for a hardback chair for his troublesome back. He was
duly ushered to one and placed on the right hand side of a
beautifully rich upholstered settee on which Larry, baby
Ruth and Dee were seated. Mgr. O' Rourke Organised
some final documents on the cardinal's panelled desk and
then excused himself from the visitors to inform the
cardinal that all was prepared.

Inside the great study the internal décor was heavily
panelled in oak wainscoting and dark polished period
furniture which belonged to another centaury. The large
study also served as a library and an office; it was designed
to both impress and foster an ambience of learning. Old
leather-bound books with gold tooling were protected
behind glass doors. Most appeared in pristine condition
as if never used and treated only with gloved-care and
respect for their cost and rarity. There was no sense of
homeliness about the room or its grand proportions.
There were many imposing portraits of stern-looking
popes, cardinals and bishops of the past posturing in all
their finery – their expressions soliciting importance and
displaying pomposity and vanity as virtue. Most were
covered with broken hairline cracks and were considered

too historically important to trash and yet an eyesore and burden to dust-gathering posterity. White marble busts of renowned pontiffs of yesteryear stood on pillared columns against opposing walls, their vying lifeless eyes staring with self-importance into a bygone time, all now appearing as the waste of history, deluded and still as the divine pharaohs and emperors of the past, all ignorant of their transient mortality and power. Even the world atlas seemed to ooze authority with its many Catholic countries rampant all over the globe marked in martyr's red. One decorated chart on the wall listed every country in the world and its estimated Catholic population. Currently, the chart boasted one billion in a world of nine billion souls. The wood floor glistened in reflected pools from the chandelier lighting – their sparkling crystal lights hanging from beautifully-moulded alabaster ceilings.

Monsignor O' Rourke entered the study with some trepidation. His alert eyes flashed momentarily on the guests and then sideways as if to look behind him in a kind of statement saying, it's him you want behind, not me. Cardinal Dwyer followed in the wake of the monsignor gliding tall and gracefully as if on air. Both clerics wore their cassock with purple piping and buttons. The cardinal's soutane had its full complement of thirty-three scarlet buttons which Larry pointed out to Baby Ruth.

'Look at tall those buttons, little Ruth …! Do you know that His Eminence, the cardinal, has been up for hours fastening them all?' Larry's baby talk seemed to take some weight from the importance of the cardinal's entrance. Father Kevin and Dee broke out into involuntary laughter at Larry's impromptu comment. The little child wrapped in a light woollen shawl smiled as she turned in Larry's arms to gaze at the cardinal in the direction of her father's pointing finger. The cardinal good-naturedly scanned the row of his red buttons and surprised both Larry and Dee when he remarked smilingly.

'All thirty three of them, they represent the years of Christ's life on earth.' The remark removed any sense of light-heartedness from the study, although he did not intend his comment to make his visitors ill at ease. He wore his scarlet zucchetto, or skull cap, which added to his distinction. He habitually fondled the large pectoral cross on his breast. It seemed to bring him confidence and remind him of his office. It too added to the sense of his graced presence. The formal attire of both clerics gave a strong sense of solemnity and authority to the ambience of the study. The company also felt a distinct sense of importance radiating from the imposing stature of the cardinal. He was six feet five inches tall, and not a pick of weight on him. Everything about him radiated the power of the Church. His bleached white hair showed below his zucchetto scarlet skull cap. Only Larry's height came close to him. Presently both clerics took their seats, the cardinal behind his heavily-panelled desk and the monsignor sharing a part of it. He felt the need to explain their position.

'I don't normally separate myself from my visitors in this formal way. It is, I fear, a necessity due to the gravity of our meeting. There are many issues to discuss from all the notes relating to your formal request to have an audience with the Holy Father, Pope Dominic X11. I hope you realise that everything we say in this office will be recorded and witnessed here by Monsignor Sean O' Rourke. Everything recorded will be made available to the Holy Father. It will be up to His Holiness to decide on the outcome of these important matters. Now I must ask all present. Do you feel the need to raise any objection to this procedure?' The cardinal looked over at the seated visitors. He continued to fondle his cross while he made a sweep of his right hand indicating the compass and magnitude of his question. The visitors looked at each other. All three dressed in their pristine best; even Larry looked as if he had just stepped out from his wedding day in his best morning grey. Dee wore a cream suit and her favourite silk green shirt. Her glistening hair falling over her shoulders like molten gold, she looked breathtakingly beautiful. The clerics were conscious of her exquisite appearance. Even father Kevin made the extra effort to look his pristine best. His black trousers pressed and sharp, his best black blazer also in pristine condition, his black shoes glistening. It was father Kevin who raised the question of the family's need for security. He knew that no one was aware, as yet, of the author of the controversial book, Larry's Law. He extended his open palms in an expression of emphasis as he said:

'You will be aware, Your Eminence, of my prior communication with Monsignor O' Rourke with regard to the need for the family's security?' There was a long pause as Cardinal Dwyer finger-read through his notes with an expression of intense scrutiny. Pages were flipped upward with a sense of urgency. Monsignor O' Rourke leaned over and pulled out the relevant paper for the cardinal regarding the point on security.

'Ah, yes! Thank you Monsignor.' The cardinal's smile to his secretary indicated his appreciation of the monsignor's sense of order and competence. 'Yes, of course, this whole thing of Mary Cassidy's healing at the police station in Cork city.' The cardinal held out the pertinent page at arms length while he studied the details.

'I quite agree that Mr. Walsh's family identity should remain anonymous. None of us need coach loads of desperate infirm pilgrims stampeding towards the possibility of miracle cures. Indeed, our sympathies are with the suffering – indeed, they are. Yet, even the good Lord himself realized that physical healing did not necessarily make for a better person or one who appreciated what was done for them. Indeed. Christ himself criticized the lake towns of Capernaum and beyond because the miracles done for their peoples advanced their faith not one iota. Even the healing of ten lepers, as St. Luke tells us, only one returned to thank God for his healing. We do not always understand why some healings take place, as in the case of your Mary Cassidy and yet thousands are not, in spite of our best efforts at prayer.' The entire company nodded in acknowledgement of the truth spoken by the cardinal.

He pulled some more papers from a buff-coloured folder. There was another long pause as he studied the contents. He passed three sheets of paper to his monsignor to hand to the guests. Each sheet listed the issues up for discussion. Some items on the list were direct concerns for the Church while others, though not directly concerned with the Church, were nonetheless social matters which did affect the lives of all peoples whether Catholics or not. The guests scanned the list of issues up for discussion. Nothing on the list surprised them since all were matters gleaned from the publication of Larry's Law. Each item for discussion was numbered and in order of importance. While the cardinal scanned the page himself Dee looked into Father Kevin's face, her eyebrows raised, her lower lip protruded in an expressions that said, crikey! This is a right barrow load! The priest made a similar response, nodding his head, impressed by the extensive list of issues. Larry let baby Ruth have his paper after scanning it briefly. The little mite began waving the paper into her daddy's face and smiling all the while with her little games. The cardinal noted the fact that Larry seemed indifferent to the listed issues. Dee too was smiling at the antics of her daughter. Father Kevin's focus was also on the antics of Larry's playfulness. It seemed to take away some of the gravity of the situation. The cardinal was none too pleased to see the company lost in domesticity as if the child was the centre of attention. He soon put an end to the domestic scene with a cutting opening remark. His face was deliberately severe, clearly dismissing the casual mood and the lack of attention that he witnessed in his visitors.

'I need to make it quite clear to all present that this request to seek an audience with Pope Dominic Ubutu X11 in Rome is no light or casual matter as if the pontiff was someone with little to do with his time and in consequence have all and sundry drop in on him at will.' The cardinal's expression was tense, even severe. Father Kevin expected no less and was certain that the pointed comment was aimed at Larry and Dee and not himself. The remark irritated Dee. The implication inherent in the cardinal's opening remark was that she and Larry were not received on trust. She glanced at Larry – he appeared totally at ease, he was not easily provoked. His sensitivities would only surface when he felt directly challenged. Dee let the remark pass for the moment. In her mind they were doing the cardinal a favour especially with their conviction that the pontiff's life revealed to Larry was in serious danger. The cardinal continued quite unaware of Dee's gathering resentment.

'I would like to draw your attention to the first issue, the question and assertion of Mr. Walsh's mother's ascension into heaven.' A tangible weight of silence gripped the room. There was no tone of mockery, not even a hint of scepticism in the cardinal's voice. Yet, when the echo and sense of his words hung exposed naked in the air they sounded ridiculous, even preposterous. The cardinal broke the silence as he spoke waving a paper in his hand and alternating his eye line from the paper's notes to the visitor's faces. 'This incident, I avoid the word, claim, since I am informed that Father Kevin has already advised the enquiry that your family make no more of Mary's disappearance than precisely that, a disappearance. Nonetheless, Mr. Walsh speaks here of his mother's return from heaven on a brief visitation bringing with her a note of instruction relating to the formation of a world government, and the return of some old bedclothes.' The litany of facts referred to in such cold formality, void of all actual experience of the event, came across as quite implausible, even to the family. The cardinal continued to wave the raised paper while looking intently at his visitors in turn. The monsignor at the cardinal's side appeared transfixed as he too seemed to have a keen interest in the question as if it was his own. Dangerous waters held the clerics in strained concentration. This was heavy stuff, a boat too far out on the lake of a gathering theological storm. 'This incident,' he repeated with his cheeks pinched and strained, as if he were a jockey considering a high fence, 'it really does assert more than a dream. As we have it here. The return of Mary Walsh, your mother, must, theologically, make her disappearance an ascension and her reappearance a resurrection, a physical reality, complete with note and bedclothes passed on to her son, here. I see no difference between the Lord's physical appearance to his followers and the appearance of Mary Walsh to her son apart from the fact, that in the Lord's case, and according to Sacred Scripture, there were witnesses!' The cardinal extended his hands in the expression of a question awaiting an answer. All the while Larry was playing with little Ruth. The cardinal put the question more directly. 'Are we to presume, I refer to the Church, are we to presume that you too interpret what has taken place to bear the same gravity and importance as Christ's resurrection and ascension into Heaven?' In truth, the family had not placed any conscious theological significance to the events that overtook Larry's life. However, to everyone's surprise Larry, who was still playing with his child, took up the question and in doing so, made the cardinal a deal more careful as to his previous assumption that Larry was not taking the enquiry seriously.

'Your Eminence, which troubles you most, the fact that the event happened at all to a person of no importance in your eyes, or because of the resemblance to our Saviour's death, resurrection, and appearances to his follower? Do you believe, Your Eminence, that I have in some way vulgarised or made common, Christ's divinity, which I must add, we all share? Was it not an important bishop and Doctor of the Church, St Basil the Great, who clarified the status of the faithful when he declared, "...that Christ bestowed on us, the dignity of divinity...?" We also have John's Gospel tell us that, '...we are God's children...' The cardinal didn't answer the question immediately. It was quite evident to the company that he was weighing the implications of the question. Larry's questioning eyes beamed unflinching into those of the cardinal. The cleric couldn't be certain as to where Larry was heading with the question. A potent silence descended on proceedings. Father Kevin and Dee were themselves uncertain as to what was moving in Larry's mind.

The cardinal's head and eyes fell to his desk staring at it distractedly. Monsignor O' Rourke also dropped his head, his corpulent face revealing an incandescent heated glow. He knew instinctively that the cardinal was flummoxed. Larry's question seemed loaded. The cardinal set about shuffling papers in the three folders before him. He deliberately took his time making a point as he done so that he was not in any hurry. All the while he was still grappling to form an answer to Larry's provoking question. It appeared to Larry that he had utterly perplexed the cardinal and so offered him some other incidents pertinent to the core of the issue raised.

'Your Eminence, you must be familiar with the ascension of Elijah into heaven taken up in a whirlwind in a chariot of fire and fiery horses, and his return to earth again?' Larry was smiling. He loved to delve into scripture – it was his garden from childhood – he knew all the stories there, they were his plants, his puzzles. He knew perfectly well that the Holy Bible was only a dangerous jungle if you didn't care to make it your home.

'To answer your question Mr. Walsh. Yes I am familiar with the account. However, Elijah did not return, as expected, did he?'

'Well, now, Your Eminence, according to Matthew's account, he has Christ's infer that Elijah did return – that he returned in the spirit of John the Baptist. Does it not seem somewhat strange to you, Your Eminence, that the Church Councils never challenged Christ's remark on the subject of reincarnation?' The cardinal couldn't make up his mind as to whether Larry was simply being provocative or what? However, the cardinal ducked the remark and looked to his monsignor as if he could enlighten him on the subject. The monsignor's expression was as perplexed as the cardinal's.

'I think we are veering away from the point here, Mr. Walsh?' The cardinal waved a paper at Larry dismissively.

'Perhaps so, Your Eminence. The point I make here is how such strange events are left unquestioned just as with the case of Enoch who was also taken up into heaven. Consider too that in both accounts of Luke and Matthew Jesus himself speaks of people who will be taken up from the earth while others close by are left behind ... Remember too, Jesus' remark to Nathaniel "that he would see the angels of God descending and ascending ..."'

'So, now we are to consider your mother as an angel?' The cardinal openly expressed his impatience. However, Larry retorted calmly:

'What are angels, Your Eminence?'

'Messengers, Mr. Walsh. Messengers,' he replied with a certain degree of contempt as though Larry's mother was very remote from such celestial reality.

'And what did my mother return with, your Eminence, if not a message?' The cardinal's expression was now one of exasperation as he looked utterly distracted at his monsignor as if to make certain that his recorder was underlining Larry's remarks. Larry could see the cardinal's vexation and so remarked further:

'Why is my mother's ascension and return to earth such a difficulty for the Church to deal with when it accepts the extraordinary accounts of Elijah's and Enoch's ascensions, which, of their kind, are far more questionable?' The cardinal looked impatiently into Larry's questioning face.

'As mentioned before, Mr. Walsh, the Church is duty bound to investigate these claims for everyone's benefit.

I'm sure you can really appreciate our difficulty. I have no jurisdiction on the events of the past as recorded in the Holy Bible. Yes, I concede that there are issues in both Testaments that are strange to our way of thinking today, that prophecy comes to us in fragmentary form as scholars understand only too well. We attempt to interpret such events as best we can as custodians of the Scriptures – otherwise every individual would seek to interpret the scriptures according to their own fancy.' The cardinal continued somewhat slyly and with the deliberate intention of putting Larry on the spot.

'Mr. Walsh, by way of emphasis, I would like to bring to your attention the massacre in Waco Texas, USA, some years back where fifty-four adults and twenty-two children who lost their lives in a shootout with the FBI and a religious sect led by one charismatic individual, David Koresh. He was also considered a scripture scholar and expert and the final prophet of the Branch Davidian sect. Ultimately, he was responsible for the horrific deaths of these innocent and gullible individuals ... individuals, some seventeen of them, under the age of seventeen. These same teenagers indoctrinated by Koresh confirmed their faith and support for their leader. During the siege the camp headquarters was burnt to the ground, some claim by the use of CS gas used by the SWAT team involved in the siege and somehow ignited. I will not go into all the horrible details of the incident or the equally gory details of Koresh's twisted life and mind. Such horrible and dangerous situations and events, Mr. Walsh, are not uncommon occurrences. I simply refer to this particular tragedy hoping it will help you to further appreciate why the Church and state take what you bring before us here today as very serious matter.'

'I don't want to kill or hurt anyone!' Larry panicked at the implications levelled at him. He voice was raised. 'Tell him, Father Kevin! Tell him! I don't want to hurt people! Tell him, Dee! Tell him!' Larry was utterly shaken by the cardinal's inference.

'Of course you don't want to hurt anyone sweetheart. You couldn't hurt a living soul.' Dee put her arm round his shoulders almost in the same action as Father Kevin, each expressing the same concern for Larry. The cardinal and monsignor noted the fear in Larry's reactions. It did not console Larry when the cardinal added further anxiety to his disturbed state.

'You may not be capable of hurting people by your own hands, Mr. Walsh. However sincere your book, Larry's Law, may be, it has been distributed across the international world and many have already taken their own lives as a direct result of the changes that your instructions have imposed on them. There is chaos out there, Mr. Walsh, due to your revolutionary ideas. You claim that all these changes are directly due to messages that you have received from Heaven. You must read and listen to the world news in spite of having it controlled by those supporting your revolution.'

'It's not my revolution! It's not! Larry was half crazed with fright. 'Tell him Dee! Tell him Father Kevin!' The cardinal remained impassive until Dee intervened. She was absolutely furious.

Dee leapt to her feet stabbing her forefinger into the cardinal's astounded face – punctuating every sentence with a forward thrust of her arm in hostile agitation. Her beauty suddenly vanished in grimacing anger.

'How dare you infer a resemblance of Larry's work with the Waco Massacre? You know, cardinal,' she deliberately ignored his formal address, 'you may frighten my husband, a simple kindly person who wouldn't hurt a soul. You know perfectly well that everything in Larry's Law has its foundation in the essence of Christ's fundamental teaching of love and care for all people. You know too that the creed of love and care of all people has always been a challenge to a world all too willing to promote individualism. All the time the world has accepted the status quo, millions, I repeat millions, have starved to death. Despotic tyrants across the world, religious included, along with their armies, have continually subjected the defenceless, terrorizing them with rape, burning of their homes and mutilating those who were supposed to be in their care. The defenceless poor forced to vote for those who sought to exploit and crush them. Yes, the Catholic Church as well as other Christian Churches spoke out on behalf of the exploited and helped with charity through their various missionary works. Yes, governments across the world spoke out and brought in sanctions where they could. However, oil-rich countries and those able to retaliate with nuclear weaponry weakened the West's resolve forcing them to prostitute the defence of the vulnerable for the favour and need of oil for the West's own benefit. Nations pleading diplomatic immunity and sacred sovereignty led the whole powers of the world in a merry old dance. Money, cardinal, enabled all those atrocities to develop and fester like a pandemic across the world. Charity doled out by Church and State, cardinal, generous and urgent as it was by caring individuals and organisation, really achieved little more than a general sense of frustration. It was like throwing a crumb to the millions dying of merciless starvation. Larry's Law, as you already know has rid the world of the need of charity. By getting rid of money the world has become richer in the love and care of all. It was never in Larry's mind to start a new religion of his own. What has occurred across the world due to the new laws is really a social upheaval not a religious one – albeit that the love and care of all people has always been expressed as religious or sacred virtues. Every meaningful faith across the world worthy of the name contains those two very virtues as fundamental to their wisdom and belief. Both prove the worthiness of true religion where complex or dogmatic theology fails.

'The unfortunate suicides of individuals across the international world because of the changes brought in by Larry's law could not be avoided. These deaths were those of individuals running Drug cartels, banking executives, sovereign leaders and royalty ... despotic leaders who were no longer in control or power ... individuals and groups who lived off the backs of the poor and powerless. You forget the millions of deaths created by the spreading of Christianity and many other faiths. You overlook the mindless slaughter of thousands of lives by Christian Crusaders, and they with the blessing of Rome's holy expedience who put to the sword with mindless slaughter and butchery before the cross and teaching of Christ. Are we to forget the terrible tortures of the Spanish inquisition ... its merciless burning of so-called heretics and unbelievers, forgetting that faith in Christ was a gift to be accepted freely with freedom and understanding and never by force against conscience? No, cardinal, I repeat, don't you even dare infer that my husband, Larry, and his efforts in changing the former cesspit of a world has the faintest resemblance to the Waco Massacre.'

The room was deathly silenced as Dee re-seated herself to regain her composure. She was trembling from rage and insult. The cardinal was already very conscious of Dee's formidable standing in political circles as an important political journalist. However, in spite of feeling steamrolled by her angry defence, the Waco reference hit home, if only as a sobering thought. The cardinal lost some confidence and dignity in the heated exchange. He hadn't reckoned on Dee's forthright character. Her raised voice still echoed in his ears as it did with the rest of the company. The cardinal regained his own composure by his usual ploy, fiddling with his papers, and his pectoral cross. He shuffled about in his seat with much discomfort. Eventually he sought to conclude with the first issue.

'We can leave aside the matter of Mary Cassidy's healing. As far as the Church is concerned the matter will simply be recorded for now. You may take that as a positive recognition for the time being. We have been into the matter in some detail with the hospital and with Miss Cassidy's home background and history. Mysterious healings, Mr. Walsh, are also not uncommon to the Church and its people. However, your Mother's disappearance and her return with the message which gives instructions for you to form a world government is quite a different matter. We have taken the liberty, with your consent I remind you, of having the paper containing the message examined by experts in forensics and carbon dating.' There was a long pause as the cardinal and monsignor appeared to be studying Larry and Dee with a sense of wonder. There was both awe and question in their gaze. The cardinal continued. 'The report back from the carbon dating experts clearly state that the paper and ink used for the message are both of no known material to exist on earth. The attempt to cut a fraction of the paper for testing and burning purposes failed to produce any further evidence of the nature of the material except to say that it was impossible to cut the paper because it acted as water, which you know cannot be cut in liquid form. The scissors simply passed through the paper as if it was water. The attempt to burn a corner of the paper was equally unhelpful. The experts could not explain why a gas jet under pressure continued to be pushed back on itself. This was attempted precisely one thousand times with precisely the same results. Their conclusion was a request to keep the material for further scientific analysis and further experiment. For now we could not agree to their request.' The cardinal held the paper aloft waving it slowly punctuating the air with an expression of utter incomprehension. Father Kevin shuddered in his chair as if a ghost had entered the stately office. The clerics opposite noted Father Kevin's unease. They looked at him directly but offered him no solace. The cardinal directed his attention once more to Larry and Dee. 'Since we could not draw any sensible conclusion for the tests done on the paper and message we can only hold onto the document and the results of the test as Recorded Matter to be held in the Vatican Archives.'

The cardinal, still feeling quite ruffled, went to the next item on the list of inquiries. 'The next issue the Church wishes to address refers to your book, Mr. Walsh, I refer to page 259 where you consider cerebral operations as appropriate procedure on the criminally insane, albeit with the aid of accomplished surgeons and doctors. How on earth did you ever come to even consider such an intrusion on a human person's mind? Do you have any practical knowledge or experience of such complex work?' The cardinal waved the opened book in the air for emphasis.

'I was shown their suffering and heard their screams; some in straightjackets and kept in padded cells throwing themselves at the padded walls in an attempt to stop their mental torment; others walked in dark corridors, their bodies limp and their faces grey in brooding depression and despair. I was shown patients attacking each other and the psychiatric doctors and lay staff. It was all so inhuman and horrible. I couldn't walk away from it all and pretend it was not happening.' Larry was in tears as he related his experience.

'Are you telling me, Mr. Walsh, that you experienced all this personally? Did you in fact spend some period of your life in psychiatric care?' The cardinal leaned well forward across the desk impassive and impervious to Larry's tearful condition, hoping with an expression of renewed vigour on his face that Larry had indeed spend a period in psychiatric care.

'No. I was never in psychiatric care myself.' His answer was empathic. He added: 'I was taken there in a vision …' Larry was attempting to explain but was quickly interrupted – too quickly in fact. Dee was getting angrier by the second.

'Do you mean in a dream, Mr. Walsh and not an actual vision? Were you awake and conscious when all this took place?' The cardinal was pressurising Larry as if he was on trial for his own sanity.

'I don't know if I was conscious.' Larry snapped his answer making his irritation plain to the cardinal. 'I only know it was a vision.'

'And you decided on the fate of these individuals based on your vision, is that correct?' The cardinal seemed to be growing in conviction that this man before him was a very disturbed individual.

'No. I did not!' Larry retaliated. 'Because of those terrible visions we visited several institutions across Ireland and the European Continent on the advice of the

Guardians of the People and in company of other professional members of the guardians of the new laws. All the doctors questioned as to their personal and professional opinion on the matter of mind-altering surgery declared unanimously, that given the choice of treatment and for the peace of the patient, they would be quite willing to surgically treat the worst of those suffering from the severest tormenting conditions of the mind. Many volunteered, without prompting, to be more than willing to perform such surgical procedures on their own suffering relatives if the need arose. These same specialists assured us that keeping patients with severe depression in a continuous drugged state was far more inhuman than the calming conditions brought about by surgical intervention. The surgeons were honest enough to state truthfully that most patients with severe depression or tormenting conditions were limited to menial servile tasks after surgery, but at least they had peace and were active in worthwhile occupation, albeit rudimentary tasks. At least they were content and free of mental persecution even though their original character was altered. Such patients were active in parks collecting the fallen leaves of autumn or picking up litter. They found a new peace. There were other simple tasks that they were capable of in factories and offices under strict supervision. All-in-all these poor unfortunate people who had been the misfortunate victims of nature's own imprecision were given a distinct degree of contentment, even if unable to experience the greater heights of happiness that were only available to those with complete mental health. That, Your Eminence, is what I have based such procedures upon.' The cardinal moved slowly back across the table crestfallen and disappointed, in spite of Larry's enlightened disclosure. Dee lowered her beautiful face. She felt every discomfort that Larry experienced. From time to time she would smile into his face and squeeze his hand to bring him confidence and comfort. Larry was all the stronger and calmer for her support. Father Kevin also kept an assuring hand on Larry's shoulder. Baby Ruth was also a comforting distraction to the family as she gurgled playfully lending a homely ambience of sound to the stressful situation.

By way of distraction Cardinal Dwyer looked over at Monsignor O' Rourke who was still confidently attending to the workings of the recorder; he also continued to speedily fill page upon page in his spiral jotters with shorthand notes. Such recording had by now taken on a new and graver importance, given all that had passed during the investigation, much of which was quite involved and unexpected. The cardinal was gradually taking Larry more seriously. He had long since realised that he was held in high regard by his wife, whom the cardinal knew was a very competent and formidable journalist. He knew also that Father Kevin had every confidence in Larry's sincerity and in the work he was undertaking in the formation of a world government. And yet for the purposes and credibility of the enquiry the cardinal had to keep these thoughts and impressions to one side. To that end he continued with a new issue and moved his immediate attention and focus back to Larry.

The cardinal turned to Item Five on the list and once more picked up the book on Larry's Law. He opened the book marked at page 300 and waved it about menacingly, his expression clearly showing his sneering contempt as if the pages were covered in filth. 'You say here,' the cardinal remarked stabbing the page with his bony finger, 'Mr. Walsh, that traditional religious leadership and authority must be curtailed ... that it be limited to the teaching of the two virtues of love and the care of all people. Do I understand the implications of this statement correctly, Mr. Walsh; that the authority of Peter given to him by Christ himself to teach and govern the Church has now been passed into your hands?' The cardinal's expression held a menacing threat. Until Larry replied.

'Did Christ order the Spanish Inquisition which Rome let loose on its people in Spain with all its barbaric and merciless tortures? Did Christ order the burning of natural healers condemned as witches? ... the martyrdom of hundreds of men and women, simply because they belonged to a different faith ... or were they the unfortunate recipients of the wrong indoctrination? Did Christ order the so-called Holy Wars of Rome's slaughtering Crusaders? Did Christ order the slaughter of those with other beliefs simply because they lived in the wrong country? Did he order the indexing of scientific knowledge because it contradicted erroneous Church teaching, which was little more than fanciful supposition? Are we now to be surprised that Science attacks the Church and all other religions considering their followers the dinosaurs of ancient times, maimed by fallacious learning and wanton superstitions? Your Eminence, before the inspired intervention of Larry's Law, for which I take no credit except as its messenger, simple people across the international world were ashamed to see the main world religions tearing each other apart, fighting for power in what came to be contemptuously referred to in Jerusalem as the Holy City. Not only were decent Christians, Muslims and Orthodox faiths scandalized by such fighting and bickering, those fighting factions became the laughing stock of every decent human being capable of grasping the utter madness of it all by their enlightened reasoning. Those people fighting over so called holy places had lost the plot. They were fighting over external and unimportant buildings. All of that nonsense was little more than the fallout of the bloody slaughter of thousands of Christians and Muslims in vying Crusading wars. Surely it was far better to visit the poor and deprived in so many other parts of the world and care for them. That is the true Holy Land, the true pilgrimage of every human being.' Larry's expression was sickened as the scenes of past religious atrocities committed in the name of Rome and its disfigurement of Christ's teaching came to him even as he spoke. He could hear their screams, see the bloody slaughter of the thousands of corpses in a city set ablaze, its ragged flags like mocking faces in the carnage of inhuman slaughter piled up in mountainous heaps before him and all set ablaze to ward off wanton disease.

The cardinal was quick to pounce. 'So you do question the divine authority of Peter given by Christ himself ... the authority passed on in succession down through the Church to this present age and now in the very capable hands of His Holiness, Pope Dominic Ubutu. X11?' The cardinal's face was now a prancing expression of smug superiority. Larry could read the cardinal's contempt as did the rest of the company.

'How is it, Your Eminence, that the Church of the Nineteenth Century declared papal infallibility when speaking on faith and morals? That, in spite of all its own shameful example concerning the depraved morality and unethical actions of its highly positioned leadership. Remember too that Paul had to go and challenge the apostle Peter in Jerusalem for his lack of learning and his hypocrisy on the matter of Jewish converts insisting on the need for circumcision which they, in their ignorance, attempted to chain convert Christians to the Law and not to the grace of faith in Jesus Christ which Paul professed. So Peter's power and authority had to be challenged and corrected by one more learned than himself. Ignorance, Your Eminence, can never legitimise its claim to infallibility. So, to answer your question directly, I do question all religious authority if it lacks true wisdom and discernment based on the very principles on which Larry's Law was founded, that of the love and care of all peoples, irrespective of their childhood indoctrination or religion. You know perfectly well, Your Eminence, that all there is to know about the faith we share in Christ is the love of love itself, which you know to be the name and life of God, and to love your neighbour as yourself. That, Your Eminence, is all that Larry's Law professes concerning religion. It is also the entire teaching of Christ wrapped up in the simplest terms for any humble person to grasp and understand; none could object to that and be called human or enlightened. That, Your Eminence, is the entire message of human salvation. That too is true worship that does not even require a building to worship in. It is the sacrifice of the Mass lived out on the streets where all are expected to live in a living communion in sacrificial service to each other. Looking after each other in Charity and love, that Your Eminence is the true consecration of the Mass by the people on the streets and in the slums of every deprived nation. That is true priesthood ... true apostolic authority.' Larry stared hard into the cardinal's furious face. Father Kevin face flinched so often when Larry challenged the cardinal. At times he ground his teeth showing them visibly in nervous expectation of some terrible response. He was more and more convinced that

Larry had no wish to court the cardinal's favour. It was also patently obvious that Larry's memory, reading and comprehension far surpassed that of Cardinal Dwyer. Dee noted Father Kevin's discomfort and awkwardness. She too sympathised with him over his main concern to reach Rome and have Larry unburden himself of his warning. Nonetheless, the cardinal was not really helping the situation forward with his personal attitude and provocations. It was certainly not neutral ground.

'So there we have it.' The cardinal snapped. 'No Petrine authority and no more need of the sacraments that Christ himself instituted. Would I be correct in that conclusion Mr. Walsh?' the cardinal asked contemptuously.

'No, you would not! I hear the contempt in your voice, Your Eminence. What I say to you in all clarity is, that when the office of Peter speaks the truth it cannot be contradicted since the truth can never be other that it is. However, when the office of Peter prostitutes its authority with commands contrary to Christ's own teaching of love of one's enemies, then the Christian is free to ignore that office and so be free to follow their informed and enlightened conscience based on the true teaching of Christ himself. The history of Peter's office, whether the chair of that authority presided in Rome or in the Avignon Papacy of France, has left a very great stench in the religious nostrils of Christendom down through the centuries. You cannot glare down on me with your blind sneering sanctimonious righteousness as if defending the virgin purity of Rome. For too often that Chair of Peter's authority was used as little more than a latrine of convenience in shameful armed crusades and international corruption. So, Your Eminence, you have no reason to belittle or be contemptuous of my lay state and lack of importance as if the garments of your high office and the privilege of this grand edifice cleanse the stench behind them.'

After these invectives the cardinal and his monsignor were puce with rage. Larry had hit back for the hurt Dee had experienced in his defense. Father Kevin's head was buried in his chest, his face a glowing ember. He didn't know what was coming next from the fuming clerics opposite. Dee was elated to hear her simple Larry kick back at them in a way that only he could when forced from his own inspired depths. She didn't encounter Larry in this way often; he was a peaceful soul – yet she knew this dept was always there.

'May I remind you, Mr. Walsh, that all you are saying is still being recorded and will be placed before His Holiness, Pope Dominic Ubutu X11 in Rome, that he would have every right and the grounds to excommunicate you from the Roman Catholic Church and community for just the half of what you are declaring and implying – Do you realize that?'

'Your, Eminence, there are two faces to Rome; the first which honestly attempts to speak truth plainly. When Christ prayed for his followers to be consecrated in truth he did not intend them to indulge in questionable or fanciful theology or to hide behind unquestionable authority.

'The second Rome, Your Eminence, is lost, entangled in its own maze of presumptuous doctrine and laws; it speaks when it should be silent and silent when it should speak. For example: for many years it denied victims of suicide a burial place among the faithful in consecrated ground, with all the torment and heartache such laws imposed on grieving families; vulnerable families who were indoctrinated to believe that their loved ones were rejected by God, Church and community alike and so lost forever. That God, Your Eminence, was a fabrication of Roman Catholic authority blinded by its own pomposity, ignorance and presumption ... lost in the mire of its own heartless and merciless law-making. Poor unlearned families left to live out their miserable existence believing that such a God really existed and had the very character that your heartless laws and presumptions ascribed to it.

'Your Eminence, when Rome fails to serve virtue, expressed in the love and care of all people, it has by that very neglect, ceased to have Petrine authority. In consequence, the people of God – God's own family, no longer have a duty to listen to it, believe in it, or follow it. Love and care, Your Eminence, is all the authority you have. Remember, Your Eminence, how Christ lampooned the authorities of his own time who occupied the Chair of Moses. He advised his followers to listen to that authority but not to follow their example because they loaded unnecessary burdens on the people without lifting a finger to help them. In fact, he went further in his criticism when he pointed out that their leaders went to the extremes to find a single proselyte and, when found, would make him twice a fit for hell as they were? Do not mistake me, Your Eminence, I do have every respect for Rome's authority to teach, guide and promulgate such teaching and guidance. However, such guidance must always put to the forefront of it laws the vulnerable nature of God's family. It must never seek to have its own authority closed to question from outside – or to have its authority held in sacred veneration as if all wisdom and insight into human understanding and learning only emerges through the institutional authority and Church of Rome.

'Remember too, Your Eminence, how Jesus was astonished at the faith of a pagan centurion who asked for his favorite servant to be healed ... how Jesus remarked that the faith of that pagan centurion was unique in the whole of Israel.'

'What point are your trying to make here, Mr. Walsh?' The cardinal was utterly lost the expression of his widely outstretched hands indicated his confusion.

'The point I make, Your Eminence, is that the pagan centurion was able to transcend the authority of his own pagan indoctrination and deities out of his love and concern for a lowly servant whom he loved. He was able to put his faith in a complete stranger for the good of a fellow human being. It is little wonder that Jesus was astonished at his faith. Put simply, Your Eminence, inflexible authority can be blinding, wayward and downright abusive.'

When Larry ceased to speak a great burst of sunlight came in a beam across his face. The entire study exploded into light as though the occupants were in a world of light. The significance was not lost on the company as all screened their eyes from its brilliance. As the beam of light slowly receded it was as if a spirit walked out of the room. All looked to each other as if to ask, what was all that about? It appeared in a strange inexplicable way to calm the cardinal. He called for a lunch break.

Cardinal Christopher Dwyer and Monsignor Sean O' Rourke dined together. They ate in their own private dining room, not as a direct hostile rebuff to their guests; they needed the space to collect their wits from the heat of the moment and to calm down.

'...Your opinion of him, Sean?' The cardinal asked, spooning a steaming broth soup after soaking it with torn bread.

'Scholar and simpleton ... as recorded by another's description, Cork University no less.'

'... But your own opinion...?' The cardinal persisted.

'As described, Chris; I would add, an idealist.'

'For heaven's sake, Sean, we're all blooming idealists – isn't that what all religion aspires to!' The cardinal smiled philosophically and added; 'you're usually more forthcoming, Sean, sharpen it man!'

'Ok, Chris. I believe him to be sincere. I'm convinced he's here strictly on the Holy Father's behalf concerning the danger he believes the pontiff to be in.'

'Sorry to interrupt, Sean. Do we have precise details of the nature of the danger in this warning of his?'

'No, Chris – just to say that it is urgent and imminent ... seems to want to keep the details to himself for some inexplicable reason, except to say that the message and its details must pass from himself directly to the Holy Father. Sorry, Chris. That's about the thick of it.'

'So... a sack full of nothing on that one, then?' The cardinal frowned resignedly, now helping himself to the main course of sliced beef, steaming buttered jacket potatoes, cabbage and turnips. He drowned the beef with gravy speaking over its flow.

'What did Cork University make of him, other than a mixture of scholar and simpleton?'

'Industrious, when left alone – a dam pest when in company.' The monsignor remarked tearing at the beef with a serrated knife and fork. Sean was responsible for chasing up such details.

'A pest ...' the cardinal paused in his own struggle with the beef.

'...Seems he just loves company ... over the top stuff, like. His colleagues loved him ... still do. The point being, he distracted everyone from their work ... wanting to chatter all the while. The staff had to virtually lock him up in his own study to force him to concentrate on his own work. What he did hand in was powerful stuff.'

'...Intellectual, then Sean?' The cardinal surmised from Sean's inference.

'No, Chris ... a visionary. That's the University's conclusion. They say that he can be penetratingly logical but that his real strength lies in his unique gift to perceive by vision the conclusion to the most exacting and perplexing conundrums.'

'He's certainly articulate,' the cardinal remarked reflectively, 'that's for sure. I begin to see the dual sides of his character now. You know, this scholar-simpleton thing, did you note how like a child he became when I poured the Waco case over him ... frightened out of his wits he was.' There was a certain sense of wonder in the cardinal's expression. The extreme contradiction of Larry's character was certainly a cause for wonder to him. 'Well let's hope the next session is less tempestuous than this morning's, Sean. It hasn't done my piles any favor, they're raw again.'

'Well. Amen to an easier session, Chris. As to the piles, you need frozen peas – that is all the hospitals advise and very effective they are indeed.' The monsignor chuckled at his vision of the cardinal in bed at night with a packet of frozen peas wedged up his backside.

Meanwhile Father Kevin and company shared a similar meal in their own make-shift dining room. They were now at the late stage of coffee, tea, cheese and fruit. Baby Ruth was smiling contentedly after being fed. The smart young housekeeper busied herself with serving and clearing, unintentionally interrupting the personal direction of the conversation by her frequent appearances. The clatter of dish-washing formed the ambience over the muted conversation.

'Bless you, Larry.' Father Kevin was speaking over his teacup, you held up well in there. I am delighted and proud of you. I could feel the pressure myself. It's important that we hold our ground until the thing is over with for your own peace of mind, Larry. Once you impart your message to the Holy Father you will have fulfilled your duty and mission to him.'

'Not before time,' Dee remarked resentfully. She still felt raw from what she experienced as the bullying nature of Cardinal Dwyer's attitude. Father Kevin's head dropped; he felt awkward since he was encouraging the family to stick it out in order to achieve Larry's peace of mind. Dee realized this. She indicated her appreciation as she leaned close to Father Kevin seated at the head of a very small improvised table and kissed his cheek. His hand caressed the back of her golden silk hair, her rich sweet perfume wafting into his relieved smile. It was father and daughter with them again. Both loved each other. That fact was not lost on the cardinal and his monsignor who had hoped that Father Kevin might have been their natural fraternal supporter, in the-cling-of-cloth-to-cloth. However, Father Kevin, because of his long association and closeness to this particular family over many years, could not even be neutral. He might just as well be classed as a member of the family. Nonetheless, he was forced to be present as the family parish priest and as the main instrument for the family's reason for being there.

It surprised no one when Larry went missing. He was on walk-about in the kitchen telling the waitress, chef and other kitchen staff all about himself and his family. He was showing off his beautiful baby to all. It was like a home-coming in spite of the fact that they didn't know Larry from the man in the moon ... he had that effect on all people. Friendliness just oozed out of him without apparent effort or design. He had all their names off by heart as he came back to his family informing them of all the intimate details of his new friends. Of course Father Kevin and Dee just smiled through the deluge of details. They were used to it all. That was Larry day and night, a natural chatterbox, when not lost in his own thoughts.

The cardinal and monsignor sauntered into their respective seats in the study. The family was on time as a mark of respect; they wanted the end of this day and supposed the clerics felt the same. All took in deep breaths, straightening their bodies in attentive postures. Monsignor O' Rourke set the sound recorder to a new chapter as Cardinal Dwyer set the agenda of the next point of discussion.

He peered at the list of enquiries. That in turn prompted him to open the book Larry's Law once more and directed the group's attention.

'Mr. Walsh, can I refer you to Item 6 on the list, marked "Married Clergy, Women Priests, Celibacy and Virginity." I am quoting from page 790. Here you cite the married state for priests as a more beneficial one for clergy. Would you care to expand on that view?' The cardinal's voice feigned indifference to the subjects, yet his face revealed his sneering contempt for what he had convinced himself to be a deliberate attack and disrespect for the state of celibacy and virginity in religious life ... a state which has always been held in the highest regard for many centuries in the Roman Catholic Church.

'It should be sufficient to quote here, Your Eminence, the Creation account of the Book of Genesis where God states that is not good for man to be on his own; so God gave him a woman for company and for continuation of human life on earth; he did not give him another man for companionship. There is great wisdom and observation in that fundamental necessity, Your Eminence.'

The cardinal responded sarcastically. 'So. The sacrifice made by thousands of unmarried, celibate priest, and the vows of chastity and virginity, dutifully preserved by countless religious sisters over the years in order to serve the Church communities by being unimpeded by personal family pressures ... to look after their Church communities, or to give their lives in service as missionaries across the world ... bringing the word of God to primitive tribal peoples in the grip of countless fears and superstitions ... bringing education and setting up schools in remote and hostile regions across the world ... all of that, then, is to be regarded by you and your supporters, Mr. Walsh, as an utter waste of their time and their sacrifice?' The cardinal's face was set in grinding hatred.

'I would never debase the sacrifice that such honorable celibate clergy and religious sisters have made. I realise too that Matthew's writing reminds us that Jesus remarked that there are "those who make themselves eunuchs for the kingdom of heaven." I simply make the point that the married clergy of other faiths managed just as well in spite of having their own families to be concerned with. Married life and personal companionship were experienced as cherished and fulfilling supports. Such things are well documented if you wish to take the trouble to look into the matter.' Here, Larry's wide learning eclipsed that of the cardinal – what's more, the cardinal knew it. Larry continued:

'Your Eminence, I regret to raise the terrible scandal and abuses of children and vulnerable adults across the Catholic world by pedophile priests and other religious. Rome's insistence on the celibate state for its clergy was always going to be an open door for sexual perversion for many clerics, even those at the very highest ranks of its institution, pontiffs and abbots included – as such evidence came to light. Your Eminence, without flogging this unsavory subject and its shameful history to death, it is enough to say that if you go against natural healthy instincts, nature will kick back in twisted perversion.

'Before the writing of Larry's Law, Your Eminence, there was much consultation with the experience of many other faiths. All agreed that celibacy as a servant of freedom to serve was simply fundamentally flawed and an open door to perversion for many lacking the moral and spiritual strength for that state ... that many who discovered their weakness too late felt too ashamed or too proud to leave their position and so faced a private unspeakable hell, an utterly botched up existence. It was agreed in the writing of the new laws in consultation with other faiths and medical opinion as well as many of our our own theologians, that celibacy on demand for clergy was an abuse in itself to human relationship. I'm surprised, Your Eminence, that you were not personally part of that consultation.'

The cardinal face was on fire. He saw no one – looked at no one – but glared with riveting eyes at the tumbling lights on the recording device beside the monsignor. He was so outraged by this turn of events he was visibly shaken. The truth was that the cardinal himself was one of the guilty parties once discovered to have covered up for several pedophile priests in his own diocese. Larry had no knowledge of that point; so there was no hint of personal malice in Larry's remarks. Monsignor O' Rourke only dared to catch a surreptitious glimpse of the cardinal's distraught face glaring at the recorder for no other reason than to cover up his cringing embarrassment. There was no hiding place in the room for the cardinal. Two members of the company knew of the cardinal's past failings in the cover-up, the monsignor beside him, and Dee in her work as a journalist – both, however, remained silent. Monsignor Sean was cringing in embarrassment and appeared with his head almost on the desk as if he wanted the ground to open up and swallow the whole proceedings.

It was with great pain and discomfiture that the cardinal raised the next point. 'You make a pressing case for the role of women priests as well as married priests to serve in the Catholic Church. Let us put aside the issue of married male priests for now. I see from your book that since you have dispensed with the use of money in the new world then the problem of cost has no bearing on the case of married clergy. However, the more important point to be considered here, Mr. Walsh is, how do you imagine that a woman priest can represent the male gender of Christ's priesthood? The prophecy concerning the coming of a Messiah to restore mankind from its fallen state of sin and so usher in mankind's redemption would be the sacrifice of God's only Son; it required a spotless sinless male not a female daughter of God, since he had not begotten one. How do you skate round that problem, Mr. Walsh?' The cardinal showed a sneering confident smile. He considered that he had Larry tied up in knots with this one. Was he going to deny Jesus as the redeeming Son of God?

'Your Eminence, why do you think Christ was put to death on the cross? Why do you think he allowed it to happen?' Larry was quite calm with his questions, all the while playing with little Ruth's hands.

'As scripture itself tells us plainly, Mr. Walsh, for the salvation of the world ... for the forgiveness of sins ... So that people could have a model of forgiveness to follow. He offered humanity another way of life to live for each other and not for personal gain and power. His resurrection, Mr. Walsh, would be the proof of whether his death was a delusion of his own making or that his divine life and sacrifice were accepted and acknowledged by the power of God! How does that answer suit you, Mr. Walsh?' The cardinal's confidence seemed to be restored in his own mind's eye. He beamed at Larry and the company in general, as if he was the superior competitor in a theological dispute.

'Well put, Your Eminence. May I just ask respectfully, and without the intention of giving you offence, was he crucified for his gender of for what he taught and for what he claimed to be?' The cardinal turned swiftly to look to his monsignor for an answer. Both clerics were stunned. Both were so tongue-tied from being institutionalized and constrained by dogma and orthodoxy that they couldn't have imagined the implications of Larry's questions. Larry could see their confusion and so offered the cardinal a lifeline.

'Your Eminence, may I put the question another way? Can a woman minister, or woman priest teach what Christ himself taught? Can a woman call on the Holy Spirit to consecrate the bread and wine on the altar so that both elements become the Body and Blood of Christ ... the Real Presence, if you wish? Or would the biological gender of a woman be such an impasse, such an insurmountable obstacle, as to render her incapable of calling on the power of the Holy Spirit, who actually does the work?' Larry waited patiently for a reply. Both clerics were so taken aback by the lucidity of Larry's reasoning that they were afraid to answer. The cardinal sensed that he was digging a very deep hole for himself in his attempts to outwit Larry on the theological front. The cardinal's mind raced for an appeal to authority in order to intimidate his opponent. He realized it was futile. He stared hard at Larry and moved his eye line to his wife and Father Kevin to gauge their reaction to his own sense of confusion. Both their heads were lowered to spare the cardinal his crushing embarrassment. Slowly his focus returned to Larry and thought, how can this individual be referred to as a simpleton? He knew plainly, now, that he was afraid of Larry's appeal to reason. The cardinal realised that as a servant of the Church of Rome he did not have the freedom to argue with Larry from the starting point of reason. Since faith was not open to or the servant of reason, the cardinal felt shackled, even resentful, since reason always seemed to be the stronger camp. He was caught in the Church's constraints of having to accept Paul's opinion ... that faith speaks of things beyond the mind of man. Larry's view on that opinion was, if any knowledge is beyond the mind of man, then the statement itself is a total nonsense, a self-contradiction. It is like saying, reason and intellect are no-go-areas to faith and religion ... that religion is so other worldly one is forced to accept anything held in the sphere of faith, no matter how ludicrous or unreasonable. Larry viewed this manner of thinking as the ghost of fear itself, a self-induced and self-perpetuating oppressor. Larry held that It was one thing to be open-minded to strange events and inexplicable mysteries in the world, yet quite another to have nonsensical doctrine imposed on the ignorant whether by Religion or by Science. This strange world of theological presumption reminded Larry of the words of the German philosopher, Ludwig Wittgenstein who remarked,

"Whereof one cannot speak, thereof one must be silent."

It is a great pity, Larry considered, that the religions of the world failed to have the grace and humility to own and treasures such advice.

The cardinal shuffled uncomfortably in his seat, several times revolving his neck and attempting, with some effort, to appear quite relaxed. From the look on his pinched features, he gave the impression of calm indifference. Yet within, he was in utter confusion as to what to make of Larry's real intellectual and Catholic position. The cardinal was duty bound to record for the Holy Father a clear impression as to where Larry stood as a practicing Roman Catholic. As far as the cardinal was concerned, at this juncture, Larry might just as well be classed as a humanist, but one still clinging to the last threads of his Catholic faith. With such thoughts swimming in his pedantic mind he put a very involved question to the unsuspecting Larry.

'Mr. Walsh, I want to raise one last important issue with you here; it concerns the Sacrifice of the Mass, as it relates to the Holy Eucharist, the Real Presence of Christ in the consecrated species of Bread and Wine, and the need to consume this food as a crucial imperative in order to receive life in Christ. Do you actually understand the Church's teaching on this vital necessity?' The cardinal leaned forward on his desk with his elbows and propped his chin on the tips of his joined hands. His eyes were riveted to Larry's face. Dee turned to Father Kevin with a questioning look as if to ask, where in heaven's name are we going now? She read the priest's face. His eyes were partially screwed in puzzlement and his brow furrowed, indicating a distinct unease with the cardinal's question and his body language. Was the cardinal attempting to entrap Larry with this hoary old chestnut which was kicked about Christendom like a football until The Council of Trent of [1545-1563] settled the rather controversial doctrine, as to what is received in the consecrated species of bread and wine from the altar? Trent stated clearly and without the slightest ambiguity, from its own point of references of course, that Scripture, Tradition, and the infallible magisterium of the Church from which it maintained that the consecrated species of bread and wine became the Real Presence of Christ, albeit a mysterious one. Father Kevin opened his hands a little, indicating to Dee his own puzzlement and discomfort. Dee became all the more alert and focused as a result of her friend's unease. The cardinal watched this exchange of quizzical expressions between them and showed a confident smirk on his thin face with its scheming expression. He could clearly sense their unease with this issue. Larry, to his credit, seemed un-phased. But did he realise that this was dangerous ground? None of the company was quite sure where the cardinal was about to run with this issue, not even Monsignor Sean who sat on his right and showed his own expression of bewilderment. In any event, Larry replied to the question calmly.

'Yes, Your Eminence, indeed I do understand the question and the need to consume the body and blood of Christ as a true and living presence.'

'I am delighted to hear you say so, Mr. Walsh.' Cardinal Dwyer gave one of his characteristic sideways bows and managed a sickly smile. 'We know from Father Kevin's communications with the Diocese, Mr. Walsh, that you regularly attend Holy Mass, even on weekdays, which I find highly commendable.'

'Thank you, Your Eminence. It is good of you to acknowledge that,' Larry replied with a beaming smile and a smart sideway's tilt of his own head. The cardinal sneered to himself. He probably didn't give a tinker's toss if Larry attended Mass ten times every day. He now revealed the real issue on his mind as he said menacingly:

'The Church is very much aware and concerned with the emphasis that your book places on the Real Presence of Christ, Body and Blood being most critically present and received on the streets of every nation in the world. Would you clarify for us exactly what you mean by that? And while you are at it can you inform us as to what you believe you receive in the Holy Eucharist from the altar in church during the Sacrifice of the Mass since you receive Holy Communion so regularly?' The penny dropped in Father Kevin's thoughts as he reflected to himself – you sneaky old rascal, Dwyer. If Larry says the wrong thing, I will be pulled apart for not instructing him properly in his faith. He smiled to himself and thought. You pay Larry a complement for his regularity at Holy Mass and his reception of the Lord on a daily basis, but only to weave a web of flattery to ensnare him and entrap his priest at the same time. Clever! – By God! – How bloody clever! –

The priest was feeling vulnerable. He could gauge from the blatant smirk on the cardinal's conniving face that he reveled in the priest's discomfort. Father Kevin was concerned for Larry; he knew the results and recordings of these meetings were going to be scrutinized in every minute detail by Rome because of Larry's widespread influence on the people and his strict emphasis of the Love and Care of all people as the most important aspects of human salvation.

'Love. Your Eminence!' Larry remarked proudly.

'What has that to do with the question, Mr. Walsh?' The cardinal's head shot back in irritation.

'It is what I receive in Holy Communion, Your Eminence,' said Larry with equal fervour.

'Not the Body, Blood, soul and Divinity, whole and entire, the Real Presence of Christ?' The Cardinal was trying to pour the whole of the Council of Trent's Dogma on top of Larry in summary form, and with all the venom of expression he could pull on his contemptuous face.

'… All of what you said, Your Eminence, and a bit more besides ….' Larry was rubbing his hands enthusiastically.

'" … and a bit more besides." What is that supposed to mean?' The scowling cardinal enquired.

'Love, Your Eminence – the whole of God entire in substance, soul, divinity, power, Spirit – everything, Your Eminence – nothing missing.' Larry continued to rub his hands in fits and starts. Unknown to him his actions were being recorded in shorthand by Monsignor Sean who was smirking to himself because he knew perfectly well, being familiar with the torturous technicalities and Dogma of Trent, that Larry was also aware of the same dogma and doctrine. His answer took in the whole of the essence of the doctrine with that one word "Love," as the entirety, purpose, and being of God.

Cardinal Dwyer sat back as one defeated as if he was in the presence of an utter lunatic or some mad mystic who was wired to the moon – uncoupled from logic, reason and incapable of a straight answer to a straight question. The cardinal put his left hand to the side of his face and looked around at every aspect of his study with his eyes looking to heaven for consolation and patience.

Father Kevin allowed himself to relax, as did Dee. They both knew now that Larry was never going to allow himself to get tangled up in the torturous labyrinth and knots of the Council of Trent's Dogmatic doctrine. Even Monsignor Sean allowed himself a few moments of calm. Sometimes it felt to him, while beside the cardinal, as if he was sitting too close to a bubbling volcano.

Presently the Cardinal calmed down sufficiently to pursue the issue in more detail. 'Let us be a little clearer, Mr. Walsh.' The cardinal was breathing noisily through his thin nostrils again. 'In what way do you believe that people on the streets of the entire world receive the Body and Blood of Christ in "Love" as you so mysteriously put it?' The cardinals wrists leaned on the desk with his hands limply apart in a pleading expression, as if to ask, just a simple answer will do, please.

'We become what we receive, what we believe, Your Eminence.' Larry gave his head an assertive nod.'

'"We become what we receive,"' the cardinal repeated in a soft tone, yet straining his patience. 'Meaning what precisely, Mr. Walsh?'

'The follower must become like his Master,'

Larry remarked boldly, with another affirming nod of his head.

'God give me patience, Mr. Walsh. Can you not give a straight forward answer to anything?'

'You mustn't blame me for what Jesus himself says or the way he speaks. Larry wagged his index finger at the cardinal as if scolding a naughty child. The cardinal raised his two hands high to heaven as he exclaimed in exasperation:

'All right, Mr. Walsh; alright; explain it in your own way in your own time, only please, in a way in which we can all understand.'

Father Kevin shielded his face from the cardinal's wretched sense of defeat; Dee had done precisely the same thing. Monsignor Sean was also shielding the side of his face from the cardinal; he half expected the volcano to bubble over at any moment.

'It's a long story, Your Eminence,' Larry began confidently.

'O please, indulge us! We are all ears.' The cardinal's eyes reached the heavens once more – his face angelic, but his piles on fire as he lifted his burning bottom a little to ease the fire below.

'It's the Baptism, you see, Your Eminence.' The cardinal lifted his left hand to shield the side of his face again to look everywhere and at nothing. He was determined not to interrupt. He was convinced that Walsh would be even more enigmatic. So he allowed him full reign.

'Yes. You see the Baptism makes us God's sons and daughters – that means everyone, Your eminence. So you see, when we become God's children in Baptism and allow our lives to become like his through our daily conversion to a life of virtue, then we become one in God in Love. We become like him, we live in him – we live his life. So we become the food of God for others because we live like Christ – we become a Real Presence in the Love and Care we show for all people. We become Christ's flesh and blood because we become what we receive, you see.' No the cardinal didn't see but he wasn't going to interrupt and allow himself to be any more confused than he already was.

'You see, Your Eminence, when we live the life of Christ as his brother or sister, we die to the old way of life of caring only for ourselves and our own interests. In order to do that, we must allow our new lives in Christ to be consumed in living a life of service to others. What we do for others in love and care we do in communion with each other. We feed God in the sick, the naked the homeless, the hungry the prisoners ... Jesus stated that clearly in Matthew's writing, as you know yourself, Your Eminence. We expend ourselves as the Body and Blood of Christ. We are the same as Jesus. He makes us Divine.

'Finally, Your Eminence, there's the Last Judgment.' Cardinal Dwyer glanced heavenward again in exasperation – If only it could be the last judgment of this bloody mystic or whatever he is. God give me patience, he thought.

'We know that Jesus says of the last Judgment in Matthew's writing, mentioned above, that what we do to others we do to him. Therefore, Your Eminence, it you neglect to love and care for others you neglect to love and care for God. And if you love and care for others, then you love and care for God. You see, Your Eminence, every sin is against Love, because Love is God.

'Remember too, Your Eminence, how Jesus gave his own definition of the Council of Trent before it ever came into being when he said that the two most important commandments are to love God with your whole being and your neighbour as yourself. And he went further with his summery when he said, that the whole of the Law and the prophets also hung on these two commands. So you see now, Your Eminence, that Love and care of others is the Holy Eucharist given out on every street in the world where people give their lives is loving communion with each other. It is even it own Baptism, Your Eminence.'

The Cardinal sprung erect from his seat in an instant, waking the whole company in shock. 'It's what? Mr. Walsh,' he screamed.

'It's own Baptism, Your Eminence, and you mustn't shout 'cause you'll frighten little Ruth.' Larry wagged his finger at the irate cardinal once more.

'Never mind Little Ruth, this is outright heresy!'

'Don't you dare dismiss our Ruth's presence as if she didn't matter.' Dee jumped to the family's defense. 'You're not fit to conduct an enquiry with such uncontrolled anger and hostility towards my husband. He's ten times the Christian you'll ever be, even if you were to live ten lifetimes in a bloody monastery full of angels.' Dee reseated feeling very ruffled. She put a comforting hand on Larry's shoulder and rubbed it. Larry responded by giving her face a big kiss. She smiled and reached over him to see if Baby Ruth was not too frightened. Finally she looked back at the cardinal giving him a contemptuous glare.

'Alright! Alright! It's been a long day. I'm sure we are all tired and worn.' The cardinal raised his hands in a begrudge gesture of conciliation. Monsignor Sean blew the breath from his mouth as one who had run a marathon. His eyes focused on Father Kevin as he shook his head slowly to indicate that he too had enough of this bloody circus.

'Baptism, Mr. Walsh, is absolutely and inescapably essential for salvation. This is Christ's own teaching, which the Holy Roman Catholic Church is duty bound to preserve and carry out.' Cardinal Dwyer stared directly and menacingly at Larry.

'But then there are the virtues of Love and care, Your Eminence,' Larry replied, his free hand gently extended away from baby Ruth in a pleading gesture.

'Meaning what, Mr. Walsh?' the cardinal retorted with an expression of utter exasperation.'

'"I haven't come to call the virtuous...." Jesus' own words, Your Eminence,' Larry offered reflectively.

'Meaning what precisely, Mr. Walsh?'

'Virtue, Your Eminence – It is its own salvation, a baptism of love.' Larry held a gaze of expectancy at the cardinal, one which seemed to say – even you must know that – it's plain enough in Jesus' teaching.

'So the Baptism that Jesus spoke of as essential for salvation, by water and the Spirit, these are no longer necessary for salvation according to you?' The cardinal Looked contemptuously at Larry and added with a stern warning. 'Mr. Walsh, you are sailing very close to the wilderness of excommunication from Holy Mother Church if you really believe that the Sacrament of Baptism is of little importance. You infer that there may be one soul alive in our fallen world who can claim to be without sin. That, Mr. Walsh, would be to call such an individual a blatant liar; as Scripture states clearly, that there is "none without sin," that the sacrament of Baptism is essential "for the forgiveness of sins," ... Jesus' own teaching, Mr. Walsh.' The cardinal waited with threatening expectancy for his adversary to give a clear denial to this vital teaching. His face was smoldering in contempt as Larry remarked calmly.

'The life of Baptism, Your Eminence, Virtuous living. That's what is necessary. Millions across the world have been baptized throughout history, thousands of despots along with them, religious included, and they never lived its life. What then did they receive, your Eminence?' Larry was tapping the backs of his fingers from one hand to the other for emphasis, while at the same time holding baby Ruth in the crook of his left arm. Little Ruth thought it was a game and so copied Larry with her own tiny hands clapping, and gurgling away contentedly into her daddy's face. This ambience of family domesticity put a warm smile on Dee's face and on Father Kevin's. Even Monsignor Sean could see the innocent humour of it all. The cardinal, however, resented this seeming casual attitude to the importance of the issue in discussion – the wrath of his fury rippled all over his face and agitated body. His two clenched fists looked ready to pound the desk in frustration as he barked out in anger.

'But the water and ritual of the celebration are necessary, Mr. Walsh, whether the child or person to be baptized is worthy of it or not. All candidates, Mr. Walsh, or their parents in the case of infant baptism, are duty bound to receive a long period of instruction. The words and promises recited by the parents for the child, or recited by the adult on his own behalf, all these are essential as a means of instruction and as moments of grace. We are commanded by Christ's authority to baptize. The words and promises to reject Satan and all evil and to be under the instruction of the Holy Catholic Church and its authority alone, which was given by Christ, all of these are necessary and essential, Mr. Walsh.'

'I don't deny any of that, Your Eminence. But the life of Baptism is not given by the Church, Your Eminence; it has to be lived out by the person who has accepted the external nature of Church ritual. The spiritual life which makes Baptism work has to be owned – the individual accepting the life of Baptism has to be in a personal communion with all the virtues of love and care for others and to mature in these virtues throughout the individual's life. Love, care, charity, mildness of character, kindness, gentleness – these have to be lived experiences, Your Eminence. They will not work by magic – personal involvement on a daily basis in a life of prayer and right actions are the very life blood of all the sacraments. The recipient of the sacraments will get nowhere and receive nothing in honouring ritual alone.' Larry finished tapping the palm of his hand as the cardinal interjected for clarity and emphasis,

'But the Church's part, ritual and all, is of critical importance?' The cardinal insisted on emphasizing the authority of the Church to minister the sacrament of Baptism as a directive and command from Christ himself.'

'Your Eminence, I agree with all of that you insist upon in that regard. The most important point I wish to stress is that in all of the Seven Sacrament of the Church which Christ instituted himself and gave authority over them to the Church, under the supreme authority of Peter and passed down through all the popes, who in turn shared that authority with legitimately ordained bishops, priests and deacons. My point is, that in spite of all that legitimate authority expressed in the rituals of the Church, Baptism, Holy Communion, Confirmation, Reconciliation, Anointing of the Sick, Holy Orders [the ordination of bishops, priest and deacons] and the Sacrament of Marriage, in all of these, it is the recipient of these sacraments who minister their internal lives. The parents are the first teachers of their children with regard to teaching them to pray and to learn by good example to live a good and holy life. Yes, Church and school have their part too. Ultimately it falls on the recipient of each sacrament to mature in virtue and in the love of God. The parents, Church and school cannot live the child's life for them. The priest cannot live the life of the couple whose marriage he celebrates, nor can he supply the love and care essential for the marriage to work. Nor can the Church live a minister's life for him. Nor can the abbot or abbess of a monastery or convent live their communitys' lives for them. In the end it comes down to each individual living a life of virtue, taking his or her responsibility. Otherwise all the celebrations of the sacraments throughout the world count for nothing but empty ritual if their internal expectations are neglected. Larry was tapping the palm of his hand throughout for emphasis with baby Ruth joining in.

Cardinal Christopher Dwyer leaned ashen-faced across his desk to Monsignor Sean O' Rourke. From what he whispered into the monsignor's ear it looked as if the Cardinal had enough of the day's proceedings. His piles were on fire. Presently and with autocratic deliberation he announced his intentions to close the entire weekly meetings.

'Mr. Walsh, I cannot say that I am completely satisfied with all the answers you have furnished at this important enquiry with regard to your faith and your mission to the world as its supposed new leader by the divine authority you claim.'

Monsignor Sean collected the scattered sheet of documents and slid them into the buff folders with some urgency to be out of the place. He would have them sorted later. He detached the recorder from its power cable and placed it into its glinting aluminium case – everything would be dispatched to Rome by air with some urgency.

Father Kevin interrupted the closing down of the enquiry. He had been very patient during what he experienced as an interrogation. He felt so strong about the attitude of Cardinal Dwyer that he felt he needed to put a more positive conclusion to the meetings.

'Your Eminence, I think you have been quite out of order to conduct this enquiry as if it were an inquisition.

We were all here in good faith, including myself. This family is in my care. They are my parishioners and they are also intimate personal friends. Larry's views on our faith and Church doctrine may seem quite radical to you since he is an absolute stranger to you. You act as if personally threatened by every point of view that comes from him. However, I know him to have a very simple faith, and more to the point, I don't know any other individual in my entire life that lives the true and essential Christian life as he does. He loves his faith, always expressed in childlike Christian simplicity, just as he loves people. As you mentioned at the beginning of our meetings, the Holy Father will have the final word on this matter. I realize that you have to be sure that Larry is not a time-waster. Surely the importance of his being here it to pass on an urgent message to the Holy Father, Pope Dominic X11 with regard to the danger that he faces in Rome. Larry has to deliver the message in person. I wish it was simpler. Unfortunately it is not. Even if Larry was a confirmed Buddhist, his message concerning the pending danger to the Holy Father's life remains paramount.'

Father Kevin's face was flushed with emotion. It gave him no pleasure to confront his superiors, indeed, quite the opposite. Yet, he was a fair man, quite humble and ordinary in his ways. Confrontation was not his way. Cardinal Dwyer, himself flushed with emotion, raised his hand towards the company, his face now bearing a more conciliatory expression. Inwardly he resented Father Kevin's siding with his parishioners against what he considered his rightful fraternal allegiance to a fellow cleric. It was a sad day for the Cloth, the cardinal thought.

'...My sincere apologies to you both.' It was an icy contrition, indeed, as he continued in cynical tone.

'We need to be certain where we are going with all Mr. Walsh's thinking, and precisely where he really stands with regards to the established tenets of our Church and our profession of Faith. This book of his, Father Noonan …' the cardinal would not deviate from formal address, not even for a fellow priest. He waved the book in his hand, slapping it with force in the air towards their faces. 'This book of his, Father Noonan,' he repeated in icy emphatic expressions, 'has spread its influence across the international world. Because of its immediate and controversial influence on all aspects of social and religious life, the Catholic Church, and no doubt most other faiths, has every right to be intimately conversant with its author's trustworthiness and ultimate claims to authority.'

'I have not objected to the serious nature of your enquiries, Your Eminence, simply to your hostile and shameful attitude to Larry, considering he is doing us the favour by alerting the Holy Father to the immediate danger he is in. He has nothing to gain by being here except his peace of mind for delivering his warning. Believe me, Your Eminence, he will prove the truth of the matter with or without the help of the Church. I believe Larry to be one of the most honest, harmless, and trustworthy individuals I have ever known in my life. When he declares that his directions and instructions have come from a higher source and power than his own, I am quite prepared to put my very life as guarantee to the authenticity of his message and his absolute trustworthiness. I can say without hesitation, that I know of very few individuals alive to whom I would give such a guarantee.'

Cardinal Dwyer's response to Father Kevin's absolute faith in Larry brought a mellowed smile to the cardinal's pinched features for the first time. It was as if everything Cardinal Dwyer hoped to achieve from this troublesome enquiry was handed to him on a plate. In his private thoughts he had a ready-made scapegoat if anything untoward should manifest itself in Rome. He had an instant guarantor to Mr. Walsh's credibility and his standing with his Church and his Faith. It was all on record, literally. The cardinal's sudden benevolent expression made the company feel uneasy. They considered his new-found calm to be another ploy to further his own perverse interrogation. Privately, he couldn't make up his own mind about Larry. Was he some kind of mystic or one given to visions, he thought? There were always plenty of those about. Or was he more lunatic than simpleton? He was certainly convinced that Larry was some kind of freak individual, a genius, perhaps …? Whatever …! Cardinal Dwyer wanted rid of him and a swift end to this dam circuitous enquiry. He felt Larry was now making him question his own faith by putting dangerous unspeakable notions into his own time-trod orthodox understanding. The enquiry had taken place over four weeks with few breaks between for meals and such like. Now Cardinal Dwyer had brought it to a premature end. He was convinced that he was not dealing with an ordinary individual. Enough was enough. Any fallout from Rome would ultimately descend on Father Kevin's reputation and reliability. And that, the cardinal considered, was a good enough outcome. Even the cardinal's piles seemed to sense relief from their burning stings.

'Well now. I think we have sufficient material here to pass on to Rome, in spite of my own reservations.' The cardinal beamed with a new satisfaction at Monsignor Sean O' Rourke who was preparing at full speed to exit the study.

The poor man was glad to see the back of the tempest ... his face puffed and glowing ... his ears on fire as one well cooked over a radiating grill. When finished, the monsignor gave a curt bow of his head to Cardinal Dwyer by way of seeking the all clear for him to depart to his usual duties in his own city parish. The cardinal bowed his head sideways, giving the bare semblance of a dismissal as if to someone quite inferior, and all the more to magnify in pomp his own superior position and self-importance.

'Thank you Monsignor, Sean. We are indebted to your labors.' The cardinal's overbearing tone portrayed a shameless lack of humility to all present.

Ultimately it was Father Kevin's unexpected and forthright willingness to act as guarantor to Mr. Walsh's spiritual character that provided Cardinal Dwyer with a satisfactory ribbon to the enquiry's closure. Monsignor O' Rourke gave a backward departing glance at the company in general. He was clutching the glinting aluminium recording case in one hand and his much scuffed black briefcase in the other. He seemed to carry all the burdens of the world on his own ill-used person. Only forced discretion held him back from dashing from the study.

'A bloody right old carnival if ever I heard one,' he muttered under his breath. 'I need a good stiff drink.'

'Well there we are.' The cardinal addressed the remaining company who were also collecting their belongings and eager to depart their torture chamber. 'You will hear from me presently with further instructions, you may rest assured.' The cardinal walked the guests to the front door of the palace. They were just in time to see Monsignor O' Rourke's Volvo kick up a spray of pebbles as he raced out of the graveled driveway. He never looked back once ... he was gone like a startled bird in flight.

'A busy priest, the monsignor....' The cardinal's remark was a feeble attempt to excuse the monsignor's graceless exit which did not reflect well on the cardinal's friendship with him. The company was shown to the door with one of the cardinal's curt, sideways bow. There was always something begrudged and superior in the controlled leaning of his head when bidding farewell, or meeting with inferiors.

'Thank you for your co-operation. I'm sure we are all pleased to have these matters come to their conclusion.'

'Indeed.' Father Kevin's brief reply spoke for all.

The guests walked out on a beautifully bright late afternoon. The fresh air felt as if they were released into the real world among real people. Pink May-blossom bedecked the trees along the private roads leading away from the cardinal's palace. Dee's silver Volvo cruised along the private roads. Her companions were captivated by the May blossom as if it was a unique discovery. Dee felt a strong urge to reach out and take a handful of the pink scented flower clusters and wash their moist petals all over her body to rid herself of the clinging staleness of the cardinal's study. They felt like prisoners being released into the real world again. All experienced a strange sense of solemnity as if still held in the grip of the cardinal's stern authority. It took time to let go the grip of the four weeks semi-detention and isolation from normality.

'Let's have a meal Father Kevin. I'm craving for normal company.' Dee was keen to kick into touch all memories of the past four weeks, she was not alone; It had been a grueling time for all concerned, the clerics included.

'Paul's; that's the spot ...! My safe haven when forced to brave the city.' Father Kevin, now in good spirits, guided Dee's Volvo to the back streets of his old city haunts. 'It's nothing fancy, mind, just good clean fare. Dublin had long since dispensed with the use of money and was all the better for it. Even small cafes and restaurants were a pleasure to use. Service and décor were excellent, no matter how small the venue. After alighting from the car Father Kevin pushed Larry and Dee from behind good naturedly and mischievously...his lighter side came flooding back. The décor had improved dramatically since he last used the restaurant. Paul Dunn and his wife Bet still ran the show. They greeted Father Kevin like a long-lost friend. They welcomed Larry, baby Ruth and Dee warmly. True to character, Bet lashed the invisible crumbs from the perfectly clean chairs with a red and white-chequered tea towel which had hung from her shoulder like a badge of trade. Father Kevin recommended stew to Larry, knowing Dee would go for something lighter. She settled for sliced smoked salmon on a bed of mixed salad, grapes and brie cheese. Larry was feeding Ruth by bottle. The little mite was forever smiling and waving her tiny hands about.

'How's that terrible city of yours, Father, has it floated away yet? I hear we whipped Cork with the sticks in the All Ireland last year. Now I might be hearing wrong, Father.'

'Bet Dunn, I've known people to be sent to purgatory for a hundred years for less ... teasing the holy priest, and him a Kerry man, not a Corkonian in case you forgot. Sure didn't the Corkonians feel sorry for keeping the Cup from the Dubs for the last two hundred years?'

'Don't priests have to go to the confessions, then, Father? Imagine not believing the Dubs to be a superior race to those terrible Corkonians, imagine that!' It was good to indulge in the banter again Father Kevin thought, not having to measure and preface his words and thoughts with religious scrutiny. Life was worth living again.

As the meal progressed with wine, fruit, more cheese, tea and coffee, so Dee asked the question uppermost in her mind. She hoped the last four weeks were not just a waste of breath and everyone's time. She turned to her friend.

'Kevin,' her voice was low since Bet was not too far away; 'what are our chances of meeting Pope Dominic in Rome? Will his nibs block the way?' She was quite concerned, given the cardinal's hostile response to the family.

'Dee, don't worry. He will be just as glad to wash his hand of all of us, myself included.'

'What makes you so sure, Kevin? I don't see him doing us any favours.'

'Two things in our favour Dee; Larry's Law, the book, has already created a storm worldwide as a very distinct challenge not just to the Catholic faith but to all faiths. Pope Dominic will want to meet the author on that issue alone. Secondly: Larry's healing of Mary Cassidy at Cork General Hospital is a confirmed and recorded fact and therefore makes Larry's warning of the Pope's impending danger too risky to ignore. I'm pretty certain of that.'

'I hope you're right, Kevin, for Larry's peace of mind – for all our sakes!'

It was never easy to leave people with Larry in tow. He just has to go and find out everything there is to know about everyone. His social hunger was insatiable; most likely attributed to his parents. They lived for the lad. They didn't regard him in his childhood as someone who was a liability, incapable of normal relationships at school or of holding down a job. They simply adored him, giving him their undivided attention above all their own interests. In consequence he now drained Paul and Bet, complete strangers to him, of their entire family history. They took an instant liking to him and to little Ruth. Larry told them all about how he was given her as a Christmas gift from Dee. He told them all about his garden at home at Garrettstown, how he, and not Dee, made everything grow. He didn't spare them the names of all the flowers and plants and what he done to make them grow. By the time he finished with them, only after being dragged away by persistent calls from Dee and Father Kevin, Paul and Bet were his new lifelong friends. You could guarantee that he would keep in touch with them. It was fortunate for all that there was no cost to his communications or he would have cost Dee a small fortune with all the people he kept in touch with. Sometimes Dee had to put a stop to such excessive antics when she deemed it inappropriate. Paul and Bet whispered to Father Kevin on the way out,

'Is he ok, Father?' Bet indicated with her head towards the departing Larry.

'Bet, one day you'll know better …. For now all I can say is that you have just met genius and humility stretching to infinity,' Father Kevin remarked, his head nodding reflectively.

'We take it the quare one is a writer, according to Larry's information?' Paul asked indirectly.

'A remarkable one, Paul, I can assure you. More I can't say. You know some things are best left without comment.' Father Kevin had his arm round Paul's shoulder conspiratorially. He knew that the true identity of Larry and Dee had to be kept secure.

Paul and Bet tapped the side of their own noses together remarking,

'Down the Liffey, Father ... down the Liffey ...' Father Kevin smiled at the implications of their remark. If the River Liffey flowing through the center of Dublin could give up its history, there would be a library indeed. As it is, all is washed into the sea – Dunn's sins and all.

'She's some beauty, though, Father.' Paul nodded towards Dee. 'How the hell did he get his hands on her? He must have been wide awake that day.'

'Ah! Sure, we can't always know about the workings of a wheelbarrow, now, can we?' Father Kevin addressed them both. Once more they tapped the sides of their noses. They were laughing aloud now as Bet remarked mischievously:

'Sure, aren't yeah well suited to the Seal, Father, like no other I know.'

'And when, my good woman, did you last grace the seal of a confession box I'd like to know?'

'Ah, sure, Father, I puts it all in the water ... all in the water, Father,' she repeated mischievously. Bet and Paul were creased with laughter.

'Maybe one day, Bet Dunn, they'll drain the Liffey or find a way to make the fish talk.'

'Ah, sure, Father, we'll be living in the Milky Way by then.'

'Now don't leave it so long next time, Father Kevin. Bring your friends along too ... always a welcome.' The couple stood waving from the open door. Larry planted a big kiss on Beth's cheek before climbing back into the Volvo with his precious bundle.

By the time they reached St. Patrick's in Cork city, they were all exhausted. Nell, the housekeeper, convinced the family to stay overnight. She received all the news of the day. She was well acquainted with Cardinal Christopher Dwyer in Dublin from his periodic appearances on television or listening to him on the radio. She knew him to be blunt, dogmatic and no stranger to controversy. From all she heard of the cardinal's manner, irritatingly regurgitated to her by Dee, he didn't seem to have changed one iota.

'There's no mellowing of some souls,' said Nell. She added mockingly: 'and him nearly a thousand years old.' The friends laughed heartily at Nell's exaggeration.

CHAPTER 17

Larry's Journey to Rome

Two weeks later a letter arrived from Cardinal Dwyer confirming arrangements with a meeting between Larry and Pope Dominic Ubutu X11. The letter was addressed to Father Kevin.

He was instructed and advised by Cardinal Dwyer of all the formalities that would be expected of Larry and Dee once they were being received by Pope Dominic. The pontiff would be no less grilling in his enquiries, the cardinal emphasized.

All these details were relayed to Dee in Garrettstown. Father Kevin hoped to spare Dee further indignities by informing her of what to expect. The family Journeyed once more to the city. Dee turned to her friend with a reassuring smile as they sat drinking coffee in the church presbytery.

'Oh don't trouble yourself further, Father Kevin; don't forget that I have a history of being grilled as a journalist. I know what we can expect. As for Larry, so long as he can amuse himself with baby Ruth, the Vatican might as well never exist.' She glanced at Larry sunk in one of Father Kevin's easy chairs with baby Ruth being bounced up and down, smiling her new world away in utter innocence, and oblivious to the troubled world of adults.

'So, you are taking baby Ruth with you, Dee?' The priest was somewhat taken aback. He had a keen concern for baby Ruth. He felt he was part of her life and family.

'I'm afraid that it's Larry and Ruth or no Rome. I have to go with him. Larry is as good a father to baby Ruth as it is possible to have. He doesn't begrudge one second of his time with her. It seems to be a family trait picked up from his doting parents.'

'I don't doubt that in the least, Dee; I couldn't expect less from Larry and his kindly loving nature. No, I am just a little surprised, given Ruth's age.'

'Ah, Father Kevin,' Nell intervened, 'sure babies are tougher that you realize. I'm sure you were one yourself at some point in history,' Nell remarked teasingly.

Dublin Airport was one of the most miserable places on God's good earth when lashed with rain and wind-swept. Larry had never flown in a plane before. He had no particular thoughts about flying or the duration of the Journey; as usual, he lived in a world of his own. He watched fascinated at the great Jets coming in to land and others roaring down the runways and climbing into the skies. All the while he was watching from the terminal windows with the rain lashing at the glass and running down in rivers. It was only when their plane took off that he let out a shrieking, terrified scream and instinctively clung to Dee in sheer terror. Dee herself was startled and worried … her heart pounding. She had never in all her knowledge of Larry known him to be afraid of anything. Ruth's eyes flinched momentarily from her daddy's scream and yet she was none the worse for the experience.

The other passengers grew very tense and alert for the duration of the flight. Most were concerned about the possibility of having a neurotic on board the aircraft and the unimaginable consequences. They need not have worried so much. A sturdy male security officer stood close to Larry's seat without making his intentions too obvious, he became a consoling presence for the duration of the flight. Dee had taken control of Ruth and gently comforted her husband. She had the window seat; she could see the runway racing towards the aircraft in the process of landing. There was a gentle thump as the wheels hit the runway. To Dee's astonishment Larry turned to her and smiled and at the same time took his white bundle, baby Ruth from her. He now acted as if they were in their lounge at home in Garrettstown. Dee smiled in relief. While they struggled with the restrictions of their seats it flashed across Dee's mind that they would have to face the flight home and wondered if Larry might refuse to fly again. Still, she shelved that thought until she could approach Larry with the difficulty, if it still remained a serious concern.

Because of the gravity of the visit to Rome the family was met off the plane by two Saint Clare Sisters. Both were natives of Ireland and were well acquainted with the Garrettstown community of elderly sisters of the same order. Much of the conversation ran in that direction. They were bubbly characters and very interested in the little community back home in Ireland. The sisters drove Dee's family to St. Peter's square for a brief visit. Occasionally Dee stopped to take photographs of Larry with Ruth; he was feeding the pigeons with bits of sandwich that he had left over from the plane journey. In turn, the sisters took pictures of the family together. Dee also included the sisters in the photographs as happy mementos of the visit. Larry was never trusted with the camera ... he was notorious for making a mess of it due to his co-ordination difficulties. His efforts usually had heads cut off or inclusions of irrelevant subject matter.

Dee felt suddenly uneasy. She had an instinctive sense of danger and foreboding. She was partly aware of being followed by several men who seemed to have encircled the family and sisters, yet keeping their distance. Dee was uncomfortable for several reasons; she was after all a very beautiful woman in spite of being in her thirties. Her incredible beauty instinctively drew unwanted attention. Larry was not one who could be depended upon to fight off possible assaults from strangers – it wasn't in his nature. Another cause for her concern was her keen intention to keep the family's identity from the press and media in general. She dare not have her family's anonymity compromised. The two sisters became aware of Dee's change of expression and her unease. Previously she seemed relaxed and happy with her beautiful angelic face smiling softly at the mad antics of Larry showing off little Ruth to the pigeons. Now she appeared severe, her jaws grinding, her brow furrowed, her eyes fiercely defensive and suspicious.

'Is there something troubling you Dee?' The sisters voiced their concern.

Dee spoke through half clenched teeth; 'I think we are being stalked or followed by several well-dressed men.' Dee pointed deliberately to them by way of letting them know that she was well aware of them. Dee's exquisite beauty and the meticulous care of her appearance, coupled with her natural elegance, invariably made her the target of un-solicitous attention. She was instinctively aware of this, which made her cautious in strange surroundings and company.

The sister's were relieved. 'Oh! That lot .... Don't concern yourself with them; we are well aware of who they are. They followed us from the airport; they are under instructions to do so.' The sisters were calm again.

'Under whose Instructions...?' Dee asked, feeling affronted – her anger all too visible.

'They are plain clothes Swiss Guards, I see them occasionally. They're no problem, they are specialist in protection. Someone in the Vatican must think your visit very important to have those boys called out.' Sister Rosemary assured Dee. She was the younger of the two Irish nuns with a fresh tanned youthful face.

'Some specialists, if I could notice their presence! They seemed to be too obvious.' Dee was still uneasy, even resentful at such conspicuous exposure.

'You're right, of course, Dee,' Sister Patricia intervened. Both sisters wore soft black head coverings with a white band in front giving shape to the covering. Their brown habits were nearly as familiar in the surrounds of the Vatican as the pigeons that flocked there; the square oozed religious-clad clerics and pigeons.

Sister Patricia continued: 'Don't worry, Dee, they have no idea of your business here, they are meant to be conspicuous; in your case, to send a message to less savory characters who may mean you harm. Unfortunately, Dee, there are unsavory characters here only too willing to rob or abuse visitors, especially women and those who go about displaying obvious naivety and affluence. It's a sad, sad reflection on what might otherwise be considered a pilgrim's city,' Sister Patricia sighed resignedly.

She looked at the bwana-covered pavement as she spoke, as if the shame of her revelation was entirely her responsibility. Dee grew a little calmer. She touched the sister's arm and commented with a more relaxed smile, 'You can't take the bird out of the cat's head no matter how much you feed it. It's the way of the world – even poor humans are also surviving animals; though we do not all stalk others with evil intentions,' Dee added philosophically.

'You have great understanding, Dee. I'm sure I have no personal responsibility or need to apologize for the dark side of Rome or any other city, pilgrim or not.'

'No indeed,' her companion rejoined in support of her older friend.

The sisters drove the family to the community house, a small convent with three older sisters including themselves and six young Irish novices from various parts of Ireland. It was midday when they reached St. Clare's Convent. It felt good to be out of the noise of the city traffic, the constant blare of motor horns and the cacophony of engines revving and hissing ... the sudden hissing of breaking commercial vehicles. The community was in the process of laying the table for lunch. The dining room was immaculately furnished in glistening rose-colored furniture. There was a distinct energetic bubble in an atmosphere of laughter and youth as the young novices were falling over themselves trying to be seen to be lending a hand at preparing the long highly-polished dining table. Sister Patricia offered Dee and family the option of eating with them or to lunch in private, the sisters providing a cooked meal for them in their quarters. Dee chose to dine with the community; the gay chatter and melodious Irish accents seemed inviting in themselves – she might never have left Ireland. The clatter of plates and the steaming dishes of potatoes, cabbage and bacon were homely and familiar. Larry was an instant favorite, as was Ruth. He took Ruth around the table and introduced her to each individual novice as if the little bundle of white was a freshly cooked salmon to be inspected and remarked upon by every member. Dee excused her yawns and apologized for her tiredness. It had been a long day even up to now. She was one of those creatures who needed to be actively involved with some interesting occupation. The flight drained her from inactivity and the early start.

The convent setup reminded her very much of home; like the small community in Garrettstown, every room, corridor, chapel, and particularly the washing facilities were glistening clean as if the convent was fairly new instead of being over four hundred years old. The meal came in large gaily-colored, floral-patterned, family-size dishes, from which all helped themselves. The younger novices were surprised that it was Larry who was left to spoon-feed the gurgling infant. They looked at each other in turn, a little taken aback as if to inwardly criticize Dee's apparent indifference to the child. They had no means of knowing Larry's obsession and love of Ruth and her Mother; in truth, he was still every bit as besotted with Dee. Whispers passed surreptitiously from one novice to the other regarding the stunning beauty of Dee. She wore a silk green shirt and light black trousers; her meticulously-groomed blond hair glistened in length and neatness. The choice of green was deliberate as a means of reminding herself of home. The combination of Light green and black was a popular combination at the moment with Irish travelers and very much in vogue. Even so, Dee would still appear stunning even if she wore a black plastic bag for a dress. Her blond silken hair fell on her shoulders like a spill of gold and her soft angelic face, so beautifully formed in flawless perfection, was breath-taking to their captivated eyes. Her full unpainted lips gave her a natural beauty that cosmetics could only cheapen. Her rich expensive perfume wafting through the air and mingling with the aromas of the freshly cooked meal, jacket potatoes, boiled bacon, and Savoy cabbage, all glistening in melting butter. The conversation came mainly from the novices; they were full of curiosity about Dee's work and background. The three older sisters kept a discreet silence but smiled at the intimate questions of their younger counterparts. They knew perfectly well that Dee was all too aware of their innocence and enthusiasm. The older sisters didn't have a clue as to the nature of Dee's business with the Holy Father. Indeed, they were not even aware that her visit involved a meeting with the pontiff at all. Certainly they were aware that the family was to be given every comfort, protection and facility. They knew only that her business was of some importance. These sketchy assumptions were not relayed to the novices for obvious reasons.

The novices addressed their guests in the familiar at Dee's invitation. She felt absolutely at home with their questions and the banter between them. Every now and again they would look at their elders to see if they were over stepping the mark with all their questions. When they realized that she wrote under the name of Dee Lamb for the City Vanguard, young faces blushed as only youth can. The community read her columns regularly having the principle Irish papers posted as essential reading to keep up with the political changes and social situation in Ireland and abroad. Even the older nuns were taken aback; whatever a journalist is supposed to look like, Dee didn't seem to fit into the profession. There was a broad unvoiced opinion that she was a film star, a model, or certainly a celebrity of some kind. Dee never mentioned her past career on the same Newspaper ... if the community only knew the half of it ...!

Dee excused herself and family; she wished to have a nap to recover from the journey. Larry went to each individual novice again and kissed each one of them on the cheek. All the while Dee was smiling at his natural propensity to express his love of people. The young novices in particular were blushing crimson as well as cringing as they were obliged, out of common courtesy, to await their turn. The older sisters were in fits of laughter; they really believed that Larry was doing it out of pure devilment to embarrass everyone. Little did they know of Larry's genuine love for people?

As the family were shown to their private quarters. Sister Patricia, the novice mistress, handed Dee a book which she thought might take her interest during her stay. As Dee looked at the cover by way of showing interest through her tiredness, she almost had a heart attack. It was a copy of Larry's Law.

Dee fought momentarily for her breath and attempted to appear nonplussed. Of all the books that this happy little community could offer her none could have been more inappropriate at this present time for her. She was trying to cope with the coming day of her audience with the Holy Father. Even a comic would have been more welcome. In the circumstances she accepted the book graciously and moved her head sideways in an expression which implied, this looks interesting.

Dee and Larry slept very deeply from exhaustion; it had been a long day. Baby Ruth was no bother to either of them during the night although Dee had a distinct feeling that the child, even if it cried during the night, wouldn't have registered with her. As things were, Ruth was alert and smiling; she showed no effects from the journey nor did she appear distressed for want of feeding or attention.

The family grew accustomed to the daily routine of the convent. Morning prayers with Mass were from 7.30am followed by breakfast. One novice remained behind each day to help the older sisters to carry out the house chores and food preparation and shopping, while the others helped out in junior schools and other appropriate community placements, according to their age and experience. There were various snack times for those remaining at home in the convent. More prayers at 12 noon; evening meal at 5pm followed by evening prayers and rosary from 6pm, followed by various courses or private tuition in art, sewing, music, singing, or directed religious study; they had time to relax in front of the TV to watch appropriate subjects of interest; then a late non-alcoholic beverage of personal choice ... followed by night prayers and then retirement. Dee was thinking to herself, there is no time for the novices to get bored in their event-packed days. There was, however, wide latitude of choice and freedom on weekends, even though they usually went out together as supporting friends and community. Sister Patricia, the novice mistress, approached Dee, rather timidly, asking, with wringing hands, if she might consider giving the novices a few talks on the world of journalism and communication in general. Dee felt honored to be asked. She had no hesitation in responding to the sensitive request. Sister Patricia continued punctuating her request with the phrase: '... only if you have time.' Dee laid her hand gently on the sister's shoulder and assured her.

'I will be glad to make time;' and added with a distinct emphasis, 'I know that the young ones will benefit greatly from learning to gauge the characters of people and build up the tools and ploys of handling various personalities; after all, one day they will be like your good self, Sister, and find themselves thrown into many demanding positions concerning communication.' It must be said that Sister Patricia never missed an opportunity to collar some talented individual to contribute to her novices' amour and tools for life. Sister also slipped in the fact that even the older sisters, including her, would feel highly privileged to sit in on any talk that Dee might give. Dee smiled and thought, 'this sister would squeeze every grace from heaven just so that she wouldn't pass any opportunity to advance the quality of her vocational role among the novices.' Dee felt a great buzz and energy about this convent. She felt in her heart that she would have loved such an opportunity when she was young to have such love, care and professional guidance, no matter what she chose to make of her life afterwards.

As events unfolded, Dee and family were to stay in Rome for five weeks during which time she was invited to join in as much of the convent's activities and prayer life as her family wished. Larry became a great favorite with all the sisters, so did baby Ruth. Dee too was very well received by the novices during her talks; she could hold them spellbound with the depth, expertise and extent of her utter professionalism. What the novices appreciated in particular was the fact that in spite of Dee's importance and status as a highly respected and widely read journalist, they never once felt in any way inferior to her; she didn't speak down to anyone. She never reveled that they were once multi-millionaires from the family's sale of the book, Larry's Law. Of course all that was useless now with money being a thing of the past. Dee also gave them lessons on touch-typing as an aid to working on computers. The entire novitiate was dazzled by her utter speed and competence on the keyboard.

The family's first audience with Pope Dominic Ubutu X11 was quite intimidating with all the security procedures put in place. The six Swiss guards dressed in plain clothes who had followed Larry's family from the airport had never left the convent grounds nor had they ever allowed Dee and family out of sight when they went out shopping or sight-seeing. Meeting the Holy Father for the first time left a lasting impression on both Larry Dee. They had to pass through innumerable marble corridors and enormous rooms with marble pillars and priceless religious paintings hanging from walls and breath-taking decorated ceilings. Even incidental tables and chairs that stood about as unused ornaments, these glinted in gold leaf and rich crimson coverings. The utter cascading luxury of the entire interior was breathtaking and intimidating. Dee loved beauty and refinement; yet here she experienced a distinct feeling of vulgarity and dripping hypocrisy. What did all this opulent extravagance say or declare to the world in need. What was its true spiritual function in the world? It seemed to Dee like a betrayal of the Faith which it professed and the teaching of the Master concerning worldliness. Here in this palatial colossus of blatant vulgarity was the accumulation of hundreds of years of scandalous misappropriation of wealth and effort, adding nothing to the credibility of its purpose for existence.

Pope Dominic on the other hand was such a gentle individual. To see an African at the head of the entire

Catholic Church gave Dee new cause for wonder and Joy; it meant that no nation had an individual claim on the Catholic Faith as of right. The Church belonged to all and was clearly open to all.

Larry all but disgraced the situation. On being introduced to Pope Dominic he said quite spontaneously,

'Gosh, you're a very black man. I've never met such a black man in all me life.'

'Sister Patricia, who had acted as guide to the family through the labyrinth of securities, corridors and procedures, nearly died of shock and embarrassment; more so because Dee seemed to take the comment in her stride. She had grown accustomed over the passing years with Larry's seemingly outrageous or inappropriate comments no matter the company. Strangely people cottoned on very quickly that Larry was without malice and responded to him as such. Pope Dominic, God bless him, threw back his head, his eyes wide and shocked as if being hit hard by the rough end of blatant ignorance and insensitivity. Yet as suddenly as the shock came, so it passed; it came rapidly to his mind concerning the documents from Cardinal Dwyer in Ireland relating to the innocent characteristics of Larry's child-like nature. Pope Dominic's response was to grab hold of Larry in a true African bear hug. He greeted Dee a little more gently as she was now holding the baby. He took to baby Ruth from the start as if she were his own child. He was nearly a match for Larry in his attention to the gurgling smiling child.

'God must love you,' Larry proclaimed in his usual forthright manner.

'I would like to believe that is true,' the Holy Father replied in all humility. 'Why would you say such a thing

Mr. Walsh?' the pontiff remarked with deliberation – his brow arched in amazement.

'Please, your Holiness, we would be honored if you would address us by or Christian names,' Dee interjected.

'By all means, if you both agree to address me as Dominic in my private residence.' This was agreed willingly.

Larry continued with a big smile on his face. 'God must love you, 'cause he is protecting you and he has brought you from Africa to look after us, hasn't he?' At this point Sister Patricia was relieved of her services. Larry and Dee kissed her goodbye by way of letting the pontiff know that she was more than a servant to them. The pontiff picked up this gesture quickly and commented in the sister's absence.

'I see you have already grown affectionate towards our dear friend, Sister Patricia.'

'We have indeed, Dominic; we have become good friends.' Dee had noted the warmth in the pontiff's expression, "… our dear friend, Sister Patricia." It did not carry a tone of cold formality or condescension. Dee was sharp to pick up such nuances. Once the Sister had disappeared Dominic took them into his private quarters – something quite rare for him because of his own security and for his need of a fox hole away from all officialdom.

Dee's first impression of Dominic's personal sitting room was how it evoked African culture and his own personal interests in music. He had a guitar and bongos lying about which he used frequently, he assured them. There were carved wooden masks hanging on the walls; Dee thought they were frightening.

'The masks trouble you, Dee?' he remarked with a curious smile.

'They're a bit scary, to be truthful.' Dee grimaced, unnerved by them. There were many other wall-hangings around the room all thematic of Africa's tribal history and culture.

'Those masks, Dee, remind me of the time when the whole of Africa was without the benefit of the Word of God in our primitive land. These masks were used by our primitive leaders who were the first stepping stones to a kind of primitive priesthood. The masks also remind me of every other nation in the world and their similar primitive beginnings and having the same need to hide behind the many masks of ignorance and fear ... masks that endeavored to empower and camouflage the vulnerable inadequacy of tribal leaders. These poor ignorant primitive peoples were forced by ignorance and circumstance to worship in terrible barbaric human and animal sacrifices at their carved totems. Souls now faded into to mists of ancient history... manipulated by ignorance ... attempting to appease their imagined gods of storm and pestilence, as if Nature itself could change its impersonal course at the behest of ragged savagery ... poor souls who were little more than creatures enslaved to their carved totem gods, equivalent to our own altars. Their elaborate dances and rituals all in an attempt to appease their own neurotic fears and convince themselves and their peoples that there was a power beyond themselves that held sway over them and kept them in fear and subjection.' The pontiff paused, smiling with an expression of irony as he added: 'now we wear the mask of affluence instead to hide behind so we can pretend to be what we clearly are not. We hide behind the mask of materialism and convince ourselves that we are what we own or what we have power over. We make gods of our own power and influence over the less privileged as if we owned our own existence and controlled that existence in an absolute way. It is so easy under the delusion of our own self-importance to forget that we all age and die, and with time, are utterly forgotten. As I say, Dee, our own delusions are merely the masks we wear in our own time and culture. We wear them over our minds and lose sight and understanding of what we really could be as truly free souls living for each as Larry's book inspires … and as Christ himself teaches as the very ordered end of humanity.' Dee was taken aback by Dominic's insight into the externals of religion. She had a distinct feeling that she was in the presence of a deeply studious and articulate person; his insights left a deep impression on her. She knew also, from his reverie, that he was familiar with Larry's Law – that he had read it and seemingly absorbed it. But what would he really make of its more controversial challenges on traditional Catholic Faith, she thought?

Larry, as always, could be depended upon to bring the company back to earth.

'Do you play the guitar, then, Dominic?' Larry's question took on the enthusiasm of an invitation.

'I love to sing and dance … it shakes away my tensions and troubles,' he replied filling the room with a hearty belly laugh. Pope Dominic was a man who laughed easily.

'Will you sing us a song, then?' Larry asked with smiling gusto and added, 'can you play the Banks?' Dee gave Larry's long leg a swift kick.

'What?'

'Don't you know that Dominic comes from Kenya? And that is nowhere near Cork City in Ireland,' Dee remarked showing a distinct degree of unease and embarrassment. She knew that Larry was well-read even though he made no effort to reveal that side of his character in public.

'Well he might know it for all you know, smarty clogs.' Dominic broke into hysterics at the banter between husband and wife. Their manner indicated their ease and comfort in his company.

'I can assure you both that I know the song and every verse off by heart. Our beloved sisters from the Saint Clare's Irish community established it in my memory from our little get-togethers. I know that the song refers to "The Banks of my own Lovely Lee" and concerns itself with the Banks of the River Lee that flows through Cork City and also immortalizes the Mardyke and its avenue of elm trees,' Dominic reminded them with delight.

'You see, clever clogs, Dominic knows all about Cork and the Mardyke.'

'Alright, Larry love, I concede to your superior authority,' she remarked teasingly.

Inwardly she was vexed with herself for being slightly embarrassed by what seemed an indiscretion and forgetting Larry's natural openness with all people.' Before any more ado, Dominic picked up the guitar and began singing The Banks. Larry joined in. His singing voice was like the raucous cry of an irate cow that was way past milking time. The private concert was made all the more painful as Larry tried to play the pontiff's bongos. The rhythm-less noise was like a countryman's effort to ward off the menacing descent of swarming bees. Dee screwed up her eyes and whispered to Larry, while Dominic was unaware of her movements,

'Let Dominic do the singing, it would be polite; and the bongos need retuning.' Larry ceased immediately from his fall from grace and raucous ache to please Dee. It was such a relief to hear the beautiful voice of Dominic and see his heartfelt expression of the sentiments of the song. Dee wanted to join in but dare not take the risk of setting anew the agony of Larry's torturous efforts. It was so comforting to Dee to realize that here was the leader of the Roman Catholic world and its faith, with God-knows-what pressures laid on his shoulders and yet he could make time to display such warmth and humility to two perfect strangers ... a family he had never met before in his life. It grieved Dee to realize that what her family had to offer in return was mind-shattering news for the pontiff personally and officially. Dee wept at the sweet closing cords of his singing – not because of the song and the memories it continued to evoke, but rather due to the family's reason for being in Rome and the utter misery of the message that had to be imparted to this most human and holy man, a pilgrim to his faith and far from his own native people and home.

Dominic rose slowly from his simple upright chair to replace the Spanish guitar by the wall on its stand. He left the family by themselves once more after settling them with refreshments. He preferred to look after his own needs in his own time and quarters, in preference to having people fussing over him. He went to fetch the folders containing the documents that were compiled in Ireland by Cardinal Dwyer and his monsignor, the details of his interrogation of Larry and family as well as Father Kevin's contributions and recommendations. He perused these with his fists leaning on a highly polished study desk. His face grimaced in concentration and from a deep sense of foreboding and uncertainty. He was summarizing the pertinent points of the message contained within the documents. Larry withdrew a sealed letter from his inside coat pocket marked "Strictly Private" and passed it to Dominic. Larry's mood and expression changed at once, knowing as he did the terrible nature of its contents.

The gist of Larry's strictly confidential instruction was a warning to evacuate Rome within the month of August as there would be a large scale earthquake due during the month of September. The evacuation would be permanent for the pontiff and for all the people of Italy, but for different reasons. There would be no city left for the people to return to; it would be totally destroyed. With regard to the pontiff, the Catholic Faith was to take on a new era and expression and reformation. The Pontiff's status was to be once again that of an itinerant nature, moving from one country to another on an annual basis. The priesthood itself would be open to married couples, male or female.

The pontiff had already listened to the recordings that were sent from Ireland concerning the family's meetings with Cardinal Dwyer and Monsignor O' Rourke.

'I was deeply troubled, by much of what was reported to me from Ireland. Such meetings I realize cannot have been easy for anyone. Of course they were essential – nevertheless their controversial nature was bound to create friction. Few of us take kindly to having our long-held traditions and teachings challenged, especially from outside of clerical circles. Anyway, that aside; I would like to deal firstly with the more worrying subject of the danger you say that I about to face here in Rome. Would you be so kind, Larry, to clarify the situation and the danger you believe that I and my people are facing?' The company had by now shifted into a more comfortable room with easy chairs and more conducive to comfort. Larry and Dee sat together sinking into a soft settee facing Pope Dominic who was seated in a richly fabricated pastel-blue covered arm chair; baby Ruth was in her natural position, in Larry's arms.

'Dominic, it gives me no pleasure whatever to pass on to you this warning of an earthquake due to take place in September. Rome and the whole of Italy will be affected. I was told to warn you to call for a total evacuation of the city and the entire land of Italy – that no one will be safe. I cannot understand why such a message had to be carried to you by a complete stranger ... why the warning could not have been revealed to you personally or by another fellow priest – I don't understand that at all, Dominic.' Larry's expression showed a sense of utter incomprehension. He continued a little more relaxed, now that he had clarified his essential message. He appeared less burdened. 'God must really love you and the people Dominic ... why else would you be given this warning?' Dee was more skeptical. She didn't voice her thoughts. She asked herself: why, if God, or whoever was revealing these messages to Larry, could foresee these dangers, why allow them to happen at all? Pope Dominic stared at Larry for some time without being conscious of seeing him. He was deeply troubled by the warning and its revelation. He was weighing up Larry's character in his mind from the notes and recordings passed on to him from Ireland. If what Larry believes to be true and yet does not manifest itself in reality, the Catholic Church would be a laughing stock across the international world. On the other hand if Larry was right about such a disaster and it became known at a later date that the Catholic Church, at its highest level, kept silent and millions died, then the Church would never be forgiven. Errors in history were not easily forgotten, nor readily forgiven. The Pontiff had to face up to his own doubts.

'This warning, Larry, is an enormous expectation for me to act upon, especially since the source is from a non professional individual. I mean this in the context of the earthquake and the total evacuation and destruction of Rome. I must be strictly honest with you both; I would have more confidence to act if these claims came from a seismologist or even an architect ... that is not to undermine the nature of your husband's integrity and sincerity, Dee, with regard to his claim to be from a higher or divine source.' Dominic had no wish to hurt their feelings. Dee could see his position and its gravity quite clearly. She offered him some small consolation when she said:

'Dominic. If you wish to consult a seismologist before you accept Larry's message as authentic, please feel free to do so. I would, if I were in your position.' Dee was perfectly at ease with Dominic's doubts.

'Dee, you have put me at ease, I cannot thank you enough. It means that if it is possible to confirm any activity below our city of such a disastrous event, then a public warning would not seem like utter madness ...'

'And make the Church a laughing stock.' She plucked the thought from his mind.

'Precisely,' he replied with a smile and much relief in the exhalation of his breath. He was further relieved to know that Dee was totally attuned and sympathetic to his concerns.

'But, Larry, how do you feel about my doubts and the practical measures I would prefer to take?' He looked under Larry's face who seemed more interested in playing faces with little Ruth, now that he had imparted his message and warning.

'You are a very holy man, Dominic, or God would not have sent us here to bring you these warnings and instructions. I don't know God's mind or how his messengers come to know what they know. All I can say is that God does not make earthquakes ... it is a fault in nature which can be so unpredictable to us most of the time. I can't explain why I was given these warnings and instructions to pass on to you; I'm just surprised that you haven't received these directly as I mentioned before. I know that strange things are revealed to certain individuals from time to time, whether such things are of an inspired scientific nature or of an inspired spiritual nature. I simply don't understand such things. Life can be so mysterious sometimes. I just know that there is a good deal about natural communications that none of us have the wherewithal to explain' Dee and Dominic were taken aback by Larry's simple honesty and his ability to state the obvious.

'But do you object to me, Larry, using the aid of professional help?'

'Yerrah, you must do as you think fit, Dominic. I have no right to dictate to your conscience on the matter. Our duty is done here ... I have brought you the warning and further instructions regarding the development of the Church. What you do with the information is entirely in your own hands and within your own integrity. I know perfectly well that you will do the right thing. At least I was told that you would know what to do and the appropriate steps to take.' Dominic felt that it was Dee doing the talking rather than her husband. Larry could be so articulate, so inspired; there was always this duel personality at work in him? Dominic couldn't make up his mind which was true. It appeared that Larry could just switch from someone caught up in a child-like world and yet on occasions seem very articulate and profound. Without a doubt, Larry was well-read over the years with no little credit due to Dee's intellectual influence and that of his own parents when he was young; yet he did not make his knowledge widely known to others. Dee, of course, was used to these characteristics in her husband but no less taken aback at times by his ability to communicate at a much higher level. It was as if he was composed of dual personalities. It was difficult to know what triggered these odd changes. Dee loved him too much to dwell for too long on his bizarre personality traits, even though at times it could disturb her and take her off guard as if she was in the company of an intruding stranger.

'I am delighted and relieved to hear you both being so frank with me and for allowing me the widest latitude possible in dealing with all this knowledge. I can assure you both concerning your wish to be kept anonymous and that I will deal with the more urgent aspect of the message immediately.'

The audience with Pope Dominic couldn't have been more generously and sensitively handled. Cardinal Dwyer's warnings and objections in Ireland hardly affected the family's audience with the pontiff at all – though it was too early to draw conclusion of Pope Dominic's real thoughts about Larry and his growing influence across the world. By the time Dee and Family were driven back to the convent by Sister Patricia, she had the bizarre feeling that the meeting had never taken place ... that she had never actually met Pope Dominic except in her dreams, such was the sudden transition from the grandeur of the Vatican and its dripping opulence to the humbler surroundings of St. Clare's Convent and its humble occupants. It might have been an informal meeting with family or an old familiar friend in her own home. Only a snapshot of his physical presence remained with her.

Pope Dominic called a meeting with Monsignor Edward Henry, a member of his own council. He was a chosen trustworthy man who had the pontiff's ear and could be relied upon for his proven discretion, and loyalty. He was a man with good judgment and had the grace to be silent in all matters concerning the pontiff'. Pope Dominic broached the subject with care. He put the question to Monsignor Edward in a straightforward manner.

'Edward I would like you to contact an architect, preferably one of our own, and ask him if he could find out, discretely of course, from a seismologist about the likelihood of Rome being affected by volcanoes or earthquakes. I have no wish for the source to be overly inquisitive beyond my concern for the archives and their unique and irreplaceable nature. You might also discover where our archives could be safely stored outside of Italy if such a disaster were ever to take place. It has struck me of recent times, that if any major disaster was to occur in Vatican City and its surroundings, the ancient history of our Church could be lost forever.' Pope Ubutu was not really concealing things from his mentor. He didn't feel it wise or appropriate at this point to say more until he was convinced that there really was imminent danger to himself, the people of Rome and Italy as a whole.

'Leave it with me, Your Holiness.'

Monsignor Henry was a very able individual, a sincere prayerful man with unpretentious humility and deeply committed to the pontiff's service. His aid to the Holy Father was not given as if in intimate friendship, it was given as a privileged duty. There was warmth between them but more out of respect for each other's genuine spiritual character. Monsignor Henry was a humble man. Many a cleric tended to walk over him even hold him in contempt, as if his silence and humility were the characteristics of his seeming inadequacy. He never pulled rank on any other cleric or religious sister; it simply was not in the man's nature. He worked away quietly, yet, like a beaver to every task … he gave his duties full attention and devotion. He was a fit man of average size carrying no extra weight. His steely gray hair put him in his mid fifties; he was invariably dressed in a crisp clean black suit or wore the traditional soutane of a monsignor when it was formally expected of him to do so. Many clerics saw him as a creep and his humble manner no more than fawning deference to curry favor with the pontiff. However, nothing could be further from the truth. He would give any one above his own office and standing the same devoted service. It was on this man's shoulders that his Holiness unburdened himself.

The monsignor was in the process of phoning a personally-known archaeologist with the intention of gleaning from him how and where he might be indirectly introduced to a seismologist. Suddenly his office and building were shaken to their very foundations. The tremor was so great that it threw him across the office and ripped the telephone from the wall which was still in the monsignor's hand as he crashed half dazed onto the gray-blue carpet. The poor cleric was absolutely terrified and ashen-faced. Three times the same day there came more tremors but none quite as dramatic as the first. He lay on the floor for what seemed an age; he was stunned and visibly trembling. What made the incident all the more frightening was the sudden darkening of the sky and the gathering mountainous clouds. There came a fierce blasting wind followed by a horrendous thunder clap that again shook the Vatican buildings causing the windows to vibrate noisily in their frames. Following on the rolling thunder, came great electric-blue flashes of lightening that seemed to tear the very heavens apart. The rain fell in sheets like pounding steel rods that actually hurt the pedestrians who ran screaming to whatever shelter they could find. Many old buildings came crashing down. It seemed like a miracle in itself that no one was actually killed.

When the trembling monsignor calmed down he made his way over the debris of fallen books, lamps and other office paraphernalia. He ran to the pontiff's private chambers to see if he was injured. He found Pope Dominic flat on his face in a pool of blood; he too was also very dazed and trembling. Monsignor Henry gentle turned the pontiff onto his back and in doing so was greatly relieved to discover that Pope Dominic had no more damage than shock and a very bloody nose. The monsignor gave him every attention and asked if he wished him to call for medical assistance. The pontiff waved away the question in slow thoughtful deliberation.

'We can manage between us, Edward.' The pontiff experienced a sudden fear arising from a sense of guilt ... a guilt arising from placing his confidence in the hands of professional people rather than relying on Larry's message. Yet he was able to put his fears aside when he remembered how Larry and Dee gave him their blessing to handle the imparted warning by his own reasoning and common sense.

There was much cleaning to do and the replacement of many office items including much of the furniture that had been cast adrift from their normal positions. Six Swiss guards came running to the pontiff's aid even though four of them were quite blooded themselves. The best they could do was help to replace the main items of heavy office furniture which were scattered all over the Pontiff's study. He dismissed the Swiss Guards, but not before expressing his sincere gratitude for putting his welfare above their own, considering the injured state of some of them.

'Edward,' the pontiff said, 'you can forget the instructions that I gave you regarding the need to contact a seismologist. We know now that we have to remove all the archives out of Rome to a safe haven. I must warn you also, Edward, in good time,' the pontiff emphasized, 'that we too and all the residents of the Vatican must flee from Rome as quickly as possible. You, Edward, will travel with me and whatever family you may have in the vicinity of our doomed city.' He explained to Monsignor Henry that there was going to be a far more catastrophic earthquake believed to befall the city and beyond sometime in September. Pope Dominic didn't elaborate on the matter nor did he reveal the source of his information. He simply requested the monsignor to attend to his requests with all speed in readiness ... that there would be the greatest need for prompt action for saving the more important contents of the archives and arrange for their transport and for a safe country to store them whether on a temporary basis or for a more permanent one. That was not going to be an easy task, given the mammoth technical problems involved in moving the material from the Vatican archives. The contents were kept in constant controlled temperatures as many of the documents came into the Vatican's possession hundreds of years ago, writings from the very dawn of Christianity from the Apostles, Desert Fathers, martyrs, and countless saints from every nation under the sun ... many secret documents among them.

'I assure you, your Holiness, your instructions will be carried out without delay I'm sorry that you had to experience such an incident without the slightest warning. Are you feeling any better now?' The monsignor asked with grave concern.

'Yes, Edward, thank you once again for putting my needs and safety above your own.' The pontiff was deeply appreciative to the dutiful monsignor who merely replied graciously to the pontiff's gratitude with a simple sideways bow of the head. The monsignor never questioned His Holiness as to how he suspected an earthquake, he presumed, rightly as it came to pass, that he had some source of professional information on the subject. But, what did professional mean in this case?

It was three days later when the full picture of destruction came to the public's attention both nationally and across the globe. There had been incalculable damage right across Italy although Rome itself took the brunt of the damage with so many old buildings scattered across its intricate streets. Electricity cables were down everywhere. Many explosions had occurred in the duration of the catastrophic tempest. Many petrol stations were set ablaze and put out of action especially those that had the misfortune to be struck by fork lightening which had continued to rip the heavens asunder. The worst of the remaining damage was caused by widespread flooding and overflowing sewage into the public streets and rivers. Rescue teams were stretched to the very limit. The city fire brigades were working twenty-four hours on shift-work mainly tackling the widespread floods. In speaking to the media they remarked that the torrential rain spared the city from total destruction by fire although the damage caused by the same torrents of rain was as big a problem due to the sheer scale of the damage and destruction. The city drainage system couldn't cope with the persistent deluge. Even as they answered the many enquiries of the media, the rain continued in blasting sheets with the demented wind. The tremors ceased and, for now, that was the only blessing among a terrified people.

Pope Ubutu need not have bothered himself with the dubious task of warning the people to evacuate the City … the national Government took that course of action itself having called in several seismologists to calculate whether or not there were soundings to cause further concern. Their reports varied in severity. Reports came in of more rumblings right across Italy. The seismologists, along with a team of building engineers and architects, advised the government to have Rome and most of its surrounding towns to stand by for immediate evacuation.

Pope Dominic was in tears with the news … not only from the government's call to evacuate Rome, which was partially under water … .Many parts were without electricity and clean drinking water…he simply couldn't believe that the disaster prophesized to occur in September could possibly be worse than what had already occurred. Was the warning he received an error by its messenger, Larry Walsh, he thought? However, he decided to act immediately with plans to permanently vacate Rome as instructed by Larry.

The needs of the terror-stricken people, and the thousands of fleeing refugees were Pope Dominic's first priority. He gave the word to throw every possible means at the situation. He pleaded personally for international help which came rapidly to the rescue of Italy's terrified and fleeing refugees. Emergency supplies and services consisting of food supplies and drinking water, life rafts, helicopters, field tents, makeshift hospitals and medical centers were set up in a safe region well outside the surrounding borders of Italy. The transportation of priceless archives were put on hold indefinitely and only now considered as a last resort.

Permission was granted by the Israeli government for Pope Dominic Ubutu and his immediate staff to be given emergency refugee statue to stay in the country until his safe return to Italy or another safe haven was guaranteed. This message was relayed to Rome to be taken up at the pontiff's earliest convenience. His Holiness expressed his heartfelt gratitude to the Israeli Government and its people for their generosity and acceptance of him and his immediate staff in their hour of desperation and need of sanctuary. Their act of generosity would never be forgotten by the Catholic Church whose very conception and birth issued forth from their very soil and people. Although many of the Israeli people rejoiced at the prospect of the return of the Catholic Church to the place of its birth, the place of the Messiah, so long prophesized in the Old Testament by the Prophet Isaiah ... many traditional Jews did not share the same jubilation because of their un-acceptance of Jesus as the promised Messiah. Nonetheless, their hearts went out to all caught up in the dilemma of the fleeing Church and Italian people. The world was in shock at the plight of European refugees and did all in its power and capacity to welcome them. In the meanwhile, the pontiff, and the whole Church scattered across the entire globe, threw every resource at the catastrophic situation. Fortunately, with the absence of money there was no issue with the resources needed – aid came flooding in from across the international world.

The pontiff contacted St. Clare's Convent where Larry and family were staying; they had escaped the worst of the general damage, mayhem and flooding, as the convent was built on high ground away from the immediate location of the Vatican. Sister Patricia took the call on her mobile phone.

'Sister, this is Pope Dominic.' His voice quavered with fear and concern. 'Are any of your sisters in need of emergency help?'

'No thank you, Your Holiness, we are all well, though shaken with fear and shock.' Her voice lacked her normal sparkle and confidence.

'Are our visitors safe and well?'

'As well as can be expected in these extreme circumstances, Your Holiness. Larry seemed to have been most affected by the terrifying situation. Baby Ruth had taken it all in her stride, God bless her.'

'Well, that is wonderful; I'm delighted to know you are all well. Listen, Patricia, you must all flee to Ireland, to Garrettstown where Larry and his family live. There is a small community of Saint Clare sisters there of your own order, as you know. They will make you welcome since the few remaining are very elderly and will be overjoyed with the extra help and young blood to support their mission and work. You all have my special blessing for your journey and new work. I will keep in touch and thank you all for your unstinting and joyful service that you have given me personally and to my predecessors. You have brought me so much Joy and friendship ... so many spiritual blessings in my short time in this awesome office. Evacuate at your earliest convenience since there is worse expected by September. I will be making a public statement to that effect for all clergy and religious to evacuate at their earliest convenience. Forget all unnecessary property that would hinder delay and prove an unwanted burden on the emergency services. God bless you all and keep you safe and happy always. Let it all be done in the spirit of a new beginning ... God speed Now please put Larry and Dee on the phone to me. God bless you, Patricia. I promise you I will be in touch personally. I am not likely to forget you and your beloved community and all that you have meant to a lonely African miles away from his own home.'

As Sister Patricia called Larry and Dee to the phone she was in a flood of uncontrollable tears. She couldn't even tell Larry or Dee who was on the other end of the mobile phone. She lost complete control of herself. Dee took the phone from the Patricia's hand with an expression of startled concern for her; she had never witnessed the terrible convulsions and tears of this jovial and confident sister. Patricia literally raced from the room without as much as a backward glance.

'This is Dee, who am I addressing?' Her voice was full of apprehension and concern.

'Dee ... Larry ... This is Pope Dominic.' She beaconed to Larry to come quickly and listen to the conversation. He arrived in his own leisurely way with baby Ruth cradled and swinging in his arms as though the tiny bundle was a human pendulum.

'Dee. Is Larry clear about the date of the earthquake meant to occur in September?' Pope Dominic's voice was filled with both resignation and apprehension. Larry took the phone from Dee.

'Dominic.' Larry thought the informal address of his Holiness was still current even outside the official grounds of the pontiff's residence. Dee gave him a kick and received the usual amazed response,

'What?'

'Address him as Your Holiness while we are not in his home.' Dee was cupping the speaker on the phone.

'But we like him ... he's our friend.' Larry was puzzled over the fuss.

'All the more reason to respect his wishes, not to be too familiar with him when away from his home and office. That is what he wants.'

'Sorry Dee, I'll remember in future.' He stroked her back and kissed her gently on the cheek. She felt full of remorse for scolding him.

'It's Larry, Your Holiness; how are yeah?' Dee was cringing; she didn't know what her innocent love was going to come out with next. 'We had a terrible storm here ... and we were all frightened. Did you hear the storm ... and feel the ground shaking ... and see the sky going dark... and all the rain lashing down?' He was giving a blow-by-blow commentary on every aspect that took place including the fact that little Ruth was braver than her hysterical daddy. His torrent of information was like the stampede of a startled heard of cattle which the pontiff knew he had to turn home again. Patiently, the pontiff repeated the question:

'Larry, my dear friend, I would ask you to my home again to talk with you but our home was very badly shaken up and is in quite a mess. Can you tell me, Larry if the message that you received regarding the earthquake was for September and not for June in which we are in at the moment. Could you have been mistaken about the month?' Pope Dominic was hoping and praying that the later date was wrong and that the city could once again be restored, albeit whenever that might be, considering the devastation now being endured.

'Absolutely not, You Holiness. The message I received and have passed on to you is exactly as I was given it. However' – there was a long awkward pause before he continued; 'the angel who gave me the message in my dreams might be wrong. I have no way of knowing that. All I can say and I know you are very frightened and concerned, is that all I have told you about the future will come to pass. I was assured on that.

'Larry, do you mind if we keep in close contact with your family, this is important. I know that you have to flee back to Ireland with your family to the safety of your home. Nevertheless, it will be of great comfort to me if your family were available to help me in the future.' Pope Dominic was eager to keep this contact even though he knew in his heart that their delivery of the message meant that their duty to him was at an end.

'You can depend on our help at anytime and anywhere, Your Holiness. We all love you, even baby Ruth is smiling 'cause she knows your voice.' This simple statement from such an innocent soul was too much for Pope Dominic, he couldn't prevent his own tears welling involuntarily from his eyes. It was as if Larry had restored his confidence in some unique way, giving him the strength to face the worst that may befall the people of Italy and God knows who else. He couldn't explain the tangible feeling of renewed strength only that he experienced it as though some unseen power had suddenly come to his aid in the worst crisis of his life.

'You know, Larry that you really do need to reveal your Identity to the world as the source of the book, Larry's Law. I know that there are risks involved. However, it is important that the world realizes that what you have written is the inspired will of God and not some new craze. I realize that this is not an appropriate moment to speak of this with all the chaos and turbulence going on about us. In spite of the book's many commands that seem at variance with Church teaching, it will require our endorsement in order that it might be more fully and officially accepted across the Christian world and particular by our own Faith. It has struck me,' the pontiff continued his attempt to convince Larry and Dee, 'that the original message that you received from heaven guaranteed your safety, in spite of those who may wish to harm you. In view of that guarantee, and the proof that God is with you, proved by the healing of Mary Cassidy and the healing of Dee herself. Surely these events and powers should be sufficient to convince you that to reveal yourself as the source of the message would more easily convince people that the contents of the book most certainly are not the designs of communist Russia or China, or any other vying political movement, or some new religion.'

'Holy Father, for my part,' Larry scratched his head vigorously to aid his concentration, 'I am certainly willing to make this message widely known, as my wife, Dee, remarked, particularly as we were sent to you not by our own will but because I was commanded to come to you. That suggests to me that heaven holds you in high regard. I was told that you were a good man, one who can be trusted and that God loves you. However, I do have my wife and child to consider and I do not want to place them in any unnecessary danger. I think you really need to speak to Dee and see what she thinks.'

Larry passed the phone to Dee; she looked concerned as she picked up the gist of the conversation.

'Holy Father, this is Dee.' She did not try to conceal the concern in her voice. 'You are asking Larry to go public as the source of his book?' The pontiff repeated the point on Larry's guaranteed protection. 'Holy Father, we cannot expose our child, Ruth, to any risks even if we wanted to … she can't give her permission … she is too young but that does not mean that she has no basic human rights to protection by those closest to her.' Dee's voice was crisp, defensive. She added: 'I must also remind you, Your Holiness, that Ruth and I were never mentioned to be included in that guarantee of divine protection.' Her latter comment could have been misconstrued for sarcasm. Dee was determined to safeguard her child – who could blame her?

'Dee, is it likely that God would guarantee your husband protection without extending that protection to you and Ruth? I think it inconceivable.' The pontiff was forcing the issue. He continued:

'The Church needs to make public those on whom God had bestowed the privilege of directing his people. It inspires the people that God can choose the most humble of us to carry out his designs. If the prophets of the past refused to pass on God's inspired directives and teaching, we would all still be in the grip of paganism with all its fears, its brutal and meaningless rituals of human sacrifice to appease natural powers as imagined gods that were capable of intervention and concern.' The pontiff was trying hard to remain calm and yet remain consistent to have this important step considered. He never mentioned the necessity of standing up for the Faith and having to take risks for it. However, that very point was strongly inferred in his reasoning. Dee wasn't slow to pick up that nuance. The inference troubled her conscience. Old memories and roots of her atheism rose within her from her former life, like roots to water; her adopted Faith gave her the best of her life up to now. It too raised a flag of battle within her vying conscience. Was her own security and self-protection and for that of her child's safety used for the expediency of self-preservation and an unwillingness to break the family cocoon she wished to live in ... to preserve her own controlled world? Her world she knew to be as fragile as a mere bubble, pending a collision at any given moment with unpredictable Nature and circumstance. Dee's penetrating mind was racing with such speculative thoughts and conscience-pricking disturbance. At last she agreed, though reluctantly. Nevertheless, she realised that Pope Dominic's seemingly secure world was falling apart around him. His kind heart was reaching out to thousands of fleeing refugees and their children ... most were not in the pontiff's privileged position of importance to receive an immediate guarantee of secure help that came only with high office, privilege and status. Dee's vacillating conscience eventually considered too ... who was she not to support her new Faith and Church when so much good could ensue from the open revelation of her husband's true identity? She was even more conscience-driven when she remembered the words of other Christian teachers that, "... the Christian Church stands erect today only by the blood of her martyrs..." She realized that going public internationally was bound to make demands on her family. There would be searching questions from the worldwide media ... financial experts and political interests of every hue would wish to tear her simple husband to pieces. He would become the God he believed he represented and his hated mouthpiece. In the end she was forced by conscience to agree to risk the security of her family's anonymity

With both their agreements verbally sealed, the pontiff added further pressure. He wished to endorse the book personally by giving it the Church's official seal of approval, the Nihil Obstat and Imprimatur. This approval from the See of Rome by the pontiff himself would always be a controversial point with many bishops, cardinals, clerics and religious orders worldwide, including hundreds of ordinary people who were deeply loyal to established doctrine and tradition. The approval by the pontiff meant that such a book as Larry's Law or any other book or pamphlet with the approved Nihil Obstat and Imprimatur ... that is was considered to be free from doctrinal and moral error. However, it is not implied that those who have granted the Nihil Obstat and Imprimatur agreed with the contents or its opinions or many of the statements expressed. Given those guarded and hesitant conditions it was a bold step for the pontiff to take without the approval of the College of Bishops and Cardinals who were at the front line of any backlash in their respective countries, their dioceses and parishes. It was one thing to ask the faithful to honor in humble submission and obedience the supreme authority of His Holiness on issues of morals, faith and doctrine that have been established for decades, even hundreds of years and then suddenly pull the carpet of established doctrine from under the feet of the common people ... especially when the Holy See's approval was established from a very questionable and controversial source.

Larry had no academic credentials from any orthodox college or institution. At best he could only be referred to as a prophetic dreamer and visionary, like so many of the Old Testament mouthpieces that had ushered in the most obnoxious notions of a warring, vengeful and jealous God, who presumably favored a Chosen People, and condemned to slaughter their so-called pagan neighbors … men, women and children who were put under the Ban … and who had their lands confiscated on the so-called prophetic dreams and messages of self-appointed prophets, who really turned the sacred notion of a loving creator God into their own image and likeness to meet the approval of a religious hierarchy who seemed to revel in petty Laws, rituals and severe punishments … how later prophets would sweep away as so much nonsense such as the slaughter of animal victims that were quite incapable of wiping our human sin and personal offences.

In spite of all this knowledge of Judaic religious history and the errors of the past, the pontiff's mind was already racing towards the perfect and ideal opportunity to promulgate the book's approval and declare that he was already warned of a worse earthquake to come in September; an opinion that was already agreed by the government's own seismologists, though only uncertain as to the precise date, and time. The pontiff knew that his own credulity as a trustworthy occupant of the Chair of Peter was put on the line. He was banking on the fact that no one in Italy or elsewhere had predicted the terrible earth tremor that had already caused so much damage and destruction. Pope Dominic couldn't fault Larry's Law on principle as its contents stood firmly in agreement on a life of virtue expressed in the love and care of all peoples. That was his definitive decision which he proclaimed to his College of Cardinals and Bishops and also promulgated to the wider Catholic world. He saw in the new laws the virtue of all that was done on behalf of the true needs of the people. He knew that such laws would never suit all people … that much limitation would be imposed with regard to the manufacture of unnecessary wasteful goods, given the ever increasing limitation of natural resources. To the credit of the new laws, it meant that there was no possibility of powerful and influential people manipulating those limitations to their own advantage.

It was now the middle of August when Pope Dominic called the attention of the viewing world to the predicament and plight of the people in the Rome and the whole of Italy in a special and urgent Vatican broadcast concerning the total pending destruction of the Vatican, Rome, and much of the outer lying regions of Italy ... that he, the Holy Father, would himself be forced to flee to the safety of Israel under the protection of the Israeli government until such time that he could establish the new itinerant Church that was set out in the directives of Larry's Law ... that he, the pontiff, would be forced to move, in time, to another Catholic country.

He further revealed the source of his information by having Larry and family in his presence during the entire broadcast. The introduction of Larry's family in the Vatican's Media Office was as dramatic as it was solemn. Outside, the pontiff was quite aware of the activities below in St. Peter's Square where hundreds of fleeing refugees, were being air lifted by helicopter and army trucks, military coaches, to makeshift refugee camps beyond the borders of their own country and to the docks. St. Peter's Square seemed like the end of a dynasty with its grandeur reduced to hideous rubble. Headless statues that once stood glorifying the triumph of Christian Rome over vanquished pagan dominance were now, from their own scattered rubble, ushering in a new era of humility, giving the dignity of all peoples a new expression and emphasis in a new way of life that would glorify the love and care of all peoples.

The whooshing sounds made by the rotor blades of descending and ascending helicopters batting in and out of the square were like a war zone of evacuating refugees. These poor terrified families, the very young and the elderly were in a wretched condition; all were scrambling in a disorderly mass to be first onto freshly-returned helicopters...or being pushed and dragged up into every conceivable military vehicle. Even military camouflage busses were drafted in. Military tanks were used on the main routes out to the docks sweeping away cars that were partially submerged in water and hindering the massive evacuation. Great ocean-going liners and cruise ships were brought into action; trucks, helicopters, and busses emptied their cargo of wearied refugees ... the screams of little children were heart-rending on the parents and troops alike. In St. Peter's Square they were all ankle deep in flood water and fetid sewage which bubbled up from the underground sewage system that was totally incapacitated due to the torrential rains and severed pipes crushed in the fiercest quakes that had struck Italy in modern times. The stench was hardly bearable. Hundreds more of UN transporters arrived by the minute. The noise was deadening. All branches of the emergency services were stretched to absolute capacity. Everyone was conscious of the government warning concerning the likelihood of another more destructive earthquake.

As the pontiff spoke so the broadcast came out over the speakers of St. Peter's Square, a continuing scene of scrambling mayhem. However, the broadcast and revelation of Pope Dominic was meant for the world media who he knew was watching and listening with baited breath on millions of TV screens, radios and computers for more news of the ongoing disaster. Families of the refugees who were scattered across the world listened and watched intently for any news of their fleeing and terrified relatives. There was no doubt in the minds of many millions of viewers that the chosen occasion for this Vatican broadcast, including its controversial revelations, was meant to give further credence and support to the directives in the book, Larry's Law. If the predicted earthquake actually occurred in September, and the pontiff had no doubts about it now, then the wider world would sit up and take notice of Larry's Law, and its credible divine source. Larry's credibility as a chosen prophetic voice in a very skeptical world would cause a new questioning wonder; all of which would in turn make people once more give credence to the existence of a living Spirit who is quite capable of communicating with humanity.

The pontiff asked Larry directly to corroborate and testify that he was the source of the world's most talked about book, Larry's Law, and further, that he had cured a Miss Mary Cassidy, a native of Cork, city in his own country … a cure that had been documented and accepted as a miracle or an unexplained cure of a lady who was a born cripple … that his own deceased mother had ascended bodily into heaven … Larry admitted to all these points though he did so reluctantly. He was not at ease with this scale of attention. He did not have the slightest notion that millions of people across the world, Catholic and non Catholic alike were listening to him and seeing him in person. He couldn't possibly know that there were also skeptic scientists and staunch Darwinists who were impatiently looking forward to all this nonsense being proved wrong or having a perfectly rational and natural origin and explanation. The farming community in Garrettstown, along with the city community belonging to Saint Patrick's Church, Cork, was animated about knowing Larry's family personally. The family was suddenly elevated to celebrity status, the most talked about family in Ireland and throughout the globe. The whole of Cork city was claiming intimate knowledge of him.

CHAPTER 18

Mafia Assassination Attempt on the lives of Larry's family and Pope Dominic

One listener riveted to his TV screen and listening to every word of Pope Dominic's broadcast was Cardinal Fabio Bellini. He was, perhaps, the most hated, feared and dangerous man in the Vatican. Prior to the installment of the present incumbent on the throne of Rome, Cardinal Bellini had been the personal aid to the previous pontiff and was hoping to replace him ... Instead, the present African pontiff could see at once the un-spiritual character of Cardinal Bellini. Pope Dominic chose instead one Monsignor Edward Henry, as his personal aid and trusted advisor and confessor. From the very moment of Bellini's fall from grace he was determined to regain his position, by whatever means.

As for Monsignor Henry, Bellini hated the very mention of his name and even displayed openly an even greater hatred for his physical presence. Bellini, a native of Italy, was alleged to have close connections with the city's underworld. No one doubted the allegations since he was a perpetual and persistent snoop into every one's affairs. He took a perverse delight in gleaning the slightest tittle-tattle from whatever quarter and from all and sundry. His menacing hatred of Monsignor Henry was founded on the monsignor's confidential and careful manner. Monsignor Henry never volunteered information even on the safest subject. The very idea of lending himself to tittle-tattle or to the breaking of a confidence would have appalled him to the very essence of his being. Cardinal Bellini on the other hand delighted in it; especially when it advanced any particular scheme he was involved in, and that was clearly a frequent occupation of his.

Bellini was a trouble-maker for other Vatican clerics and staff. The only ones spared his menacing attention were those already forced into his deferential service ... students who were caught out by him in some compromising fault that if exposed, would mean the end of their religious career. Bellini's tongue was an insatiable source of poison to further advance his cause for the pontiff's throne. He was the most able and skilled devil's advocate in any argument or discussion. His mind was quick-witted, widely knowledgeable and as sharp as razors. This was a man who despised the current pontiff and all things African. No one who knew Bellini well, not many did ... except on the surface ... would not have been shocked to know that he would do all in his power to have Pope Ubutu assassinated in the hope that he would occupy the throne of Rome himself, or at least have it clear for another son of Italy. However, they would be very surprised to know that in fact this scheme of his was already very advanced. He could endure a son of Italy on the throne of Rome at a push ... however; it was his greatest ambition to capture that prize for himself. He had already many important and influential cardinals in his camp ... men who hated the very ground that Bellini trod but were chained by personal compromise ... bearing serious misgivings and abuses that would end their religious careers if revealed. How Pope Dominic Ubutu X11 ever slipped past him to be voted to the seat of Rome was something that enraged him. He felt that he could not have given the voting procedures his full attention or at least that there were traitors among those he believed he had in his sadistic grip of compromise. He didn't believe that any pontiff was chosen by God or the Spirit, but rather by internal politics and back-scratching deals, gerrymandering, compromise and favoritism.

Bellini was a tall figure-of-a-man with imposing stature that drew everyone's attention to himself. He had the very charisma of evil. His sickly smiling face amounted to no more than sweet dripping poison to greet his prey into false confidence and friendship. The more you were in his company the more you were striped of your dignity, self-confidence and integrity. The seal of confession was for him no more than a door of opportunity to compromise the trusting and gullible clergy or laity who didn't know him. He listened at the doors of private offices making pretence of smoking his pipe. He was both hated and feared. His plans to have Pope Dominic Ubutu assassinated were well advanced. He realized that the plot to destroy the pontiff would have to be moved forward because of the current crisis in Rome. If the pontiff was to make it to Israel before Bellini's plot was put into action, then he may have lost his opportunity altogether or at least made more difficult, more dangerous and complicated even though his father's hired killers would stop at nothing to claim the four million dollars agreed for the contract killing. If the assassins failed to kill the pontiff and the Walsh family along with him, then the money promised would be forever useless, since Larry's Law had already succeeded in ridding the rest of the world of money outside of the Mafia. There were still sufficient powerful individuals only too willing to back the Mafia's urgent efforts to reinstate a world dependence on money.

Now, the plot to have Pope Dominic assassinated grew even more complicated, and expensive for Bellini. After realizing the implications of the pontiff's broadcast, he was convinced that Larry Walsh and family would have to be additions to the contract killing since they were at the heart of the nonsense that Pope Ubutu was acting upon. If Pope Dominic was to carry out the new directives written up as instructions in Walsh's book, Larry's Law, then it meant that even if Cardinal Fabio Bellini was ever to sit as the supreme head of the Catholic Church, he would have to leave his native beloved Italy and be moved about annually to God-knows-where. Such a situation was never going to be allowed to happen; Bellini and his hired assassins would make sure of that.

It was important to understand Bellini's background. He was born in Sicily of parents closely tied up with Mafia families and their organizations. He had just the one sister Angelina whom he loved dearly. She was beautiful, loving, and indeed, an angelic person. Both children were loved by their parents in a way that was almost unique to the older Mafia families. Papa Bellini was the fountainhead of the family from which all honor and benefits flowed. His legitimate business was growing and dealing with the very best virgin olive oil. However, his more lucrative and shady business was a mixture of service to the drug's trade; he and his armed staff ran a drug's purification plant that was heavily guarded day and night. He was also tied up with contract killing. His connections ran right across the international world. No place on earth was beyond the reach of his notorious assassins; and more importantly, no one was beyond the reach of his international syndicate. He had corrupt politicians in the highest positions on his payroll. His syndicate of crime made Papa Bellini one of the richest members of the currently known Mafia organization. He was a much feared man.

Angelina, the angelic apple of the eye of all the family fell madly in love with Paulo, a handsome young worker from the olive plantation. A pregnancy soon resulted from this wild, frenzied love affair. Angelina was only fifteen then and her farm lover, Paulo, just sixteen. She was eventually forced to abort the baby. The sixteen year old farm boy disappeared never to be seen again by Angelina. However, from her own circle of friends among the young farm workers, she found out that her young lover died the most gruesome death by being castrated and having his genitals shoved into his screaming mouth and then having his throat cut and his body dumped into a local sewer. Angelina was devastated by this news and mentioned it to the only friend she considered to have left in the family, her brother Fabio. However, because the flower of her virginity was taken out of wedlock, and by a common farmhand, she lost all family esteem in which she had been formally held and cherished. Brother Fabio tried his level best to console his beloved sister. He too had been a close friend of Paulo. Both siblings had shared their love for each other from the very beginning. Yet over the pursuing months, the horrific death of the young Paulo played on brother Fabio's mind. He was forced under the directives of his parents to distance himself from support of his disgraced sister. She was now considered to be beyond a respectable marriage. As far as her parents were concerned she no longer existed. Through parental pressure, and through fear of them, Fabio too showed a distinct aloofness towards Angelina. She now felt that he had put a knife into her heart. She needed his love and support at this critical time in her young and inexperienced life. On the other hand, the incident made Fabio think in a more searching way as to the kind of parents who really loved him but could be as merciless to a youth the same age as himself. He didn't make his feelings known on the matter; his fear was greater than his liberty to do so. Although his father's love for him grew even stronger, seemingly by the day, Fabio questioned this love to himself. He had befriended the murdered youth on several occasions because of the age and generation they shared in common. They became close friends though the friendship was never mentioned in the Bellini household as they held themselves aloof from common olive-grove farmhands.

The young Bellini was indoctrinated into believing that Family was everything ... that blood ties mattered most of all ... that you must love dearly your own flesh and blood. Brother Fabio couldn't quite comprehend why his parents didn't practice what they taught him ... after all, they all but disowned their fallen daughter whom they held in perpetual disgrace.

It was Angelina's eventual suicide that turned brother Fabio's head and began in him a festering hatred for his parents and all they stood for, especially his father. Angelina couldn't bear the disgrace of falling from grace with regard to her father in particular. However, the fact that he made certain of having the child aborted was the final display of his true feelings for her. She was left with nothing of her young love. She realized by now that her parental love meant nothing at all. She realized too that she was no more than dirt to all the family – she experienced contempt from all of them, including Fabio, her once loved brother. He had shown her as much as the others what betrayal felt like. As this festering hatred took hold of her mind she planned an act of revenge on them in the only way she felt left open to her.

One evening when both her parents were out visiting, Angelina, in an absolute state of depression, misery and tears, took a bottle of whiskey from the family bar and a bottle of her mother's anti-depressant tablets from her parent's bedroom. While still sober she went outside the house to retrieve a length of rope from the tractor shed and arranged it to be tied on an old beam directly over the dining room table. She also took a large kitchen knife from its block. When all was prepared, she stripped herself naked in her parent's bedroom, leaving her clothes where they dropped. She wrote out a final message for her parents, sneering and grimacing at her own final words of indescribable passion and hate. She drew back the bed sheets of her parent's bed and poured a bucketful of her own excrement and urine, which she had purposely saved over several days. She poured the bucketful of excrement over the entire bedding and then replaced the bedding neatly. She placed the note carefully on her parent's bedcover in the hope that they would have at least one disturbed night. Every action was arranged with slow deliberation, and in her dark despair she returned to the dining room. It was a tragic and ghostly sight to see such a beautiful young teenage girl walking about her home naked and with such gruesome intentions. The knife she lodged in her thick hair until needed. She climbed carefully onto the dining room table and onto the chair she had placed for the purpose of her own execution. She drew the noose of the rope over her head, arranging it with measured deliberation. She winced at the first taste of the neat whiskey and swallowed the tablets with urgency. Tears streamed from her sad dejected face. Once she felt the whiskey and tablets taking effect, which was swift, due to the fact that she was not accustomed to strong drink ... the half empty bottle dropped involuntary from her hand along with the empty bottle of tablets, the remains of the whiskey splashing all over the highly polished table below. She took the knife from her hair ... plunged it with all her remaining strength into her lower abdomen and ripped upward with the knife. Her guts fell out, hanging in a disgusting, horrific mess ... she slashed the knife across her throat and at the same time kicked the dining chair with her heals. She dropped ... swinging like a macabre bloody pendulum – a butchered carcass. The teenager's blood spattered all over the table, furniture and carpet.

When Angelina's family returned from their night's entertainment, which was really no more than business-as-usual in the company of some of the most unsavory characters one could imagine, the horrific discovery of their teenage daughter was too much for the mother. The instant collapse of her heavy body into her husband's unprepared arms caused both to be thrown against the blood-drenched dining table. The furniture was sent skidding in all directions. The fall of the parents also collided with Angelina's hanging carcass sending her swinging once more like a macabre swinging pendulum, a hellish sight for any eyes. Both parents were soaked in their daughter's blood.

Old Bellini hurried frantically to the bedroom to change into working clothes. It was then that he spotted the note on the bedspread. The letter of itself was gruesome enough as Papa Bellini read it in the absence of his unconscious wife. Angelina's address to her parents was a diatribe of cursing hatred.

"Parents! Huh!

You both deserve each other. You, mother, had influence. You could have intervened to save Paulo his horrible end. You could have allowed me to have his child at least, so that I had some memory of his love. Don't you remember, dear mother, how you told me that you had married your husband when you fell in love with him – when he was nothing but a youth from the gutter, a no-hoper. [This detail was news to the father; He now put the letter at arm's length in disbelief at what he was reading...he winced at the revelation] Well, dearest, mother, you may have had your piece of shit from the gutter to wed, but you couldn't separate the gutter from the shit. There isn't enough water in all the oceans of the world to cleanse the both of you. You treated me like shit; so now I give you back the crap of your body with my everlasting curse upon all the family including the apple of your eye, Fabio. May you never again know a moment's peace and may the very horrors of hell visit you to the ends of your rotten existence.

The shit of your eyes,

Angelina."

The curse of Angelina certainly had its desired effect. It split the family asunder. Her parents were hoping for a restful night to help them bear up to the tragedy. It didn't happen. Papa Bellini had his wife sleep downstairs. He hadn't the strength to carry her upstairs. There were no servants in the house at that time of night. Old Bellini wouldn't call the police to the incident nor did he call out the doctor for his wife. His own son was away visiting friends. It was a strange irony and an unplanned bonus for the departed Angelina, as if her curse had taken immediate effect. Old Bellini had to sort out the entire mess on his own. It took hours to clear the dining room. The bloody corpse of Angelina he wrapped in several black plastic bags and then covered it all with a clean sheet. He fetched a trolley from the tractor shed and wheeled the covered corpse to one of the tractor sheds, ready for burial the following day. It was a very weary and drained Bellini who reached the bedroom. He switched off the light after undressing and threw the bedding apart and flopped into the stinking mess of his daughter's final present. He screamed frantically as he reached across to his bedside light. The revelation and the stench caused him to throw up his night's entertainment. He was too shocked and exhausted to deal with the mess. He showered, locked the bedroom and slept in one of the guests' rooms.

His wife's hair turned snow white overnight. After six months she had to be sectioned in an asylum for the insane. Eighteen months later she was buried on the family estate. Angelina's body was buried separately in the woods of the estate. Bellini noticed to his horror, after several weeks that nothing ever grew within ten meters of her grave. It was as if Angelina had cursed the very ground in which her father had dug her grave. Papa Bellini was forced to reveal this gruesome revelation to his beloved son Fabio. Though he only revealed a highly censured version of the details. He simply had to explain Angelina's suicide since he couldn't explain her disappearance without incurring innumerable and irritating complications. He couldn't take the risk of fobbing off his son with an unexplained disappearance. He made certain to tell Fabio of his sister's hatred for all the family including Fabio himself.

Fabio began to realize that blood ties were not all they were claimed to be; after all, he gleaned from his own self-perception that his parents didn't marry into their own blood for very good natural reasons. To young Fabio the whole blood-tie thing was a contradiction ... you made of it what you wanted to believe yourself.

The sixteen year old Fabio turned to religion for some kind of solace ... his family being regular highly respected church-goers. Young Fabio realized quite early on during this period that his father, in particular, was the greatest hypocrite he knew. Young Bellini listened to the gospels of Christ concerning the need to love one another as we would have ourselves loved ... and to forgive the offences committed against us ... that we are all God's children...that the rich would never see heaven ... that one of the prime commandments of God and the Church was, that you shall not kill .... With all these teachings forming in young Fabio's conscience he grew more sanctimonious at first and more and more fed his festering hatred of all the hypocrisy that his father stood for. It never dawned on him that his own father, in spite of the evil man he had become, was also in need of forgiveness. However, his son was too afraid of his father to confront him concerning the death of his friend, Paulo, Angelina's murdered lover.

Young Fabio's initial vocation was sincere enough when he approached his parish priest Father Paulo Pinto. The priest greeted him with enthusiasm; so much so, that the priest could hardly wait for Sunday to come so that he could introduce the good news to his congregation. To understand the priest's initial jubilation it was essential to understand that it had been over seventy five years since anyone could remember a new vocation to the priesthood from Bellini's rural parish. Fabio, now two years on, was introduced to the congregation. The parishioners were ecstatic with Joy; it was as if an angel from heaven had descended to visit their little parish church.

However, one elderly lady in the parish was not so enthusiastic ... she had seen such a vocation before, some twenty or so years ago, in another parish where she once lived. A young lad of no more than fifteen years approached the then parish priest. Once he was introduced to the congregation the people were equally as jubilant. The unfortunate thing was, as they were to learn later, the fifteen year old was only making initial enquiries in order to find out what was involved and how long the training in college would take. The then priest dismissed the boy's hesitations and virtually steamrolled him off to college. The Sunday before he set out for college the parishioners hoisted the boy on their shoulders and filled his pockets with money.

The result of all the hype and pressure meant that the lad couldn't any longer hesitate. He spent just under one year in the seminary when he realized that the environment of the college was not for him. He found out that some of the other young students were being abused and sexually compromised. The young lad's parents were an understanding and loving family. When they realized what their young son was experiencing, they looked for a face-saving way out of the situation, which wasn't easy in those days when priests were treated almost like gods. Unfortunately, the young lad himself couldn't see any easy way out of the situation. With the pressures of academia in the seminary and the stress from his fear, in a severe fit of anxiety and depression he took his own life by throwing himself headlong from the ninth floor of the city seminary. The boy's parents never got over the shock and in the end their marriage fell apart ... that poor, once happy and loving family, was totally ruined by a priest whose commitment to vocations overruled common sense and responsibility to one so young. The congregation at the time had a lot to mull over in the passing years, when the memory, the terrible unnecessary tragedy, remained raw in their minds. They found out the whole story from an article written in the local press which was revealed by the boy's distraught parents ... they felt that the only peace they might have for their hesitation in removing their son instantly from such a dangerous and evil situation might in some way compensate and appease their conscience in the hope too that the exposure might save some other innocent victim.

Returning to the young Bellini's situation, Catherina Tullio, the old lady with the long memory would not share in this present enthusiasm and she made a point of reminding the present parish priest and the people of the earlier forgotten tragedy. Catherina Tullio couldn't save the new potential vocation. As matters began to progress with the new recruit Bellini's father took control of the situation, as might have been expected. Like all events that involved his son, papa Bellini threw money at the situation [while it was still in circulation in Mafia circles only] and which had the ability of giveing priority to all his ventures. He also made indirect threats to the clergy running the city seminary. His accent was deep and strong when he met the rector of the seminary and expressed his immediate concern for Fabio's education and future vocation.

'You will look after my, beautiful son Fabio, eh? I will know if he makes unhappy, eh?' It was a statement and a threat combined. He passed a brown packet of banknotes across the rector's office desk. 'I hear you have all kinds of building problems with your college, eh? Well, is no good to have the college come a-down on my a-son, eh? 'cause I would be very angry and maybe I blow all the buildings up in my grief, eh?' Papa Bellini roared with laughter to veil the threat. He had a sinister smile on his face when he made such veiled threats … his smile, a teeth-bearing grin … a distinct sneer. The rector, who desperately needed the money, couldn't mistake the warning. He wasn't ignorant of the Bellini family and its connections. Yet he couldn't refuse to take Fabio based on newspaper claims of his father's connections with the Mafia.

Once Fabio was accepted and installed in the best bed-sit in the old seminary his advancement was rapid. Certainly he was a scholar and a studious one in his early days. As he progressed and advanced he began to feel empty … he couldn't quite make out the cause of the emptiness until one day when the seminary broke up for its quarter session, when all the seminarians went home to their families. It was then that the young Bellini discovered the source of his emptiness. He discovered that he had never consciously taken note of his position on his father's extensive estate. The olive groves of the estate seemed to go for kilometers; the workforce, though massive, always gave deference to the children of the Bellini family. The children grew up with this deferential respect shown to them. Most of the workforce tried to avoid getting into conversation with the children. All were terrified of Papa Bellini. He didn't encourage polite conversation from any of them. His labourers, like most of the surrounding rural villages, were well aware of the newspaper reports and their accusations against the old man and his sinister connections with the Mafia. The reports claimed that he was actually the Godfather of the organization ... that his billions of dollars were really made from the purification of drug's for his agents. His lucrative business from the production of the very best pure virgin olive oil was more of a means to cover up the nature of his vast wealth. The olive business was also used to launder dirty money cascading in from drug sales. The olive grove workers also remembered what had happened to the young hansom labouring lad who had befriended Fabio and fell in love with his sister, Angelina, which ultimately became her downfall and disgrace. Her young lover's death was a constant reminder to all the hired hands, if they needed reminding, to keep one's self to one's self, salute in silence and in deference when the family passed by among the groves; other than that, give the family as wide a latitude as possible. Young Fabio had now discovered, or become conscious of, this lack of respect and deference from the other students in the seminary. To them, he was just another classmate. Certainly he received the respect and deference from all his tutors, but that was not what he yearned for. He wanted to be respected by his fellow students; that was his consuming need, the very roots and food of his upbringing. Eventually he knew that there was only one way that he was going to get the deference and respect he demanded from them.

Now in his fourth year of study, his year group was reduced to forty percent of its original intake. There was now only fourteen of his original group left; and that was considered about the average figure of student survival in most seminaries. The dropout rate was fairly consistent over the years. Bellini developed his skills at domineering and compromising his colleagues He managed to set one against the other for no other purpose than to see them squirm in their own exposed scandals. One student was compromised by a sexual indiscretion; another was discovered to be using drugs, another discovered to be indulging in excessive alcohol. He would use these student and their compromised positions to force them to snoop on their fellow students. It was easy to see how and why he was the most feared and hated student in the city seminary among all the year groups, both above and below him. The young Bellini was considered a walking disease ... a man whose mind should have been turned to holiness, but instead, had deliberately chosen another master – he was, without being consciously aware of it, a slave to his own vanity and neurotic obsession with instinctive powerful feelings of his own superiority. His need for the deference of others and their subjection to his needs consumed him. In his sinister ferreting exploits, he had uncovered several older students compromised in homosexual activities. He also uncovered others who were sharing hard drugs; three others who had a drink problem and the remainder who were actually either courting women outside of the college grounds or being uncovered by acts of sexual self-abuse. The only innocent and clean-living students over which he had no power he hated most of all for their impenetrable piety; and he let such students experience his hatred by his endless displays of open hostilities towards them. He would open and destroy their private mail, strip their rooms of furniture while they were off for the day. They would come back late at night to find that they had to go and hunt all over the college for their beds, furniture and other property. He had their personal study books ripped up and scattered across their rooms. All these acts of vandalism and harassment were actually carried out by groups devoted to and compromised by Bellini himself. He never involved himself in any of these hate campaigns – he would just instigate them. He was too astute to be caught. Those genuine priestly students were certainly tested to the extreme … they had to bear a heavy cross indeed from this sinister, counterfeit religious student. There was no redeemable virtue about him whatsoever. Spiritual, he was not … he mouthed prayers loud and mockingly as if to tell all that prayer and priestly vocation was utter nonsense. There was no feeling to his prayers, not the slightest attempt to reach their ordered end. It seemed to all who experienced his presence, that God was a-no-go-area on Bellini's highway. God, to him became a permanent no parking zone.

This, then, was the nature of the beast that was ordained priest after five years of study. With regard to his academic abilities, he was streets ahead of any other student in the entire college. Even so, he used to get other students whom he held in his sinister power to type up his essays for him. He was by no means a lazy individual … he had inherited his father's genes for enterprise. Unfortunately it was not the only gene he inherited from Papa Bellini. It seemed that his father's evil streak had to manifest itself at some point in his life.

His ordination ceremony was the most elaborate ever held in Sicily. There were flowers flown in by private jets from the four corners of the earth to decorate Sicily's St. Francis Cathedral. The sanctuary, large and elaborate as it stood, was almost obscured by the most incredible floral designs; there were pedestals as tall as small trees; flowers intertwined and climbing to cover the full height of the marble cathedral pillars. The entrance of the cathedral was more like a florist's shop. The quality of the flowers was the very best that money could buy. [Money at this stage was only used by the Mafia. Their organization was using every means and influence to have a monetary system reinstated] For Papa Bellini his son's ordination was more important than his own wedding day. It was really a marriage of his beautiful boy to the goddess of respect he imagined existed in some mysterious way in the minds of important people such as his own dark brethren who flooded in from many parts of the international trading world ... men and their wives who packed the cathedral wearing pure white suits and dark glasses. They had to let Papa Bellini know that they were present even though code names were the order of the day. Gift envelopes were passed to Papa himself for the use of his beautiful holy son. Millions of dollars were passed that day for young Fabio's use. Outwardly the entire razzmatazz appeared as though a new pontiff was being installed to the See of Rome. Yet every representative of the underworld, the international cartels who formed the bulk of the chosen congregation knew perfectly well that the entire event was no more than an elaborate circus, a showcase of respect and wealth. Not to be present was not an option.

Usually only one bishop performed the celebration of ordination to the priesthood. Yet even in this case Papa Bellini managed to grace the occasion by inviting Cardinal Antonio Russo, a personal friend of the family, to be the main celebrant. Seven other bishops from across the international world concelebrated the event. Each bishop was surprised to see their colleagues. Each figured out from their own compromised presence why the others came. Normally the ordination of a priest would take place in the parish of the candidate. However, because Bellini's parish was a small rural church, and because it was considered too small and too unimportant, Papa Bellini insisted on using St. Francis' Cathedral as the proper and fitting venue for what was to become the Bellini show. One hundred and fifty priests concelebrated Fabio's Mass of Ordination. Most of Fabio's student year group was also invited with no refusal taken. The same students were sickened to the heart at what they saw as a whore's wedding to Satan. The elaborate decoration of the cathedral decked in the most exquisite and costly flowers were to them emblematic of blatant hypocrisy ... their perfume, which engulfed every square molecule of air space was nothing more than a vain attempt to cover the stench of utter rottenness. The music was exquisite, glorious, triumphant, and numinous. The organist was hired by Papa Bellini himself from a specialist, usually at the services of a classical orchestra. The playing was pure genius ... notes and cords seemed to have a life of their own as though they were solid spheres, musical planets that hung and spun in the cosmos of the cathedral. Every organ pipe became a member of a specter choir. Even the choir itself was hired. Papa Bellini left nothing to chance, irrespective of the cathedral's own virtuosity. For Fabio's father this was a-once-in-a-lifetime occasion … one never to be repeated in his family history. Needless to say the cathedral's own organist and seasoned choir were more than a little put out by the insensitive insult of being considered incapable of doing justice to the grand occasion. The insult was somewhat softened by the generous donation given to be shared amongst their own organist and choir. Each member received over three hundred thousand dollars each as a face-saving sweetener. Most felt that the insult was more than handsomely compensated and breathed a deep sigh of relief to have been spared the many hours of practice and rehearsals demanded of such a great occasion. All invited clergy were duly rewarded with specially decorated envelopes, each containing thousands of dollars according to rank and degree of compromise, position and value of their general service. Each envelope had a photo of Father Fabio placing both his hands in blessing over the head of a kneeling bishop. Although the act was a traditional one, it was highly inappropriate. It would have been more in the true spirit of ordination to have the focus of the bishop blessing his newly ordained. That would never suit Papa Bellini – not likely!

Papa's highly honored son, now a fully empowered man of the Cloth was driven from the cathedral in a brand new gleaming cream Mercedes limousine with a long black faring; white had been considered too vulgar for the occasion. The black fairing seemed an apt feature to the new priest's character and vocation. The sparkling luxurious limousine was to be given to Father Fabio as a matter of course. Apart from the immaculately-dressed chauffeur the only passengers allowed in the limousine were Papa and the newly anointed Fabio himself. The cortège of black sparkling limousines that followed in the wake of the cream Mercedes seemed more like a party that couldn't be certain if they were celebrating a wedding or a funeral. The family and invited business fraternity celebrated the grand festivities in one of the most luxurious marquees that were possible to manufacture. The long white table with its silk covering was decked out in a breath-taking banquet; the food and drinks were elaborate and attended by an army of waiters serving from silver platters by well established caterers who were immaculately turned out for the occasion. Papa Bellini felt that his own family home among the olive groves was the most fitting place to celebrate the wonderful and deeply personal occasion. A grand orchestra supplied the beautiful soothing music which allowed comfortable conversation among the chosen two hundred guests. The guests saw the flaming sunset make the marquee glow as though they were about to be consumed by fire. Then a wall of darkness came as the shadows of night ran across the marquee as if specters of the night had come to join the weary souls. Each guest was instructed to go down on both knees to receive Father Fabio's blessing. Each one receiving the blessing was instructed to join his hands and bow his head as Father Fabio gave his blessing. Papa Bellini stood by his son as each guest stepped forward to be blessed. Papa acted as a kind of MC-come-altar boy to his son during the entire performance. He was out of his skin with pride from his imagined ascendency onto the celestial heights of numinous power now radiating in beneficence from his son's divine anointing. All the guests slipped away after paying their respects to Papa and Fabio. Only then did Papa Bellini consider it sufficiently safe to belch and fart from all the rich food and heightened solemnity. He waved his hand at his behind pulling a grimaced face from the stench. His holy son gave him a withering look ... his own face revealing utter disgust as he remarked, 'Pa....pa,' in drawn out syllables.

So was launched the young man of God. His first and only parish was in Rome itself where he served the people, or, it should be stated more precisely, where the people served the young Bellini. From the very onset of his vocation he found every available opportunity to be involved in Vatican activities and affairs. His climb to the ranks of cardinal was rapid. Needless to say it was a mucky climb up a ladder of compromise and gerrymandering from every quarter. Dirt, backhanders, presents, outright threats and blackmail; these were the rungs of which Bellini's ladder was composed in order to reach his final goal, the throne of the See of Rome ... the jewel in the Bellini crown. It seems incredulous to think that any young priest would seriously make the aim of his priestly vocation to aspire to become the pope of Rome, the highest power and authority of the Catholic world. Such incredulity was not to understand or grasp the nature of Cardinal Bellini's ambition, his neurotic need for absolute adulation and deference. For him, humility was an unknown concept, a word that only seemed to define someone to be dismissed from the mind as one would dismiss an irritating fly, a thing to be crushed or swatted.

The tragic situation that continued in St. Peter's Square on Vatican grounds gave Cardinal Bellini the ideal opportunity to achieve his burning urgency to rid Rome of Pope Dominic Ubutu and the world of the Walsh family and their book, Larry's Law. The spirit of the book was now being widely implemented across the international world. Again, it must be stressed, it was the poorest of the peoples who were driving Larry's Laws into a living reality. There continued to be much resistance to such forced laws by former governments ... however, the international leaders of the military were fighting a losing battle as more and more unranked and un-commission service men and women who made up the bulk of all the armed forces refused to stand against their own peoples. These ordinary fighting men and women knew all too well that they had more to gain from Larry's Law than they had from their service careers and their paltry pay packet. They realized that Just to own their own homes would take the best part of their lives to do so, and then when they grew too old to care for themselves they would be forced to sell their homes to pay exorbitant costs to care homes whose owners lived in luxury at their expense. More and more common people were realizing the utter futility of working for money. It had only ever been a social philosophy, and that is all money ever was – it had its day. Bellini, however, by the very design of his own mind and nature was having none of that utopian lunacy. It didn't fit into his definition of utopia where the powerful and influential did their level best to keep the common classes in their places by every means possible.

Cardinal Bellini noticed several news teams with their television crews using mobile broadcasting units to cover the tragic events for the international media. Bellini realized that here was the perfect solution to arrange his evil intention. He knew that Pope Dominic Ubutu would appear on the balcony of the Vatican overlooking St. Peter's Square as a means of showing his solidarity with the plight of his people. Pope Dominic changed his daily routine and instead of saying his prayers in private or in the company of other chosen clerics as he frequently did, he chose instead to do so in full view of the scrambling crowds below him who were still fighting to get drafted out of the stricken city. The refugees were bundled into the various military vehicle and civilian busses to drop them off at the waiting ships of every sort and size, As soon as one batch of refugees was removed so more and more people took their places. It seemed to the exhausted military and other civilian personnel that their impossible task was like trying to empty the Mediterranean Ocean with a thimble.

None of these unfortunate souls appeared to take the slightest interest in the white figure praying on the balcony above them. Nor did they notice the two other figures praying the rosary with the pope. Most refugees were too spooked, too shocked to care about anything except the hope of being evacuated from their hell-hole. However, Bellini was well aware of this new routine of Pope Ubutu and his special guests, the Walsh family. The pontiff and his guests were at this new routine now for a week; they were as regular as time itself; always from 11am to 12 noon before they disappeared for lunch.

This breach of protocol stuck in Bellini's craw. He was thinking aloud. 'It was just typical of the African Pope to appear openly with common people at the most inappropriate times and places. Who could respect such a man and his habit of breaking all the presidential norms of high office? Hasn't common experience taught even this tribal upstart that familiarity only gives way to contempt in the end?' What was even more aggravating to Cardinal Bellini's agitated mind was that the camera crews were beaming the praying pontiff's pictures and his guests across the entire viewing world; the pontiff was clearly sending out messages that he not only gave Larry's Law the Nihil Obstat and Imprimatur but that he was openly declaring to the same world of Catholics that he considered the Walsh family as worthy of special status and as honored guests. It was all too much for Bellini.

Within days Bellini had hired a camouflaged mobile news-transmitting unit. Papa Bellini, now an old and physically fading man in his eighties, hired five professional assassins. He spoke to his son, the cardinal, in whispers, his voice straining from his croaking throat as though he might die at any moment. However, his mind lost nothing of its edge and control.

'I've hired two assassins from USA ... one from Sicily ... another from Columbia and the last from Holland.' Papa Bellini's arrangements were that four of the assassins would take one target each, Pope Ubutu, Larry Walsh, Dee Walsh and the other to kill baby Ruth. Each of the four assassins was to be paid two million dollars to carry out their contracts with another two million dollars on completion of the contract. The initial two million dollars as part payment would be delivered to the camouflaged mobile TV transmitter unit ready for the assassin's arrival in the unit. The money would be delivered to the transmitter by Cardinal Bellini himself. The final payment to the assassins would also be delivered by the cardinal. That meant eight million dollars up front and another eight million on completion of the contract. The fifth assassin was given the most dangerous target of all. Papa Bellini held this man, a Sicilian, in the strictest confidence, telling him that the other four assassins were to be shot after the job was completed. He attempted to convince the Sicilian that he was settling an old score with these four deliberately chosen assassins; that all four had crossed his path before when each had screwed up important contracts. The Sicilian knew perfectly well that he was being fed a load of bullshit. Old Bellini wanted nothing to be traced back to himself or his son. Papa Bellini knew the Sicilian from his boyhood days. Rossi, the Sicilian, was one of the most ruthless and reliable contract killers known personally to Papa Bellini. In spite of that, Rossi was terrified of old Bellini. Rossi's duty was to return the money to Papa Bellini after dispatching the four assassins. His payment would be made by old Bellini himself at his home. Since the Sicilian had always been paid anonymously he could smell a rat in the overall scheme. Old Bellini made it quite clear that his son, the cardinal, would accompany the five assassins in the mobile TV transmitter unit. He was to be responsible for contacting his father to inform him that the job was complete in all details. The final twist in these sinister arrangements was that his son was given the order to kill the Sicilian after the job was done and to return the money to his father's olive farm.

The bogus, camouflaged transmitter unit pulled into St. Peter's square in the dark of night. The four assassins responsible for the contract on Pope Ubutu and the Walsh family set up their specialized long range sniper rifles ... all weapons being camouflaged to form extended blocks of microphones on the top of the unit's roof. The fake camera was a perfect painted replica of the real thing. All five assassins wore dark glasses and off-the-peg clothing without telltale designer labels. These professional killers left nothing to chance.

The plan to carry out the sequence of the assassinations was clear in the minds of the four killers; the assassin from Holland was to target Pope Ubutu ... the Columbian was to target Larry Walsh ... and the taller of the two American assassins was to target Mrs. Walsh. That left the smaller American to target baby Ruth. The bullets being used were the exploding kind; there would be no chance of the mother or baby surviving. The sequence for firing the bullets was to be on the count of five allowing for the slow careful squeezing of the sniper triggers; the slightest movement of the rifles would mean a miss by kilometers. On the count all shots were to be fired at once so that there was no time for any of the targets to flee from the scene. The fifth assassin, the Sicilian, appeared to the others to be no more than a messenger boy for the cardinal.

By 10.45am the transmitter unit was in place. The crew of assassins had slept in the vehicle overnight having their food packed in the unit also. Unknown to the cardinal who also slept in the unit, the Sicilian informed the others of the double-cross that old Bellini had planned. The reason why the Sicilian whispered this information to the rest of the crew was that he intended to kill the cardinal before carrying out the actual contracts on Pope Ubutu and the Walsh family. The killers themselves had a vestige interest in carrying out the contracts ... since as Larry's Law gained more and more momentum across the world their livelihood and money would be gone forever. That, in their minds, was never going to happen.

The atmosphere in the vehicle was poisonous. Only the cardinal, now dressed in civilian clothes, displayed a composed but sickly smile. He was seated on one of the long bench seats that ran the length of the vehicle. The Killers were jumpy about each other, each eying the other surreptitiously. None of them were at ease with group assassinations. None of them had total control over the situation. The four killers stood on a stepped-platform behind the front seats enabling them to give their upper body clear space on the open roof of the vehicle. The dummy Camera was behind the killers on the roof. The four sniper rifles were placed in a neat row on the foremost part of the roof. All four weapons were covered and fixed with silencers. The rail on which the weapons rested was disguised with spotlights and cabling. The setup allowed the assassins to have a clear view of their respective targets without exposing themselves. Rossi, The Sicilian, was seated on the other bench seat opposite the sinister presence of Cardinal Bellini. From time to time all five occupants used a bucket for their toilet, dumping the contents outside into the flood of bubbling sewage that covered St. Peter's Square.

True to form, Pope Dominic Ubutu appeared as a tiny white figure on the balcony overlooking St. Peter's Square, and alongside him, the Walsh Family. As usual the group was praying the rosary together – Pope Dominic leading and the family responding. Meanwhile the crowds below were still scrambling onto all available vehicles. There was a constant cacophony of mayhem from the people – military personal barking orders over the constant sound of revving trucks and busses. The thumping thudding sound of several helicopters and their rotor blades ... the loud cries of hysterical children all contributed to a terrible sense of doom. While all this pandemonium was taking place, and with the pontiff and his guests deeply concentrated in prayer, the four killers had their camouflaged weapons accurately trained on their individual targets. There was no possibility of missing their victims. Each killer had their respective targets fixed in their rifle sights.

Just before the assassinations were to take place The Sicilian stepped up on the platform and whispered to his four companions to grab the cardinal and remove his automatic revolver. All five killers descended their prepared posts with the ploy of taking a drink. There was another ten more minutes before the Pontiff and the Walsh family would be finished their prayers. The four assassins grabbed Bellini while the Sicilian relieved him of his automatic. Bellini was taken in utter surprise and bewilderment. He had never been manhandled in his life by anyone. His own revolver was fitted with a silencer. The Sicilian forced the nose of the weapon into the cardinal's mouth and pulled the trigger. There was a heavy dull thud, no more. Bellini's skull splashed off the side of the mobile unit leaving a stream of blood, flesh and bone splinters running down its side. The cardinal's body fell in an ungainly heap and was kicked aside to the rear of the vehicle as so much trash. That done, the two Americans, the Dutchman, and the Columbian resumed their positions to deal with their primary targets. The Sicilian examined the four large hold-alls containing the eight million dollars; he flicked swiftly through various bundles of money leaving the wrapped up bundles intact. He whispered to his comrades in heavy, broken English:

'... Is all there, eh!' The other four scrutinized the money and smiled sickly ... all were very suspicious and wary of the middle-aged Sicilian. He was a very trim healthy looking individual without a hint of gray in his raven-black hair. All four saw how calmly and swiftly he dispatched the cardinal, albeit that he had their help. These were ruthless paid killers. The Sicilian, however, seemed to take the matter personal. Of course he had every reason to take the killing of Old Bellini's son personal since the cardinal's presence, apart from delivering the money to the four assassins, was to finish off the Sicilian once the latter had betrayed the other four. None of the company knew each other by name, nor did they want to know any such irrelevant details. The younger of the two Americans asked the question that was uppermost in the minds of the four assassins:

'Your share of the cash doesn't seem to be here, buddy, isn't that a little strange?' The speaker never turned to face the Sicilian instead he was training his eye on his target. His face was thin and grimaced as he stiffened his jaw bones. None of these killers were really at ease with the situation; each had an automatic revolver at the ready. All were fitted with silencers. They insisted that the Sicilian stood up front on the platform with them. Any sudden move, even by the Sicilian's shadow would mean his end. Each killer knew that as soon as the count of five was uttered by the Sicilian and when each killer's bullet hit its target, then all would instantly spin about with handguns pointed into the face of the Sicilian. The latter was well aware of this; he understood their discomfort and said,

'Eh! My friends; you no worries, eh! I return to old man Bellini with the present of his holy son, eh! He wish to pay me personally, eh; I'm a handy, eh. 'cause I live no more than the twenty of kilometers from he homes, eh! Oh, yes, my friends … I will get my pays, eh! And you will come with me, eh, to collect the other part of you monies, eh! And my friends, we will take the bonus, eh, for the dirty trick he planned for our short futures, eh!'

'You say you want us to travel back with you to drop off his son in that condition, the grim-faced, young American pointed behind him without taking his eye off his target, baby Ruth, now held in the arms of her mother on the balcony. Do you think we're f...n crazy?' The other three killers kept their eyes fixed on their respective targets. However, all three nodded their heads in agreement with the younger American who seemed to take on the role of mouthpiece for the others. The Sicilian was perfectly genuine in his attempt to reassure them of their safety. He pulled out his own automatic snub-nosed repeater to place it close to the young grim-faced American. However, before the well-meaning Sicilian could carry out his innocent intentions, four automatic revolvers were thrust into his face. He backed off with such a start that the entire vehicle shook. He was not very taken with their mistrust. It seemed too as if the killers had eyes in the back of their heads or understood the significance of moving shadows.

'Christ-a-mighty, eh! You all full of the bloody nervous; you a-keep on like this and you will shoot the bloody stars, eh, and miss you bloody targets, eh!' He waved all their guns aside as he held his own automatic gun by its barrel, to emphasize his neutrality and lack of threat. He passed it to the small American who was nearest to him. There was venomous displeasure grinding in the Sicilian's facial expression as he said: 'Better I-never-a- warn you at all but carry out my - a- previous instructions. What you bloody lot of the spooked hens you take me for? Next you shit yourselves if I do the fart, eh! Maybe you think I have the bomb up my arse, eh? Bloody contract killers ... I shit them-for-the-breakfast.' The four killers lowered their weapons and burst into hysterics. The small American handed back the automatic to the enraged Sicilian who felt he had to have the last word, 'So. You no trust me for my word, eh? I must put myself in the dangers first? Bloody contract killers, I shit them!'

The four assassins felt more at ease when they turned to sight up their targets. The time for clowning around was past. The Sicilian asked the killers in unison, 'You-a-ready for-count of five, eh?' Beads of perspiration appeared on the killers' foreheads from all the tension. They concentrated their aim. The count began. 'A one – a two – a three – a four – a five. The vehicle rocked violently on the call of five. It was another big earth tremor. The four shots exploded millimeters above the Pontiff and his guests sending exploding debris spraying all over the targets …. The five assassins were thrown about in the vehicle. The result of the tremor caused the Pontiff and his guests to dart from the exploding building debris. They were quite unaware of what had really caused the external explosions on the stonework of the building just above them. As the targets failed to reappear, the Assassins took it for granted that their task was a success. For now they sped away in the vehicle to Papa Bellini's olive farm … the Sicilian speeding away causing a great wave of sewage water on the flooded square.

'Where the f…n hell do you think you are taking us?' The smaller of the two Americans spoke through his teeth, his voice full of anger and venom. He was not accustomed to being led anywhere that had not been explained to him or agreed upon by precise negotiations. He was by nature a defensive, distrusting, cautious man – a man who measured his actions and options in a precise and level-headed manner.

'Christ, a might! Is the bloody President of America again … he think he negotiations with the f … n Russians, eh! Like a bloody war is coming?' The Sicilian, now driving the vehicle erratically, began twisting about in the seat in his characteristic agitated manner. He continued. 'Maybe, Mr. President, you forget, eh, that you all have to collect two more of millions each, eh? Well Mr. President, I no forget, eh! No. Giuseppe Rossi he never forget the pay day.' The agitated Sicilian stabbed vigorously at his own temple with his middle finger and banged his chest for good measure to emphasize his intentions and determination. 'Maybe, Mr. President he is quite happies with half the pay, eh, and he expect Giuseppe Rossi to have no pay at all, eh? Well Mr. President, you go f ...k yourself and your bloody donkeys and all, eh! Giuseppe Rossi comes to collect his honest debts, eh! Maybe we drop Mr. President off here, eh.' The Sicilian, his eyes and face contorted in rage and contempt, leaned forward across the other passengers to have a look at the smaller American as a challenge to his presumption to be the spokesman for the five assassins. The smaller American sat on the extreme end of passenger's seats. The expression on his face was grim and defensive. He too returned an equally vicious expression at the Sicilian. The atmosphere in the speeding vehicle was developing into a poisonous, dangerous situation for all concerned. It was the Columbian who saved the day; he sat at the back of the others and suggested a vote of hands to collect their remaining two million and at the same time to help the Sicilian to get his dues. Or just be satisfied with the money they had and leave the Sicilian to sort out his own problems. As the Colombian made the suggestion so he was the first to raise his hand in favour of collecting the rest of the contract money. All but the smaller American agreed verbally and with a show of hands. The Sicilian grinned from ear to ear and said,

'Now we- a- drop off Mr. President of America and we go-a-collect-eh?' He shuffled about in his seat like an excited dog wagging its tail.

'Ok! Ok! So I'll go along. But mark my words, Rossi,' he deliberately dragged out the name sneeringly and contemptuously as he added menacingly, 'if there is a shoot out at the olive farm, you'll be the first to get it.' The Sicilian just waved the back of his hand at the grim-faced American as if to dismiss the prattling mouthpiece out of hand; he considered him as nothing more than an insignificant passing fly with a lot of buzz and nothing more. It was strange to witness this personality clash between two complete strangers. Both hated the other from their first meeting. It might have been nothing more than bad chemistry. On the other hand it seemed as if it was some primitive ritual – like two rutting male stags locking horns to establish dominance, which seemed the more likely. Presently the tall American, who was by now pig sick of his countryman's provocations turned to him and said calmly:

'Listen buddy, put a bloody sock in it. You're beginning to be an irritating pain in the ass with your loud mouth; either that, or just f ...k off with what you've got. You don't speak for anyone here.' Having said his piece, which had been on his mind for some time, he turned his attention to the smirking Sicilian, who was delighted to hear that he was not the only one who was irritated by the small American. He posed a measured question rationally in a matter-of-fact way. 'What kind of trouble can we expect to encounter at this Bellini's farm, or olive grove, or whatever you call it?'

The Sicilian replied mockingly. 'What war will eighty-year old man start, eh? All he do now is to piss he nappy. Yes, all the time he piss himself; Papa Bellini, the great fountain I call him; the great fountain,' he repeated. The

Sicilian broke into hysterics before he calmed down and continued in a more sober contemptuous vein. 'I tell you, my friends; I know his house from I be a boy, eh! One day, I am only the twelve years eh, and he show me into his metal wardrobe; how you call a walk-in-a-safety, eh? A bloody great-a-safety room, full from the floor to the ceiling, eh! Billions of bloody monies, eh; all packs wrapped up, eh! I tell you I shit myself that day, 'cause I know from holy church school, eh, that to see the face of God you die, eh! Is the same – no? To see Bellini's monies you becoming the walking dead, eh! I say to h m, and I trembling and shitting together, Mr. Bellini, sir, I no want to see your monies, is all yours; I no want your monies. Oh, yes, my friend, I rob many things when I just a poor boys in the street, eh! But to rob from Papa Bellini, no sirs, I not that brave then, cause I still a-shit myself when old Bellini be around. Yes, my friends, everyone who have the brain give Papa Bellini the wide spaces, eh!' The Sicilian tapped his temple vigorously and continued, 'He run from that man as fast as the legs go whoosh – you gone, like the antelopes, eh! Old Bellini he tell me that day: "Giuseppe, my dear boy, you no be afraid of Papa Bellini." He smile at me like the snakes; I still shaking and full of the shits. When he use my name is like he take off all my clothes and leaves me in the nakeds, eh!' The Sicilian seemed to be reliving a boyhood nightmare; his tanned face grew a little paler. 'Old Bellini he put his arm around my shoulders and I get the creepers like someone is walking over my graves, eh!' The Sicilian, whenever he passed an opinion, or was in general conversation, turning him back to the point was like turning a stampeding heard of cattle – you had to run ahead of them to turn them home.

'Ok;' the taller American cut in on the Italian's reverie. 'We have established he was a dangerous man then.

However, how many soldiers are protecting him just now?' The question was to the point.

'Oh he have hundreds of the soldiers, eh! Hundreds,' he emphasized. 'You no worries; they not at his home, eh! They not even guarding the bloody olives. No my friend, they have more important things to guard.'

'What?' The tall American asked impatiently.'

'They busy with the white factory, eh.'

'What white factory?' The vehicle's engine droned on while the Sicilian continued.

'Is where they clean the drugs and make snow packs for Christmas, eh' He smiled at his own pun and continued. 'The planes, they come, eh, and they fly off into the skies. Then he use the ships, the lorries, the trucks; whatever transport is wants, eh; even the bloody donkies and the carts he use, eh.'

'But Bellini has only to call his soldiers and we are in deep shit?' the American remarked questioningly.

'But he no do that, eh! You all stay in the vans and I speak to him alone, eh? I tell him that I kill all of you, eh! But how the earthquake it-a-shakes your beautiful son, the cardinal off his feets and he hit his head off the seat in the TV unit, eh! and that I take him to the hospital, eh! ... and that right now he sleeping like the baby, eh! Is good plan, eh?'

'Then what happens?' The tall American got the knack of jumping in with questions just at the right moment to curtail the Sicilian's meandering rivers of thought.

'Is a simple, eh! While he thinking what he want to do, I grab him and make him open his a-walk-in safety wardrobe. I put my gun to his head, eh! And I say to him, is my pay day, you shit; maybe you forget ... but Giuseppe Rossi, he never forget, you pissy fountain. Once he open the wardrobe, eh, I drag him out, eh! Then I knock on the vans and you meet the great Papa Bellini, the great pissy fountain. We show him his beautiful cardinal, eh! And then we kick all his shit out of him for how he betray us, eh! Then we take our monies and a little few millions as the bonus for our troubles, eh! Is good plans, eh?'

'Ok, buddy. That sounds straightforward enough for me anyway.' All agreed even the smaller mouthy American, who was now brooding and deferential – not that he was any less dangerous. The Sicilian would most certainly have to watch his back.

None of the assassins were entirely comfortable with the Sicilian since he kept repeating his own name in boastful elation. It was understandable why they were all, in their own way, more than a bit skittish about the Sicilian.

It was a merciless end for old Papa Bellini. He was dragged out from his mansion by the ear after being forced at gun point to open the walk-in-safe. Giuseppe came to the parked vehicle and knocked on the outside door panel with the butt of his automatic. All four assassins jumped out smartly from the stinking confines of the van, their automatics in hand. The Sicilian smiled triumphantly as he held his boyhood nightmares by the ear.

'My good friends – eh! You meet in the very flesh, the devil himself, eh! Look at he trousers, eh! He wet from the piss; the great Bellini fountains, eh! Now, you old bastard, you ask me to kill my brother assassins, eh! Then you have your beautiful Fabio, to kill me, eh! So we all get nothings for doing your dirty laundries, eh! Well my childhood night-horses, and all my bloody horrors, you give to the poor boy, Giuseppe Rossi. Now he give you some night-horses especially for yourself, eh.' With this vindictive tirade the Sicilian pushed the old man into the vehicle to see his son with his head blown open and lying in a pool of his own blood. His feeble hands went to his thin gray hair and pulled at it hysterically with his skeletal fingers. He screamed as one utterly out of their senses. Here was the highlight of his life, the holy boy that had become a cardinal in the Vatican. The old man was in floods of hysterical tears, his hands moving involuntary from pulling on his hair to making fists and pressing them into his horror-struck eyes.

'Fabio! – Fabio! What have they done to you? What have they done to me? What have they done to us?' Old Bellini was dragged back out of the vehicle by the back of his shirt collar like a limp sack still screaming hysterically. His voice was frail as he spoke in forced fragile whispers from his croaking throat.

'Giuseppe Rossi, you and your friends have signed your own death warrants. You will not see a week of life – none of you – eh! The world itself cannot hide you from this day's work ... eh! I will make certain of that if it is the last thing I do, eh!'

'Listen to the fountain piss, eh! You make the threats to me and my friends, eh!' The Sicilian gave the old man a forceful kick in the behind almost making him topple over. 'You days are over, mister pissy fountains. You think that this mess be traced back to us, eh?' Rossi waved his hand in a sweeping motion to his fellow assassins as if to show how hale and hearty they all were and how full of victory they were over the old man's botched plans. 'Listen well, pissy fountains – you see the number plates on the van, eh? Who you think they belongs to – eh? I tell you 'cause I want you to eat you own heart of maggots, eh! You can twists in you grave and realize that the numbers plates belong to your precious Fabio, mister pissy fountains. And the number plates of this vans they on you private car, eh! So what you think of that, mister pissy fountains? Is that not the good plans, eh? This latest revelation bit into the old man's heart. He knew for certain that Rossi was right. The only consolation for old Bellini would be the realization from the grave that all four of the hired killers would be traced for the botched job having failed to assassinate Pope Ubutu and the Walsh family. The four killers couldn't know this information until they got home. Only the Sicilian was safe since he was hired directly by old Bellini. He didn't have to go through the Agency. The other four assassins would be blamed for the deaths of Papa Bellini and his son, Fabio.

'Now I shows you what we do with you mister pissy fountains, Bellini. He kicked the old man to the gravel-covered ground and continued to kick him in the body rather than in the head. He didn't want to kill him too quickly. For every kick on the fragile body he would shout more vindictive remarks.

'This is for the night-horses you give to Giuseppe when he only a boys, eh! This one for making me have the fears and the shits.' As the merciless kicking continued so the others also put in their boots for good measure. In the end old Bellini lay dead in a pool of his own blood. His body was completely misshapen and his face was an unrecognizable mashed up mess of flesh and blood. It was a horrendous brutal and merciless end, even for one who had been responsible for hundreds of deaths. No one really deserved such an end – it was pure vindictive and neurotic rage and revenge. The horror the old man had to endure to see the bloody end of his own beloved son was torture enough for anyone. It would have been a kindness to have shot the old man and given him a quick end. Unfortunately the five remaining assassins, because of their precarious occupation, lived and matured on merciless killing.

The Sicilian took one of the tractors from the olive grove's massive barns. All the workers had long since gone home. He coupled the tractor up to a long deep trailer which was used for loading and unloading large sack of olives. All five killers went into old Bellini's mansion and down to the walk-in safe. It was really an elaborate room packed from floor to ceiling with new and used packets of dollar bills in their highest denominations. In spite of that it was impossible for any of the assassins to estimate what the strong-room held; it had to run into billions. All this money was used both for cash deals and housing laundered money. Only a particular unnamed Mafia-run bank knew of Bellini's stock pile; and that bank did not do business with the general public; it traded only with the established Brotherhood; here again only the inner sanctum of the Mafia were allowed to trade with the anonymous bank.

It took three hours with the five killers working flat out to fill the trailer with the money. There was only room for one more layer of sacks on the trailer. Rossi, the Sicilian, left his four comrades to carry out the last four sacks of money. As they approached the trailer to discharge their burdens, the Sicilian sprayed all four assassins in the back with his snub-nosed automatic, killing all four. They never knew what hit them. They wouldn't even have heard his final words to them.

'Contract killers … Huh, I shit them for the breakfast, eh!' He searched the pockets of all four killers. All they had between them were their wallets containing Italian money and American dollars in high currency bills ... None of them had any identity of any description, not even the makers' names on their clothes. There were no photos of family. It was as if they were aliens from another planet. The Sicilian understood this perfectly well, since he took the same precautions with his own identity. All five had been dressed in off-the-peg suits that were sufficiently smart to pose as respectable professional business people. They all avoided the expensive handmade suits because such quality outfits had a unique identity in the very quality of their tailoring. They could be traced back to their tailor and eventually to a description of the purchasers.

The Sicilian turned the trailer away from the bodies but not before his spat down on them and remarked triumphantly, 'Contract killers, eh! I shit them for the breakfast.' He had to turn the tractor round in a circle to leave the olive farm. He was elated and overjoyed with his day's work. He thumped his chest with his sweaty fist and said, 'Giuseppe, you more than the match, eh, for all the world of Bellinies, eh! Is the best pay days ever!' He punched his fist into the roof of the tractor making a resounding bang, grinding his brilliant white teeth in victorious elation.

The sun was setting in all its glory. It appeared as one great disc of blazing fire with streaks of blood and flame across its lower horizon. Great shafts of golden beams fanned out through broken purple clouds, the same clouds edged in crimson blood. The evening was deathly quiet except for a gentle breeze still causing the olive trees to move in dancing shadows. Only the noise of the tractor engine and the evening chorus of roosting birds filled the descending darkness. The tractor made its way homeward, having to pass the Bellini Mansion once again. The Sicilian was feeling very secure and self-assured. It would be a life of absolute security for him until the day he died. He entertained himself with such thoughts. They were like a fall of delightful confetti cascading on the head of a hero returning victoriously from battle.

As the tractor came closer and closer to the Bellini mansion, he was completely unaware of the small American still lying on the ground where he had dropped. He was in the grip of perspiring agony from the several bullets that had hit his spine. He was still alive! It could only have been the adrenaline and neurotic hatred for the Sicilian that kept him alive in the desperate hope of revenge. He managed to move both arms forward with his snub-nosed automatic in one hand which lay fixed in the palm of his other hand to steady his aim. The extreme effort made him wince in new spears of shooting pain from his spine. Sweat poured from his forehead into his blinking eyes. With grim determination he lined the gun's sight to the Sicilian's forehead. Slowly and gently he squeezed the trigger. He only managed one shot since the pain was too overpowering. The screen of the tractor shattered like a sudden sunburst. The bullet went straight through the Sicilian's forehead. The American killer saw the figure of the Sicilian slump over the wheel and vaguely heard the horn of the tractor go off. He passed out never to recover again. His one consolation was that he died with a smile on his sick face. The tractor was now racing towards a great reservoir of water used for the irrigation of the massive acreage of olives. It plunged headlong into the lake causing a great tidal wave before bubbling its way down to its depths.

It was early morning before the macabre scene was discovered after the arrival of the olive grove farm workers. The charge hand contacted the police. They arrived at speed once the gravity of the scene was reported. During the process of the investigation one of the police inspectors in charge of the incident, one who was all too familiar with the family, remarked to a colleague,

'Well, you've heard the old saying, "What goes around comes around." This family was always going to produce a stench. You can't live and work in a sewer and avoid the stink forever. You know, it's going to be one hell of a job identifying this lot, if we ever manage it at all. Our one consolation is that someone has done us a great favor.' Within weeks of the Bellini assassination their drug's plantations and their massive purification factory were torched, bombed and raised to the ground.

CHAPTER 19

Italy totally Destroyed
by Earthquake –
Evacuation of Refugees

It was now just two weeks away from September – the month of the expected earthquake that would devastate Italy completely and Rome itself. By now the entire population of Rome was evacuated to transit camps, mainly in European countries. The last of the emergency services was evacuating. The only souls remaining were the very old who refused to budge and couldn't be persuaded to move. Those poor souls took their decisions with stubborn insistence. '...I was born here ... I grew up here ... I lived my entire life here ... and I intend to die here ... earthquake or no earthquake.' The men and women of the emergency services had pleaded with these stubborn individuals to no avail. They knew the big earthquake was coming – there had been too many minor tremors within the month of August. It was not easy for the service men and women to leave them behind, it was as one service woman commented in the last news broadcast, "...It felt like abandoning a baby or a young stubborn child to their fate." Removing such souls by force was not an option ...

time was against the overstretched services and their patience; most were exhausted to the point of total collapse. Sadly those doomed souls were left to whatever might befall them.

The Israeli government pulled out ever stop to make Pope Dominic's flight to Israel safe, comfortable and welcoming. He was given the maximum respect appropriate to any international visitor of high office. The pontiff's aircraft, once inside Israeli airspace, was escorted by six fighter jets two leading the aircraft as escorts in the front, another two at the rear and two more at each wing. The Pontiff's pilot never felt more important in his life with all the attention lavished on his VIP passengers, Pope Dominic and his cardinal-secretary, Monsignor Edward Henry. When the private jet landed, the airport was a hive of activity with fully armed military scurrying everywhere. The Israeli president was there in person to greet the pontiff and his aid which he did warmly and apologized for the plight of the people of Italy, now scattered across the globe with family, friends, or for the unfortunate packed in temporary transit camps. The warm greeting and compassion showed him by the president brought tears to the pontiff's eyes. He was a man who gave way easily to tears, being a kind and emotional soul. It was not difficult to see that this was a man who was brought up on the intimate love of his parents and tribal members.

The Israeli president, Ishmael Cohen, was a tall well-built individual; he was overweight with a rather obvious protruding stomach. His natural disposition was given to a calm smiling countenance. However, in these troubled times of strained relations with his close neighbors, the Palestinian people, he had little reason to be his calm self.

In spite of all the troubles of his demanding office he put every need of the pontiff at his immediate disposal. He invited the pontiff and Monsignor Henry to his own private and well-guarded family home to have lunch and talks about his plans for his stay in Israel. The pontiff had only two basic needs that he could not manage by his own immediate means, given the hurried departure from his home and all the organizational trappings that came with the highly organized structure of the Vatican. His immediate need was the ability to communicate with the Catholic world. This was duly arranged and given urgent priority given the plight of devastation suffered by the people of Italy. His other immediate needs were a secure place of worship and home to reside in for the duration of a year; after which he intended to move from country to country as requested by the message given to him from the messenger of Larry's Law. The pontiff believed in this as a command, an absolute order. In the end the pontiff settled down in a highly secured military zone.

It was a rather happy accident that the temporary place of worship was to be set up in an elaborate Marquee, one that was well guarded. It reminded the pontiff of his home in Kenya where so many of his poor tribal people had once depended on canvas and tent-dwelling for shelter. More appropriate still was the fact that Peter's Great Marquee, as it came to be known, was a reminder of the early life of the Israelites when Yahweh, their God was said to accompanied his tent-dwelling people. Peter's Great Marquee became another Tent of Meeting like the one used in the time of Moses.

President Cohen was generosity itself in allowing the pontiff every opportunity to use Israel's national network

TV and radio to communicate with the outside Catholic world. The pontiff was incapable of showing sufficient gratitude for this unprecedented and extremely generous assistance. The president informed his people in a TV broadcast:

' ... I considered the pontiff not only a welcome refugee, and visitor, to Israel, I also considered him a citizen entitled to every security and hospitality that our government and people can afford him and whatever staff he needs for his sojourn in our land.' The people across the world listening to this live broadcast saw the tears flow freely from Pope Dominic's eyes – he made no attempt to hide them. The millions of viewers were choked with emotion themselves. To them it was a question of a refugee far from his own native people in Kenya, a refugee for his Faith – but also a refugee from the pending devastation of Rome. In spite of his high office, he stood as a symbol for all the homeless and refugees of Rome and from every other part of Italy. The viewers were well aware by now of worse to come if the predicted earthquake for September became an actual event. Many people across the world were very anxious to see the outcome of the expected event which Pope Dominic made public in his address to the nations before fleeing Rome.

A team of workers had set up four large adequate pre-assembled dwellings for the pontiff and his immediate staff. Up to now only Monsignor Edward Henry accompanied him from Rome. Two sisters from Saint Clare's community arrived later. Other clerical staff and general help occupied the other three prefabricated dwellings. The dwellings were made of concrete and stone-cladding; these materials were in common use and demand in parts of Israel that had suffered rocket attacks from the Palestinian borders. Even the pontiff's official aircraft was housed by the Israeli military. Vehicles for the pontiff's personal use were immediately placed at his disposal.

It must be said that not all of the Israeli people were pleased to have the Pope of Rome on their soil. For many of them held on to the old prejudices of past history passed down to them by their forebears or by some of the old folk still alive. The pontiff was already well aware of this fact. In consequence, he avoided any occasion that might be likely to rake up the simmering embers of past historical conflicts, differences and resentments. He was after all only a temporary visitor and a refugee. Strange to say, the ordinary people who comprised the Israeli population were actually grateful to the pontiff, or at least for his association with the directives of Larry's Law – in particular for the universal abandonment of the use of money and bartering as an outmoded and destructive force in the moral, spiritual, freedom, and future advancement of humanity.

This opinion was creating havoc for the Israeli defense of their country. As more and more soldiers turned away from the army and other world military forces, there was real concern for the immediate and ongoing need to defend their country. Military resources were drying up as more and more nations refused to manufacture arms or have any dealings with money, weapons and wars. Although countries who normally chose to support the Palestinian cause against Israel and against their greatest ally, the USA., these too were struggling to continue to manufacture and supply arms as the ordinary workers turned more and more to the principles of Larry's Law as their real investment for a more peaceful and meaningful future for all nations and peoples.

The peoples of many volatile nations, like the Middle East, tribal Africa, and the satellite towns and cities of Soviet Russia took more and more control of their own destiny as they were encouraged by the gathering success of other nations that had already taken control of their own future. Efforts at Intimidation by the Kremlin, the KGB and secret police became ineffectual. Governments were falling like skittles as taxes were drying up and refused to be paid ... more and more people refused to pay bills of any description. New organizations were springing up that were supporting the general population of peoples. Farming, housing, travel, food production, all the basic essentials for life became reorganized thereby eliminating all ownership and any possibility of compensation .... New courts of law were being organized by able people who devoted themselves and made it their business to carry forward the principles laid down by Larry's Law. The world's media and printed press were now in the hands of the common people. The Newspaper industry was cut to its essential and relevant needs. Many superfluous glossy magazines disappeared from the shelves and with them all the perversions expressed in pornography.

All gambling ceased to exist though racing in most of its forms continued. The world of sport began to change drastically as teams that once dominated most others with bought-talent now fell by the wayside. All contestants were on a par with each other. The art of sport was now more widely appreciated, literally as an art form. Sport as a whole was played as armature entertainment secondary to the life of work. In spite of this radical change there was no lack of enthusiasm on the part of players and supporters.

The predicted earthquake took place with devastating punctuality. It ripped Rome apart as though the city was made of wax. Solid roads rippled as though liquefied ... they floated in waves along their length ... houses, bridges, skyscrapers, the Vatican buildings, all were swept away like so much liquid wax. Powerful hurricanes demolished everything in their paths. Great trees were uprooted and flung miles into the air only to fall as matchsticks swirling about in a dense and extensive storm of debris. The noise was deafening, demonic and relentless. Ocean waves one hundred meters high smashed the city of Rome and ground its debris to little more than graveled stones that were sent bursting into the air like high velocity missiles which went clean through anything standing in their path. It was a blessing that most of Rome and its outer regions had been evacuated. The elderly people who had decided to stay knew very little of the horrendous tempest – most died instantly of fright while the remainder was crushed in their own devastated dwellings. The city was like another undiscovered violent planet ... the whole of its land and outer reaches were as dark as night except when lit with the constant tearing violence of fork lightening that ripped the very skies as if it was a devouring monster, Explosion after explosion of electrical power stations barely competed with the utter mind-shattering thunder bolts and ripping cracks of lightening. It was difficult to believe that it was rain coming down. At times the rains were more like gigantic steel rods; waterfalls thundered down with demonic force. It was like giant waves from an upper ocean descending on the Land of Italy. You couldn't speak meaningfully of the land being flooded – it was literally being submerged in an ocean. From its four compass points, the entire land of Italy was submerged into a sea of water with only the tips of its highest mountains visible.

Worst of all was the fact that no emergency services were possible not even from the countries closest to its land. Visibility was at zero with repeated hurricanes causing more and more deafening, pounding gigantic waves. This freakish demonic event continued to tear at the land and oceans for the entire month of September. The only survivors were those families of refugees who had already been evacuated to other countries. No one ever gave a true account of the disaster … not even the satellites that swept the earth could quite penetrate the dense atmosphere of the area at the zenith of that hellish upheaval. It took the better part of three years to see any recognizable shape to the land that had been completely stripped of every living thing. It was as if the land of Italy had just emerged from the depths of the ocean as a new mountain range.

The world now watching the aftermath of Italy's devastation grew ever more conscious of how vulnerable our planet had become under the stewardship of humanity. The tiresome, outworn debates concerning the need to take urgent action on global warming went into the old stew pot of debate once again – the usual international experts were given air time to voice their opinions of the need to take matters seriously. None of the so-called scientific experts could agree with each other. Some claimed that the melting of the last Ice Age could not be attributed to abuses in human industry – some claimed that human activity in modern times was definitely to blame for the present climatic upheavals.

In the meantime Italy remained an uninhabited mountain range of bare rock – the very earth of its entire surface was jet-blasted into the sea from the pounding ocean. It was strange to witness, and even harder to imagine that a once great land, a great conquering nation that once ruled as an empire, was now uninhabited except by colonies of sea birds. It was thought a strange irony that its mountains were covered in guano, sea-bird excrement ... all that was left of a once great empire. Of course the cynics said it wasn't the first civilization to be destroyed by time and the inevitable follies of humanity at variance with nature and itself. It would take years, decades for the land of Italy to re-establish itself. Many visitors came to witness the damage for themselves. It was impossible to say which city, town or village used to be situated in any recognizable location? Only the old maps, films and photographs of the land and its former inhabitants could be relied upon as archaeological and geological references. Books and photographs covering Italian life and history were prized possessions for the curious.

Pope Dominic Ubutu wrote a long letter addressed to Larry and Dee. He greeted the family in intimate terms. He also asked to be remembered to all the sisters and staff at Saint Clare's Retreat Centre. He gave a general synopsis of his life and events in the Holy Land. However, the main thrust of his communication was a heartfelt request for the family to visit him in Israel. The pontiff expressed a deep concern for the age old conflict between the people of Israel and Palestine which never seemed to get any further than constant acts of aggression on both sides. He believed that there had to be a workable solution to this age old conflict that grew worse and more violent by the passing years. He hoped in his heart that he could make some small contribution to their peoples even if it seemed like a drop in a vast ocean of difficulties. Pope Dominic felt that with Larry's gift of being in a special communion and favour with some divine influence, that they, Larry and the family, might join with him in some special prayers for that very purpose. Not that he, Pope Dominic, was not already making the needs of these people in conflict the second most important subject of his prayerful intercessions, after the needs of the Italian refugees scattered among the nations and now without a nation or land to call their own. The pontiff finished his letter using the expression, "Love Dominic."

Dee perused the letter for some considerable time. She considered why Larry could not simply pray for Dominic's concerns here at home; indeed she was quite well aware as a Catholic family, always to include the Pope's intentions in their own daily prayers as any good Catholic family would. If their prayers here in Ireland, were ineffectual, or if Devine power was not listening to them, then why should they be any more effective by a visit to the Holy Father in the in the so-called, Holy Land? She also thought hard about the fact that her family had already joined Dominic in prayer for the people of Italy ... were those prayers any more effective for Larry's presence? Was God, or whatever powerful influences that seemed to favour and communicate with Larry, going to make favourable choices for one nation over another? Were there not other terrible natural disasters across the world? Were God and the mysterious powers of Nature two incompatible realities? Was God no more than a human aspiration, a discernible power emerging out a developed moral and ethical conscience, which of its nature demanded virtue? Just as mathematics was to science and which demanded measurable truth in order for the discipline and its reality to exact its power and influence. These thoughts ran like springs of water bubbling up from Dee's atheist roots and questioning mind.

Such thoughts disturbed Dee's conscience regularly and deeply. She did not believe that the Jews were a chosen race no more than she believed in any race to be chosen by God. At least not by the god of the old Jewish nation, whom she was convinced, was really made in the image and likeness of themselves. Yes, she believed there was a chosen way to live a good life ... but that applied to all people of every nation without distinction or prejudice. Such a notion as a "chosen people," to her, was no more than a weapon used in national propaganda as their ancient forebears wrestled with the superstitions and competing powers that permeated their neighboring cultures. Many kings of the surrounding nations pronounced themselves as the anointed of God and yet caused more wars for the purpose of retaining or extending their own position and power over others. Even the USA still cry out the old worn out cliché, "God bless America," and yet one is left to ask what God are they referring to? It most certainly isn't the God who Christ proclaimed who preached forgiveness of enemies while the USA rain down bombs in retaliation for enemy attacks. It is like having God's message of love for all on your tongue but a bigger or better bomb than your enemy, ever ready to strike. Again Dee saw the same hypocrisy in The USSR and nations allied to them who would not countenance sanctions against nations favourable to their expression of socialism and the iron rod of state control. Dee was deeply skeptical about the whole God question. She seriously considered all religions having a divine intervening God as no more than the superstitious baggage of many contributing ancient civilizations. She accepted that some religions, even the more bizarre of them, were capable of producing outstanding and genuine spiritual individuals. And yet all were capable of the most blatant hypocrisy, and capable of teaching the crassest nonsense. Many seemed to scorn the use of reason preferring instead to hold rigidly to speculative doctrine as if it were sacred and irrefutable truth. Although Dee was very fond of Pope Dominic, Father Kevin, the sisters of Saint Clare's and many other religious individuals and communities besides, nonetheless, she sincerely considered all religious people as being part and parcel of ancient baggage, all indoctrinated over eons of time. These good souls would have given themselves generously to any worthwhile cause, even if the world had never come to establish the hypothesis, the notion of God at all. Dee felt that she, like many in her situation, were colluding with what they really doubted about religion in order to keep a certain harmony because of living with someone very loving and special. To Dee, good just comes out of being good, just as bad just comes out of being bad.

Once the invitation from Pope Dominic had been discussed with Larry, who was very keen to revisit his friend Dominic, as he called him, he agreed without hesitation even though the family had never visited the Holy Land. He hadn't reckoned on the long flight in the plane until Dee purposely brought that detail to his attention. She didn't want a repeat performance of his trip to Rome. He managed to convince Dee that he would be fine ... that he never expected to suddenly go soaring up into the air or be aware that there was nothing under his feet if he happened to fall out of the plane. Dee didn't laugh at the comment; she knew that it was an instinctive discomfort for Larry. Dee's other immediate concern was for little Ruth, how she might cope with such a long flight. Lastly, there was the matter of her writing for The City Vanguard; the latter was not a major problem as long as she was not delayed in the Holy Land for too long, whatever the reason. When all these details were considered, the family decided to go in support of the Holy Father. Dee realized that this was a very demanding time for him. In the long term, the pontiff would have no settled home. The itinerant nature of what he had taken on as a direct intervention of Larry's message for the restructuring of the Catholic Church of the future was very acute for Pope Dominic, considering that the poor man already had an early upbringing of being burnt out of his own village in Kenya as intertribal conflicts seemed to flare up every two years or so. One could not get used to such upheavals no matter one's age. For all concerned it meant hunger, violence, rape of men and women, young and old; homelessness, disease and, all too frequently, even death by merciless, brutal hacking machetes. Dee knew all those details better than most other people from her daily political coverage and her in-depth editorials on such matters.

It was agreed between Pope Dominic and Dee's family to invite Sister Patricia, the novice mistress from St. Clare's Convent who once served in Rome. She was, by now, a firm friend to Larry's little family at Garrettstown, county Cork. She was also a firm friend to the pontiff from the onset of his election to the See of Rome. The proposed visit had all the feeling of a very special reunion. Sister Patricia had no detailed knowledge of the entire purpose of Dee's visit beyond the fact that it had been the Pontiff's own request. It was not that Sister Patricia could not be trusted, far from it – it was simply a question of discretion. Dee always held the view that what she heard at the convent stayed in the convent and what communication she had with the pontiff remained with him and the family. Such things were never the subject of idle talk, gossip or speculation. Patricia was also a wonderful travelling companion – a dynamo of conversation on every topic imaginable. She was deceptively well-read and full of surprising insight for her years, comparatively young in her middle forties. Her thin face was always warm and inviting ... the fine lines present at the corners of her eyes were formed from her constant smile. Her face wore an expression that drew you into itself like an open door with a friend standing there to greet you. She had a very sprightly slim figure ... her tailored habit revealed softly the contours of her body. In all, she was such a rounded, well-developed character that it was hardly surprising that she was one of the pontiff's favorite entertaining companions in the best sense of that expression.

The plane journey to the Holy Land took off without incident. Dee relaxed and allowed her heart to replace itself to its normal calm. She had fully expected a scream of fright from Larry ... to her delight and surprise there was no more discomfort to him than the sudden grasp of the seat in front of him as the powerful jet engines roared and thrust the aircraft like a rocket into the heights. Once the aircraft leveled out he let go of the seat in front to the relief of all. Once he relaxed himself he sat calmly as if he was in the lounge at home. It was then that Dee passed him his favorite toy, the one he never tired of playing with, adorable Ruth. His face lit up once he had her in his arms ... the little child gurgled away contentedly, her natural disposition with Larry.

As the plane flew low over the Holy Land Larry shouted aloud for all the passengers to hear: 'Look, Jesus' hometown. Look at all the domes ... the same as you see on the Christmas cards ... there's no snow though ... King

Herod used to live there, you know.' Larry was giving one of his running commentaries and with assured authority. All the while his hand was shielding the glare of the sun from his eyes as he pressed his face and hand as close as possible to the window. Dee put her hand discreetly on the side of her face to shield her embarrassment. Sister Patricia did likewise but with great humor as she whispered to Dee from the side of her mouth:

'He's priceless. I bet the passengers never expected to be catechized on the plane for free.' Both of them broke into fits of laughter at the very idea of it and partly from relief of what must have seemed outrageous to all onboard. The plane was full to capacity. Most of the passengers wore Eastern headdress of one kind or another. They ceased to look with outrage and fear at each other. They could gauge that Larry wasn't a dangerous lunatic, but simply an eccentric innocent soul. The fact that someone trusted him enough to hold a baby seemed to season their benevolent credulity. Now Larry seemed to concentrate his narrative on little Ruth exclusively as he began to quote every character from the bible that ever lived in the land of Israel and beyond. Little Ruth continued to sparkle through it all.

'See down there, little Ruth ... Samson lived there ... he had magic hair .... He was so strong that he had to eat a whole cow for breakfast to keep up his strength ... But then, there came along a terrible witch named Delilah and cut off all his hair and so he lost all his strength.' Dee was mortified when she heard her real name and all the dark memories that clung to it. Sister Patricia was intrigued at how simple and dramatic he related the stories to the child. Larry streamed on as more and more characters leapt to his mind from the pages of the Bible. 'King David lived there once ... he had lots of wives and was always at war .... He stole another man's wife and God said to him: 'King David, you are a bad lot, indeed. You must go to confession to Father Kevin in Cork as soon as you can, 'cause you have committed a grievous mortal sin. You will have to scrub the million steps to heaven every day with your own tears for six billion years ....That's a lot of steps, little Ruth,' he added with stern expression. Little Ruth just gurgled on like a happy laughing stream.

Larry continued his rambling as the mighty jet touched down its wheels bouncing and screeching on the tarmac jolting its passengers. He smiled at little Ruth and said, 'Whoops!' It was plain to Dee and Sister Patricia to see that Larry had overcome his earlier terror of air travel. Even when all the passengers were shuffling down the isle of the aircraft he was still telling bible stories to his precious daughter. Most of the passengers smiled at him and the child as they pushed forward – though some thought him quite mad and hurried away from him as soon as they could in case whatever ailed him was infectious.

'Come on you two, David and Goliath – it's time to go before you end up back in Cork.' Larry just screwed his eyes shut and stuck out his tongue at Dee while grinning and shaking his head from side to side in a rocking motion. 'Come on with yeah, yeah daft lump. I swear there's more sense in little Ruth.'

'Did yeah hear your mammy, little Ruth, isn't she the bold brat.?'

'Come on, yeah beanstalk, shift yourself.' When the giggling Larry eased himself and the child out of the seat he gave Dee a big Kiss.

Sister Patricia looked away shaking her head in wonder. She had never been so close to and intrigued by such a happy trio. It was not always easy to believe how God had made this family the instruments of a new world. She began to appreciate more how it must have been for Mary and for Joseph to be chosen to foster-father the infant Jesus, who himself would drastically change the world in his own day and usher in the dawn of Christianity right across the world. The thing that struck Patricia's mind, or sense of awe, was the fact that while others were intimately connected with Jesus in his own time, few if any could accept his extraordinary claims to be the Son of God and Savior of the world. He was only a little child as Ruth is now. Sister Patricia was aware that the teaching of Jesus in his own day, and even up to the present time, was not widely accepted and the consequence of that lack of acceptance of his basic message of love and concern for all people was a world in constant conflict with itself, since Jesus' basic and simple teaching was all too frequently ignored as Utopian and unworkable. Yet what was he asking in its simplest form but love and care for others, for forgiveness of past hurts ... for love of Love itself which was the same as loving God. No one needed a complex theology to figure that one out. And here we are in precisely the same situation with Larry's Law. The fact that Patricia was an intimate friend of the family made her feel especially privileged to be accepted as their intimate soul friend. It was their very ordinariness that was hard to get her head round. To any who didn't know Larry better, he could seem even a bit of an unhinged simpleton at times. Sure he was serious about his faith and belief, and yet, he was so humble, loving and full of fun. He could even make fun of the characters of the Bible that he so often read about and yet still respect the fact that there was always an ocean of meaning and far-reaching implications to their lives. It was all a great wonder to Sister Patricia. Perhaps it was her own openness and devotion to her faith that graced her mind to see the extraordinary in the ordinary ... much as we take the earth for granted and we invariably fail to see how awesome it really is in the context of so many lifeless planets and stars surrounding us. Such were her thoughts in her reverie and awe of Larry and family. There was an instinctive Eastern spirituality about Larry's character even though he seemed to be oblivious to the fact. Larry, like most children, lived in the Now, an Eastern spiritual expression and one frequently adopted by doctors and counselors involved with mental health. Sister Patricia was well aware of this feature of his character since the study of Eastern spirituality was an important aspect of her own training and ongoing studies.

The meeting with Pope Dominic was embarrassing to the extreme. The party from Ireland was met by a broad-smiling pontiff who was surrounded by an army of scurrying military security. The pontiff stood close to a glistening two-tone Rolls Royce, a subdued rich grey and sparkling black. The doors of the Rolls were wide open awaiting the visitors. This luxury gave them an uncomfortable feeling for a family not used to such a high degree of attention and diplomatic attention. Sister Patricia was the first to remark on the scene before them. She invariably turned to humor when nervous. She whispered to her companion from the corner of her mouth, her hand shielding her lips.

'Will they remove the ten bottles of whiskey I slipped into your suitcase, Dee, do you think? Shall we confess now and hope they may be lenient on our prison sentence?

Or do you think they might torture us and find out the hard way?' Dee looked full into Sister Patricia's face not knowing if she had taken leave of her senses. The sister for her part kept an exaggerated worried face until she burst into nervous laughter to see the horror on her friend's face. Dee gave the sister a hefty bump with her hip.

'Don't do that to me Sister Patricia,' she remarked with exaggerated seriousness. In the end they both relaxed. Dee always addressed her friend with the formal title of Sister. It was for Dee a mark of respect for Sister Patricia's dedication to her life's calling and because she was a genuinely devout and holy person for all her bantering humour.

Larry was now waving franticly to Pope Dominic as though he had known him all his life. He was so animated, lifting little Ruth high above his head showing her off to the pontiff. The white-robed figure himself expressed great joy with his smiling animated face and his two waving hands. He was also delighted to see the entire group. Pope Dominic drew great strength and confidence from Larry's presence even though Larry was utterly oblivious to any such effect.

The pontiff was not allowed to walk to his visitors until they were screened for security clearance. This was done beside a heavily armored military truck in bright, high visibility faring. The blue and amber lights on the vehicle were revolving and flashing. The scene was scary. The fact that the pontiff himself was fixed to the spot created the horrible sensation of being involved in something much better avoided. It was one thing understanding the need for high profile security for his Holiness, it was quite another experiencing the gravity and seriousness of the reality of that security. One security guard in full uniform remarked in solemn tones,

'We regret this search and disturbance to your guests, Holy Father. We have no reason to doubt their good character and innocence. However, it is to such innocent individuals that terrorists turn and use to plant explosive materials in their luggage or on their person.' Once these procedures were ended there was, what seemed like, a massive step down of tension by the military as their vehicles and helicopter sped away. Only two of the heavily-armored military vehicles remained behind to act as front and rear escorts for the pontiff's Rolls with his guests.

There was a great sigh of relief all round as a greater semblance of normality helped to overcome the extraordinary ambience of strict military procedures. Although he never complained about such extreme security measures Pope Dominic realized that his presence and status as a temporary refugee and high profile international dignitary was demanding on the already over-stretched Israeli security forces. The truth was they could have done without the highly sensitive situation. Israel was after all very much a country always on the alert for the unexpected. They had many faceless enemies.

Once back in his own quarters, Pope Dominic was more at ease. Refreshments were brought in from the kitchen by Monsignor Edward Henry. He smiled brightly at the guests over the tray he was carrying – the china cups rattling as he moved spritely forward in the prefabricated dwelling. His smile was infectious – his greeting enthusiastic. The guests were like living news from home. Without intending it, his ebullient face betrayed a homesick-heart. The good man ever sought to make his home wherever his service to the pontiff called him. Dee, above all people, could sense this from his sudden sparkling face and enthusiastic greeting. What she saw on his face was not meant for her in any personal way. Any yet his sparkle was way beyond politeness.

Larry broke in, 'What is life like in Israel, Your Holiness?' He asked excitedly in his sing-song Cork city accent, which sounded even stranger in this remote part of the world. And yet his voice was like music to Pope Dominic ... after all he was frequently in the company of Irish people in his Vatican days, which now seemed so long ago ... and yet it was only December, a matter of three months since the Italian disaster and his refugee status in Israel. Larry kept rubbing his hands together excitedly with an intense enthusiasm rippling on his animated face.

'Please, Larry, we are among familiar friends here, so it's first names again.' The white-robed pontiff beamed his familiar smile on all the guests.

'Sorry, your Dominic; I mean Dominic.' A sudden roar of laughter filled the room at the expense of Larry's confused slip. He looked at everyone with an expression of incomprehension.

'What?'

'I fear I have confused you, Larry; it's of no consequence,' the pontiff remarked still smiling while he passed refreshments to his friends.

'Well, Larry, I must say it is both wearing and lonely much of the time.' The entire company, including Monsignor Edward, were kept busy with so many aspects of the pontiff's temporary existence being juggled in the air all at once. Pope Dominic continued. 'It is hard to facilitate international leaders of the Church and the many leading

lay people who needed to be attended to for one urgent
need or another. It is too dangerous to move about the
countryside and cities at present – the army are constantly
on red alert and my presence is an extra burden at the
moment. So long as I remain in our temporary location it
is possible to give us maximum security and a very
welcome degree of personal comfort for myself and all the
staff. However, the itinerant nature of my position is
taking a good deal of getting used to.' It was easy for the
pontiff's guests to see the strain on him; he appeared ill
at ease and quite tense, which was not his normal
disposition. However, most of the evening passed in
relaxed conversation, all catching up on each other's news.
Yet the pontiff seemed to be forever called to the phone to
sort out some urgent Church-related matter across the
international Catholic world. More and more he became
the spiritual father-figure of thousands of Italian refugees
scattered across the globe. Special Italian communities
were set up and organised by their own people. It was to
these that Pope Dominic would give much of his
immediate time and thoughts in regular broadcasts in an
effort to keep some semblance of national identity
considering that these poor people were now permanent
exiles struggling for any real sense of themselves. Most
clung to each other in tight communities which were
generally considered by the indigenous peoples as
ghettos. Some had sympathy for their forced exile status
others referred negatively to them as displaced persons.
Such labels did nothing to help their efforts at integration.
Pope Dominic held them in his heart like a mother bird
keenly concerned for her fledging souls, not yet ready for
the hard world of survival. Fortunately the establishment
of Larry's Law which was gaining in its global influence
was helping the world to rid itself of the narrow and

destructive notions of nationhood along with its primitive tribal psyche. Pope Dominic was always encouraging this very effort in his worldwide broadcasts. All five continents of the world needed unification ever more urgently so that every individual would grow into a world identity void of degenerative national identities and prejudices which all too often gave the narrow minds of ignorance a false sense of their own inflated superiority.

The following day, Pope Dominic turned his attention to Larry and Dee, excusing himself for temporally leaving Sister Patricia out of his immediate attention.

'Larry, I am very conscious of the fact that although the principles of your message contained in your book, Larry's Law, are now very widely accepted internationally, even so, there really is a need to be a focal point for the tens of millions of people who wish to hear from the person responsible for these tremendous changes to their lives. At the moment I am informed that the majority of the people worldwide have organized themselves to work with all the changes ... I feel that there is a need for you to be more widely known as a kind of figurehead, much as myself or as any president represents the government and leadership of his nation. In your case we need to be talking about a worldwide representative of the new world government. People need to be frequently addressed, supported and encouraged with a vision of where all these new changes are taking them and what the future of humanity should aim for. For my part, I can only address the issues related to the specific faith of the Catholic Church. However, there is a much wider social need that I cannot address since there are many faiths other than our own to be addressed. I feel that a lay person addressing the international world of so many denominations, and others with no belief in God at all, would be more effective since the message of your book covers such a wide social network of human activity, I feel certain that if you address the nations, the people will feel that they have a more solid ground and identity in the dawn of this new age ... and a new age it is, with so much change already imposed and the radical nature of such change.' Pope Ubutu awaited Larry's reaction. The poor lad just looked bewildered as if Pope Dominic was addressing him in a foreign language.

The sun streamed into the simply-furnished room composed mainly of cushioned settees and several hardback chairs. Some simple pine tables were gaily ornamented with bowls and vases of fresh cut yellow and powder-blue roses; other displays comprising a mixture of beautifully scented freesia and wild daisies. It was Dee who took the initiative for Larry.

'Dominic! Surely you cannot possibly suggest that Larry fit into such an important and demanding role, even if he had the power and the gifts to articulate such an extreme demanding office.' Dee's face was suddenly flushed and furrowed with concern.

'I don't suggest it, Dee. I must remind you of who did suggest it.' The pontiff turned his face directly into Dee's.

'Well, Dominic, who else suggested that Larry was capable of taking on such a mantle of responsibility? Larry really is not capable of such a mammoth task. I couldn't manage it without an army of professional help behind me.'

'I agree wholeheartedly with your last point, Dee; Larry will need an army of professional help behind him; and with regard to that very point, he has indeed a vast army of professional help behind him, all too eager to assist him.' The pontiff was absolutely certain of that. 'However,' he continued to answer the first part of Dee's question, as to who suggested that Larry was to head the first world government.

'Was it not some heavenly influence, according to Larry's own book, which made that very command crystal clear?' Dee was caught off guard by the pontiff's revelation and by his quoting of Larry's sources. She realized that she had not read the book for several months now. In fact, she was so pleased to realize its completion and to have the mammoth labour of it out of her mind that she avoided it as something out of bounds. But yes, Pope Dominic was quite correct, now that she allowed this irksome detail to be fished out of the depths of her mind. She also fished out another important detail which both reassured her of God's protection of Larry from all efforts to pervert his work and to assure him that he would not be harmed personally in any way. That was reassuring; however, that very reassurance only served to emphasize the pontiff's point, namely, that Larry was indeed nominated, no, commanded to carry out that awesome office! But how? God alone knows. As Dee looked from the floor of her thoughts to face Pope Dominic she realized he was right. He even emphasized that knowledge by splaying his hands out to her. There was nothing in his expression to indicate that he was particularly happy about the knowledge; he too realized the position in which Larry would soon be placed. Dee just nodded her head in deference to the truth and to the gravity of the situation and to all the unseen implications for her family. Where were all these demands and expectations going to take them? What was it going to do to their settled life of comparative contentment in their little rural sanctuary far off in the rolling hills and seaside of sleepy Ireland and Garrettstown? She looked across at Larry seated opposite; he was totally oblivious to the gravity of the conversation at hand as he continued to play with little Ruth. Tears flowed from Dee's eyes; no one was aware of it as the pontiff and Sister Patricia were staring at the floor, their minds and expressions occupied and grappling with the gravity of their unsettled thoughts.

'You mentioned earlier, Dominic, that we already have an army of professional helpers to assist us in this effort, could you be more precise?' Dee asked with a bewildered expression on her face. The pontiff now realized how badly shaken she was; he noticed too that she had been in tears; her eyes were glazed and her beautiful face quite red around her blue eyes. He felt deeply sorry for her and for the family; he knew from the result of taking Larry's message to heart that he had become an itinerant refugee himself; even though that same message actually saved his life from the earthquake and the violent storms that had devastated Rome and the whole of Italy. Of course, he could not have known about the escape from the Mafia's attempt on his life and that of Larry's family.

'It is the world's population,' Pope Dominic continued, 'that is your limitless army of helpers, the common people, who in their various ways have forced Larry's Law into a living reality in all major parts of the world. Most of the task is already completed as you well know yourself from the network of broadcasts on radio and TV that are now in the control of the people themselves. It seems to me that all Larry has to do is become the voice of the people on a reasonably regular basis. He has already had some exposure in the media from Vatican Radio. He was well received worldwide ... in fact he was an inspired speaker who had no need to lean on rhetorical pretence. People loved his simplicity and common sense.' Dee was reassured by Dominic's assessment of the situation as it stood.

'But from where could Larry address the entire world ...? Which nation should he begin with ...? How would he continue ...? Surely it would mean an itinerant's existence for all the family ...?' Instead of answering Dee's questions verbally, Pope Dominic pointed the open palms of his two hands towards himself; the gesture signifying his own predicament. He added for emphasis:

'We are both only servants of a greater cause than our own. We must never forget the upheaval that Larry's message meant for the initial security of millions of ordinary people who risked the initial steps of living without money ... millions of people across the world risked their lives by abandoning the armed forces so that they would not be used as the pawns of the old world, preferring instead, the security and dignity of a better more meaningful future for all.'

'I am aware of all that the people have achieved in the first decade of organizing their own government. However, where is Larry to begin?' Dee had no experience of being the focus of attention that Pope Dominic had grown accustom to with his high office and status. Although she had some international exposure with Larry and family with Pope Dominic while in the Vatican during the first tremors and storms that shook Rome, that was hardly sufficient to help her feel comfortable with the present expectations. She couldn't imagine herself leaving this awesome responsibility to fall on Larry's shoulders alone. She knew that he was capable of flashes of incredible insight and inspiration; however, consistency was not a quality she could comfortably ascribe to her fun-loving and innocent husband ... most of his time was spent as a ten-year-old. When he was wrenched out of that world he appeared to act and speak as if he was a complete stranger to Dee. Pope Dominic could see Dee's unease and put a calming hand on her shoulder. She could feel the heat from his hand.

'Look, Dee; you are in Israel; what better place to address the international world with its focus on their internal problems. I am sure that Larry will not say anything to cause offence to our hosts, the Israeli government, and its people. They too are a people, along with their immediate neighbors the Palestinians, who desperately desire a realistic solution for peace and harmony.' Pope Dominic added with some reassurance the words of a previous pontiff, Pope Gregory the Great, and of the need to move out of our comfort zone for the greater benefit of all. Pope Gregory the Great opened his sermon from the words of God to Ezekiel:

'"Son of man, I have appointed you as watchman
to the House Of Israel.
Note that Ezekiel, whom the Lord sent to
preach his word,
is described as a watchman. Now a watchman
always takes
up his position on the heights so
that he can see from a distance whatever approaches.
likewise, whoever is appointed watchman to a
people should
live a life on the heights so that he can help them
by taking a wide survey

These words are hard to utter, for when I speak
it is myself that I am reproaching.
I do not preach as I should
nor does my life follow the principles I preach so
inadequately.

I do not deny that I am guilty, for I see my torpor
and my negligence. Perhaps my very recognition
of failure will win me pardon from a sympathetic judge.
When I lived in a monastic community I was able
to keep my tongue from idle topics and to devote
my mind almost continually to the discipline of prayer.
Since taking on my shoulders the burden of pastoral
care, I have been unable to keep steadily recollected
because my
mind is distracted by many responsibilities.

I am forced to consider questions affecting churches
and monasteries and often I must judge the
lives and actions of individuals; at one
moment I am forced to take part in certain civil affairs,
next I must worry over the incursions of barbarians
and fear the wolves who menace the flock entrusted to
my care;
now I must accept political responsibility
in order to give support to those who preserve the rule of
law,
now I must bear patiently the villainies of brigands,
and then I must confront them in all charity.

My mind is sundered and torn to pieces by
the many and serious things I have to think about.
When I try to concentrate and gather all my
Intellectual resources for preaching,

how can I do justice to the sacred ministry of the word?
I am often compelled by the nature of my position to
associate with men of the world and
sometimes I relax the discipline of my speech.
If I preserved the rigorously inflexible mode
of utterance that my conscience dictates,
I know that the weaker sort of men
would recoil from me
and that I could never attract them to the goal
I desire for them.
So I must frequently listen patiently to their aimless
chatter.
Because I am weak myself I am drawn gradually
into idle talk and I find myself saying
the kind of thing that I didn't even care
to listen to before. I enjoy lying
back where I once was loath to stumble.

Who am I - what kind of watchman am I?
I do not stand on the principle
of achievement, I languish rather in the depths of my
weakness.
and yet the creator and redeemer of
mankind can give me,
unworthy though I be, the grace to see
life whole and power to speak effectively of it.
It is for love of him
that I do not spare myself in preaching him.""

When Pope Dominic finished quoting from the sermon of
St. Gregory the Great on the role of a watchman he closed
the well-thumbed, colorless book with a resounding thud
... a book which he had put together in his student days. He
remarked to his guests, and in particular to Larry and Dee,

'I have always treasured that sermon since my student days …. I have read it frequently in all the parishes that I served in at one time or another. That sermon, its humility, its truthfulness, its very insights into the lot of any poor soul struggling in high office has been a great comfort and consolation to me over the years.' The pontiff waved his hand upward holding the ragged-worn book, with its faded yellowing pages. He was full of pride and smiles as he commented further. 'Kings have read that sermon down through the years and quoted it liberally. Even Saint Paul came to a similar conclusion … how he tried his level best to be all things to all people … to share their lot in suffering or in joy. All this he did in the same spirit as Saint Gregory the Great … that he might turn as many souls as he could to God through the spirit of Christ … this they perceived as a higher order and possibility for all humanity. That was their Faith and we share in that same Faith. At times it may seem like turning a stampeding heard home before it destroys itself.'

Pope Dominic made a further point of reminding his guests, '… that they are not on their own in this mission … that no individual could manage such as task. Fortunately for you, Larry and Dee, you already have all the help you need, as mentioned earlier, in the millions of humble and wise souls who have already and willingly committed themselves to the codes and principles of Larry's Law. Of course, we are really speaking here of God's law since our concern is for the love and care of all people, irrespective of their origin or faith.'

The guests sat silently as they dined on a late meal of curry chicken, rice, vegetables and fruit, the aromas wafting about in the air-conditioned dining room. There was much to chew over besides the meal. All had rested including the pontiff himself. He was not at his best in the afternoons; he usually went for a long rest at 1pm in the afternoon whenever he could; it was a habit developed from the force of the heat and the idleness of imposed poverty on all without work in his homeland in Kenya. There he was naturally forced to respect the sun and the blistering heat of the day. However, he was a livewire in the early mornings and early evening; he tried his utmost to be in his bed by 10pm each night after many prayers, writings and meditations. He was a very genuine spiritual man committed to his calling and above all to the attention of his demanding office. It was difficult to imagine any other cardinal in the Vatican of the time who would have seriously entertained the many changes in the Church and be obedient to the demands that Christianity be once more an itinerant Church, especially on the dubious claims of an unimportant lay person as Larry Walsh, God's assumed messenger, and considering the odd personality of that messenger. Yet Pope Dominic Ubutu, a highly intelligent and insightful person, as well as being an extremely cautious one, accepted everything that was demanded of Larry's messages after careful deliberation and examination of both the probable source and his scrutiny of the messenger.

What Larry was to say to the world from Israel gave Dee much concern and unease. After all, she thought the people have Larry's Law which is already being widely and enthusiastically accepted by some ninety nine percent of the world's population. Dee felt heavy in heart. She knew that Larry had been through enough. His message had spread worldwide and been accepted, people had organized themselves. True, Dee considered, there was no accepted physical head of the now established world government. The people themselves were loath to accept any claims from any individual or nation to take such a position; and yet Pope Dominic was quite correct ... he had his ear to the ground and heard the same question constantly repeated:

"Why does Larry not speak to us more frequently? We want him and no other to claim that role of head of the world government, if any one individual was to hold the role at all."

Human leadership and development up to the inception of Larry's Law, was inevitably a natural instinctive development of man's animal nature, with the characteristics of might is right ... the dominance of the strong ... the virtual enslavement of the weak. Historically, altruism in leadership rarely endured ... self-interest and the innate instinct for dominance were far too deep-rooted in the human animal's psyche and reinforced spanning thousands of years.

For all Dee's knowledge of Larry's deeper understanding as a person and as her loving and adoring husband, and father of Ruth, she was still very nervous of him standing in front of a bank of microphones in communication with the entire world. However, for all her anxiety, there remained in her alert mind the promise that God would not allow anyone to hurt Larry or to obstruct the message that God wanted the world to hear. This was, without doubt, God's final message for the world. It was a case of listen and act or experience our own self-destruction by own hands. If humanity was to refuse to love and care for each other, as a first and final principle, then we would have inevitably ushered in our own self-made hell, a chaos that certainly could not be considered another myth, but a terrible appalling truth.

Dee wasn't sure if she should write out an address to the people for Larry to read. The difficulty was that Larry never spoke from notes. He had a remarkable memory if what he spoke about was sufficiently interesting to him personally. The other problem with drafting a talk for Larry was an important one, the address and its contents would not be his and he, after all, was the one to whom the divine messages had been revealed. Yet, Dee was not sure that this divine source would still be active. Her only hope of divine inspiration lay in the fact that the original message clearly stated that it was Larry who was to form a world government and that he alone was to be its head. Dee chewed on that one for some considerable time. Finally she decided to leave things with Divine jurisdiction, whatever its real source, and hope that Larry could cope. He had been perfectly calm and able for his exposure to the media in Rome. Fortunately Larry had no fear of the media simply because he had no real comprehension of the size of international media and its millions of viewers and radio audience; if he had, it never showed and he never spoke anxiously about it.

It was now time for Larry to address the nations as its supreme head. He stood in a military-controlled communication's studio oblivious to the frantic tensions from the broadcasting crew and military securities milling about the dazzling lights before several cameras and a bank of microphones. The studio technicians began the transition countdown. Larry opened with a very simple statement:

'Greetings to you all, people of Israel and Palestine and, indeed, to the entire world ...' His interjection with the phrase... "to the entire world ..." whether by intention or accident, made the viewing, listening world nod their heads in agreement as if to say, you are right there, Larry ... there is a world beyond the fragmented lives of these two vying nations. Larry continued. 'As you are aware from another broadcast, my name is Larry, Larry Walsh. Pope Dominic Ubutu has asked me to greet you with a few words of comfort in the sincere hope that our combined message may, in some inspired way, bring both peoples of Israel and Palestine more fully together in a true spirit of trust and concord with each other and with the world beyond. You are already aware that Pope Dominic himself is a refugee in Israel since the fall and destruction of Rome and the entire land that was once known as Italy. Israel opened its arms to give sanctuary and security to Pope Dominic until he is able to rearrange his new life and office ... this in spite of the historical religious divisions between the Holy See and Israel. This act of generosity between two former divided adversaries is really the central focus of my words with you today. Pope Dominic admitted that he was at a loss for words to bring you some meaningful comfort and encouragement concerning the divisions and hostilities that still plague and create havoc among your peoples. Many other nations of influence have attempted to bring peace and harmony to your divided borders; all have failed, without exception. The central question today that I am forced to ask is, will I or any other individual or nation do any better to unify your peoples and bring peace and harmony among you. The plain truth is, no. Only both of you can help each other since all avenues of aid and reconciliation have been utterly exhausted. Many offers of help and sympathy have really favoured one side at the expense of the other as many offers of help have come from those who endeavoured to manipulate your historical divisions for their own self-interest and advantage, taking sides with one or the other of you. My dear peoples, the solution to your divisions is in your hands alone. There is no possibility of security for either of your peoples in clinging to your historical identities.

'We know from our own experience that there are those among you who seek peace, harmony and mutual co-operation, and continue heroically to work towards that end in spite of the constant set backs and seeming insurmountable problems of division. We also know that there are many who do not work for those highly laudable ends. On both sides of the divide there are those who seek only personal power, the betterment of self, position and status for themselves ... those who insist on clinging to historical wrongs, inciting the gullible and inexperienced into renewed acts of hatred, acts of blind merciless terrorism, violence and revenge. The enemies of the people perversely setting the seeds of historical divisions of wrong-doing and planting them in the minds of the innocent young to germinate, generating more powerful mutating diseases forever fuelling new atrocities. The world beyond you has marched on through integration; this, in spite of all the tyrannical influences once forced upon it by all the great but fallen empires of the world.

'Where are all the great conquering empires now? What gains were there for all their bloody vying wars and destruction? Was it not the voice of wisdom itself that said, "... what gain is it for a man win the world but lose his soul ...?" These words of wisdom should haunt and inspire all of us across the nations; since in losing our soul, the very essence of what is noble and deeply virtuous in us, is to usher in a living hell on earth. My new laws have demanded that all countries surrender erroneous identities of nationhood ... to put aside our indoctrinated fallacious notions of religious supremacies, the sovereignties of nationhood and royal prerogatives ... powers of state ... all these I have pushed aside and have created in their stead a world family with only one head, one direction and one set of parents for all, and that is the love and care of all people, of every single individual. The lands we occupy for our mutual survival will not be what give us ultimate security and meaning to our pilgrim lives ... only the insistence of loving and caring for each other in genuine persistent effort will bring ultimate peace and mutual harmony to us all.

'Many thousands of Jews, Palestinians, Muslins, Islamists, Hindu, Shinto, Buddhists, Shenists, Taoists, Confucians, Sikhists, Jainist, Syncretists, and the Mohammed's of Africa and beyond, Christians ... the countless folk religions of backwater peoples ... the peoples from all these faiths and their lands are scattered all over the various nations of the world ... are all these peoples to be forced back onto the lands of their birth, cultures, and religions because some ignorant individuals insist on the supposed purity and superiority of their religious prophets, or the purity of their own nationhood ...? The result would be utter chaos. Integration, over time, adds richness, diversity and new gifts and insights to all cultures. We can only be diminished by small-mindedness and blinding prejudices that fester in the mould of ignorance. We are forced to move from our primitive instincts of defending cave-space. If we insist on marking out our territorial boundaries with the excrement of history, or like dogs pissing out their identities, we can never hope to reach out to each other in love and care as mature developing beings … we can only live the lives of dogs and vying animals without the ability to visualise how we can all live together in a spirit of sharing.

'National identities and ingrained culture all too often lose their meaning and relevance over time. The clothes we wear, the food we eat, the religious buildings and practices of our various faiths … our dominance … our ill treatment and suppression of gender and children have all been imposed on us without choice. There are many ways in which we have all been shackled to what is dubiously received as the wisdom, norms of culture and national identity. Even within tribes and communities, let alone nations. Persistence in tribal marks and identities, clothing, dominance, rule, all our reinforced norms … these can and do prostitute and blind reason in so many, and especially destructive when insisted upon by tyrannical leaders or by the bullying mentality of blind authority, whether that authority be meted out by institution or by abusive parenting or culture.

'My dear people, it is as I have mentioned earlier, the answer for your troubles and divisions are in the hands of each individual among your respective communities. Following cruel, circuitous dictatorship blindly is not about loyalty to your two peoples, it is a betrayal of self. Was Hitler alone responsible for the death, havoc and destruction across the nations? Or was the blame to be shared by every man woman and child who allowed their own fears and conscience to be compromised for a false gain that ultimately recoiled on the millions who sold their souls, who sold their conscience for a bloody demonic ideology ... a fallacious peace? National leadership and power must, in the end, either reach out to neighbours delivering love and care to all, or it will throw a switch of darkness and chaos across the world. This message is no grandiose impossible ideology. There is no new prophet or prophecy to come into our troubled word. Either we listen to the voice of the last and ultimate prophet, that of love and care of all, or we condemn ourselves to hell on earth which each one of us perpetuates and reinforce by our own personal contribution in blinding prejudice.

'I would like now to focus on the wider communities of the world. I feel that the role of a modern-day prophet has been placed on my shoulders. I would like to think that it was imposed on me against my will. However, that is not entirely true because I firmly believe in the contents of the new laws that are primary and essential for our future. What is vital for all of us to understand as a fundamental and indisputable truth for the well being of every human person and nation, is that there has only ever been one authentic prophet in the entire historical existence of humanity, in spite of the many thousand expressions of faith and religion that have been handed down or imposed on us through indoctrination, whether by cave-dwelling primitives, or by manipulating witchdoctors, or by some of the torturous theologians of our own times. The authentic prophet I speak of is the Love and Care of all people. That is who or what God is. It is a truth incorporated in many religions and yet all too often obscured by reams of irrelevant rituals, superfluous traditions and theological verbosity.'

Dee was, by now, cringing in her seat …what was he going to come out with next? So far he has all but swept every religion aside in order to promote virtue in the place of all traditional notions of God as a Supreme Being. To Dee it meant that god was given lower case status, a mere adjective in order to describe the attributes of the two concomitant virtues, Love and Care of all. Pope Dominic was also cringing in his seat as he sat glued to his TV set.

'This is Israel we are broadcasting from, for heaven sake,' he was talking to himself and feeling mortified. 'Will there be a Church at all after he is finished?'

Larry continued: 'Now I realize that we are not in a perfect world … that our histories across the nations have been bitter and cruel as one nation stood in opposition to another in terrible and shameful conflict. Sometimes nations experienced the merciless butchery of bloody warfare, blatant struggles for power and dominance …. The worst excesses of greed, barbarity, and moral decadence have visited all of us in one form or another. What land across the nations can lay claim to have known total peace and freedom from war, disaster, or being the conquered hostages of marauding savage power, or merciless warlords? Kings in their thousands have sat in great palaces and in shameful luxury and decadence, on thrones won by the blood of poverty-stricken minions … mere serfs forced and driven from the squalor of their rickety huts to be driven like fodder into the front line of war and barbarism in the name of the so-called anointed of God. Many lands have been taken by force to be given as gifts or given as wages to the victors of battle … privileged leaders. Great empires have come and gone. What have all the futile gains and suffering achieved but to poison the human spirit and divide the very souls of the nations against each other? We have been indoctrinated too long by the corrupt leaders of our nations and by many of our so-called institutions to be most proud of what is really most shameful. We have ignored for too long the prophetic voice of love and care for all ... that divine voice ... never sleeping ... but guiding us...pleading with us to turn lovingly and caringly towards each other.

'That prophetic voice continues to plead with us, to leave our past histories behind us least the resentments and endless acts of hatred, revenge and retaliation become the very spades that will bury us in our own time.

'Every fluttering flag of every nation must be torn from every pole and burnt. Every national anthem must cease to divide us one from the other. We are not a different species to each other, like flocks of birds calling out to defend the trees they believe to be their own. There has to be a new beginning. I am telling you, pleading with you to create a new tomorrow this very day for our people across the world. In the new world that we must build ... must achieve at all costs ... there will be no need for borders, nor will a separate identity and loyalty to any individual nation serve us in the end. We must grow up and free ourselves from the separation of other peoples and from clinging blindly to the limitations of tribe, nation, state or land. We must live with the needs of the living in the critical Now of our own time not with the ghosts of our bloody histories. We can only ever live as a united world if we obey and serve the only true concomitant parents of Love and Care of all.'

The viewing public across the nations were on their feet screaming wildly and cheering; their fists punching the air in frenzied triumph for the overthrow of perverted democracy. Larry continued.

'What was democracy? It was never more than a game with numbers; an agreement among the privileged to maintain their own advantage. What was freedom to vote for the common man or woman? What has it ever been but the seduction of the poor and underclass by the privileged? The vulnerable powerless, disillusioned by promises of equality that died in the graveyard of the ballot box where the people were habitually deluded, compromised, seduced and forever betrayed'

'Yes! Yes! Yes.' The viewing public was ecstatic. Unknown to Larry, he was intoxicating the people with what they knew to be universally true. Here was the true historical experience and conscience of the nations … their true thoughts that had until the arrival of Larry's Law and his rousing words been the smoldering resentment and apathy from centuries past to the present times. No one in their wildest dreams could ever believe that one day a real and selfless spokesman would arise out of the ranks and misery of the common people – a voice which spoke for all without fear or favour for any single nation – not even for his own nation. Larry continued.

'All that went before, including all the religions and their institutions, had been little more than totem authorities reigning in fear and called into existence by the expedience of the powerful and devious to harness and harass the ignorant of humanity with the tools of oppression and the falsification of reality and truth. There is only one true religion in the world; only one true Church – only one authentic priesthood – the love and care of each person fulfills each category. It makes every individual a priest to serve Love alone. Love is its own altar and the only one true universal Church.'

Pope Dominic was in terror and trepidation of what was coming next. The damage already done by Larry's references and dismissal of all religions and institutions would probably end up with himself and his guests being thrown out of Israel or locked up in one of the Israeli goals. Larry hadn't the slightest awareness that his friends, Father Kevin and Nell, sat mortified wondering what real damage all these statements of Larry were doing. His other friends in Ireland, Seamus, Lil and family were equally flabbergasted at what they were hearing. Lil had her hand covering her gaping mouth while Seamus' furrowed brow and startled eyes were wide with shock and incredulity.

'This can't be our Larry, surely?' It was difficult for any of his true friends to realize that he was one and the same person. Father Kevin, though flabbergasted by the sheer depth and controversial nature of Larry's thoughts, was speaking softly to Nell.

'This global address, Nell, is inspirational; it is Larry's voice, but he is not himself ... someone is speaking through him.'

'I know that Larry has always been a good and committed Catholic. However, I do agree with you, Father Kevin ... these are not his words.' Nell was caught up with her full undivided attention on the address.

'If this has a divine source, Nell, the Church is about to undergo some very radical and unprecedented changes. Don't get me wrong, I trust Larry; I always have; but this side of him ... it's not him at all. For the want of a better expression, it is pure idealism.'

Nell remarked in answer, 'perhaps the call for all to a common active priesthood might demean the status of the Church's ancient concept of what it is to be a priest.' Nell was being honest even if more than a little controversial herself. Certainly she would never purposefully demean nor dismiss the wonderful example of traditional priesthood that had always been the hallmark of Father Kevin's vocation and devotion to his people. Her own unstinting and unselfish support for him and his honorable position was proof of her own devotion and love for him, if any was needed. Yet she felt in her heart that all things move on as greater understanding comes to dawn on all aspects of human life and its progression.

'It sounds, Nell, that you too are drawn into the spirit of his radical idealism?'

'I can see that I am, Father ... and I can see how traditionalists would see such radicalism as potentially dangerous ... it could be seen to dismiss the great edifice of Church tradition.'

Father Kevin turned to her, not with any expression of hurt; it was just that Nell was always a very deep-thinking contemplative individual ... she had a unique gift for it. It was more a case of him being taken aback once more by the very depth of her openness even to such radical thinking at her time of life. Most people of her age, at least most regular Church-goers, would feel very threatened and insulted by a fraction of what Larry was claiming to be the divine will of God.

Larry continued with his address.

'Is the common man said to be glorified by great cathedrals, great temples ... supposedly the dwelling place of God? What God could dwell in peace and indifference while millions across the world have no home or permanent dignified shelter? Who could really praise the so-called great architects and craftsmen and women of such edifices when the scandal of the homeless poor is a sacrilegious mockery of our greatest buildings? Have we failed to learn the lessons of ancient times? We know from Christ's own teaching in Matthew's writing that he is immediately and desperately present in the hungry, thirsty, naked, homeless and imprisoned. Such presences are our opportunities to care for the Divine life of God in the desperate struggling poor and need around us. We are Love's children and as such we all need to be fed nourished and sustained by the love of others in every expression and need. We need to be housed or sheltered by love, educated by love, employed by love....'

The viewers of the broadcast were jumping up and down, cheering wildly, screaming into the walls of their own homes and offices, punching the air, their red faces bursting with wild delight and support.

Larry continued.
'Some stand in awe of the ancient pyramids built at the behest of self-deluded fools who promoted their own self-regarding grandeur by deluding their minions into believing the pharaohs' self-appointed status as being of divine origin ... that in fact they were really gods. What did the terrible enslaved labor amount to, when we who stand on the dust of their futile miserable and crumbling history see the madness and futility of it all? Then in such ancient times when the voice of the common people was trammeled into slavish neurotic obedience by fear and merciless cruelty from those who could never understand that we are all Love's family. Had human love and care

been a virtue for the powerful and influential alone while living in decadence and perversion? Seeking from incestuous marriage a diseased lineage for blood's occupancy sake? Such occupation on golden thrones of blind perversion ...pharaohs ... self-appointed kings across the nations, who considered themselves as the holy anointed of God? Those blind and perverted fools who became the dumb idols of their own self-worship, not even allowing the trammeled minions to look upon the faces of their so-called divine leaders. Those whose minds were so corrupt and disfigured by pride and self-importance that they took the belief into their own sick minds that no one could see their face and live ... they who considered their own mortal faces as divine, to be looked upon only by the privileged few ... thus reinforcing falsification and delusion in the minds of their unread and unlearned minions.'

Larry's voice seemed very remote from his normal gentle character. He was now overflowing with rage and anger, even outright hatred for the terrible blindness and for authority's litany of abuses on the common people. It was all so unlike Larry. Yet he could see it all flashing before his racing mind, the terrible abuses on the peoples of all nations throughout the world's turbulent and disfigured history. History's sins, images of ancient civilizations were flashing before his mind in terrible visions.

He spurred on:
'Think back, good people, to the royal families of the past who once considered themselves as the holy anointed of God and yet their fraudulent claims revealed their lie. Their thrones secured alone by force of their own self-serving laws ... laws to fit and make secure thrones won in

bloody wars instigated by conniving mercenaries and worse ... to raise such brutes to knight or lord by mocking sword in kneeling rite of scheming subjection and murderous alliance. To conscript their workless minions to front the ranks of bloody slaughter, no matter the war, no matter the enemy. And to sacrifice those lowly serfs on the mocking altar of bloody conquest and heartless expediency ... to leave their ragged loved ones bereft in shameful penury, in workhouses left to forage on strained, begrudged charity and rag-torn indignity. So were the empires made ... lands conquered ... natives enslaved ... The graves of the fallen given due honor with noble words and grand epitaphs ... the forlorn call of the bugle and fluttering flags paying questionable respect and honor to bloody murder .... The high and mighty decked in glamour and strutting regalia ... cheered on in their mocking parades by royal deception ... strutting the martyr's carpet as if on the face of their own vanquished pawns .... And they to have this thought of as veneration to the sacrifice of nationhood. So, we in our time, under our new laws, have, by universal consent, put all these lies and mockeries away and marked them all as betrayal. We too must know with more certainty who or what we nominate by reason and freedom to serve as God or nation.

'The primary human virtues of Love and the Care of others are not authenticated by worship with great choirs in magnificent cathedrals, churches or temples, while all around us, far and wide, we see wanton poverty and injustice, people struggling to find the security of basic shelter, food, warmth and meaningful occupation. Such buildings have their place of merit, when grace inspires the souls within to act on love's appeal to reach out to each other's dire needs? True love authenticates itself, so does care; both concomitant to each other; they are their own indisputable truths; neither has being or existence of their own ... they only find expression in vital human activity. Love and care are the highest first principles of human existence and advancement ... they are their own Christ, their own Guru, and their own Mohammad ... their own Allah ... Call the divine what you will. Love and care are our only true salvation ... they are their own messenger ... they speak their own indisputable truth in such a way that even the youngest child can understand them and live in and with them without the need for crass and superfluous indoctrination. They grow within us ... they do their own pruning ... cutting away the disease of all our self-deluding hypocrisy and all that we falsely serve up as true religion. Love and care of others, then, are the true authentic Christ or prophets of all human salvation. They are their own universal Church not confined to any particular building or institution.

'We become what we accept ... just as the fool reinforces foolishness in his own life by choosing to live like a fool. We evolve by the beliefs that we act upon; because we bring into being what did not formally exist in reality, except as pure potential. We evolve into people of care or destroyers by our own act of will not by our genetic makeup acting against our intentions.

'Our very being is activated by acceptance. That is, if we accept that love can be held universally as sacred and holy, a divine source of interaction requiring absolute devotion to its reality. Love and care take on the very sacredness of human existence and achievement. What gain is there for the human race if it eventually inhabits the entire universe or discovers multi-verses beyond what we grapple with now, if we remain divided and at variance with each other? Our new law proposes that we build our own heaven on earth with our own sense of caring hearts and minds. We must never forget that we are only pilgrims in the world passed on to us by our forebears. We too must in our turn pass on the world to our children. We can leave them a heaven or a hell.'

Larry concluded:
'Together we have achieved much in a short span of time with our new laws. We can go on to greater things ... greater advances. There is nothing too difficult for us to achieve as we continue to love and care for each other as our primary purpose and our greatest and highest good. No more can we excuse ourselves as unguided wanderers, serfs to unscrupulous use ... meaningless in our direction, when we have seen the marvelous works of these two concomitant shepherds, Love and Care for all. I thank you all for your patience for having listened to this heartfelt appeal. May the love and care of each one of us continue to parent and foster each individual across the whole world.'

There was deafening silence for what seemed an eternity. The people in general seemed frozen, hypnotized in deep contemplation. Then the delayed response came across the airwaves like a thunderbolt. Larry waved to the cameras after taking little Ruth in his arms and waved her little hand to the viewing public across the world. He also put his arm around Dee and kissed her for all her patience. She was delighted that the whole broadcast was over. She was without doubt very impressed by the scale of the address although she was utterly convinced that it was not Larry speaking; it was not his character at all. She knew him over the years of their marriage to be a person of fun and simple friendliness to all people. He had never shown any signs of such confidence in public oratory, or of being as deeply articulate as he had expressed his ideas in his lengthy address. She knew Larry to be widely read – he seemed to eat books in the silence of their home and yet never felt the need to discuss them at length with company except with her in the quiet hours of their evenings. He forged a passion for learning for its own sake from his reading and contemplative questioning of the Holy Bible and his own Faith, all of which were the result of his parent's influence. What remained for Dee now was how many pieces were left for the family to pick up? How much damage had his controversial address caused?

The reaction to Larry's address had moved and motivated the people even more. There was great jubilation across the world as all the nations tore down all the traditional flags from every pole and sea-going ship. The material of these millions of flags were collected by each nation and recycled and made into all kinds of clothing and bedding and in turn distributed among the poor and needy. The people made a formal request to Larry as to what kind of flag might be fitting for use among all the nations. Larry's advisors were swift to remind him of his address to the people and his use of the phrase, "the face of Love." This was considered a perfect solution as a fitting emblem that would honor all nations at once and be a constant reminder of what is meant by the essence of what it really means to be considered human. Dee too was delighted with the choice and its international significance. What neither of them knew was that the people themselves decided to personalize the flag by making it represent a family. The picture they chose was one taken from the broadcast of Larry's address to the nations. The finished flag had a perfect snapshot of Larry waving little Ruth's tiny hand to the people while Dee was portrayed with one arm on the child and the other hand on Larry's shoulder. Above the portrait in bold red letters were the words, "The Face of Love." Later the same picture was distributed to every home by every nation. It would immortalize Larry's family in the minds of the people for thousands of years to come. Later still it came as quite a shock to Larry and family, including Pope Dominic to witness the new flag fluttering both in Israel and Palestine. Larry and Dee were taken aback when they saw their own family portrait smiling and waving from the flag with bold red letters proclaiming "The Face of Love." Dee was more shocked than Larry; she covered her open mouth with her hand and exclaimed:

'My God, Larry ...! Look at that flag fluttering over Pope Dominic's dwellings. Who organized that?' She didn't expect an answer from Larry, yet he did manage to say:

'Well I did agree to the words as you already know, but the picture of our family is a big surprise to me. I think little Ruth looks cute though, and you, Dee ... you look so beautiful. How on earth could they have organized something so beautiful, so soon?'

'That is the easy part, Larry, love. We are in a very advanced technological age ... and in a time where people are only too delighted to give their best effort to any worthwhile project that has love's stamp on it.' When Larry and family met Pope Dominic he was none the wiser as to who raised the flag over his dwellings.

'Well, Dee, if that has shocked you as it has me, you just wait until you watch the news. That flag is fluttering on every significant building and ship worldwide. Every dwelling has hung a copy of your family's portrait in their homes ... that is true in both Israel and Palestine. I simply can't believe it myself. To be quite honest with you, I expected to be thrown out of Israel along with your family and all my staff. Larry all but said that there is no legitimate religion in the world except Christ's definition of Love and Care. My office here has been swamped with letters and e-mails congratulating me. Me, I ask you? As if I were the origin of all Larry's messages. All were thanking me for introducing Larry to the wider world. Most of these messages have come from Islamists, Hindus, Chinese, even the Communist countries have congratulated me for the acceptance of Larry's Law and The Face of Love as the one and only true creed for humanity.' Pope Dominic was visibly shaken. In fact none of the family or the pontiff's staff could take in the scale and speed of events since that last broadcast.

There was something quite frightening in the early days when Larry's Law was in its geneses. The very speed and efficiency of the organizations responsible for the production and circulation of the flags and images promoting Larry's Family as world government leaders was difficult to take in. Their images were carried in procession ahead of every important event imaginable, and dominated the opening of all sports events and tournaments worldwide in stately processions with great bands and groups of teenage majorettes dancing in breathtaking agility and grace with baton-twirling and dazzling artistry. Huge framed images of Larry's family were paraded everywhere. Poster-portraits were pasted up in every workplace and on street hoardings. It appeared that no street corner was without a reminder of the now glorified world leaders. They were given god-like adulation.

Teenagers rushed to the hairdressers to have their hair styled in Larry's nondescript style, and Dee's of spilling gold. Teenagers had their families machine their clothes in the fashions favored by Larry and Dee, who were now given royal homage. Larry's Law of Love and Care became a kind of disturbing mantra shouted at their hero's images in factory and street by their more radical devotees who made it their business to see that all which Larry's Law required was carried out to the letter. There was a certain tyrannical element creeping into the early revolutionary changes. Many of the more aggressive devotees half believed that the new regime might not last ... that the changes were too good and too fast to last, too good to be true. For their part, they were trying to help the situation along to make certain that the new changes would be permanent and by every means possible. These radical individuals invariably came from the poorest of the poor right across the international world – they had most to gain from the new laws. They were making sure that the shantytowns which were being pulled down with remarkable speed and efficiency were going to stay down and not spring up again. Such groups displayed a kind of desperation to hang on to any little new advantage that removed them from the gutter and oppression of their past – who could blame them? Nonetheless, they were dangerous and needed carful control. All new radical leadership was inherently exposed to such dangers ... vying for power and position was written into the entire genetics of physical existence, especially in the animal world, the human animal included. Even the very planets had to have order and position to keep in place; it was written into the very essence of life itself.

These radical groups need not have worried. The true officials of Larry's Law, the Guardians of the People, as they came to be known officially, these called for moderation and a more calm approach to the changes; they were dependable and able people, who in dialogue with Larry's family and professional groups worldwide, were determined and devoted to the very ideals of love and care of all peoples. In consequence, they were damned if they were going to allow the past mistakes made by dictatorial and tyrannical groups which had once germinated in Communist-infested Russia, China, North Korea, Cuba and other tyrannical states to take over and undo all the good so sacrificially won by the common people. These also included the Capitalist states with their own brand of oppressive control, using money as a God to be served rather than have it serve all the people. Communism only purported to be there for the people when it simply perpetuated tyrannical control and power for their own ends with all its tools of secrecy and willing informers on every street corner. Such powers put in place their machinery of propaganda denouncing resisters from every class and used Siberian solutions for those daring to speak out against their creed or daring to challenge their authority at any level. Doctors, teachers, writers, many from professional classes were hauled in by the KGB or secret police and made to disappear without trace. Accounts of cold-blooded murder at the hands of the secret police were officially categorized as unfortunate suicides. Such incidents, while numerous, were only spoken of in whispers by family members or friends who knew better. In such police states fear became a creed whereby the oppressed people became the instruments of their own indoctrination and oppression ... inadvertently serving fear itself but naming it peace. To speak out against authority or to challenge it at any level was considered blasphemous in spite of such states being utterly Godless. No. The new Laws now racing and widespread across the world realized that caution and scrutiny was vital. They had to be absolutely certain that even religious tyrants of any creed or hue would never be allowed to control, oppress or indoctrinate the people of the new world – even if it meant using the same securities of police states to achieve their desired ends. If the terrible examples of the Congo tribal wars and butchery of their own people and those of the Communist states taught the new world any lesson, it was that the spores of social disintegration leading to tyranny must be burnt out by all means. It meant never again allowing human armies to develop, not even small groups of possible contenders or even allowing any form of weaponry to be manufactured. Total control was absolutely essential even though it aimed for a worthy and just cause for all. Just as all tyrannical leadership controlled the media, public literature, including creative writing, all would have to be controlled and scrutinized for the good and safety of all. Long experience taught the new world that it only took the radical literature of one charismatic individual to set an entire nation against itself with systematic tyranny. This was no less true of world religions. The good intentions and directives of well-meaning pious individuals were all too often, in the experience of human history, used as the stepping stones to a more insidious creation of abusive and disfigured authority.

As Larry and family settled down to look at the news with Pope Dominic they thought that the world had gone mad. The myriad of city streets across the nations were covered in bunting. All were wild with dancing and celebrations. Every conceivable gadget that could make a noise or be blown by mouth was contributing to a mad frenzy of sound ... drums ... church bells ... motor horns ... whistles ... wild music ... There were floats full of flowers, rotating caravels on the backs of huge lorries that went slowly through the cities of the nations with young children within carriages constructed to imitate giant loafs of bread, tractors, cows, pigs and giant hens. The children were waving their little flags enthusiastically and showing their beaming smiles to all. Men and women walking on tall stilts and dressed in fancy costumes, some dressed as scarecrows to represent the saving of the harvest ... hundreds of celebrants dressed in imitation fruits and vegetables ... men and women dressed in colorful material representing all the farm animals; some dressed as giant teddy bears and pandas; there were even people made up of walking food tins. Millions danced and screamed in wild carnival atmosphere. The color and scale of the celebrations were spectacular. It was, as the media commentators chorused, "organized Chaos ... pandemonium ... bedlam on an unparalleled scale." And yet, for all the commotion, cacophony and blare, the bobbing and weaving of the blue helmets of the civic guards were in control of the miles of snaking, dancing crowds as they passed jubilantly in conga formation through every side street to be sure that every waving window-watcher was given their fair share of the wild celebrations. Small flags were waved form every window by the elderly and others who could not join the celebrations below in the streets; little children joined in the fun, waving form windows. The little flags also bore the picture of Larry's family portrait with the title, "The Face of Love." To Dee the scale of the spectacle was actually disturbing. It wasn't so much the scale of the world in some mad celebration of the seasons and a new liberty and unity among the world's populations; it was the question of her family's notoriety ... the very scale of it ... literally billions of flags and pictures of her family everywhere. She had always been a very private individual from her earliest days, especially away from her occupation as a young aspiring journalist; there had always been a reason to avoid people when she had been a person to be despised, feared and avoided at all costs.

These past fears did surface from time to time with the result that she was not always comfortable with too much public exposure. Here it was in the extreme. Larry on the other hand got up and joined in the dancing round the room with little Ruth in his arms. He managed to drag Pope Dominic and Sister Patricia out onto the floor to join in a conga dance of their own ... snaking round the furniture and into the various rooms, even the domestic and kitchen staff joined in. Pope Dominic was in hysterics, so was Sister Patricia. In the end Dee was shamed into joining in the madness, though her face was red enough to fry eggs. Pope Dominic felt a great sense of relief, Larry always had that effect on him. What was all his worrying about, he thought? Was he not under the protection of heaven's messenger, here?

While the pontiff and his guests, as well as his several staff were doing their best to cope with the whole upheaval going on in the world, a few more personal friends of Larry's family were equally shaken to their roots. The

Madden family back in Ireland, Larry's most treasured friends along with Father Kevin and Nell, all thought it was the end of the world ... that indeed the second coming of Christ, once prophesized was here happening on every street throughout the world. Judgment Day had come ... the good rewarded by new life ... evil to their own self-destruction. Cork city, once Larry's own home wasn't recognizable through the oceans of bunting in every street and with the thronging crowds in wild celebration. The noise was deafening. It carried everyone along with it in wild ecstatic, fun and joy. The world it seemed was a sea of joy-filled faces. The Maddens were standing by the windows of the priest's house along with Father Kevin and Nell. All were riveted to the windows watching the bedlam, the wild carnivals snaking and erupting in the main road passing their house and church. Even the bells of their own church joined in the wild, vying melee to be heard. Great whizzing and exploding fireworks rocketed into the skies bursting into billions of sparkling orbs delighting the "wow" of thousands of jubilant faces all mesmerized by the exploding colors.

'I suppose you all realize that it's the end of the world.' The voice of Nell was exaggeratingly formal, as it always was with her dry sense of humor. Yet there was an irony in her humor. It was the beginning of the end of the exploiting world as it was. Nell's head now nodding up and down in mock solemnity and severity while staring through the window; she had the rest of the company in hysterics.

'Nell, will you shut up, you old Kerry goat; 'tis a heart attack you'll be giving the lot of us.' The priest and the Maddens were spluttering with laughter, all the more in consequence of Nell's poker-like face. She seemed to be showing her age these days, but of course, Father Kevin didn't like to dwell on the truth of that.

'Do you think they might know about all this, I mean what is taking place in the cities and countryside across the world?' Lil asked, after a moment of composure.

'Does who know?' Seamus inquired.

'Larry and herself, of course, who else would I be talking about, yeah great eejit?'

'Well, unless they're living in caves in Israel! Of course they'll know – Israel is a highly advanced country, may I add, in case you think that they are still living in biblical times, madam.'

'Oh alright, professor; I was only wondering as to how they may be reacting to all these celebrations and changes across the nations.' Lil screwed up her nose at him and added, 'blooming cleaver git.'

Nell came to Lil's support with an interjection of her own.

'Of course, Lil, men don't always consider the more intimate need to know what anxieties others may be experiencing. Tunnel vision … the curse of men … comes from primitive spear-throwing and is loath to leave them.' Nell wore a wry smile as she continued to hold back the net curtain gazing at the passing, bustling carnival.

'Shall we go into another room out of the way, Seamus, and leave the two ladies to their wonderings?' Father Kevin's playful banter was more directed at Nell whom he loved to tease.

'You know, we are experiencing something of a miracle here.' Father Kevin was speaking with more sincerity. 'We are taking all these changes in our stride as though they were all perfectly normal rather than the radical worldwide upheaval that they really represent. The magnitude of the organization is truly staggering. If you remember how we used to think that the demands put on Larry's shoulders would crush an army of better equipped people. Yet here we are witnessing another army entirely motivated by Larry's Law and his public addresses. We have heard of many uprisings in the old world, "springs" they once called them, if you remember the phrase! Yet here we have one on a world scale. It is all very incredible. It is as though the people themselves, worldwide, have become as possessed by God's message as Larry himself is still possessed. And yet it is all happening so naturally.

'True, many bankers, high-earning professional, land and property owners have taken their own lives as a result of all the radical changes. Many farms and commercially-run enterprises have been taken over by force by the people. However, all this was inevitable, given the self-centered characteristics and self-preservation woven into centuries of self-interest and power-grasping private enterprise.

'How are you affected by it all?' Father Kevin was addressing his question to Seamus and Lil. The speculative discussion took place while all four present returned to holding back the net curtains of the windows as the thundering dancing carnival rumble along. All four seemed to be speaking at the windows rather than to each other.

'As you know, Father Kevin, there is no longer any need for my old occupation to exist since there is no longer a need to insure anything and all the banks have been converted, as it were, to more practical uses for the people. I've gone back to my old profession ...'

'Ah, yes! Teacher ...' the priest interjected.

'Just so,' Seamus agreed and added, 'it has changed out of all recognition.' Seamus' face lined in awe, his own thoughts and mind on his school, his eyes distracted following the dancing carnival beyond the window.

'So, how are you coping with it in your old age?' the priest asked speculatively.

'Less of the old age, now, Father Kevin; you know, you can go off people, especially Kerry priests who only say Mass on a Sunday and then have a holiday for the rest of the week.' Everyone laughed at the good-natured banter. The remark, indeed, was so opposite to the truth of Father Kevin's busy parish life. Seamus grew more serious as he filled in the company on his real experiences.

'You know, it is a great pleasure to be back in the teaching world today; the secondary schools which used to be like torture chambers to work in with the youngsters' cheek and arrogant attitudes have simply disappeared. We know, and they know, that they are not being trained as objects for the marketplace as in former years; now they know that they are subjects of our nation's love and care; and by God, don't we know the difference! The youngsters actually love coming to school, not just to relate to their school friends, but to relate in friendship to the teachers as well. It's like you're working from home with your own family. What used to be the old national curriculum is now the international curriculum. The top priority and emphases is on how to love and care for all people; how to respect all peoples, no matter their nationality. Certainly they have to learn all the other basics, reading, writing, mathematics .... However, these subjects are made far more interesting than in former times since they are linked to practical issues like the building of homes, and how you need to know what to order and so on. History too is taught in a more holistic way; being truthful about past abuses and their consequences on the peoples affected by such abuses. The heroes of the past, the great warlords and men of battle have been put in a new context and measured against what real good or bad they advanced to the world in general. The seizing of lands, the oppression of the vanquished, the gift of properties and position ... all these were now understood in a new light. And since we no longer countenance wars or strife among the nations, it appears to the new generation how awful the wars, destruction and the violence of the past had been. At times the youngsters ask with a sense of horror and disbelief.

"Was it really as terrible as that?"

'You can understand their disbelief since, as you know, we no longer have a military presence in any nation. Nor do we have any violence allowed on the TV or glorified in the media as in former times. No. Now our youngsters are gentler in their ways; in fact, they are like a new species altogether.'

Lil agreed with her husband's experiences. Her role as an aid to pupils with special needs in her junior school confirmed these unique experience from all children in general. Certainly there had to be discipline; however, it was more family-orientated and responded to in like manner by the children.Teaching,' said Lil, 'is no longer a job that has to be done by someone, a chore to be got through for much needed wages. Now it is a real vocation once more for all teachers, a highly respected, appreciated and fulfilling role in the care and love of the wider community.'

'School,' Seamus added, 'is a mixture of practical learning of trades and many other professional callings. These are carried out, by exposing the young to the various trades and professions. The world of work is now taught in vocational terms. These ventures are not taken lightly, they are considered as serious steps and opportunities to expose the young to the working world of the community at large. All these obligations are taken from the guidelines found in Larry's Law. By the time a young person had reached their sixteenth year of school life, he or she will have been exposed to the widest choice of occupations before choosing an apprenticeship to a trade or profession. From their very earliest years all exposure to the life of work was in the form of hands-on experience. Trades and professions could be changed as a young person grew in maturity and experience, and knew their own mind better. The whole point of the world of work was to help the young person to fit into a trade or profession that he or she would feel at home with. Adult workers and parents now take the future of the young very much to heart, their happiness was to the forefront of our minds and efforts. All training is very much family-orientated. Children were now in the habit of discussing the world of work not only with their teachers but also with their parents. Because of the extreme care and handling of young workers, it meant that they grew in confidence and enthusiasm for their occupations. Having said all that ... our young people are allowed to have a happy childhood without pressurizing them too early with an overzealous emphasis on them as objects of work but rather to experience themselves as subjects of love and care by the whole community. You only have to look at the real meaning of that fun-jostling carnival as it continues to pass, to understand what underlies it and what it really is celebrating. It isn't just the celebration of a general harvest; it is a celebration of togetherness, love, care, happiness and contentment: all of these are its true beating soul.'

'That's well spoken, Seamus,' said Nell, nodding her wise old white head and allowing the net curtain to fall on the carnival. 'Well spoken indeed,' she repeated. 'God, How my own young days could have known these happy times,' Nell said with sad reflection. 'Well,' she added more cheerily, 'Let's celebrate with a drink before the calendar of our time buries the lot of us.'

'Bury you, you old Kerry goat … sure you'll have to be shot to get rid of yeah.' Father Kevin's remark brought a hearty laugh to Seamus and Lil. But for all the priest's light-hearted banter, something was nagging at him. He loved Nell dearly. However, of recent times he had seen her grow feebler. Nell took the remark in her stride; she knew her friend all too well. She also knew from her own intimate experience that Father Kevin was deeply concerned for her. She perceived also that he had spotted her slow deterioration, even though she tried to remain cheerful when it was patently obvious to both of them that she was struggling. She was tired, worn out by the calendar of her years … now she lived only to serve Father Kevin with her last ounce of her energy and love.

President Ishmael Cohen phoned Pope Dominic to congratulate him on the international address given by Larry. He seemed to think that the pontiff was actually the author of the address.

'Ishmael, I can promise and assure you that I had no part in the narrative of that address; in fact, I have been quite shocked by the idealism of it and by its radical nature. I am left wondering now, having watched world reaction to the address and the celebrations that followed, if any traditional authority can ever suffice for the people of the future.' The pontiff wanted to apologies for Larry's references to the dismissal of all institutionalized religions and for the dismissal of Israel's early conviction that they were indeed a "Chosen Race" of people ... he also apologized for the tearing down of every national flag including Israel's. Pope Dominic half expected to be bawled at down the telephone line and to be told to pack his bags and have his staff and guests ready for the next plane out of Israel. Instead, the president actually congratulated him for the profound sentiments contained in the very impressive address. 'You should witness the jubilations being celebrated here and in Palestine as well. I can't believe it myself. It is like a living miracle. I truly believe that there is a new hope for all of us here on both sides of the divide ... the people want it ... they are ready for it. If you think you have concerns for your own faith and institutions, our own authorities and those of the Islamic authorities are left drifting on our own, just as you are. The people are more determined than ever to heed only the voice of this Larry, chap. The Palestinian people have now ousted their own national leaders and taken hold of their own futures. They are already in negotiations with our own people. I simply cannot believe what is taking place ... so soon ... so suddenly and so overpowering. You no longer need my assistance to stay in our country ... you are free to stay as long as you wish. Maybe all that is left for both of us is to scratch each other's head.' Ishmael laughed heartily and added, 'We will both have to face tomorrow as best we can. We might even be out of work as natural wastage.'

Pope Dominic laughed with the president and remarked.
'You may prove to be your own prophet yet, Ishmael.
Good bye for now, and thank you for your call and
greetings. You are ever in my prayers; although I may
have to sort out a new God before the night is over after
Larry's address.' It was Ishmael's turn to break into
laughter. In some ways, the pontiff thought, it was a good
note on which to end the call. He also had the satisfaction
of realizing that his stay in Israel with his staff was
still secure.

CHAPTER 20

The Guardians of the People. – Broadcasting. The Case Against Bankers and shareholders

The main work demanded of Larry and Dee came in the form of communications through Government Broadcasting both for Television and Radio. The Israeli Government set aside this special time to accommodate Both Larry's family in their work and Pope Dominic in his. Both made themselves available giving their time generously when requested to deal with important issues which could not be dealt with directly by other authorized guardians. It was a regular slot in international broadcasting which was highly valued and appreciated by all and relayed worldwide in all the main world languages as a Government Broadcast. It was a kind of government question time dealing with important issues of the day ... discussing points of view on every conceivable issue that was considered important enough to demand their personal time.

It was brought to Larry's attention the case of several elderly ex-bankers and shareholders who met frequently in each others' homes. They were discovered to be playing, very enthusiastically, a game which they had devised between them with very complicated rules for investing in stocks, shares and private property. The game itself was not unlike monopoly, a board game that was now outlawed under Larry's Law because of its dangers of reintroducing, by stealth, an unhealthy return and preference for private ownership and personal wealth. There was a certain degree of sadness to these poor individuals, so the enquiry went on:

> "These elderly men, who from their
> earliest days, had been
> conditioned and indoctrinated into
> the old world of money."

The question posed by a spoke's person for the Guardians of Larry's Law was:

"Are these individuals to be prevented from continuing this dangerous infectious pastime, yet having due consideration for their great ages?

All were past their eightieth year ... and with due consideration to the fact that no money or real properties changed hands only picture cards of shops, industries and houses printed on them. Also to be considered was the fact that they played the game with such earnestness, gusto, that they seemed no more harmful than schoolchildren playing in a puddle of water. Our most serious concern is the fact that the report of these events was related to us indirectly by a girl of ten years of age. She in turn related the event to her parents. The elderly gentlemen had explained the entire game to the child and related its past history. How are we to judge this sensitive situation?"

Larry and Dee gave some considerable time to this incident and other similar enquiries that came before the People's Court. The court comprised of a group of specialists. There were chosen groups of specialist in every nation in order to represent their peoples and most pointedly, the preservation of Larry's Law itself. Such groups consulted personally with Larry and Dee when there was serious need. These specialists were chosen for their absolute commitment to ensuring that any accusation brought by a member of the public concerning another individual was given a fair and in-depth hearing. The old system of Law had long since being abolished, where there were professionally paid lawyers, solicitor and barristers both for the defense and for the prosecution. Those days, were by now long gone. Instead, the People's Courts were very much conducted in the spirit of an extended family, whereby the one bringing the fault to the court and the one accused of the fault were treated with equal compassion and concern. Much of the time this procedure usually resolved the situation amicably by helping those with a grievance to be more compassionate and understanding towards each other. Obviously the People's Court had to deal with very difficult cases at times, especially where serious physical or mental harm was caused. Such cases bearing those extremes were already well catered for in the more severe punishments contained within the directives of Larry's Law and the codifications that were added to it when necessary. Cases that were brought to Larry or Dee for judgment were usually the kind stated above concerning the aged bankers and shareholders.

The conclusion reached by Larry and Dee concerning the elderly bankers, after more advise from the People's Court

and other experts in their fields, doctors, psychiatrists
and social services, was that these elderly people must be
made to desist in the game because it was not worthy of
their age nor did it contribute in any way to the spirit of
love for all people; in fact, it was a serious disfigurement
of it; considering that they had, even if inadvertently,
sown their disfigured seed into the vulnerable and
impressionable mind of the ten year old child who had
revealed the story to her parents. How could they do such
a thing against her parents and the wider community
whose duty it was to install in their child's mind the love,
care and consideration for everyone's good and well
being? It was recommended that the elderly group take
up a healthier pastime or face being prevented from
meeting in the future ... that they be considered as
deviants incapable of being responsible citizens. Age,
indeed, had no excuse for planting weeds in the cornfield
of human love and care. It was a case, Larry and Dee
concluded, with further deliberation with all concerned,
for the need to be cruel to be kind for the greater good
of all. One did not allow children to indulge in pursuits
and games from which they derived enthusiasm and joy
if their activities harmed others. No. These deviant old
timers may be the product of a world that had now all
but gone; nonetheless, either they bring themselves to
find more healthy pursuits or risk being separated from
each other by force. It was cases such as this that made
everyone realize that perfection and the pursuit of the
good for all peoples would not be accomplished in a
single lifetime. However, there was nothing to be gained
from not pursuing the new world with every ounce of
energy, opportunity and effort that the international
world was capable of. Larry and his army of helpers,
along with the people themselves, came to common

agreement on this and many other sensitive issues. There would always be storms in the lives of nature's imperfect children. This new world would not come about as a matter of course, we had to discover and build it ourselves and the good people of the world grew to know that instinctively.

Chapter 21

The World of Entertainment

Larry and Dee were asked to take on the task of passing their judgment on the world of entertainment ... the arts and crafts that might be considered beneficial to the new world. Under the scrutiny of the Guardian's of Larry's Law certain entertainments, including sports, were recommended to be discontinued as being unworthy of the new world of love and care for all. One such activity brought to their attention was that of heavyweight boxing. Several protagonists from across the international boxing world expressed their points of view with fierce argument. The advisors and protectors of Larry's Law defended their reasoning why the activity was unworthy of our present age and pursuit of the care of all people. They were adamant in their position stating that heavyweight boxing was no longer to be regarded as a suitable sport for modern civilized people endeavoring to lead the gentler spirit of humanity in a more commendable direction. After all, what was boxing? A question put to the boxing protagonists. What was its history? It was a kind of war reduced to two individuals attempting to punch their opponents into submission. It did not have a happy or commendable history. So-called gentry, the upper class of the past generations ... the privileged ... a class that considered its lordly standing in terms of enlightened gentlefolk ... a superior breed .... These sorted out their own private differences and questionable honor by having two cash-stuck unfortunates use their bare knuckles to punch each other into blooded slabs of meat for a purse of money that wouldn't keep a pigeon in corn for a month. It drew out the worst primitive instincts in the crowds that bayed for blood. Its proponents who made or lost small fortunes from the shameful activity argued for its continued establishment since it was a contact sport demanding great courage, skill, self-control and devotion to fitness. Certainly it had all of these attributes as the Guardians of the new laws agreed. The protective gloves, a much later invention, did less injury than bare-knuckle fighting. And yet the latter expression of fighting was only changed to the advantage of the fighter's own hands as a means of giving each contender a longer fighting future since bare-knuckle fighting was too injurious to their long term fighting careers.

"... My hands are my bread ..." was the brutal cliché. Now instead of the gentry being responsible for this bloody pursuit, it fell into the hands of money-making promoters and further scandalized by the infiltration of the Mafia. These competitors trained in gymnasiums punching as hard as possible into heavy, hanging punch bags in order to be proficient at inflicting as much damage as possible ... to batter their opponents into submission or win by knocking out their opponent.

In spite of a referee's duty to intervene to save unnecessary damage to an opponent who had no intention of surrendering ... and when to continue was obvious to all

that serious and unnecessary injury would follow, in spite
of these minimal safety measures, the new laws were very
much against the continuation of such a cruel sport. The
international Board of Boxing Control fought with all its
own weight and authority to keep the sport intact.
However, the history of injuries, corruption and the
offensive nature and impact of its brutality on viewing
crowds or on spectators at the various venues eventually
agreed, reluctantly, that indeed, it was not a fitting
activity in the new world of love and care of all people.
Contenders have been known to lose their lives in the ring
or be reduced to vegetating imbeciles – others to be put
unconscious and end up in hospital and remain in a coma
for days on end ... others suffered broken noses, broken
fingers and wrists, cauliflower ears, flashbacks.

One commentator, a protagonist for the sport condemned
his own argument when on being asked what kind of
damage could these well-trained boxers inflict on each
other in the general run of the sport? His reply, which was
designed to glamorize the great strength and ability of the
competitors, was:

"... that one had only to imagine that the average
fit and well-trained heavyweight boxer carried a punch of
10,000 pounds of impact ... that since the human brain was
only encased in a light veneer of skull material, that the
effect of a blow to the temple, or to the head in general, was
equivalent to placing a mould of jelly in a biscuit tin and
kicking it with all one's strength against a wall. Of course
some boxers suffer from brain damage over their fighting
careers. That is just a sad fact of life," he added with sinister
indifference. Hence his arrogant attempt to justify the so-
called sport fell apart by his own stupidity. Ultimately,
Larry's advisors had no qualms or compunctions in

banning the so-called "sport" indefinitely. With all considered, heavyweight boxing passed into history. In the same way all sports were scrutinized for their merit and contribution to the beneficial long term good of all peoples.

The game of soccer or national and international football was to continue much as it is in the present time. A few small details were to be introduced at all levels of the game. Concerning the game itself, the deliberate fouling of an opponent was to result in a ten match ban and the culprit to answer for his actions in the Court of the People. Persistent fouling would mean that the offending competitor be suspended indefinitely. The offender would also be forced to attend a psychiatric hospital or similar place of correction to stabilize his or her behavior and attitude to people in general. All tackling from behind was to be considered too dangerous and risky to a competitor's well being. It was therefore banned. Deliberate shirt pulling, if committed against a member of the losing team, and if proven to be the case later on TV, then the points would be given to the losing side ... thus insuring rightful compensation for bringing the art and game into disrepute and for degrading the spirit, skill and true comradely nature of the game played for the benefit and the achievement of excellence for competitors and spectators alike. Punishments for all deliberate offences in the pursuit of any sport was to be considered most serious not only because it was an offence against another competitor and the spirit of sport and leisure, but, because the activities of competing sports between men and women had an immediate effect and long term influence on the attitude of our vulnerable young, since they are by nature readily inclined to imitate what they see and hear without having the benefit, wit, discernment or maturity to realize the consequences of unacceptable bad example.

Using the shoulder to push a competitor off the ball while in pursuit of it is to be considered acceptable with one exception. If, when shouldering a competitor off the ball excessive force is used, or where elbows are used to deliberately wind or cause deliberate physical injury to a competitor, then a deliberate foul will be seen to have been committed. Excessive force in this case would be considered when the competitor shouldering his or her opponent is clearly too aggressive and ill-tempered in their actions.

All dubious decisions by the referee and his assistances are to be left unchallenged by the participants of the game. However, to be fair to all, the use of technology as a second referee or umpire during a game will be used where there is distinct room for doubt.

Concerning the makeup of local teams, no players outside of a given city or county may be used to the detriment and development of local talent. To deprive local talent of the opportunity to develop the art and skill of the game will not be countenanced under any circumstance whatever. The spirit of all sports must be considered in the light of the development of its own home-grown talent as a duty to developing a family spirit in sport. All sport must be considered as armature pastime but creatively competitive at the highest level.

The world of theatre is to be open to all without cost, as with all leisure activities. It was one of the benefits of the new world without the burden and disparity of money.

The new world of theatre and film was now able to extend its world of entertainment into great epics once more. With cost no longer an issue for those employed as entertainers and no charge to the audiences who could now attend in their thousands. The world of theatre and film reached unimaginable expressions of excellence. People the world over became more discerning. The slop and the banal that were once served up as soap entertainment fell naturally by the wayside. Television and radio advertisements were purely for information purposes only in keeping with newspaper notices. Commercial advertising was now a thing of the past – to the relief of all.

In more creative hands the advancement of our higher ideals and aspirations could be equally as dramatic and compelling viewing, or more so than the mundane slop once served up as a proper meal. Many of the old soaps had put too much emphasis on the portrayal of common street life as though it was the be-all and end-all of every viewer's life. The actions of the worst of all characters could rightly be accused of wallowing in what could best be described, as self-regarding frivolity. The worst of soaps were selling the viewers or audience the worst extremes of filth, violence, licentiousness ... drug-taking ... and the language of the gutter, so openly vulgar and hostile. All this, and more, served on a plate purporting to be real life.

"... this is how it is ... life in the raw ... life on the streets!" Such were the old worn out clichés in defense of banality. Of course the streets usually chosen for soaps were often those bereft of meaningful culture and wider opportunities and facilities that would most certainly develop far more discerning individuals and families. As mentioned so often in the past: "... whatever is glorified or edified in entertainment has its influence on all of us for better or for worse."

What was the function of theatre in the new world to be? At its best or most excellent, it was to be a celebration of our highest and meaningful ideals ... a life elevating excellence. Good theatre may be defined as excellent, when its actors are not attempting to glorify their own personalities but are faithful to the theme and character which needs to be portrayed in an authentic way. True stardom, true excellence in a performer may be understood when the actor's own personal character is completely overshadowed by who he or she strives to portray.

Whatever is glorified or edified in theatre has its influence on all of us. We are, after all, social creatures often deeply affected by the influences of others by the power and influence of their personalities. If we care for each other we grow to be able to carry the weaknesses and natural faults in each other. That said, when we cease to care how we influence others we have, by neglect, given birth to pain and ultimate destruction of our vulnerable social and spiritual cohesion. Such attitude has no part in the new world. The old world experienced for itself, over thousands of years, how lack of love, care and concern for all had ripped human cohesion to the point of complete and absolute self-destruction; and that same destruction did not spare the good and innocent, such as they were, no more than it spared the culprits mainly responsible. The culprits in government, the Media, every single individual's neglect, whether unintentional or consciously designed, caused the ultimate rejection and collapse of the old world.

Like all other influences on the human spirit, music too was brought into debate ... what was its part in the advancement of the new world of Larry's Law? Frivolity in music had infiltrated all cultures across the nations due to the influence of its youth. It was the power and influence of their money, their willingness to buy the latest Hit, which was responsible for saturating the international music world with screaming banality. Those who preferred excellence in music were in the minority and so their financial support was less influential.

When the Guardians of the new laws focused their attention on the world of music it became clear to all how many of us were, without being conscious of it, being conditioned to type and genre from early childhood. Family, location, peer group, all these had strong conditioning influences on each of us. Our locations and immediate influences generated in us a conditioning sense of the familiar. From the cavemen banging on rocks ... the blacksmith on his anvil ... the song of birds ... the timeless rise and fall of the pounding ocean ... the wind whistling and gusting through all its fluting paths ... all these sounds were capable of moving and conversing with our senses.

It seemed like a deep insight to the Guardians of Larry Law how yelling and music came to be used in war and battle ... sound, as music, could inspire ... give courage ... edify and terrify together. They discovered too the powerful drive for variety ... for the new ... how over exposure to any music, lyric or song ceased to inspire and became lost to time and tedium. The need for the new was a strong motivator for change.

Rap music was understood as little more than stylized rhyming ... depending on who was observing it and from what appreciative or prejudicial point of view. Some saw it as a mere concoction, best described as a poverty-stricken lunch hatched or brewed by an indifferent chef of limited resources and ingredients ... a stew pot of glorified stylization for strutting-style sake ... a mere mirror of self-regarding piffle lost in the craving for personal attention and edification ... a kind of immature childishness, neurotically in communion with self as the centerpiece of its own imagined importance. It may simply belong to Trend. Again, it can be seen as a badge, a kind of tribal belonging ... rising as it does form a culture given over heavily to stylized hand-slapping and arm-pointing ... stylized walking and dance. One singer in the past highlighted this world in his song, "... Putting on the Agony; putting on the style ..." No class or group was found to be without these very characteristics. The Guardians came see in the fashion houses of the past ... the cat-walks of the world ... or in the past elitist gatherings for the hunt ... or how the rich of the past ate at table in full regalia with a bucketful of silver cutlery to choose from. You were not a true member of the tribe unless you knew the Form ... displayed the required actions ... had the accepted polished tribal accent ... had been to the right university, comprehensive, or grammar school or elitist establishment of the highly privileged ... and belonged to the same club and had oodles of cash and informed investment.

Then there was the world of Jazz. Some judged it as nothing more than an indulgence in a frivolous abstraction ... the random juggling of notes and cords in a lottery ... a game of chance ... to indulge the ear in pure novelty for novelty sake. However, much of the African communities considered Jazz as a source of freedom from the conventions of white music and their claims to musical academic authority. Many Africans thought of Jazz as "black and slack," where white music was "too white and tight" ... too controlled. Jazz epitomized a break from slavish control over others. Indeed Jazz came bursting out with Black freedom from the white-man's slave-driving of the African worker. The Whites saw in Jazz at first, the Black's sticking up their middle finger at the White-man's face and everything the controlling Whites stood for. The Blacks didn't even like White worship, it was too solemn ... too controlled ... too slavish and too conforming. The Whites bowed their heads in respect and solemnity, the Blacks threw their bodies all over the show in wild ecstasy and joy. Their hearts were full of freedom ... they didn't fear the Lord ... they joyed in Him. It was not to be wondered at that their hymns were uniquely their own ... so uninhibited ... so full of soul and ecstasy. In many ways they even freed God to be Black as well as any other color ... God belonged to all.

During the discussion on music ... delving into its depths, meaning and function, one old soldier in his nineties appeared on Government Broadcast to express his opinion on music devoted to the military. He spoke of being tricked into joining the Scots Guards, a Highland regiment, serving England's military interests abroad. He was recruited from the streets of Liverpool as a fifteen-year-old scavenging lad who couldn't find paid work. He related how he was befriended by one of the many recruiting sergeants that combed the streets of Liverpool, London and other major cities, usually targeting the more poverty-stricken areas and the unemployed and

uneducated. The lad explained how he was half starving
with hunger and how the recruiting sergeant treated him
to a big meal in a local café. 'As a lad I was very much
taken in by the importance of this man in the full glory of
his bright scarlet uniform. After plying me with whiskey
and beer he had me sign up for the Scots Guards and gave
me the infamous shilling, which for me was riches indeed.

'The long and the short of it was that once I was dumped
into one of the army training barracks I found myself
treated like the hundreds of other raw recruits who had
been conned in the same way. We soon found out that we
were the scum of the earth, dispensable fodder thrown
into the front line of the war with the Boer farmers, a
people who were said to be a great pain and nuisance to
the British Empire. Thousand of us were marched
directionless and exposed by the din of our own bagpipes
and drums. The territory was quite unknown even by
the privileged officers that pushed us forward. We were
sitting ducks. Yes, we were driven and inspired by
bagpipes and drums ... energized by their rallying sound
... they inspired in us the valor of fools. We were
advertising our own presence and thousands paid the
price with their lives.

'So much for military music, I thought to myself for years
afterwards. I was one of the lucky ones to escape with
only one leg amputated and the loss of one eye. Few came
back from the bloody slaughter ... we didn't stand a
chance. For years after I hated myself for my own
stupidity ... for being conned into that shambles of an
army ... it ruined my entire life. I was no longer
employable ... at times I was pressurized to find work in
my condition, anything that might save paying me the

pittance that I received from welfare. Whenever I hear military music or their marches now, and in particular, those bloody bagpipes, I realize the lie they blare out. They sicken me to the heart.'

This old soldier's account was repeated by many others with the same experience during the programme. Larry and Dee were very moved and saddened by the old soldier's account. It was yet another reason to be grateful to the new world where war and soldiering had no more part.

It was due to such awful accounts that came regularly to be publicly debated, in one form or another, that spurred the common people on to greater determination and committed support of Larry's new world government. It scrutinized how all human expressions either contributed to the common good of all or detracted from it, even in the smallest detail; remembering the metaphor of the rotten apple in a barrel "It only takes one to destroy the rest."

The world of Art, here painting placed in the category of Fine Art was also scrutinized ... examined for its contribution to the nations as a whole. Larry and Dee were surprised at the criticisms of this world; a world that was often shrouded in mystery and controversy. The loss of the priceless works of art destroyed with the city of Rome, and in particular the priceless works of the Sistine Chapel, caused many controversial opinions as to the true value of the loss. Obviously their value in monetary terms didn't apply in this case since money and its former influence no longer existed.

The Sistine Chapel, which was once the private place of worship of Pope Sixtus the Second in the Vatican, Dating from the 15c, was rich in great works of art. These were remarkable works by two world-renowned artists, Michael Angelo and a fellow artist, Raphael, the latter who painted the picture of the Madonna with Pope Sixtus the Second [c127-8] 'How were their loss, the originals of course, to be understood? Some academics spoke of their loss as "irreplaceable." Yet, was that opinion really strictly true in the broader sense? Consider the fact, as many did, that the loss of the originals were not worth losing any sleep over .... The technique and every facet of all the ancient Vatican works were readily available on computer with free access to every minute detail concerning the preparations of the grounds on which they were painted, the use of primer or ground stabilizers ... their preliminary drawings ... the color pigments used and the source and composition from where some of the most scarce pigments were quarried ... the characteristics of the brushstrokes ... the mediums used in the mix of colors and tones ... the ultimate use of retouching and finishing varnishes. As Dee had remarked when all these manifold details were put before Larry and herself, 'Crikey! They nearly know what the blinking artists had for breakfast,' she muttered to herself and to Larry with a gesture of her hand at the monitor's screen adding an expression of amazement and incredulity.

Dee was no art critic, it was not her field, and yet her views were valuable for that precise reason; she represented millions of people internationally who fell into the same category as herself; such as those who no longer turned to the old established so-called academic authorities or experts on art to form their own opinion ... since these pseudo authoritative voices were themselves indoctrinated into a set of established prescriptive, prejudicial principals and academic criteria. The true merit of any work of art would never reach a definitive conclusion since all such work was open to a very broad latitude of personal preference and interpretation .... Naturally, all criticism was peculiar to the particular focus of each individual or group.

The question posed concerning the loss of the originals, was why were the originals more important than all the expertise that continued to give them new life? One could almost say ... given them an eternal life ... although it was not known for certain how long digital memory could endure, given the fact that computerized memory was still comparatively new and still in its infancy.

Consider too the fact, as Larry and Dee were informed, that most, if not all, of the old masters' paintings have been cleaned, retouched and restored, over-painted by expert craftsmen and women, that to speak meaningfully about them as being original was really pushing the boat of credulity too far out ... that seemed to be the general opinion of the common, well-informed people with an enthusiastic interest in the world of painting ... now these various interests were asking another important question...making another point in the world of art:

'Why should our galleries, which belong to the people, be the preserve of famous names, since many of these well known artists were only held in high esteem because their patrons chose to invest in their works in particular to the detriment of less known and often far more accomplished artists, who unfortunately were not well known in the accepted canon of academia ... thus making an investment in their work rather risky in terms of their long term monetary value? 'How', they asked, 'could this state of prejudicial preference be allowed to continue when other artists were given no exposure to the public in general?'

Of course Abstract art had its own pretentious individuals, as Larry was given to understand in the course of his many judgments. How was it to be defined in its relevance in the new world? What kind of visual importance did it have, if any, to a world that grew to prize and praise what is authentic and meritorious to its people? It was pointed out, to Larry and Dee, the case of a renowned American abstract artist who had his painting accepted for the summer exhibition in one of the USA's Premier Academies. Most of the critics were falling over themselves to worship at the shrine of this magnificent work of art. Reams of print lavished hallowed reverence on the work with all the superlatives pretentious experts could plaster on it.

Now consider carefully, that when the artist in question read all the favorable reviews of his work, he decided to fly the two thousand mile journey to view the exhibition and to hear at first hand whether the viewing public was really in agreement with the generous claims of the expert critics. When he stepped into the section of the gallery that had, by now, given his highly acclaimed work an even more advantageous position, he was met by a thundering round of applause from the well-packed exhibition chamber. He was immediately recognized by a photograph of himself that hung beside his world-acclaimed masterpiece. Turning to his painting to make doubly sure that, indeed, it was his painting and not that of another artist ... [mistakes were not infrequent over the years] To his great horror, amazement and fury, he stormed out of the gallery carrying with him his own work, and with a volcanic expression on his face, strode out of the gallery in a fit of rage. When the poor creature had eventually calmed down sufficiently for the experts and critics to question his motives for his extreme displeasure and actions, he enlightened them in no uncertain terms, and with pure venom in his voice.

'The bloody idiots had hung my painting upside-down.'

Dee nearly fell off her chair; she was in fits of laughter.

Dee thought of the artist's one redeeming feature ... at least he was sincere about his work. The trouble was that only he knew that his painting was upside-down. The most controversial and general criticism concerning abstract art, was its annoying habit of leaning too heavily on intellectual interpretation and special pleading, as noted in the case above; virtual rivers of ink came cascading from so many self-appointed pseudo experts.

Another side to the vexed question of abstract art and its near neighbor, pop or trivial novelty; such as a pile of bricks placed in a heap on the floor of a discerning public gallery ... or a lone toilet as an exhibit ... a single light bulb hanging from a ceiling ... abstractions painted by monkeys ... or by using car tires .... What did all these really mean?

Larry and Dee had to consider the case of a forty year old woman who went to a well known school of art to present her work with a view to be taken on as a late developer. Her appointment was for 10.30am in the morning. She arrived fifteen minutes early in order to settle her nerves since she hadn't a clue as to how she might be received or even what she was likely to expect. She brought a wide range of her drawings and paintings with her in a large maroon portfolio. As she waited she noticed a very skeletal-looking lady, of about forty years. She was as thin as a strand of spaghetti ... dressed as if she was trying to make up her mind whether she wished to practice ballet dancing in her black tights or ride a motorbike wearing a black, scruffy, scuffed-up leather jacket. Her long, stringy, over-dyed, jet- black hair might have suited an acting witch in a horror movie. She was staring at a small mound of dirt on the red carpeted floor in front of her desk where she leaned back, one hand studiously gripping her skeletal chin the other folded sagaciously across her skeletal body. As she focused intently at the dirt, her visitor felt like offering to help her to clear the offending mess for her. In all events, the dark creature noticed the visitor's shadow pass over her, which moved the strange figure to look upward from her contemplation.

'Can I be of assistance?' The dark creature inquired, viewing the visitor as if she had interrupted her morning's meditation. Her manner and tone were curt; her heavily-painted coal black eyelids batting each other like slamming doors and her expression irritated, even hostile, that her morning reverie was so untimely interrupted.

'I have an appointment to see Miss Needle. My name is Felicity Rivers. I have brought the portfolio of some examples of my work and progress.'

'Oh, Yes. You're early,' she commented with irritation, glancing at the wall clock to emphasize the point. 'No matter, now you're here; drop that lot on the table.'

'You mean my portfolio,' replied Mrs. Rivers, her voice and tone were defensive; she would not allow herself to be bullied by this freak of darkness and hostility before her. She considered her manner downright rude to the extreme.

'Whatever!' The skeleton replied, still pondering on the heap of dirt on the carpet. On the stroke of 10.30am precisely, the dark vision condescended to flip through the highly organized, presented drawings and paintings, some works were painted on oil paper for the purpose and convenience of such an interview.

'Oh God!' the dark vision exclaimed. 'Figurative work! Reality! I thought all that went out when we left the caves! You know, the Neolithic Period …?' Her remark was a complete dismissal of all the effort that Mrs. Rivers had put into her presentations which covered a whole eighteen months of devoted work. Mrs. Rivers was raging inwardly by now, given the short period of the interview and the utter disrespect shown both for her person and for her work. The disappointment sapped her life's energy from her. She had set her heart on a career in art for years. Her husband had believed from her enterprise, her devotion to her efforts, that the final and most important step that she was now taking this very morning would be the making of her and her long sought after dreams. Now her precious world was pulled from under her feet. She fought back the tears … she wouldn't give this skeletal bitch the satisfaction of believing that she would now abandon her world of recognizable beauty and that which gave her soul so much exhilaration life and meaning. Before she left the company of the dark self-regarding and neurotically absentminded freak, she put a question to her as calmly and as measured as her distraught emotions allowed her:

'Would it be possible to view some of your own work; I would be most interested to see it?'

The dark vision simply nodded to the heap of dirt on the floor and declared with all the intellectual weight that her discerning mind could muster and remarked with great solemnity:

'It's from the Hoover ...' and added with equal solemnity, 'I'm into dust at the moment.'

Mrs. Rivers commented as she closed her portfolio with a bang and declared in white rage,

'And no doubt you will be in deep shit tomorrow.' It need hardly be stated that her remark was meant to be insulting and vengeful – and who could blame her? However, and this seems hardly credible, the dark vision smiled beamingly and took the insult as a complement. The irony of it all was that Felicity Rivers went on to become a renowned artist after enduring the frustrating efforts of being self-taught ... while the dark vision who was so caught up with her own importance took her own life five years later after a long period of severe depression. It was indeed a sad case in the rise and fall of human enterprise. The old worn out cliché had an evergreen truth to it, the need to "lighten up." Perhaps it was true also, the words of a wise man; "... Where your treasures are so will be your heart." In the case of Felicity Rivers, her appreciation of beauty, whether in landscape or the human form, elevated her to heights that she never thought possible. In contrast, the Master of Arts that she hoped might help to direct her artistic future was to fall wretched and abandoned by her own blind self-obsession. Who could gloat over such a tragic end? Who or what had brought her down that road, perhaps another well-meaning, but pretentious, abstractionist tutor?

A very heated debate came to the fore in the TV studio concerning the denial of Larry's Law that the Jews were a "Chosen Race" called and favored by God.

'A Mr. Joseph Bloom wishes to address you personally, Larry, concerning an important religious issue.' The presenter splayed his hands deferentially, his face lined in an expression of uncertainty as he remarked, 'the man is quite irate,' the presenter warned. 'Do you wish to debate the controversial matter with him?'

'By all means, please allow him to express his views.' Dee took the child from Larry with one of her disarming smiles. She had a gut feeling that he might have to give this new guest his full undivided attention.

'Mr. Joseph Bloom, good day to you, sir. How may I be of help to you?' The guest appeared on a large studio TV screen.

'Mr. Walsh, sir.' The tone of the man's voice was cold. His sallow round face carried a frowning hostility. The deep black pupils of his grimaced eyes and the furrows above them seemed fixed like a plaster cast or mask with anger in every line.

'Mr. Walsh,' he repeated. 'I am deeply grieved and angered by the implications of your book, "Larry's Law."' Larry was by now acclimatized to challenges made to his prophetic claims although he wasn't always comfortable with them. It was against his nature to deliberately hurt anyone; it was as though he felt their pain too. Larry's face grimaced as if struck by a blow. 'Your book and laws, Mr. Walsh,' Larry winced again at the man's deliberate, cold formality, 'imply that there is no such thing as a Chosen People, which we Jews know to be absolutely true. We are and have always been God's Chosen people … that truth is fundamental to our faith and tradition. It seems to us that you have deliberately dismissed that truth as mere propaganda on the part of our ancient prophets. You also refute the fact that the land we occupy was given to us by God himself.' The speaker was absolutely convinced of this as irrefutable truth.

'My dear sir, our laws do indeed refute your claim since, even if it was actually true, the new world under the guidance of our laws wouldn't want anything to do with such an outrageous claim. In fact, we would have nothing to do with such a God that would discriminate with the rest of humanity ... such a being would not be worthy of human interest or attention; he, she or it, could only be known as a monster ... a demon given to division and strife between nations and peoples.

'As to your claim that God gave you the lands that you took from other so-called pagan neighbors, my dear, sir, any nation can make the same claim by referring to their own divine right and their own prophetic voice to do so. If we all went about making such untenable claims, why, we would be in endless conflict with each other throughout the entire world! The deliberate occupation of any nations' lands by another is always wrong and has no justification or compliance with the laws of the new world that cares for the justice, love and protection of all peoples. What you insist upon, sir is nothing short of an insane claim to any caring, reasoning person?

'The laws that were given to me to promulgate across all nations are not my own; they too are the inspired directives from God. Look across the wider histories of the nations and see that such abuses and arrogance have taken place time and time again. Consider too, sir, that your people were once a nomadic landless people consisting of tribes ... that you were not a nation at all. You had no lands of your own to speak of. Look at the histories of all conquering nations who came to occupy the lands of indigenous peoples ... the pharaohs of Egypt who took you into slavery ... the Greek and Roman empires that came to occupy your lands and to consider their own leaders as having divine status ... consider too the conquered lands of the British Empire and their brutal occupation and exploitation of their conquered lands ... they who once conquered my very own nation of Ireland and almost succeeded in the obliteration of our own language, the expression of our faith, culture and religious rituals ... they, who in their occupation and exploitation of our lands and people almost brought us to a state of extinction by starvation and brutality ... they who followed the dictates of their own supposed holy anointed kings and queens, and with the willing brutal aid of their indoctrinated minions ... the pawns of poverty and ugly necessity. Are you then denying their rights to own the lands that they came to occupy by force?

'Consider too the French, sir, the Portuguese, the Saxons, the Vikings, The Normans, the Americans, the Russians, the German nation under Hitler who claimed a divine right to mercilessly slaughter your own people with the hope of your extinction and extermination ... the list is endless, sir. All of them in their different ways giving themselves the divine right to march on the lands of other peoples and then imposing their own brand of exploitation and brutality on the less powerful and less advanced indigenous peoples. The poor and helpless, sir, have had to eat the scraps left over by such conquering and brutal occupations and have the Creed of strangers forced upon them ... and they to accuse the indigenous of savagery and ignorance only to be exploited and brutally treated by an even greater savagery and ignorance. What nation, sir, has not been guilty of what you yourselves must share in such blame and accusation?

'You, sir, Joseph Bloom, and the leaders of your religion, eat from the loaf you claim to be sacred and inspired tradition just as we do from ours. Indeed, we have gathered the good wheat from the finest harvest of your faith, your traditions, and have made our own loaf which is supplied by Christ the Baker who baked the loaf in his own suffering for all. We eat from his bread, you from the manna of Moses, his Laws and rituals. With Christ, the Baker, there is no Jew, Greek, male or female ... all are made family to Love ... a love born in humble obscurity because his family was considered of no particular importance or consequence.

'As a member of the Jewish faith you claim that God would not want any human person to die for human sin and that human blood sacrifice is detestable to God, as in the case of Christ's death. What you seem not to understand is that it is Love that made his sacrifice necessary. As enlightened people we realize that much of so-called sacred scripture, is little more than the moral guidance of self-appointed, self-declared prophets claiming to speak for God, thus giving themselves a form of divine authority and superiority over their neighbors and generally instilling fear and mere propaganda into the gullible and ignorant of their time. Much of their moral guidance was indeed worthy of instruction and benefit. It was all the other fear-ridden threats that invariably came with their menu that was so objectionable.

'Ancient prophecy, sir, the cabbalists of your own ancient tradition, were no more to be relied upon for divine truth as they read animal entrails, from smoking caldrons or dark dreams or from the raving dances of occult madness and opium ecstasies. Only plain unobtrusive virtue could stand unchallenged for reliable prophecy. Listening to the many imagined voices of man-made gods, sir, has invariably been the voice of deference and servitude to power and royal expediency. At its most dubious, it came in whispered riddles from cupped hands into the ears of fear-ridden royals, desperately clinging to transient power … demented minds divining in the dark of night, gleaning from the position and motion of stars such wide latitude of chance so as to deem falsehood and royal deferential predictions as prophecy. One of your own truly inspired prophets exposed the false prophets for what they really were, a bunch of ineffectual cabbalists dabbling in nothing more than occult witchery. The contest between Elijah and the slaughter of four hundred Baal prophets recorded in your own scriptural writing tells us quite enough about the rampant delusional voices claiming to speak for God. Certainly, sir, many humble prophets from your times were inspired. All had one irrefutable truth and virtue to their inspired voices, that God, or more precisely, Love, hears the cry of the poor, their pleas for justice, the care of the orphan and widow … hospitality for the stranger …. Through all these inspired insights, sir, lay the shadow of the greatest prophecy of all …. That all the virtues essential for the moral, spiritual and physical care of all humanity, irrespective of nation, religion or gender, emanated from one source, sir, Love itself. That, sir, if you will believe me, is the total wisdom and key to human direction, harmony, existence and future. It is the only true covenant that all humanity has with its Creator. It is the Love and Care of all people, sir, and only those two virtues, which will fulfill humanity and remold its imperfect nature. That, sir, is our one and only everlasting covenant. It is quite unlike all the covenants that your race broke with its own perceived notion of

God.' Here Larry paused and read out just a few examples of the broken covenants that he referred to. They were numerous in the Books of Jeremiah, Judges Kings, Isaiah, and so on ....

Joseph Bloom seemed to clarify his stance when he remarked quite candidly and with indifference to all that Larry had said:

'Mr. Walsh, sir, am I correct in assuming that you have a background in the Christian Faith? That your claims of prophetic inspiration emanate from that source?'

'You most certainly can make that assumption, sir. Although I make no precise claim to know precisely who inspired the work. All I can vouch for is that the Laws I was inspired to promulgate to the world were indeed of a Christian ethos. However, I would like to go beyond that and say that the same inspiration can be reasoned to exist in essence in many other religious faiths with similar virtuous teachings including your own.' Joseph Bloom was not content with the broad latitude of Larry's inferences to other faiths; his attack was squarely aimed at Christianity's total reliance on Christ as the mediator between God and mankind.

'Our faith,' said Mr. Bloom, 'does not require a mediator between God and man. We go direct to God for our own needs and concerns.'

'In that case, sir, why on earth did you need Moses at all? What was his role, if not one as mediator between your people and God? Or are we reading from different scriptures? Did you not occupy foreign lands on his words that he professed as coming from his God? I fail to see why Christ the Messenger who was revealed to be the light of the nations beginning with his supposed own people, your people ... that you do not understand why we have embraced his teaching. Christ, Mr. Bloom, is not simply a person. Like all of us he is what he lives. He is only as good as his teaching and how he lived what he taught. We have simply to take on his way of life. It is his life we look to not some invisible power isolated from what he lived and revealed. What other individual in human history served the love and care of all people as he did? Such a love was entirely new in the world. That was not a love confined to personal family members or to one's own nation as national love is. This love we have taken on, Mr. Bloom, could not walk away from the cross and still claim to love. The grain of his love that was set in the field of the human harvest was to provide the only true source of human food expressed in the love and service of all peoples. That, Mr. Bloom, is the harvest we are about in the new world.'

'We as traditional Jews, Mr. Walsh, are loyal to our faith. We find the need for a human being to be crucified for the forgiveness of human sin a deeply offensive concept to put before the human race as something essential for human salvation. We ask for forgiveness for our faults directly from God and we know we receive it.'

'How is it then, Mr. Joseph Bloom that the notion of the sacrifice of animals for the forgiveness of sin comes directly from your own scriptures? How your own later inspired prophets or teachers spoke of the utter futility of such practice ...? That it took Christ himself to give such sacrificial practice its true significance and power? That, sir, was an act of love for humanity not an act to appease the wrath of a vengeful God. Sin, sir, left unchecked, as everyone with a grain of wisdom knows, is a destroyer; whereas the love of others is a forgiving powerful creative force. Love, sir, when related to humanity or even to poor animals, demands self intervention and unavoidable self-sacrifice.

'Love is the true Mediator between mankind and his true sense of being and security. Surely, sir, the division of your nation with the Palestinians and with the divisions of all nations has taught us that entire irrefutable truth? Both of your peoples sacrifice their own lives from time to time, as well as other nations have done in war. Surely you could not declare the spirit and reality of their self-sacrifice as obnoxious or futile! The imperfection of humanity, sir, demands a powerful intervention if we are not all going to end up destroying each other. The big difference between the sacrifice of one nation in conflict with another and that of Christ's sacrifice for all in a sinful world is that the latter is for everyone ... it goes beyond gender and nationalism ... it is universal and for all. The reality of the message, sir, is what counts; the biology, gender and nationality of the messenger are secondary. We are not our biology, sir; we are only what we mean to achieve in loving concordance with each other ... that is our true being. We are the measure of our direction. How you fail to see that is quite beyond me, sir. Perhaps your own bigotry against Christianity blinds your better judgment, sir!

'Your fixation and preoccupation with the coming of some unique Jewish Messiah will never be something so Jewish nor so absolute. After all, Christ hasn't done away with your Law, even if Paul speaks of it as being under the curse. Christ came to fulfill it ... to disentangle it from empty ritual and to encapsulate all the Law and prophetic voices into two related and simple-to-understand commands ... that of our complete love of God and neighbor. He, or more precisely Love, is the new and everlasting covenant for all peoples.

'No, sir, your own prophets over a period of time began to understand that prophecy, all prophecy, is little more than a deeper development in humanity's understanding of itself, as it comes more and more to discern for itself through the higher virtues contained in the concept of love and care of all peoples. I'm afraid, Mr. Bloom, sir, that we could be exchanging the polemics of our own positions forever without benefit to either of our understanding and appreciation of the other. All I can say is that we have found our own prophetic voice from the contributions and development of your own prophetic voice and from the prophetic voices far more ancient that your own. We all have to move on and leave the irrelevance of primitive, cultic history, ritual and half truths behind us.'

Joseph Bloom broke in on Larry's commentary.

'Mr. Walsh, sir, for all your utopian directives and philosophy of a completely integrated and caring world where all peoples love and care for each other, it's never going to happen. For God's sake …! It's not the Palestinians that we fear but the Islamic creed behind them that intends to wipe our nation off the face of the earth. They have boasted that intention often enough to keep their threats alive in the generations as yet unborn. How on earth do you expect us or any other nation in similar circumstances to reach out with the hand of friendship and trust? I repeat, sir, it's never going to happen, Mr. Walsh. You're a bloody dreamer! And I have no further intention of discussing the matter with you.'

Joseph Bloom suddenly cut off their communication without further ado. Larry sat bolt upright and turned to Dee with his extended hands directed to the blank screen as if to ask, what was all that about?

'Don't worry about it, love;' Dee remarked, 'it was obviously a very sensitive subject for him.'

'But why be so rude, to switch off with such arrogance and hostility?' Larry's face grimaced.

Dee pressed on Larry's shoulder by way of comfort and consolation as she remarked with one of her familiar compendious pearls of brevity, 'Ladders have steps, sweetheart; that's why they are called ladders. I'm sure he will have much to think about. Changing loyalties from the doctrine of our childhood is not always easy for anyone; it can take the feet from under us; it can strip our sense of identity and security. And yet Dreamers do change the world In spite of Mr. Bloom's opposition to you. After all what is prophecy – if not the dreams and visions of a new day? Nonetheless, sweetheart, truth, can't be hurried ... no more can we rush childhood into adulthood. Things are really changing around him, sweetheart, but he doesn't want to acknowledge those changes; he prefers the mould of his old identity, it's not for sharing.'

'You're right of course, Dee. I should know better than to expect new insight or teaching to be accepted too readily. The Lord himself knows that I have had to relearn much about my own understanding of the Catholic faith since receiving all these messages.'

Pope Dominic never interfered with Larry's broadcasts while he was in Israel. Nonetheless he was often torn between his loyalties to traditional Catholic teaching and Larry's controversial messages. He was not at ease with

Larry's last debate with Mr. Joseph Bloom. Larry's frequent dismissal of ancient prophecy was deeply disturbing. The pontiff knew of Christ's own references to prophecy concerning his own coming and the kind of life and death that he would encountered on Earth. Who could fail to appreciate the prophet Isaiah's account of the coming of the Suffering Servant in the Old Testament and the life and suffering of Christ in the New Testament? The likeness and closeness were too remarkable to dismiss; although some would claim that Christ deliberately chose to live out the prophecy of Isaiah and other passages of scripture referring to him and the type of Messiah he would be. Matthew's account of Christ's life explains why Christ did the things he did by using the phrase, "... this was to fulfill the prophecy of .... Or this was to fulfill the scriptures...."

It was Larry's honest contention that the entire scriptures were the work of mankind itself working out its own self-understanding. Mankind's reference to a sacred source to life was both unavoidable and inspired at the same time. Larry was widely read and well-acquainted with ancient pagan history ... pagan belief systems ... and their sacrificial rituals of both children and animals to appease the gods. The Hebrew Scriptures and their rituals were not free of these same superstitions and their need to appease the wrath of their notion of God ... the Old Testament is full of examples of need to appease God's anger. Larry's prayerful study of scripture convinced him that humanity developed its moral and spiritual sensibility from utter necessity and new insights into the world and its peoples, and from the universe above his head. It was as if the universe surrounding man and the awesome powers of Nature itself demanded to be questioned, where did we come from? The role of prophets and prophecy can be clearly traced in their progress and self-understanding from prophet to prophet ... from book to book. Until in the end the entire mish-mash of all the scripture's wisdom and human direction came to be encapsulated in two simple and universal truths, the Love and Care of all peoples. That was the entire aim, meaning and direction of the Scriptures. In one word, Love was humanity's purpose for existence. No matter what man might achieve in the future, he will amount to nothing worthwhile without the love and care of each other.

CHAPTER 22

The Death of Nell

Sometime after Larry's international address he grew weary and tired. He couldn't explain how he felt. Dee, however, had experienced this effect on Larry before. It had been the same when he was receiving all the messages that would eventually result in the writing of the book, Larry's Law. He usually did end up with exhaustion after receiving visions and messages. He fell into a deep sleep where he sat. Pope Dominic looked directly into Dee's beautiful but troubled face, he was deeply concerned. She had to reassure him that Larry's condition was not that unusual.

'Don't be too concerned, Dominic. I would, however, be much obliged if you could help me to move him into our sleeping quarters. He will be fine, I'm sure, once he has slept off all the stress of his public broadcasts. It is like power sapped out of him. I am familiar with it, I can assure you.' As an aside she said to Pope Dominic with a reflective smiling expression. 'Can you recall, Dominic, the story in Matthew where a woman in the crowd touched Jesus' cloak and he wanted to know who touched him? How his disciples thought that he was being ridiculous because it could have been any one of hundreds from the crowd. The point being made by the account was that he felt power going out of him?'

'Yes I recall the passage,' Pope Dominic replied, leaning his head questioningly at Dee's face.

'Well that is how Larry feels when he has these revelations of his, or when he is involved in healing. I am convinced that he acts light-heartedly most of the time because he is afraid of this gift of his. He doesn't like the suffering that comes with it.' Dee reminded Dominic of the dramatic effects of her own healing, and of the burnt triangle on both their palms, and the trauma that followed the healing of Mary Cassidy in the police station in Ireland.

Presently, they both carried Larry into his sleeping quarters. In the meantime, Sister Patricia, to her delight, was left holding sweet little Ruth whom she cradled so fondly. She was standing with the white bundle in sharp contrast to her own brown habit and dark headdress. This was the picture that Dee and Pope Dominic captured on their return to the lounge, the smiling face of Sister in adoration of the little child. Dee knew the face of genuine love when she saw it so warmly expressed … it was wonderful to behold. She couldn't avoid her own thoughts imagining Sister Patricia as a gentle loving mother.

'Isn't she just adorable, Dee?' Sister Patricia remarked, her face radiating absolute bliss and delight as she reluctantly offered the white gurgling bundle back to her mother. Dee, who had by now changed from her cream suit to her green silk shirt and black slacks, was so struck with the effect that the child had on Sister that she insisted that she continue to hold onto the child for a while longer, using the convenient excuse that Larry usually relieved her of the weight most of the time. Pope Dominic looked in on the playful child as if looking into a little white-hooded window which framed little Ruth's head.

'She's Larry's daughter alright and no mistake; she is always gurgling with a constant smile on her little face and twinkling blue eyes; she has a kind of playful, mischievous character.' However, like all seemingly perfect things, they usually have their natural interruptions, as Sister Patricia discovered when she felt the palm of her hand that held Ruth's bottom grow suddenly hot. Sister offered to change Ruth's nappy but Dee declined; she preferred to leave her close friend with Ruth's better moments. Dee knew that nappy-changing was not new ground for her religious friend; Sister Patricia had infant nephews and nieces of her own.

Dee looked in on the sleeping figure of Larry. She was more concerned for him than she allowed the others to believe. He was tossing in his sleep and perspiring profusely. She knew that he was dreaming ... that his dreams were relaying images and voices to him. His grimaced face and furrowed brow, the perspiration falling in beads from his skin all indicated something foreboding. He was mumbling incoherently. Dee finished cleaning and changing the child. She intended to hand the bundle back to Sister Patricia. However, Sister had moved to the kitchen facilities to order the evening meal for the pontiff and guests. Pope Dominic took the child from Dee since she wanted to look in on Larry for a little while. Once back in the bedroom she sat on the bed holding Larry's sweaty hand, it calmed him instantly. A little later, she joined the rest of the company for the evening meal which comprised of a beautiful pot of Lamb casserole and mixed vegetables of honey-coated roast parsnips, crisp roast potatoes and Savoy cabbage. Bowls of mixed fruit bedecked the table along with a generous board of various cheeses and savory biscuits. Various bottles of wine and fruit drinks glistened on the white tablecloth. Evening meals were always long drawn-out affairs; it was very much the African way.

Pope Dominic had wanted very much to include Larry and Dee in evening and night prayers. He was a little disappointed that she was preoccupied with her sleeping husband. Dominic was always strengthened by Larry's presence and especially reinvigorated when both Larry and Dee prayed with him. It was as if it was meant to be that way; that he was given this sense of faith and trust in Larry and his wife to grace his own trust and confidence in Larry's directions. All of this took nothing away for the efficacy of the company and prayers of Sister Patricia and Monsignor Edward Henry, his secretary and personal friend. The pontiff also requested all the other domestic staff to join in the night prayers together. He was missing the order and grand celebrations of high liturgy in Rome. Certainly, he was instinctively more at ease with lots of friends round him – it was his tribal way – sharing was innate to him.

Dee continued to sit by Larry's as he tossed and turned in his bed. She was heavy with sleep herself and kept nodding off in fits and starts. After several draining hours that were more like a vigil over the sick, Dee was suddenly startled into consciousness by Larry's piercing scream.

'N............O' His body jack-knifed involuntary into life as he sat rigidly upright in terror.

'Larry; for God's sake! What's wrong? What's wrong?' Dee repeated. He turned quickly to look at Dee. The expression on his thin, heavily-perspiring face was that of someone demented, it was horrible and frightening. Dee was more than a little scared of him. He didn't recognize her. His expression appeared to be accusing her of being his imagined tormentor. Dee began crying with fright and confusion. The noise of her crying and the sight of her tears brought some distant recognition into Larry's tormented and swirling consciousness. After several more confused moments, during which time he surveyed their sleeping quarters, slowly he became more fully present to himself and Dee.

'Why are you crying, Dee?' He took her in his arms and cradled her soothingly and lovingly. The involuntary scream had awoken baby Ruth from a deep sleep; however, she was none the worse for her disturbance. Her little eyes fluttered as she lay in the safety and comfort of her wooden crib with a light white covering over her little body. She soon dropped off again into a warm sleep. She had not noticed her parents, which was a relief to both. Larry repeated the question, only his voice was softer than before, with more concern in its tone.

'Why are you crying Dee? Did I do something? Did I hurt you? Please speak to me.' Dee kept sobbing. She couldn't really say for sure why she was uncertain of her distraught condition.

'You scared me Larry.' Her words emerged in heart-rending heaving sobs. 'You terrified me … . You didn't seem to know me. You looked as if you hated me.' Larry could feel her warm soft body pulsating in involuntary sobbing rhythms. It was many hours later, after a long exhausted sleep, before she could express her emotions and thoughts more calmly and more clearly; in many ways she was clarifying her own understanding of it to herself as well as to her loving husband. Larry explained to her, as best he could, what seemed to him a horrible nightmare.

'I saw her coffin .... We were at her funeral .... It was terrible .... Father Kevin was taken away; it was all terrible! Terrible! Terrible! Nell's coffin came at me as if I had to get into it.' It had been at that point when Larry had suddenly sat up terrified, screaming from what seemed to him a most gruesome and terrifying nightmare.

'For heaven's sake Larry, stop frightening me again. Whose coffin ...? Whose funeral ...?'

'Nell! Our Nell, she's dead and all alone.' Larry was not hysterical anymore; yet he was full of concern and absolute in his conviction as to the certainty of events in Ireland. He added with even greater insistence. 'We must go back at once. We must,' he repeated.

'But, Larry, love, isn't Father Kevin in control of things there, if what you say is true?'

'No, Dee. You don't understand; he doesn't even know that she is dead.' Larry was as certain and clear about what he said as he was as clear and as capable of seeing Dee and baby Ruth on either side of him.

'But, Larry, love, how can Father Kevin not know – he lives with her!'

'He isn't there in the house.'

'Well, where is he, then, Larry?'

'He was rushed to hospital three days ago with a heart attack; he has had an emergency heart operation and is intensified, I mean in intensive care.' In his haste Larry was getting his words and expressions somewhat out of kilter.

'Ok, Larry. So you are absolutely convinced that all you say is true.' Dee was willing to believe Larry. She had every reason to believe him from her own past experience. These vivid visions had been a great gift and a kind of curse in their lives. It had brought them together in an indescribable love for each other; and yet, it made huge demands on both their lives. After all, it was not out of pure friendship and pleasure alone that they were now inexorably bound up with the life of Pope Dominic and international affairs and concerns. She felt strongly at times that their lives didn't belong to them anymore. Yet her new understanding concerning all the upheavals was given much support and consolation in the fact that Pope Dominic, Sister Patricia, her community, Monsignor Edward Henry, all of them shared in this human enterprise in their own unique way ... new demands were invariably placed on all of them. This knowledge did, in time, give Dee an even greater spirit of generosity and willingness to continue; it was, as she eventually came to understand, a yoke of faith. She recalled the words of Jesus which she had often pondered over to make sense of the changes in her life: how his yoke was not one of burden or oppression. The service and commitment to the needs beyond her particular existence was far richer and more meaningful than the miserable existence and self-interest of her former life.

For all her conviction as to the truth concerning Nell's sudden death, Dee felt that she had to approach the situation with sensitivity and great caution. After all, dreams, visions and nightmares, though usually only valves to release and help us all to face our deeper and hidden fears and concerns, can frequently be Just that, valves in the service of the human mind preparing to face the worst of what we believed may occur and affect our sense of security. The point here for Dee was the fact that they, Larry, herself, the baby and Sister Patricia would be forced into abandoning their post in the service of Pope Dominic Ubutu; he was still feeling very vulnerable in what he considered to be a kind of outpost and without any real sense of a stable future. He was, after all, a man grounded in a tribal culture and upbringing; this meant that he was not comfortable with the developed world's sense of independence; an independence that had developed out of riches and the impersonal world that came with it. There was more of a brotherhood and sisterhood in the tribal situation. Tribal leaders were closer to their peoples' needs than their faceless conniving governments. The material development and infrastructure of developing nations were forced by sheer complexity to put their trust in governing parties ever weighed down by bureaucracy and officialdom ... parties who did not share in the intimacies of the families that they purported to represent ... parties of individuals who, all too frequently, served their own families, careers and personal aspirations. All this was alien to a tribal member who was ingrained with a distinct need for the personal. The social environment of the developed nations did not feel instinctively right. Dee in particular was frequently reminded of Pope Dominic's need of personal company around him. This need could be demanding at times since the tribe was not brought up with self-management and independence; it depended completely on local interaction rather than on the complexity of nationhood and responsible government. Governments in poorer and less developed parts of the tribal world rarely took meaningful responsibility for its peoples; they often denied them the basics of shelter, food and schooling. Much alleviation from poverty and hopelessness depended on local responsible volunteers to make any difference at all in order to advance their own future and spare their tribal existence from utter fragmentation. The generosity of the tribe in their poverty forged a distinct intimate bond of sharing which was in contrast to the more developed world's self-reliance and independence. This ingrained reality was deeply felt and expressed by Pope Dominic, for all his education. The truth of the old adage was most appropriate here, "... You can take the man out of the tribe; but you cannot take the tribe out of the man." All this knowledge troubled Dee. Larry's instincts were more intimately closer to Pope Dominic's needs; Larry's personality was grounded in such paternal intimacy – Dee's was not. She was by and large a product of the impersonal world and a loveless detached background. She did not need a large group around her since she had developed in isolation from a caring responsible, intimate family. In consequence, she could face her departure from Pope Dominic and Israel with the minimum of regret; for Larry it was very different; intimate friendship was instinctively the only way he was brought up to understand. He felt deeply hurt by any form of personal separation. Worse of all was his inability to cope with the death of anyone close to him; that just sent him into prolonged depression. It was as if his intimate friendship with others grew physical adhering tendrils or roots into his very body. Loss through death severed these physical connections, seriously damaging his very sense of self, leaving him to feel so utterly disconnected and abandoned.

The decision to leave for Ireland immediately shocked and hurt Pope Dominic. His only consolation came with the promise, which he all but extracted from Dee and Larry, to visit as often as their positions allowed. Many tears were shed by all at their decision and ultimate departure. Dee shed her own tears for the weeping Larry who was in turn cut to the heart by Pope Dominic's pain and upset. Sister Patricia, always a very emotional soul and a genuine long term friend of the pontiff's, was not spared her tears.

It was a deeply upsetting sight to see Pope Dominic's white figure waving farewell from the windows of the air terminal with its windows now streaming in lashing rain.

The arrival in Ireland at Cork airport brought with it new concerns that inadvertently caused the family to put their minds to the issue of Father Kevin and Nell's situation. Dee had discovered with the help of Sister Patricia's convent in Garrettstown that Father Kevin was, indeed, in intensive care in Cork city's General Hospital. That fact told her instinctively that since Larry's nightmare was correct in one part, most likely it was true concerning Nell's situation.

No one had a key to the priest's house. There was never any need for a third party to have a key since Nell was available night and day except, for the normal domestic needs such as shopping or attendance at church, which took her from the presbytery. The situation was reported to the Garda. Their questions seemed interminable, which was understandable, but no less a nuisance, prolonging, as it did, the urgent need to have the situation resolved one way or the other. Was Nell in the presbytery or not? Was it all just Larry's imagination, or what? The Garda would not allow the Walsh and Madden families to enter the presbytery even though they knew both of them from several years or so back when they came in search of Larry's missing mother. It was these two families that had informed the Garda of the potential situation.

'We are sorry that we cannot allow you to enter the house until we ourselves have carried out our duties. The house will be out of bounds to all but the forensic team and other members of the Gardai. We just don't know what we may find in this situation.' The male and female officers made every effort not to appear dismissive or ungrateful for the help of the two families. The officers were already aware that the families were personal friends of both priest and housekeeper.

What the officers discovered once inside the house was, indeed, a slowly decomposing body on the bed; the smell, though pronounced, was just about bearable. There was no immediate means of identifying the body. Fortunately the officers were themselves familiar with Nell from previous calls to the priest's house on other matters concerning Father Kevin's parishioners.

There were always the drunks and conmen and women who came to the presbytery. That was usually the case when money was still a part of the old world before Larry's Law took hold. Many rogues came from time to time making threats and demands for money using the feeblest excuses for their own ends. There was always the women who came to the door asking for a loaf of bread because their family was homeless and starving for days on end; these creatures usually turned out to be professional artful scroungers forever attempting to solicit anything they could by their interminable badgering of soft-hearted priests or naïve housekeepers. One needed the patience of Job to cope with them; not all priests could. There were the more aspiring callers who came with a cock-and-bull story claiming that they had a wife or brother, a husband, small children in intensive care in an English hospital ... how desperate their necessity to get to England by the night's sailing. Was it possible to lend them the fare? That story was so frequently used in varied form and only differed in detail and incredible imagination. It was claimed by most priests and their housekeepers that if they were to write an account of all the hard luck stories ever invented, they would produce a best seller. Most of these infamous characters would usually be discovered in the various pubs around the city bragging about their exploits. Al too often they were discovered for what they truly were, having fallen over their own lies and stories which were full of holes and self-contradiction. It was all part and parcel of a priest's daily life in a big city – one of its more ugly sides.

When the Garda emerged from the house with folded handkerchiefs covering their mouths and noses, they mumbled through muffled hands, 'It is Nell as far as we are concerned; however, keep that information between you. Her identity will have to come from family or from the priest himself. I hope you appreciate our dilemma.' The two waiting families nodded in understanding, grateful at least to know that Larry's strange knowledge of events was completely accurate. It was Seamus and Lil who addressed the two officers now.

'I don't know if you are aware that Nell has no remaining family who could confirm her identity. The one who could, her priest, he now lies in intensive care in the City General Hospital, and by all accounts, he is not capable of seeing visitors. I thought you should know that, given the odd circumstances of the situation.'

'I'm much obliged to you both for your information … else we could be chasing our own tails for days on end. Thanks once again for your invaluable help.' All the Garda could do now was to have a glazier fit a new pain of glass to the side window which they smashed in order to gain entry to the house. They had inadvertently discovered a spare key to the front door after gaining entry. The Key was marked with a label clearly stating, "spare, front door." It was a key belonging to a mortise Lock. To avoid any further complications the officers removed the workings of the Yale lock in case some bright spark decide to break into the presbytery and walk out from the front door pulling the door back onto its Yale lock-keep. The Garda were trained to keep in mind that, …"the unlikely was always likely." Now they could only monitor the Priest's situation and make sure that if and when he is released from hospital, that the relevant authorities be informed at once. The Garda were left in another dilemma as they considered the very real likelihood of Nell's funeral and burial before Father Kevin would be free to leave hospital. They were trying to avoid imagining the worst scenario … the shock of Nell's death and unattended funeral could finish the priest off altogether – given his critical condition.

'Poor Father Kevin, lying in hospital completely unaware of Nell's death,' Lil Madden voiced the thoughts of the little group of friends as they stood outside the presbytery door. 'How on earth is he going to face it when he recovers?'

'Let's hope he does recover,' Seamus remarked, and added, 'a triple bypass is a serious operation, when all said and done.'

'It doesn't bear thinking about,' Dee interjected with tears in her eyes. 'Gosh! He's been there for everyone. Who is going to look after him now? Nell was everything to him, mother, sister, soul friend, housekeeper. Their worlds revolved round each other. We're going to have to support him more closely from now on. However, I know he likes his own privacy …'

'We all do, Dee.' Seamus remarked with a distant expression. The group nodded their agreement.

All the while the group of friends shared their thoughts Dee was consoling Larry who was in tears and in a most distraught state. His tears dropped in streams onto little Ruth's covering as she lay in her pram playing with the little row of toy ducks attached to a line that hung across her pram. Every time she spun one of the colored toys with her little hands she looked up to her daddy. She didn't smile now; it was as if she had an instinctive understanding that daddy didn't want to play with her. It was a sad picture of the group of friends all comforting each other. Lil was doing her best in her own tears to comfort her friends Dee and Larry, while Seamus rubbed Lil's back. It was rare to see Seamus in tears it was obvious to all that he had a great fondness for Father Kevin and Nell over the years; in fact, ever since the family moved into the parish. Father Kevin, as busy as he was with the needs of the parish and its parishioners, was in the habit of dropping in at Mardyke Road, the Madden's home. There usually followed a lot of light-hearted banter, a shared meal and "...the nip or a glass or two of beer." It was like a second home to his friend. Father Kevin was forever ribbing Lisa and Andrew. The children loved his light-hearted nature even when he ribbed them something fierce. Andrew would punch him after a bout of tussling. Father Kevin would turn to his parents saying in mock amazement:

'Did you see that, Lil, this bold son of yours hit the holy priest?' Then he would inevitably turn back to the laughing Andrew and say, 'There's no heaven for you ... imagine hitting the holy priest.' Seamus more often than not would remark:

"I don't know which of you is the bigger child, you or him." It was such intimate reveries that replayed themselves in the thoughts of the friends as they stood reflectively on the gravel driveway outside the house.

Another problem concerning Nell's death was where her burial or cremation was to take place? Who would be likely to know about these details? The Garda contacted Father Kevin's bishop; he in turn informed them that the priest and his housekeeper used the same firm of solicitors; they would hold those details. The diocese kept a sealed copy of each priest's will or where such a will was to be found; this was an absolute expectation demanded from all the clergy. However, no one had access to the personal contents of such important and sensitive documents. The firm of solicitors named by the Bishop was Burke and Morris; they did, indeed, hold Nell's will as wells as the priest's. The Garda contacted the firm of solicitors and came straight to the point concerning their particular interest and duty. In spite of the delay of several days of Nell's funeral by forensics and the coroner's office, the funeral directors were given the go ahead to carry out the funeral arrangements by the city coroner. It was established that there were no surviving relatives of Nell and that Father Kevin was not direct family. Given the priest's situation, it was decided by the coroner to spare him further problems. He gave the Garda the power of attorney to act on the funeral arrangements. They visited the solicitors. The main solicitor dealing with Nell's funeral arrangements was a Mr. Morris from Morris and Burke Solicitors. The Garda came straight to the point.

'...The funeral and internment of Nell Snee, Mr. Morris; where is it to take place?'

'Ah Yes! Miss Snee.' It was strange to hear Nell's surname; it sounded quite alien since she was never known as anything else but Nell. 'How sad that there is no family left to make arrangements.' The old weary solicitor, Patrick Morris remarked. He was gnarled in body and tired in mind. He was uncomfortable with all the changes to his former partnership with Burke since the sweeping changes to the traditional role and functions of his office. Larry's Law had taken hold of city life. There was no question of paying for the funeral or for solicitor's fees since the abolition of commercial business and the use of money that had driven it. All the old firms of solicitors and their functions had taken on a holding role for the time being while all their information was in the process of being computerized and simplified for future reference. It surprised many a former client to know that that they were to inherit vast sums of money and property; only to learn that under Larry's Law all such wills were now null and void. For the moment the final burial place and service arrangements were to be respected.

'Well, officer, I can tell you for certain that she is to be buried in County Kerry in the grounds of St. Joseph The Worker, in the area or village known as Hogan's Cross; 'tis an isolated setting used by the local inhabitants and their families only, given the restrictions of its size. A small plot has been arranged for her there to be interned and rest beside one Reverend Kevin Noonan, whom she served as housekeeper and intimate friend for many years. She wishes the funeral service to be celebrated by Reverend Noonan himself. There is no will, as such, only a private letter for Reverend Noonan's personal attention. She had no property or wealth of her own.'

'Out as born, then,' the Garda remarked philosophically.

'Out as born, indeed,' old Morris agreed, and added with some regret for the better days of the past, ''tis the very same for us all now, with this new fangled Larry's Law carry on.' He closed the old buff-colored dusty folder as if it were the lid on his own coffin. To the Garda in his bright light blue modern uniform, old Morris looked like a man just awaiting his own death.

There was no more for it but to carry out the last service for this faithful servant, Nell, who had given her life in the service of her dearest friend and beloved priest in his absence. It was a sad end bereft of any glory as the familiar bells of her much loved church, St. Patrick's, tolled out over the busy city of Cork for the last time over this saintly and wise woman. One would have hoped for a packed church for so meaningful a departure, given her closeness and unstinting service to the parish priest who now lay unconscious in the intensive care unit in the city's General Hospital and quite oblivious to the passing of his dearest and most treasured friend, Nell.

'My God...!' Seamus remarked, 'at lest he was spared this.'

'...If, indeed, anyone could express it in those terms.' Lil added, uncertain which was the better option was for the poor priest.

Since it was Wednesday, it was believed that the church would be relatively sparse of parishioners. However, for all the wrong reasons, the church was packed to capacity. The vast majority of the congregation had come because they had read the newspapers which informed them of the presence of Larry and Dee Walsh at the requiem Mass. It was difficult to criticize the public's motives for their presence; albeit that Nell's funeral meant little or nothing to most of them, save the normal general respect they would show at any funeral. It was a rare opportunity and privilege for them to see such highly renowned figureheads of world importance, to see them in the flesh was too good an opportunity to pass by.

Everyone stood as the Rite of Entry into the church was said and the coffin blessed with holy water. The altar servers led the procession in their well-rehearsed formation, the thurifer; cross bearer; two acolytes; servers for the altar, followed by an elderly priest. The elderly supply priest walked so slowly that it gave the entire gathering the greater advantage of seeing Larry, Dee and little Ruth. The child was wheeled in her pram since it was thought safer with Larry being in such a shocking state of grief. Heads craned along the lengthy pews to get a good glimpse at Cork's famous son, his wife and child. Few could take in the heart-rending wretchedness of their hero who was the main purpose of their attention and interest. Their hearts went out to him; many in tears of sympathy for his own all too visible crushing grief. There was little thought for Nell from those strangers except some tenuous curiosity as to how Larry and family were connected to this obscure priest's housekeeper. The four men in black carried the coffin on their shoulders, inching their way slowly along the long isle in procession to the Hymn, "O Sacred, heart our home lies deep in thee; on earth thou art an exile's rest, in heav'n the glory of the blest, O Sacred heart ...."

Nell's coffin was a very simple affair. It seemed to reflect the humility and simplicity of her life and loving service to the priest she loved. There had never been a pretentious act or thought in her long, adult, faithful service. The hymn had meant so much to Nell and to many of the old folk; its words and sentiments having a deep meaning ... a consolation in faith and comfort for all. It was, as it were, an anthem of hope and promise that life had a higher meaning and that life on earth lived by Christ's directives of love and care for all had ultimate meaning and divine purpose.

Larry's little family and the Madden family, including their children, Lisa and Andrew, was afforded the privilege of following the simple coffin to the altar. They too were all in black, their solemn expressions tearful, their faces like pallid masks drained in grief. Larry was inconsolable as Dee and Lil hung onto him for fear he would collapse; he insisted on holding onto the pram with baby Ruth inside; the child still swinging and rattling her little line of toy ducks stretched across the pram. In some unspoken way the rattle of her toys and her gurgling sounds gave daddy an unconscious strength that held him together with delicate threads; they seemed to hold out a future of tenuous hope and light in the darkness of his dense wall of depression.

Because the temporary supply priest did not know Father Kevin or Nell, except from various accounts related to him by the parishioners, he had arranged for Seamus and Lil to do the chosen readings and for Dee to do a eulogy. All three accepted their roles, although Dee was not overly keen since she had Larry to care for and console. Lil and Seamus agreed to comfort Larry as best they could when Dee would be called forward to the lectern to give the eulogy. The first reading read by Seamus was from St. Paul's First letter to the Corinthians in which Love was the zenith and meaning of all human life.

The Psalm, read by Lil, contained the important verse:
    "If God doesn't build the house, then the laborer's toil is in vain...."

The Gospel was replaced by John's first Letter to his community. This was a special request by Dee herself and was quite a remove from the rubrics of the Church.

However, the supply priest, a kindly elderly man saddled out of retirement, allowed it; believing it was a pastoral concession for the deeply grieving Larry, and how he was sure that it would be of inestimable comfort to him. He also felt that he was too old to be sacked or to be pulled over the coals for his breach of rubrics. This reading too emphasized the theme of Love; that anyone who has never loved has never known God...since God and Love are one and the same thing.

Dee's eulogy or tribute centered round the theme of love also.

'I have been given the undeserved privilege of standing here before you in the absence of your parish priest, who, as some of you are aware, lies critically ill in the intensive care unit in the City General Hospital.' Few people in the congregation would have been aware of that information. She continued; 'I am not a parishioner of your church, though I do use it from time to time when I come to visit Father Kevin and Nell. Why do I undertake this task? I will clarify this in a moment. Today I have lost a mother. I will speak of one day in her long lifetime, one day only, so that you will be better able to get an insight into both Nell and myself and why I stand here today before you.'

All ears were straining to hang onto every word; not to benefit from what she might mean but only to hear her voice – to speak later of her as if she were a collector's item. She was, after all, a world-wide celebrity, part-head of the new world government.

'Many of you will agree that you know very little about Nell's life because she will have appeared to you only as the parish priest's housekeeper and in that capacity kept herself very much to herself, for good reason. In such a responsible position she was forced to keep what happened in the parish and presbytery and to its troubled parishioners as a strictly private and confidential matter ... as if she too had taken a solemn vow to keep the seal of confession. In such a capacity gossiping and over familiarity were two extreme dangers to be avoided at all costs. In her capacity as housekeeper she was also an intimate and supportive friend of Father Kevin. They were both natives of County Kerry, both from farming communities; both shared an innate rural wisdom. In Nell's case, her insight into the troubles and needs of others was nothing short of the miraculous. In short, they had much in common. Nell never married but devoted most of her later life to the welfare and concerns of her friend and parish priest. I know, as a close friend to both, how close they really were to each other in mutual support and deep respect and appreciation.

'When I first set eyes on Nell in my capacity as a journalist, I was covering the story of the disappearance of Mary Walsh, the mother of Larry Walsh, who, as you are aware, is my loving husband. As I recall that day, which seems light years ago now, a day that fills me with mind-wrenching shame and sorrow since it still reminds me of the bitter and self-opinionated person I was then. I had insulted Father Kevin and Nell most despicably and shamefully. My bitter language and expressions, my taunting criticism used on that day pains me still. I cannot go into the details of what passed between us since it was, on my part, a venomous attack on their faith. In those days I was proud to profess myself as a confessed and enlightened atheist and a very embittered one at that. In spite of my outrageous and spiteful disrespect for both

Father Kevin and Nell, within two or so hours after our meeting I found myself a sobbing wretch held in the eager and open arms of Nell, the woman I had so intentionally insulted only moments previously. As Nell held me in her loving motherly arms in her kitchen, her words of comfort and consolation have meaning for me still to this day. Prior to that first meeting I had never set eyes on her before. Yet within the space of those two short hours she had unraveled the dark secrets of my soul; secrets I scarcely knew or understood about myself. I can still hear her consoling and loving voice speak:

'"Hush, dear child, you have been badly wronged as many have by nature's imprecision. How many of us have had to bear with the misfortunes imposed on us by nature's unpredictability! And yet, if we allow ourselves to be in the service of fault and personal disfigurement, it can only offer us a devouring wasting disease, a bitterness that never sleeps as we allow our troubled lives to feed on disfigurement. How many suffering souls have had to live with nature's imperfections and wanton deformity in a lifetime of disadvantage ... looked down upon by those favored by chance alone ... yet sneering in mindless mockery at another's hapless disadvantage. In the end, dear child, we all have the choice to lean on the wisdom of what is possible for each one of us, as we look to the greatest and highest good that is attainable and beneficial to the given circumstances of our disadvantage."'

'Nell went on to clarify her thoughts. "The blind," she said, "have the choice of cursing their darkness or accepting the hand of another to direct their way safely avoiding the obstacles before them. The cripple too can take a hand offered to him from another's compassion and concern, or sit about in despair judging and begrudging help, considering another's concern as cold pity and condescension.

"No individual has total freedom or separation from the need of others. There is no total independence or total self-reliance for any of us. Indeed, if we have the grace and wisdom to understand it, we are more than we can ever be by the companionship, dependence and reliance on others. Not even our own families can supply all that our hearts crave or reach out to. The parents of every family were once strangers to each other. We all leave one family circle to discover a deeper sense of fulfillment in another. Let the mind pray, dear child, not curse. Prayer at its most profound and beneficial is a communion with wisdom. It is a wisdom that constantly seeks to reach out to the greatest and highest good in each circumstance of our lives."

'Nell's words of comfort, her inexhaustible depths of wisdom and warmth, gave birth in me that day; I was no longer being judged for my bitter misfortune; and more importantly, was given the grace form her love and willing understanding to cast aside my own wretched judgment and self-hatred. By God's loving grace she had taken the measure of what I was and what was possible for me in the future. She became my true mother and the most important anchor to my future that very day.

'How was it, you may ask, that I was so wretched before I had, by God's grace, been given the lifeline from so dear a soul as Nell? To this I must relate a shameful confession that may speak more forcefully of my life and bitter communion with one so far adrift from grace; that in my blind conviction and feelings of superiority I had with deliberation caused the destruction of so many lives by my merciless judgments and festering hatred for the world. I recall one poor soul, out of the countless I have hurt, a soul who had crossed my path in all innocence and paid a terrible price for his misfortune and presumption to have considered me his friend.

'He was merely a shy young man in his early twenties, a work colleague. He was so taken, besotted by passion, a passion that for him might be mistaken for the love of someone of whom he knew precisely nothing. His besotted love was directed at me. He dared to make his feelings known in the form of a poem that might have been considered wonderful if composed for anyone else but me. I looked into the depth of his words and considered them no more than a blind besotted craving for someone who was a complete stranger to him in terms of friendship.

His poem made me realize how nature is such a cunning and devious matchmaker, willing to parent life by fair means or foul. By Nature's cunning – an artistry of chemistry, that uses the ploy of colored feathers and seeming deceptive trivialities to form its tenuous bonds that serve its urge for the generation of life without any great purpose other than its own replicating force. This same nature which all too often throws together, often by vision alone, two unsuspecting souls caught up in its web and chemistry of blind passion, simply to generate life. Such life, to drop like seeds blown in the hope that they might find some fertile soil in which to thrive and continue to repopulate in blind pursuit of its own abundance. So did the poor soul's poem flow in blind pursuit and passion:

'"I would that I could soft embrace
such beauty rare in form sublime –
Yet must I dare to bare my hand
to will your own in mine.
All giddy in your perfume's wake –
besotted – smitten – and trembling swoon,
So wide expanse between our hearts –
so far apart as sun to moon.

All too aware that I must breach
my hapless rank where beggars dream –
A speck beyond your galaxy
of nobler cast and high esteem;
Yet I solicit honor's cause –
would keep you safe in truth's embrace;
Nor act on passion's rising horn –
nor pluck your flower in lust's disgrace.

Could you for humble honor stoop –
to take a lowly soul's poor heart?
So lost and tossed in fate's cruel whims –
So wayward in disordered charts ....
Bear with me then most cherished soul –
nor let true love be put aside ...
Nor fall within less honored arms –
where love turns sour to rank and pride."

'For many more appreciative souls such a poem would be appreciated, if only for its exaggerated sense of flattery and well meaning intentions; a kind of first love ... an imagined mutual bond that could, perhaps, given its un-solicitous hand on my part, never be returned nor requited. Most who would receive such lavish attention from one so young in the spirit in which it was meant might feel a certain flattery and so keep the poem to themselves, even surreptitiously treasuring it? Yet my reaction, God forgive my shameful arrogance, was to expose his words by having a copy of it given to all our other colleagues at the office of my place of work. They in turn took a perverse delight in throwing his indiscretion back in his face in a mocking mimicry that was so prolonged over the next months ... motivated as it was by their own artless jealousy at the young man's foolish daring presumption. In the end he failed to show up at the office; my rejection and his disgraced standing and wretchedness were too much to bear. He was discovered by his own inconsolable parents, hanged in the bedroom of his own home ... a home, his parents remarked later, "... that had always been a sanctuary of love for him." I can only confess now that I have been haunted by his death and ask his poor family for forgiveness. It is small wonder that the new world established by Larry's Law, of love and care for all people was so wanting in the broken wretchedness of so many disfigured souls as my own.

'So, I was the creature that surrendered my life in the un-censorious arms and heart of Nell ... who all too willingly saw beyond the darkness of my wretched and disfigured existence, and her, God bless the good soul that she was, chose there and then to become a loving mother to me. All that remains for me to say now to all present and beyond these walls of prayer, is to ask your forgiveness and understanding for my past heartless character. God bless you, Nell. Thank you for being there for me in the ugliness of my wretchedness. I know I will feel forever the embrace of your kindly and compassionate love.'

Dee moved away from the lectern and stepped down from the sanctuary, her head bowed with emotion and from the self-abasement of her own exposure and confession. She felt naked, her beautiful face aglow with fervor and the consequence of her own revelation. The silence in the body of the cathedral was tangible in its weight. Many were shocked; others uncertain as to what to make of her revelation and image; and yet in a general embarrassed awkwardness, most partially admired her unwarranted self-exposure.

Up to the moment of her confession she was held in the highest regard; after all, she was a world figurehead, the very image of the face of love hung in every public space and home. Could her endearing image now remain intact? Was her confession wise? Only time would tell what damage her disfigured image might cause among the world's peoples who came to adore and worship what she and her family grew to represent. The entire world would have heard this confession, since any public appearance of the family held immediate interest for all. Only Seamus' family among the congregation really understood the truth of Dee's past life. And yet, there was a general realization and hope in the family's mind that others would come to understand Dee. This hope arose in the familys' thoughts when the supply priest taking the service remarked in private to Seamus and Lil after the service:

'...Her words, you know, were the most honest and moving that I have heard in many a long day. I do hope her image might survive their controversial impact; she deserves all our admiration. It is all too easy to speak of how loving we can be and yet fail to spare the time to reflect on the very real damage of our past failings and sinfulness. Sometimes we have to crawl through a swamp in our development. Hopefully it will only be a few self-righteous cynics who hold on to her disfigured past.'

The internment of Nell was a strictly private affair. This restriction was no hardship or disappointment for the heaving crowds that spilled out of the church after the service. The majority of the people got what they came for, to gaze on the world's greatest and most honored celebrities. Only Dee's family and the Maddens were allowed to attend the burial, along with the elderly supply priest who had celebrated the requiem Mass. The cemetery was built on a very high mound of earth and stone. It was well kept, evidenced by the mown grass and fresh flowers shuddering in the wind over so many graves. The setting of the cemetery was strangely chosen. It seemed to appear miles away from any human habitation. It seemed to hang in the air on an old bog road that further along revealed the signs of turf-cutting with many rows of fresh sods leaning against each other to dry. The small gathering by the graveside could smell the scent of the turf wafting over them. There was a deathly silence that surrounded the remote bog land; only the sound of a distant church bell tolled for Nell, as it would for any other soul. There came on the wind the distant sound of a crowing cockerel drifting up from Hogan's Cross, a remote homestead. The internment service was brief. All that needed to be said and done had already taken place in the city church. The coffin was lowered by three coffin-bearers and Seamus acting as a fourth. It was something he wanted to do. Larry refused the offer to help; he was too far gone emotionally and in uncontrollable heaving tears. Dee's heart was broken with the loss of Nell and with the terrible state of Larry. She felt pulled apart. Lil, Seamus' wife, was also cut to pieces by all the overpowering emotions around her; and yet she was a rock for both Dee and Larry. It was small wonder that all of them were inconsolable with their own deep and personal sense of emptiness, loss and grief.

At the words, " Earth to earth, ashes to ashes, dust to dust, The Lord gave; the Lord has taken away ... " Larry could take no more of it and ran from the hill with baby Ruth in the pram. Dee flew after him followed swiftly by Lil. Their immediate concern was for the safety of baby Ruth, her pram and father racing blindly among tightly packed graves. Only Seamus remained – he too was in tears. Nell was not a character that he could push from his mind – she meant so much to him over the years. There was a ghostliness about the droning voice of the old priest as the solemnity of his words seemed to leave a sense of the sacred lingering in the air itself. The meaning and sound of his words were like living specters blowing in the wind ... a kind of celestial blessing. They seemed like the words spoken by angels and not belonging to the priest at all. Their meaning gave them form and a real sense of a sacred presence. Seamus looked down on the coffin six feet below. The glinting brass cross on the coffin seemed to speak of her loving service to her Lord in a fellow human being, her priest and the Lord's own friend and fellow shepherd. It seemed like a badge of honor, a medal for faithful service rendered to a dear friend. Seamus' last words were spoken aloud without affectation or self-consciousness and with a deep and solemn sincerity,

'Thank you, Nell, for all you meant to all of us and in particular to your dearest friend Father Kevin who can't be here to bid his farewell and gratitude.' The grave diggers who were eager to backfill the grave pulled back for a few moments, their heads bowed; Seamus' words had touched them. His words were not the formal and ritual lines of the well-meaning supply priest. Seamus' personal farewell commanded a kind of manly respect from them. He noted before moving away the names of the Noonan family. So Nell had her wish at last to be buried alongside Father

Kevin, albeit there would be a delay, hopefully a long one, Seamus thought. He shook hands with all four grave diggers in turn and with the funeral director and the coffin bearers. Lastly he shook hands with the old priest whose wind-blasted vestments wrapped against his frail form. Seamus, true to his character, instinctively and without a trace of affectation made a point of acknowledging everyone; it was more than polite formality on his part. He just took an instinctive interest in meeting people in general, no matter the situation; it was one of the reasons why he was usually called upon to lead and organize in social events.

Father Kevin was released from hospital after two months. However, he was not allowed to return to his church and parishioners. He was ordered by his bishop to spend a further six months in convalescence. He read the solicitor's note over and over, Nell's final words to her beloved priest and dearest friend.

"Dearest Father Kevin,

It is hard for me to compose these few words in advance of my own death.

It is hard to imagine never hearing the comfort of your loving voice again, or of not seeing the face that was the very sunshine of my waking hours. It is not a welcome thought never again to share the intimacies of our meals together, our long unhurried conversations. I hope I can say now without fear of excommunication and the wrath of our Bishop, that I love you so much – I always have. You have made my life, my years, so full of meaning and richness. If there is anything I can do, or have the power to do beyond the grave, you can consider it done. Forgive the tears that have fallen and stained this little note. God Keep you safe and happy always, my most beloved friend and spiritual Father. Truly, you have been my world. Remember me always in the same affectionate way as your old Kerry goat. God keep you now. Remember me fondly at the altar where no better hands than your own called down so often the sweet communion of our dear Lord.

Farewell dearest of friends, farewell. Please God we may meet again and be to each other what we always were.

Love as always, Nell."

When Father Kevin had finished reading the farewell note in the silence of the empty presbytery, he burst into heaving tears, like those of a young grief-stricken child without the experience of years to dull the pain. The bond between them was as deep and as intimately shared as if they had been one flesh and one spirit. He would have accepted the haunting of his home by Nell's endearing presence; instead, he was haunted and weighed down by a terrible oppressive emptiness. For days, he would find himself in tears; they came involuntary and without warning. Only his closest parishioners guessed at the cause. It was difficult for them also to stand by the priest of their affections and realise that they were incapable of easing his pain and grief.

He was a much weakened man from his confinement. His gradual return to the city parish was but a brief one. Although he could not be considered an old man by the standards of the day, his early life of hard physical work had taken its toll on him. He asked the bishop to move him to Garrettstown to live near Saint Clare's convent as their chaplain, and to be among his dearest personal friends, Larry, Dee and Ruth.

CHAPTER 23

Father Kevin's Retirement

'My dear, Father Kevin, you cannot know how delighted your humble request means to me,' Bishop Mark McCann, of Cork, remarked with visible relief. He smiled as he sat opposite Father Kevin in Saint Patrick's Church presbytery. The bishop was dressed in a simple black suit and could well be taken for any other priest, except for the pectoral cross and chain of his office which hung on his chest.

'You know, Kevin, I was dreading this day for some months now while you were away in hospital and followed by your time in convalescence. I was very aware of your growing frailty and of the demands the city parish would continue to put on you. God knows,' he added with firsthand knowledge, 'Saint Patrick's city parish is really one in need of three priests let alone a younger one who is fit and healthy. Of course we don't have the luxury of placing three priests in your absence, we can only supply one. God alone knows we will have to keep an eye on his workload. My hope is that I can give the younger man the assistance of one or two relatively fit retired priest to help out occasionally.

'Kevin, it is a sad day for Ireland and its many churches, many built from the pennies of the poor and generous benefactors, that we can no longer supply them all with the priests they deserve.' Bishop Mark paused as Father Kevin nodded in regret and agreement to the present sorry state of things.

'I do hold out hope though, Mark,' Father Kevin intervened. 'I get the strong impression from the current and more friendly attitude of the people in general that they are less hostile to the past mistakes and faults of our priests and the Church in general. My only doubt is that the wider implications of Larry's Law may mean that the new generation of young people, now well grounded in the sentiments of that Law will feel quite comfortable with the new directives, accepting all the new changes which seem so alien to us, married clergy, women priests, celibacy as a thing of the past....' Father Kevin was staring at the tired old red carpeted floor which had bourn Nell's footsteps and his own over the years. He looked up resignedly into Bishop Mark's face.

'Well at least we still have the Church and her guiding Sacraments intact. That's something that cannot and will not be changed.' Bishop Mark spoke with self-assurance. So much was happening so fast. Bishop Mark was grateful for the comforting stability of those things at least.'

'It can't be easy for the older ones among us to feel at home with the new beginnings,' Father Kevin remarked. 'There is one small consolation, though, if you might consider it a consolation at all.' The bishop held out two begging hands to the priest with a mocking smile on his face and remarked,

'Please, Kevin, fill them up with any consolation you can glean from this merger harvest of yours, put me out of my misery.'

'It is just a thought Mark ...'

'Anything will do, Kevin, don't hold back now, for pity sake.' Father Kevin smiled at the exaggerated pretence of the bishop's desperation.

'Do you recall the passage in scripture where Jesus inferred the need for the best of both the old and the new to coexist with each other, taken as they are from the storeroom of proven experience?'

'So, Kevin, what are you making of that?' The bishop asked eagerly.

'Well, some believe, as Matthew is inclined, that it a reference to those who take to the best of the old religion as well as embracing the advancement of the new teachings of Christ. The new, if you like, demands a fresh start or acceptance. It is similar to Jesus' reference to sewing a new patch onto an old cloak; the one is incompatible with the other so that both are destroyed. His reference to the danger of putting new wine into old skins so that both destroy each other has a similar lesson.'

'Meaning what, Kevin?'

'Simply that it is often very difficult for many elderly people to change from one established doctrine or supposed truth that they have been loyal to since their youth and then be expected to take on what seems to them an entirely new doctrine void of established authority. Many just feel threatened and disorientated by such change. They experience feelings of disloyalty and even outright betrayal. It can be very difficult to consider the true value of the new. The trouble seems to stem from the inability to be free to think and judge for oneself. People generally follow a common line of indoctrination and institutionalization.

The machinery of human conditioning has always been a powerful weapon used to subject peoples in fear by threat of punishment or of isolation. Most people latch on to someone else's thinking and authority without ever attempting to evaluate the claims of others to see if their own conscience, experience and comprehension really do concur with each other. It appears to come down to the question that is often asked, how free are any of us to believe by our own reason and efforts of understanding? The early roots of conditioning run very deep in every aspect of our character and psyche, even when we drift from our traditional moorings – we are never really quite free of our early conditioning. Human conditioning is akin to living as a tenant in a house someone else paid for and built. In order to remain secure the tenant must abide by all the rules of the landlord. To rebel against the rules is to find oneself homeless and worse, considered an outcast from one's neighbors and community. That can be very threatening, and lonely. Some would not consider that freedom at all but a kind of enslavement to wanton individualism.

'If you remember, Mark, the many problems Paul encountered with Jewish converts both in Rome under Peter's jurisdiction, and among the Jewish converts living the Galicia. They were convincing the pagan converts that circumcision was absolutely essential and that they had to come under the authority of the Law. Whereas Paul pointed out that the Christian was not subject to either. The Law, he said, was given to show up sin. It was not capable of taking it away. It was only by the grace of faith in Christ, working through love, that sin could be removed. Paul had to clear up this situation in Rome, clearly demonstrating to the Apostle Peter, of his own hypocrisy for giving in to his Jewish converts.

The point I am making here, Mark, is that it was not a simple matter for the Jewish converts to let go of their traditions which were ingrained in them from their childhood.'

The bishop rubbed his jaw studiously. 'Well, I must say, Kevin, there is a lot of truth in what you say.'

'It seems a strange contradiction, Father Kevin added, that Paul had Timothy circumcised in order that his ministry be accepted among the local Jews.'

'Sometimes wisdom has to sleep with hypocrisy, Kevin, for a greater good, do you not think?'

'You may be right, Mark. Yet such actions can give way to troublesome presidents afterwards when the heat of the moment is past thus leaving wisdom and truth to bow to the whims of convenience.'

'What do you mean, Kevin?'

'Just take the case of Moses allowing divorce by a writ of dismissal; which then left Christ the troublesome task of having to clear up the mess by insisting how divorce was fundamentally unacceptable in the eyes of God or in the reality of love itself. Even Larry agrees with that, since he insists that Love cannot divorce Love. It is a gross contradiction. Though even he does concede in one of his statements when he says that those who divorce never knew what real love was or what it embraced In which case, he maintained that there never was a marriage to begin with. Since God is Love and only love puts a marriage together as an inseparable bond. It is not the sexual act of itself that is love, Mark, otherwise there never would be a divorce or separation. The Love which Larry speaks of is the total absorption of a person, warts and all. It loves lovingly by absorbing lovingly in every circumstance.'

'Surely, Kevin, that could never be achieved by the average human being, not even in a lifetime?' Bishop

Mark's expression was one of incredulity. 'It's all very idealistic and utopian,' he added, as if affronted by the very impossibility of such a love, given his wide experience of people, even among his own clergy and religious.

'Yet it is real enough, Mark, and achievable. I realise that it is usually only experienced in very advanced and gifted individuals. Yes, for all of us poor primitives, it has to be worked at and meditated on day and night. The trouble is, Mark, love is one of the least understood universal virtues among us humans. Kindness, gentleness, patience, forgiveness, mildness, all of these we understand and attain to some degree in most of us, like steps on the ladder to universal love. However, the love Larry speaks of, that which was ushered into the world by Christ himself is such a powerful and unique reality and ultimately the only saving grace for humanity and for our most meaningful and fulfilling way of being in the world. If we are to continue as a Church in the future, Mark, we are going to have to insist on love and care for all people as the only virtues that can possibly authenticate us as a teaching practicing, and credible ministry. That, Mark is the complete essence of Larry's message to the world.'

'I still say it's a grand ideal, Kevin; a slippery board on which to ride the thundering waves of our storm-battered world. It seems we slip off all too easily, even in little trials.' Bishop Mark smiled philosophically and added: 'I say we ride the waves of the other attainable virtues and hope this universal love you defend on Larry's account might come eventually, slip in through the back door as it were!'

'No doubt your right, Mark,' Father Kevin agreed good humouredly. 'However, Larry knows of no different love than that ushered in and revealed by Christ himself.' Father Kevin was smiling also as he added without malice, 'you're a minimalist, Bishop Mark, well-meaning, yes; but still a minimalist. You have to raise the bar in the mind of the world and especially among our own congregations.'

'Why are you so persistent, Kevin? You're no fool. I have always known you to a practical priest. Why demand such extremes of half-civilized humanity?' Bishop Mark insisted on holding the lower ground until Father Kevin reminded him of Christ's own call to perfection.

'Mark can you recall Jesus' question concerning Peter's love for him?'

'I do, indeed,' Bishop Mark replied affably and added, 'what lesson have you got for me now, Kevin?' Both laughed together good naturedly. The discussion between the two religious was like bringing shamrock to Ireland. And yet Father Kevin was making an important point.

'Three times, Mark …' Father Kevin slapped the palm of left hand with the backs of his right hand fingers for emphasis and added, 'three times, Mark, Jesus asked Peter if he loved him. We know that Peter answered yes three times and was told each time to "feed my Sheep." Peter wanted to say, you know perfectly well that I love you. Why can't you understand a simple yes? You see Peter couldn't grasp what Jesus was getting at, Jesus was saying to him indirectly, "Prove it."

'What point are you making here Kevin? You've lost me a bit?'

'The point I'm making, Mark, is a very important one; and I take it from one of Larry's conversations; it is that Jesus was turning Peter's exclusive love for Jesus away from himself and redirecting it towards everyone else in the world. "Feed my sheep," meant that Peter had to redirect his intimate and exclusive love for Jesus towards every other individual. Only by doing so could he prove his true love of Christ who lives as "needing love" in each individual. Christ, as Larry insists, Mark, is Love manifest. The need to be loved in each individual can only be fulfilled by love from all others, not just from a few special people. Peter, like all the rest of us Christians, as Larry states, only prove our love for Christ and for God by turning that same love towards other people by being more inclusive. The more immediate point as it concerns all of us in the here and now, Mark, is that we have to move the focus of our personal and exclusive, indulgent love, our possessive love of family and friends in order to embrace, to reach out to others as if all were family and friends.' Father Kevin kept an emphatic gaze on the Bishop to see his reaction.

'It is still a very tall order, Kevin. A grand ideal, I admit. But nonetheless very utopian.'

Bishop Mark had a wide experience of people in the extensive diocese of Cork city and its sprawling county. Many personal problems were brought continually to his busy office from around his diocese for him to give judgement or instruction. He knew as well as any other, the fickle nature of his fellow human beings, even among his own clergy. Hence his practical approach to the spiritual welfare of his people. His lower expectations of others, though, could at times forget the radical nature and demands of Christ's teaching and insistence of turning away from exclusive love of family and all you love dearly to focus on his inclusive love of all. As Christ himself said, "What thanks can you expect for helping and loving those who help and love you in return ... even criminals do that much."

'I must say, Kevin, You do your college proud. Where did you say you studied? You certainly have a way of clarifying things, Kevin. I must admit to my shame that I never did grasp that point before now.'

'Ouch, I can't give my college the credit for that, nor are such insight my own. When you have been in Larry's company and exposed to his private discussions you get some wonderful insights into his interpretation of Christ's teaching; he has a unique gift for it.'

'Well, Kevin, I must say that you have the humility and grace to leave credit with its proper owner. Of course, Larry is almost a son to you,' Bishop Mark added thoughtfully as he nodded his head knowingly.

'He certainly keeps me on my toes. I must be honest, Mark; though, much of what he discusses I get second hand from his wife, Dee. In any event, I am always grateful for these insights, no matter their source,' Father Kevin smiled philosophically.

'Amen, to that Kevin.' The bishop raised his joined hands to heaven and bowed in a kind of reverent good-natured smile. 'I am familiar with his writing, of course, who isn't these days? Where do you think he really got all his ideas from, Kevin? He has put love and care at the very heart of his world guidance, which none could fault him for in principle, I'm sure.'

'According to himself and his wife, Dee, Mark, he is convinced that all his directives are not new nor are they his own imagined instructions but soundly based on a passage from Hebrews and from the writings of the Evangelist John. Both these sources make similar statements that "everyone will be taught by God," the greatest no less than the least. It also states that brother or neighbour will no longer be the teachers of each other ... that to learn from God is to turn to Christ himself. All Larry concludes from these sources is that to be taught by God or Christ is to be taught by the internal voice of Love in each one of us, if we care to listen with understanding. Love, Larry insists, is the world's only authentic teacher.'

'Well, I couldn't possibly contest that, Kevin; he certainly has set the world ablaze with it, I will say that for him,' the Bishop remarked.

'Well, Kevin, my dear friend, you have left we with a mighty lot to chew over. So now we turn to the issue in hand …. We are agreed on your move to St. Clare's Convent, then, Kevin.'

Before their parting many little details were aired with regard to the timescale of the pending move. Both embraced in brotherly affection and with the bishop's sincere gratitude for all Father Kevin's hard work in the past and for his cooperation with the present changes. The bishop left the presbytery with a distinct sense of relief and gratitude even though his mind was spinning with the many questions left unanswered for the Church of the future. He heard Father Kevin close the presbytery door behind him. His eyes stared distractedly at the graveled ground outside. His bent head and stooped body expressed the countenance of a much troubled man. In his disturbed thoughts he knew that he would need to put more trust in God's hands.

The news of Father Kevin's departure from Saint Patrick's came as a blow to the parishioners who had grown to love him over the years. This was no surprise to him since he had experience the same sense of loss by the people from other parishes where he had served. Nonetheless, moving permanently from a parish after many years of service and intimate involvement with all the parishioners' families was always a disruptive upheaval all round. From the point of view of the parishioners, they were going to have to get used to a new priest over time. It would be a test on both priest and parishioners – it was a kind of marriage breakup. Although moving a priest from one parish to another was part of his vocation, nonetheless it was also a great upheaval for him also. The Parishioners didn't have to leave their own homes – the priest did ... lock, stock and barrel, and most likely be sent to the far-flung reaches of the diocese.

A great celebration was held in Father Kevin's honor and many words of heartfelt thanks and appreciation were spoken by those who were given the privilege of doing so on behalf of the people. He was not one to feel at home with all the sincere plaudits heaped upon him. He knew in his heart that there were many helpers in his ministry who had carried him along the way with their unstinting generosity and dependability. His reply to the people, brief as it was, gave that very point his special emphasis and importance as he spoke softly and with controlled emotion.

'No priest could ever hope to serve in such a large city parish as ours, here in the city of Cork, without the generous and unstinting reliance on the good parishioners themselves. To that end we have all shared in a common ministry here. It is your priesthood too that has made my years here a privilege and a pleasure. We have all worked hard. I avoid giving special thanks to any particular group or individual for whom words alone could never suffice for gratitude; you know who you are already and what in good times and bad we have shared together. However, I feel that I can be forgiven if I mention one particular individual who cannot be compromised or embarrassed by the mentions of her name.' Before he continued, tears streamed from his eyes.

'Nell is no longer with us in person. She, in no small way, has been the backbone and spirit of my priesthood here. I cannot find the words that could adequately express my heartfelt gratitude for her unfailing and dearest friendship ... for her deep love that held me together through the many unavoidable storms of parish life. Her final resting place is alongside our family grave in the bog-lands of Kerry, our shared birthplace.' The last remark brought a peal of laughter from the parishioners. 'There is just one vacant plot beside her that awaits my own end. It only remains for me to say, thank you, dearest Nell, for being there and for all you meant to me. Sleep on good friend, sleep on dearest soul – till we meet again, I pray for the grace to be good enough to be granted a new home with you – a new table to share – and a safe lodging together.' His words drew haunting heaving sobs which echoed throughout the Hall.

He strode way in hurried steps and blinding tears to the company of Larry's family and the Maddens who had come to take part in the celebrations. There was hardly a dry eye in the hall which was packed to capacity; the only free room was taken up with rows of tables weighed down with a lavish variety of savory foods, cakes and drinks. A very heavy and tangible sense of sadness and loss engulfed the people. It was painful and yet unavoidable, given the much-loved character of the man and his long kindly service to his people.

Father Kevin's move to Garrettstown went smoothly enough. For all his years in the priesthood he had nothing of his own by way of furniture – all belonged to the presbytery. Larry and Dee offered Father Kevin a home with them which he accepted gladly. There was plenty of room for him at the convent. However, he chose to take up Dee's offer. He knew their house well from his many visits and overnight stays. More to the point, he loved Dee as a daughter and as an intimate soul friend. He always felt enthused by her quick and wide intelligence. He was used to conversing with her for hours on end on every conceivable subject and interest. Larry too he treated as both son and dearest friend. Larry was also capable of keeping him entertained when he had a mind to. Usually Larry liked to go out socializing with the whole community. His international profile and importance might as well never have existed. His simple child-like character always remained with him and the locals of Garrettstown loved him for it.

'We are delighted that you have accepted, Father Kevin; it will be the greatest pleasure for us to look after you here. You have your own room with an onsite; the house is a large one, as you know from when you stayed before. You have the same room as always. Larry was beside himself with joy at the thought of having Father Kevin to stay, to live and eat with them. There was no awkwardness on the priest's part he had grown quite used to the family from all their visits to the city.

Dee remarked with further enthusiasm, 'With regard to your temporary driving restrictions, don't worry in the least; I will drive you to the convent each morning, or at any time you feel that you wish to celebrate Mass there for the sisters. I know that they will not expect too much until you are stronger and more fully you old self again.' Larry was rubbing Father Kevin's back in between pauses to clap his two hands together and doing his little excited Jig. Dee smiled to Father Kevin and shook her head at the excited antics of Larry. He picked up little Ruth from the blue carpeted floor in the sitting room and brought her over to Father Kevin.

'Look, little angel, you have two daddies now.' The priest broke into laughter and was handed little Ruth as if she was offered as a present.

'Isn't she the very dote, all the same.' The infant was pulling at his fingers. The priest marveled at the fragility of one so little.

'She's a very doting child, Dee, don't you think?'

'And why wouldn't she be with that great eejit playing with her all day; I swear he has her spoiled already.'

'No I don't, then; she loves to play; you ask Father Kevin; look, she is sucking his fingers.' Dee shook her head smiling affectionately.

They all settled down to their first meal together. It seemed like a long time since they were all together in the family home. Inadvertently, Larry began the grace before meals. Father Kevin put his head on his chest in like manner with Dee; both wanted to laugh at Larry's form of blessing, his sign of the cross swept across the room and seemingly over their heads with the exaggerated sweep of his arm. He had never quite moved on from his first childhood efforts which were exaggerated to the extreme in an effort to show his daddy and mammy how well he was able to sign the cross on himself. Dee had to remind him, in subtle whispers, that the blessing and privilege were usually reserved for the priest as a matter of respect and recognition of his sacred office, to which Larry expressed his usual sense of surprise.

'Oh!' He leapt across to Father Kevin's chair and gave him a cuddle by way of apology for his forgetfulness.

Dee remarked with a strong sense of relief, 'You know, Father Kevin, it's good to hear the clatter of plates and cutlery again in our own home. Don't mistake me; we enjoyed Israel with Pope Dominic. Yet, you couldn't help feeling insecure there, surrounded by so much security and military.'

'Yes,' Larry chimed in, furrowing his brow; we could hear bombs or rockets explode in the distance; I wouldn't like to live there all the time. I'm pleased that Pope Dominic's year of sanctuary is almost come to an end. However, he has told us since in his last e-mail that there has been a remarkable improvement since God's Law has been taken up more fully on both sides.'

'God's Law, Larry, whatever can you mean?' The priest expression was quizzical.

'Ah! He always refers to Larry's Law as God's Law.' Dee interjected.

'And so it is too; you know that I didn't make it up myself; you helped me to write it,' said Larry defensively.

'Alright, sweetheart, I am only explaining to Father Kevin what you mean; it can be confusing calling it by two names.

'Oh!' He exclaimed – 'sorry.' He continued to wolf down his meal in between feeding baby Ruth with her milk bottle.

'What is Pope Dominic's plan after he moves from Israel?' Father Kevin asked as he rested his knife and fork temporally on the meal of bacon, cabbage and jacket potatoes, a favorite meal of his.

'Oh! I told him that he is to return to Kenya,' Larry replied in a matter-of-fact tone.

'You told him, Larry!' The priest's face seriously startled.

'Oh, yes; I wasn't going to leave my friend in that frightening situation. It was not as if his presence was contributing in any peaceful way to the situation there. Do you know, Father Kevin, that he hasn't seen his own people and his own family for over ten years? Ten years, I tell yeah!'

'But surely, Larry, does he not make his own decisions as to where he moves?'

'Absolutely. However, he asked my advice and I told him that holy God says that he must go to visit and stay with his own people for three years and then he is to move from nation to nation where he is to be the guide of his own people in their Catholic faith and make all the new changes that must follow.' This latter remark was not left unnoticed by the priest. He left it unquestioned for the moment but with every intention of coming back to it. In the meantime, Larry continued.

'Did you know, Father Kevin, he lost two brothers and three sisters before the new Laws brought liberation to the people?' Father Kevin looked across the table at Dee while Larry kept his head down engaged, forking his food. She nodded to the priest in agreement, confirming the personal information about Pope Dominic that Larry had imparted. He wouldn't normally divulge such personal and intimate details to anyone other than family. Larry was certainly slow in many ways but he wasn't completely indiscreet, he had his own sensitivities.

'Larry. Does Pope Dominic consult you on all his moves and intentions?' Father Kevin was somewhat taken aback with the sense of his own question; there was no offence behind it, just a certain sense of incredulity. Traditionally it was the pontiff who took the initiative concerning his own moves and directives, albeit with regard to due process and wide consultation from many quarters; his was always the final decision; he was, after all, occupying the Chair of Peter, a position of presidential authority over the Faith.

'No, Kevin, he doesn't have to; he invites me to do so. Sometimes holy God or his angels, or whoever brings these messages, tell me what to say and what is going to happen, or what is best in the circumstances of the time.' The priest was inwardly skeptical; his face still tense and quizzical. Dee could trace his mind from his expressions. She was used to these intimacies of Larry, so much so, that it was not always easy for her to understand how others in the priest's position were not similarly at ease with his revelations. The priest knew, better than most that Dee was a highly intelligent and educated person. She was ironing some sheets in leisurely fashion after the meal, the expression on her face was calm in quietude; this was every day conversation for her, when Larry had the form on him.

'No, Larry, I didn't know that he lost family; indeed I am so sorry to hear it; I know how close tribal families can be to each other.'

'Oh yes, Father Kevin; not only that, he still has several of his family missing among the thousands of refugees in the relief camps. They were in contact from the camps with their mobile phone some months ago now; however, they lost the phone in the squallier, bustle and overcrowded conditions of the camp. Dominic; pardon the familiarity, Larry threw a quick glance at Dee before she had a chance to remind him not to use the familiar form of the pontiff's name beyond his office as agreed. Dee smiled and looked teasingly down her nose at him as she continued with the ironing. Her expression inferred: you watch it, Mr. Walsh.

Larry gave a mischievous smile. His use of the pontiff's Christian name, without the formal title of his office was an indirect compliment to Father Kevin; it inferred and further emphasized the priest as family. Father Kevin was quick to notice the exchange of facial signals between them; he spoke without any trace of condescension as he proposed a personal intimacy of his own.

'I would be pleased if you would afford me the same privilege by using my Christian name when we are not in public or in the company of others.'

'Larry stuck out his tongue at Dee as if to say, Now, then, smarty boots, what have yeah to say about that, then? Dee smiled as she wrinkled her nose at him playfully.

'Larry, you mentioned earlier that Pope Dominic is to move from country to country and to oversee the changes that are to take place in the Catholic Church; have you any Idea of what these changes are?'

'Oh, Yes. Sure aren't many of the changes already laid out in the new Book of Guidance!'

'Book of Guidance!' the priest exclaimed.

'Larry's Law,' Dee interjected.

'Ah!' said the priest, 'would you care to elaborate on some of the changes?'

'Have you not got a copy of the book yet, Kevin?'

'Indeed I have,' the priest answered, with a sudden upward thrust of his head as if caught out. The expression of Larry's incredulity and surprise within the question half startled the priest and left him with a distinct sense of guilt and embarrassment for not having read the book. In fact there was hardly a soul in the international world capable of reading who didn't keep it as both friend and reference. It contained every conceivable aspect on social and spiritual matters; that, coupled with an extended codified commentary written by the Guardians of its laws, the Latter approved by Larry himself. The priest lowered his head in apology and offered an explanation.

'What with the latter pressures of parish life, the countless meetings that were meant to cover some of the implications of your book on the local churches and the priesthood in general; meetings that usually ended up with so many diversions and irrelevances, that we were going nowhere fast with the whole situation. Ultimately, the old ticker, and the hospital, coupled with the convalescence put paid to the rest of my time.'

By way of apology, Larry went across to Father Kevin and gave him a big hug; it spoke volumes about Larry's sensitivity and his utter inability to deliberately hurt anyone, least of all his old tried and trusted friend. Father Kevin stroked Larry's arm with swift movements indicating that there was no offence taken from the question or its unintended implications.

Larry took up the question of the major changes to the Catholic Church in particular and to other Christian Churches in a general way as the one imposed its influence on the other. 'The Church, Kevin, if you will forgive my directness, was never given the authority to pronounce or promote wanton speculation and then to serve it up as gospel fact for no other reason than because it was imagined and publically promulgated.'

'And yet, Larry, the Church was given authority by Christ through Peter to teach by agreement with others and so make public, to promulgate, its decisions on various aspects of faith.' Father Kevin was thinking that Larry was going too far in his criticism of Church teaching and doctrine.

'That isn't in dispute, Kevin,' Larry assured him. 'Can you recall when we were being interrogated by Cardinal Christopher Dwyer in Dublin? That time when we requested to go to Rome to warn Pope Dominic of the danger he was in?'

'Yes, Larry, I recall the occasion very well ... A difficult time for us all.'

'Indeed. But do you remember I told him that the authority given to Peter and in consequence, passed on after his death, did not give him the authority to distort truth or to prevent further understanding, other ways and insights into what we believe to be doctrine and faith? It is such changes as these that need to be made for the clarity and benefit to all.

'Kevin, Let me give you just one example of ill-founded teaching and doctrine. Let us take the teaching of the "Assumption of Mary into Heaven." Such a doctrine is based primarily on the fact that her grave was never discovered. Surely it should have dawned on the early writers of the infant Church that Mary's overriding importance was simply her lack of status. She was nobody of importance in her own time. Why would her burial place matter to anyone except her immediate family and friends?

'The Magnificat professed by Mary when told that she was to be the mother of Jesus, the Savior, revealed quite clearly how she considered herself unworthy of so great a consideration and privilege. She reflects her own humble status, her "nothingness." That, Kevin, surely was all the teaching required without constructing a great edifice of doctrine about Mary being ever virgin and without stain of sin. It is as if her physical intimate relationship within her marriage to Joseph was somehow dirty, a kind of inappropriate vulgarity as though the both of them were celestial beings and not naturally subject to essential carnal needs.

'Consider too, Kevin, that if we accept the teaching that God made marriage into a unique bond where two consenting people become one body, how can such a relationship be considered sexually and physically sinful or inappropriate? It demeans Mary's physical nature and her marriage to Joseph, her husband. This is particularly true when the Church speaks of Mary's immaculate state, whatever that might mean? It also brings into question the state of Mary which is said to be "ever virgin." That too claims too much and again demeans the natural love between Joseph and Mary. It degrades what the Church sought to elevate; it degraded her humanity. Denial of their physical intimacies does nothing to elevate their status. It is as if the Church separates Joseph from Mary physically in spite of the fact that Jesus teaches the indivisibility of marriage. The whole point here, Kevin, is that none of these claims or such teaching is either warranted or necessary. Elevating Mary to such sterile heights makes it impossible to appreciate her humble status and simple healthy and common humanity. Jesus answers those who inform him that his family is asking after him. Jesus' reply was to say that his real family is those who listen to his teaching and act on it.

'The miraculous birth of Jesus is a mystery and therefore cannot be challenged as an article of faith – we accept it on faith, or reject it from reason. It is all this other stuff and nonsense tacked onto it instead of leaving well alone. What is really elevated to a heavenly state from Mary's life is her humility, her ordinariness, or nothingness; it is those virtues we should be honoring. Such virtues give our own ordinary lives their true dignity. Joseph too shares in that same virtue and honor since he too was nobody of importance in the world of his own time. The whole teaching on the assumption of Mary into heaven, if indeed it has to remain at all, should be changed so that both Mary and Joseph's humility are assumed together through the concomitance and true dignity of their marriage, as a humble marital bond – what happens to one must happen to the other. Their humility is the whole and most important point. It is that which becomes a heavenly state or virtue for our admiration and praise. Many Christian writers, including some recorded in the Roman Canon of saints, obscured Mary's humble statues by plastering her humble state with impossible pious platitudes and then adding wild exaggerations about her supposed piety, and were praised by Rome for doing so; when in fact they hadn't the slightest experience or knowledge of her actual life in its historical context and lifetime, except that she was recorded to have been with the disciples in prayer after her Son's death and resurrection. Prayer was common to all, an essential expectation to all Jews worthy of their faith. There was nothing exceptional recorded concerning her prayer life. Such writers do no one a favor, least of all Mary and Joseph. We should remember Jesus' words to the Father whom he petitioned in prayer for his disciples' advancement, that they be consecrated in truth.'

Father Kevin had his head lowered, a glass of white wine before him on the table as he sat engrossed, listening to the changes that Larry envisioned for the Church of the future. From time to time he became aware of the sound of hissing steam rising from the clothes being ironed by Dee.

He knew that she too was engrossed in the discussion, in spite of her domestic, tasks which she carried out with quiet efficiency. Outside the gulls were wheeling about crying out to each other, ever reminding the family of the proximity of the sea close by. Baby Ruth was visible from the open plan kitchen-come-lounge. She was tumbling about contentedly sucking her many colorful plastic toys.

'Alright, Larry, so we have assumed Mary and Joseph into heaven together, on the merit of their marriage, which makes them one according to Christ's teaching regarding the importance of their humility, a most important and primary virtue. So we have a new feast in our Church calendar?' Father Kevin remarked in summary, without any trace of mockery, though he smiled resignedly and with a mischievous glint in his eyes. Although Larry was serious, the notion had a certain novelty about it for Father Kevin. Larry and Dee smiled realizing that their friend was taking it all in his stride.

The priest couldn't be sure if these were divinely inspired ideas or Larry's own. He was well aware of Larry's great love for his parents and for his own besotted love of Dee. Was Larry, then, simply giving marriage a divine status to an extent never consciously emphasized by the Church before – not in the way Larry was doing so now? The Church has always held that marriage was made by God and is an inseparable union between one man and one woman. If his views simply emanated from his personal view and experience of marriage, then he could not even be faulted on that score, since the Church has always held that marriage was both a sacrament instituted by Christ. It was brought about by love in its most authentic form and since Love is another name for God, it follows theologically that marriage brought about by authentic love was and is a divine inseparable bond where two people, a man and woman, become one person. The difficulty for Father Kevin to accept was that such love among most married people was not experienced in Larry's idealistic way. The massive divorce and separation rate throughout the entire world was at staggering proportions with all the hardships and damage as a result, in most cases. The love Larry knew personally to be divine or inseparable was not as widespread as he experienced love. Father Kevin was in a position to know the general status of marriage from the many divorces and separations that had taken place in all the parishes in which he had served for over forty years.

'You know, Larry, the love you speak of that needs to coexist in a true loving relationship must be seen as an ideal to strive for. At best, it is really a call to perfection in love, or as close to perfection as it is possible for two individuals to strive for.' Father Kevin was perfectly aware of the main thrust of Larry definition of universal love. He had the same discussion several days ago with **Bishop Mark McCann**. To some extent Father Kevin was playing the role of Bishop Mark who had himself played the role of devil's advocate in their own discussion on the same matter. He was attempting to keep Larry on terra firma.

Larry continued.

'That is precisely my point, Kevin. I know Christ insistence on ushering in the universal love of all cannot come about as a matter of course. There has to be a dying to self, a surrender of self for a greater good. Such love is sacrificial by its very nature. Yet in such sacrifice made in love, by love, for love, something new and wonderful comes about that did not exist before except as pure potential.

Such a love can only come about unconditionally by both individuals.'

'But real life on the sod, Larry, is far too complicated and pressurized for your average couple. Many have other aspiration beyond their immediate relationships ... work, other friendships, enterprise, health...the list has endless diversions.'

'Yes, Kevin, I agree. But all those diversions that you relate to can be made as graced realities, more meaningful, when the love of the one you are committed to in marriage is placed as having far greater importance that the individual pursuit of one's own self-indulgence. We separate ourselves from each other bit by bit over time, sometimes in imperceptible ways, when we allow ourselves to drift from our real moorings. Remember the teaching: "... where is the profit to gain the whole world and lose one's soul in the process and end up in a state of misery and pain in the end?" That, Kevin, was the real problem of the old world before the law of Love and Care became established in abundance in the new world.

'Most of your objections, Kevin, harp back to the old ways. In the old days many marriages were simply marriages of conveniences, a kind of understood bargain, both individuals being useful to each other, so they allowed themselves to become the object of each others use rather than be the subject or worship of each other's love. You get what you feed, Kevin.'

'Now, you're being cryptic Larry.' Father Kevin remarked smiling and sipping his wine.'

'He's not you know, Kevin. Dee interjected. She was now at the table feeding little Ruth.

'So, Dee, you might enlighten a poor ignorant old priest.'

'Ignorant! I don't think so, that will never be thought of you Kevin. No, what he refers to is the old story about an old Indian who was seated outside his tent when his little granddaughter came up to him and asked.

'Why are you so sad-looking granddad?'

He replied solemnly, 'There are two wolves fighting in my head, little one,' Came the reply

'And which one will win, granddad?' she asked in all innocence.

'The one I feed,' the old man replied in great solemnity.

'... A wise man Dee, eh?'

'The Lord's own sentiments,' Larry interjected with a big exaggerated nod of the head and once again remarked – you get what you feed.'

'So, there we have it.' Father Kevin remarked appreciatively, 'a thoughtful lesson for us all in many avenues of relationships, even beyond marriage. So true friendship, true marriage, true care, it is all at best a communion served in love.'

'I couldn't put it better myself, Kevin, God bless, you.' Larry remarked. Dee added to Larry's remark:

'You know, Kevin, while we were discussing the implications of love in marriage, it suddenly struck me how love in marriage, though indisputably special and unique to the relationship, does not actually define all there is to know about love, even within the experience of marriage itself.' Dee's face was intense and thoughtful.

'I'm not quite with you, Dee.' Father Kevin put his head to one side as if to look under Dee's face, hers now lowered reflectively. Larry too was puzzled.

'It suddenly struck me how much love yourself and Nell brought into our lives – into our marriage. Our love for each other is all the richer for what both of you have been to us and still remain as part of us. What I'm trying to say is what you and Nell added was not there to begin with. In fact I learned to really love Larry the way I do through the love I found in Nell and you first – bolt of lightning apart.' She lifted her beautiful smiling face to look affectionately into Father Kevin's face. Larry said aloud.

'Amen to that.' He too was smiling. Father Kevin's face was on his chest. Dee rushed to his side. He was in a flood of tears. It was the first time in their friendship that she had seen him so upset within their home.

'Kevin! Kevin! Kevin! Whatever is the matter? Have I said something wrong? What is it?' Larry too went to his side and put his arms round his shoulders. The poor priest was in a terrible state. It was all so unexpected. All he could manage through his heaving tears was to cry out hysterically 'God Nell, I miss you! I miss you, Nell!'

'It's alright Kevin, it's alright.' Larry and Dee were talking as one – both their faces lined in shock and concern. It took some time for Father Kevin to compose himself. All the while he held onto Dee's waste with one hand and onto Larry's hand with the other, his head still in his chest, his face awash in tears.

'I'm so sorry. It's plain that I'm not quite over Nell yet. You know,' he said looking up at each face in turn, 'she would love to see this day – all of us here together.'

Larry and Dee were now in tears. This was all so unexpected. They now realized how much he loved and missed Nell's company. Both were greatly relieved when he said to them,

'You know, you have both brought a lot of love into our lives also which was never there before. We too were the richer for your love and I certainly am still.

'It was such a profound insight of yours Dee. I suppose it is only when you delve into the depths of love and relationship, how we all become far more than we can be on our own – cocooned in our own little world. Strange how even friendship can have a profound love attached to it. I should have been far more aware of that from all the instructions on marriage which I have had to give to others that Christian marriage has to reach out beyond itself to all. And here I am nearly engulfed by it.' He was now more himself again.

'You don't regret moving here, then, Kevin, do you?' Dee was not yet convinced until he remarked teasingly:

'If that long rascal hadn't married yeah, and I was half my years, I would have married yeah meself, so I would.' Larry towered over his friend rubbing his hands and doing one of his excited jigs, so happy to see his friend more himself. Dee sat on Father Kevin's lap with her arms round his neck and gave him the biggest kiss on the lips that he ever had in his life. His face was even redder than before.

'You see,' said Larry, 'It's exactly like I said before all this excitement happened.'

'What's that, Larry?' Dee asked smiling, still sitting on Father Kevin's lap.

'It's what you feed. Bad food brings bad relationships.'

'Oh, don't you go all over that ground again – Mr. Solomon Walsh. We've heard enough of your wisdom for one day. They all joined in the laughter. And yet Dee's sudden insight really did act in a forceful way to prove or to bring home the truly wonderful and life-changing power of love as something not at all utopian when considered deeply enough. Personal effort is not beyond anyone, even though such effort requires a life of meditation and grace. Mindlessness can never serve any individual as virtue.

Further questions concerning the changes in the Church of the future were put on hold as the family was forced to focus more and more on events beyond the home. Life in Garrettstown followed a general pattern. Morning Mass in Saint Clare's Convent began at 7am to facilitate the working day of the sisters. Father Kevin liked to get up early – a habit of a lifetime and he was at his best in the mornings, as was Dee. Larry always took some waking. He usually slept like an ancient lichen-covered boulder pressed into a field and down to the maker's name. Dee had the patience of Job with him in the mornings – he could be worse than waking an exhausted child. Ruth too was carried off to the convent church in the family Volvo. The routine helped in giving their lives a distinct pattern. Dee was usually involved with her political writing; from time to time having to Jet off to some foreign land to gather the latest political development from across the globe. Most of her writing these days concerned itself with the deepening development and influence of Larry's Law. National upheavals had all but ceased as the new world settled more and more into more peaceful ways and pressing developments. Father Kevin busied himself with his favorite past time, fishing off the rocks at the far end of Garrettstown shoreline; or else trying his hand in one of the distant lakes or rivers. Larry and Dee were never far from his mind when out and about on his own. He often pondered on their lives and on their involved discussions. Larry often joined his friend on walks taking baby Ruth with them in the pram. They were frequently forced to press themselves into ditches along the country roads while flocks of sheep or herds of cattle took over the country lanes while being shifted from one pasture to another or while the cows were being herded for milking. The strong scents and smells came wafting from the wind-tossed fields and farms about their home. The crying gulls and toneless crows were forever wheeling about the salt-wet air high over the rolling fields; these were the ambience of their waking days and gave them a deep sense of contentment.

From time to time the family were forced to journey into Cork city to attend Question Time, referred to as "Government Broadcast", which was sent out worldwide four days a week and in the event of emergency or crisis. Sometimes Father Kevin would go along with them to call on past friends. The communication centre in Ireland was a massive forty story glass-sided building, a hive of world-wide communications with teams of native-speaking interpreters. The building was staffed by over two thousand specialists in their own social fields. There was a department for every social or specialist need, Farming, Fisheries, Roads and Travel, Health and Safety, Industrial and Manufacturing Standards, Police, Shipping, Employment, Sports. These and many other social departments had their counterparts worldwide.

On this particular occasion, a Russian scientist, Ivan Kriukov, appeared on the studio screen in a white laboratory coat. He kept lifting his wire-frame spectacles up and down every few seconds displaying a fidgeting unease. He appeared to be a dancing, hyper individual. As he was speaking in Russian from a broadcasting station in Moscow, the Irish broadcasting station gave him an English voice-over; English being one of the most widely used second languages worldwide. Larry and the Russian guest were linked up. The broadcasting presenter, Orla Jordan, gave the cue to Larry and the guest speaker.

'Go ahead, Mr. Kriukov, you are live to Mr. Walsh at Government Broadcast.' The red light signifying recording mode reflected on Larry's skin. He was sitting with baby Ruth in his arms. It was un-nerving to watch the fidgeting Russian even though Larry was fascinated by the complex dome buildings in the background of the screen. The Russian posed his question, constantly moving his wire spectacles, his face severe, and his voice irritated as he posed his question.

'Mr. Walsh, sir. I work as a scientist here in Russia. I have many years experience of Space travel and research. Why has most of your government support for space research and space travel been suddenly withdrawn not only from us but from all the countries across the world at your insistence? Surely,' he added, 'this has to be a retrograde step in the advancement of human knowledge and experience, not worthy of our modern age. We were well on our way to colonizing the moon and using is as a sustainable base for further penetration into deep space. I repeat, why has your government withdrawn its material support?'

'Good day to you Mr. Kriukov and good morning Russia, greetings from Government Broadcast.' Larry had placed baby Ruth on a studio table beside him. She was playing contentedly with some plastic color bricks, plates and balls as he spoke to the studio screen. The little tot gave the studio an ambience of domesticity. There was no hint of world problems here. Larry withdrew his attention from Ruth for the moment, giving his immediate attention to the fidgeting Russian.

'You are quite correct, Mr. Kriukov, we have indeed withdrawn government material support from Space Travel and Space Research. However, you must have also been informed as to why this critical decision was taken. The massive material and fuel cost once lavished on your science, Mr. Kriukov, is being redirected to the construction of dignified homes and for slum clearance in several parts of the world.

That takes into account rural poverty and some of the city back streets of Russia, India, and the continent of Africa. We are also diverting material aid and labour to all slum and poverty-ridden inner cities areas across the globe, which also includes China and the USA. It is our intention to make absolute certain that every individual family across the globe has proper dignified secure housing, food, medical care and a good education and vocational training. To that end we have directed the efforts of science to be at the immediate service of people's basic needs and comfort. As you must be aware, Mr. Kriukov, the world population growth is beginning to be a major concern for the supply of sustainable building metals and other precious materials, even timber is close to being classed as precious building and construction material and in real danger of running out across the world due to past exploitation.

'We have not completely abandoned all material expenditure on space exploration and travel, simply put it on hold until every individual across the world is able to live a comfortable and meaningful life and be in worthwhile employment in the service of others. A recent group of space scientist, sir, based in China, USSR, India, Germany, USA, France and England, have informed us that to reach any possible life-sustaining planet in our solar system that the bones of the human body in a weightless environment would simply waste away before we reached any life-sustaining planet. Colonizing the moon, sir, would still leave you with the major headache as to how you get over the zero gravity problem and its dire effects on human bone structure. That being the case, Mr. Kriukov, according to the advice given to my Government, we have decided to keep to attainable and urgent needs here on our vulnerable Earth. Once all our fundamental needs on Earth are met we most certainly will reconsider your needs. In the meantime do whatever you can to help us here to make the world a better place. One last point, Mr. Kriukov: as a race of people we are far from ready to occupy outer space. We must first develop to be truly committed to each other's absolute care. We cannot have a divided people blast off into the outer reaches of space and bring division and strife along with them. We are still dismantling nuclear weaponry across the world. We are simply not developed enough for space travel yet. We are getting their under our new Laws. We need more time.

'Well, Mr. Kriukov, I sincerely hope that I have gone some way to answering your question. Goodbye Sir, Goodbye Russia.' Many people listening to the late news across the world agreed wholeheartedly with Larry's sentiments. Though others posed the scenario, what if there is some cataclysmic upheaval on earth, like the destruction and obliteration of Italy? That disaster was still fresh in peoples' minds. Some complained as if there was some safe haven in outer space to escape to, even if it was possible to build some kind of gravity-making machine.

Orla Jordan, the Question Time presenter, turned to Larry and asked, 'Are you able to take another call, this one is from Anita Gutherez, a school girl of thirteen years speaking from La Paz, Bolivia?'
'By all means, Orla, please put her through.' Anita appeared on the screen, a beautiful young lady, dressed in

a bright white open-neck shirt and wearing a burgundy-colored school blazer with the emblem of an acorn as the school badge. Her deep brown eyes danced with the freshness of youth that expressed so much of her energy and vitality. Her voice was louder than usual. She thought that because she was speaking to Ireland so far away from Bolivia that her voice might be diminished. She needn't have worried. Both Larry and Anita were given the cue to speak.

'Go ahead, Anita, from La Paz, Bolivia; you are through to Government Broadcast. We hear you loud and clear, Anita; you might even consider lowering your voice a little to your own natural pitch.' Her English was reasonably good so it was decided not to voiceover.

'Greetings from La Paz, Senor Walsh, may I call you Senor Larry? I like you very much; I all the time to listen to you talks. I am the thirteen years of old.'

'Greetings from Ireland and from Government Broadcast Anita. I like you too. You are very pretty. Maybe I come over to La Paz and bring you home with me.'

'Maybe I like that, Senor Larry. I think you jokers with me. I know you wife Dee. She no like the two pretty senoritas in you house.'

'... Your question, Anita, before we run out of time?' The presenter was attempting to curb frivolous chatter, she was very aware that the world was listening to these broadcasts. Even Larry had to toe the line – it was in his best interest too. After all, this special time devoted to world-wide Question Time was not designed nor meant to be a low-key chat show. It was meant to answer serious questions and promote serious debate from the worldwide public. Of course Larry was well aware of that. Yet it was in his very nature to be light-hearted, especially with the young.

'Good, Senora Orla. I make my question. Senor Larry, in school la profesorna speaks about our Law of love and the care for all the peoples.' This was the first time that Larry had heard of Larry's Law referenced as "our Law." It pleased him greatly. It meant that the younger generation was making his law their own.

'Yes, Anita, I am listening.' She could see that Larry was playing with little Ruth on the table, passing her colored plastic toys or stroking her cheeks.

'Well, Senor Larry, is not easy to love and care for people when they very bad. La profesorna, she say that some people have evil. I no understand what is only bad and what is evil. What I ask, is how is evil in our world when you teach your Law to be love and care for all peoples? Where the evil is coming from?' Her youthful face seemed to take on the whole worries of the world – her expression, straining to understand the mystery of it all.

'Anita, Anita! You have asked a very big troublesome question. Your professor is right to say that some people have evil in them. However, evil does not exist outside of human existence as many used to believe in the olden days, long before you were born. The simplest way I can explain what evil is and how it comes to be in some people, Anita, is explain the difference between good and bad. Let us take the example of a little pussy cat that jumps up onto the table and licks all the milk in your cornflakes. The little cat doesn't know that what it is doing is wrong or bad. Only you can say that it is bad. But, it is your own fault for allowing the cat to jump up on the table in the first place. We could say that you are bad for not taking more care of the cat or your food. You have to teach it better or restrict it more. Let us keep with the example of the cat. Suppose after feeding your cat and you let it outside to play or wander around as cats do, and you discover that it has killed a bird in spite of feeding the cat earlier. Now, Anita, I ask you, has the cat done something bad or not?'

'Maybe the little bird think the cat a very bad thing?' Anita replied.

'I'm sure if we could read a bird's brain you could be right, Anita. However it is a cat's right by natural evolution to kill for its own survival. The cat can't help killing. It evolved to prefer to hunt no matter how much you feed it; it has been programmed that way over thousands of years of hunting. Now, Anita; that is an example of what seems to be bad but is not in the animal world, no matter how savage many wild animal may be even when they remain in captivity.

Are you with me so far Anita? I hope I am not being too complicate for you?'

'No problems, Senor, Larry. You always making the good sense.' Anita was smiling with a keen interest in Larry's insights into the reality of evil, good and bad. Larry continued, all the while attempting to keep things as simple but as relevant as possible.

'You know, Anita, that we as human eat the meat of animals, birds and fish of every kind. Do you think that we are bad to do that, after all these creatures have a life they want to live also?'

'No, I no think to eat the meat of the animal is the bad act.'

'Why are you so sure, Anita?' Larry was testing her comprehension to be sure that she was grasping the main gist of the examples.

'I be sure, because we be like to the wild animals. La profesorna she say to eat red meats and white meats when she speak for good diet – that our granddaddy parents have hunted for many of the years so we bodies need the special things in the red meats that are not in the white meats. La profesorna, she say we also animals.'

'Once again, Anita, you and your professor are quite right. We are human animals with very special needs. We too have evolved to be able to kill. However, Anita, the big difference between us, the human animal, and the wild animals is that we have developed to know a good action from a bad action. That in turn has helped us to know when killing is necessary to eat and when it is not to our advantage or best interest. Are your still following me, Anita?'

'Si Senor Larry, I am know about the good-for-me things. Sometime I no like to go to the school because I like to play in the parks and to give the head the rest from all the learning things. But mama and papa they say, if I no go to the schools, no hansom senor will want to marry me because I be as stupid as the dumb, dumb. So is better to do the difficult things if something is better in the end because we do the difficult.'

'You understand, good, Anita. We have developed, Anita to take more control over ourselves for a greater purpose, a greater good. For example, if we were to kill every animal we came across just for the excitement of killing, we would eventually run out of animals and for many that could mean starvation. This very problem makes the fox one of the most hated animal by farmers who keep chickens or small lambs. The fox has not evolved to know that killing all the chickens in one go is against its own best interest. It only knows right and wrong, good and bad on its own terms. Let me explain that, Anita.

'The fox knows it is bad to get caught or trapped. Similarly, it knows that to escape or avoid capture is good.

Yet it only knows this at a very low level of understanding. It is very clever in its own world at hunting down food, but very stupid in our world because we understand that it acts against its own long term interests. We could be forgiven to presume that the mass killing instincts of the fox is a throwback to the time when it hunted in packs ... that the consequences of that is still in its genetic makeup. We become how we live over a long period of time, whether as animal or as humans, Anita.'

Larry was well aware that he was probably more interested in these phenomenon than the young Bolivian school child and so, for her sake, he tried hard to be as brief as possible – which wasn't easy for him once he had launched himself out in to the stratosphere of a point of interest. 'I hope I have not confused you so far, Anita, we are in some deep water here,'

'You no stop now, Senor Larry. I like the rivers. Please, now you tell me if the animal have no evil in them because they evolve to be wild. How can evil be in a human persons when we all animals?'

'O Anita, Anita! I am glad to hear you are still following me although you may find this interesting, the waters are going to get very deep in order to speak of how evil comes to be in some people and not in others.

Nature, Anita, is neither good nor bad. It is what it is. We cannot, for example, call a volcanic eruption evil even when it spills lava down its mountain sides and destroys all the dwellings in its path, killing thousands of people in the process. Nor are the many tsunamis that have destroyed thousands called acts of evil. However, as highly developed human animals we have learned to distinguish between a human act that is bad, like hurting someone by an act of neglect, as in a car crash, and by an act that can be distinguished as evil, as in using a car to deliberately kill someone. The first example of injury by neglect can be classed as bad, even very bad, depending on the seriousness of the injury or damage done. The second example of deliberately taking an innocent life had for thousands of years in our moral development been described as an act of evil. Why do you think that is, Anita? Can you understand the distinction?'

'Si Senor Larry. We all make the accidents from the time to the time. Sometimes, it no our faults. Like my mama she leave open the cupboard door and I bang my head to it. Mama, you trying to kill me, you lovely daughter? Now I get Lump on the head and all the children at school laugh at the lump. The calling me the egg heads. Is no funnies. But I forgive my mama when the egg he is gone. But maybe not for the week. But, yes, for the killing, is evil because he no have to done it. And if he is put to the death or in the horrible prison for the life – what he family can do? They crying all the time and maybe the family of the person who has dead, they come and make bad things for us.' Anita finished. The studio crew were laughing at Anita's vivid portrayal of events as she imagined them unfold. Larry Smiled and remarked,

'Well said, Anita. You have given us a good picture of the consequence of an evil act. However I would like to stress one point that may have got lost in your understanding, which is the word "deliberate." When someone who commits a deliberate act of evil it is judged and referred to as an act of will. It only applies to human beings. There is a further distinction to be made, Anita, and that is the pleasure an act of evil gives to the one causing the hurt. There is also the pleasure in the power that the offender enjoys from such a cruel act of suffering. Let me clarify that still further. Anita. In the past, before my laws prevented all armies from going to war with some other country, there used to be many wars, many terrible killings. Sometimes enemy soldiers were captured and kept in very bad conditions in prison camps, even though all soldiers had the right to protect their country or tribe from an unprovoked attack by another tribe or army. Yet some prison camp guards didn't want to know about the need to be fair with their prisoners and so took pleasure in using all kinds of terrible tortures, because they were trained to believe that all armies that fight against another army are natural enemies and therefore should be hated and made to suffer and call them bad names so that they can hate them even more, because you use bad names for those you hate. Do you still follow me, Anita?'

'Yes, Senor Larry. I am understanding. We have bad peoples in La Paz who do bad things against Larry's nice laws of the love and the care. Is no good they be like that. They make sadness.' Anita's face was very cross as she reflected on her personal experiences. From time to time Larry would go into broken English himself as if to help Anita to understand better – which of course was of no particular help. He did it out of pure instinct as some people do when speaking to those with broken English. Anita, however was quite articulate and easy enough to follow.

'You quite right, Anita. Bad people make sadness. You not be bad lady, Anita.'

'No Senor, Larry, I good persons. Except when my mama give big egg to the head and the other school children call me the egg head. But I no fighting. La profesorna she say, Larry's Law of the love and the care for all the peoples is very good law – that we must make these good laws the most important best things all the time and for all the life, forever and ever. Yes, Senor Larry, I good persons for Larry's Law.' Anita's smile beamed across the studio screen.

'I sure too, Anita, that you a good person. Now you try to understand this a bit more.

'Since it was right to kill your enemy in battle in a just war or be killed yourself if you fail to do so. Such fighting when done fairly could not be counted as evil. The real evil in these circumstances was committed by those who were to blame for the war in the first place – or those who provoked a peaceful people into a war that their enemy knew they could never win because of the enemy's superior power. Such wars, or uprisings against deliberate abuses such as starving and oppressing a people under occupation, that is real evil in people, Anita. It comes out of deliberate choices – acts of will that could be prevented.'

'La Profesorna, she say that in many of the years gone past that they was very good peoples who no fight, they only to live for peace. These good peoples, she say, no join the army for fighting. Some of them die rather than to fight. So, Senor Larry, are they bad not to fight to save their own families, their homes from the bombs, and all these terrible things?'

'They are not bad people, Anita, if they prefer to live in peace. Such people who die for love of peace they called martyrs, Anita.'

'But, Senor Larry, La profesorna she say there be good martyrs and bad martyrs.'

'Ah, yes, Anita, it can be very difficult to understand sometimes.' Again your Professor is correct. Let me try to explain as simply as I can, Anita.

'Do you understand the difference between what is national, international and universal?'

'Si Senor Larry, I know these things. There is my lovely country, the Bolivia. Then there is all the other countries in the big world, and especially the Ireland with my friends, Senor Larry, the Dee and the little Ruth. The universal is all the nations join together.'

'Very good, Anita. You show you do the understanding. Well to die for you nation for the good reason is a good act. That is what we call a good national martyr. However, a good national martyr does not mean that he or she is good for all the other nations. A soldier, who is a martyr for the lovely nation of Bolivia has not died for the Ireland or for the Larry's family, Anita. He only died for the Bolivia. But suppose that same soldier died for a universal reason, such as dying to save the freedom of all nations then he is called a universal martyr. He or she is not just thinking of his or her own nation. Do you understand that difference, Anita?'

'Si Senor Larry. I die for the Larry's good Law of the love and the care for all the peoples all over the big world. Only I no can do it today, 'cause I promised the mama that I take the shoppings when the school be finished.' Larry and all the studio crew laughed at the disappointed expression on Anita's young face.'

'Oh, dear, Anita you mustn't worry over such things today and hopefully not for a very long time. You are a very beautiful and good lady for saying all the nice things. I hope I have helped you understand a bit better about the things we have talked about. May God bless you and all your family, Anita. It was a pleasure to talk to you. Goodbye La Paz, Goodbye Bolivia.'

'Goodbye, Senor Larry. I love to you. Please to come to our home to visit my family in the La Paz. And bring the beautiful Dee and the beautiful baby Ruth. I so excited I have met the Senor Larry in the person.' The screen died on La Paz, but not before Anita blew a big kiss to Larry off the outstretched palm of her hand. Larry looked at little Ruth still playing away contentedly. Tears fell from his eyes as he said to his child, 'what a beautiful young lady we have been speaking to little Ruth. I hope you growing to be like her.' The echoes of Anita's broken English were still echoing in his words.

CHAPTER 24

Evening Fishing at Garrettstown

The days and weeks of Father Kevin's retirement raced by. Larry took him out fishing frequently to meet up with Mack's Brigade. These were a diverse conglomeration of local characters, farmers, hotel workers from Oakley's Hotel, the local lifeboat crew and many of the local families round about. Many of them took delight instructing Father Kevin and Larry on the finer points of mackerel fishing. Most of the motley crew was comprised of native Cork men and women who had a keen appetite for the mackerel – a fishing tradition handed down for generations. There were many young people of all ages among them. It was a case of all hands on deck. There was always a kind of frenzied madness to the pursuit – Gulls dive-bombing the broiling water – the crazed roars of the fishermen and women, 'Come on son … go for it!' The silvery beach was decked out with several smoking braziers fed by charcoal; the smoke swirling in a crazy dance, being whipped about by the wind coming in from the sea. The waves fell in on the beach and on the welly-clad boots of the anglers. There was no real art to the fray in spite of all the friendly and well-intentioned instructions to the novices. For bait, most used simple bits of silver paper which were supposed to represent the little sprats that the thrashing mackerel demolished. Some wily old characters used small bits of white cable as bait others used what was commonly referred to as plugs that resembled small silvery imitation sprats. It seemed that no matter what was cast into the tumbling waves and thrashing activity of the hungry mackerel, a catch was guaranteed. The only real art to the simple pleasure was to unhook the catch with all speed and cast back into the fray as quickly as possible in frenzied haste. The fishermen and women never tired in their enthusiasm. It was a ritual. The thrashing would gradually peter out after a couple of hours, or less, once the darting sprats found a route out from the frenzied giddy mackerel, leaving only half-fed stragglers behind to be caught by the more enthusiastic of the fishers. Some of Mack's army stood by the smoking braziers with large frying pans gutting and cooking the fish with great gusto. It was by no means an everyday occurrence.

'Ah!' said one old codger, to Father Kevin, the priest himself dressed in ordinary garb and also welly-clad, 'did you ever eat anything more heavenly than the taste of fresh mackerel cooked in pan or grilled?' Father Kevin roared with laughter at the unintended association in his own mind that might have been aimed at his profession. The old country codger didn't have a breeze as to the connection at all. Larry who was now beside the fire wolfing greedily on the steaming fish, stopped with his mouth open, the fish half in and out of his mouth with an expression of utter puzzlement on his wind-blown face and thinking that Father Kevin had taken leave of his senses, since no one else seemed to grasp the meaning of his amusement. He put a hand on Larry's shoulder.

'Don't worry, Larry, it's just an odd thought that a foolish priest might amuse himself with.' Father Kevin was thinking of the Eucharist – that it might be better thought of as the best food ever tasted. He considered the real Eucharist, as did Larry, as the giving and receiving of love. Mackerel didn't quite fit the bill, Father Kevin thought light-heartedly.

Most of Mack's army went home in great spirits, each with a good catch carried in plastic buckets. All were babbling at once on the evening's excitement. They always expressed the same enthusiasm, no doubt like their grandparents before them. If they lived to be a thousand years, you had the impression that their utter joy of landing Mackerel would never wane. All were usually clad in heavy clothes, as they were now. They knew from experience that the evening breeze coming off the sea in the evening or early morning could bite and chill to the marrow, even in summer months. A few hardy souls stayed on by the fires smoking their pipes and having the craic. The aroma of grilled mackerel and salty sea was a constant fragrance to their days and thoughts. Howling winds or fine, they took it all as the sounds and music of their honorable craft. For hundreds of years these old codgers were forced to live off land and sea together, in good times and bad. They were simple people with a simple pride in their own worth. Some took out flasks of tea to wash down the taste of the salty fish; one or two took a few nips of 'the golden dew,' the local jargon for the whiskey. Dusk fell on the noisy screams of the wheeling gulls who continued to dive-bomb the unsuspecting, distracted mackerel. The rolling tide pushed further in onto the silver sands until at last its waters reached the piles of large grey stones that ran along the length of the beach making them glisten.

The fiery sun was descending like a great ball of fire into the distant horizon turning the waters, beach and rocks into the crimson coals of a great fire. All was quiet as Father Kevin and Larry finally made their way home; they too with their bucketful of fresh mackerel and their rods held high victoriously and with an instinctive primitive pride as though time had encapsulated them in the ancient ritual of man's unity and bond with the sea.

Dee was used to the sound of their approaching voices, of their trudging home and landing at the door – the amber lights of home falling on their shapes now ritually divesting themselves of their heavy coats, hats and wellies. Dee liked the fishing herself and either Larry or Father Kevin gave her the opportunity from time to time to join Mack's army on the beach. Usually they received a phone call from the locals to alert them when the mackerel were there for the taking.

Larry's most important interest once he landed home, and after kissing and hugging the life out of Dee, was to pick up his favorite toy, the adorable baby Ruth who was now sprouting up like a spring flower. She was also speaking her first words, 'da-da, ma-ma.' Even Father Kevin was referred to as, 'da-da.' Though Ruth was still in nappies, Larry, Dee and Father Kevin took great pleasure in holding onto her tiny podgy arms as she tried her first tottering steps. The little child beamed into their faces with big bright saucer eyes. She had a smile for everyone. Larry used to cry over her growing, he loved her so much. Dee adored her also but she was more concerned with the practical needs that came with her growth.

The family, including Father Kevin, was very popular. Their fame as international celebrities was no longer a novelty to the locals. All fitted into the quite haven of Garrettstown as if they had been part of it for a lifetime. Father Kevin was a regular visitor to their homes. He was frequently invited to say Mass in one of the homes and all the surrounding neighbors would come together to share in the privilege. The locals took it in turns to open their homes for the same purpose. Sometime they went with him to the convent to attend Mass on Sunday and on other special celebrations. The Saint Clare Sisters also encouraged the local community to come to the convent for their important services. They loved the priest for his simple comradelier nature. He was at ease with the families that gathered together just as they were at ease with him. He would always say Mass on the Sunday at the Saint Clare's Convent for the sisters, except when the winter days made his journey there too dangerous or impossible.

He was spoilt at the convent as he was everywhere else where he offered his humble service. He usually heard confession walking on the roads much to the delight and convenience of the people. He usually walked for two miles each day keeping to the instructions that he had received after his heart operation and recovery.

"Don't mollycoddle yourself, Father Kevin, just because the old ticker went into recession." Those were the surgeon's instructions and to which he enlightened him further. "Many believe, wrongly, that if they take it easy and sit at home all day, or take excessive sleep, that they will last longer. Don't take that old wives' tale seriously; it would be disastrous. The old adage holds good here, ...If you don't use it you lose it. It's all down to moderation and common sense." Father Kevin knew those instructions instinctively; bouts of flu that kept him in bed in his younger days were proof enough, if any was needed. He experienced how the body weakened after enforced rest. Both Larry and Dee often accompanied him on his walks along with Ruth who was growing fast and was now at the stage of being wheeled about in a buggy instead of being enclosed in the old pram. Sometimes they used the family car as a means of going further afield to get to know the countryside better. They would park up and discover a new walk. Life for them all was as close to the heavenly as they could have wished. The lives of the people they met too were so much more fulfilling since the establishment and greater development of Larry's Law.

Larry's work in many ways was complete. Apart from his weekly broadcasts in the city, life in Garrettstown was lived at a snail's pace. None of the family would have it any other way. Dee herself ceased to work full time for The City Vanguard. Although she continued to write for the newspaper, she was more involved with Larry's work at Government Broadcast. The City Vanguard was a much altered news media. All the remaining newspapers and magazines were free. It was hardly coincidental that their content was far more widely read and appreciated as a general service to the public worldwide. It still carried all the sport's news, several crosswords and puzzles offering varying degrees of challenge.

CHAPTER 25

Church Leadership

As the weeks sped past in their idyllic world and the chill of winter winds kept the family more and more at home. Their minds returned to the topic of how the new world was to cope with religious life in general. What was the real role of religion and the priest in these changing times when people locally and internationally felt that the ongoing development of Larry's Law seemed to be sufficient in itself without the need for the old clerical model of priesthood or for the authority of the old leaders of other non-Christian religions? It was commonly held internationally, at this juncture, that the most praiseworthy and meritorious direction for humanity's development for the future was indisputably bound up in the commendable ideals and achievements of Larry's Law itself. Why would any religion be necessary? What would any religion have to offer that was not already given in the essence of Love and Care as the primary principles, directives and expectations of Larry's Law that was now embraced by the entire world? True there were always stubborn reprobates for who even perfection would be considered an imposition. It was Father Kevin who opened up the discussion.

'Larry, your book examines the role of the priest, in the new world. Surly there has to be some kind of religious leadership, people trained to combat the dangers of allowing people to simply believe in any old mumbo jumbo they want to? You remember our meetings with Cardinal Dwyer in Dublin before you set out for Rome. He was quite right regarding the need for trained leadership. After all, Larry, even the scriptures, with their many flaws, saw a critical need to be the voice of dignified direction and social conscience. If Judaic religious history and social development taught our modern world anything, it taught us the need for a leadership that was truly a guardian over all its people and bearing down with much of its weight on the side of the poor and marginalized of their nation. It read the moral signs of the times and placed moral and ethical conduct onto a godly plane. Virtue for them was the true life of God – It read the human heart and spirit. It saw how rampant paganism had the tribes of their surrounding neighbors at the mercy and fear of imposed idolatry. Primitive peoples showed their fear of nature in many of their rituals, wearing the masks of animals and worshipping them as demigods. Fear and superstition are still with us, Larry, in spite of your Laws. Fear and superstition are powerful controlling forces over vulnerable people, especially those subjected to accident or natural disasters such as extreme drought, harvest failure, flooding, disease and other natural disasters. Informed spiritual leadership is an absolute necessity for a more meaningful development and freedom for all people. The ancient prophets acted as the voice of the Church, much as the Dail, Parliament, Science, or enlightened presidential governorship does for our time. There has to be trained leaders to act as guides against error; to scrutinize and evaluate the dignity and worthiness of human direction. Our own history of wandering monks coming among communities and preaching error, not with deliberate intention, but because they had no proper training or understanding of the scriptures ... these well-meaning wandering monks had done untold damage to the communities they fell upon. That was the reason why the role of bishops was given the guardianship of scripture to prevent a repetition of the past. As you know, Larry, we have been over this ground before with Cardinal Dwyer.'

'I hear all you are saying Kevin. However, prophecy in our own time is not so much in the hands of single religious individuals as in was in the days of the founding and guidance of the tribes of Israel. The various disciplines of learning of our time, science, psychiatry, psychology, biology, chemistry, archeology, chemistry, logic, moral theology, ethics, all these and others have a distinct guiding influence over human and spiritual understanding. Chemistry knows that you cannot drug yourself into moral or spiritual advancement. It is only critical to healing and to the ease of suffering. We don't allow the priests of our own time to diagnose cases of leprosy as in the Hebrew past. Similarly, in the role of spiritual leadership we must look to the dignity of both men and women to share the role of priestly ministry. For years our own Catholic Church has reminded our people that they share in a common priesthood with us all. And yet that same Church always kept the people at arm's length. I mentioned all this to Pope Dominic while we were in Israel and he has agreed since to make changes to accommodate the priesthood of the people by allowing them to serves as married and women priests. I do agree that we will always have to have trustworthy and trained leaders in the community to keep Peter's Church on an even Keel.

'As things stand Kevin, the new laws of love and care for all people are the only essential and ultimate prophecy and true authority needed for humanity's dignified direction. Whatever we achieve together, no matter how we might advance in travel to deep space, we have to be able to live with each other and depend on each other. The leadership of Larry's Law and the leadership of religious sensibility are not at variance with each other. I know your concern for Church leadership in local communities, Kevin, is what really concerns you. I don't think you will have any need to worry about that. The message of human salvation through the sacrifice of Jesus Christ taught in Christian churches throughout the world is not going to change or suddenly go away. Each new generation needs that same unchangeable message passed onto them. And the church community is the most appropriate place for that to take place for many commendable reasons. As my own dear parents used to tell me, "Repetition is the mother of learning."'

'Well I'm delighted to hear you say that Larry. With Pope Dominic in Kenya at the moment, coupled with the itinerant nature of his future, the old ship and the captaincy of Peter is in danger of being tossed about.'

'Well as I discussed that point with His Holiness before. However, it might be as well to repeat it for your benefit Kevin. It was fundamental to the message I brought to the Holy Father. The message was for his ears only and so you would not have been aware of the instructions I was told to pass onto him.

'Firstly the gist of the more urgent instructions of the message informed him that there was a warning to evacuate Rome within the month of August as there would be a large scale earthquake due during the month of September. The evacuation would be permanent for himself and for all the people of Italy, but for different reasons. There would be no city left for the people to return to; it would be totally destroyed. With regard to the Holy Father himself, the Catholic Faith was to take on a new era and expression and reformation. The Pontiff's status was to be once again that of an itinerant nature, moving from one country to another on an annual basis. The purpose of this important step is to emphasize the point that every individual Christian is only a pilgrim in this passing world. The pontiff's office will no longer be the preserve of the clergy ... that this important office was to fall on proven holy men or women from any nation whether married or single, or without restrictions to background. Obviously the one chosen has to be of the same Faith and fundamental beliefs of the Petrine Church. A worthy and reliable Catholic candidate, male or female, would be chosen from any country having a sufficient population of Catholics. The country will be chosen at random from all other Catholic-populated nations. Every parish in every diocese of the chosen nation would make their choice. Voting would take place via the internet, thus avoiding the mammoth mountain of paper that would be necessary to achieve the task. A profile form will be supplied online. The profile form will contain a list of categories denoting the virtues desired and critical for the suitability of each candidate. There will be tic boxes after each category with a scale of 1-10 choice for each category. Categories will include questions such as, is the candidate a person who loves and cares for others? – not one to judge others – one who cares for his own family – a person with a forgiving disposition – a person of humility – of deep prayer – of gentleness – wise in learning – not self-opinionated – not a dictator over others – a person of sincerity yet having a sense of fun – yet not frivolous – a person of peace – active in local needs outside his or her own work – a sober person who drinks in moderation – not a drunkard, nor a glutton …. ?

'The leaders of each diocese, men and women, already chosen and established, will computerize the parish results. A random choice will be made where several candidates score the same desired virtues. The second stage of the voting will examine all the results of each diocese. Where several candidates have the same desired virtues and scales, the final choice will be a random one. The chosen candidate will be announced at Government Broadcast by the Walsh family. A special Mass of thanksgiving will be held in ever parish across the world. Each parish is to organize a party celebration. My family will express its thanks for all the work involved. The new Pope will be installed in a residence suitably constructed for the need of that great office. The new location of the Holy See will be will be centered in Clonmacanoise in Southern Ireland as a tribute to the many monks who spread their learning and Catholic Faith across the far-flung reaches of the globe in perilous times and across vast turbulent seas. At the death of any Pope the same procedure will follow. A new country will be chosen. No nation will be allowed to be chosen twice until all remaining nations have had a candidate on the seat of the See of Peter.

'In the case of local diocesan leadership a similar process for choosing a man or woman worthy of the position will take place. The chosen candidate will receive his ordination from the Holy Father and confirm his allegiance to him above his own authority. He or she will wear the humble clothes akin to the dress of ordinary people, with one single exception, the new diocesan leader will continue to wear the traditional pectoral cross hung from a simple chain to remind the candidate that his or her first service is to the salvation of souls expressed in the love and care of the community who have placed their trust in the newly anointed.'

'Well, Larry, I'm delighted to hear that Peter's ship will continue to be captained at least, in spite of the new order of selection and a mainly lay priesthood – That is all very new and challenging.' Father Kevin spoke over a steaming cup of tea while seated in his old hardback chair. He was now in the need of having a table in front of him to ease his weakened back. He was not in any kind of pain; it was simply a matter of extra comfort and ease to his back. He always kept some reading material and writing paper on the table. He was positioned in his usual place by the window wall that looked out onto the front garden and front entrance porch to the house. Larry was seated away from him in a three-seat settee with his beloved Ruth wheeling about in a walking frame travelling over the powder-blue carpet to Father Kevin, then to Dee in the kitchen and back to Larry again. Larry wanted to hold her all the time but Dee insisted that she needed to develop her walking and gain in strength. The lounge in which he was seated was a very large room both in length and breath. The kitchen was a very modern affair able to cater for several guests with comfort. The family used Larry's old floorboard-table, taken and treasured from his parent's home, when only the four of them dined in a casual way. The main dining room used for visitors was elegantly furnished with a highly polished mahogany table and beautiful chairs elegantly formed with a rich blue cushion fabric to their seats. The table was capable of seating sixteen including the family. The small family usually dined at one end of the table. Dee loved beautiful things. The entire house sparkled and yet she never seemed to fuss over any chore, It seemed at times to Father Kevin, anyway, that the house cleaned itself – Dee was always so upbeat and yet so calm. Larry on the other hand could live in a shed and be happy – he was, at one level, the most lovable, uncomplicated soul in the universe – his strange messianic nature apart. The latter side of his character was too mysterious even for Dee to understand. To that end it was like living with two different people when he was plagued by these strange messages.

Dee was forever calling from the kitchen to Ruth,
'I can hear someone. Is it little Ruth.'
'Ma-ma.' The child answered
'Is that a little sheep, or is that my little Ruth.'
'Ma-ma.' She cried again.
'Of course she's not a little sheep. She's our lovely precious daughter, Ruth. You mustn't call her a sheep.' Larry remarked sternly.
'Oh, shush you great pillock. I'm trying to encourage her to talk, to get beyond, ma-ma; da-da.'
'But I like to hear her say, ma-ma; da-da.'
'I know you do, Larry, love. But we can't keep her as a baby forever.'
'Oh.' Larry remarked, comprehension suddenly dawning. Larry shook his head mockingly towards Father Kevin and making faces then pointing his head in the direction of the kitchen, mischievously soliciting his support. All he got from his friend was a roar of laughter and a voice coming from the kitchen.

'Is that long-drink-of-water, mocking me, Father Kevin? You have my permission to give him a good slap.'

Father Kevin laughed all the more because Larry continued to shake his head and pull faces at her voice. It was Larry all over, one minute he was in serious discussion, the next he was full of fun and mischief. And Dee, for all her remarks worshipped him. Father Kevin was so at home with it all. He grew to love his adopted family more and more and also felt a deep intimate sense of belonging to it and the surrounding community with its seascape and rolling farmlands.

CHAPTER 26

A Visit from Old Friends, the Maddens

There was a sudden heavy sound of crunching gravel on the driveway to the house. All bodies and eyes moved towards the front windows, drawing back the net curtains to identify the callers. The house was set deep in a rural landscape where there was no passing traffic close by. The family was not expecting visitors.

'Larry! Larry! Larry! By the grace of God and a couple of stout policemen, how the Dickens are yeah?' The family members were smiling at Seamus' greeting, all suddenly more animated than usual. Larry grabbed Lil in a bear hug as if he hadn't seen her for twenty years or more; in fact their last visit was a matter of weeks past.

'Will yeah put me down, yeah great lump before yeah squeeze the teeth out of me mouth.' Larry then proceeded to do one of his gliding dances which usually came on him involuntary when over excited. He ran in a circle round the company with his long arms outstretched dipping and diving like an aeroplane. The results had the entire company in hysterics, including Dee, who was the more sober of the friends. They all embraced enthusiastically and fondly, delighted to see each other. Andrew was acting a little self-consciously as there were no children of his own age about. In spite of that significant disadvantage to his wild ways and active nature, he was delighted to reacquaint himself with the family, the house and the surrounding countryside. It wouldn't be too long before he would make his way to the beach or surrounding woodlands to see if there was any adventure to be had. Oh!, he was cute enough to greet all with his usual openness and charming smile, but Dee and Father Kevin knew him all too well … they knew that he would soon be straining at the bit of polite cordiality but ever eager to be away with his wild gallivanting.

'Boy!' Andrew exclaimed, 'that cooking smell's good. What's on the hob?'

'You'll be on the hob, master, Andrew, if you don't watch your manners.' Andrew gave one of his uncertain, mischievous smiles to his father's warning.

'Are you hungry, then, after your journey, Andrew?' Dee embraced him gently as she asked the rather obvious question.'

'That thing – hungry!' Lisa, his sister, turned on him. 'He's no better than a savage … the city dustbin we call him. He'd eat yeah out of house and home … and then eat all the occupants. It isn't fair; he eats like a savage and never puts on a feather's weight. I eat like a mouse any yet put on pounds – it isn't fair,' Lisa repeated, scowling.

'And greetings to you too, Lisa.' Father Kevin remarked humorously halting her tirade at Andrew.

'Some things never change, Father Kevin, as you can gather, the brats are here again.' Seamus threw another warning glance at both children … he loved them both, yet they were the better for his discipline and well-intentioned control over them. Both were allowed sufficient slack in company with a view to encouraging their own sense of responsibility, self-control and politeness towards others. Both knew how much slack they had to play with. Both parents would not tolerate neglectful impoliteness – the two growing children were all the better for the discipline. Andrew was now twelve years and Lisa fourteen.

Andrew was fascinated watching little Ruth scrambling about the lounge carpet. She seemed to be growing taller by the week and more mobile than Andrew had seen her on his last visit. He loved the little child and it wasn't long before he had her in his arms as he played with her on the powder-blue carpet. The aroma of the cooking wafted into the lounge from the kitchen. Andrew's hunger grew more intense as his thoughts were more and more seduced by the wafting aroma of cooking and from his growing impatience for the meal. His rumbling stomach knew no politeness.

Lisa seemed to have that sprawling loose nature ... she was a little ill at ease with Dee's almost clinical neatness. Lisa was a strongly-built lass; very girly in her ways. Her mammy's wardrobe was often subject to her adventures. Still, she had a very obliging nature. The more she developed the more enthusiastic she became to be involved in the frequent social life of her city home. Her enthusiastic willingness to help was a great benefit to both parents in their social lives and entertainment. Partying for the Maddens was a frequent indulgence, given their large circle of acquaintances and family members. Party arrangements were often made at the drop of a hat.

Father Kevin's gentle nature never seemed to change. He had that happy disposition of being at ease in all company. Now, however, the Maddens noted how much greyer his hair had become. Whereas the last visit showed some remaining signs of his grayish-black hair, now all trace of black was gone. The jowls of his face sagged noticeably and his skin color had taken on a notable creamy pallor in spite of his frequent walks. Indeed, he walked more slowly even though he walked more frequently than he had done in his busy city parish. As he moved about in the house, there was a distinct shuffle to his movements, like that of some older people who were more conscious of falling over. His sincerity mingled with his ready wit remained with him. It was hard to believe that he was now in his seventy fourth year. Larry too was showing his age in his hair and his gain in weight. His friends figured out his age to be about fifty six. There was obviously a lot of years left in him, they hoped silently. He never lost a spark of his love for his dearest of neighbours and life-long friends who were every bit family to him from his most impressionable years.

Seamus and family enjoyed a delightful meal of fresh cooked lamb chops which were butchered locally. All the vegetables were also locally grown. Lil and Dee caught up on all the latest news and events on city life and shared in the local news at Garrettstown. Seamus chatted away to Father Kevin covering all the more important sporting news. Before the visitors set off for the city again Father Kevin and Larry went through all the news and changes concerning the local convent, Saint Clare's.

CHAPTER 27

Changes at St. Clare's Convent

The focus and ethos of the convent had changed beyond all recognition. Now, with all the elderly sisters gone to their reward, the entire focus of the convent was given over to being a very advance retreat centre which was in constant use. It could cater for twelve pilgrims self-catering or for meals prepared by some local lay staff. The entire staff comprised a mixture of four sisters and six young novices with Sister Patricia and her dear friend Sister Rosemarie the leading lights. Mass was still an important feature of the convent's life, however, its doors were open to all, even to visitors of other denominations and none. The ethos of the pilgrim retreat centre was to offer a quiet place for prayer, meditation or to simply absorb its tranquility and to go for long walks or savor life by the sea and tumbling waves and its local fishermen and women. Its main focus as a retreat centre was to allow pilgrims on retreat from the busy world to find an inner peace.

All forms of counseling were available – these were conducted principally by Sister Patricia who was highly trained for this work. It involved the grieving process of those who lost loved ones; she also comforted and counseled those with no faith from a purely psychological perspective. Her work also involved the very young in the family situation who were experiencing various traumatic experience of loss or maturing difficulties. Grieving for the young was often very different and difficult. Older people could often cope with the loss of an elder husband or wife where the same loss could crush the young who were lovingly attached to an elderly parent or grandparent. In these circumstances age meant nothing where love meant everything. Sister Patricia was acutely aware that love was not a tap which could be switched on and off at will as if the grieving person was a mere robot – There were so many stages of grief to consider and work through. Each stage had to be dealt with patient and insightful understanding. Sister Patricia's training prepared her to be sensitive and careful not to come in too quickly with talk of heaven and resurrection or that all would be well once we were safely in God's hands. A reference to the spiritual was no less important to people of Faith. However, the time had to be sensitively chosen to go down that path. Sister had to bear the draining emotions and pains of those poor souls arriving at her door, often shattered and in deep depression.

Many of the earlier novices left the convent when Larry's Law ruled that the life of celibacy and virginity were no longer essential to the priesthood or to the religious life of the sisters. The guardians of Larry's Law considered these virtues to be left entirely in the hands of those priest and sisters who had given the matter long reflection and consideration before making their choice. It was Celibacy and Virginity that were considered by the guardians of Larry's Law to be out of kilter with the older and more

balanced prophetic view of scripture which stated: "...
that it was not good for man to be alone ..." The guardians
considered from their own experience of life and in the
history of religious celibacy and virginity how those
imposed conditions had been the cause of much scandal
and disfigurement among so many priest and religious
alike. There was also a sense too in the past that love
expressed in sexual activity was somehow an inferior state
to that of religious life. Celibacy and Virginity were looked
upon as something sacrificial and therefore raised on a
higher plane than married life – as if married life and the
rearing of children was less sacrificial than religious life.

When Larry and Dee were asked by the guardians of the
people to give this ruling due consideration, both contacted
Pope Dominic Ubutu to see what he made of the situation.
The pontiff was the one who considered the position of
leaving it up to the free choice of the priest and sisters. He
admitted that significant difficulties and scandals had
arisen over the years with regard to priestly celibacy and
religious virginity. On the other hand, married priests and
sisters posed significant problems when cost of their upkeep
by the parishioners was taken into account. Now, however,
with money and cost taken out of the equation, he could see
no practical or religious reason for either state to remain
except by long and deliberate personal consideration. There
was also the opportunity for those who wished to remain
celibate or virgin to opt out of that state when an individual
felt the need to do so – in which case the pontiff ruled that
no official vows of celibacy or virginity were to be made
except in the individual's own mind. Whatever choice was
made, the Church of the future would no longer consider
the celibate or virgin state to be considered more virtuous
than life within the marital union. The long history of the

Church, both ancient and modern had experienced great elevation and sanctity in its many married saints just at it had experienced the most shameful scandals that had arisen from those who had taken vows of celibacy and virginity.

The pontiff reminded Larry and Dee that the guardians of the laws of Love and care must never forget the other side of priestly celibacy and religious virginity which were the stepping stones of many missionaries across primitive lands and cultures; how devout and holy individuals who were unencumbered by the pressures of marriage and family life and so enabled them to be free to bring the first notions of a loving God to primitives living in fear and superstition. Such primitives, who through the generosity and selflessness of dedicated pioneers, had eventually prepared them to face the modern world that was annually encroaching on their lands and destroying their simple way of life. He was also made aware that many married ministers from other faiths had managed to evangelise primitive communities across the world with great sacrifice to themselves in selfless service. Ultimately Pope Dominic made the decision to agree with the Guardians and so with his advice and blessing the new law was included in the wider aspect of Larry's Law and the Roman Catholic Church.

CHAPTER 28

Ruth's Development

During her school years Ruth had never made the connection between her father's preoccupation with his daily communications and his connections with Larry's Law. She developed the widest understanding of that law since it was fundamental to every school throughout the world and an essential part of global basic curriculum. From her enrolment in preparatory infant's class, through to first and secondary education she was none the wiser of her parent's international standing. She was immersed in the world with children her age and interests. Certainly she saw the flags and posters of her family everywhere she looked. These were so common that she took no real notice of them, except to remark to people how the posters and flags were quite like her parents. However, since such an observation could be misconstrued by other children to be attention-seeking and an indulgence in self-importance, Ruth kept all such thoughts to herself. Most of her school friends and teachers were so familiar, so over-exposed to the portraits and flags of her family that they seemed no more to them than a national emblem, ignored yet cherished unconsciously. Her friends, especially the older ones, were too engrossed in her wardrobe, friendship, and her gallivanting playfulness, and such like, to be troubled with her international standing as the child of her world-renowned parents. The fact that her portrait showed only a babe in arms wrapped up in a white-lace shawl with her father waving her little hand made the connection to her very remote indeed.

She proved to be a highly intelligent child, popular with school mates and teachers alike. Her intelligence and quick wit she inherited in abundance from her mother. Her lovable accommodating nature expressed itself in a constant smile on her beautiful face, this she inherited from her father. She was growing in height, seemingly by the month, no doubt from the inheritance of her father's height. She inherited the beautiful blond hair of her mother along with her sparkling blue eyes. She was rather thin in her teenage years, which was also due to her father's genetics. She also inherited her father's deep love of people. Just as her father had a terrible problem with grieving over the death of close friends, Ruth too could get herself into the most dreadful state of depression when any of her friends were hurt. Fortunately up to now she had not lost any family or friends through death. Secretly her mother was dreading such an event since her experience with the extent of Larry's grieving was so difficult to cope with. Dee had tried, without success, to coax Larry to have a stay at Saint Clare's under Sister Patricia's guidance; unfortunately Larry was too defensive and frightened to even consider it. He could spend months in the deepest state of depression, tears and silence ... a time when he shut himself away from Dee and all his close friends. At such times Dee was forced to avoid having visitors which made her misery all the more difficult to bear. Ruth had also developed her father's characteristic of prolonged physical contact with her associates. She would caress the faces of her friends as though they were uniquely precious; she would rub their arms and back as if she might never see them again. Not everyone was comfortable with such physical intimacies; to that end, some thought her a bit odd until they realized that she was the same with boys and girlfriends. Put simply, she was just a touchy-feely person, just like her father.

Now at the age of eighteen years Ruth decided on her initial career studying Family Care which also entailed child protection. At the heart of this career was the ability to keep difficult families together whenever possible. Obviously this president did not always work; in which case, the child or children of proven inadequate or dysfunctional parents were removed from them and lodged or adopted by parents who were considered suitable to adopt or give temporary refuge to vulnerable children – while at the same time committing inadequate or dysfunctional parents to a prolonged period of intensive training and correction under strict supervision in specialized psychiatric facilities. Inadequate parenting was not considered deliberate neglect until such a condition was proven. Every effort was taken in the long term to reunite families. Sometimes this would mean that parents removed from their blood offspring could only become spectators to their children's upbringing and welfare. Of the many experiences that resulted in these sad situations was the conclusion that blood relationship was not of itself a criterion for good parenting. Secondly, that parenthood was not always a natural consequence of physically giving birth to children. There were many unfortunate reasons and circumstances for this phenomenon. As mentioned earlier, just because we all have the ability to produce children, does not automatically follow that we have the wherewithal to care for them in a wholesome, loving, and caring way. It was established from long experience from the work of Family Care that many parents lacked the ability to bond, to show love, or to protect their offspring. It may be that in many cases poor parenting may have had its roots in the upbringing of the parents themselves; it may be a case of the children being no more than an appendage to married life or to the act of procreation itself. Parental indifference to their childrens' needs was considered as crass selfishness.

Ruth learned that the reasons for inadequate parenting were manifold and not always simple or straightforward. Even the animal world displayed such traits at times. Although no parents were condemned outright as useless to the wider community, every effort was taken to help them and to care for and protect their children from neglect and abuse of any kind. At the back of Family Care was the knowledge that none of us are perfect ... that none of us choose our nature or the circumstances of our birth, or the community in which we find ourselves ... the parents to whom we belong ... or the conditions and influence of our nation into which we are born by fate's indifference.

Ruth's principle lecturer, Miss Susan Baker, was principle lecturer for the subject at Larry's Family Care University in Cork City. Miss Baker warned her students, with great emphasis:

'When you come to assess the factors that may result in the separation of children from their natural parents, keep it well in mind that you will have to trawl through a mountain of reports from the courts of the Guardians of the

People who are responsible for the upholding of the strict codes of Larry's Law ... they will scrutinize your decisions through its prism. As you know from your studies, that Law considers all aspects of every individual's needs. Your decisions will have to be made with the greatest care and scrutiny of all reports including your own. There can be no short cuts. Once you come before the panel of professional doctors, psychiatrists and other professional care workers, any shoddy decisions on your part will come to the fore and reveal your own incompetence. So be warned. One or two members of the panel, or all of them, may test the precision of your reasoning, so be alert.

'To digress for a moment – I would like to give you an anecdotal example of my own early experience when I first left university after my initial training. I had taken the decision, after careful consideration that a particular family in our care was unsuitable to be allowed to keep its child. The parents left the protection of our house on several occasions at night without permission. They invariably returned in a terrible state of drunkenness. The father was a very violent man – the mother was in the habit of taking drugs. Both screamed the house down with senseless circuitous and aggressive arguments. Several times we had to call the police in to have them removed for the protection of their own child and that of the other families in care. Normally we were given six to eight weeks to assess the progress of such families before we came to the decision that they were fit to return home and look after their child in a safe and caring manner. However, in the case of the parents I refer to, I felt that their child was too much at risk. It was agreed by my own superiors, after careful appraisal, that the child should be put into care for its own protection and that the parents should be sent to one of the people's specialized psychiatric facilities which catered for such parents in accordance with the recommendations of Larry's Law. Obviously the case for separation was brought before the Guardians of the People – the People's Court, which was under the jurisdictions of the Guardians of Larry's Law. While I was being cross examined by representatives of the parents and those of our own work, the defense for the parents put this question to me:

'Miss Baker ... you are not married, are you?'

'No, sir, I am not.'

'Do you have any children of your own?'

'No, I do not.'

'Can you honestly consider yourself competent to take a decision to separate a child from its parents since you have no intimate experience of married life?' Miss Baker looked into the speakers face quite calmly and then turned her eyes to the panel of assessors.

'There is no necessity, sir, to catch a disease in order to become a doctor.'

The court fell silent, 'I thought I might have been disciplined for sarcasm. Fortunately the principle leader of the panel rallied to my side when he said,

'That is wisely put, Miss Baker. May I remind you, sir,' the leader addressed the counsel for the parents, 'that it is not Miss Baker's marital status that we are considering here. I would ask you, sir, to be more respectful for her position and professionalism. Just stick to the issues in hand, sir. I should not have to remind you that her decision had been a joint one, taken with due consideration with the help and experience of her own authorities. Please read your notes more carefully in future before your resort to methods of intimidation. You were not paying sufficient attention to the details of the case but allowing your prejudice to move in favor of the parents and so distort your own questionable judgment and competence, sir.'

'Needless to say, the offending representative for the parents sat down burning in his own embarrassment. 'Unfortunately', the lecturer continued, 'even our court representatives are only human. Again I say to you, be very careful about your decisions, and leave your emotions and prejudices where they belong when reason and wisdom call for courtesy and professional impartiality.'

Ruth, as well as the lecturer's other students were very much taken with Miss Baker's insights and professional competence. The lecturer continued to reveal the complexity of the work of Family Care.

'Much of poor inadequate or dysfunctional parenting is usually, but not always, the result of the parent's background. There are usually early indicators like that of parents screaming, shouting, swearing, violent shaking of children and other abuses. We may summaries these conditions as verbal or physical bullying of the child. In the short term children exposed to such abusive treatment may show early signs of being overly fearful and overly sensitive – bed-wetting, lack of confidence – depression – lack of communication or of their inability to play with other children. Other indicators may reveal themselves such as screaming, shouting and swearing, and generally displaying aggressive reactions towards other children and adults. These traits can all too often be direct instinctive means of copying their parent's behavior. Extreme aggressive behavior will inevitably seem normal to the child ...which may well be the only life they have ever known.

Such children seem always to turn calm situations into stress in order to achieve dominance over other children or even their teachers. Learning at school can become extremely difficult and in some cases impossible. School and teachers in areas of deprivation have invariably resulted in poor teaching as teachers who come to be employed in such areas become frustrated and eventually are reduced to no more than containing forces put in impossible positions. Teaching as vocation in such extremes over a prolonged period gets ground down so that survival by inadequate teaching takes root. To be asked a question in class is usually taken as a form of personal challenge or unwanted attention. Although the child is physically present at school, in its mind it is still defending itself at home. Such children carry the home environment with them everywhere including into the streets and into all their relationships. They may not be able to relate to anyone except in a confrontational, aggressive way.

'Dysfunctional parenting,' Miss Baker continued, 'is more often than not the result of extreme environmental pressures imposed on young parents in a hostile environment which has gradually built itself up around them. Areas formally at the mercy of historical financial deprivation and the lack of investment and leisure facilities … areas noted to be black-spots for unemployment … areas noted for their violent gangland hotspots, where drugs, alcohol abuse, prostitution and crimes of extreme violence develop and thrive … where gun and knife-crimes are all too common. These become the breeding grounds of an underclass. Normal language becomes stylized and coded to such an extent that their native tongue becomes so distorted that children exposed to such conditions lose the basic abilities to read, spell or construct a proper grammatical sentence or hold an intelligent conversation. All too often such children leave school unable to read or write and are quite incapable of finding worthwhile employment. The adults formed in such an environment soon find themselves in a vicious cycle where every twist and turn of their miserable existence militates against them. They invariably marry into their own culture because the more advance privileged classes steer well clear of them.

'This old cycle of poverty and deprivation could sometimes be partially broken by those, who for want of gainful employment, turn to the military forces in the hope of making something of their own wretched existence. However, rarely do adults from such areas of deprivation advance in the military or defensive forces. It is the privileged classes that invariably form the higher ranks and authority over them. In these situations the poorer classes, the underprivileged, form the front line of aggressive dangerous situations in hostile foreign wars and conflicts. They often do make good soldiers and killing machines. Their early bullying upbringing and their rebellious reactions to it all too often make them immune to conflict situations; compassion and moderation of behavior do not come natural to them. The military identity and its uniforms, and all the paraphernalia that go with them, serve to give their hyperactive and hypersensitivity some kind of outlet to their instinctive aggression. A career in the forces can often serve to give them a meaningful identity and comradely belonging. Boisterous aggressive situations seem to hold few natural fears for them; they are able to rise above such situations as a result of their early defensive conditioning. Reaction to events come more natural to them rather than reasoning and calm deliberation.

'Before the establishment of Larry's Law,' the lecturer continued, 'one of the main contributing factors that had led to a general breakdown in family life and family welfare was the dominance of the existence of money. It was far easier for the privileged classed to make and accumulate riches for themselves through personal investments. The privileged classes were the main controlling factors and were the principle reason for the general deprivation of the underprivileged classes in the dark days of the Twentieth Century. It was calculated that 80% of most nations' wealth lay in the iron grip of 10% of that privileged group. It meant that 80% of the population was struggling worldwide to make a meaningful comfortable living. Within that struggling 80% it was not uncommon to experience every degree of impoverishment. Virtually every city in the world had its own ghettos where poverty and squalor existed in unimaginable horror. It is hard for us to imagine it now with all the achievements and developments since the establishment of Larry's Law. No city of past years was exempt from ghetto experience and ghetto mentality.

'In order to escape the miseries of wanton poverty and deprivation many impoverished families took to emigration from one country to another. Yet such moves invariably left the immigrants exposed and exploited, often by their own native people who had become established in their new adopted countries. Indians exploiting Indians, Polish immigrants exploiting their own, the Irish of America exploiting their own ... the Italians, Latinos, Africans, Chinese, Arabs, Jews, Spanish, Germans, Philippines ... the list is endless. This movement of displaced peoples often created worse conditions for the native or indigenous peoples already established in any given country. If we spread the net more widely and go back much further to learn the lessons of the exploitation of the indigenous Indian tribes of America, Canada, or the Aborigines of Australia and so forth ... people who lived and thrived without the curse of money, these too were cornered and exploited, hounded and warehoused on reservations while their lands were plundered for their minerals and for the ownership of the land itself. Such reservations in time became ghettos with the introduction of alcohol, drugs, money and the breaking down of indigenous cultures and language and their ancient ways of life. Some would call such exploitation progress. Naturally that would depend on which horse one rode in such a discussion.

'The ghetto experience in the cities of the past meant that more and more corruption took root. Corrupt officials and police, the former guardians of the people, added to the miseries of the general plague of poverty. The workhouses of many impoverished nations bore witness to so much wanton misery and horrific conditions. Many diseases spread like wildfire in such institutions. And yet, the greatest of all diseases to inflict most nations was the exploitation of humanity by humanity itself, with heartless cruelty and wanton neglect of their own kind.

'Areas of comparative stability meant that the movement of the poor into such areas soon brought along a new vicious cycle of poverty. Good families were forced to move away from the homes that may have seen several generations of relative peace and relative stability. Once decent families moved out and poverty-stricken families moved in, the vacated houses lost their monitory value which unscrupulous landlords bought up and let them to overcrowded families. Such ghettoes eventually became no go areas for police or social workers as crime and gangland cultures took hold. In these situations the usual pattern of gun and knife-crimes became common and escalated from the introduction of drug supply, prostitution, and general gangland warfare. Police and social workers were all too frequently attacked or harassed preventing them from carrying on their duties. In the end few were brave enough to venture into such criminal ghettoes. Rent collectors were attacked and brutally assaulted. Criminal gangs followed their own laws and in the process a culture of silence and fear flourished resulting in the ghettoes being virtually impenetrable with regard to law and order. Vying gangs meted out their own forms of protection and justice.'

Miss Baker returned to the main focus of her lecture. 'What we have looked at here are the traditional and historical experiences of past deprivations once so common to the city ghettoes of our distant past. There are no excuses now for the development of subcultures since the inception of Larry's Law and the removal of money with its many direct causes of injustices from the equation. Nonetheless, we are far from being a perfect world. It will be your duty in the future to be able to spot the early symptoms of child abuse by parents or other relations. In doing so you will invariably manage to nip the embryo of systemic abuses in the bud before a similar vicious cycle repeats itself.'

Ruth Walsh was very impressed at the knowledge of her lecturer, both became staunch friends as Susan, the principle of the university, became Ruth's ear and mentor long after Ruth had take up her position with Family Care. Ruth's work, as she gained in experience, was mainly taking on new recruits into the care service. She found her work rewarding and demanding at times. The world of Larry's Law, was far from being complete or perfect. The old adage held true: "... You can take the man out of the slum but you can take the slum out of the man." Just as the civilization of mankind could not remove us from animal nature – albeit that through our struggles at virtuous behavior, one could believe we were seeing the building blocks of a new and more graced evolution. The words of Julian of Norwich, a mystic and seer in her own time, gave our future a real sense of hope in her words:

"...All shall be well ... and all shall be well ... and all manner of things shall be well...."

CHAPTER 29

The Death of Father Kevin

A great pall of oppressive grief continued to hang over Larry's home at the sudden death of Father Kevin at the age of eighty five. He had been a lifelong friend of Larry and his family. His death was the dreaded situation that had rooted itself in Dee's mind for several years. She knew without the slightest doubt that whenever Father Kevin would pass on that Larry would inevitably descend into one of his extended periods of depression. It was going to mean a prolonged period of silence and inactivity for Larry and a very depressing time for Dee as a result. Fortunately the expected situation was somewhat eased by Ruth's influence on Larry and as a great support to her mother. In grief Larry could not abide people around him but for some unexplained reason Ruth could comfort him and even managed to take away some of the pain that held him in its grip. It was as if he could never ignore or neglect the little infant that he felt was in need of his constant attention. Naturally that very bond hurt Dee very deeply even though it worked for her benefit also. It seemed to Dee that Larry was free to make choices as to who he allowed into his life at the time of his depression. Yet Dee's reasoning didn't seem to be true. It seemed more likely that his dependence on his wife all through their marriage, and coupled with Dee's seeming unshakable confidence, left Larry with some innate unspoken sense that she could endure without his temporary lack of support. Larry would only discover the depth of her hurt when he recovered from his state of depression and grief. Thankfully Ruth was such a comfort to them both during this difficult period. It wasn't easy for Ruth either as Father Kevin was virtual family to her from her very conception. She too needed to let go her own sobbing tears when she could be on her own to do so.

The city vigil Mass was celebrated in the presence of a great throng of clergy and people. The church was by no means packed to capacity. This was due to Father Kevin's age and his departure from the parish some fifteen years previous. Many new priest and parishioners had come and gone in the natural way of things. Even so, he was well represented by those who had known him from childhood experiences in the life of the church. Bishop Mark spoke of Father Kevin's humility and simple piety. His words, though meant sincerely, were a little like importing shamrock to Ireland. Those who were familiar with Father Kevin's priestly ministry knew all this with far greater intimacy than the bishop. Nonetheless the acknowledgement of these characteristics was a comfort to those who knew him, including the many priests and religious of the diocese. The humble and sincere tributes paid to him by the bishop seemed to the people the very sentiments that they would like to have expressed themselves. To that end Bishop Mark had further endeared himself to the people, priests and religious alike. The elaborate celebration with its outstanding contribution from the old organist and choir, along with the up-lifted voices of the congregation, sent a shiver to the very spines of those who were there to witness the celebration. An elderly couple sat whispering to each other – the husband remarked with tears in his eyes:

'Poor Father Kevin, such a kindly soul; 'tis hard to believe he has been taken from us.' And so it was, his sacred remains were carried out of the church in solemn procession with most of the congregation in tears. Still they endeavored to sing in heartfelt salutation, the spiritual interpretation of the song, O Danny Boy....

The church bell tolled mournfully over the city as the simple coffin was covered with wafting incense and blessed with holy water in the sign of the cross as it was placed in the glinting hearse. Floral tributes softened the bare nakedness of the carriage. The bishop remarked softly and with sadness to his chauffeur-secretary:

'He takes a great deal with him, Father Anthony.'

'I'm sorry bishop; I don't take your meaning.'

'We only take with us what we have given away to others – and believe me, Father Anthony, he has given so much to all who knew him. God bless his kindly soul.'

The requiem Mass at Saint Clair's Retreat Centre in Garrettstown could not compete with the city celebration; perhaps that was exactly what Father Kevin envisaged when he made the final arrangements for his departure. It was a simple affair and out of respect for Father Kevin's wishes, Bishop Mark kept the service as simple as possible. The Madden family did the readings; Dee read out the eulogy which the family and intimate friends had composed between them. Ruth, Lisa and Andrew read the prayers of intercession.

As ever, Dee could always be counted upon to deliver a meaningful eulogy as she faced the small local congregation that filled the small convent Chapel to capacity:

'All of us, I feel sure, consider our own priest to be head and shoulders above others; and why not! Since it is those who touch our lives so intimately that we take deeply into our hearts – they become so much the foundation on which we build our spiritual existence. Kevin, if the bishop will forgive my familiarity,' the bishop waved the remark aside with the sweep of a hand, a sign to continue, 'was for me personally an exceptional priest, an exceptional friend. I cannot help but think of him as a priest among priests, blinded no doubt by my own prejudices and all our own special closeness to him and his ministry. I know that he has touched the lives of all here, all the locals that he came among and shared in our lives. He never once separated himself from any of us; he never allowed his sacred office and ministry to rise above our heads; instead, he seemed more humble than the most humble of any of us. He laughed with us on the seashore with Mack's Army of fishermen and women; he shared our fun, our pleasures and our pains. Many found comfort from his inexhaustible patience, kindness, compassion and understanding in our times of trouble. I don't stand in front of you and your hurting hearts with insincere and empty platitudes. You knew the man, you knew the priest in him. Yet in truth I think I may be allowed the privilege to give him due honor and remember Kevin as the main mast of the spiritual ship in our small community since his arrival here.

'Perhaps too I can speak with greater insight than most as part of the family he lived with over the past fifteen years or so in the intimacy of our own home in which he was always considered an intimate member of the family.

And yet his connection with my family goes back much further to the time when he was Parish priest of Saint Patrick's in Cork city with his beloved and dearest of all friends, the unforgettable Nell. Father Kevin even then, was everything to us. Our lives are all the richer for the knowing of so dear a friend and humble, loving priest. I feel sure that Bishop Mark will forgive me using his own words related to me in my own tears when he whispered to his secretary as Father Kevin's body was placed in the hearse to be carried off in the last benediction of incense over his sacred remains:

"He takes a great deal with him, Father Anthony ....

We only take with us what we have given away to others; and believe me, Father Anthony, he has given so much to all who knew him. God bless his kindly soul."

'I can't improve on those final words of our bishop nor do I intend to except to say what is in all your hearts at the present moment. Thank you so much, Father Kevin, for being there for all of us. Your kindly spirit and all you meant to each soul here will never be far from us.'

The congregation erupted into spontaneous applause. It gave release to their emotions as well as a token of their appreciation for being addressed as a community and having their collective sense of loss addressed.

When the coffin was carried out after the service to be placed in the hearse once more, Bishop Mark didn't know whether a sacrilege was being committed; for there before him in a arch of fishing rods was a gathering of eighteen of Mack's Army, a mixture of men and women. The bishop's face was a stage of utter confusion. It needed Sister Patricia from the convent to whisper discretely into his ear,

'Don't worry, Bishop Mark, they are his second family.' It seemed on first impression to the bishop that the guard of honor composed of a motley crew of fishermen and women was a bit frivolous – out of keeping with the solemnity of the death of a priest. It was plain to see from his face, in spite of Sister Patricia's efforts to put him at ease, that it was not the time or place for such sentiment. Only when he saw their tears did he begin to realize the depth of esteem in which Father Kevin was held locally and how he had endeared himself to the people and become an intimate part of the lives of these simple farming and seaside people and their activities. He was informed by one of Mack's army that it was a very old tradition. The bishop's surprise and horror was removed, he realized the true meaning and significance of their gesture. As the funeral bell tolled out from the convent over his kindly soul it was a strange but fitting event ... a great flock of wheeling and crying seagulls flew over the departing hearse. Even Mack's Army read the significance and appropriateness of what they considered a fitting salutation and final benediction from the sea that he had grown to love. Dee was thankful for the great comfort of poor Larry shown to him by his beloved Ruth. Dee also had to comfort Andrew and Lisa, Seamus' children. Father Kevin had been like a second father to them as well as to Larry and Dee.

A strong gale blasted over the small exposed hill-cemetery forcing the clothing of the family and the entire gathering to cling like flapping flags to their bodies. Large white clouds swept scurrying across the summer sky. Tufts of bog grass and bog cotton shuddered all round the lower edges of the gravestones with the force of the gale. The clamber up the terrace-like structure of the cemetery made the coffin- bearers thread very cautiously. The words of the internment, now familiar to all present, were carried away on the wind. The funeral bell tolled intermittently like the voice of some invisible haunting specter echoing across the wind-blown scene. A flock of calling crows swept speedily across the wild-blown skies. Somewhere down the ancient and rutted donkey track came the distant bark of a dog, no doubt from Hogan's cottage, which was set deep in Kerry bog-land. Ruth clung to her father who was in a terrible state of tears and with his tall frame wracked in heaving spasms. Fortunately he too clung to Ruth; she was now much taller than her mother, taking her height from her father. Dee was in tears and yet she comforted the forty year old Andrew, Seamus' son along with Lisa. Lil also clung to Larry for his own safety. Seamus too was in tears with his head buried in his chest and gazing distractedly down onto the interned coffin. It was Dee who spoke the last words of farewell over the open grave:

'Thank you once again Father Kevin and Nell for being there for all of us. Our hearts and minds will ever embrace you both. We are sad now because we are left with only words to give you both one final embrace. There will always be a place in our home for you both in the recalling of your love and fond memories and all that you both have meant to us over the years. May God's love embrace you and keep you both safe and happy always.'

All present took on her final gesture throwing single red roses into the grave. Flowers were also placed on Nell's grave. The family and their friends, the Maddens, knew for certain that they would be back in turns to pray by their graves. There were wooden benches placed strategically around the cemetery for visitors. The family had learned long ago, from Father Kevin himself, that to visit the graves of loved ones, friends and neighbors, was to reopen the book of their lives, their wisdom and receive a renewed communion with them. There was nothing macabre about such visits. There, many graces would be received in such a holy and contemplative communion. The family and friends looked back for the last time as they suffered the blasting gale to take, as it were, a snapshot of the cemetery. They agreed that the cemetery was well kept by the locals responsible for its maintenance. This pleased the family as they took their seats in the black glinting funeral car to take them home.

Father Kevin had few belongings of his own. His priestly clothes where removed by Seamus and Lil at Dee's earnest request. Dee was determined to remove them while Larry was still in his depressed state. She hoped that by doing so she might prevent an additional recurrence of depression if Larry was exposed the clothing.

Father Kevin had many notebooks filled with prayers. It became evident to Dee that he was indeed a very profound and spiritual man from the many alterations and crossings out that were self-evident of his thoughts. She noted that he had transformed The Chaplet of the Divine Mercy Rosary introduced to the Catholic world by the late Sister Faustina Kowalska, a Polish nun who died in 1938. He had mentioned to the family in private that he could not accept the notion of the need for God's Mercy. He considered the word as belonging to the old Hebrew-Jewish world that identified with God as one capable of terrible vengeance and punishment – that this image of God got passed down through the ages and into Christianity itself. Father Kevin had explained to the family that he would not ask anyone he loved for mercy – that the very notion of it was so utterly self-contradictory. Therefore he always used the word love in place of mercy. God, to Father Kevin, was Love … he came to realize that very early on in his priesthood and the New Testament emphasized to the same conclusion particularly in John's account of Jesus' teachings. That conclusion was by no means immediately obvious form the early beginnings of scriptural prophecy – it was arrived at developmentally in the progress of prophetic human understanding.

It was also obvious from his writings that Father Kevin had never been at ease with attributing any gender to God but made the compromise for those with whom he prayed. He never related these words to his congregations in any church since he was not there to represent his own understanding of God nor was he at liberty to do so and still stay in office. Nonetheless, with regard to his own private prayers and with those of his close friends he made his opinions clear to them but never asked their acceptance of his understanding of the prayer. His friends were perfectly happy to join him with the words of his understanding which they all came to agree with and see the sense of it. As he took some pains to explain: '… We must pray with our own words, our own understanding and conscience, but never force them on anyone since many require the authority of others to form their conscience for them. For many souls moving out of their comfort zone and trusting to their own conscience and understanding was too threatening and left them with a distinct sense of betrayal to their faith and Church authority – even when such a position only perpetuated self-inflicted ignorance and blind, fear-based indoctrination. These were the very conditions with which Jesus had to confront the authorities of his own time. As Jesus inferred ... tradition is man-made – it is not guaranteed truth.

Father Kevin usually led the morning and evening prayers for the family he considered his own. Many of his prayers were originals and the family was well acquainted with saying them with him. Yet it was only now that Dee could see from his notebooks how he came to the conclusions and expressions of his prayers. He had obviously "dug deep into the garden of scriptures" as Larry aptly put it. Dee was to treasure his notebooks which she considered to be sacred to his memory. Her deep personal love for Father Kevin, coupled with the journalist in her, saw a significant future for the contents of her friend's notebooks. She had every intention of producing a biography to his memory. She saw in him a rich meaningful life – one worthy of record and for sharing with others. For now, she only shared them with Ruth, the Maddens, Susan Baker, a dear friend and Ruth's former lecturer from Larry's Family Care University. Dee avoided allowing the note books to come into contact with Larry since death to him was far too painful; he simply couldn't cope with it. In short, death was a-no-go-area for him. It struck Dee forcibly and quite suddenly some time back when she tried to figure out why death was such a dreadful and prolonged psychiatric condition for Larry. Her best guess was that it had something to do with his vulnerable childhood and his need of extra parental protection. Added to her thoughts was the fact that his parents lived for him – devoting their entire love and energies to protecting him. Was this healthy? Had it developed into a suffocating-dependence? Time and time again she asked herself the same question in her more sober and reflective moments. She was angry because she felt pushed out of his life when close friends died. Was possessive love for a wounded individual, or for any individual, real love at all? Did it keep such an individual too remote from the needs of others? Was parental need to possess a kind of selfishness on their part? In making Larry's world did they inadvertently cripple him from dealing with death or any kind of permanent separation? It was then that these reveries struck her when she remembered that Jesus himself referred to death as the last enemy of man. This insight, or puzzle, made Dee once more look more deeply at Saint Paul's writing in Corinthian's regarding the character of Love as something all consuming. It wasn't enough, as Paul emphasized, to sacrifice oneself for another or for the entire world as something noble and worthwhile, as in an ideal. Real Love at its most profound and meaningful, at its most complete, was to take the subject of who or what is loved totally into one's self. It amounts to a deep sense of unconditional belonging. Dee now realized that she also felt intensely possessive of Larry. She had taken him into herself in a total way including all his awkwardness – she loved him through it all. She admitted to herself that it had taken her a total conversion of a life of grace to do so. But then that applied to every individual. Grace was the lifeblood of Love. Now she didn't even allow the thoughts of his death to enter into her mind – not even for a conscious second.

CHAPTER 30

The Wedding of Ruth and Andrew – New World Leaders

Over the next few months, due to Father Kevin's death and absence from the family home, Dee and family felt a very oppressive sense of loss and quality vanished from their home. Andrew took two weeks off work to stay with Dee and family. Lisa was away most of the time she had become a song writer and poet of some standing. She was also engage to be married. Andrew was often seen in tears. Father Kevin was for him someone who was around forever and gave him that sense of happiness and permanence. He had baptized and confirmed Andrew as well as Ruth. Andrew's decision to spend the entire two week break with the family proved to be the very opportunity that Ruth hoped might come about one day, when she might express her deep love for him. Andrew on his part was completely unaware of her feelings and designs on him. Inwardly he had always been besotted with her remarkable beauty and kindly affection towards all people. She was approachable to all, in spite of her almost royal status as part of her family's world leadership. Ruth had many admirers any many offers of marriage locally and from her work, communicating with the international public. She never considered any of these. Her heart and love throbbed for Andrew only. Unfortunately, and completely unknown to Ruth, Andrew always felt that she was in an orbit far above him. Inwardly he craved for her but his natural modesty and feelings of inadequacy made him act with seeming indifference to Ruth's love ... and that was the message she struggled to live with. Andrew was also a man's man; he seemed never to be in the company of women for long. There was an instinctive wildness to his nature – he couldn't be kept indoors for too long, particularly in his boyhood years. He had a wonderful considerate and mature nature in many ways. Certainly, he felt more at ease in adult company. Even so, he would always draw other children into his games and antics especially when such children seemed to be alone or lacking in confidence. He was instinctively generous; no doubt he had caught that instinct from his parents, Seamus and Lil, since that character was with them in abundance.

Ruth considered it fortuitous that Andrew was still smarting from the loss of his friend Father Kevin. She realized that these were twisted thoughts in her mind. Yet it was his grief for Father Kevin that gave her the opportunities to take Andrew in her arms by way of comforting him in his grief. Gradually her kisses on his tear-run cheeks came to slip in deliberation to his lips. She weighed his response with care. In the end she had to break the deadlock between them. And with a few days left of his holiday she was determined not to waste any more years than she had already. She was sharply aware of her age in relation to her growing desperation to know whether Andrew might have the slightest interest in marriage and if she might be considered on any grounds at all. She made up her mind to have him at any price, even if it meant that they could only be together permanently in marriage with herself doing all the giving. Three days before he was due back to work Ruth held him once again in her arms; he wasn't in tears but she pretended that she thought he was and clung to him tightly and kissed him on the lips with a kiss that couldn't any longer be mistaken for simple comforting. She paused to move her soft silky lips to his ear and whispered in trembling words:

'Andrew. I love you so much; I always have from the time I was old enough to appreciate my own inner feelings. I would love to marry you but fear that you have other plans for your life....' Andrew began to tremble physically with tears gushing from his eyes. He held Ruth back from him at arm's length.'

'O – Ruth! Don't mock me. Don't!' Ruth was devastated from the way she felt pushed aside from him.

'I'm not mocking you, Andrew. Surely you can tell I love you? How many boys or men have you seen me kiss as I have kissed you?'

'I don't know Ruth. I have never seen you kiss anyone on the lips before.' Andrew was trembling even more now because he knew from the unusual sternness of Ruth's expression and the look of exasperation with her gesturing hands that she meant ever word she was saying. Andrew fell into the large settee in the lounge. He was still trembling and barely able to speak. He couldn't take it all in as a million thoughts and impressions flew through his mind which was already in turmoil.

'You're an international celebrity, for God's sake.' He now spoke only to his own churning mind: 'I know you have been offered countless proposals ... you are much taller than me ... God, what am I to look at in comparison to your indescribable beauty! ...' All these and countless other thoughts and impression raced incoherently through his mind. As he calmed down he looked up at Ruth's tear-stained face. Her sparkling bright blue eyes had turned into fountains from the torrent and pain of so many frustrating years of waiting, hoping and craving. Andrew sprung suddenly to his feet. There was no more room for doubt as he said without a notion of romance in his voice:

'O God! What a couple of prize eejits we have been. I have always tried to avoid expressing my personal love for you. I didn't want to spoil the friendship we had. I never believed that I ever stood a chance of being loved by you except in my own dreams and fantasies. I dared not even countenance the thought of speaking out about my obsession about you. Every time we ever embraced I felt giddy with passion and emotion. Sometimes I just wanted to go away and be sick with all the churning and stress of my own strangled emotions. You cannot imagine the shame I felt inwardly because of my passionate cravings for you .... All those bloody wasted years ... All those bloody pain-racking and tormented years ....' Ruth stopped his anger with himself as she kissed him more passionately than ever. She held nothing back now there was no calm dignity left between them.

'We will marry, then?' said Ruth sobbing with relief.

'Of course we'll bloody marry – and not a minute too soon. Just name the hour, never mind a day away .... Even that's too far off.'

'We can do it right now,' said Ruth in a rush of passion.

'But the church ... The arrangements ....?'

'They're upstairs,' Ruth replied with urgency.

'What are?'

'The arrangements she replied,' impatiently.

'Will you love me for the rest of your life?' Ruth was holding him tightly as he blurted out his answer.

'Of course I will. You know I will.' The echo of his words, his blurted agreement, was still travelling through the air when she replied with the same frenzied response:

'So will I love you as I always have loved you all my conscious life.' With her answer swiftly ended she dragged Andrew upstairs with such speed that he was stumbling on the carpeted stairs as if he were no more to Ruth than a feather's weight. She locked the door. They all but ripped the clothes off each other in a mad fit of passion as if they had only the next few seconds to live. You couldn't call the next bliss-shattering minutes an act of love. It was unadulterated passion the result of years of their own self-inflicted physical and mental flagellation of their mutual longing and sexual yearnings.

Roars of ecstasy from the bedroom came to Dee's ears – she was busy in the kitchen. She reacted instantly and bounded up the stairs like a demented woman to see if someone was attacking Ruth. She tried the door frantically turning the knob and shouldering the door, to no avail. The screams were unrelenting from the two voices climaxing in a body-throbbing experience totally new to their entire senses.

'What's wrong Ruth …? Are you in there Andrew …? For heaven's sake, will one of you answer me? What's wrong?' Dee was trying to shout over their screams. Finally, and with her protective instincts at their wit's end she began pummeling the door with her fists. 'Let me in, Andrew …. Is that you in there …? Let me in, I tell you!'

Ruth unlocked the door and stood there gasping for breath and with only a bath towel half covering her nakedness.

She appeared, flushed, exhausted and her beautiful blond hair wildly tossed. She stood before her mother, a corner of the powder-blue bath towel pressed to her mouth with sheepish embarrassed innocence and awkwardness. Her bare shoulders glowed with tiny beads of perspiration. She was using both hands to keep the bath towel in some semblance of modesty. She looked downwards on the mother she loved so much with eyes that seemed to have grown calm and yet bearing a trusting expression and half pleading for her mother's understanding. The expression in Ruth's eyes looking upward from her lowered face saw the beaming love and smile in her mother's kindly eyes. Dee's expression was all embracing …. She could see the ecstasy of love in her daughter's eyes and happy face. They embraced and held each other for what seemed an eternity. Dee moved Ruth aside from the open door and passed into the bedroom and looked calmly at the tossed bed. Andrew was hiding under the light duvet which he had retrieved swiftly from the carpet. Dee was careful to remove only the upper part of the powder blue cover in an effort to spare Andrew his natural shyness and the indignity of pointless compromise and embarrassment. His two half-frightened eyes gazed up into Dee's smirking, teasing expression.

'It's alright, Andrew. I just want to satisfy myself that neither of you have bloody murdered the other with all your screams. You terrified the very wits out of me. Perhaps the next time you two decide to show your love to each other would you please go about ten fields away and there you can scream all you like out of my earshot.' She stooped down to kiss Andrew but before her lips touched his cheek Andrew grabbed her in a wild embrace, taking Dee off her feet to land on top of him. Ruth stood there in hysterics while her mother struggled like a netted fish to be free and calling to Andrew:

'Oh no you don't, master Madden ...! You may not have the mother as well, you great tinker. You control yourself now.' As Dee struggled to regain her dignity and composure she was smiling and beaming with pride. She always did love the wild Andrew, and now he was family she thought; not that he had ever been anything else to her since the first day she had become friends with the Maddens. Andrew tried to explain himself; how he didn't mean anything compromising by his wild embrace of Dee.

'I only meant to tell you I love you and ...' Ruth cut him short.

'Oh, shut up you great eejit! Mammy knows perfectly well what you meant.'

Andrew remarked: 'I mean, we are married now and that makes you my mother by law, Doesn't it, Dee?' There was innocence in Andrew's remark as he continued to keep only his face exposed to the two women now smiling at him in a teasing manner.

'What's all this about being married?' Dee's eyes and face lined quizzically.

'We made our vows,' said Andrew with a justifying tone to his voice as though to say their actions were all above board.

'Vows ...! What vows?' Dee couldn't understand.

'She said...' Andrew's head indicated to Ruth as if he was acting out the story of Adam and Eve in the Garden of Eden.

'What's all this, Ruth, about vows been taken?' Dee was persistent. Is there something I don't understand here, Ruth?'

'It's alright mammy. I told Andrew that I loved him and he said the same. We made the promises of our marriage in the bedroom; I told him that I was taking him up to the church in the bedroom. There wasn't time to explain.'

Ruth thought it all quite reasonable in view of her understanding of Larry's Law on the matter.

'I bet there wasn't time to explain, you pair of wild cats. Now, listen here you two besotted-cats. You will not get away with a private marriage no matter your own understanding of the way things are between you. You Ruth have an international responsibility to the people as well as you have to yourself and our dear, besotted Andrew.

'But, mammy; we have always been taught by daddy, that Love is the true Church. We made our vows to each other because love has made our marriage. What else needs to be done? Surely love is its own priest and Church ... That's daddy's understanding of it?' Ruth couldn't understands her mother's need for the old ways.

'Look my dear Ruth; and I hope you are listening Mr. Madden.' Dee's smile was calm and patient as she continued. 'Now listen carefully you pair of brats – vows indeed. You two are no longer your own private property. The people across the nations have taken our family to their hearts. We owe them a wedding for their sake. They will expect it and rightly so. The nations have been loyal and supportive to all that our family led them through. The very least we can do in return is to consider them as our family also and allow them to know that our special day is theirs also. Now I demand that we have a public wedding for their sake. It will further cement the privilege and responsibility of world authority that they have freely and willing placed in trust on our shoulders. Consider too that you have no right to kick the significance and importance of the Church up the ass, and Father Kevin hardly cold in his grave. Finally, I will only say this once: Larry and I are growing old .... We will not be around forever.'

Ruth cut in on her and said with tears in her eyes: 'Mammy please don't say things like that – we both love you and daddy, you know we do ... don't we Andrew?' He could only nod his head fitfully in agreement, though for the life of him he couldn't quite grasp the wider implication of what Dee was implying.

'It's all right, Ruth; hush now; don't make things harder for me than they are already, having to face the truth of Larry's age and my own. The people respect and almost worship our family for freeing them for the tyranny of money and all the unnecessary oppression that held the nations in a grip of poverty and meaningless existence. We have always honored our responsibility by keeping in communion with the nations through Government Broadcast. The guidance of our new laws, the freedom they eventually brought would never have been possible without the peoples' own personal sacrifices and the great upheavals of their lives in a bid to establish all that Larry's Law recommended to them. You must now continue what Larry and I established. Don't fret. I don't intend abandoning anything at the moment. That goes for you too, Mr. Madden,' Dee remarked, smiling. You will need to support Ruth in this work.' Andrew's eyes popped out in terror. He knew that the family had international status and responsibility ... They knew what they were doing, he hadn't a breeze.

'Dee! I'm just an ordinary builder. I don't know about international affairs.' He was clearly terrified by the prospect of having to communicate on Government Broadcast with the entire world looking on at him.

'You are little more that a figurehead, you rumskull. The Guardians of Larry's Law will know that. Nonetheless, it is important that you are seen to represent the authority of the people. That is what we stand for now. Larry and I have done all the groundwork years ago. So get up out of that nest of yours and come downstairs to have your dinner ... and try doing it without making any more screams.' There was a teasing smile on Dee's face as Andrew stuffed a corner of the duvet into his face to cover the burning color of his embarrassment. Ruth, still half covered stood laughing at him until her mother smacked her bare backside with a telling slap that resounded in the room.

'Ouch, Mammy ...!'

'Never mind, ouch, Mammy! Marriage and vows indeed ....' Dee closed the bedroom door muttering again as she descended the stairs. '... Marriage vows indeed....' She wasn't slow to have noticed a little blood on the exposed side of the bed where Ruth had lain.

It was something of a wonder to the mother that her thirty-three year old daughter had saved herself for Andrew all those years when she could have had the pick of the entire world. Her mother was proud of her even though she thought she had left things somewhat late. Secretly, she had always hoped that Andrew might be that special one to win her over. She wondered too, as she set about preparing the table for their meal, how long ago was it that Andrew realized that he was in love with Ruth in that intimate way? He certainly never let on; in fact, he seemed to avoid all intimate contact with her. Dee always knew that Ruth had a special fondness for him. She was only a baby when he was twelve years old. Here he is now at forty-five. I could murder him, she thought reflectively, if I thought he knew he loved her more than just as a childhood friend. To leave matters this late. She would only learn the truth much later when Andrew had the confidence to reveal that he always thought that Ruth and her world were far beyond his. He believed that he would never have stood a chance. He also revealed how the terrible crippling pain of his shyness and uncertainty had blinded and distorted his judgment of Ruth's true feelings …. How he had suffered in particular when he sometimes had the opportunity of holding her and kissing her cheek when they met from time to time when his own parents traveled up from Cork city. Now he realized that he should have been able to read the expressions of her face and body. 'God, Dee! I have been such a dumb fool all those years suffering as the mute fool of my own stupidity.' He had Dee in tears when all was revealed. She just held him and held him until it was made quite certain that he was one of their own – belonging to the family entirely and forever and that her embracing of Andrew meant that the entire Madden family were included. They had been friends for a lifetime.

Dee got the wedding she insisted on. It took place in Cork City with the world media represented. Pope Domenic Ubutu X11 was the principle celebrant of the wedding with Monsignor Edward Henry, his faithful servant beside him. The Cathedral of S.S. Mary Anne Shandon was used for the ceremony. The cathedral was packed to the rafters with people and officials from many other faiths and none. The very best of choirs were represented from across the nations via massive great television screens to facilitate the auspicious occasion and ceremony. International choirs were cued in to sing the various parts of the High Mass. The solemnity and grandeur of the occasion was awe-inspiring, gripping congregation and viewers alike across the world. Pope Dominic's homily spoke of all that had been achieved under Larry's Law – how Larry and his family had been given the privilege of being the voice of Love and Care for all the nations ... nations which were now totally at peace with one another. 'He had,' the pontiff emphasized, '... achieved what no other Church in the long history of our divided faiths and nations had achieved, namely, to put Love and Care of all people at the very heart of human meaning and expression to life – that Love chose the most humble and least able of souls to establish the true foundation of human interrelationship and dignity for us all. We all know now that over the last thirty or so years, ever since Larry's Law took its true place in the human heart across the nations, that what has been achieved by international cooperation across world was nothing short of a miracle. There was a simple but profound foundation to it all – that Love itself had freed us from every form of slavery that was the cause of so much injustice and neglect – neglect that was all too often perpetuated by the rich and powerful and all vying authority.

'Now, my good people you are witnesses to what has been achieved. Even our own Church, with Peter's authority behind it, must feel its own shame and no little portion of blame for obscuring the true meaning and direction of human freedom and dignity. For all our learning and influence we failed to bring the people of the world together in concord and international cohesion. Now at last, thanks to the humility and clarity of Larry's Law, we have, at last, achieved our true direction and an evergreen faith that all nations have embraced freely and without reservation. No Faith or religion in our long history had achieved this. Together we have discovered the true God of our lives that all our ancient forebears sought through the jungle of human understanding and our precarious development. We had all lost the plot, our true direction, as each nation battled against each other for supremacy and control but never quite managing to find it, not even with the great empires of the ancient and modern world which have come and gone like a puff of wind in our long histories. All failed to bludgeon the entire civilization into a common unity even with by the use of force, fear and dictatorship.

'Larry who stands before us,' a deafening thunderous applause followed across the nations and from the cathedral's congregation, 'now an old and tired soul like myself, is overjoyed to know that he is handing over his guiding hand to that of Ruth and Andrew now on this happy and momentous occasion of their marriage. Andrew too, is one of those humble souls who will serve us well in his devoted love of Ruth as well as to all her family and friends.' More applause thundered for Andrew – the poor lad was terrified, literally quaking. He was dressed in a beautifully-tailored morning-grey suit; the pockets and collar of his coat in black velvet ... his Shirt and tie both crisp and new, his black shoes glinting in the summer sun.

Dee had a hand placed on Andrew's shoulder to let him know that the family stood behind him. Ruth was dressed in full wedding attire – a beautiful cream silk long flowing wedding dress and a simple silver crown on her immaculately groomed golden hair. She wore a veil over her face as she held onto the terrified Andrew. All the attention lavished on Ruth and family was received with calm yet respectful and dignified familiarity. No matter where the family appeared in public, hands waved, fingers pointed, applause and cheering for them were as frequent as the rising and setting of the sun; and yet such lavish attention, no matter how frequent or familiar, was always acknowledged and shown to be acknowledged. The family knew perfectly well that their international position and importance was really an office of the human heart. Of themselves they had no power but that of the people who loved them for what they stood for, the love and care of all.

Although Dee was still beautiful for her fifty-five or so years she had long since been eclipsed by the exquisite and near goddess perfection of Ruth's beauty and graceful elegance. Dee was dressed in a simple white suit. She still retained her slim figure in spite of her years. Larry too, like Andrew, wore a morning-grey outfit both trimmed with black velvet to the collar and pockets. Such outfits were freely supplied from a specialist outfitters devoted to wedding attire and for other special occasions. This same service was available freely to all as a matter of course. In fact everything supplied for this momentous wedding was available free to all. It was again one of the many benefits of living in a world without the use and burden of money.

With the official ceremony at an end, the nations across the world thundered out in one voice for speeches from Larry, Dee, Ruth and Andrew. The poor lad was, by now, beside himself for want of the toilet to sit on. His face was puce with the strain. He whispered to Ruth concerning his predicament. Ruth was ready to crack up in hysterics until Andrew forced her attention to the severity and urgency of the matter. The message was relayed along a string of controlling officials. When Larry stood in front of the microphones to speak first, Andrew was discretely hurried off to a toilet in the conveniences of the cathedral without any embarrassing attention. He quite literally had the runs as a result of all the attention and from his own unfamiliarity with such lavish attention and solemnity. Larry addressed the world in his familiar Cork city accent; the international world had become familiar with it over the years of his broadcasting and many addresses.

'My dear people, Dee and I have held this awesome office as head of the world government for many years now. It has been an awesome duty but also a privileged one. It is an office first and foremost that belongs to you, the people. Personally speaking, I never dreamt in my wildest dreams that I might still be here at your kind insistence. Dee has always been the rock and love of my life.' More thundering cheers and chanting followed across the nations and TV screens. Larry continued. 'The only way that we have managed to keep our heads and sanity was from something Dee had said to me many years ago as we took on this awesome duty for the first time. "Remember, Larry, we are not talking to the people or inviting them to implement a philosophy or messages that is of our own connivance; we too had to sift through all the masses of details and instructions to discover for ourselves that it was the voice of Love and Care for all people that was speaking through you for the benefit of all the people." 'That is who we were doing this for; it was for the oppressed people of the world that we were trying to liberate and give them their true dignity and reason for living. We do not represent ourselves except to the extent that we too must be seen to comply with what we were instructed to put before all the nations and their peoples. We are simply your willing servants. Our privileged position is always and ever will be the voice of the people.' [More thunderous applause and cheers]

'Now as you can see, I am bent with the accumulation of years needing a stick to walk with, and love alone knows what creams and medications I am forced to indulge in to keep my old weary bones alive. In short; I am an old creature.'

Shouts and screams followed: 'Never! Never! Never! Long live Larry and his family; long live them all forever in our hearts.'

Their words and sentiments brought tears to Larry's tired eyes. He was unable to say more so that Dee had to step up in front of the demanding crowds. Cheers thundered out for her.

'Thank you so much for all your support. You have carried our family a long way all these years.' More thunderous applause followed along with more wild chanting at Dee's appearance. She was still the darling of the people.

'We never thought that our message to the world would ever be accepted in the universal way that it has. Of course we hoped that it would. As Larry has made clear before, it wasn't our message but the prophetic message that was gleaned from so many world religions of the past, if anyone took the trouble to do the gleaning of the essential message that was brought to you. We are rightly proud of the cooperation that has turned the old world of money and oppressive powers on its head and vanquished that world never to be repeated or to rear its ugly face again.'

More cheers across the world and from the cathedral congregation.

'We have many people to thank who have worked with us in the background. Not least of these is our own dear Pope, Dominic Ubutu, who has travelled here today from Kenya to give our daughter to Andrew in marriage with his blessing. He has been a great inspiration to us and so generous in promoting our cause from the very onset. He saw in our simple message only what he essentially understood by his own reasoning and learning – that there was no contradiction to the faith we share with Christianity, the Muslims, Sufism, Buddhism or any of the world faiths that have love and care of all people at their core and the absolute essential message of what we refer to as sacred scripture. Yes our message has stripped the scriptures of so much of its dross and ancient superstitions. Many of the old prophets, not just in the scriptures of Christianity but in many other faiths, have spoken falsely of their knowledge of God and of the decrees that were fabricated as coming from him. Their words came from their own hearts to flatter pharaohs, kings and emperors with nothing more than royal expedience, nationalism and propaganda to curry favor and self importance for their own fraudulent office. The test for all we have put before you concerning world scriptures and their supposed wisdom was to see how it corresponded to the essential and universal prism of the Love and Care for all people. What did not correspond to this filtering test, we dismissed as dross and irrelevance, unworthy of human concern. Although Larry was never quite certain of the true person or voice speaking to him in his dreams, we have come to agree and understand that it was the voice of Love itself.

We realized that after hundreds of years of human indoctrination by many faiths which served up speculation and superstition as gospel truth how much the nations of the world were truly oppressed. Some speculative theologians spoke of a First Mover or the Unmoved Mover of creation and human existence ... we realized that all of this was pure speculation and of no practical use or progress for the universal peoples of the world.

Mysteries of the origin of life will have to wait for more enlightened minds to pursue over time. In the meantime, we concluded that we had to live by what can be clearly understood by the simplest child or mind. Yes, some prophets came close to the mark when they said that "God is Love ... that we all have a duty to love and care for each other." However, this conclusion was never a true reality until Larry's Law insisted on it as the absolute datum of our lives and our futures.'

More chanting followed. 'Long live Larry's Law ... Long live the Face of Love'

Dee continued. 'All of us can see what we have achieved over the past thirty years or so, which is almost miraculous in so brief a time. Yet the work of our hands, our united cooperation with one another was no miracle arising from beyond ourselves. It is all our own work, our universal effort. We can never begin to thank you enough for your selfless help. Thank you all once again.'

More thunderous cheers followed. 'More! More! More,' the people roared. 'We want Ruth and Andrew .... We want Ruth and Andrew .... We want Ruth and Andrew ....'

As Ruth moved forward to the banks of microphones the volume of thunderous applause and banging shook the cathedral to its foundations. On the streets of Cork city and on the streets of the countless cities across the nations the same thundering chorus resounded shaking the very buildings. Andrew had by now, slipped back unseen behind Ruth as she addressed the people.

'This is a very happy day in my short lifetime and that of Andrew's, my dearest husband. I know we have won your hearts on the proven service of mammy and daddy.' The people responded immediately,

'We love you too, Ruth and Andrew …. Long live Ruth and Andrew.' The roars were deafening from the people in the cathedral and across the viewing world. While Ruth took the calls of the people in her stride, though quite exhilarated by them, poor Andrew was bewildered and terrified. He knew beyond all shadow of doubt now that he was going to be forced to stand in front of the microphones and face the entire world. He felt sick and faint; his knees knocking together involuntary as though they had a life of their own, a life as incompetent as his own deranged, terror-racked mind He could neither hear the thundering roars of the people no more than he could hear what Ruth was saying. So deranged was his state he could not even take the cue or learn from what Ruth was saying. She continued:

'The family has come to realize and accept that daddy has become weak and struggles to continue with the task that was demanded of him. So it was agreed that Andrew and myself would take over the office of World Government with mammy and daddy to advise us in this awesome service and duty to the people. However, both mammy and daddy have assured us that the principle work of government is already carried out by the Guardians of Larry's Law right across the nations; we owe those countless groups of professional men and women a very great depth of gratitude which words of appreciation, though necessary to be spoken, can never express what we and the entire united peoples of the world feel in the wake of all we benefit from by their selfless generosity. Only their joint achievement and the great benefits that issue from their guidance can of themselves glorify and praise their work. Andrew and I can only hope to continue the work that daddy and mammy, along with the Guardians of our laws, have so far achieved. We are determined to give our utmost efforts to this momentous achievement.' Andrew kept telling himself fitfully, 'Keep on talking Ruth, maybe night time will fall early and we can all go home. Please! Please! Please! Ruth, don't stop now.'

'We have only to look across the nations, even at this early juncture of our worldwide achievements to realize and appreciate what a very simple message has advanced. We are no longer at the mercy of a divided world. There have been no wars or armies to serve them. Not one individual is without work, home or food. Even though we all have to do our work, it is done with good grace .... All the trades have accelerated in quality and immense personal satisfaction for all concerned. Look at the quality of our modes of travel; no other age has ever considered giving the peoples the very best of comfort and dignity. Our hospitals and the world of medicine have advanced to such a degree that even our elderly citizens cannot believe what has been achieved. All weaponry of war and conflict has become a thing of the past; all melted down to manufacture the machinery and means of prosperity right across the world. All the barbaric prisons of the past are gone forever, replaced by dignified hospitals and psychiatric institutions dedicated to the healing and dignified lives of so many unfortunate and disadvantaged souls. Our homes and schools have replaced the old concepts of preparing our children in the service of a marketplace, where our nations were once the slaves of money and its countless abuses. Our own institutions have devoted themselves to the love and care of all peoples, and removing from the minds of the young all the dividing instruments of indoctrinated nationalism. We have become a universal people for the first time in our long and ancient history. We have done away with all borders and national sovereignties. There is no longer any need for diplomatic immunity and back-scratching perversion. All are held responsible for any deviation from the principles of love and care of all people. Kingdoms, the dark cartels of power, and palatial luxury built at the expense of the poor and struggling have all been exposed for what they really were, the mocking thrones and institutions of the privileged and powerful.'

More thunderous clamor followed.

'Long live the voice of the people! Long live Larry's Law! Long live Ruth and Andrew.' Andrew became even more wretched and white with fear. His guts told him that Ruth had finished her inspired recollections of the nation's achievements. He was dreading the inevitable call for him to step forward. It would be like an emperor calling a court jester forward for mere mockery and the entertainment of the people.

Larry spotted Andrew's terrified condition and moved imperceptibly towards him. Up to now Larry had never used his healing powers knowingly since the healing of Mary Cassidy in the city police station all those years ago and the healing of Dee herself. Larry was advised in a dream that healing rarely achieved its desired end in the healed … that all too frequently it was received selfishly and as a deserved right from the consequences of dumb nature that had caused disease and deformity in the first place with indiscriminate indifference. It was also given to Larry to realize that those who suffer from the severity and disadvantage of deformity were the indirect cause of inducing in those good caring souls untold graces of love and concern for the suffering. Handicap, physical deformity and mental disfigurement, with all their outward ugliness and disadvantage, very often overshadowed the quiet saintliness of the misfortunate. In fact many a severely physically and mentally disadvantaged man or woman has been known to be the fountain of great genius. However, in this case Larry felt called to heal Andrew. Without show or observance, Larry put his hand on Andrew's shoulder and whispered softly:

'Don't worry Andrew. Be calm. You will be fine. You will not have to depend on yourself I assure you.' Their heads were hung as in private conversation with each other. As Ruth gestured to Andrew to come forward to address the people she too whispered:

'Just greet the people and tell them something about yourself.' She was not being condescending; she knew Andrew to be a man of action not of words; he was a builder after all, not an orator capable of ground-breaking speeches. As he stepped up to face the media with its forest of news cameras and microphones everywhere in the great cathedral, the thunderous applause and cheers seemed to draw him forward. His earlier wretched state of crippling apprehension had all dissolved as if a miracle had taken place. Larry alone would have known the source of the calm that had utterly transformed him from an incompetent wreck to a person who might have been reared on the stage and at perfect ease in its limelight. There was elegance in the waving of his hand to the people and viewers. The sickly, white terror had vanished from his face and his usual healthy outdoor color restored. His flaxen hair was smartly cut and combed to perfection. The borrowed powder-grey morning suit with its black velvet collar and pocket trimmings gave him an air of sophistication normally alien to his workman-like personality. However, this day was special in so many wonderful ways for him. Not alone had he married into a family of international importance, he was to belong to those very ranks himself. Suddenly – a tangible silence fell over the cathedral as Andrew began to speak.

'Like my beautiful wife, Ruth,' Cheers erupted and Andrew had to wait for it to subside. 'I am so moved by the welcome you have expressed to me on this most wonderful occasion for us both. I cannot begin to express my thanks or compete with Ruth's grace and elegance. She grew up with the world's media in her life. I just hope that I can learn to feel the same degree of comfort and ease with time.' More cheers of encouragement.

'We love you too, Andrew.'

'This day will always be special for both of us …. That goes without saying; we love each other. Even so, you, the people, have made the day even more special. Yes, it is your day too. I know that our marriage is not going to be self-serving – I realized that from the very time Ruth and I decided to marry. I know the love we have for each other is meant to reach out to all the people in selfless service to all. Thankfully I have been well prepared for that extension of our love by my wonderful parents, Seamus and Lil. I also owe a tremendous debt of gratitude to Larry and Dee as I have seen their love extended freely and generously in their untiring service to all the nations across the world. At the moment all of it seems very daunting and challenging for me, a humble building-trade worker.' More cheers.

'God bless the builders …. Long life to our Andrew …. Long life to our Ruth'

'Many of you may think that it was the luckiest day of my life when I entered into this wonderful family and became the husband of such an adorable and loving wife. All of that is true of course. It has indeed been very fortuitous. And yet there is another side to this fairytale. I did not step into this family with any degree of suddenness. Ruth stepped into my life, or I should say crawled, when I was twelve years old and she a little infant crawling on all fours on the carpet of her parents home. I loved Ruth as a baby and often held her in my arms. In truth, she has never left my arms since.' [More cheers and applause]

'I have also loved Ruth's mother, Dee, from the moment I first met her, again, when I was twelve years old. I loved her too and continue to love her to this day. Larry too – he has been a childhood friend and is now like a second father to me. Larry has always looked out for me from my childhood and in truth, I have never been without his love and influence in my life; he was like a second father and older brother. He was always like a guardian watching over me and always the most playful of companions. The child in Larry has never deserted him, not even today though he may seem old to himself. All that he has meant to me and all the family will remain with us forever. It has been my undeserved privilege and good fortune to have been blessed by his enduring presence in my life.' [More cheers and applause]

'As a humble builder and tradesman I have witnessed what I could never have believed possible, even in our building industries across the nations. A new pride in craftsmanship in the workshops of the nations and general industry has replaced the shoddy workmanship of former times when money linked to time degraded craftsmanship especially among the poorer classes who could not afford to pay for good work. All the advances of the present have only been made possible when Larry's law separated itself from the curse of money which had been linked to every aspect of trading. Now the building and manufacturing industries take delight in the pursuit of excellence in craftsmanship and technical advances that is appreciated by all. The days of bodge-it-and-flog-it are gone forever.

'Gone too are the days of waste when what was considered not worth repairing due to the restrictions of money and time are now repaired and renewed. Together we have won back time and the repairing of broken household goods since they have been unshackled from time and cost imposed on labor. The result has been a massive increase in employment in the repair industry for which we have all witnessed the benefits. We are the richer in our skills and contentment and reliability. We have ceased to manufacture for the dictates of a whimsical market economy. Yet we have lost nothing of the essentials but continue to devote our efforts to all that is desirable and for the real benefit to all. Work no longer belongs to the slavish drudgery of the past – drudgery that only served the privileged and maintained the few in a life of palatial luxury at the expense of the less positioned and less privileged. There is no longer a split or segregation of people into classes. We all work happily together for the greater good and benefit for all.'

A long pause as the viewers and listeners applauded and cheered their approval and appreciation of what was clearly the experience of all.

'It seemed like a strange irony to me when my dear and childhood friend Danny asked me rather philosophically recently, what I think heaven must be like. My answer was simple: we are living it now in our own times in so far that our liberated working lives allow. There are no exclusive areas of privilege for any particular persons, groups or classes – there are no more no-go-areas, whether we speak of modes of travel, holidays, housing, schools, colleges or sporting activities, or universities – all are given the same opportunities, the less able no less than the extremely gifted. The slums and shantytowns of once impoverished nations and peoples have disappeared forever.'

More cheers of approval and concordance with the truth of Andrew's reflections.

'I have little more to say beyond thanking my own parents, Seamus and Lil and my sister Lisa for all the help and love they have lavished unstintingly on me over the years. Many of you will know my sister, Lisa, and her husband, Raymond Doyle. We are all familiar with Lisa's songs and poems and with Raymond's musical compositions that are known the world over.

'It only remains for me to repeat my sincere thanks for your kind support and encouragement in my new role as part of the world's governing family. Thank you for making this day so very special for Ruth, myself and all the family.'

Cheers and applause thundered in the cathedral and across the watching nations.

Every street, every nook and cranny, across the nations were decked out for street parties. Millions of lines of bunting fluttered from every conceivable space. Trestle tables were bedecked with every kind of food and drink.

Andrew, Ruth and both their families were carried away in the same horse -drawn golden coaches that had driven them to the cathedral. Now they passed down every main street where there was room enough for the gleaming golden carriages; the horses loaned for the occasion trotting with grace and elegance in their glistening harnesses and decorated shafts. The newly-weds waved enthusiastically to all the crowds. The cacophony of the cheering crowds was deafening. Bands played in every street. The city of Cork would never be allowed to forget this spectacular and momentous occasion. Virgin history was being made and recorded for all posterity. The magnificent city scenes were decked out in blazing colors; the exploding fireworks and fluttering flag were relayed across the world in deafening jubilation. The entire festivities were repeated across the nations. The people knew in their hearts and souls that the world of the future and its leadership was well and truly established in the safe hands of Andrew and Ruth. Neither knew that at this very moment that the seed of another generation and future leadership of the nations was already growing inside Ruth's fertile womb.

Six months after the wedding it was clear to all that Ruth was with child. Be it boy or girl Ruth would welcome either. When Larry and all the family discovered this happy news he decided to address the nations for the last time, half aware that his own death was imminent. The family travelled from Garrettstown for the last time to Government Broadcast in Cork City. Larry addressed the nations and a crowd facing him in the studio.

'My dear people, today we have the delightful news that Ruth, my own dearest baby, is now with child herself.'

Great Jubilant cheers followed.

'Just as Dee and I have been the figureheads of our great enterprise steering the nations through many obstacles, so now we pass on that responsibility to the youth of our family. I know that you are in good hands. Just as we, together with all the nations, have removed many abusive tyrants from the leadership of the past, I have every confidence that you will give that same generous support to Andrew and Ruth. The awesome task that was set upon the shoulders of Dee and I is now laid on the shoulders of these young parents. I am assured and confident that you will afford them the same generous support that you have given us in such devoted abundance and selflessness.

'I realize that I must face the inevitability of my own death.' The nation's murmured a distressing groan at the mention of such a prospect. Larry raised his hand to calm the studio audience and no doubt, the watching and listening peoples of the nations.

'I know this saddens you as it does me. For I too will leave my loved ones behind and that distresses me.' Dee, Ruth and family friends were in tears just as the many listening nations shed their tears at the sad prospect.

'However, I do leave you with this prophecy. The days are coming when every individual of humanity will no longer give way to physical death. This has always been the final enemy of mankind. Yes, death can be a happy blessing and release for all poor souls born to disadvantage ... for all who have struggled with the pain of deformity and disease as a consequence of Nature's imperfections. But for those of us who leave loved ones behind, death remains the curse it always has been ... that dark and terrible appointment ... that destroyer and separator of love and of our dearest friendships. For now our knowledge and physical advances fail us. However, I do sincerely believe that as our minds and hearts cry out for extension to life, such noble and desired sentiments will be given the new regeneration of our heartfelt yearnings. With all the development of science, in concordance with Nature's limitless creative being – giving time, we will see the dawn of so great a day and wonder. But for our generation we must face the inescapable consequences of the, not yet.

'As a token of my love and gratitude for every individual in the nations I have requested not to be buried in the grave of my beloved daddy, Bernard, who sleeps alone in Cork city. As you also know by now, Mary, his wife, my dearest mammy, was taken from me in mysterious circumstance and ascended into heaven – a place so mysterious to me that I have not the words or concepts to speak sensibly about such a state or place. And yet, it was through a visitation from my dear mammy that I was given the privilege and power to begin and continue our enterprise that has enfolded the entire world with such incredible benefits of peace happiness and the loving care for all. No. I wish to be buried on a remote hillside cemetery with two of the greatest and dearest friends whose love for me and all the family have strengthened us with their generosity and guardianship of my life. I wish to be buried with Father Kevin, the most loving and wonderful priest that any soul could desire to have known – to lay down beside his loving housekeeper and my second mother Nell. I do this, as I have mentioned earlier, as a token of my love not just for them but for you also. It means that it is not our bloodline that regenerates love in the world. It is rather the loving hearts and minds of those outside of the family that build the nations to love and care for each other. It hurts me deeply to know that I must leave behind my beloved wife, Dee and my cherished Daughter, Ruth, and Andrew and Lisa – two of the loved children of my life. I must part from many friends also, too many to name …. I owe a deep debt of gratitude to the Madden family in particular who have been my treasured friends and my saviors when I was lost and alone after losing my parents. God bless you Seamus, Lil, Andrew and Lisa for all you have meant to me and my family over the years.' Tears poured from Larry's eyes – his voice and body shook and trembled involuntary. His family rushed to take hold of him in his enfeebled state but he halted them with his raised hand and took some moments to calm himself. He clung only to Dee. Both had their arms around each other – both sobbing painfully. The people gathered in the streets and by their TV screens were themselves is convulsing tears. The Madden family was at home watching the TV – they too were in a terrible state of upset. They felt like something was tearing their family apart. Presently, Larry continued.

'I realize that many of you might wish to make a pilgrimage to my grave as a means of remembrance and celebration of what we have achieved together. However, I ask this most sincerely: do not make a pilgrimage to my burial place, nor make it a shrine for the nations. I will not be there – nor will I thank you for doing so. If you continue to build on what we have begun in your name, that will be the greatest honor that you can attribute to my name and the memory of all my family and the meaning of our lives. Make your pilgrimages into the living hearts of those in need around you … in that way we will always be together. Make the love and care of each other the true shrine and meaning of your lives.

'I must now say farewell to you all. My heart goes out to every individual across the nations. I wish to thank the Guardians of the People for their loyalty to my family and the duties imposed on us from the very beginning. My sincere gratitude is also extended to the Peoples' Courts across the nations who have ministered to our laws and guarded them from every abuse. God bless you all and may your love and care for each other be my final blessing over each and every one of you. Do not fret for the future.... All shall be well.'

A terrible feeling of deep foreboding fell over the people. There was no cheering now in Broadcast House. The people across the world were convulsed in wailing grief.

CHAPTER 31

The Death of Larry and Dee

Within six months of Larry's final address to the nations the news of a double tragedy was released to the world. Larry had died peacefully in his bed. When Dee awoke in the morning and discovered that Larry's body lay cold and rigid beside her, she collapsed with the shock. The family doctor stated publicly that there was no natural reason for the sixty year old Dee to have died. He presumed from his own experience in such matters that Dee had died of a broken heart. The nations mourned as never before for the loss of two of the dearest leaders that the world had ever known. Their only consolation would come with time when their terrible sadness would subside and the knowledge that Larry and Dee had left the nations the legacy of their life's work and united achievements as well as the heirs of a new tomorrow.

Cork city, the birth place of Larry, fell into a deep mourning and tragic sense of personal loss for one of its dearest and greatest sons and for his beloved wife, Dee; both later to be called by all, "the true parents of the nations."

Larry had requested one last privilege from the people to be carried out at his funeral ... that it be as simple as possible ... that his body be taken by donkey and cart to and from Saint Patrick's church in the city in loving memory of Father Kevin and Nell. The gentle beast of burden was to stop for five minutes outside his parent's home and that of his loving neighbors, the Madden family, in Shandon Rise, off the Mardyke Road. This was in salutation of his love for his humble parents, Bernard and Mary, and his dearest neighbors, the Madden family; but most of all, for the most loving of all priestly individuals who rode a donkey into another city two thousand years ago, to face his own death for preaching the love and care of all peoples, and from which Larry's own simple faith would be born and flourish across the nations in the simple creed of Larry's Law.

As the little animal and open cart passed through the city streets bearing the simple caskets of Larry and Dee side by side, the people were inconsolable, sobbing with rending tears and grief. Although the city streets were lined with millions, four and five abreast, the silence was all but deafening. The rumbling wheels of the humble donkey-cart passed slowly by. The flag of the nations hung to the ground from the sides of the cart with the portrait of Larry's family clearly seen over the emblazoned crimson words: "The Face of Love."

Only the family attended the committal at Hogan's Cross, the burial place of Father Kevin and Nell. The final, stuttering words of committal were said in flowing tears by Pope Dominic Ubutu X11.

'What a friend you have been to all of us – what a humble example – through your simple creed the whole of humanity has ascended into heaven. You will never be forgotten dear Larry, and you, beloved Dee. Until we meet again, sleep on dear souls, sleep on good friends.'

A forlorn single peal of a distant funeral bell carried across on the wind-blown bog-land cemetery. The ever-faithful Seamus and Lil, both now weakened with age themselves, were trembling with the heavy burden of their loss. Ruth and Andrew were also distraught in grief as well as Lisa and her husband, Raymond. Brother and sister held on tightly to their feeble parents. A terrible weight of darkness descended upon the family. Their senses numbed in a heavy weight of darkness and loss. They stood reflecting on the meaning of their lives together – loving faces and voices carried on the wings of precious times and golden days. They could see a vision of their loving friends pass before them.

And so it was that Larry, the simplest of all souls, along with his beloved Dee, was now lowered together into the bosom of the earth. Four simple graves in a row – four of the dearest friends: Father Kevin and Nell, Larry and Dee whom love had brought together and now would remain forever in a sacred bond of love for all eternity.

The End

Lightning Source UK Ltd.
Milton Keynes UK
UKOW040449061212

203254UK00001B/1/P